PENGUIN BOOKS

MURTAGH

WORLD of ERAGON

CHRISTOPHER PAOLINI

PENGUIN BOOKS

PENGUIN BOOKS

UK | USA | Canada | Ireland | Australia
India | New Zealand | South Africa

Penguin Books is part of the Penguin Random House group of companies
whose addresses can be found at global.penguinrandomhouse.com

www.penguin.co.uk
www.puffin.co.uk
www.ladybird.co.uk

First published in the USA by Alfred a. Knopf, an imprint of Random House Children's Book 2023
This edition published in the UK by Penguin Books 2023

001

Text copyright © Christopher Paolini, 2023
Jacket art copyright © John Jude Palencar, 2023
Map art and interior illustrations copyright © Christopher Paolini, 2006, 2023

The moral right of the author and illustrator has been asserted

Printed and bound in Great Britain by Clays Ltd, Elcograf S.p.A.

The authorized representative in the EEA is Penguin Random House Ireland,
Morrison Chambers, 32 Nassau Street, Dublin D02 YH68

A CIP catalogue record for this book is available from the British Library

HARDBACK
ISBN: 978–0–241–65131–5

INTERNATIONAL PAPERBACK
ISBN: 978–0–241–65134–6

EXCLUSIVE HARDBACK
ISBN: 978–0–241–68781–9

All correspondence to:
Penguin Books
Penguin Random House Children's
One Embassy Gardens, 8 Viaduct Gardens, London SW11 7BW

As always, this is for my family.

And also for those who stand on the outside, looking in.

CONTENTS

PART III: NAL GORGOTH

PART IV: OTH ORUM

PART V: REUNION

ADDENDUM

WORLD OF ERAGON

Argument

✦ ✦ ✦ ✦ ✦ ✦ ✦

Behold, the land of Alagaësia, vast and verdant, full of mystery. Here stand mountains that scrape the stars, forests as fathomless as an ocean, deserts scorched to barrenness, and more besides. Throughout, one will find divers peoples and creatures, from hardy humans to long-lived elves to deep-dwelling dwarves to war-wedded Urgals. And above all else, dragons—bright and brilliant and terrifying in their ancient glory.

For the past century, King Galbatorix reigned as tyrant over most of the human-settled lands and was a terror to the other races as well. By his will, the dragons were broken, and their numbers much reduced until only few remained.

Those brave folk who opposed Galbatorix fled into the hinterlands, where they came to call themselves the Varden. There they dwelt, with little hope for victory, until the dragon Saphira hatched for the human Eragon.

Together—and under the wise leadership of the Lady Nasuada—they marched against Galbatorix's Empire.

Now the king is slain, and the war to overthrow him is ended, and the land entered a state of renewal.

Yet even in this peace, shadows stir, and there are whispers of strange happenings about the edges of Alagaësia, and of these, one man seeks to know the truth. . . .

To hold the center amid a storm,
To cleave or cling or seize the standard?
'Tis a question troubles even
The broadest mind. A stand of aspen
Grows as tall and strong as the lonely
Oak. Honor demands, duty compels,
And love cajoles, but the self insists.

—*Quandaries* 14–20
Atten the Red

CEUNON

~~~~~~~~~~~~ ❖ ~~~~~~~~~~~~

KEVNOR

BAY OF FUNDOR

Stormcloud Isle

Fulsome Feast

Shipyard

CHAPTER I

✦ ✦ ✦ ✦ ✦ ✦ ✦

Maddentide

Will you go alone?

Murtagh gave Thorn a quizzical look. The red dragon sat crouched next to him atop the rocky hill where they had landed. In the fading dusk, the sparkle of the dragon's scales was subdued, tamped down like coals in a banked fire, waiting for a breath of wind to flare back to brilliance.

"What? You'd go with me?"

A wolfish grin split Thorn's jaws, showing rows of sharp white teeth, each as long as a dagger. *Why not? They already fear us. Let them scream and scurry at our arrival.*

The dragon's thoughts resonated like a bell in Murtagh's mind. He shook his head as he unbuckled his sword, Zar'roc, from his waist. "You'd like that, wouldn't you?"

Thorn's jaws hung open wider, and his burred tongue ran across his chops. *Maybe.*

Murtagh could just picture Thorn stalking down a narrow street, scraping the sides of buildings with his armored shoulders, breaking beams and shutters and cornices while folks fled before him. Murtagh knew how that would end, with fire and blood and a flattened circle of destruction.

"I think you'd best wait here."

Thorn shuffled his velvet wings and coughed deep in his throat. His way of laughing. *Then perhaps you should use magic to change the color of my scales, and we could pretend to be Eragon and Saphira. Wouldn't that be fine sport?*

Murtagh snorted as he laid Zar'roc across a patch of dry grass. He'd been surprised to discover that Thorn had a trenchant sense of humor. It hadn't been readily apparent when they'd been bonded, partly because of Thorn's youth and partly because of . . . attending circumstances.

For a moment, Murtagh's mood darkened.

No? Well then, if you change your mind—

"You'll be the first to know."

Mmm. With the tip of his snout, Thorn nudged the sword. *I wish you would take your fang. Your claw. Your sharpened affliction.*

Murtagh knew Thorn was nervous. He always was when Murtagh left, even for a short while. "Don't worry. I'll be fine."

A puff of pale smoke rose from the dragon's flared nostrils. *I don't trust that shark-mouthed skulker.*

"I don't trust anyone. Except for you."

And her.

Murtagh faltered as he went to one of the saddlebags that hung along Thorn's side. An image of Nasuada's almond eyes flashed before him. Cheekbones. Teeth. Parts and pieces that failed to sum the whole. A memory of her scent, accompanied by a yearning and a sorrow, an aching absence for what might have been and now was lost.

"Yes." He couldn't have lied to Thorn even if he wanted to. They were too closely joined for that.

The dragon was kind enough to return the conversation to safer ground. *Do you think Sarros has scented anything of interest?*

"It would be better if he hasn't." Murtagh excavated a ball of brown twine from the saddlebag.

But if he has? Do we fly toward the storm or away?

A thin smile stretched Murtagh's lips. "That depends on how violent the storm."

It may not be obvious. The wind can lie.

He measured a length of twine. "Then we'll continue sniffing about until it becomes obvious."

Hmm. As long as we can still change course if need be.

"One hopes."

Thorn's near eye—a deep-set ruby that gleamed with a fierce inner light—remained fixed on Murtagh as he cut the twine and used it to tie Zar'roc's crossguard to belt and scabbard so the crimson sword couldn't slide free. Then he placed Zar'roc in the saddlebag, where it would be safe and hidden, and returned to stand before Thorn.

"I'll be back before dawn."

The dragon hunkered low on his haunches, as if braced to take a blow. He kneaded the ground with his curved claws, like a great cat kneading a blanket, and small rocks popped and cracked with explosive force between his talons. A low hum, almost a whine, came from his chest.

Murtagh laid a hand on Thorn's jagged forehead and strove to impress a sense of calm and confidence on him. Dark chords of distress echoed in the depths of Thorn's mindscape.

"I'll be fine."

If you need me—

"You'll be there. I know."

Thorn bent his neck, and his claws grew still. From his mind, Murtagh felt a hard—if brittle—resolve.

They understood each other.

"Be careful. Watch for any who might try to sneak up on you."

Another bone-vibrating hum emanated from the center of Thorn's chest.

Then Murtagh pulled the hood of his cloak over his head and started down the side of the hill, picking a path between jags of solitary stone and clusters of prickly hordebrush.

He looked back once to see Thorn still crouched atop the crest of the hill, watching with slitted eyes.

~~~~~~~~~~~~~~~~ ❖ ~~~~~~~~~~~~~~~~

A man with a dragon was never truly alone.

So thought Murtagh as he headed west with a long, loose-limbed stride. No matter how many leagues separated him and Thorn, a part of them would always remain connected, even if the distance kept them from hearing each other's thoughts or feeling each other's emotions. Magic of the oldest kind joined them, and never would they be quit of it until one of them died.

Yet magic was not their only bond. The experiences he and Thorn had shared—the hardships, the mental attacks, the torture—had been so intense, so singular in nature, Murtagh didn't think that anyone else could truly understand what they had endured.

There was a certain comfort in the knowledge. Wherever he went, and whatever he did, Thorn would always be there for him. What's more, Thorn would understand. On occasion disapprove, perhaps, but even then with empathy and compassion. And the same was true in reverse.

There was also a sense of confinement to the knowledge. Never could they escape one another. Not really. But Murtagh didn't mind. He was well sick of being alone.

The land sloped away beneath him until, after several miles, it arrived at the Bay of Fundor. There, at the water's edge, lay the city of Ceunon: a rough-walled collection of buildings, dark with shadow, save for the occasional lamp or candle—warm gems set against the encroaching night. Rows of fishing boats with furled sails floated alongside the stone wharves, and with them, three deep-sea vessels with tall masts and broad hulls, ships capable of surviving passage around the northern tip of the peninsula that separated the bay from the open ocean.

Across the bay stood the mountains of the Spine, sawtoothed and ridge-backed behind a bank of obscuring haze, and the salt water between appeared deep and cold and unfriendly.

Grey clouds lay low upon bay and land alike, and a muffled stillness softened the sound of Murtagh's steps.

A cold touch on his hand caused him to look up.

Thick flakes of snow drifted downward: the first snow of the year. He opened his mouth and caught a flake on his tongue; it melted like a pleasant memory, fleeting and insubstantial.

Even this far north, it was unseasonably early for snow. Maddentide had been two days past, and that marked the first run of bergenhed, the silvery, hard-scaled fish that invaded the bay every autumn. The shoals were so large and dense you could nearly walk on them, and Murtagh had heard that, during their height, the fish would throw themselves onto the decks of the boats, driven to insanity by the intensity of their spawning urge.

There was a lesson in that, he felt.

Snow didn't usually arrive until a month or two after Maddentide. For it to be this early meant a bitter, brutal winter was on the way.

Still, Murtagh enjoyed the soft fall of flakes, and he appreciated the coolness of the air. It was the perfect temperature for walking, running, or fighting.

Few things were worse than struggling for your life while so hot as to pass out.

His pulse quickened, and he tossed back his hood and broke into a quick trot, feeling the need to move faster.

He kept a steady pace as he ran onto the flats surrounding Ceunon, past creeks and copses, over stone fences and through fields of barley and rye ripe for harvest. No one marked his passage save a hound at a farmhouse gate, who gave him a perfunctory howl.

And the same to you, Murtagh thought.

His connection with Thorn thinned as he ran, but it never vanished. Which was a comfort for Murtagh. He felt as nervous as Thorn when they were apart, although he worked to hide the feeling, not wanting to worsen the dragon's concern.

Murtagh would have preferred to land closer to Ceunon. If he needed help, every second would count. However, the risk of someone spotting Thorn was too great. Best to keep their distance and avoid a potential confrontation with local forces.

Murtagh rolled his neck. Being on his feet—lungs full of clean, crisp air, pulse pounding at a quick, sustainable beat—felt good after spending most of the day on dragonback. His knees and hips ached slightly; he wasn't bowlegged like so many of the cavalrymen of Galbatorix's army, but if he continued to spend most of his time on Thorn, it could yet happen. Was that an inevitable part of being a Dragon Rider?

A crooked smile lifted his lips.

The thought of far-famed Riders—especially the elven ones—walking around with legs as bent as those of a twenty-year veteran lancer was amusing. But he doubted that had been the case. The Riders likely had a way to counter the effect of being in the saddle, and at any rate, once a dragon was large enough, it became impossible to sit on like a horse. Shruikan—Galbatorix's mountainous black dragon—had been like that. Instead of a saddle, the king had installed a small pavilion on the hump of Shruikan's enormous shoulders.

Murtagh shivered and stopped by a lightning-struck tree. A sudden chill washed his arms and legs.

He took a deep breath. And another. Galbatorix was dead. Shruikan was dead. They had no hold on him or anyone still living.

"We're free," he whispered.

From Thorn came a sense of comforting warmth, like a distant embrace.

He pulled his hood back over his head and continued on.

When Murtagh arrived at the coastal road south of Ceunon, he paused behind a nearby hedgerow and poked his head over the top. To his relief, the road was empty.

He pushed through the hedge and hurried north, toward the wide, slumped bulk of the city. The faint light that penetrated the clouds had nearly vanished, and he wanted to be in Ceunon before full dark fell.

Deep wagon tracks ridged the well-worn road, and pats of cow dung forced him to switch lanes every few steps. The snow was gathering on the ground in a soft, thin layer that reminded him of the decorative lace that ladies would wear to high events at court.

He slowed as he approached Ceunon's outer wall. The fortifications were stout and well built, if not so high as those of Teirm or Dras-Leona. The blocks of rude-surfaced blackstone were mortared without gaps, and the wall had a properly angled batter at the bottom, which he noted with approval.

Not that any of it mattered if you were facing a dragon or Rider.

A pair of watchmen leaned on their pikes on either side of Ceunon's southern gate. Murtagh glanced at the battlements and machicolations above. No archers were posted on the wall walk. *Sloppy.*

The watchmen straightened as he neared, and Murtagh let his cloak fall open to show that he was unarmed.

A *clink* sounded as the watchmen crossed their pikes. "Who goes?" asked the man on the left. He had a face like a winter rutabaga, with a fat nose cobwebbed with burst blood vessels and a yellow bruise under his right eye.

"Just a Maddentide traveler," said Murtagh in an easy tone. "Come to purchase smoked bergenhed for my master."

The man on the right gave him a suspicious once-over. He looked as if he could be the cousin of fat-nose. "Says you. Where do you hail from, traveler? An' what name might you use?"

"Tornac son of Tereth, and I hail from Ilirea."

Mention of the capital put some stiffness into the watchmen's backs. They glanced at each other, and then fat-nose hacked and spat on the ground. The gob melted a patch of snow. "That's an awful long way on foot w' no pack an' no horse fer a few bushels of fish."

"It would be," Murtagh agreed, "but my horse broke her leg last night. Stepped in a badger hole, poor thing."

"An' you left yer saddle?" said the right-hand man.

Murtagh shrugged. "My master pays well, but he's not paying me to lug a saddle and bags halfway across Alagaësia, if you follow."

The watchmen smirked, and fat-nose said, "Aye. We follow. Have you lodging secured? Coin fer a bed?"

"Coin enough."

Fat-nose nodded. "Aight. We're not wanting strangers sleep'n on our streets. We find you mak'n use of 'em, we'll see the backside of you. We find you mak'n trouble, out you go. From midnight t' the fourth watch, the gates are closed, an' they'll not open for aught but Queen Nasuada herself."

"That seems reasonable," said Murtagh.

Fat-nose grunted, and the watchmen moved their pikes aside. Murtagh gave them a respectful nod and passed between them to enter the city.

~~~~~~~~~~~~~ ❖ ~~~~~~~~~~~~~

Murtagh scratched his chin as he moved deeper into Ceunon.

He had grown a beard at the beginning of the year, to help conceal his identity. He thought it was working; so far no one had accosted him. The beard was itchy, though, and he wasn't willing to let it get long enough that the hair became soft and pliable. Untidiness bothered him.

Trimming the beard with his dagger had proved impractical, and he was reluctant to resort to magic, as shaping the beard with nothing more than a word and an imagined outcome was an uncertain prospect. Besides, he didn't trust a spell to remove the hairs but not his skin, and there was a craftsman-like satisfaction in attending to the task by hand.

He'd bought a pair of iron clippers from a tinker outside Narda. They worked well enough, as long as he kept them sharp, oiled, and free of rust. Even so, he found maintaining the beard almost as much trouble as shaving.

Maybe he would remove it after leaving Ceunon.

The main street was a muddy strip twice the width of the southern road. The buildings were half-timbered, cruck-framed structures with lapstrake siding between the wooden beams. The beams themselves were stained black with pine tar, which protected them against salt from the bay, and many were decorated with carvings of sea serpents, birds, and Svartlings. Iron weather vanes sat idle atop every shingled, steep-sided roof, and a carved dragon head decorated the peak of most houses.

Murtagh forced himself to stop scratching.

He could have recited the whole history of the city, from its founding until the present. He knew that the carvings were in the style commonly called *kysk*, which had been invented by some anonymous craftsperson over a century past. That the blackstone in the outer walls came from a quarry not two dozen miles northeast. And that the good folk of Ceunon had a deathly fear of the elves' forest, Du Weldenvarden, and went to great lengths to keep the ranks of dark-needled pinetrees from encroaching on their fields. All that and more he knew.

But to what end? He'd received the finest education in the land, and then some, and yet his life was now one of rough travel, where sharpness of hearing and quickness of hand meant more than any scholarly learning. Besides, understanding what *was* and what one should *do* were two very different things. He had seen that with Galbatorix. The king had known more than most— more even than some of the oldest elves or dragons—but in the end, his knowledge had brought with it no wisdom.

Few people were out on the streets. It was late, and the days following Maddentide were full of feasting, and most of the citizens were inside, celebrating another successful harvest of bergenhed.

A trio of laborers staggered past, stinking of cheap beer and fish guts. Murtagh held his course, and they diverted around him. Once they turned a corner, the main thoroughfare again fell silent, and he didn't see another person until he crossed the city's market square and a pair of feathered merchants burst out of a warehouse door, arguing vociferously. A short, bearded figure followed them into the square, and his voice bellowed loudest of all.

A *dwarf!* Murtagh ducked his head. Ever since the death of Galbatorix and the fall of the Empire over a year ago, dwarves had become increasingly common throughout human-settled lands. Most were traders selling stones and metals and weapons, but he'd also seen dwarves working as armed guards (short as they were, their prowess in battle was not to be underestimated). Murtagh couldn't help but wonder how many of them were acting as eyes and ears for their king, Orik, who sat upon the marble throne in the city-mountain of Tronjheim.

The backlit dwarf seemed to look his way, and Murtagh reeled slightly—another Maddentide drunk on his way home.

The ruse worked, and the dwarf returned his attention to the squabbling merchants.

Murtagh hurried on. The spread of the dwarves had made travel even more difficult for him and Thorn. Murtagh had nothing against the dwarves as a race or culture—indeed, he quite liked Orik, and their feats of architecture were astonishing. However, they held a deep and abiding hatred of him for killing King Hrothgar, Orik's predecessor . . . and uncle. And dwarves were known for the tenacity with which they held their grudges.

Could he ever make amends to Orik, his clan, and the dwarves as a whole? Were it possible, Murtagh had yet to think of the means.

Unfortunately, his situation with the dwarves wasn't unique. The elves maintained a similar animosity toward him and Thorn, on account of the role they had played in killing Oromis and Glaedr, the last surviving Rider and dragon from before Galbatorix's rise to power.

Murtagh could hardly blame them.

The average human was no fonder of them, as it was widely believed they had betrayed the Varden to Galbatorix during the war. Traitors earned only contempt from both sides in a conflict, and rightly so—Murtagh himself had no sympathy for snake-tongued oathbreakers like his father—but that did not make it easy to be falsely branded as one.

No safe harbor for us, thought Murtagh. A hard, humorless smile formed on his lips. So it had been his whole life. Why should it be any different now?

The stench of fish, seaweed, and salt grew stronger as he moved along the wharves and past rows of drying racks set beside the street.

He glanced up. Midnight was still three or four hours away. Plenty of time to conclude his business and depart Ceunon. After so long spent out of doors, in the wild reaches of the land, the closeness of the buildings felt uncomfortably constraining. In that, he was becoming more and more like Thorn.

Music and voices sounded ahead of him, and he saw the common house that was his destination: the Fulsome Feast. The low, dark-beamed building had crystal windows set in its front-facing wall—a rare luxury in this part of the world—and petals of yellow light spread across the paving stones on the street: a welcome invitation to enter, rest, and make merry.

Sarros had picked the place as the location of their next meeting, and that alone made Murtagh wary. Still, the Fulsome Feast seemed innocuous enough—just one more disheveled, hard-run establishment like so many others. Aside from the crystal windows, the common house could have been in any seaside town or village throughout the land. But then, Murtagh had learned long ago that appearances were rarely to be trusted.

He steeled himself against the noise to follow and pushed open the door.

CHAPTER II

+ + + + + + +

The Fulsome Feast

The inn was a warm, homey place, neat and well tended. Fresh-cut rushes covered the floor, the tables were clean, and the casks, bottles, and mugs behind the polished bar were arranged in mannered rows. A crackling fire warmed the great room from behind a blackstone hearth free of soot, and by the fire, a goateed man with extravagant, double-belled sleeves was plucking at a lute.

Whatever he sang was hard to hear over the clamor of conversation rising from the packed room. Maddentide was over, and the folk of Ceunon were happy of it.

The innkeep was a short, balding man with a dirty apron and a sweaty forehead who bustled from table to table, delivering drinks and plates of smoked herring. Not, Murtagh noted, smoked bergenhed.

They must have eaten enough of it to last the year, he thought.

He shook a scattering of snow from his cape and moved toward the one open table by the fire. As he sat, the innkeep hurried over and said, "Sigling Orefsson at yer service, Master . . ."

"Tornac son of Tereth."

Sigling wiped his hands on his apron. "Honored, t' be sure. An' what might I get fer you?"

"Something hot from your kitchen. My stomach is stuck to my spine." Murtagh wasn't about to miss an opportunity for a hot meal, not when *he* didn't have to cook it for once.

"An' fer drink?"

"A mug of ale. Not too strong, if you please." And Murtagh pressed three copper coins into the innkeep's hand.

Sigling was already moving toward the back room. "Won't take more 'n two shakes of a lamb's tail, Master Tornac."

Master Tornac. Hearing the name said back to him always gave Murtagh pause. He hoped his old fencing instructor wouldn't have minded him using it, given how tarnished Murtagh's reputation was at the moment. He only meant to honor Tornac's memory, same as when he'd given the name to his stallion after Tornac died during their escape from Urû'baen. . . .

Annoyance caused Murtagh's brows to narrow. He never *had* found out what happened to the horse when Galbatorix had arranged for him to be ambushed and kidnapped in Tronjheim.

He looked around the room. The dockworkers, fishers, and other inhabitants of Ceunon were a boisterous lot. Many an absent father returned from weeks at ship and sea to celebrate the Maddentide bounty. They seemed friendly enough. Still, Murtagh made sure he'd worked out the shortest path to the front and back entrances.

It never hurt to be prepared.

Sarros was nowhere to be seen, but Murtagh wasn't concerned. The trader was the one who had decided on the day of their meeting, and Murtagh knew Sarros would sooner cut off his own hand as miss a chance to earn more of Murtagh's coin.

A pair of laborers—masons, if their leather aprons and thick, mortar-smeared arms were anything to go by—bumped into the chairs on the other side of Murtagh's table. They pulled the chairs out, and he said, "Sorry, but I'm expecting a friend." And he smiled in what he hoped was an inoffensive way.

One mason looked like he wanted to argue, while the other seemed to see something he didn't like in Murtagh's face. He tugged on his friend's arm. "Comeon, Herk. Lemme get you a beer a' the bar."

"Ah, fine. Aight. Hands off." But his friend kept tugging on his arm until the other man followed him toward the bar.

Murtagh relaxed slightly. He really didn't want to get caught in a meaningless brawl.

Then a name leaped out at him from the general hubbub of the common room: "—*Eragon*—"

Murtagh stiffened and twisted in his seat as he searched for the source of the word. There. The goateed troubadour plucking on his lute. At first the words of his song were hard to make out, but Murtagh watched the man's lips and concentrated, and by and by, he made sense of them.

And the troubadour sang:

—and so to dread Urû'baen.
Rejoice! Rejoice! The dauntless Dragon Rider flew to fight,
To free our land from danger and fright.
Then mighty Eragon faced the king in bloody conquest,
In a great and terrible contest.
And with flaming blade and blinding light,
He slew that horrid tyrant, that ageless blight,
Galbatorix, bane of dragons and Riders alike.

Murtagh's lip curled, and he felt an urge to throw a boot at the man. Not only were the verses badly composed and badly sung—no bard would have dared sing so off-key at court for fear of being beaten—but they were *wrong*.

"He would have lost if not for me," Murtagh muttered, thinking of Eragon. And yet, aside from those who had been present in Galbatorix's throne room at the end, no one knew and no one cared. He and Thorn had quit the capital following the king's death, preferring to remove themselves from civilization rather than contend with the hostility of an ignorant public.

It had been the right choice. Murtagh still believed that. But it meant they lost the opportunity to defend themselves in the court of popular opinion. And if Eragon or Nasuada or the elves' queen, Arya, had spoken in defense of him or Thorn, to explain the role they had played in killing Galbatorix and Shruikan, word of it had yet to reach Murtagh. The fact sat badly with him. Perhaps the truth needed more time to spread among the common folk. Or perhaps Eragon, Nasuada, and Arya were content to let the world think the worst of him, to use him as a convenient scapegoat, a monster in the dark that might focus people's fears and leave the three of them free to govern as they pleased.

The thought made his stomach twist.

Either way, as far as most folk were concerned, Eragon was the greatest hero who had ever lived, and none could stand before him.

Murtagh snorted softly. *Hardly*. But there was no fighting a song or story once it became popular. So often the truth bent to what felt right. At least the troubadour hadn't bothered to describe Eragon's supposed triumph over Murtagh and Thorn. At that, Murtagh really did think he would have thrown his boot.

"An' there you go, Master Tornac!" proclaimed Sigling as he slid a plate and mug under his nose. "You need aught else, you shout my name, an' I'll be back right quick-like."

Before Murtagh could thank him, the innkeep rushed off to tend another table.

Murtagh picked up the wrought-iron fork on the side of the plate and started eating. Roast mutton and turnips with half a loaf of black rye bread on the side. Humble fare, but it tasted better than anything he'd cooked in the past three months. And though, as he'd requested, the ale was hardly stronger than water, that was all right too. He wanted his wits about him in Ceunon.

While he ate, he balanced the plate on his knee and leaned back in the chair, stretching out his legs as he would before a campfire.

It felt strange to be around so many other people. He'd gotten used to being alone with Thorn over the past twelvemonth. To the sound of the wind and the calls of the birds. To hunting his food and being hunted. Talking to the watchmen and Sigling—and even the masons—had been like trying to play a badly tuned instrument.

He sopped up the juice from the mutton with a piece of rye bread and popped it in his mouth.

The door to the inn swung open, and a young girl rushed in. Her dark hair was done up nicely in a pair of curled plaits, her dress was embroidered with bright patterns, and she looked as if she'd been crying.

Murtagh watched as the girl moved across the great room, light as feather down. She slipped around the end of the bar, and Sigling said something to her. Standing one next to the other, Murtagh saw a family resemblance. The girl had the innkeep's mouth and chin.

The girl reappeared around the end of the bar, carrying a plate loaded with bread, cheese, and an apple. She lifted the plate over her head and, with practiced skill, wove between the crowded tables until she arrived in front of the great stone fireplace. Without asking, she plopped herself into the chair across the table from Murtagh.

He opened his mouth and then closed it.

The girl was no older than ten and perhaps as young as six (he had never been good at judging children's ages).

She tore a piece off the heel of bread on her plate and chewed with determined ferocity. Murtagh watched, curious. It had been years since he'd been around a child, and he found himself unexpectedly fascinated. *We all start like this*, he thought. So young, so pure. Where did it all go wrong?

The girl looked as if she were about to cry again. She bit into the apple and made a noise of frustration as the stem caught in the gap between her front teeth.

"You seem upset," Murtagh said in a mild tone.

The girl scowled. She plucked out the stem and flung it into the fire. "It's all Hjordis's fault!" She had the same strong northern accent as her father.

Murtagh glanced around. He still didn't see Sarros, so he decided it was safe to talk a bit. But carefully. Words could be as treacherous as a bear trap.

"Oh?" He put down his fork and turned in his seat to better look at her. "And who is this Hjordis?"

"She's the daughter of Jarek. He's the earl's chief mason," said the girl, sullen.

Murtagh wondered if the earl was still Lord Tarrant, or if the elves had installed someone else in his place when they captured the city. He'd met Tarrant at court years ago: a tall, self-contained man who rarely spoke more than a few words at a time. The earl had seemed decent enough, but anyone who stayed in Galbatorix's good graces for years on end had ice in their heart and blood on their hands.

"I see. Does that make her important?"

The girl shook her head. "It makes her *think* she's important."

"What did she do to upset you, then?"

"Everything!" The girl took a savage bite out of the apple and chewed hard and quick. Murtagh saw her wince as she bit the inside of her cheek. A film of tears filled her eyes, and she swallowed.

Murtagh sipped of the ale. "Most interesting." He dabbed a fleck of foam off his mustache. "Well then, is it a tale you feel like telling? Perhaps talking about it will make you feel better."

The girl looked at him, suspicion in her pale blue eyes. For a moment, Murtagh thought she was going to get up and leave. Then: "Papa wouldn't want me t' bother you."

"I have some time. I'm just waiting for a certain associate of mine who, alas, happens to be habitually late. If you wish to share your tale of woe, then please, consider me your devoted audience."

As he spoke, Murtagh found himself reverting to the language and phrasing he would have used at court. The formality of it felt safer, and besides, it amused him to talk to the girl as if she were a noble lady.

She bounced her feet off the legs of the chair. "Well . . . I'd like t' tell you, but I can't possibly 'less we're friends."

"Is that so? And how do we become friends?"

"You have t' tell me your name! Silly!"

Murtagh smiled. "Of course. How foolish of me. In that case, my name is Tornac." And he held out his hand.

"Essie Siglingsdaughter."

Her palm and fingers were startlingly smooth and small against his own as they shook. Murtagh felt the need to be gentle, as if he were touching a delicate flower.

"Very nice to meet you, Essie. Now then, what seems to be bothering you?"

Essie stared at the partially eaten apple in her hand. She sighed and put it back on the plate. "It's all Hjordis's fault."

"So you said."

"She's always being mean t' me an' making her friends tease me."

Murtagh assumed a solemn expression. "That's not good at all."

The girl shook her head, eyes bright with outrage. "No! I mean . . . sometimes they tease me anyway, but, um, Hjordis— When she's there, it gets really bad."

"Is that what happened today?"

"Yes. Sort of." She broke off a piece of cheese and nibbled on it, seeming lost in thought. Murtagh waited patiently. He decided that, as with horses, gentleness would go a lot further than force.

Finally, in a low voice, Essie said, " 'Fore harvest, Hjordis started bein' nicer to me. I thought—I thought maybe things were going t' be better. She even invited me t' her house." Essie gave him a shy, sideways glance. "It's right by the castle."

"Impressive." He was starting to understand. The richer tradesmen always cozied up to the nobles, like ticks to dogs. Envy was a universal human trait (and the other races weren't exempt from it either).

Essie nodded. "She gave me one of her ribbons, a yellow one, an' said that I could come t' her Maddentide party."

"And did you?"

Another bob of her head. "It—it was today." Tears filled her eyes, and she blinked furiously.

Concerned, Murtagh produced a worn kerchief from inside his vest. He might be living like a beast in the wilderness, but he still had *some* standards. "Here now."

The girl hesitated. But then the tears spilled down her cheeks, and she grabbed the kerchief and wiped her eyes. "Thank you, mister."

Murtagh allowed himself another small smile. "It's been a long time since I've been called *mister*, but you're very welcome. I take it the party didn't go well?"

Essie scowled and pushed the kerchief back toward him, though she still seemed to be on the verge of crying. "The party was fine. It was Hjordis. She got mean again, after, and . . . and"—she took a deep breath, as if searching for the courage to continue—"an' she said that if I din't do what she wanted, she would tell her father not t' use our inn during the solstice celebration." She peered at Murtagh, as if to check whether he was following. "All the masons come here t' drink an'—" she hiccupped, "they drink a lot, an' it means they spend stacks an' stacks of coppers."

Her story filled Murtagh with a host of uncomfortable memories of the mistreatment he'd suffered at the hands of the older children while growing up in Galbatorix's court. Before he'd learned to be careful, before Tornac had taught him how to protect himself.

Serious, he put his plate on the table and leaned toward Essie. "What did she want you to do?"

Essie dropped her gaze and bounced her muddy shoes against the chair. When she spoke again, the words came tripping out in a crowded rush: "She wanted me t' push Carth into a horse trough."

"Carth is a friend of yours?"

She nodded, miserable. "He lives on the docks. His father is a fisher."

Murtagh felt a sudden and intense dislike for Hjordis. He'd known plenty like her at court: horrible, petty people bent on improving their position and making life miserable for everyone beneath them.

"So he wouldn't get invited to a party like this."

"No, but Hjordis sent her handmaid t' bring him t' the house an' . . ." Essie stared at him, her expression fierce. "I din't have no choice! If I hadn't pushed him, then she would have told her father not t' come t' the Fulsome Feast."

"I understand," Murtagh said, forcing a soothing tone despite a rising sense of anger and injustice. It was a familiar aggravation. "So you pushed your friend. Were you able to apologize to him?"

"No," said Essie, and her face crumpled. "I—I ran. But everyone saw. He won't want t' be friends with me anymore. No one will. Hjordis just meant t' trick me, an' I *hate* her." She grabbed the apple and took another quick bite. Her teeth clacked together.

Murtagh started to respond, but Sigling came by on his way to deliver a pair of mugs to a table along the wall. He gave Essie a disapproving look. "My daughter isn't mak'n a nuisance of herself, is she, Master Tornac? She has a bad habit of pester'n guests when they're try'n t' eat."

"Not at all," said Murtagh, smiling. "I've been on the road for far too long, with nothing but the sun and the moon for company. A bit of conversation is exactly what I need. In fact—" He reached into the pouch under his belt and passed two silver pieces to the innkeep. "Perhaps you can see to it that the tables next to us remain clear. I'm expecting an associate of mine, and we have some, ah, business to discuss."

The coins disappeared into Sigling's apron, and he bobbed his head. "Of course, Master Tornac." He glanced at Essie again, his expression concerned, and then continued on his way.

For her part, the girl seemed somewhat abashed.

"Now then," said Murtagh, stretching his legs out toward the fire. "You were telling me your tale of woe, Essie Siglingsdaughter. Was that the full accounting?"

"That was it," she said in a small voice.

He picked up the fork from his plate and began to twirl it between his fingers. The girl watched, entranced. "Things can't be as bad as you think. I'm sure if you explain to your friend—"

"No," she said, firm. "He won't understand. He won't trust me again. They'll hate me fer it."

A cutting edge formed in Murtagh's voice. "Then maybe they aren't really your friends."

She shook her head, braids swinging. "They are! You don't understand!" And she brought her fist down on the arm of the chair in an impatient little gesture. "Carth is . . . He's really nice. Everyone likes him, an' now they won't like me. You wouldn't know. You're all big an' . . . an' old."

Murtagh raised his eyebrows. "You might be surprised what I know. So they won't like you. What are you going to do about it?"

"I'm going to run away," blurted the girl. The moment she realized what she'd said, she gave him a panicked look. "Don't tell Papa, please!"

Murtagh took another sip of ale and smoothed his beard while his mind raced. The conversation had gone from amusing to deadly serious. If he said the wrong thing, he could send Essie careening down a path she would regret—and he knew *he* would regret it if he didn't try to talk her back onto the straight and narrow.

Careful now, he thought. "And where would you go?"

"South," said Essie firmly. She'd obviously already considered the question. "Where it's warm. There's a caravan leaving tomorrow. The foreman comes here. He's nice. I can sneak out, an' then ride with 'em to Gil'ead."

Murtagh picked at the tines of his fork. "And then?"

The girl sat up straighter. "I want t' visit the Beor Mountains an' see the dwarves! They made our windows. Aren't they pretty?" She pointed.

"They certainly are."

"Have you ever visited the Beor Mountains?"

"I have," said Murtagh. "Once, long ago."

Essie looked at him with renewed interest. "Really? Are they as tall as everyone says?"

"So tall the peaks aren't even visible."

She leaned back in the chair, tilting her head toward the ceiling as if imagining the sight. "How wonderful."

A snort escaped him. "If you don't count being shot at with arrows, then yes. . . . You do realize, Essie Siglingsdaughter, that running away won't solve your problems here."

"Of course not." *Silly*, her expression said. "But if I leave, then Hjordis can't bother me anymore."

The utter conviction of her tone nearly made Murtagh laugh. He hid his amusement by taking a long drink from his mug, and by the time he finished, he'd regained his composure. "Or, and this is just a suggestion, you could try to fix the problem instead of running away."

"It can't be fixed," she said, stubborn.

"What about your parents? I'm sure they would miss you terribly. Do you really want to make them suffer like that?"

Essie crossed her arms. "They have my brother and my sister and Olfa. He's only two." She pouted. "They wouldn't miss me."

"I very much doubt that," said Murtagh. "Besides, think what you did with Hjordis. You helped protect the Fulsome Feast. If your parents understood the sacrifice you made, I'm sure they would be very proud."

"Uh-huh," said Essie. She didn't seem convinced. "There wouldn't have been a problem if it wasn't fer me. I'm the problem. If I go away, everything will be aight." And she picked up the apple core and threw it into the fireplace.

A whirl of sparks flew up the chimney, and the sizzle of water boiling into steam sounded above the crackling of the logs.

The girl's sleeve had ridden up, and on her left wrist, Murtagh saw a twisted scar, red and raised and thick as a rope. His lips pulled back from his teeth, and in an overly casual tone, he said, "What is that?"

"What?" she said.

"There, on your arm."

Essie looked down, and a flush darkened her cheeks and ears. "Nothing," she mumbled, tugging the cuff down.

"May I?" Murtagh asked as kindly as he could, and held out a hand.

The girl hesitated, but at last she nodded, timid, and let him take her arm.

She turned her head away as he gently pulled back the cuff of her sleeve. The scar crawled up her forearm all the way to her elbow, a long, angry testament to pain. The sight of it put cold fire in Murtagh's veins, and he felt a sympathetic pang from his own furious mark, on his back.

He lowered Essie's sleeve. "That . . . is a very impressive scar. You should be proud of it."

She looked back at him, confusion lurking in her eyes. "Why? It's ugly, an' I hate it."

A faint smile lifted his lips. "Because a scar means you survived. It means you're tough and hard to kill. It means you *lived*. A scar is something to admire."

"You're wrong," said Essie. She pointed at a pot with painted bluebells on the mantel. A long crack ran from the lip of the pot to the base. "It just means you're broken."

"Ah," said Murtagh in a soft voice. "But sometimes, if you work very hard, you can mend a break so that it's stronger than before."

The girl crossed her arms, tucking her left hand into her armpit. "Hjordis an' the others always make fun of me fer it," she mumbled. "They say my arm is as red as a snapper, an' that I'll never get a husband because of it."

"And what do your parents say?"

Essie made a face. "That it din't matter. But that's not true, is it?"

Murtagh inclined his head. "No. I suppose it isn't. Your parents are doing their best to protect you, though."

"Well, they can't," she said, and huffed.

No, they probably can't, he thought, his mood darkening even further.

She glanced at him and seemed to shrink in her seat. "Do you have any scars?" she asked, soft, uncertain.

A humorless laugh escaped him. "Oh yes." He pointed at the small white mark on his chin, a gap in his otherwise full beard. "This one is only a few months old. A friend of mine gave it to me by accident while we were playing around, the big oaf." The tip of a scale on Thorn's left foreleg had caught Murtagh's chin, tearing the skin. It hadn't been a serious injury, but it had hurt badly and bled worse. Then he said, "What happened to your arm?"

Essie picked at the edge of the table. "It was an accident," she mumbled. "A pot with hot water fell on my arm."

Murtagh's eyes narrowed. "It just *fell* on you?"

The girl nodded.

"Mmm." Murtagh stared into the fire, at the jumping sparks and throbbing embers. He didn't believe the girl. Accidents were common enough, but the way she was acting hinted at something worse.

His jaw flexed, teeth clenched. A warning throb sank down the root of his bottom right molar. There were many injustices he was willing to tolerate, but a mother or father hurting their child wasn't one of them.

He glanced toward the bar. Maybe he needed to have a talk with Sigling, to put the fear of a Dragon Rider in the man.

Essie shifted. "Where are you from?"

"A long, long way from here."

"In the south?"

"Yes, in the south."

She kicked her feet against the chair again. "What's it like there?"

Murtagh inhaled slowly and tilted his head back so he was looking at the ceiling. The fire in his blood still burned. "It depends where you go. There are hot places and cold places, and places where the wind never stops blowing. Forests seemingly without end. Caves that burrow into the deepest parts of the earth, and plains full of vast herds of red deer."

"Are there monsters?"

"Of course." He returned his gaze to her. "There are always monsters. Some of them even look like humans. . . . I ran away from home myself, you know."

"You did?"

He nodded. "I was older than you, but yes. I ran, but I didn't escape what I was running from. . . . Listen to me, Essie. I know you think leaving will make everything better, but—"

"There you are, Tornac of the Road," said a sly, slithering voice that Murtagh recognized at once. *Sarros.*

The trader stepped forward from between the nearby tables. He was thin and stooped, with a patched cloak draped over his shoulders and ragged clothes underneath. Rings glittered on his fingers. He smelled of wet fur, and there was an unsettling, catlike slink to his steps.

Murtagh suppressed a curse. Of all the times for the man to show up . . . "Sarros. I've been waiting for you."

"The reaches are dangerous these days," said Sarros. He pulled out the empty chair from the table, shifted it until it was exactly between Essie and Murtagh, and sat facing them both.

The girl edged away in her seat, wary.

Murtagh glanced around the room. He spotted six men who

had entered the inn while he wasn't paying attention. They were rough-looking fellows, but not like the local fishermen; they wore furs and leathers and had cloaks wrapped about them in a way that told Murtagh they were concealing swords strapped to their belts.

Sarros's guards. Murtagh was annoyed that he had lost track of his surroundings while talking with Essie. He knew better than that. A lapse in focus was a good way to end up dead or in prison.

By the bar, Sigling kept close watch on the newcomers. The innkeep pulled out a leather-wrapped truncheon and laid it next to his washcloth as a silent warning.

Despite Murtagh's reservations as to Sigling's character, he approved of his caution. The man was no fool, that was for sure.

His attention returned to Sarros as the trader pointed one long finger at Essie. "We have business to discuss. Send the youngling away."

No, I don't think so, decided Murtagh. He hadn't finished talking with the girl, and in any case, keeping her around might have a civilizing influence on Sarros. The man was uncultured at best and downright offensive at worst.

"I have nothing to hide," Murtagh said. "She can stay." He glanced at her. "If you're interested. You might learn something useful of the world by it."

Essie shrank back in her chair, but she didn't leave.

A long hiss sounded between Sarros's teeth as he shook his head. "Foolish, Wanderer. Do as you wish, then. I'll not argue, even if you put your foot crosswise."

Murtagh let his gaze harden. "No, you won't. Tell me, then, what have you found? It's been three months, and—"

Sarros waved a hand. "Yes, yes. Three months. I told you; the reaches are dangerous. But I found word of what you seek. Better than word, I found *this*—" From the leather wallet on his belt, he produced a fist-sized chunk of black *something* that he thumped down on the table.

Murtagh leaned forward, as did Essie.

The something was a piece of rock, but there was a deep shine to it, as if a smoldering coal were buried in the center. A strong, sulfurous smell clung to the rock, as pungent as a rotting egg.

Essie sniffed and wrinkled her nose.

A coil of tension formed in Murtagh's chest. He'd hoped he was wrong. He'd hoped the whispers and warnings had meant nothing. . . . *Beware the deeps, and tread not where the ground grows black and brittle and the air smells of brimstone, for in those places evil lurks.* So the ancient dragon Umaroth had said to him ere he and Thorn had left on their self-imposed exile.

Murtagh had prayed that Umaroth was mistaken, that there wasn't some new danger rising in the unsettled regions of the land.

He should have known better than to question the wisdom of a dragon as old as Umaroth.

Without taking his gaze off the rock, he said, "What exactly is that?"

Sarros lifted his shoulders. "Suspicions of shadows are all I have, but you sought the unusual, the out-of-place, and that there doesn't fit in the normal frame."

"Were there more, or . . ."

Sarros nodded. "I am told. A whole field scattered with stones."

The coil tightened in Murtagh's chest. "Black and burnt?"

"As if seared by fire, but with no sign of flame or smoke."

Essie said, "Where is it from?"

Sarros smiled, and the girl shied back. As with so many of the horse folk from the central plains of Alagaësia, Sarros's teeth were filed to points.

For Murtagh, the sight was an unpleasant reminder of another, even less pleasant man with similar teeth. *Durza.*

"Well now," said Sarros, "that there is the nub of it, youngling. Yes indeed." Murtagh reached for the rock, and Sarros dropped a hand over the shiny chunk, caging it behind his fingers. "No," he said. "Coin first, Wanderer."

Displeased, Murtagh fished out a small leather pouch from the inner pocket of his cloak. The pouch clinked as he put it on the table.

Sarros's jagged smile widened. He tugged loose the pouch's drawstring to reveal a gleam of gold coins inside. Essie sucked in a sharp breath. Murtagh doubted she'd ever seen a whole crown before.

"Half now," said Murtagh. "And the rest when you tell me where you found that." He poked the rock with the tip of a finger.

A strange choking sound came from Sarros. Laughter. Then he said, "Oh no, Wanderer. No indeed. I think instead you should give us the rest of your coin, and perhaps then we'll let you keep your head."

Across the common room, the fur-clad men slipped hands under their cloaks, and Murtagh saw the hilts of swords, half hidden beneath.

He wasn't surprised, but he *was* disappointed. Was Sarros really breaking their deal for nothing more than greed?

How common.

Essie spotted the swords, and her eyes widened. *Blast.* Before Murtagh could intervene, she leaned forward and was about to say or do something loud when Sarros drew a thin-bladed knife and pressed it against her throat.

"Ah-ah," he said. "Not a peep from you, youngling, or I'll open your throat from stem to stern."

CHAPTER III

✦ ✦ ✦ ✦ ✦ ✦

Fork and Blade

The loaded spring in Murtagh's chest felt fit to burst. At that moment, he ceased to think of Sarros as a person. Rather, the man became a *thing*, a *problem* to be solved, quickly and without hesitation.

Essie froze at the touch of the trader's knife. It was the smartest action she could have taken.

A spike of distant concern reached Murtagh as Thorn prepared to fly to his aid. Murtagh responded with a fierce *No! Don't!* The last thing he needed was for the dragon to come barging into Ceunon.

Doing his best to keep his emotions hidden, Murtagh said, "Why the turn of face, Sarros? I'm paying you good money."

"Yesss. That's the point." Sarros leaned in closer, lips pulled wide. His breath stank of rotting meat. "If you are willing to pay thiswise-much for hints and rumors, then you must have more coin than sense. *Much* more coin."

Stupid, Murtagh thought. He should have realized that spreading around so much gold might cause a problem. It wasn't a mistake he would make again.

The truth was, he'd already spent nearly all of the coin he'd brought with him when he and Thorn fled into the wilderness. He'd been greedy for information, and now that gluttonous desire was costing him more than money.

He muttered a single, harsh curse and then said, "This isn't a fight you want. Tell me the location, take the gold you're owed, and no one has to get hurt."

"What fight?" Sarros cackled. "You have no sword on you. We are seven, and you are one. The coin is ours whether you wish it or not." The steel bit a tiny amount into Essie's neck, and she tensed. "See? I make the choice easy for you, Wanderer. Hand over the rest of your gold, or the youngling here will pay with blood."

The girl kept her eyes fixed on Murtagh. He could feel her desperate fear, and he knew she was waiting—hoping—for him to help her. She seemed so terribly young, so terribly vulnerable, and an overpowering affinity welled up within him.

Resolve girded him.

He smiled faintly. Had he really expected to visit Ceunon without getting wound up in some form of trouble? *Oh well.* So it was.

Then Murtagh gathered his mental reserves, focused his will, and poured his fierce intent into a single line of words drawn from the ancient language—the language of truth and power and magic.

"Thrífa sem knífr un huildr sem konr."

The air between them seemed to shiver. That and nothing more.

Murtagh blinked, caught by surprise. The spell had failed. The trader had wards protecting him? And strong ones too, for the strength of the spell would have cut through any lesser charm. It was an unexpected and entirely unwelcome development.

Sarros chuckled again. "Foolish. Very foolish." With his free hand, he pulled a bird-skull amulet from under his jerkin. "Do you see this, Wanderer? The witch-woman Bachel charmed a necklace for each of us. Your weirding ways won't help you now. We're protected against all evilness."

"Is that so?" said Murtagh, deadly quiet. The trader had just gone from a nuisance to a genuine danger. Moderation was no longer a desirable option. Not if one wanted to win, and Murtagh had long since decided that he was willing to go to the furthest extremes in order to avoid—again—losing.

Then he spoke the Word, and such a word it was. It rang like a bell, and in the sound were contained all possible meanings, for it was the most powerful word of all: the name of the ancient language. The Name of Names. The most secret of all spells, known only to him, Eragon, and Arya. With it he could break or alter any spell. With it he could change the very meaning of the language itself.

In the Name of Names, he imbued three intents: a desire to remove Sarros's wards, a wish to seize and hold the man's knife, and, last of all, a command to prohibit the people who heard the Word from remembering it.

A dull silence followed. Everyone in the common room looked at him, many of the guests with a dazed expression, as if they'd just woken from a dream.

Essie stared wide-eyed, fear seemingly forgotten.

To Murtagh's astonishment, Sarros appeared entirely unaffected. Concern chilled his core. The only way to defy the Name of Names was with wordless magic—magic cast without the guiding safety of the ancient language. It was the riskiest and wildest form of spellcasting. Even the most skilled of enchanters would shy from attempting it.

Murtagh had underestimated Sarros and whomever the man had dealings with. The situation had become dangerously unpredictable. And Murtagh didn't like unpredictable.

"Essie!" cried Sigling, finally noticing her plight. He grabbed his truncheon and sprang over the bar with more alacrity than Murtagh would have given the balding innkeep credit for. "You let her go now!"

Before Sigling could take more than a step, two of the fur-clad ruffians charged and knocked him to the floor. A *thunk* sounded as one of them struck Sigling on the head with the pommel of a sword.

He moaned and dropped the truncheon.

No one else dared move.

That's enough of that, thought Murtagh.

"Papa!" Essie cried, and she squirmed beneath Sarros's knife.

The trader chuckled again, louder than before. "Your tricks will not help you, Wanderer. No enchantments are as strong as Bachel's. No magic is as deep."

"Perhaps you're right." Murtagh's voice was calm as a windless pond. He picked up the fork and turned it between his fingers. "Well then. It appears I have no choice in the matter."

"None whatsoever," said Sarros, smug.

A stout, red-cheeked woman with her hair tied in a bun appeared in the doorway to the kitchen, wiping her hands on her skirt. "What is all this—" she started to say, and then saw Sarros holding the knife and Sigling lying on the floor, and her face went pale.

"Don't cause no trouble, or your man gets stuck," said one of the fur-clad men, pointing his blade at Sigling.

While everyone was distracted by Sigling's wife, Murtagh spoke without voice, and he said, "Halfa utan thornessa fra jierda." A glassy, flame-like ripple ran the length of the fork.

Essie's eyes widened, but she didn't otherwise react.

Sarros slapped the table. "Enough with the yapping. Your coin, now."

Murtagh tipped his head and, with his left hand, again reached under his cloak. He kept himself relaxed until the last possible instant.

In a single motion, he swept the cloak through the air while striking with the fork. He caught Sarros's knife between the tines and used the fork to toss the knife across the room.

Ting! The knife bounced against the wall.

Sarros blinked and froze as Murtagh pressed the points of the fork against the fleshy underside of the man's chin. The shark-toothed man swallowed, and a sheen of sweat broke out on his face, but his hand remained next to the girl's neck, fingers spread wide as if to tear out her throat.

"Then again," said Murtagh, savoring the reversal, "there's nothing in your charm to stop me from using magic on something else. Like this fork, for example." He pressed the tines deeper into Sarros's flesh. "Do you really think I need a sword to defeat you, you tumorous sack of filth?"

Sarros hissed. Then he shoved Essie into Murtagh's lap and sprang backward, knocking his chair over.

Murtagh jumped to his feet, and Essie fell to the floor. She scrambled away on all fours beneath the tables.

The six fur-clad men drew their blades, and the great room became a sea of thrashing bodies as the fishermen, laborers, and other guests rushed to escape through the front door. The lute player stumbled and fell, and there were shouts and crashes and breaking mugs.

Murtagh threw off his cloak so he could move freely. He risked a glance at the floor, looking for Sarros's knife. It was nowhere to be seen. A snarl curled his lips. He wished he had Zar'roc or even a camp knife to defend himself. But no, he'd been too confident, too clever. All he had was the fork.

The cutthroats tried to box him in by the fireplace, but he was having none of that. He slipped between the tables, circling to get a good angle.

Sarros had retreated to a corner and was shouting, "Slice him crosswise! Kill him! Cut open his belly and spill his guts."

I'll deal with you directly, Murtagh thought.

By the back of the great room, the girl reached her mother. The woman pulled Essie behind her skirts and grabbed a chair, which she held in front of them as a shield.

The nearest ruffian charged Murtagh, swinging his blade. *Clumsy fool.* Murtagh parried with the fork and then stepped inside the man's guard and buried the fork in the man's chest.

The tines punctured bone and muscle as well as Murtagh could have wanted. The man convulsed against him and collapsed with a wet, blood-choked gasp as his heart gave out.

A tidal surge of fearful rage emanated from Thorn, and Murtagh felt the dragon's sudden resolve to join him. STAY! he bellowed in his mind before armoring his thoughts against possible intrusion. Thorn held, but barely.

Three more of Sarros's hired swords moved in. All three jabbed and slashed with their blades, not waiting for the others to take their turn.

Murtagh grabbed a chair and, one-handed, smashed it over the man to his left. At the same time, he used the fork to deflect the attacks from the other two brutes. He matched each of their blows, fencing with effortless ease as they tried to break his guard. None of them were well trained; he could tell that much.

The men had the advantage of reach with their swords, but Murtagh sidestepped their blades and slipped into striking range. Faster than the eye could see, he stabbed with the fork: one, two, three, four hard impacts that dropped the men to the floor, where they lay silent or groaning.

His blood ran hot, and a slick of sweat coated his forehead, and crimson crept in around the edges of his vision. But his breathing remained measured. He was still in control, even as the thrill of violent triumph coursed through him.

Across the room, Sigling pulled himself up the bar into a standing position. He had regained the truncheon, not that Murtagh thought the leather-wrapped stick would do much good against the ruffians' swords.

The innkeep's wife said, "Essie, Olfa is in the kitchen. I want you to go—"

Before she could finish, one of Sarros's guards ran up to them. In his off hand, he held a mace, which he swung at the chair the woman held.

The impact knocked the chair out of her hands, breaking it.

The girl screamed as the fur-clad man drew back the sword in his other hand—

Murtagh knew he couldn't cross the great room in time to save them. So he gambled on fate's goodwill and threw the fork—

Thud.

The fork embedded itself in the back of the man's skull. He collapsed, boneless as a sack of flour.

Relief washed through Murtagh, but only for a second. Sarros and his last remaining companion attempted to flank him. Murtagh kicked a table into the swordsman's stomach and, when he stumbled, jumped on him and knocked his head against the floor.

Sarros cursed and fled toward the door. As he turned, he threw a handful of glittering crystals at Murtagh.

"Sving!" cried Murtagh.

The crystals swerved in midair and flew into the flames of the fire. A series of loud *pops!* sounded, and a fountain of crimson embers sprayed the stone hearth.

Before Sarros could reach the door, Murtagh overtook him. He grabbed the back of Sarros's jerkin and—with a grunt and heave—lifted Sarros off the floor and overhead and then slammed him back down onto the wooden boards.

Sarros's left elbow bent at an unnatural angle. The man bellowed with pain.

"Essie," said the innkeep's wife. "Stay behind me."

Murtagh planted a foot on Sarros's chest and, with a growl, said, "Now then, you bastard. Where did you find that stone?"

Sigling left the bar and staggered across the room to his wife and daughter. They didn't say anything, but his wife put an arm around him, and he did the same to her.

A burbling laugh escaped Sarros. There was a wild note to his voice that reminded Murtagh of Galbatorix's more demented moments. Sarros licked his sharpened teeth and said, "You do not know what you seek, Wanderer. You're moon-addled and nose-blind. The sleeper stirs, and you and me—we're all ants waiting to be crushed."

"The *stone*," said Murtagh from between clenched teeth. "Where?"

Sarros's voice grew even higher, a mad shriek that pierced the night air. "You don't understand. The Dreamers! The Dreamers! They get inside your head, and they twist your thoughts. Ahh! They twist them all out of joint." He started to thrash, drumming his heels against the floor. Yellow foam bubbled at the corners of his mouth. "They'll come for you, Wanderer, and then you'll see. They'll . . ." His voice trailed off into a hoarse croak, and, with one final jerk, he fell still.

Disquiet wormed in Murtagh's gut. The man shouldn't have died. Magic or poison was at work here, and neither explanation was particularly appealing. In fact, the whole situation left a bad taste in his mouth. He felt as if he'd been caught in an invisible snare, and he didn't know who—or what—had set it.

For a moment, no one in the great room stirred.

Murtagh could feel eyes on him as he yanked the bird-skull amulet off Sarros's neck, retrieved his cloak, and walked back to the table by the fire. He pocketed the stone with the inner shine, picked up his pouch of coins, and then paused, considering.

Bouncing the pouch in his hand, he went over to where Sigling and his wife stood shielding Essie. The girl looked terrified. Murtagh couldn't blame her.

"Please . . . ," said Sigling.

"My apologies for the trouble," said Murtagh. He could smell the stink of sweat on himself, and the front of his linen shirt was splattered with blood. "Here, this should make up for the mess." He held out the pouch, and after a moment's hesitation, Sigling accepted it.

The innkeep licked his lips. "The watch will be here any minute. If'n you leave out the back . . . you can make it t' the gate before they see you."

Murtagh nodded. *Thoughtful of him.*

Then he knelt and yanked the fork out of the head of the ruffian lying on the nearby boards. The girl shrank back as Murtagh looked at her. "Sometimes," he said, "you have to stand and fight. Sometimes running away isn't an option. Now do you understand?"

"Yes," Essie whispered.

Murtagh shifted his attention to her parents. "One last question: Do you need the patronage of the masons' guild to keep this inn open?"

Confusion furrowed Sigling's brow. "No, not if it came to such. Why?"

"That's what I thought," said Murtagh. Then he presented Essie with the fork. It looked perfectly clean, without so much as a drop of blood on it. "I'm giving this to you. It has a spell on it to keep it from breaking. If Hjordis bothers you again, give her a good poke, and she'll leave you alone."

"Essie," her mother said in a low, warning voice.

But Murtagh could see that the girl had already made her decision. She nodded in a firm manner and took the fork. "Thank you," she said, solemn.

"All good weapons deserve a name," said Murtagh. "Especially magical ones. What would you call this one?"

Essie thought for a second and then said, "Mister Stabby!"

Murtagh couldn't help it; a broad smile split his face, and he laughed, a loud, hearty laugh. "Mister Stabby. I like it. Very apt. May Mister Stabby always bring you good fortune."

And Essie smiled as well, if somewhat uncertainly.

Then the girl's mother said, "Who . . . who are you, really?"

"Just another person looking for answers," said Murtagh.

He was about to leave when, on a sudden impulse, he reached out and put a hand on the girl's arm. He spoke the words of a healing spell, and the girl stiffened as the magic took effect, reshaping the scarred tissue on her arm.

Cold crept into Murtagh's limbs, the spell extracting its price in energy, drawing off the strength of his body to make the change he willed.

"Leave her be!" said Sigling, and pulled Essie away, but the spell had already done its work, and Murtagh swept past them, cloak winged out behind him.

As he moved through the kitchen at the back of the inn, he heard Sigling and his wife utter sounds of astonishment, and then they and Essie started crying, but with joy, not grief.

Murtagh wasn't done. While Essie's parents were so distracted, he reached out with his mind and slipped unnoticed into their stream of thoughts. He was subtle, and no probing was needed. The very thing he sought was forefront in each consciousness: the moment, three years ago, when Essie had bumped into her father in the kitchen while he was carrying the dented iron stewpot with the crooked handle that had been full of water boiled for washing. Essie had been running about, not looking, not paying attention, and she had been where she wasn't expected. From Sigling now, guilt and relief intermixed. From his wife, relief and sorrow and a relaxation of close-held resentment over how her husband had caused, though unintentionally, the accident.

Murtagh withdrew. His fears had been unfounded, and for that, he was glad. Essie and her siblings were safe with their family. There was nothing more he needed to do here.

He felt tears in his own eyes. At least he'd been able to accomplish some good today. No child should have to grow up with a scar like Essie's . . . or his own. For an instant, he imagined smoothing his back with magic as he'd smoothed Essie's arm, but he shook off the thought. Some hurts went too deep to heal.

He was his father's son, and he could never pretend otherwise.

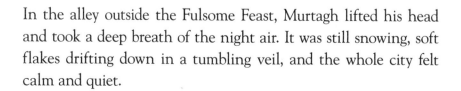

In the alley outside the Fulsome Feast, Murtagh lifted his head and took a deep breath of the night air. It was still snowing, soft flakes drifting down in a tumbling veil, and the whole city felt calm and quiet.

His pulse began to slow.

How long had it been since he'd last killed a man? Over a year. A pair of bandits had jumped him as he was returning to camp one evening—foolish, uneducated louts who hadn't the slightest chance of taking him down. He'd fought back out of reflex, and by the time he knew what was happening, the two unfortunates were already lying on the ground. He could still hear the whimpers the younger one had made as he died. . . .

Murtagh grimaced. Some people went their whole lives without killing. He wondered what that was like.

A drop of blood—not his own—trickled down the back of his hand. Disgusted, he scraped it off against the side of the building. The splinters bothered him less than the gore.

Even though he hadn't gotten a specific location from Sarros, at least he now knew that the place Umaroth had warned him of existed. He would have far preferred disappointment. Whatever truth lay hidden beneath the field of blackened earth, he doubted it would herald anything good. Life was never so simple.

A questioning thought reached him from outside Ceunon: Thorn fearful for his safety.

I'm fine, Murtagh told him. *Just a bit of trouble.*

Do I need to come?

I don't think so, but stand by in any case.

Always.

Thorn subsided with cautious watchfulness, but Murtagh still felt the thread of connection that joined them: a comforting closeness that had become the one unchanging reality in their lives.

He started down the alley. Time to go. The city watch would soon arrive to investigate the disturbance, and he'd lingered long enough.

A flicker of motion high above caught his attention.

At first Murtagh wasn't sure what he was seeing.

Sailing down from the underside of the firelit clouds was a

small ship of grass, no more than a hand or two in length. The hull and sail were made of woven blades, and the mast and spars built from lengths of stem.

No crew—however diminutive—was to be seen; the ship moved of its own accord, driven and sustained by an invisible force. It circled him twice, and he saw a tiny pennant fluttering above the equally tiny crow's nest.

Then the ship turned westward and vanished within the veil of descending snow, leaving behind no trace of its existence.

Murtagh smiled and shook his head. He didn't know who had made the ship or what it signified, but the fact that something so whimsical, so singular, could exist filled him with an unaccustomed joy.

He thought back to what he'd told the girl, Essie. Perhaps he should take his own advice. Perhaps it was time to stop running and return to old friends.

His smile faded. Wherever he'd gone in the year since Galbatorix's death, he had heard the poison in people's voices when they spoke his name. Few there were, aside from Nasuada, who would trust him after his actions in service to the king. It was a bitter, unfair truth—one that circumstances had long since forced him to accept.

Because of it, he had hidden his face, changed his name, and kept to the fringes of settled land, never walking where others might know him. And while the time alone had done both him and Thorn good, it was no way to live the rest of their lives.

So again he wondered. Had the time come to turn and face their past?

No. The thought arrived with decisive immediacy. He wasn't sure if the conviction was his own or Thorn's or a combination thereof. Even if they attempted to rejoin polite society, Murtagh couldn't imagine how they would ever be seen as anything more than murderers and traitors.

Besides . . . Murtagh looked down at the object he was holding: the bird-skull amulet he'd taken off Sarros's neck. A crow's skull, by the look of it.

Who was the witch-woman Bachel? Murtagh had never heard of her. Casting spells without words was a wild, dangerous thing, and rare was the magician brave, foolish, or talented enough to risk it. Even with the proper training, he wouldn't have dared do so in the Fulsome Feast, not with so many innocent bystanders nearby. And what of the Dreamers that Sarros had mentioned? Were they associates of Bachel? Always more mysteries.

No, before anything else, Murtagh wanted to know where the gleaming stone had come from, and he wanted to find the witch-woman Bachel and ask her a few questions.

The answers, he suspected, would be most interesting.

A brassy alarm bell sounded elsewhere in Ceunon, jarring him from his reverie. He tucked the amulet into his cloak and set off at a quick pace for the southern gates, determined to escape the city before the watch found him and he had to kill someone he would regret.

CHAPTER IV

✦ ✦ ✦ ✦ ✦ ✦

Conclave

Fugitives again, thought Murtagh as he ran through Ceunon's open gatehouse. It seemed like he and Thorn were always having to flee one place or another. *Unwanted. That's what we are.*

A horn rang out within the city, and he ducked his head, half expecting a flight of angry arrows to land about him. He heard such horns in his dreams: dread-inducing clarions that heralded the approach of faceless hunters, relentless in their pursuit.

He ran faster.

Past the stables outside the city walls, he swung off the road and into rows of snow-dusted barley, heading east toward where Thorn waited for him.

The night was descending into total blackness. Even once his eyes adjusted to the dark, he could barely see where to put his feet. Nevertheless, he maintained his pace as best he could, determined to put distance between him and Ceunon.

Several molehills caused him to stumble, and he nearly twisted his ankle in a badger hole.

"Son of an Urgal," he muttered.

At the far end of the fields, he paused to look back. The city gate had been closed, and lamps bobbed along the outer walls as soldiers patrolled the battlements, but he saw no sign that anyone had left Ceunon to give chase.

He started to relax. But only slightly.

As he continued on his way, he risked summoning a small werelight with a whispered "Brisingr."

The werelight was a drop of bloody flame wavering in the night, just bright enough for him to see the ground. It hung several feet in front of him and held its distance no matter how fast he ran.

Brisingr. Eragon had taught him that word of power, as he had many of the words in the ancient language during their travels together, in the brief period when they had been friends and allies. For all the stresses of that time—they had been evading the Empire the whole while—it had been one of the most enjoyable chapters of Murtagh's life. He remembered it with a curious mixture of gratitude, regret, and resentment: a short, shining span of freedom, bracketed by his initial escape from Galbatorix's tyranny in Urû'baen and his subsequent recapture at the hands of the king's minions outside of Tronjheim. Following which, Galbatorix had bound him with the ancient language and forced brother to fight brother.

Murtagh found himself clenching his teeth. *Brother.* It was still strange to think of Eragon as such. Half brother, in truth, for while they shared a mother, Murtagh was the son of Morzan, first and foremost among the Forsworn—the thirteen Dragon Riders who had betrayed their order to aid Galbatorix in his campaign against the Riders over a century ago. *I am the traitor son of a traitor,* thought Murtagh, and the knowledge burned like acid dripped upon his heart.

Eragon was also the son of a Rider, but in contrast, his father, Brom, had bitterly opposed Galbatorix and all his servants. A fact that had a deeply personal outcome, for it was Brom who had slain Morzan and his dragon when Murtagh was still a young child.

His lip curled. Their family history was as tangled as a briar patch and just as painful to wade through. He wished their mother were still alive that he might question her about it, but she had died shortly after giving birth to Eragon. And while Murtagh knew it was irrational, he could not help but blame Eragon for the loss: one more reason for resentment among so many others.

With an extra-deep breath, Murtagh cleared his lungs and lengthened his strides. It was true that stepping outside the main current of events in Alagaësia had helped calm his mind, but he still felt twisted up inside, him and Thorn both.

It might take years for either of them to unknot, if ever they did.

An owl hooted from a nearby tree, and somewhere in the brush, an animal darted away. Maybe a rabbit. Maybe something worse. A Svartling perhaps. The small, dark-skinned creatures were said to help with household chores if given gifts of bread and milk, but they were also said to treat travelers with cruel and often dangerous tricks.

Whatever the sound, Murtagh didn't want to meet its author in the middle of a night-bound field.

He slowed as he climbed the hill where they'd landed earlier, weaving between the crags of rock and the thickets of hordebrush.

At the crest, he found Thorn crouched, ready to spring into the air. The dragon's eyes outshone the werelight, and his scales flashed and flared with renewed brilliance. Great furrows scarred the earth around him: the tufts of grass torn, hordebrush uprooted, rocks split.

Thorn's tail twitched when he saw Murtagh, and he shivered with an excess of unburnt energy. A snarl wrinkled his muzzle.

Murtagh eyed the furrows but made no comment.

"I'm fine," he said. "Seriously." He turned in a circle, arms outstretched. "The blood isn't mine."

Thorn sniffed him and growled slightly before settling back on his haunches. His muzzle smoothed, but Murtagh could still feel his fear, frustration, and anger. *I should have come to help you.*

"It's all right. Really." He stroked Thorn's neck before continuing to the saddlebags, where he removed Zar'roc, unwrapped the crimson sword, and—with a sense of relief—strapped the weapon to his waist.

"We'd best find somewhere else for the night," he said, climbing up Thorn's back to the saddle strapped between the large spikes on the dragon's shoulders. Once in place, he snuffed the werelight.

Always you stir up the ant-nest cities, said Thorn.

"I know. It's a bad habit. Let's go."

Another growl, and with a great gust of wind and surge of steely muscles, Thorn leaped into the night air, the *thud* of his wings an invisible hammer blow.

Three more beats carried them into the clouds. The mist was cold against Murtagh's cheeks, but not unpleasantly so after his run. It tasted of moss and fresh-cut grass and new beginnings.

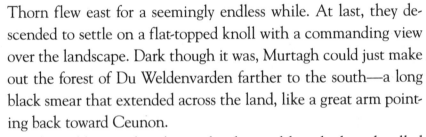

Thorn flew east for a seemingly endless while. At last, they descended to settle on a flat-topped knoll with a commanding view over the landscape. Dark though it was, Murtagh could just make out the forest of Du Weldenvarden farther to the south—a long black smear that extended across the land, like a great arm pointing back toward Ceunon.

The cold stung his skin as he dropped his cloak and pulled off his bloodstained shirt, trying to avoid touching the spots of gore. "Hvitra," he murmured as he imposed his will on the garment.

The cloth shimmered slightly, and the blotches of red faded.

Murtagh stroked the linen. It looked clean enough, but he still intended to wash the shirt before he wore it again.

He stored the shirt in a saddlebag and removed his one other garment: a thick woolen top—knitted, not woven—dyed a dark brown with interlaced patterns of red along the wrists and neck. The wool was itchy, but it was his preferred wear for flying, as it was far warmer than the linen.

Eager to cover his skin, he donned the top and again wrapped himself in his cloak.

Since a fire might draw attention, Thorn curled into a tight ball, nose to tail, and Murtagh crawled under his right wing and laid out his bedroll next to the smooth scales of Thorn's underbelly.

Was it worth it? Thorn asked.

"I think so," said Murtagh. Opening his mind more than felt safe around strangers, he shared his full memories of Ceunon.

They were not very good, said Thorn, fixing on an image of Sarros's guards.

"No, they weren't. Lucky for me."

A faint growl, and the dragon drew his wing tighter around Murtagh. *I see now there is a storm set before us.*

"But how big, how bad? We still don't know."

But it exists.

"Yes."

Thorn's plated eyelid closed and opened with a slight *nack. You wish to fly into the storm.*

"Maybe not into it, but toward it, yes. What say you?"

The dragon coughed with his peculiar laugh. *That we should take the stone to Tronjheim and have the dwarves carve it into something pretty for us.*

Murtagh snorted. "With our heads on pikes to watch?"

A faint scent of dragon smoke filled the space around them as a thread of crimson flame flickered in Thorn's nostrils. *No? Then I say we should sleep and speak of it in the morning.*

"I suppose you're right."

Behind him, Thorn's belly vibrated with a low hum, and Murtagh crossed his arms and let his chin sink to his chest. Underneath the wing, all was still, and it felt as if he and Thorn were the only two creatures in existence.

Before sleep took him, Murtagh did as was his nightly habit and, in a silent voice, spoke the words in the ancient language that were his true name. Hearing them was never easy; to know your true name was to know your faults as surely as your virtues.

Yet he said the name every day so as to be assured that he still understood his own nature and that no one besides Thorn held claim over him. For a true name granted power to those who heard it, and even as a magician might command an object with the proper words, so too might they command a person.

As Murtagh and Thorn had learned to their sorrow and despair during their subjugation in Urû'baen.

Thorn too spoke his true name, a deep singing sound that made Murtagh's skin feel as if laved with warm water. Then the day's tensions ebbed from their limbs, and they fell into close slumber.

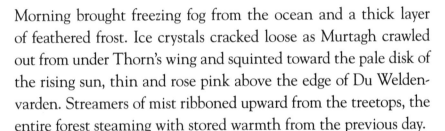

Morning brought freezing fog from the ocean and a thick layer of feathered frost. Ice crystals cracked loose as Murtagh crawled out from under Thorn's wing and squinted toward the pale disk of the rising sun, thin and rose pink above the edge of Du Weldenvarden. Streamers of mist ribboned upward from the treetops, the entire forest steaming with stored warmth from the previous day.

Murtagh shivered and pulled his cloak closer. The morning cold never got any easier.

He checked their surroundings and was pleased to see no sign of search or pursuit.

Confident that they'd escaped detection, he allowed himself the luxury of a small fire, built with scraps of dry hordebrush he foraged from the top and sides of the knoll.

Thorn lit the fire for him, igniting the woody stems with a single, tiny puff of flame from his nostrils.

"Thank you," said Murtagh, and he meant it. Fiddling with flint and tinder when your fingers were half numb wasn't fun, and he preferred to avoid using magic for everyday tasks. Magic made its own sort of noise for those with the ears to hear it, and it was impossible to know who might be listening.

Breakfast was flatbread and bacon and two dried apples, with a cup of elderberry tea to warm his insides. Thorn watched as he ate but had no food of his own; the dragon had devoured several deer not three days earlier and wouldn't need to feed again for the better part of a week.

By the time Murtagh finished, the morning had warmed enough to melt the frost and dissipate the morning haze.

He took out the bird-skull amulet and the coal-like stone and laid them on a scrap of cloth between himself and Thorn.

Thorn sniffed the two objects, and the tip of his tongue flicked out between his teeth. As he scented the stone, the scales along the back of his head and neck flared, like those of a pinecone opening in a fire.

"What?" said Murtagh, leaning forward. "What is it?"

A shiver ran Thorn's sinuous length, and he cowered in a way that Murtagh had only ever seen him do before Shruikan. *The stone smells wrong.*

"How so?"

Like . . . blood and hate and anger.

Murtagh scratched his cheek. His beard was prickling again. "Could it be magic?"

Another flicker of Thorn's tongue. *Maybe. But then it should affect you as well.*

"Unless it's meant only for dragons." Murtagh picked up the rock, bounced it in his hand. On a whim, he extended his mind toward the piece of stone, thinking perhaps it held some secret spark of consciousness bound within. But he felt nothing. He frowned and returned it to the cloth. "We need to find out where it came from."

Thorn hissed like a snake. *No. You* want *to find out where it came from. There is a difference. We should destroy the rock or else bury it where none will find it. There is evil here. Leave it, forget it, do not pursue it.*

"You know I can't."

A growl rumbled in Thorn's throat, and his scales rippled. *You can! Listen to Umaroth. He warned us for good reason.*

"And what reason is that?"

It matters not!

Thorn released a huff of black smoke and reached with one taloned paw toward the rock and amulet, as if to sweep them aside.

"No!" Murtagh cried, and sprang to his feet so he blocked Thorn's way. They stared at each other, neither backing down. The air between them seemed to vibrate with the force of the dragon's glittering glare.

Move aside.

"No."

This hunt will bring nothing but sorrow.

"I don't believe that."

Fingerling flames danced along Thorn's tongue, and the inside of his mouth glowed like a bellowed forge. *When has fate ever gone as we wish? Let this go.*

"I can't," said Murtagh. A familiar grimness descended upon him. "I can't sleep easy knowing there's a wolf stalking around in the dark. Something so dangerous Umaroth won't even give us its name."

Some secrets are better left buried.

"No! No, no, no. Do you want to wake up one morning to find out that we've been outmatched, outmaneuvered, and outsmarted? Not me. Not *ever again*." Murtagh stopped, hands clenched, and his nostrils flared as he steadied his breathing. He fixed Thorn with an iron gaze. "*Never*."

The dragon released a long, snaking *hiss* and said, *Isn't what we have enough? All the earth and sky is ours to travel. We sleep when we want, eat as we will. We paid our price, we shed our blood.*

"And we're still not safe!" With a conscious effort, Murtagh lowered his voice, though his words remained as intense as before.

"We never will be, but perhaps we can catch our enemies unaware. Umaroth is hiding something from us, and I won't rest until I know what it is."

Thorn breathed out a stream of black smoke that enveloped the stone and the bird-skull amulet. *Were you to take those to Eragon or Arya—*

"This has nothing to do with them!" Murtagh ran a hand through his hair. It was getting long again. "I want answers. And I want to be useful."

Being yourself is use enough. We do not need to prove ourselves to anyone.

He laughed bitterly. "Maybe if you're a dragon. But I've always had to prove myself, and I always will. There's no easy path through life when you're born as Morzan's son."

He went to Thorn and put his hands on either side of the dragon's scaled snout. "Besides, you and I, we are Dragon and Rider. We swore no oaths to the Riders—"

Thorn arched his neck in a proud curve, though he left his head in Murtagh's hands. *And I will swear no more oaths of fealty. No words will bind me, nor shackles or fetters.*

"No," Murtagh agreed. "Nor me. But we owe a debt to those who came before. We wear their mantle, whether we wish it or not, and I find myself reluctant to dishonor their memory by ignoring this."

Thorn snuffed. *No one would know if we chose another path.*

"*We* would know, and that is enough." He gestured toward the rock and bird-skull amulet. "That there is work for a Rider and Dragon, as it was of old."

The dragon turned his head then, to better see Murtagh. *So shall we fly about fighting evil and righting wrongs wherever we find them? Is that how you wish to spend your days?*

Murtagh's lips quirked. "Not entirely, but perhaps we can do some good here and there while we attend to our own interests."

As you did with the girl.

"As I did with the girl." He put a hand on Thorn's cheek then, and opened his mind as much as he could to the dragon's inner eye. *Look,* he said, and let Thorn feel the fullness of his heart.

Finally, Thorn uttered a soft growl and pulled his head away. *I understand.*

"But you don't agree."

The last few feet of Thorn's tail slapped the ground. Once. Twice. Three times. *What you want isn't what I want.* A wave of his hot breath rolled over Murtagh. *But where you go, I will go.*

He nodded, grateful. Their relationship wasn't as smooth as Eragon and Saphira's, and Murtagh didn't think it ever would be. But that was all right. A dull thorn was no thorn at all.

Besides, Murtagh knew that he wasn't the easiest person to get along with, even for a dragon.

Thorn must have sensed his mood, because a faint hum of amusement came from the dragon, and he curled his neck and tail around Murtagh's legs.

What then?

Kneeling, Murtagh touched the bird skull. "We need to find someone who can tell us about the witch-woman Bachel, and about this stone."

Umaroth?

He shook his head. "Too far away, and he would just warn us off the stone again."

Thorn snapped his jaws together, quick and sharp as a steel trap. *Would he? I still think you should speak with Umaroth. He is wiser than most.*

It was a fair point. Not only was Umaroth old and learned, but he and his dead Rider, Vrael, had been the last leaders of their order. That alone was reason enough to give weight to the drag-on's words. Yet Murtagh remained wary. "I respect Umaroth," he said. "But I'm not sure if I trust him."

You think he lies?

"No. I think his goals and aims may not be our own. We don't know. How long did we speak with him outside Urû'baen? Barely a few minutes, if that." Murtagh picked a breadcrumb out of his beard. Annoyed, he flicked it at the ground.

So you wish to find the truth of this yourself.

"I do."

Thorn nodded toward the amulet. *Then whom shall we seek out instead?*

"I'm not sure. We need someone here in Alagaësia, someone who is familiar with the secret doings of the land."

Thorn's eyes narrowed to knife-thin slits. *What of Yarek?*

The back of Murtagh's neck prickled, and a fist seemed to close around his chest, making it difficult to breathe. Yarek Lackhand, tight-mouthed, hard-eyed, clever as an elf and cruel as a torturer— Murtagh could see him still, standing in the stone hallways of Galbatorix's citadel, a drably dressed man with an iron cap strapped over the stump of his right wrist. Yarek had been Galbatorix's spymaster, and from what Murtagh had seen, he'd excelled in the position. It was he who had arranged for the Twins to kidnap Murtagh from the Varden so the king could break him, bend him to his will.

Thorn touched his snout to Murtagh's elbow.

He patted the dragon. If not for Yarek, he wouldn't have ended up bonded with Thorn, and Murtagh had to count that as a good thing. However, the spymaster had been the very definition of ruthless. And he kicked dogs, which Murtagh disapproved of. "Even if he's still alive—"

You know he is.

Murtagh inclined his head. "Probably. But I'm sure he's disappeared down some hole, and if I start poking around, asking questions, it'll attract attention."

Thorn made a deep, coughing sound.

"What?"

If not Yarek, why not the female, Ilenna?

"Ilenna—" Murtagh gave Thorn a quizzical look. Of all the folk who had passed through Galbatorix's court, Ilenna had been one of the more unusual. She was a younger daughter of a merchant family based out of the city of Gil'ead. Her father's cargo trains had helped supply the king's army during the war, and the family had made a fortune because of it. Despite her lowborn station, the girl had pursued him most *assiduously* whenever she was at court, so much so that Murtagh had taken to actively avoiding her. That alone was hardly unique, but what had caught his attention was how particularly well informed she was. As he'd later learned, her family had done more than just shift supplies for Galbatorix. They had also served as gleaners and sifters of information on Yarek's behalf, and Ilenna no less than her father or brothers.

"There's no telling if she knows anything about Bachel or the stone."

Thorn coughed again and tapped the ground with the tip of one razor-sharp claw. *She is more likely to than most. And if not, no doubt she would be eager to ask questions on behalf of the great Dragon Rider Murtagh.*

He grunted, unamused. "Even if that's true— No. We're not going there. We'll find someone else, somewhere else."

Who? Where? If you want to track down Bachel and the source of this rock, then Gil'ead is the answer. If not, how long will it be before you catch their trail?

"You never know," Murtagh mumbled. "It could happen. Maybe one of the tinkers or—"

A puff of acrid smoke blew over him as Thorn snorted.

Murtagh stopped. The dragon was right; he was being ridiculous. Grim, he crossed his arms and stared out over hill and dale toward the horizon.

The weight of unspoken memories hung between them.

"Gil'ead is dangerous."

More dangerous than Ceunon? More closely guarded than Ilirea?

Murtagh shifted his shoulders, as if he had an itch in the

middle of his back. He still wasn't used to Urû'baen's new name. Every time he heard it said—*Ilirea*—he felt as if he'd missed a step on a flight of stairs.

Finally, he answered, with his mind, not his mouth, *I don't want to.* There was no dissembling when it came to mental communication, no barriers to understanding. It was the most vulnerable form of connection two beings could share, and he shared it with Thorn.

The dragon hummed a soothing note and lowered his head until it rested on the ground by Murtagh's feet.

Then leave it, said Thorn. *Or hold the course. What is this hunt worth to you?*

Murtagh let out his breath and uncrossed his arms, forcing himself to stand straight. He put a hand in the middle of Thorn's forehead. The scales were hot against his palm.

"All right. We'll go to Gil'ead and find Ilenna."

~~~~~~~~~~~~~~~~~~~ ❖ ~~~~~~~~~~~~~~~~~~~

Before they departed the knoll, Murtagh sharpened his dagger on the bit of dwarven whetstone he carried with him. He stropped it on his sword belt and then made a mirror from water poured in a plate and stilled with the word *entha*.

Peering into the silvery grey surface, he was struck by how gaunt he looked. He hadn't been eating enough. They were always moving, walking, flying, often in inclement weather. Meals were intermittent at best, and more than once he'd gone a full day without so much as a bite.

Not good, he thought. The thinner he was, the less reserves he had for spells when the need arose. The magicians with the most raw power were always the heaviest.

He pulled the skin on his jaw flat and tight, lifted the dagger, and started to shave.

The dagger wasn't as sharp as a barber's razor, but it did the job. Even after the first pass, his face felt colder, and Murtagh half regretted his decision. Still, he persisted, and soon enough, he was finished.

He only cut himself three times, which he counted a success.

Afterward, he studied himself in the makeshift mirror. Without the beard, he appeared younger but also leaner, harsher, like a starveling wolf.

He dashed the water aside with the flat of his hand.

You are yourself again, said Thorn.

Murtagh grunted. Maybe he should have waited until after Gil'ead to shave, but he couldn't bear to have crumbs on his chin. Not to mention the constant itching.

He dried off the plate and tucked it into the saddlebags. Then he bounded up into Thorn's saddle and strapped down his legs so he wouldn't fall. "Let's fly!"

Thorn growled in a fierce, pleased tone and sprang into the sky, wings sweeping overhead.

The world lurched around Murtagh, and he gripped the neck spike in front of him, squinting against the rush of cold wind. For better or worse, they were going to Gil'ead.

CHAPTER V

✦ ✦ ✦ ✦ ✦ ✦ ✦

Dragonflight

The map Murtagh had—which he had bought off a fur merchant near Teirm—wasn't detailed enough to tell him where exactly in Alagaësia he and Thorn were. Like most maps intended for use by traders, it was mainly concerned with land and sea routes and not, for example, the exact shape, location, and scale of Du Weldenvarden.

He knew that the forest extended westward in a great tongue of trees. South of it lay Isenstar Lake, and south of Isenstar lay the city of Gil'ead. The shortest path to Gil'ead would have been straight across the wooded expanse, but that would entail entering the elves' territory, which they protected with fierce devotion. Moreover, there was a range of high-topped mountains somewhere in that section of the forest, and mountains always made flying difficult.

So, instead, he and Thorn decided to skirt the forest as they worked their way westward and south, until they caught sight of Isenstar. Then they would know their location and could turn toward Gil'ead.

As had become habit, Murtagh used a simple spell to hide Thorn from the eyes of those on the ground, human or otherwise. Simple though it was, the spell took energy, and by the end of every day, Murtagh felt a dull fatigue, which was exacerbated by the effort needed to ride Thorn. The dragon flapped slowly compared with a bird, but each beat of his wings was still a jarring experience. Murtagh wasn't able to doze as he might have on a horse during a long march.

To pass the time, he thought. Mostly about magic. He had long since realized that magic was the key to mastering the world, to controlling circumstances and protecting himself and those he cared for, few as they were. Galbatorix had not trained him in enchanting as Murtagh was growing up at court, for the king had guarded such knowledge most jealously. And while Eragon had taught Murtagh his first words of power, he had not been able to make use of them at the time, no matter how hard he tried. It was only months later, after Thorn hatched for him while imprisoned beneath Urû'baen, that he succeeded in breaking the glass-like barrier in his mind and, through force of will, enacting his first piece of magic.

It had been a simple spell—*lyftha*—with which he had raised a single gold crown from Galbatorix's seamless palm.

The king had been miserly with his instruction thereafter, teaching Murtagh the bare minimum of the art. A slave armed was a man freed, and Galbatorix had made it clear that he had every intention of maintaining a close hold over Murtagh and Thorn, even as he had chained his dread servants the Forsworn.

Including my father.

Murtagh scowled and wrenched his thoughts into a different track.

He'd grown increasingly obsessed with understanding what was and wasn't possible with gramarye. As a result, he spent a great deal of time thinking about the intricacies of the ancient language, and how the ancient language *wasn't* magic itself, but rather a means of guiding and constraining one's intent. Without it, a random thought whilst casting a spell might result in an entirely different—and potentially devastating—outcome. Which was exactly why wordless magic was so dangerous.

The study of the ancient language was the work of a lifetime. And yet . . . the language itself was insufficient to explain the true nature of magic, for at its heart, magic was the act of manipulating energy. And it was energy that really interested Murtagh. What *was* it? Where did it come from? How could it be gathered and used?

It was a perplexing question.

He sighed and looked at the dark apex of the sky. The elves might know the truth of the matter; they'd spent centuries studying the mysteries of magic. Magic ran in their blood, even as it did with the dragons.

If only he could ask them.

At times, he wished he and Thorn had kept the Eldunarí whom Galbatorix had given them. Then they would never have to worry about a lack of energy, for the Eldunarí's crystalline structure contained more motive force than a dragon contained in their normal flesh-and-blood body.

Murtagh still found it strange to think that dragons grew the large, gemlike stones within their chests. Up until Galbatorix showed him one, he had not even suspected their existence, much less that it was possible for dragons to transfer their minds into the Eldunarí and thus live on even after their flesh perished.

Just one more mystery among many relating to dragons.

The king had often lent them the Eldunarí of an old male dragon by the name of Yngmar. Like most of the Eldunarí whom Galbatorix had acquired, Yngmar was quite mad, tortured into incoherency by the king. Murtagh had barely been able to make sense of the dragon's thoughts; trying usually left him with a throbbing headache.

Yet, on occasion, he missed Yngmar and the other Eldunarí. He knew Thorn felt the same. The flesh-dead dragons had given Murtagh strength and speed beyond that of a normal human, enough to match that of an elf. (A not-always-welcome gift, as the resulting soreness had often been crippling.) More importantly, having the Eldunarí nearby had provided a certain companionship during the time he and Thorn spent enslaved to Galbatorix.

And he'd learned from them too. The Eldunarí had often ranted in the ancient language, and he'd managed to pick up a word here, a word there, although the exact meaning often eluded him.

He had left the Eldunarí with Nasuada outside the citadel in Urû'baen following Galbatorix's explosive demise. It had been the right choice; the dragons needed care, and Murtagh had felt inadequate to it, as had Thorn. So far as Murtagh knew, all of the existing Eldunarí—including Yngmar and Umaroth—were now with Eragon in the far east, beyond the borders of Alagaësia, where he'd gone to establish a hold for the next generation of dragons and Riders.

Which was as it should be. And yet, in his darker moments, Murtagh found himself chewing on discontent that Eragon should have so much, even though life had been far harder for him and Thorn. It wasn't fair. Not that Murtagh believed life had anything to do with fairness. Nevertheless, the discontent remained, although he tried not to feed it, tried to focus on more helpful thoughts.

No remembering!

Murtagh dug his nails into his palms and spent a few long minutes watching the slow parade of the land below. Rows of long, thin clouds straked diagonally beneath Thorn, breaking up the ground into discrete stripes of green-brown spectacle.

What do you think magic is? he asked Thorn.

Potential.

When he tired of thinking about magic, Murtagh occupied himself by composing poems in the fashion of Galbatorix's court, in a form known as Attenwrack, after its originator, Atten the Red—a minor earl from the far south, near the city of Aroughs.

Murtagh had never been one for scholarly pursuits. Growing up, he had played the obedient student, but he'd had little interest in math, logic, or astronomy. History had been a carefully metered account approved by Galbatorix, a repetitive cycle of self-praise that bored him even in the first telling. He learned his letters and practiced his reading, but the books that might have interested him were locked in Galbatorix's great vault, forbidden to everyone but the king himself.

Always Murtagh had found himself drawn more to physical activities: sparring, dancing, climbing, hunting. They cleared his mind, gave him a sense of well-being and accomplishment and, most importantly, control.

And yet now, in the empty wilderness, with nothing but the sky and the earth to behold, and a vast and dangerous silence constantly tempting him to retrospection, he had found a new enjoyment in arranging words according to the patterns of the Attenwrack. It was a strange experience, but he persisted, confused and intrigued by the satisfaction that the process gave him.

As it was too difficult to put pen to parchment while riding Thorn, he spoke the words out loud and did his best to hold them in his mind.

It wasn't easy. Sometimes he forgot what he'd composed, and that was frustrating. Other times he couldn't think of the right word—even when he knew it existed—and that was frustrating too. The hardest part was fitting the words into a pleasing shape while still saying what he wanted to say.

Speaking slowly so as to avoid mistakes, he recited his latest stanza:

> Eagle soars, eagle hunts, a king of air.
> Sparrows dart, sparrows flock, no crown to wear.
> Ever at odds, the many against the one.
> In equal combat, the eagle prevails.
> Unequal and harried, the sovereign fails.
> Fly as you are told or fly alone, the
> End of each is still the same. The chilled
> Embrace of death will calm your final care.

And dragons eat them all, said Thorn.

Murtagh scratched his neck and stared at the horizon, somber.

He wished Thorn *could* eat every living thing, should the need arise. But it still would not save either of them from their fated end, for the doom of all things was to die and be forgotten. Even dragons.

~~~~~~~~~~~~~~~~~~~ ❖ ~~~~~~~~~~~~~~~~~~~

That evening, they made camp in a field by a grove of alder trees. Murtagh would have preferred the cover of the trees—he hated sleeping out in the open—but as he always did when it came to where they stopped, he deferred to Thorn.

The alders stood along the banks of a small stream that poured out of Du Weldenvarden some leagues distant. While he waited for the campfire to build to full heat, Murtagh went to fill their waterskins.

The white bark of the alders almost seemed to glow in the fading light, and it felt cool and still and sacred beneath the arching branches. The leaves were starting to turn red and gold, and the smell of dewy moss freshened the air.

Murtagh knelt by the trilling stream. The water ran cold across his wrists as he submerged the skins, one after another. Once filled, the skins were heavy, awkward, and slippery. Murtagh had only packed two originally, but he found that flying made him unaccountably thirsty, and so he'd bought another three off a trapper in the Spine.

As he lifted the skins, the carrying strap on one broke, and the skin fell to the ground.

"Barzûl," he swore in Dwarvish.

He tried to pick up the skin, but it kept slipping out of his hand, and the four other skins kept pulling him off-balance.

Without thinking, he called out, "Thorn! Can you help? I can't carry them all!"

A snuffling sound came from the edge of the grove. He looked back to see Thorn crouched in front of the trees, sniffing and swinging his head back and forth.

Murtagh realized the problem at once. There was enough room between the alders for the dragon to fit—a game trail led down to the stream—but only barely. The space was too confined for Thorn to spread his wings, lift his head, or easily turn around.

"You don't have to—"

The words died in his mouth as Thorn took a step forward. Then another. Hope began to form within Murtagh.

A gust of wind ransacked the branches over Thorn's head. The wood creaked and groaned with uncanny complaints, the grove seeming come alive with hostile intent. Thorn cowered, and his lip curled to bare his fangs. Still snarling, he retreated to the edge of the alders and shrank against his haunches.

A curious mixture of sadness and anger displaced Murtagh's hope. He set his jaw and adjusted his grip on the skins.

Thorn extended his left foreleg beneath the trees, reaching out with extended claws. *Give them thisways. I will carry them back.*

"It's all right," he said, and kept his gaze on the skins. "I'll manage. Go. I'll be there directly."

Thorn growled, but there was a plaintive quality to the sound. After a moment, he turned and, with heavy steps, crawled back to their camp.

Murtagh's breath hitched in his chest. He ignored it and contorted his right hand until he was able to grip the mouth of the fallen skin.

Then he trudged out of the grove.

The fire had died down, leaving a bed of smoldering coals.

Murtagh stared at the glowing rubies and compared them in his mind to the stone Sarros had found.

He scratched his forearm where it ached. He was more tired than usual. The excitement at Ceunon and the flight thence had taken their toll.

From his bags, he fetched the leather packet that held his quills and parchment and a bottle of oak-gall ink. He took the piece of parchment half covered with his upright script and carefully lettered the lines he'd composed earlier.

The result left him unsatisfied, feeling as if he could have done better.

While he waited for the strokes of ink to dry, he used his finger to draw a narrow furrow in the ground. Then, from one end, a fork branching left and right.

He cocked his head, studying the sight.

During the hours he'd spent contemplating magic, he had begun to consider the possibilities of *if* spells. They held more potential than most realized, he believed.

He touched the point where the furrows forked and whispered, "Ílf adurna fithren, sving raehta." Or, in rough translation, *If water touches, turn right.* Then he unstoppered the skin by his side and poured a measure of water into the opposite end of the furrow.

The water ran along the course until the way divided. Then, as if guided by an invisible hand, it flowed into the rightward branch of the shallow ditch he'd dug. And Murtagh felt a slight—but proportional—expenditure of energy. He brought the enchantment to an end.

He frowned as he stoppered the skin.

How many *ifs* could he stack in a spell? And how close did he need to be to the point of action? Could he bind a conditioned spell to an object, like a gem, and leave it to do his bidding? As a trap for a foe or to signal him in the event of a certain happening? The possibilities were myriad. Could he build an edifice of *ifs* that would protect Thorn and himself from every conceivable threat?

All things to experiment with.

Across the bedded fire, Thorn stirred and uttered a whimpering sound. He was sleeping, but it was an uneasy slumber. Always it was so.

Murtagh watched him, troubled, and rubbed his left forearm,

rubbed the old hurt away. He sighed and looked at the great arc of stars splattered across the night sky, and he wished for the wisdom to calm and comfort, to heal wounded minds.

If the thought were a prayer, he knew not to whom he prayed. The dwarf gods weren't his own, and the superstitions of the common folk held no appeal to him. But he hoped that perhaps someone or something might hear his plea. And if not—if, as he suspected, no one was there to respond—then the task of improving was his and his alone. The prospect was daunting in the extreme, but there was solace in it too. Whatever he accomplished—good or evil—he might rightfully claim without apportioned dues. If chance dictated the events of his life, *he* was the master of his responses, and no king or god could infringe upon that right.

He packed away the parchment, quills, and ink, and then laid himself down on his blanket. He looked to Thorn and decided to let the dragon sleep rather than wake him for their nightly ritual. Thorn needed the rest after a long day of flying, and Murtagh was well familiar with Thorn's true name. It was as dear to him as his own, and as the incident at the alders had shown, another telling of it would teach him nothing new.

Tomorrow will serve, Murtagh thought.

Too soft to hear, he spoke his true name, and the back of his neck prickled, and his heart quickened at the flood of self-knowledge, harsh and uncompromising.

Then he pulled the blanket closer around his shoulders and watched the pulsing of the coals while he waited for his heart to slow and sleep to take him.

~~~~~~~~~~~~~~~~~~~~ ❖ ~~~~~~~~~~~~~~~~~~~~

Murtagh dreamt, and they were difficult dreams.

He found himself reliving his ambush and capture in Tronjheim. Being bound hand and foot, the Twins forcing him to ride through countless miles of dark tunnels and then across the better part of Alagaësia to Urû'baen and Galbatorix. Never had he felt so helpless. . . .

Then he was fighting Eragon upon the Burning Plains. The hosts of men and dwarves clashed about them while the dwarven king lay dead in his golden armor amid the field of eternal flame. And regret mixed with rage.

When the battle receded from mind, his vision shifted:

Nasuada standing before him. Nasuada, as he had first seen her in Tronjheim. Young and untested by the rigors of command, not yet risen to the leadership of the Varden nor yet to her queenship, but tall and regal nonetheless.

And he, by contrast, a prisoner in a cell, sequestered there by the Varden as they attempted to determine where his true loyalties lay.

Even from that moment, he admired her, for he could see that her resolve was a match for his own. And she showed him kindness when no kindness was warranted; she spoke with him without prejudice, out of a sincere desire to understand what had brought him and Eragon to the Varden. She spoke with him as the person he was, not the person others believed him to be.

She shifted then: her dress changed to that which she had been wearing when, much later and at Galbatorix's orders, Murtagh had seized her from the Varden's encampment. Her expression of defiance tore at his heart. He could see her fear beneath, and the monstrous unfairness of the situation broke him.

He saw her chained to the ashen altar within the Hall of the Sooth-sayer, in the ancient chamber beneath Urû'baen, where Galbatorix had kept her prisoner. Stains and tears appeared on her dress, and her hair grew frazzled, her eyes haunted. Livid marks disfigured her arms. But never did her defiance vanish throughout the tortures Galbatorix had him inflict on her. And still, she showed him understanding.

Then they were together in the rubble-strewn courtyard outside the citadel in Urû'baen. Smoke darkened the sky, and ash fell like snow. The king was dead. The war was won. Nasuada was looking up at

him, all defiance gone, her dark eyes round and vulnerable. And the
only words he could manage were "I'm sorry."

They weren't enough. How could they be?

Starlings and magpies were arguing in the alder tops as Murtagh
woke. His forehead was sweaty, and under his arms too, and his
pulse was racing like a frightened horse.

He sat up and wiped his forehead.

The sun hadn't risen yet, and Thorn was still asleep.

His heart felt hollow. There had been a brief time, after the
battle for Tronjheim, where he had been a free man, and Nasuada
as yet unburdened by the responsibilities of command. The possibility of a courtship had just begun to form between them when
fate had intervened. Had they continued uninterrupted . . .

He shook his head. It was bootless to consider *what if*s and
*might have been*s. What was, was, and it was the lot of the living to
deal with it as best they could.

But knowing that did nothing to ease his pain.

Careful to be quiet, Murtagh stood, picked up Zar'roc from by
his blanket, and walked a ways from their camp.

The frost-laden grass crunched under his boots, a crisp, dry sound.

He stood in an expanse of empty sward. Chest up, shoulders
back, staring forward into the future.

An intake of frozen air, and he swept Zar'roc from its crimson
sheath. In dawn's grey light, the sword's blade was a sharpened
shard of iridescent red—a shimmering thorn of frozen blood,
eager to cut and stab and kill. The blade of a Rider, forged out of
brightsteel by an elven smith over a century past and imbued with
spells of strength and keenness and resistance. The finest weapon
a warrior could hope to wield, and yet he regarded it with as much
aversion as appreciation. A Rider's blade, yes, but that Rider had

been Morzan. His father. And Morzan had used Zar'roc for many a black and bloody deed . . . as had Murtagh after him.

Not for nothing had Morzan named the blade *Misery* in the ancient language, and true to its name, the sword had brought pain to many throughout the land, including Murtagh himself.

Sometimes he wondered if he should have ever taken Zar'roc from Eragon.

He shook off the thought. Whether he wanted it or not, Morzan's shadow would always lie upon him, and aside from his name and the scar on his back, Zar'roc was all he had from his father. It was a meager and hateful inheritance, but it was his alone, and for that he clung to it.

He held the sheath in his off hand as he flowed through the familiar forms. Step, cut, parry, turn. Block, swing, lunge. He moved without thinking, his mind as still and empty as a windless lake on a cloudless day.

Attack, defend, escape. Beat and break, search the opening, make the cut, risk the stab. He used the sheath as a dagger, blocking, deflecting, rapping the wrist, creating opportunities for a lethal blow.

His skin warmed, and his pulse steadied. He moved faster, pushing himself to maintain the pace of battle, every movement a whip-snap of life-preserving, life-ending action.

His lungs gave out before his arms. Unable to continue, he fell to his knees and braced the sheath against the ground. Zar'roc he placed across his thighs.

As the first rays of light crept across the frozen grass, the egg-shaped ruby in Zar'roc's pommel refracted the beams, splitting them into glowing darts of red.

Once his breath steadied, he stood, sheathed the blade, and staggered back to camp.

Across the dead fire, Thorn watched. He sniffed as Murtagh came close. *You stink of fear.*

Murtagh grunted. "I know. I'll wash." He flinched as Thorn

licked his elbow. Then he forced himself to relax and patted the dragon's head.

~~~~~~~~~~~~~~~~~~~~ ❖ ~~~~~~~~~~~~~~~~~~~

The days followed the same pattern. They flew, being careful to avoid detection. Murtagh thought and wrote and thought some more. At camp, he recorded whatever was worth saving and sometimes cast a few spells. And every evening, he and Thorn spoke their true names together in silent confession.

Nights he dreamt, and neither he nor Thorn spoke of what they saw in the small hours.

Throughout, Du Weldenvarden remained a seemingly endless sea of trees to their left. The forest's dark depths filled Murtagh with foreboding; he disliked the idea of losing himself among the trackless ranks of pines. Still, he wondered what it would be like to walk the ancient forest. He and Thorn had never had an opportunity to visit the ancestral home of the first Riders.

The thought reminded him of Vroengard Island, and he shivered. *That* had been one place he and Thorn had been glad to leave. The whole island had felt wrong, tainted by the deaths of dragons, poisoned by the magics loosed in the Riders' fall.

Sometimes it felt to Murtagh as if the whole of Alagaësia were a graveyard, laden with history's sorrows.

During the third evening, Thorn was in a playful mood, so they sparred together, or as well as a man and dragon could. Murtagh ran and darted and jumped around Thorn, trying to touch him with the tip of Zar'roc (dulled for the moment with magic). And Thorn in turn did his best to keep Murtagh at bay and to catch him and pin him to the ground.

It was great fun, even if Murtagh ended up bruised and cut. He left a few bruises of his own, but Thorn didn't mind; the dragon's eyes sparkled with fierce enjoyment every time Murtagh landed a hit or made him dodge.

Afterward, Murtagh lay against Thorn's heaving belly as they both caught their breath. "You were as slow as a turtle," he said in a playful tone.

Thorn nudged his bruised arm. *And you were as obvious as an ox.*

Murtagh smirked. "Maybe, but I still managed to mark you."

A small, good-humored growl was his answer.

~~~~~~~~~~~~~~~~~~~ ❖ ~~~~~~~~~~~~~~~~~~~

On the morning of the fourth day, a sheet of silver appeared stretched along the southern horizon. "Isenstar!" said Murtagh, and Thorn banked into a gentle turn.

The lake was one of the largest in Alagaësia. Under normal circumstances, they would have stuck to the shore, keeping land beneath them in case they needed to alight. However, there were sure to be folk along the water's edge, and the spell Murtagh used to hide Thorn from prying eyes did nothing to conceal the sound of his wings or the feel of their minds. So Thorn struck out straight over the rippling expanse.

There were herons at Isenstar, and gulls and terns, flown inland to feast on the lake fish. A V-formation of herons joined Thorn in the sky; the birds showed no fear of the larger, slower dragon.

Murtagh amused himself by shouting at the herons, and they responded with an appalling barking scream that made him think of a donkey crossed with a pig.

All day Thorn flew, maintaining a steady pace with slow, powerful flaps. At noontime the reflected light from below was so bright, Murtagh had to avert his eyes to keep from being blinded. Later, the water acquired a startling clarity; even from far above, he could see great fishes and swaths of swaying weeds.

There were boats too, fishermen competing with the birds for the bounty of the lake. Also trappers and merchants transporting goods north or south between Gil'ead and Ceunon.

But what caught Murtagh's attention the most was a slim, two-person rowboat that had a white hull and an unmistakably elegant shape. "Elves," he said, and pointed with his mind.

Thorn swerved west, away from the rowboat.

"Guard your thoughts," said Murtagh. "If they haven't noticed us, we might sneak by."

Thorn hummed in response.

The rowboat shrank behind them more slowly than Murtagh would have liked. He watched until it was a tiny, undistinguished speck, and only then did he relax.

Of all the races, elves were the most skilled with magic and mental communication. If the elves had decided to reach out with their thoughts and test the sky, well . . . Murtagh allowed himself a wry smile. The day would have become unpleasantly interesting.

He scratched around the spikes on Thorn's neck. "Well done."

Sharp eyes, was all the dragon said in return.

The sky had darkened to purple, and a scrim of golden clouds hung above the lake when Gil'ead entered into view, past the shoreline ahead of them.

The city was much as Murtagh remembered. Low and rough, with log-walled structures and—near the center—a sprawling fortress. It was there Lord Relgin, the city's current governor, would reside, and there Murtagh suspected he would find Ilenna, currying favor and gathering secrets. Assuming, that was, her family hadn't been exiled from favor for their association with the Empire. But Murtagh doubted it. Her father's shipping concern was too useful for whoever held power, whether that was Galbatorix, Nasuada, or Lord Relgin.

Murtagh was glad to have arrived, but the sight of Gil'ead brought him little pleasure. The last time he and Thorn had been at the city, they had been fighting at Galbatorix's behest, in a desperate and failed attempt to defend the place from the elves. It had been a bloody, miserable battle. And the time before *that* had been little better: an ambush and then him having to sneak into the fortress to rescue Eragon from the clutches of the Shade Durza.

He looked for it and saw: the roof above the fortress banquet hall, rebuilt and newly shingled. The people of Gil'ead had been busy since the end of the war.

In his mind, Murtagh heard the mighty *crack* that had sounded when Saphira ripped off the banquet hall's original roof during their escape. He made a face. That had been a dire night. Nor had it been the first such night in Gil'ead for his family.

We've had an unhappy history here, he thought. *Best not to add to the tally.*

Then don't get into any more fights, said Thorn.

You know I can't promise that.

Murtagh turned his gaze westward. In that direction, tucked somewhere among the hills surrounding Gil'ead, was the hollow where he'd hidden with Saphira while they plotted to rescue Eragon. . . .

"That way," he said, pointing.

The horizon tilted as Thorn angled westward, and Murtagh returned to studying the layout of the city while he considered how best to approach Ilenna.

GIL'EAD

CHAPTER I

✦ ✦ ✦ ✦ ✦ ✦ ✦

Hostile Territory

Thorn's wings knocked loose a flurry of leaves as he descended amid willows and poplars into the secluded hollow. The clearing was barely big enough for him, and Murtagh could already feel his discomfort.

As the leaves settled, Thorn glanced around at the confined space. He growled, and a brace of ravens sprang cawing from within the poplars.

"It's all right," said Murtagh in a soothing tone. "We have to hide, and this is a good place for it. If anything happens, you can take off."

Thorn rolled his eyes but held his position.

After unstrapping his legs, Murtagh slid to the ground. It felt strange to be back in the hollow, as if it were a place from a half-remembered dream.

He shook himself and searched the area with his mind. To his relief, the only living creatures he felt were mice and rabbits, two weasels, and a small herd of deer grazing on a nearby hill.

Satisfied, he said, "It's safe."

The day was already near an end, so they made camp and soon enough were fast asleep.

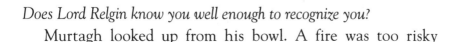

Does Lord Relgin know you well enough to recognize you?

Murtagh looked up from his bowl. A fire was too risky

so close to Gil'ead, which meant breakfast of cold porridge and jerky.

Thorn was watching from the center of the clearing. He refused to crawl under the edge of the canopy, where Murtagh had placed his bedroll.

"He knows *of* me, but I don't think we've met. In any case, I shouldn't cross paths with him."

And if you do?

"I'll lie, and if lies aren't enough, I'll run."

Thorn blinked.

A sparrow darted past over the clearing, chasing morning insects.

Murtagh scooped the last of the porridge into his mouth. "Either way, I'll be back by sundown. If not—" The soft soil squished between Thorn's claws as he kneaded the ground. "If not," Murtagh repeated with gentle emphasis, "I'll let you know."

Will you take Zar'roc with you this time?

Murtagh looked at the sword propped against the log he was sitting on. He wanted to. Entering Gil'ead unarmed wasn't an appealing prospect. "It'll attract too much attention. I'll bring my dagger instead."

Thorn uttered a hiss of disapproval. *Always this problem. You should get another sword, one that you can carry wherever you go.*

"That's not a bad idea," said Murtagh, wiping his mouth. "I'd have to enchant it, though, so it didn't break."

Then do so, insisted Thorn.

Murtagh eyed him. "All right. Gil'ead has a large weapons market. Or it did. I'll see what I can find there."

Good. Thorn dug his claws deeper into the ground.

"But in the meantime . . ." Murtagh hopped to his feet and walked among the trees until he found a poplar sapling—as thick as his wrist—that had died from lack of light, shadowed by the branches of the full-grown trees. He pried the sapling loose from the loam and carried it back to camp.

There, he stripped it of bark and cut it so it was a head taller than himself. "Done," he said, hefting the staff. "Not the best wood, but it'll do for now."

You can fight with this? Thorn asked.

"Better, I can walk with it," said Murtagh, and he leaned on the staff as if he had a bad knee. "If anyone looks, they'll see my leg, not my face."

Thorn sniffed the staff. *Dull stick-claw is improvement on no dull stick-claw, I suppose. Still, try not to kick up a hive of hornets as you did at Ceunon.*

"That wasn't on purpose."

It never is. Perhaps Ilenna can keep you from getting into trouble, hmm?

Murtagh raised an eyebrow. "If I didn't know better, I'd think you wanted her to catch me."

Thorn's mouth spread in an approximation of a smile. *Maybe you should let her. It might ease the fire in your belly.*

Murtagh snorted. "You know what that leads to. Children."

Hatchlings are not a bad thing.

He eyed Thorn, serious. "They are if you can't give them the care they need. I wouldn't inflict that on any child of mine. I'd sooner die."

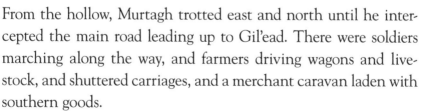

From the hollow, Murtagh trotted east and north until he intercepted the main road leading up to Gil'ead. There were soldiers marching along the way, and farmers driving wagons and livestock, and shuttered carriages, and a merchant caravan laden with southern goods.

Murtagh slipped onto the road and fell in behind the caravan, making no attempt to avoid the cloud of dust kicked up by the line of mules. He pulled his hood over his face, lowered his head, and adopted a limping step.

As he walked, he practiced his lies. Yes, he was Tornac son of Tereth, come from Ilirea to purchase swords and spears and shields for his master's men. His master? One Burdock Marrisson, who had served honorably as captain in Nasuada's army and been awarded a minor title as reward. No, he didn't have any letters of recommendation. Why should he? Yes, he had a letter of credit to make his purchases. His horse? Stabled at the Cattail Inn, south of Gil'ead.

And so forth and so on. The story wouldn't stand close inspection, but Murtagh hoped it would be enough to avoid trouble if trouble came looking.

In the fields alongside the road, he saw traces of the battle for Gil'ead, ghosts of past bloodshed. There along a hedgerow was where the Empire's cavalry had massed, and even now a circle of ground was bare where horses had trampled the dirt until it was hard as fired brick. Half a ruined wagon lay rotting along the lip of a nearby ditch, the wood burnt black by spellfire. Farther to the east was where the elves had broken through the army's defensive lines and begun to drive them away from Gil'ead.

Murtagh forced himself to stop looking, but he couldn't stop remembering. *It must have been terrifying*, he thought. To be stuck on foot, with dragons fighting overhead, and ranks of elves descending upon your position . . . He could hardly imagine a worse situation.

As he drew closer to Gil'ead, he noticed an odd thing. Half a mile ahead of him, there was a narrow side path that ran west some distance to a large oak tree on a hilly crest. At least a third of the travelers turned aside from the road and walked to the oak, which they looked at for a long time before doing an about-face and returning to the road.

Murtagh couldn't make sense of it. There were no stands beside the oak. No merchants or tinkers plying their trade. It was just . . . a tree.

He stopped next to the road and waited until an oxen-pulled wagon came up alongside him. The man holding the reins was rawboned, sun-darkened, and had a stalk of green grass hanging from the corner of his mouth. Next to him sat a pair of boys who couldn't have been older than ten or twelve.

"Pardon me, neighbor," said Murtagh, putting on a northern accent. "What might be happening over at that there tree?"

The farmer glanced at him sideways and twitched the stalk between his lips. "Tha's where the dragon's buried."

A knot formed in Murtagh's stomach. "A dragon?"

"Ayuh. An' an elf too, if'n you believe it." The two boys peered curiously around the farmer at Murtagh, and the oxen lowed. "Th' elves burned th' dragon's body, an' grew that tree over th' ashes."

Then the wagon rolled past, leaving Murtagh standing alone.

With heavy steps, he resumed walking. He didn't look at the tree again, and he tried not to think about it. But when he reached the intersection, where the path diverged from the road, he muttered, "I'm sorry."

He could still see Glaedr's battered body falling from on high, a burning meteor plummeting toward the bloody mire that footed the world, wings fluttering like wind-torn flags.

Thorn's mind touched his, and the dragon said, *Their fate was not our fault.*

Murtagh tensed as he recalled the feeling of Galbatorix entering and seizing control of his mind. The king had used him to kill Oromis, and Thorn to kill Glaedr, although Glaedr still lived on in his Eldunarí. *No, but Galbatorix wouldn't have succeeded without us. Not then. Not there.*

A sense of reluctant agreement came from Thorn. *I would have liked to have known Glaedr as a friend, not a foe.*

And I Oromis. It's possible we might still have a chance with Glaedr, if ever he allows it.

The memories of dragons run as long and deep as the roots of the mountains. He will not forgive us for killing his Rider.

I suppose not. Murtagh sighed. He couldn't help but resent Eragon and Saphira for having the chance to study under Oromis and Glaedr. *If only we'd had the same opportunities, what could we have become?* A useless line of thought, and he knew it, but the sentiment weighed on him all the same.

We have become strong, said Thorn. *No one has survived what we have.*

Which was true. But despite what Murtagh had told Essie, he believed that some wounds, some scars, were too great to overcome and did nothing to make a person stronger. Quite the opposite. A truly severe injury only left you weakened, imperfect, and there was no fixing most of it.

He kept the feeling to himself. He didn't want Thorn to ever believe that he viewed the dragon as irrevocably damaged. If anything, Murtagh thought the dragon had a better chance of becoming whole than he did. By the standards of both humans and dragons, Thorn was hardly more than a hatchling, despite how Galbatorix had accelerated his physical growth. He was *young,* and like magic, youth meant potential. But it would take time for Thorn to heal. Years and years, if not the entire span of their existence.

The pattern of our lives is set so early, he thought. If ever he did have children—and the thought filled him with the deepest trepidation—he knew he would do everything within his power to ensure that their first few years were full of love and joy. If nothing else, then, the children would have those first bright memories to sustain them during the darkness. What better gift from a parent?

Soft as a shadow came words that he felt almost more than heard: ". . . *beautiful boy. What a strong boy. You make me so proud.*" His mother's voice, half remembered, as she'd spoken to him in the hall of Morzan's castle.

Murtagh's steps faltered. He leaned on his staff for real then, and stared at the net of cracks in the bare dirt as he waited for the surge of emotion to pass. Was it grief, anger, longing for what he never had? . . . He couldn't tell.

Setting aside his feelings, he continued forward. It was all he could do.

~~~~~~~~~~~~~~~~~~~~ ❖ ~~~~~~~~~~~~~~~~~~~~

Gil'ead didn't have a proper city wall, as did Ceunon and Dras-Leona—in the event of an attack, the commoners were expected to shelter inside the central fortress—but there was still a gatehouse along the main road.

The guards, Murtagh was relieved to see, were just keeping a general watch and made no effort to inspect those who entered.

He lowered his head and hurried past, trying to blend in with the caravan he'd followed.

The city proper was a loud, boisterous place, earthy and muscular. The smell of manure was strong in the air, and people shouted across the streets and from the balconies of their houses. There were minstrels by the squares and tinkers in the streets, and dozens of buildings were being raised across the city, which surprised Murtagh; they'd have to hurry to get the roofs on before winter descended in earnest.

He saw even more evidence of the war. The buildings along the main thoroughfare were scorched on their beams, and broken-off shafts of embedded arrows stuck out from the walls, like thorns on a rosebush. A rowdy band of dwarves was arguing with a stablemaster near the city entrance as they tried to agree on terms for housing the dwarves' ponies. Close to the center of Gil'ead, Murtagh saw a pair of elves—one male, one female, both with ink-black hair—standing inside the gate of an ostentatious stone-walled house, talking in the front garden while purple-edged butterflies fluttered about their heads and shoulders.

Murtagh suppressed a snort. *How like them. We're all true to our own natures, I suppose.*

He made sure to keep well away from the stone house.

After the quiet of the past four days, the smells and sounds of the city were overwhelming. Murtagh fought the urge to plug his ears—and nose—and he found himself flinching at unexpected noises.

You're turning into a wild animal, he thought. Skittish and untamed. He wasn't sure if it was a bad thing.

He made his way to the main market, which indeed had many weapons on display. He gave them a pass for the time being, as he felt that a sword would attract more attention than his staff, and wandered among the other stalls, inspecting the wares. A few discreet questions about the origins of a soft woolen scarf and a cask of southern wine and a set of carved necklaces were enough for him to learn that Ilenna's family still plied their trade. Further inquiry with a seller of cloth revealed that, as he suspected, Ilenna was most often to be found at Lord Relgin's court, advising the earl on her father's behalf.

Satisfied with his findings, Murtagh stopped at a small tent decked with wicker cages containing doves, pigeons, and songbirds of various sorts. The owner was a gruff, mustachioed man who more resembled a military quartermaster than a merchant.

After some brief haggling, Murtagh bought the brightest, sweetest-sounding finch. With a cloth over the cage to keep the bird silent, he hurried through the busy streets to the fortress entrance.

The main gates were open, the cross-barred portcullis raised high, but Murtagh didn't head toward them. The guards standing on either side of the gates *would* inspect anyone who tried to walk straight in.

That had never been his plan. Instead, he positioned himself behind the corner of a nearby house, where the guards couldn't see him but he could watch everyone who entered and exited the fortress. Murtagh knew his time was limited. Someone was sure to notice if he kept loitering there, but he didn't think he would need to wait very long.

He was right.

Not half an hour after he settled into place, a red-haired page with tasseled sleeves hurried out the front gate and rushed off in the direction of the market. Murtagh perked up. *Perfect.*

He slipped through an alleyway stinking of night soil and placed himself by the side of the street where he guessed the page would return.

A tug on his cloak caused him to start. He looked down to see a pair of dirty faces staring up at him, urchins barely half his height, dressed in rags that had seen more years than their owners.

"Please, master, sir," they said in unison, and held out cupped hands.

Murtagh couldn't tell if the children were male or female. He decided it didn't matter. He also decided it didn't matter if they were making a fool of him, if they had a house with family and food and a warm hearth.

"Here. Go buy something to eat," he said, fishing two coppers out of his purse.

They laughed and bobbed their heads. "Thank you, sir! Red, red, red, an' dragon get'cha!" Then, quick as rats, they scurried down the alley and disappeared among the buildings.

Murtagh checked his belt. His purse was still where it should be, which he counted a victory. He smiled. Whatever happened with Ilenna, he'd done *some* good that day.

His smile faded as he spotted the page heading back along the street. The youth was dawdling along, eating a hand pie, enjoying the sun, and watching the ladies on the street. *Not so eager to return to your master or mistress, eh?*

As the youth passed the alley mouth, Murtagh swept aside his cloak and, in a voice from the past, said, "Boy! Hold there. I would speak with you."

The page froze, and Murtagh could see panic in his eyes as the youth tried to figure out whether he was in trouble and, if so, how much.

"Y-y-yes, sir?" The page bowed slightly, and then looked askance at Murtagh's travel-stained clothes. A line of gravy ran from the page's half-eaten pie and down his hand.

Hesitation would lose the day. Assuming a haughty air, Murtagh beckoned him closer. "Come here, boy. You are a page of Lord Relgin's court, yes? I have need of a courier to deliver a message of mine."

The youth glanced back at the fortress and shifted on his feet, as if to turn and run. "My master—"

"Speak not to me of your master! This is of the highest importance." Murtagh tapped the side of his nose. "The *highest* importance." The page's expression sharpened into interest. Intrigue always had that effect. "You know the goodwoman Ilenna who attends Lord Relgin's court?"

"I know *of* Ilenna, sir."

Murtagh gestured as if that were of no matter. "And you no doubt might command her attention, by reason of your position, yes?"

The youth puffed out his chest slightly. "Why yes, sir. I suppose I might."

"Excellent." Murtagh held out a square of folded parchment sealed with a blob of melted tallow. "Then I charge you to convey this message to the estimable Ilenna, and with it my urgent desire to have words with her at the soonest convenience. Along with my request, I offer this gift to Ilenna, as a sign of my deep respect." He motioned to the cage by his feet.

The page eyed the cage and parchment. "If I do find her, sir—"

"Then return with alacrity, boy, and let me know her response. This is a matter of urgency." The page hesitantly accepted the parchment, and Murtagh said, as if he'd forgotten until that very moment, "Oh yes, and for your troubles." He handed over a tarnished coin. "A silver now, and a crown when you return."

The page's face brightened. "Sir, *yes sir!*"

A crown was more than the youth likely saw in a year. An expensive bribe, but worth it, although the cost left Murtagh's purse sadly depleted.

If this keeps up, I might have to seek gainful employment, he thought, sardonic. *Perhaps as a mercenary or a chirurgeon.*

As the youth scooped up the cage, the finch inside warbled with sleepy protest. "I'll be back as soon as I can, sir."

Murtagh nodded, again wrapping himself in his cloak. "I shall wait until such time as I hear Ilenna's response. Now go! And swift fate guide you."

The page turned and trotted toward the castle, holding the cage in one hand and his half-eaten pie in the other.

Murtagh shook his head as he watched the youth depart. Pages had formed an essential, if inefficient, means of communication in Galbatorix's court. Not only that, they usually knew more of what was going on than even the spymaster himself. He just hoped that the promise of gold would keep the youth focused on his task.

While he waited, Murtagh passed the time by watching the people of Gil'ead. There were soldiers in shirts of rusted mail, with spears resting at a jaunty angle on their shoulders. Officers trotting past on well-groomed horses with braided manes. Merchants with plumed hats and clothes made of rich fabrics. Nobles—or would-be nobles drawn from the upper ranks of the Varden—attempting to avoid splattering mud on their finery, often with a line of trailing servants carrying bundles of purchases. Many of the more important personages made use of covered chairs carried by porters who trotted through the streets at a brisk pace, conveying the impression that whoever was inside had the most urgent business.

In reality, Murtagh knew the porters couldn't maintain such a pace, and most of the trips were of the most mundane variety. But as always, appearances had to be upheld.

He glanced at the muddy hem of his cloak. As much as he liked order and cleanliness, he didn't miss the never-ending drive to present a perfect image to the world. Now that he'd had time away from court, that pressure seemed a form of temporary insanity.

At the end of the street, opposite the fortress, he could see into the main square. Lively music sounded among the buildings, and through a crowd of shifting bodies, he caught glimpses of a harvest dance: men and women circling each other, arms interlinked, feet lifting high to the rapid beat.

Murtagh found himself tapping his own foot. Dancing had been the one thing he'd enjoyed at court, although everything surrounding the dances—the politics and machinations and general villainy—had been miserable. But the dances themselves, ah, those had been a special pleasure. He'd mastered even the most complicated sequence of steps, and it had served him in good stead in his swordplay. Footwork was everything in dance and war, whether on an individual level or on the level of armies and nations. The right move at the right moment was the difference between victory and defeat, and the right move wasn't always the expected one.

A face across the street caught Murtagh's attention. A flash of pale cheek, the line of a jaw, the distinctive silhouette of a nose . . . Murtagh stiffened as he eyed the profile of a youngish man walking amid a knot of five guards.

It can't be. Lyreth? The oldest son of Lord Thaven, who had served as commander of Galbatorix's navy? Lyreth was four years older than Murtagh. He'd always been larger and stronger while growing up and hadn't been shy about using that to his advantage.

Now that Murtagh thought about it, he hadn't seen Lyreth in Urû'baen during his last stay in the capital. Thaven's son had been smart enough to avoid appearing at court while Murtagh was there as a Rider.

What's he doing here now? Lyreth turned his head to look at something on the other side of the street, and Murtagh sank farther back into the alley. Lyreth, of all people, would have no difficulty recognizing him. *I shouldn't have shaved.*

But no reaction altered Lyreth's expression, and he continued on his way at the same brisk pace.

Murtagh let out his breath and retreated to the corner of the building. Lyreth probably had even more cause to avoid being recognized in public. All of the noble families who had served under Galbatorix—families who had accumulated enormous wealth and power during his century-long tenure on the throne—had lost their positions, and many of them had been executed or exiled. But loyalties ran deep, and wealth bought protection. As with Yarek, Murtagh knew that some not-inconsiderable number of Galbatorix's followers were living in gilded secrecy.

He didn't envy Nasuada having to deal with their undermining influence.

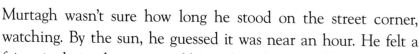

Murtagh wasn't sure how long he stood on the street corner, watching. By the sun, he guessed it was near an hour. He felt a faint tingle in the center of his right palm—as if his hand had fallen partially asleep—and he scratched it without thinking.

He froze. His right palm was where his gedwëy ignasia lay: the silvery, scar-like blotch that marked where he'd first touched Thorn as a hatchling. And it often itched or tingled when there was danger nearby.

The feeling wasn't infallible, but it had saved his skin more than once.

Again alert, he glanced around. *There.* Soldiers slipping out of the fortress entrance and gathering by the corner of a house. He'd been too distracted; he'd missed the first few.

And with the soldiers . . . a man in a black, purple-trimmed robe, hood thrown back to reveal a head of hair so pale it was nearly white. On the breast of his robe was embroidered a golden symbol, a heraldic standard: in the top half, a crown with rays spreading from the points. A fess, then, dividing the standard in half, and below it, a cockatrice statant, with an iron band around each scaled ankle.

Murtagh knew it well. The coat of arms of Du Vrangr Gata, the guild of magicians who served Nasuada, and who enforced her laws prohibiting unauthorized and unaffiliated magic throughout not just her realm but also the southern kingdom of Surda. Every human spellcaster was required to join the guild, or else submit to drugs and spells that would prevent them from using magic without permission.

Murtagh had yet to agree to either provision, and he never would.

Which meant the blond-haired man was a threat. Given the opportunity, he would seek to chain Murtagh in one manner or another, and even a weak magician could prove to be a formidable opponent in one-on-one combat, for fights between magicians were rarely resolved with spells alone. Mental prowess mattered, and if you could gain control of your foe's mind, they would be at your mercy, no matter their skill, strength, or wards.

"Curse you," he muttered, meaning the page. It wasn't the betrayal itself that bothered him—Murtagh was well acquainted with betrayal—it was the inconsistency. Pages weren't supposed to rat out those who came to them in confidence! How could a court function otherwise?

A feather-light touch brushed Murtagh's mind.

He recoiled, retreating deep within himself and armoring his mind with a wall of iron determination. "You shall not have me," he muttered again and again, using the words to focus his thoughts. The emptier his mind, the less there would be for the magician to find.

The robed man frowned and said something to the soldiers. He pointed down the street.

Murtagh moved. Time to leave before the soldiers cornered him.

He'd just reached the other end of the alley when a thickset man in a sleeveless jerkin stepped in front of him. The man's bare arms were as heavily muscled as a smith's, and he carried a cudgel in one hand.

Murtagh nearly struck the stranger, but the man backed off, arms spread wide, and in a low, gruff voice said, "Are you Tornac?"

"Who asks?" He had made no mention of Tornac to the page, although he had used the name on the note for Ilenna. Was the man her servant? If not . . .

A flicker of annoyance crossed the man's face. "The werecat Carabel has sent me. She requests the company of this Tornac."

A *werecat!* Alarm and curiosity coursed through Murtagh. He glanced back. The magician and soldiers were nearly to the mouth of the alleyway. He had to decide. "That's me," he said, curt.

"This way, then. Right quicklike, if you please."

The bare-armed man hurried up the side street, and Murtagh followed close behind, carrying his staff sideways in his hand. There was no reason for subterfuge now.

For a few minutes, the only sounds were their breath and the soft pad of their boots on the ground.

Murtagh's mind whirled with puzzlement. How had Carabel ended up with his note? Of all the creatures in Alagaësia, were-cats were the most secretive. Always they kept apart from others, although in the final press of the war, they had joined forces with the Varden against Galbatorix. But on the whole, they weren't partisan as the other races were.

Since the fall of the Empire, Murtagh had heard tell that a werecat sat on a velvet cushion next to Nasuada's throne. And likewise in King Orrin's court in Surda, and in the courts of all the great cities. Murtagh assumed Carabel served in a similar fashion at Gil'ead. But what did she want with *him*?

She can't know who I really am, he thought. Unless, of course, she was a confederate of Ilenna's. He supposed he would find out soon enough.

Murtagh felt another faint touch against his mind, but it was so soft as to be nearly imperceptible, and it slid past without stopping.

Not so skilled, are you? he thought. But he didn't allow himself to relax. Not yet.

The man led him to a narrow house built close to the fortress, through the house's gated yard, and down a flight of mossy stairs set against the fortress's outer wall. At the bottom was a well situated within an alcove adorned with carved flowers. Murtagh was entirely unsurprised when the man pushed on a petal and a small stone door swung open.

A breath of cold air washed over them.

Most castles had bolt-holes or the like. Escape routes for the nobles who lived within. Such things compromised the fortifications, but when needed, nothing else would suffice.

"After you, sir," said the man, holding the door open. A low, dark tunnel ran under the fortress, its far end hidden in shadow. "Carabel awaits."

"And what does she wish with me?"

"Wouldn't be my place t' say. You'll have to ask her yourself."

Murtagh hesitated. Once he entered the fortress, it would be far, far harder to leave, even with all of his magical prowess. It was a risk. A big one. How likely was it that he was walking into a trap?

The man shifted with impatience.

Murtagh wished he could tell Thorn what was happening, but he didn't dare expose his consciousness for the equivalent of a mental shout.

He spared a glance for the open sky and wondered when he would see it again. Then he gathered his cloak close and ducked inside.

The door shut behind them with a soft *thud*, and the sound echoed the length of the tunnel.

CHAPTER II

✦ ✦ ✦ ✦ ✦ ✦ ✦

Questions for a Cat

The tunnel smelled of wet stone, mold, and the sweat of the man shuffling along behind him. It was pitch-black.

Murtagh felt an uncomfortable prickle along his spine: not a premonition, but a concern. It would be easy for the man to hit him in the head with the cudgel. Too easy. Murtagh had wards to fend off attacks, but there was no knowing what enchantments your opponent had, if any.

The mark on his palm no longer itched, which gave him some comfort. Nevertheless, he remained tense.

"Keep straight," said the man, rough. "'Bout a hundred feet there's a turn to the right. Be careful, there are stairs going up directly after."

"Understood."

Murtagh was tempted to summon a werelight, but there was no point in revealing that he could use magic.

As he felt his way through the dark, a profusion of possibilities bedeviled him. A thousand likely—and unlikely—fates, each worse than the last. It was fruitless speculation, so he wrenched his thoughts away and instead reviewed his answers to every question he could imagine.

He wasn't about to allow Carabel to catch him out, even if she were the cleverest of werecats.

In the blackness beneath the ground, the hundred feet seemed more like a thousand. Murtagh would have sworn they had crossed the fortress yard and were under the houses on the other side.

Just when he was about to ask how much farther they had to

go, the hand he had on the wall slipped around a corner. *Finally!* He breathed a sigh of relief as he turned. Another stride, and his left foot bumped into the bottom of a step.

Using his staff for balance, he climbed.

One . . .

Two . . .

Three . . .

Four . . .

Fi— He slipped on the fifth step; a patch of water caused his boot to lose its grip. He caught himself on his staff and then continued, heart pounding.

Five . . .

Six . . .

Seven. A dim thread of light appeared before him, tall and straight.

"Give it a good push," said the man. "It'll open right fine."

Murtagh put his hand out and pushed. An arched door swung open, revealing a small storeroom. A lit candle sat in a sconce on the wall, and after the profound blackness of the tunnel, the flickering flame was almost blinding. Several barrels were stacked in one corner, and dried hams and chains of sausages hung from hooks in the ceiling.

"Nasty business that," said the man. Murtagh turned to see him closing the door behind them; when shut, the outline of the door was practically invisible. The man brushed cobwebs from his shoulders and made a face. "Too many spiders down there. Right, she'll be wanting to see you directly. This way."

Murtagh followed as the man led him through several side passages in the fortress—retreating behind corners whenever they heard voices—until they arrived at a dark wood door somewhere on the eastern side of the complex.

The sleeveless man bowed in what Murtagh thought was a slightly mocking fashion and opened the door for him.

Murtagh stepped through it.

He found himself in a sumptuously appointed study. Rows of polished bookcases lined the walls; thick dwarven rugs, rich with reds, greens, and blues, covered the floor; and a beautiful map of Alagaësia, painstakingly annotated with thousands of names, was framed as a centerpiece above a stone fireplace, wherein a stack of logs merrily burned.

Facing the door was a great desk of carved wood. And sitting behind the desk, propped up on a green velvet cushion, was none other than the werecat Carabel.

She was in her human form, which meant she appeared to Murtagh as a slim, grey-haired woman no taller than four foot. A loose white shift left her lean arms uncovered. Murtagh guessed the shift made it easy for her to change shape if she wished. Although she had the same general contours as a human, there was no doubt that Carabel *wasn't*. Her cheekbones were too wide, her emerald eyes too angled, her pupils too slitted, and there were small tufts of white hair on the tips of her ears. Murtagh wasn't sure if the tufts were because Carabel hadn't fully transformed or if they were a normal feature of her race.

Until then, he had never actually seen a werecat, and he found himself unexpectedly hesitant.

On the desk in front of Carabel were three things: the cage with the finch he'd bought, now empty save for a few yellow feathers; a plate with cuts of cold meat; and the parchment he'd given the page, unfolded to reveal the lines of runes written within.

The sight puzzled Murtagh. If the werecat had intercepted his message to Ilenna, was she acting as Lord Relgin's spymaster? And did that mean she had used the magician and soldiers as a ploy to force him into her clutches? Or were things as they appeared, and she really had been trying to save him from Relgin's forces?

Murtagh forced himself to remain relaxed even as he realized his understanding of the situation was woefully inadequate. *I'm going to have to step carefully. Very, very carefully.*

The door shut behind him, and he was conscious of his guide taking up a position in the back corner, cudgel still in hand.

Carabel cocked her head and watched Murtagh in exactly the same way he had seen yard cats watch a bird or mouse they were stalking. He had a sense that she would happily sit in silence for the rest of the day.

Or until she got bored, and Murtagh didn't think he wanted to deal with a bored werecat.

He motioned toward the wicker cage. "You enjoyed the bird, I take it."

Carabel lifted one perfectly sharp eyebrow. "It was acceptable, man of the road." She had a plummy, purring voice that oozed self-satisfied confidence. And yet, Murtagh detected a note of underlying strain. Her gaze shifted to the sleeveless brute at the back of the room. "Was there trouble on the way?"

"Close, ma'am, but none worth mentioning."

"Good." She smiled, revealing sharp little fangs. "You have met Bertolf, yes? He is a most excellent help. He fetches me meats and morsels and tasty mysteries such as yourself."

Murtagh wasn't sure if he liked being referred to as *tasty*. He allowed himself an expression of cultured amusement, as he would have used at court, and made a sweeping bow. A bit of theatrics never hurt, especially with cats. "My apologies, Lady Carabel, but the finch was intended for another. Or perhaps you didn't know?"

With one long, needle-tipped nail, she pricked the center of the parchment square. "Oh yes, I knew. You sought to speak with Ilenna Erithsdaughter, did you not?"

"That's right." Murtagh felt glad he'd couched his message to Ilenna in deliberately vague language that, he hoped, would mean little to others.

Carabel gestured at the chair in front of the desk. "Sit, human. We have much to speak of."

"Do we, now?" But Murtagh pulled his cloak to one side and sat. He leaned his staff against his right knee, where he could grab it in an instant. "Might I ask why you seized my letter and gift? I have broken no law and caused no trouble."

"That is the wrong question. You should instead ask *how* I knew to seize your letter and gift. The page's master is Lord Relgin's chamberlain, and the page told him of the strange man offering coin to speak with Ilenna Erithsdaughter. No doubt the chamberlain rewarded him far in excess of your bribe."

Murtagh winced. He should have quizzed the page more closely. "And the chamberlain then came to you. I see, but—"

"Not quite," said Carabel. "The chamberlain went to Lord Relgin, and Lord Relgin dispatched a number of his men to apprehend you, O Tornac. Most unusual. Such court intrigues are usually beneath Relgin."

So the soldiers *had* been after him. A sour taste formed in Murtagh's mouth. It seemed like he wouldn't be getting near Ilenna anytime soon. He put the thought aside. That wasn't his immediate problem. "I admit, I am confused, Lady Carabel. Did Lord Relgin tell you all this? If so, why bring me here in defiance of him? And why should any of you highborn folk care about my doings? I am no one of importance."

Carabel licked the points of her teeth. Her tongue was small and pink. "That's not exactly true, now is it . . . Murtagh son of Morzan?"

A coal popped in the fireplace, startlingly loud.

Murtagh felt his eyes narrow. He gripped the staff, ready to fight. "How did you find out?"

A cruel little smile curved Carabel's dark lips. It unsettled him to think how often they touched raw meat and blood. "The name

Tornac is not unknown to us werecats, human. Besides, you smell of dragon."

Her explanation did nothing to ease his mind. "All right," he said. "What do you want?"

A frown pinched Carabel's delicate features, and a dark aspect settled upon her face. "A question for you first, human. What business had you with Ilenna Erithsdaughter?"

Had. Murtagh didn't like her use of the past tense. He affected an abashed look. "In truth, no business. It is a private matter between us. I'm sure you understand."

Again Carabel paused. *She's uncertain,* he realized. *Why?* He decided to take the initiative. "Is there a problem with Ilenna? Has something happened to her?"

The tufts on Carabel's ears swayed as she shook her head. "Ilenna is unharmed. The problem lies . . . elsewhere. I will ask you again, Murtagh son of Morzan. What business had you with her?"

"Am I speaking to you or to Lord Relgin?"

She inspected the nails on her left hand, holding them up to the light so the tips gleamed red-gold from the flames. "Werecats answer to no one but ourselves. You speak to me and me alone."

"And him." Murtagh jerked a thumb back over his shoulder.

A slight purr escaped Carabel. "Bertolf is trusted."

"Maybe by you." Murtagh adjusted his grip on the staff. "Why should I tell you, werecat? There's nothing you can do to stop me from leaving."

Carabel's slitted pupils constricted. If her tail had been present, he thought it would have twitched. "No, but you want information, human. Why else would you wish to talk with Ilenna? Oh yes, I know of her family's *activities.* Great clumsy oafs they are. Not like cats. But I can promise you this: there is no way you can speak to Ilenna or her father without Lord Relgin finding out. If you don't mind revealing yourself, then go to them. Leave now. But I think you prefer to remain hidden, you and your dragon."

Murtagh turned his staff in his hand. What was the werecat getting at? He felt as if he were fighting a duel and he was two steps behind his opponent.

"Maybe you're right," he said. "You still haven't given me a reason why I should share anything with you."

Carabel's thin shoulders rose and fell. "If it is secrets you seek, then who better to ask than a cat? Ask of me, Murtagh son of Morzan, and if I do not know, I will speak to Ilenna on your behalf."

"You're offering to help me," said Murtagh, wary.

Her eyelids lowered until they were half closed, and she nestled in on herself, as if to brace against inclement wind. "I am."

"In exchange for what?"

She blinked. "The smallest of favors."

In an instant, things became clear to Murtagh. A cynical laugh escaped him. "Of course. And what is this *smallest of favors?*"

The werecat lifted her pointed chin, defiant. "A task that needs doing, and none there are in Gil'ead who can do it, save you."

"Somehow I doubt that." He frowned at her; she was trying to manipulate him. "I'm not your errand boy, cat. No one gets to order me about. Not you, not Relgin, not even Nasuada."

"I would not think to tell a Dragon Rider what to do. This is an offer, not a command."

Murtagh growled and ran his fingers through his hair. "And what is it you need doing?"

"You will agree to it?"

"That depends on the nature of the task and whether or not you have the answers I seek."

With a seemingly uninterested air, Carabel licked a fleck of blood off the middle finger of her left hand. "That is hardly fair, human. What if I must confer with Ilenna? Shall I hunt for you out of nothing but the goodness of my heart while I await your agreement?"

"Shall I help you out of nothing but the goodness of my own?"

Carabel flexed her fingers, as if to extend and retract claws. "Trust is a sword with a blade for a hilt. It cuts all equally."

"That is far from a convincing, or comforting, argument."

"For a human."

"Human I am."

She gave him a flat, humorless stare. "I have not told Lord Relgin of your presence here. Is that not enough reason to trust me?"

Despite the werecat's seemingly relaxed pose, Murtagh saw hints of coiled tension throughout her body. *Something's seriously amiss, or she wouldn't have gone to so much trouble.*

He lifted the staff a few inches and let it rap against the floor. Once. Twice. Three times. He decided. The cat was right; he wouldn't be able to talk with Ilenna without attracting attention. Regardless of the *favor* Carabel had in mind, he might learn something by putting his questions to her. Even if she knew nothing helpful, that itself was a useful piece of information. And in any case, it could be prudent to forewarn Carabel and, by extension, Lord Relgin about the strange doings in the land.

"It's not," said Murtagh, "but let us both cut ourselves." From inside his cloak, he removed the bird-skull amulet and the stone with the inner shine and placed them on the desk.

A sulfurous smell began to taint the air.

Carabel hissed and scooted backward on her velvet cushion, her spine arched as if she were about to spring into the air. Her grey hair nearly stood on end. "Where did you find those *thingsss?*"

Once again, Murtagh had the disconcerting realization that he wasn't talking with another human, but something entirely different. "Ceunon. I took them off a rather disreputable trader by the name of Sarros."

Carabel extended a clawed hand and touched the tip of her index nail to the amulet. She snatched her hand back as if burned, and then shivered and straightened, again assuming a dignified air. It was a false front; Murtagh could see that the werecat was shaken, and that likewise disturbed him. Werecats were many things, but cowards they were not.

"Tell the full tale, human, and leave nothing out."

He didn't do as she asked. Not entirely. There were some secrets he didn't feel like sharing, such as his use of the Name of Names. (Even if the werecats were aware the Name existed, he saw no advantage in revealing that he knew the word.) But aside from that, he told the truth.

As he talked, Murtagh was conscious of Bertolf listening behind him. He hoped the man was more discreet than the page.

The crackling of the fire was the only sound in the room when he finished.

Carabel stretched and shivered, and Murtagh noticed for the first time that her feet were bare. "*Sssah.* You ask questions you may not want answering, human."

"Then you know where to find the witch-woman Bachel?"

"*Yesss.*"

"And the origin of the stone? And also the Dreamers that Sarros mentioned?"

Her lips retracted, showing more of her pointed teeth. "Yes and *yesss.*"

"And you will tell me?"

Carabel's gaze went to the map over the fireplace before returning to the coal-like stone. "If you will complete the task I set before you . . . yes."

"What guarantee have I that you actually possess the information I seek? Tell me first."

Her tufted ears pressed flat against the sides of her head. "After, human. After. We must both grasp the sword."

Murtagh still wasn't convinced. "Maybe I should talk to Ilenna instead. I'm sure I could find a way to approach her unseen."

An unpleasant scraping filled the study as Carabel drew her nails across the surface of the desk, leaving thin lines in the wood.

"You would be disappointed, human. She has no knowledge of these things. I swear it."

"But you do."

"*Yesss.*"

He tapped the butt of the staff against the floor. "And how is that?"

"Because I am a cat, human. I hear many things, and I know more. I hunt in shadows, and I dance in moonbeams, and wherever I walk, I walk alone."

Nonsense and riddles, but what else had he expected? "What is the task?"

A tense stillness settled upon Carabel, and her eyes flared with dark anger. She looked ready to fight or spring after her prey. "Over the past six moons, three of our younglings have been taken in Gil'ead. One of them was later found lost along the shore of the lake with no memory of how he got there. The others have never been seen again. Most recently, another youngling was seized, not three days past."

A sympathetic anger formed in Murtagh. "Seized by whom?"

"Men. Humans. But I cannot say why."

"And you want me to find the ones responsible?"

Carabel shook her head. "No. I want you to find the youngling who was taken. *All* of the younglings, if possible, but I fear only the one may yet be saved. Silna is her name. We tracked her through the city—a werecat's nose is hard to fool—and we know where she might be."

"But you can't get to her."

The werecat blinked. Her lashes were as long and fine as the silk atop summer grass. "There is a certain captain of the city guard. Captain Wren. In the barracks he has command over, there is a set of stairs that lead underground to a room where he and his officers meet once every sevenday. Past that room are certain other chambers, and at the end of them is a door that never opens. We suspect Silna might be found therein."

Murtagh frowned. *A captain of the city guard* . . . The implications were unpleasant. "Do you think this Captain Wren is responsible for taking Silna?"

"We do not know."

"And just how many werecats are in Gil'ead?"

The tips of her ears twitched. "More than you might think, human."

He let that pass. "Who else has access to those chambers?"

"Again, we do not know. There may be an entrance from the other side, some secret tunnel we have yet to discover."

His frown deepened. "Have you spoken to Lord Relgin about this? I assume not."

Carabel let out a sharp breath. "We are werecats, but still, at heart, we are cats. We are the ones who walk through doors. Always and ever. But we cannot walk through the door beneath the barracks, which means there is magic at work, and none there are in Relgin's service fit to deal with such things. It is a task for a Rider. Besides . . . there is always a chance that Wren or someone in his command was given orders from above."

The more she spoke, the more troubled Murtagh felt. He turned the staff in his hand. "What about Du Vrangr Gata? Surely they could help."

A low coughing, spitting sound issued from Carabel. "I would not trust them to catch a mouse with three broken legs. *Pah!*"

"And you need someone you can trust."

She met his gaze and held it. "Yes."

Murtagh wondered about the elves. That Carabel had not mentioned them was answer enough, but he was curious as to the reason. Elves and werecats did not seem entirely dissimilar, and if bad blood lay between them—or even just a basic dislike—he was interested in knowing why. *A question for another time.*

His thoughts returned to Silna. In his mind, he pictured a child huddled alone in a bare stone cell. He could imagine all too well the cold, the pain, the anger, and the despair she might be feeling.

Had he not shared those same torments when the Twins had deposited him in the dungeon beneath the citadel at Urû'baen? Worst of all had been the uncertainty, not knowing what fresh outrages one moment or the next might bring.

Nor had that been his only experience in such a helpless, dire situation. He still remembered with painful vividness when, at fourteen, he'd snuck out of Urû'baen without permission or accompaniment. That evening, he'd tried to slip back in through the main gates, and the soldiers standing watch had caught him. Not recognizing him, they threw him into one of the cells buried beneath the guard tower. Galbatorix had been absent from the city at the time, along with his entire retinue. No one remained whom Murtagh could call upon to confirm his identity. So there he had languished for a week and three days, convinced he would die in sunless confinement and that no one would know or care.

In the end, Galbatorix returned, and word of Murtagh's plight somehow reached the court, for the king's then chamberlain had come to see to his release. After which the chamberlain promptly had Murtagh soundly beaten for the trouble he had caused.

Murtagh suppressed a shiver. He could still smell the dampness of the cell and feel the cold of the stones seeping into his bones. And yet, despite his familiarity with the distressing realities of Silna's likely plight—and his compassion for her—he resented Carabel using the youngling to secure his help. Doubly so because he knew he would hate himself if he walked away.

"Fine," he ground out from between his teeth. "I'll do it. But not for you, nor even for myself. For Silna."

Carabel nodded. "Whatever you find behind that door, the race of werecats will be grateful and count you as a friend, Murtagh son of Morzan."

Stop calling me that! "Where are the barracks?"

Her hair bristled slightly. "It is not that simple."

"Why shouldn't it be? I'll walk in and open the door, magic or no, and if anyone dares stop me, I'll—"

"No!" She dug her claws into the arms of her chair, and for a moment, Murtagh thought she might leap across the desk. "If you rouse the alarm, Silna might be spirited away before you can reach her. Or worse, killed. The risk is too great. And you do not know what spells may have been deployed in that place."

Murtagh inclined his head. "So how am I supposed to gain entrance without attracting unwanted attention?"

Carabel settled back on her cushion and smoothed the tassels on her ears. "You must become a member of the city guard and join Captain Wren's company."

He allowed his eyebrows to rise. "Oh, is that all? . . . Well, I suppose I can talk my way into their ranks, if need be."

"Alas, that will not suffice." Carabel was somber, but she seemed to take a subtle delight in confounding him. "Captain Wren no longer accepts general recruits into his company. At Lord Relgin's indulgence, Wren selects his men from among the rest of the guard, and it is counted a high honor to be so chosen. But Wren only seeks out men whose service he trusts."

"And that's not suspicious at all."

Carabel flicked her ears. "But not uncommon for officers of distinction."

"True enough. So how do I earn Captain Wren's trust?"

"It is not possible, not in the time we have. Instead, you will have to impress him."

Murtagh nearly growled. "And how am I to accomplish that? A feat of arms?"

A sly smile curled Carabel's sharp lips. "It is very simple, human. To impress him, you must kill a fish."

"A fish? A *fish*? Do you take me for a fool?"

"Not at all. But, alas, to kill the fish, you will need a special lure."

"Bah!" With an expression of disgust, Murtagh fell back in the chair. How deep of a hole had he fallen in? If he hadn't already given his word, and if it weren't for the vanished youngling, he would have gotten up and left. "Enough of these riddles, cat! Explain, and you'd best do a good job of it."

"Of course, human. It goes as such. In Isenstar Lake lives a great cunning fish the men of this place have named Muckmaw. He is fierce, hungry, and cruel, and over the years, he has sunk many a boat and eaten many a fisherman. There is a reward in Gil'ead for whosoever can dispatch Muckmaw and present his head as proof of the deed. Four gold coins and a promise of a position in the guards, if so desired. I have no doubt that if you bring Muckmaw's head to Captain Wren, he will welcome you into the ranks of his men."

"Killing a fish is no great challenge," said Murtagh.

"Were that was true. Muckmaw is no ordinary beast." Carabel gestured at herself. "And a werecat should know. No common bait or cloth or colored thread will attract him, only something of special significance."

"Or I could just find him with my mind." Murtagh gave her a dangerous smile. "A quick spell, and that will be the end of Muckmaw."

The werecat matched his smile. "And how will you pick out the thoughts of a single fish amongst all the fish in Isenstar Lake? . . . No, you will need a lure, one that he cannot resist."

"What sort of lure is that?"

"A scale of the dragon Glaedr, whose body lies burned and buried outside this city."

Murtagh's immediate reaction was outrage. "You must be jesting!"

"I would not jest about such a thing," said Carabel, deadly quiet. "Not when one of our younglings is in danger. Trust me, human, only the scale of a dragon will suffice for Muckmaw."

Again, Murtagh saw Oromis and Glaedr falling limply through the air while ranks of men and elves clashed on the ground below. He rubbed his knuckles as he stared at the floor. "I'm not happy about this, cat."

The slightest bit of sympathy entered Carabel's voice: "It is a hard thing I ask you for, I know. But there is a rightness to it also."

"I fail to see any *rightness* in grave robbery."

"You slew Glaedr. Now, by fate's design, you may use a part of him to help save an innocent. What could be more right than that?"

The question struck him to his core. He forced his hands apart. "The elves will have set wards around Glaedr's tomb to prevent exactly this sort of desecration."

A shrug from Carabel. "Yes. Probably. That is why we haven't tried. That is why we must ask *you*, Rider."

"And what if I hadn't come to Gil'ead?"

When she answered, he heard no pretense in her voice, only honest emotion, raw and vulnerable and shot through with determination. "Then I and all the werecats in Gil'ead would have stormed the barracks and attempted to breach the door." She met his gaze. "If that meant we had to fight an entire company of guards, then so be it. We will not abandon our young."

". . . No." Murtagh frowned and looked at the wood-braced ceiling. *I should have known better than to give my word.* Another thought followed close behind: *Thorn won't like that I did.* But he knew he couldn't ignore Carabel's request, even if, right then, he rather hated the werecat. "Get the scale, catch the fish, find out what's behind the door. Is that it?"

Carabel nodded. "Exactly. But you must be quick about it, human. We have heard whispers of men moving in the night, wagons readied, horses freshly shod. . . . By tomorrow evening, Silna may no longer be in the city."

Murtagh silently cursed. *This isn't going to be easy.* Then his resolve hardened, and he leaned forward with his elbows on his knees. If the werecat child was in Gil'ead, he'd find her, even if it meant pulling the city apart beam by beam.

"Then we'd best not waste any time."

A savage, toothy smile spread across Carabel's face.

CHAPTER III

✦ ✦ ✦ ✦ ✦ ✦ ✦

Barrow-Wights

It was late afternoon when Murtagh exited the secret tunnel underneath Gil'ead's fortress. Shadows had filled the streets, and only the rooftops remained bathed in light warm and gold.

The stone door closed behind him with a grinding sound as Bertolf, the sleeveless servant, pulled it shut.

Cautious, Murtagh climbed the stairs from the hidden entrance, half expecting a band of soldiers to jump him at any moment. At the top, he paused long enough to make sure no one was watching, and then he slipped through the garden, through the front gate, and into the street.

He had to force himself to pay attention to his surroundings as he hurried back toward Gil'ead's southern entrance, but his mind kept returning to his encounter with Carabel. A wry chuckle escaped him. *Quests from a werecat.* It was the sort of thing one heard about in stories, where the earnest young hero proved his doughtiness and won the hand of a princess.

Only Murtagh knew the world didn't work like that. More often than not, the hero ended up dead in a ditch, or else forced to carry out orders from the king he hated. . . .

His mood soured as he arrived at the edge of Gil'ead. With long strides, he hurried away from the buildings until he felt himself a safe distance. Then he moved off the road, to the top of a small hummock, and focused his mind in the direction of the hollow where Thorn lay hiding.

Can you hear me? he asked.

Thorn's response was immediate: a rush of concern and aggravation. *Of course. Are you safe?*

Safe enough.

Where are you?

Murtagh impressed an image of his surroundings onto Thorn. The dragon huffed, and Murtagh heard the sound in his mind. *Were you able to speak with Ilenna?*

Not quite. Opening his memories, Murtagh shared his recollection of his conversation with Carabel. It was faster than using words to explain every little detail.

Afterward, Thorn snorted. *The cat got the best of you, I think.*

I know, he agreed mildly. *There wasn't much I could do about it.*

Still, it will be good if you can help the hatchling.

I'll do my best. You don't mind about Glaedr's scale, do you?

Why should I? His scale is not my scale. Besides, Glaedr's body is dead. Why should a dragon care what happens to them when they are gone?

Many people do.

Thorn made the equivalent of a mental shrug. *If I am not here to know or feel, what does it matter? It is fear that drives such care, and I do not fear the worms.*

No. There are far worse things than death.

Murtagh could almost feel Thorn staring at him. *You are part dragon, I sometimes think.*

Of course. We are joined, you and I, aren't we? He looked at the sky, gauged how much time until nightfall. *I'm going to get the scale, and then I might need your help with the fish.*

Rainbow flecks of excitement colored Thorn's thoughts. *We will hunt together?*

Yes.

The flecks brightened, variegated lights sparking as Thorn imagined the successful conclusion of the chase, of teeth sinking into fishy flesh.

Soon, Murtagh promised.

With a purposeful stride, Murtagh headed west, toward the oak tree grown atop the mound where Oromis and Glaedr's remains were buried. As it grew near, he saw numerous people gathered about the oak, some kneeling, others standing, and he heard distant singing.

Among the people, he saw what looked to be a white-robed elf next to the twisted tree trunk.

"Barzûl," Murtagh swore, and turned aside. There was no sure way to conceal himself or what he was doing from elven eyes, which were the keenest and most perceptive of all the races'.

He hated to delay—every hour that passed lessened the chances that he could rescue Silna—but there was no help for it. He would have to wait.

Frustrated, Murtagh studied the fields around him. *There.* A small stand of willows near a bowl-like depression filled with lush grass, cattails, and a few crabapple trees heavy with their sour fruit.

He glanced at the road to make sure it was clear, and then trotted over to the stand of willows. There were midges and biting flies flitting about the grass, and his boots sank into marshy ground, but Murtagh was willing to put up with the annoyance in order to have some cover.

A fly bit his neck, and he slapped it away.

He wedged himself into the willows in an angled position that would keep him from falling onto the wet ground. Then, from the purse on his belt, he took some dried apple and a piece of cold bacon and chewed them slowly, savoring every bite. It was all the food he was going to get for a while.

He was thirsty too, but he didn't want to drink whatever stagnant water he could find in the depression. That was a good way to end up bent over sick for the next few days.

There has to be a way to make water safe with a spell. He remembered something of the like from Yngmar's memories, but the details had been vague.

Still thinking on it, he crossed his arms over the staff, pulled his hood over his face, and closed his eyes.

The hum of busy insects soon lulled him to sleep.

~~~~~~~~~~~~~~~~~~~~ ❖ ~~~~~~~~~~~~~~~~~~~~

Soft flesh fumbling at his skin, teeth scraping, unwelcome wetness along his hand, then a flare of yellow pain bright enough to make him yelp.

Murtagh jolted awake, shouting, wild-eyed. He thrashed with the staff, hoping to knock back whatever was hurting him.

A bony, dolorous face hung before him. Sideways pupils rimmed with dirty gold, cruel, inhuman; a profusion of black and white bristles; grasping lips searching like blind worms for food; splayed, flat-topped teeth yellowed around the bases, grinding, gnashing, snapping only inches from his cheek; breath like a putrid pond.

Murtagh recoiled. The face was a terrifying, uncaring hunger set to devour the world.

The yellowed teeth closed on his hand again, hard and painful. Repulsed, Murtagh reacted without thinking and shouted, "Thrysta!" while funneling his strength into the spell.

A full-body blow knocked him against a willow trunk as the creature in front of him went tumbling through the air with an outraged bray.

The animal landed several paces away and scrambled to its feet.

A goat. It was nothing more than a goat.

Murtagh blinked, still disoriented. He worked his mouth, tongue thick and dry, and looked around. No one else was in sight. He and the goat were alone in the shadowed depression.

The goat shook itself and gave Murtagh an angry, disapproving look. It lowered its head and scraped the marshy ground with a front hoof, as if preparing to charge.

"Letta," Murtagh said with a note of finality. The word wasn't a spell as such, but it contained the authority of the ancient language, and the goat—like all animals—understood the intent behind the command and stopped.

The goat pulled back its neck and shook its head as if a wasp had stung its nose, upper lip curled with unmistakable anger. Then it went "*Maaah*" in a disgusted tone and trotted away, flicking its tail.

Murtagh slumped against the willow. The image of the goat's open-mouthed face still filled him with revulsion. If he hadn't woken, he felt sure the beast would have kept eating and eating and eating until it consumed him alive.

Fresh alarm flooded his mind; his fear had woken Thorn from the dragon's own nap. For a few seconds, confusion reigned as their emotions overlapped and Murtagh attempted to calm Thorn.

It was just a goat, Murtagh said, extricating himself from the willow. *Just a goat.*

You scared me, said Thorn. Not an accusation, more of a plaintive statement.

I scared myself. I'm sorry. Everything is all right.

Do you want me to eat the goat?

For a moment, Murtagh seriously considered accepting. *No, but I appreciate the offer.*

Be careful. Even four-legs-no-fangs can be dangerous.

I know. I will.

Making a face, Murtagh brushed off his clothes. His back was sore from where the spell had slammed him into the willow tree. He berated himself for not setting a ward to wake him if someone or something came near . . . and for overreacting so strongly. Too many dangerous encounters had left him more twitchy than was good.

And yet his reactions had kept him alive.

He rubbed his hand where the goat had bitten him. The skin was red and bruised but unbroken.

The wards he *had* placed around himself only went so far. Too much protection and he wouldn't be able to interact with the world in a normal fashion—touching a sharpened edge or an overly hot pot, for example—and powering wards all the time would exhaust him, as they fed off the strength of his body. Which meant he'd never set a ward to specifically prevent an animal from biting him. Nor had the goat's teeth met any of the conditions he'd built into his wards.

I'll have to fix that, he thought. It would be a tricky bit of spellcraft, but he wasn't about to let some thrice-cursed goat eat him either.

The horizon was a hazy line bisecting the gold half dome of the setting sun. Purple shadows streaked the land, and nightjars darted overhead, chasing insects as the first stars appeared in the sky beyond.

At Glaedr's burial mound, orange lights bobbed and flickered around the base of the rise. Murtagh cursed. *Have you nothing better to do?* he wondered, eyeing the distant mourners. They showed no signs of leaving; if anything, their numbers had grown. He had a horrible suspicion that some of them intended to hold vigil at the tomb throughout the whole night.

Hopefully the elf had departed. Either way, Murtagh dared not wait any longer. Time was tight, and he feared that catching Muckmaw might be a more involved process than Carabel had made it seem. If the fish slept, as most animals did, he would not show himself until the following day.

"Let's get this over with," Murtagh muttered, and set out for the barrow. He wished he'd brought a waterskin. He was even more thirsty now.

The walk allowed him to plan. The elves were sure to have placed spells on the location to prevent anyone from desecrating Oromis and Glaedr's remains. That was the first difficulty. The second was finding a scale. If the farmer he'd spoken to was right and the elves had burned Glaedr's body, there wouldn't be many scales left—and the barrow made for a decently sized hill, so actually locating a scale amid all the dirt would be tricky even with magic. Third was the need to do so without attracting attention.

At least the dusk would help hide his actions.

The fourth and final difficulty was Murtagh's own reluctance. He didn't want to visit the barrow, and he didn't want to dig up anything of Glaedr's body, and he worried about why a dragon scale was needed to lure in Muckmaw. Why not something else equally large and shiny? Was there some quality to dragon scales that he was ignorant of? Or was Muckmaw drawn to arcane objects specifically? Either possibility was concerning.

He slowed as he came onto the path leading to the barrow. From there, he moved at a measured pace, another travel-weary pilgrim at the end of a long day of walking.

It wasn't so far from the truth.

Around the barrow, he counted twelve people: all humans, five women, seven men. They were commoners, dressed in rough smocks, caps, and loosely gathered trousers. Most appeared to be farmers from the countryside or laborers from the city. Two of the women smelled of Gil'ead's dock, and one of the men, a thin, bristle-haired fellow, wore a blacksmith's leather apron.

Some knelt, some stood—lanterns in hand—and a low murmur of sad voices floated through the evening air. They were praying for the dead, Murtagh realized. Praying, pleading, or simply remembering.

The path continued up the side of the grass-draped barrow to the oak tree at its crest. Flagstones had been set into the soil to make the climb easier. By the tree, two more people knelt: women in shawls of black lace. From them came a soft keening.

Murtagh felt deeply uncomfortable. Merely being there seemed like an intrusion and an insult to their grief.

As he edged around the barrow to the shadow side, he came upon a standing stone planted by the base of the mound. It was as high as his waist, and two more of similar height stood in line. Rows of chiseled runes covered all three stones, along with patterns of decorative knots.

Curious, he paused and read.

His blood chilled. The first stone told the whole sorry story of the Dragon Riders, starting with their formation as a means to keep the peace between the different races of Alagaësia—which they had succeeded at for centuries—and following through to their destruction at the hands of Galbatorix, then a young, untested Rider who had turned against his order after losing his dragon and going mad with grief.

Murtagh's stomach cramped as he scanned the lines. The Forsworn were mentioned, of course, and Morzan specifically.

The second stone recounted how Galbatorix had established the Empire following the defeat of the Riders and, with the Forsworn by his side, ruled as sovereign absolute over the greater part of humanity. *Galbatorix the Deathless*, the runes called him, as the king indeed had aged but little over the hundred years since, a remnant of his bond as Rider.

Murtagh wondered who had carved and placed the stones. Not the elves, for it was not their writing, but someone who knew of the true history of the land. That which Galbatorix had forbidden the common folks to share.

The third and final stone told of Oromis and Glaedr. How they had taught among the Riders. How they had been last surviving of all their order, hidden for the past century among the elves in Du Weldenvarden. And how they had died during the Varden's rebellious war against the Empire, cut down at Gil'ead by the son of Morzan. Cut down by the betrayer, Murtagh.

He stood for a time, feeling as if he'd taken a blow to the chest. Then a nightjar swooped past with a soft brush of wings and a trill, and he started, as if waking from a reverie.

With slow steps, Murtagh moved past the stones and leaned

on his staff. He stared at the ground, hood over his face, and did his best to look like the other mourners. In a way, it was the truth.

Forgive me, he thought. At the back of his mind, he could feel Thorn watching, and the dragon's regret added to his own.

The ground beneath his boots was soft with scythed clover. He closed his eyes and let himself sway back and forth to match the keening from above.

If he tried to use magic to pull a scale straight out of the barrow, he'd be sure to trigger whatever protective magic lay within. The key, as ever, would be to accomplish what he wanted in an indirect, sideways manner. Such was the way to defeat wards. As Eragon had with Galbatorix . . .

He thought about it for some minutes. In the end, it was his thirst that gave him the answer. He looked for flaws in his logic and, finding no obvious ones, assembled the words he needed and murmured, "Reisa adurna fra undir, un ílf fithren skul skulblaka flutningr skul eom edtha."

And he fed a thin thread of energy into the ground beneath the barrow, searching for whatever water there was to find.

The idea was relatively simple. Instead of casting a spell directly on the barrow, he would use magic to push water up through the soil, and *if* the water touched a scale, it would carry the scale through the dirt to his hand. However, he would confine the motive energy for the water to an area deep underground so that no part of the strength he spent would directly affect the scale or anything else within the mound.

Whether that would be enough to circumvent whatever wards the elves had placed upon the tomb, he didn't know.

We might have to make a hasty retreat, he thought.

As he stood there, concentrating on the trickle of his own strength draining into the depths of the earth, a shuffling footstep sounded nearby.

He glanced over. The bristle-haired blacksmith had for some forsaken reason moved over to join him.

Worse yet, the man began to talk. "I haven't seen you here before, stranger. You're not from thesewise parts, I take it?"

Murtagh struggled to split his attention between his spell and the blacksmith. For a moment, he nearly ended the magic, but he didn't. Every attempt would increase the risk of discovery.

"No," he said, keeping his face down.

"Ayuh. I thought as much," said the man, satisfied. He rubbed his corded arms against the evening chill. "Iverston is m' name. Iverston Varisson. Although everyone round th' lake calls me Mallet, on account of, well, that's a story that'd take a jug of cider to tell, if y' follow. Were I to start, I'd be talking from now to sunup."

Murtagh knew what was expected of him. "Tornac son of Tereth."

Mallet peered at him with a somewhat concerned look. "You're not an elf, are you? No . . . I see not. There's someth'n elfish 'bout your face, though, if'n you don't mind me saying."

Murtagh did mind, but he held his tongue. The barrow was too large for him to bring up water underneath the whole thing; he had to start in one quarter and slowly work his way across.

Another pause, and Mallet rubbed his arms again while looking at the women at the crest of the mound. He gestured at them. "They're always up there, y' know? Sisters, come from the city. Lost their father during th' battle. Their brother too, I think. Everyone here lost someone. Most of 'em, leastwise. Couple folks are just enamored with th' idea of dragons." He tapped his temple. "Something a bit crooked in their heads, I reckon. No offense intended, if'n that applies."

"It doesn't," said Murtagh, keeping his voice low.

Mallet nodded wisely. "That's good. Ain't right t' be worshipping a dragon, if'n you ask me. . . . I don't come most nights, y' know. Only when work at th' forge is low. It's been a few weeks since m' last visit. Harvest time's full up w' pitchforks an' shoeing an' scythes an' chains needin' mending, an' then there's always nails t' be making. Never enough nails in th' world, you know?"

Murtagh nodded and made a noise as if he did. Still nothing from his spell, but he could feel the cold water oozing through the dark soil.

"Why . . . ," he said, and then stopped. Mallet stooped slightly, as if to look under the edge of Murtagh's hood. "Why do they grieve here, if . . . if . . ." He wasn't sure how to phrase the question in a diplomatic way.

He was relieved when Mallet picked up the thread. "If it were th' dragon and th' elves that killed those as they cared f'r?" His knobby shoulders lifted under his shift. "I couldn't rightwise tell you f'r most. Might be they hated th' Empire, and th' death of th' dragon and his Rider makes 'em feel right bad. 'Course might also be th' Rider helped 'em during the battle. I know it to be th' case with Neldrick over there. Buncha soldiers set fire to his farmhouse on their way t' flank the elves. Th' dragon came down and put out th' fire with his wings, something like a storm or a force of nature is what I heard."

The blacksmith crossed his arms and buried his chin in his chest. "Me? I ain't got no story as epic as that. Nothing th' bards would sing about, nothing like that. My son, y' see, Ervos—we named him after his mother's father—my eldest, my only son, he got it in his head a few summers back t' join the Varden. Always was a headstrong boy, that one. Thought he'd do well 'cause of it, but . . . he ran off without telling us, and we didn't hear nothing of him till the war was over. Couple of the Varden came by t' tell us they'd fought with him on th' Burning Plains. Th' Burning Plains! Can you imagine?" Mallet shook his head. "Ain't never seen anything like that, I can tell you. Whole wide swath of land that burns and burns forever. Crazy t' think of. . . . Anyways, the men who came by were footsore and battle-weary. They'd been at Feinster and Ilirea after. Saw Roran Stronghammer fight, they said. And anyways, they said, well, they said Ervos had been with 'em when th' Empire charged 'em, and, well . . ."

Mallet's chest rose and fell several times. Then he stared up at the stars, and though Murtagh didn't want to see, he looked over, and he caught the silvered glimmer of tears in the man's eyes.

"It's funny, y' know," said the blacksmith. "Y' take all that time t' feed and clothe a child. Take care of 'em. Keep 'em from killing themselves on every such thing. But y' can't protect 'em from themselves. Ervos . . . he wanted to belong t' something bigger than himself, I think. He wanted a cause t' believe in, t' fight for, and there was no giving him that in a forge, y' see. . . . He always was a headstrong boy."

He shook his head. "Never even got t' see his body. That's the hardest part, would y' believe. Can't say goodbye proper without a body." He gestured at the barrow. "So this'll have to serve till a body shows, if ever it does."

Murtagh's mouth and throat were so dry, it was difficult to talk. He thought he knew the charge Mallet spoke of; he'd been the one to lead it. "I'm sorry."

"It's the way of the world, and no sorrow will fix it, but thank y' all the same, stranger." Keeping his eyes fixed on the stars, the bristle-haired man said, "If'n you want, it can help t' talk about such things. And if'n you're not so inclined, that's fine too, y'see."

The shadowed privacy of the gloaming loosened Murtagh's tongue, made him feel as if he could speak of subjects that normally were too painful to give voice. But he knew it was a false sense of anonymity, so he chose his words with care.

"I lost . . . I lost a friend. More like a father. Killed by Galbatorix's men."

"Ah now, that's hard, and there's no denying it."

"Not as hard as others have it."

Mallet looked down from the sky. "Well, far as I see it, there's no putting a price on pain, if'n you follow. Everyone's entitled to their own. Would be a strange thing t' say that some pain is easier 'an others without knowin' what it's like in another's shoes, if'n that makes sense."

"It does."

Mallet harrumphed and nodded, and then surprised Murtagh by patting him on the shoulder. "Y' seem like a man who wants his space, so I'll leave y' to it, but if y' change your mind, I'll be over thatwise."

And the blacksmith moved off around the base of the mound until he was a dark outline at the far side, leaving Murtagh standing alone in the shadow of the barrow.

Murtagh let out a small, choked laugh that was nearly a cry. Faint from distance, Thorn said in a carefully neutral tone, *What a strange man.*

Not really, said Murtagh.

He concentrated on his spell then, working the water through the ground with greater speed. So far, it didn't seem to have triggered any protective spells.

Foot by careful foot, he pressed the water past stone and pebble, worked it into interstitial spaces, penetrated mud and clay and packed layers of ash—the mortal remains of the great dragon Glaedr. The dragon had been enormous by most standards. Smaller than Shruikan but still several times the size of Thorn or Saphira. And his pyre had left a thick stratum of incinerated muscle, organs, bones, and scales.

Murtagh wasn't sure if any scales had survived. The fires elves made with their magic burned hotter than those of a forge.

But he kept searching. Every inch of progress felt like a transgression. He was not by nature weak of stomach—blood did not sicken him, nor did the gore and viscera of battle—but knowing that the tendrils of water were passing through what had once been the innards of a creature such as Thorn made Murtagh increasingly queasy.

He fervently wished to be quit of the task, and he cursed the werecat with what energy he could afford.

Then, just as he began to despair . . . *there!* A shift in the flow of water as it touched an object near the center of the barrow. A scale, he hoped. The water caressed the object, formed a pocket around it, and, gentle as a mother's touch, drew it forth from the womb of the earth.

It was hardly an unlabored process. Rocks and bones blocked the way, and every few inches, an obstacle forced the water to divert. Each time, he struggled to return the scale to its intended course, and each time, he succeeded. That was, until the scale met an enormous stone that defied his every effort to bypass.

"Barzûl," he swore. He couldn't seem to find the edges of the stone; the scale kept getting caught on unseen ridges.

With no other option, he increased the flow of water, pushed more and more into the barrow until it softened the soil beneath the stone, turned it into a pool of mud.

Thin rivulets of water seeped out by his feet, and the belly of the barrow sagged slightly, as if to collapse.

"*Hold,*" he muttered, willing the mound to stand.

Within the ground, he felt the stone sink into the morass he'd created. The scale slid forward in a rush of pressure released, and he quickly reduced the amount of water to the bare minimum needed to keep the scale moving.

Like a mountain spring burst to life, a patch of dew welled from the surface of the grassy barrow, and then the soil parted. From within the dark interior a gleaming, golden scale emerged, bright as a faceted gem of topaz. In the dusk, the scale was a shield-shaped piece of evening sunlight, a condensed pool of illumination, still possessed of a sense of life and motion.

Wonderstruck, he ended his spell and took the palm-sized scale from the ground.

The instant his hand touched the scale, a foreign mind touched his, and a mental attack struck him with such strength, he staggered and clung to the staff in order to remain standing.

Murtagh reacted without thinking, old reflexes taking charge. He recoiled deep within himself, armoring his mind and focusing on the phrase he used to block out any other thoughts. "You shall not have me. You shall not have me. You shall not have me," he muttered, over and over.

Despite his speed, he wasn't fast enough. The other mind bore down upon him with implacable force. Whoever it was possessed incredible mental discipline and, it seemed, complete mastery of their emotions, for Murtagh felt nothing but fiercely controlled intent.

He tried to move, tried to drop the scale, but the invading consciousness held him in place through sheer overwhelming strength.

Murtagh assumed his assailant was an elf, one from Gil'ead set to guard the barrow. Normally a mental projection of such intensity required the magician to be relatively close. At least within half a mile. However, Murtagh guessed that the scale was somehow enchanted to act as a scrying mirror or a magnifier—a conduit between whoever touched it and the ones protecting the barrow.

Even so, time was short. It wouldn't take an elf long to ride from Gil'ead to the barrow. Minutes, if that.

If Thorn were trying to help, Murtagh couldn't tell. He hoped the dragon wouldn't leave the hollow.

Between the words of his defensive chant, he again tried to move the hand touching the scale. Nothing.

"You shall not have me. You shall not have me."

As determined and disciplined as the other mind was, Murtagh knew he was stronger. When it came to resolve, he could hold his own with the largest, oldest, and wisest creatures in Alagaësia. Galbatorix may have been able to break Murtagh's defenses, but he had never broken his will—and that gave Murtagh courage that, no matter how dire the situation, his self would prevail.

Then from the intruding mind came a questing thought, in both the human tongue and in the ancient language: *Who are you?*

Alarm threatened to disrupt Murtagh's focus. He couldn't wait any longer. If his attacker learned his name . . . He had to find a way to disrupt the elf's attention and slip away.

With his off hand, he fumbled at his belt until he found the hilt of his dagger. He drew it, and then—with grim-minded determination—stabbed his right forearm.

Not deeply. Not enough to cause major damage but enough to cause pain, and it was pain he wanted.

His face contorted with agony, and the dagger fell from his fingers. The unexpected spike of pain passed through his mind into the elf's, and as Murtagh had hoped, it broke his attacker's focus.

Freed from the immobilizing influence, Murtagh dropped the scale. As it left his hand, the mental contact vanished, and with it a sense of oppressive weight.

The reprieve would be short-lived.

Using the corner of his cloak as a protective mitten, he again picked up the scale. The layer of cloth was enough to avoid triggering whatever spell had been placed on it. He dropped the scale into the purse on his belt and then went to retrieve the dagger.

A few paces away, Mallet was watching, a look of horror on his face. The smith sputtered and pointed and said, "That's . . . you're . . . You're no friend. Graverobber! Desecrator!" His voice rang out in the evening air, cutting through the lamentations of those around the barrow. The men and women turned, their expressions alarmed and hostile. Mallet was still shouting. "He took a scale of th' dragon! I saw it! Thief! Graverobber!"

The smith swiped at him, trying to grab Murtagh with his long, hooked arms.

Murtagh spun and ran. He ran like a common thief, and he hated himself for it with every step.

I shouldn't have told him my name was Tornac, he thought. The elves might know enough to realize who he was. And if not they, then perhaps the magician from Du Vrangr Gata.

A pulse of pain from his forearm caused him to look down

as he sprinted across the landscape. A blot of blood had soaked through his sleeve, and his whole forearm was hard, knotted, as if cramped.

He pressed his left hand over the wound. "Waíse heill," he growled. *Be healed.* It was a risky spell to cast without knowing the exact nature of the damage he was attempting to repair, but he trusted it wasn't *too* much, and his guess proved correct. His arm burned and stung, and he felt lightheaded for a moment, enough to make him stumble a few steps. But the pain vanished and his muscles relaxed, and he was able to open and close his hand as before.

Losing the dagger hurt nearly as much as stabbing himself. He'd had the weapon since Galbatorix had armed him in Urû'baen, and it had served him well in the years after. Moreover, Murtagh had set spells on it—spells to strengthen it, to protect the sharpness of the edge, and to help it pierce the wards of other magicians.

I'll have to get another one and start all over. It was a matter of practicality, if nothing else. He needed a knife for many of the tasks around camp.

He threw back his hood, slung his cloak over the crook of his left arm, and concentrated on running. Behind him, the angry shouts of the mourners faded into the night.

A *bad start*, Murtagh thought. But he couldn't stop. Silna was still in danger, and there were answers to be had from Carabel.

Grim, he quickened his pace.

CHAPTER IV

✦ ✦ ✦ ✦ ✦ ✦

Fish Tales

Murtagh ran until the burning in his lungs forced him to slow to a quick walk. Then he ran again, then walked, then ran. In like fashion, he hurried back to the hollow where Thorn was waiting.

Always you stir people up, like a hill of ants. Thorn was crouched, tense and ready to take off from within the ring of willows and poplars.

"I know," said Murtagh, leaning over with his hands on his knees. "It seems to be a bad habit."

Will the elves find us here?

"I don't know," he said, straightening. "But I don't think it's safe to stay." He went to the waterskin he'd left hanging on a branch by his bedding, unstoppered it, and drank his fill. The water was warm and somewhat stale, but it was a welcome treat after a day of thirst.

Thorn watched, unblinking. *Let me see the scale.*

Murtagh wiped his mouth. He tossed the empty skin onto his blankets, fetched his gloves, and then carefully removed the gleaming scale from his purse.

With an excited hum, Thorn crept forward until his nose nearly touched the topaz plate. The dragon's hot breath created droplets of moisture on the scale, and they reflected its inner light in a dazzling display.

The stubbed end of Thorn's tail slapped the ground. A crow rose cawing from the top of a poplar.

Murtagh studied the puckered white scar that marked where Glaedr had bitten off the last three feet of Thorn's tail. His tail was a normal length now—Galbatorix had seen to that—but the healing had been a forced, imperfect thing. What had been lost could not be replaced, so instead the king had set spells on Thorn to stretch the bones and muscles left to him. It had taken Thorn weeks to relearn how to balance himself in flight.

Thorn let out a long breath. *Glaedr was a worthy foe.*

"Yes, he was," said Murtagh.

He died as every dragon should: fighting on wing, in the sky.

"He's not entirely dead."

Thorn blinked. *But he can no longer fly. He cannot move. He can only think. I would sooner crash myself into the side of a mountain than live like that.*

"I know," said Murtagh, soft. They had been fortunate Galbatorix hadn't forced Thorn to disgorge his Eldunarí. Young as he was, Thorn would have ended up with a severe mismatch between the size of his mind and the size of his body.

After Murtagh wrapped the scale in cloth and carefully stowed it in a saddlebag, Thorn said, *What now?*

Murtagh checked the sky. The stars were fully out, and the horns of a crescent moon were peeking over the horizon. *Perfect.* Just dark enough to help conceal them from watching eyes, but not so dark they couldn't see their work.

"Now," he said, rolling up his blankets, "we go fishing."

~~~~~~~~~~~~~~~~~ ❖ ~~~~~~~~~~~~~~~~~

Murtagh let out a sound of frustration and slumped back in Thorn's saddle.

An hour of flying around and across Isenstar Lake had proved fruitless. The lake was huge, and they had no idea where to look for Muckmaw. Moreover, it was impossible to see anything useful in the dark water, even with the help of the crescent moon, and

Thorn didn't dare fly too close to the surface, lest night fishermen spot them. Murtagh had used his mind to search for creatures in the water, but from high above and at speed, it was easy to overlook the cold thoughts of a fish. Especially if it were sleeping. In any case, he didn't know what Muckmaw's consciousness felt like.

They landed upon several sections of isolated shore and he dangled Glaedr's scale in the still waters, hoping it would attract the fish's attention, as Carabel had claimed. But the waters remained smooth and untroubled, and the hoots of sleepy loons echoing across Isenstar were the only sign of animal life.

Frustrated, they took to the air again.

This isn't going to work, said Murtagh, using his mind so the sound of his voice wouldn't carry over the moonlit water. *We could spend days patrolling Isenstar and have nothing to show for it but flies in our teeth and elves on our tail.*

Thorn gave an irritated shake of his head. *It is a good night for hunting, but only if we know where to hunt.*

Exactly. . . . Murtagh glanced back toward Gil'ead. A scattered constellation of lanterns and torches lit the city, forming a warm welcome in the darkness. If he were a fisherman, he thought the sight would have been comforting indeed. He tapped Thorn on the shoulder. *Turn around. I have an idea.*

Why do I have a feeling in my belly that your idea will be dangerous?

Because you can read my mind, that's why. And it won't be that dangerous. Not if I'm clever.

Try not to be too clever. Clever fails more often than simple.

Mmh.

At Murtagh's direction, Thorn landed behind a small hill half a mile from the northeastern side of Gil'ead. Hopefully the elves wouldn't be looking there. Surrounding the hill was a dense patchwork of cultivated fields: clover, wheat, and close-planted rows of various root vegetables.

Murtagh slid to the ground and took a moment to study the

land. There was a farmhouse to the north, closer than he would have liked. "You'll have to be careful. There could be dogs."

I know how to hide, said Thorn, sounding vaguely offended.

He smiled. "Yes, you do. But listen, if I'm not back in a few hours, leave. Don't wait for dawn. Farmers rise early, and if they see you—"

They'll cause no more trouble than we've faced before. Thorn huffed, and white smoke billowed up from his muzzle.

"Let's avoid it all the same."

Squatting, Murtagh dug a handful of moist dirt out from under the grass and rubbed it into his hands and onto his face. He hated the feel of the grime, but it would help age him and make him look more like a commoner.

He had a sudden, intense sense of familiarity, as if he'd already lived this moment. In a way he had, he supposed. Before entering Gil'ead to help rescue Eragon, he'd done exactly the same.

"The more things change, the more they stay the same."

Thorn cocked his head. *And what help is it knowing that?*

"Not sure. Maybe we'll learn to recognize the patterns, and we can avoid making the same mistakes twice." He stood. "I'll be back soon."

And he set out at a steady trot, again heading toward Gil'ead.

Behind him, Thorn let out a concerned growl.

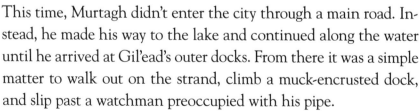

This time, Murtagh didn't enter the city through a main road. Instead, he made his way to the lake and continued along the water until he arrived at Gil'ead's outer docks. From there it was a simple matter to walk out on the strand, climb a muck-encrusted dock, and slip past a watchman preoccupied with his pipe.

The docks had a very different smell from those at Ceunon. Isenstar was a freshwater lake, and the absence of salt resulted in a cleaner, fresher scent. Even the odor of fish was more mild, inoffensive.

Murtagh skulked along the lakeside buildings—past sorting houses and storage barns and dry goods stores—searching for what he knew had to exist. But all of the taverns and common houses he found were already shuttered for the night, and dogs, not drunks, ambled across the packed dirt of the street, sniffing and snapping at one another in a desultory manner.

The patter of light footsteps passed behind him.

He turned fast, only to see the same two ragged urchins who had accosted him outside Gil'ead's fortress. They held up their dirty hands, their faces pale and wide-eyed beneath their poorly cropped hair. "Please, master, sir," they said in a pleading tone.

Murtagh frowned, his senses alert for an ambush. "What are you doing about at this time of night?"

The two glanced at each other with bright, impish expressions. They were brothers, he thought, only a year or two apart. The taller one said, "Oh, nothing much, sir. Just trying to find food."

The shorter one piped up: "That's right, sir. Food for our poor mum, that is."

The brothers exchanged delighted glances again. Then, from both of them: "Please, master, sir."

Trouble, that's what you are, Murtagh thought. He eyed the length of dark street. A watchman appeared between a pair of buildings some distance away; the man's lantern cast a key of yellow light across the street before he walked on and a corner cut off the glow.

Murtagh looked back at the two incorrigibles. He fished out a pair of coppers. The boys reached for them, and he lifted the coppers over their heads. "Ah-ah. Not so fast. Tell me first, are there any taverns still open at this ghastly hour?"

The boys bobbed their heads. "Oh yes! Several."

"And where might I find the nearest?"

"Right down thataways, sir!" said the shorter one without the slightest hesitation, and he pointed along the lakeside buildings.

"Right past th' stables and to the left. The Rusty Anchor. You can't miss it."

Murtagh dropped the coins, and the boys caught them out of the air, fast as birds. "My thanks. Now off to bed with the both of you, and don't let me catch you out here again."

"Yessir! Thank you, sir!" they said, bowing and laughing. And then they ran off into the dark city, the shorter leading the taller.

Murtagh shook his head and continued in the direction they'd indicated.

The way was farther than he expected. He had nearly lost faith in the boys' instructions when he spotted a battered old tavern with light in the windows at the western end of Gil'ead, where the buildings were low and shabby. True to its name, the Rusty Anchor had a ship's anchor hung over the front door, along with a sign featuring a pair of beer mugs clinking together.

"The more things change . . ." Out of habit, Murtagh touched his belt to check on the position of his dagger. But, of course, it wasn't there, only the empty sheath.

He scowled. He was running a risk going to a place like this unarmed. It was the sort of disreputable establishment where strangers often woke up the next day with a lump on their head and a purse empty of coin. If they were lucky enough to wake up at all. More than once, he'd heard about the sons of nobles who had gone out drinking in such establishments and ended up robbed, bruised, or worse.

Of course, now *he* was the sort of person that others needed to be afraid of. He couldn't lie to himself: the thought wasn't entirely unpleasant. After the past few years, Murtagh would settle for inspiring fear if it would keep him and Thorn safe.

He took a moment to set his mind and assume the needed persona. Then he moved forward with a rough stride and entered the tavern.

Unlike the Fulsome Feast in Ceunon, the Rusty Anchor was a

dark, grim place that smelled of smoke, sweat, stale urine, and despair. The floor was a mess of muddy boards, and there were only a few bottles and cups on the shelf behind the bar. The barkeep himself sat in a corner, next to a cask of tapped beer, head against the wall, snoring loud enough to wake a dragon (and Murtagh knew exactly how loud that was).

The patrons of the establishment were a mix of fishermen, laborers, and several men who Murtagh guessed were either swords for hire or—if they didn't get hired—footpads looking for their next object of prey.

He could feel them watching him as he made his way across the room. The barkeep woke the instant he placed coppers on the scarred wood counter.

"Beer," said Murtagh. "Cheapest you've got."

"Cheap is all we 'ave got," said the barkeep, slowly getting to his feet. He had a pregnant paunch that stretched his apron as tight as a drum. He made the coppers disappear in his pudgy hands and gave Murtagh half a copper in return. Then he grabbed a mug that looked none too clean and filled it from the cask.

Murtagh eyed the beer. It was totally flat. He decided not to press the point and carried the mug to a table by the small stone hearth. The fire was almost dead, barely more than a bed of despondent coals.

As Murtagh settled into a chair, one of the hired swords—a short, bird-chested man with a nervous tic in his left eye—cleared his throat and said, "Yuh come in w' one of th' caravans?"

Murtagh nodded. "Straight from Ilirea. We got in two hours before dark, but it took this long to shift everything out of the wagons."

A man with a dwarflike beard and a scar through his left eyebrow spoke up: "What news of the road?"

The beer had all the flavor of thinned barley water. Murtagh grimaced and put it back down. "The road is fine. Dusty, that's for sure. We made do without anyone waylaying us, so I reckon the queen's men are doing a good job of keeping order."

The bird-chested man and his bearded companion exchanged a glance that seemed somewhat conspiratorial. Bird-chest said, "Were yuh working as protection for this said caravan?"

Murtagh nodded. "Didn't even have to draw my sword none. Can't complain with that."

"Always a good day's work when you don't have to work," said the bearded man.

"There's a truth worth drinking to." Murtagh raised his mug and took a quaff. Then he looked over at the fishermen in their cabled sweaters and woolen caps, which they kept on even indoors. "I heard tell there's good fishing in Isenstar Lake."

"Passable good," said the near fisherman, keeping his gaze on his mug.

"One of the men I stood watch with wouldn't shut his gob about it. Kept going on and on about the summer pike. That and the eels. Always the eels."

"The eels is fine enough eating," the fisherman allowed. "Long as you ain't overcook 'em."

Murtagh nodded, as if this confirmed what he'd heard. "Seeing as that's the case, I might try my luck with a hook and line while I'm here. I used to be a dab hand at fishing." He lifted his mug again and then shook his head and put it down. "Only . . . It's a silly thing, and I'm dead sure this watchmate of mine was tozing me, but, well, he kept talking about how it was right dangerous to drop a line hereabouts. On account of some fish called Muckmaw. Said it was the biggest, meanest fish in the whole lake. I figured he was talking out his ear an' it were all stuff and nonsense. Right has to be, no?"

The fishermen tensed, and one of them made a motion to ward off the evil eye and leaned over and spat on the floor. The spittle was dark green from a plug of cardus weed tucked in his cheek. "Blasted thing."

Murtagh raised an eyebrow. "So there's something to it, then?"

"Maybe," said the near man, surly.

"That sounds like a story worth telling."

No one volunteered. The fishermen stared with sullen gazes at the fireplace, while bird-chest and dwarf-beard smirked at each other at the lack of response. The man who had spat pushed back his chair. "Horvath. Merrik. I'll be off. Anra will be a-waiting."

Murtagh raised a hand. "Barkeep. A round for everyone. My coin."

The barkeep forced his eyes open and blinked, bleary. He nodded and shuffled off toward the cask.

After a moment's hesitation, the fisherman settled back in his chair. "Suppose she can wait a mug longer," he muttered.

They sat in silence while the barkeep filled the mugs and made his rounds to the tables. As Murtagh handed over the last of his coppers, bird-chest raised his mug in an appreciative gesture.

"Thanks, stranger," said one of the fishermen. He had a scar on his forearm that reminded Murtagh of Essie. "Mighty kind of you."

"Oreth son of Brock," said Murtagh. He figured it wise to start using a name other than Tornac around Gil'ead.

The cardus chewer scratched the red stubble on his chin. "Muckmaw, eh? If you really want to know the truth of th' matter, you'd best be talk'n to old Haugin, but he's long since asleep if'n I know aught about him."

"He'll sleep th' whole winter through," said the scarred fisherman.

"Ain't that right," said cardus-chewer, nodding. "Can't rightly blame him, though. He's got three and seventy winters. A man's due some sleep after that long working."

Murtagh took another sip of the flat beer. "And what would he tell me about Muckmaw?" he asked, trying to hurry them along.

Cardus-chewer and his companions exchanged significant looks. "Well now, it's a curious thing. Might be you think I'm whistling in the wind if I say the truth, but y' asked, and since you paid the beer, you'll get the tale, if'n you pardon the expression."

Murtagh smiled. "Of course."

"So. You have t' understand what Muckmaw is afore I start."

"Do tell."

The scarred fisherman burst out: "He's a right mean old bastard, is what he is. You see this mark on my arm? There is where he bit me four summers ago. Bastard. I'd like as to gut him and smoke him up for dinner one of these days."

"We all would," said cardus-chewer. The hired swords were listening intently now, eyes gleaming in the dull red light of the coals. "You see, Oreth, th' blasted fish is near as long as one of our sailboats. A good ten paces from tip to butt, I'd reckon, and 'bout three paces 'cross the beam."

Murtagh felt a frown forming between his brows as he listened. *What didn't Carabel tell me?* "That's . . . a big fish." Even if they were exaggerating, Muckmaw was clearly enormous.

Cardus-chewer snorted. "You could say that. The blasted thing is nearabouts a small whale. It's a sturgeon, see, or someth'n like a sturgeon. Armored plates th' size of a buckler on its sides, razor spines along its back, big old barbels coming off its mouth. The mouth is what gave 'im his name. *Muckmaw*. He trawls th' bottom of th' lake, scooping up everything, feeding off it. Whenever he comes up, he has silt an' mud streaming from his mouth, like smoke from a charcoal burner. He's been lurking about Isenstar for the past sixty years. And it's true, he's *mean*. He fouls our lines and cuts our nets whenever he has th' chance. We've seen him scoop up herons, cave in the sides of boats. . . . Not last year he knocked poor old Brennock right out of his skiff an' thrashed him near to death with his tail."

"Muckmaw's tail, not Brennock's," the scarred fisherman clarified.

A bark of laughter escaped cardus-chewer. "Yah. Brennock wouldn't know what to do with a tail even if he had one."

Murtagh's frown deepened. "Come now. You're yanking my cap, aren't you? You can't expect me to believe—"

"Every word of it's honest truth, swear on me ma's grave," said cardus-chewer.

As he spoke, Murtagh saw a pair of boys slip into the Rusty Anchor from the scullery: the two urchins from earlier. The brothers took up on the hearth and sat together, bent in close conversation. Here in the tavern, Murtagh noticed an undeniable resemblance to the bird-chested man. He snorted. *I should have figured as much.* He wondered what sort of arrangement the brothers and father had with the barkeep.

Putting it from his mind, he said, "Well . . . if that's really how things stand, why hasn't anyone caught or killed Muckmaw by now?"

Cardus-chewer leaned forward with his elbows on the table, eyes strangely bright. "The tale's in the answering, so listen close-like, and don't be doubting a word of it. Those sixty years ago, Haugin was 'bout ten summers old. As he tells it, he an' two other boys were out fishing from th' shore, couple miles north a' here. It were him, Sharg Troutnose, and Nolf the Short. Both Sharg and Nolf are buried now, but they told th' same story while they were 'round and kicking."

He adjusted the plug of cardus in his cheek and downed a mouthful of beer. "Anyways—"

The third fisherman—a thin, gaunt-faced man who had been silent until then—said, "Tell him about the—"

"Aight. I'm getting to it!" said cardus-chewer, visibly annoyed. He rolled his shoulders, taking an extra moment before resuming. The gaunt-faced man glared. "*Anyways*, th' boys were fishing, and they'd caught a couple of trout, couple of sturgeon, and they'd put 'em out on th' shore. Only, instead of giving 'em a rap on the head to stop 'em from thrashing, they decided they'd sit and watch and see how long it took 'em to stop wiggling about and which one lasted longest. It weren't right, but, well, you know how boys can be."

Murtagh did. He stared into the depths of his beer.

"So there they are, sitting and watching th' fish gasp on th' rocks, and a man walks up from behind 'em. No horse, no ox, just walks on out of the wilds. Haugin says he were a strange-looking man. His hair were red, not red like my whiskers but proper red, like a cut ruby. An' his teeth were sharp and pointed like cat teeth."

A cold prickle crawled up the back of Murtagh's neck as he listened. *Durza.* What had the spirit-possessed mage been doing in Gil'ead all those years ago? Carrying out some miserable, blood-soaked mission for Galbatorix, no doubt—or at least, so Murtagh assumed. Much of Durza's history remained a mystery to him. Galbatorix had kept the existence of the Shade a secret from his court, and Murtagh had only learned of Durza during his travels with Eragon. Later, after the Twins had dragged him back to the capital and Thorn had hatched, Galbatorix had told Murtagh a few details about Durza's service, but only a few.

In retrospect, Murtagh was astounded by his own ignorance. And by the stupidity of his overconfidence. He had truly believed he could defeat Durza in Gil'ead, without magic and without the enhanced strength and speed that came with being a Dragon Rider. *Idiocy. Durza would have killed me before he realized who I was. . . . At least I managed to put an arrow between his eyes.* Although even that hadn't been enough to kill the Shade. Only a blade through the heart could do that, as Eragon had later proved in Tronjheim.

Cardus-chewer was still talking: "Soon as they see him, th' kids jumped up, tried to go after th' fish. They *knew* what they were doing weren't right, you see. But the man tells them t' hold, an' he asks 'em what they're about. So they lay it out, all shamefaced like. And Haugin says the man smiled then, and he sat down by 'em with his hand on th' hilt of his sword and asks 'em to watch and wait, 'cause *he's* curious too. Only it weren't a real ask, if'n you follow, but more of an order. Leastways, that's how Haugin tells it. So they sit, an' they wait, and th' fish go on gasping an' flopping until they've had their last mortal breath. All but one of 'em."

"Let me guess," said Murtagh. "A sturgeon."

By the hearth, the brothers laughed as they played a game of jacks with colored pebbles.

"Or something as like a sturgeon," said cardus-chewer. He nodded sagely. "An' here's where it goes strange. The man, he picks up th' fish, and he says words over it, only not in any tongue as makes sense. Old Haugin, he swears on his mam's grave, *swears*, that he could feel the words in his bones, an' Sharg and Nolf always accounted the same."

"Magic," said the scarred fisherman.

"Aye, magic. So the red-haired devil says his piece, and then he tosses the fish back in th' lake, and he tells Haugin an' Sharg an' Nolf, he tells 'em that since they were wanting to know which fish was the strongest, it were only fair to reward th' survivor. An' he tells 'em that since they were such naughty, naughty boys, they'd have the fish afflicting 'em and tormenting 'em for th' rest of their days. Then he walked off into th' brush, an' from that day since, th' fish has been a terror to us all."

The scarred fisherman poked cardus-chewer in the shoulder. "Tell him the rest."

"I'm a-gettin' to it! A tale has to be done proper. . . . Anyways, Muckmaw grows into his fearsome self, and once folks round here took notice, we tried t' kill him, Oreth. Oh, we tried. But 'tweren't no good. Hooks won't set in his mouth, y'see, an' spears just a-skate off th' side of his armored plates, an' arrows—"

"Arrows bounce right off him," said the scarred fisherman.

Cardus-chewer scowled at him for a second. "Aye. An' the blasted fish is too smart t' catch in nets or weirs. Before th' war, Lord Ulreth set a bounty on Muckmaw. Two whole gold coins. An' our current lord, Lord Relgin, increased th' bounty to four gold coins, if'n you can believe it. Four! That an' you get a chance to join the guards if'n you're so inclined." Cardus-chewer shook his head. "Won't do no good, though. Muckmaw is a curse on our lake, a punishment for mistreating th' fish, and that's th' truth of it."

Murtagh silently swore at Carabel for not telling him the full story. Catching and killing Muckmaw was going to be far more involved than he'd first thought.

"Why haven't you found a spellcaster to kill the fish for you?" he asked.

The scarred fisherman snorted. "What? Them of th' Du Vrangr Gata? They've no time for our concerns. An' Frithva, th' hedge-witch down th' way, wouldn't be much help. Y' need a wart taken off or a compress for a boil, she'll fix you up just fine. But an enchanted fish set on murdering you? No, sir. For that y' need an elf or a Rider."

"An' they're all busy elsewhere," said cardus-chewer sadly.

"Be glad of it," replied his friend. "Their kind only cause rack and ruin."

Cardus-chewer shrugged and drained the last of his beer. "An' now y' know th' truth about Muckmaw. Believe what y' want, Oreth, but we'll swear to every word." He pushed back his chair and stood. "Now I'd best be off. Anra's waiting for me, and she'll not be pleased I tarried so late."

Murtagh raised a hand in a casual, careless gesture. "My thanks for the story. I'll admit, it seems unlikely, but I've heard stranger things on the road. If a man wanted to avoid getting eaten by Muckmaw, where ought he *not* go fishing?"

The scarred fisherman snorted. "As if. Th' whole lake is his hunting ground. Wher'er you go, y' have to watch, lest he chomp you."

Cardus-chewer said, "That's not quite th' whole of it, and you know it, Horvath. There's a marshy area just west of here, along th' shore, nearwise where th' elves cleared out th' last of Galbatorix's soldiers. It goes from cattails to water weeds, an' there are rocks large enough for Muckmaw t' lurk beneath. Most times he's somewhere in the vicinity during mornings an' evenings."

"Much obliged," said Murtagh.

The fisherman nodded. "You're still a young man. Wouldn't want t' see ol' Rove measuring for your coffin 'cause you tangled with Muckmaw, if'n you take my meaning."

And with that, he left.

Murtagh stayed to finish his mug of beer. It would have been odd if he hadn't. While he sat and drank and thought about what he'd heard, bird-chest and his bearded friend bent together in close conversation. Then the hired swords slipped out of their chairs and quietly departed the tavern, keeping behind him the whole time.

He pretended not to notice. And he hoped his suspicions were misplaced.

By the fire, the two boys were beginning to appear sleepy, though they were still laughing and playing. The taller had won the last three games of jacks, and the shorter was arguing the fairness of his pebble snatching.

Murtagh put down his mug and went to the fireplace. The boys gave him a furtive look and then pretended to ignore him. He held out his hands, as if to warm them, and then checked to see if the barkeep had fallen back asleep.

The man slumped limp against the cask, his head lolled to one side on a boneless neck.

Good. As Murtagh turned to leave, he used his cloak as cover to pilfer a length of split pine from the woodbox next to the fireplace. With the pine hidden against his side, he left the tavern.

The night air was a fresh respite after the stuffy interior. He stood a moment and enjoyed a view of the stars while he cleared his lungs.

He kept a firm grip on the hidden piece of wood as he started down the dark docks. Carefully, ever so carefully, he allowed his mind to open and spread out, feeling for the touch of other people's thoughts.

He noticed the two men just as they charged: one coming at him from the front, and the other out of an alley to his right. Bird-chest and his bearded friend, clubs in hand.

Murtagh hitched his step, throwing off the timing of his stride, ducked sideways, and drove his shoulder into the chest and stomach of the bearded man. The footpad's breath left him with a *whoof* as Murtagh knocked him against the wall of the near building, a dry goods store with shuttered display windows.

Without waiting to see what happened to the man, Murtagh spun around and, with the length of pine, knocked aside bird-chest's club and struck him on the collarbone.

The thin man collapsed with a gurgle and a clatter of jarred teeth.

The bearded man was still moving; he'd gotten onto his hands and knees and was struggling to stand.

A quick forward step, and Murtagh rapped him near the back of his skull. A rabbit blow, but not hard enough to kill.

"Ahh!" cried the bearded man, and he curled up, covering the back of his neck and head with his hands.

Murtagh paused for a moment to check for more enemies. Finding none, he looked back at the two unfortunate would-be thieves.

His teeth drew back in a snarl, his blood molten in his veins. He strode back to bird-chest and kicked him in the side. And again. And again. A shout of rage and frustration burst forth from him as he swung his leg.

One or more ribs cracked against his shin.

He knelt and grabbed the man by the hair. Bird-chest's eyes rolled, and red bubbles popped at the corners of his mouth. His lips moved in a mute attempt to plead for mercy.

"Be a better father," Murtagh growled. "Or next time, I'll beat you worse than this, you worthless sack of filth."

The man groaned as Murtagh dropped his head.

A purse on bird-chest's belt caught his eye. He grabbed it, as well as the man's dagger. It wasn't a particularly nice dagger, but the blade appeared sound enough, so Murtagh transferred the weapon into his empty sheath.

"Da!"

The cry sent a chill through Murtagh. He looked up to see the two urchins standing by the door of the tavern, anger and fright on their dirty faces.

"Get away from him!" the smaller one shouted, and threw a handful of pebbles. Several bounced off Murtagh's shoulders.

He stood. "Your father needs your help. See to him." Then he hurried away.

Halfway up the docks, with the tavern well out of sight, Murtagh's gut clenched and his heart seemed to flutter. He half stumbled before his stomach relaxed and his pulse resumed its usual pace. He swore.

He almost wished he'd killed the man. The children might have been better off because of it. Or maybe not. It was impossible to know. All he could be certain of was that he hated the man and his brutish stupidity.

He quickly made his way out of the city and hurried back across the dark land toward where Thorn was waiting. Once he was no longer concerned about any watching minds, he reached out to Thorn and told him what he'd learned.

Thorn's first comment was, *Can you go anywhere without getting into a fight?*

Doesn't seem like it. It wasn't my fault, though.

Is it ever?

Sometimes. Anyway, we'd best find Muckmaw, and then I can go open the door that's always closed. If anyone of note is listening to the rumors and gossip around the city, they might realize something is amiss and start looking for us.

What about the fish?

Murtagh hopped a slat fence as he continued across a field

toward Thorn's hiding place. *I can break the wards Durza placed on Muckmaw. That won't be a problem. For that matter, I'm sure you could bite right through its protective spells.* The idea seemed to please Thorn. *We just have to find the fish.*

Then let's go find it!

As soon as I get there. I'm not— Before he could finish, Murtagh felt a surge of motion and excitement from Thorn as the dragon took flight. *No, wait!*

CHAPTER V

✦ ✦ ✦ ✦ ✦ ✦

Muckmaw

Murtagh's cry was too late. Ahead of him, he saw the dim sparkle of Thorn's shape rise above the hill where they'd landed, and he heard the dull *thud* of the dragon's wings.

"Blast it," he muttered between clenched teeth. He quickly read the lay of the land and then sprinted toward a flat patch of wheat stubble a few hundred feet away.

He arrived just as Thorn drifted down from above. The gust of wind from the dragon's velvet wings staggered Murtagh, forced him to spread his feet and brace himself against the press of air.

"Did you *have* to?" he said.

An amused sparkle lit Thorn's eyes. *No, but I* wanted *to.*

"Gah. Let's get out of here before someone notices." He scrambled up Thorn's side, the dragon's scales sharp against his palms.

He grabbed the neck spike in front of the saddle and held on tight—not bothering to strap down his legs—as Thorn took off.

The crescent moon was near the top of the sky as Thorn sailed over the southern edge of Isenstar Lake, looking for the marshy area the fisherman had mentioned. Murtagh considered casting the spell he normally used to hide Thorn from people on the ground but decided against it. No boats lay on the dark water below, and he wanted to save his strength.

He thought as they flew, and the more he thought, the more uneasy he felt.

What's wrong? Thorn asked.

I'm worried that Durza might have done something unreasonably clever with Muckmaw.

How so?

Spells take energy, yes? And that energy has to come from somewhere. Durza couldn't sustain the wards he set on the fish when he wasn't here. So the energy has to come from Muckmaw.

Where is the problem in that?

Murtagh shrugged, feeling an itch between his shoulder blades. *Maybe there isn't one. Only, when Muckmaw was small, how could it have maintained wards strong enough to deflect spears and swords and the like?*

For a moment, the only sound was the sweep of Thorn's wings. *Perhaps no one tried to kill the fish until it was bigger.*

Maybe.

. . . Do you think Durza used the same spell to grow Muckmaw that Galbatorix used on me?

A sudden tiredness came over Murtagh. Remembering the past always left him feeling old and sad. *There's no way to know, but I wouldn't be surprised.*

Mmh.

They flew in silence until a patch of bright-tipped reeds appeared along the shore: the tops of the cattails catching the moon and starlight.

Thorn descended on silent wings and landed on a wide slab of slate that hung over the edge of the lake. Murtagh slid to the stone and looked across the silvered water. In other circumstances, he would have found the sight beautiful, but knowing that a creature such as Muckmaw lurked beneath the surface gave it a dread feeling—the water a great, dark unknown.

Murtagh shivered and rubbed his hands. His breath showed in a pale plume.

From the saddlebags, he fetched the bow Galbatorix had given him. Murtagh hooked the nocked end of one limb behind his right ankle and, with effort, bent the bow until he could slide the string's loop over the tip of the other end.

He checked the alignment of the string and, satisfied, slung his quiver over his shoulder.

The bow was made of dark yew bound with magic. Most men, and perhaps even some Urgals, would have found it too strong to draw. The white-fletched arrows were appropriately heavy and crafted of solid oak, for any lighter, weaker material would have shattered when the string was released. And as with his lost dagger, Murtagh had set spells on the arrows: spells to make them easier to find should he miss his mark, spells to help them buck the wind, and spells to help them drive deep into their target, no matter what protection, arcane or otherwise, guarded it.

Also from the saddlebags, he dug out Glaedr's golden scale—still in its protective wrapping of cloth—as well as a skein of cord. With deft fingers, he tied a foursquare knot, the strands of which he kept loose and open and laid out on the ground like an iron bear trap. Then he donned his gloves and removed the scale from the cloth.

Even by the marble light of the moon, the scale glowed with an inner flame, as if part of Glaedr's fire yet flickered within its faceted depths.

Murtagh placed it in the center of the foursquare knot and pulled tight the strands until they locked the scale into place.

Satisfied that it was secure, he removed his gloves. "Right, let's find this fish," he muttered, and walked to the end of the slate. He spun the scale about his head and let the cord play out of his hand a fair extent. Then he loosed the scale out over the water. It landed with a splash that echoed along the shore and sent up a fountain of droplets before sinking from sight like a dying ember extinguished in the depths of the abyss.

"Maybe I should have tied a log as a float."

I can get one, said Thorn, settling on his haunches.

"Let's wait a bit first. Here, hold this."

Thorn obliged by lifting his left forefoot, and Murtagh looped the loose end of the cord around the dragon's middle toe. Then Thorn made a fist of his foot and secured what remained of the skein.

"Give it a tug on occasion." Murtagh fit an arrow to bowstring. All of the fishing he'd done during their travels had been with the aid of magic, and never for anything larger than a trout, so he wondered about how best to attract the beast.

He stared into the inky mass of the lake and pushed out with his thoughts. This far from Gil'ead, he didn't worry about being noticed by another spellcaster and so used the full force of his mind.

He closed his eyes to better concentrate on what he felt.

Behind his eyes, darkness reigned. But then he looked to the side, and Thorn appeared as a burning blaze of heat and life, a radiant star amid the void.

In the lake, he beheld many lesser stars, tiny spots of warmth that marked the location of a myriad of different creatures. Fish floating in safe crevices and by the base of swaying water weeds, resting the night away. Eels burrowed into the lakebed mud—their minds faint and indistinct, dominated by the baser instincts: cold, hunger, fatigue. Fainter still were the hundreds, if not thousands, of insects that swarmed the water, darting about, or else resting beneath rocks and sticks or cocooned in shells. And Murtagh felt sure that if his inner eye were sharper still, he would continue to see the life force of smaller and smaller creatures until he came to the smallest iota of matter.

But among the many animals he sensed, and even among the barely perceptible warmth of the water weeds and other lake-born plants, there was no creature big enough to be Muckmaw. Not even close.

He let out his breath in frustration and exchanged mental sight for physical. The tips of the low waves were like chips of metal across the lake.

"Nothing," he said to Thorn. "There isn't even a hint of something. . . . Pull in the scale. We'll have to try another spot." He turned back to the dragon, discouraged. "Blast it. This is going to take days, and we don't have—"

Look! Thorn nudged him with his nose, pointing toward the lake.

Murtagh spun about, lifting his bow.

Fifty-some feet from shore, the water swelled, thinning and smoothing as it went, like a wave passing over a capsized boat. A huge, bulbous mass pressed the water upward, and in the shadow beneath, Murtagh caught a hint of white-rimmed eyes as large as his fist rolling in their sockets.

Then the swell subsided, leaving only a trail of ripples behind.

"I swear, I didn't feel anything," said Murtagh, tracking the ripples. *It's huge!* Cardus-chewer's description had failed to adequately convey the true size of the fish. Muckmaw was bigger than a cave bear, bigger even than a three-month-old dragon (if one ignored the wings).

Murtagh marshaled his mental resources and then stabbed outward with his thoughts, aiming to locate and immobilize the gigantic animal, even as the elf had immobilized him at the barrow.

"I still don't feel anything," he whispered. "Thorn, can you—"

A faint growl escaped the dragon. *It's like claws on ice. I can't catch hold.*

Murtagh swore under his breath. "I'm going to have words with that werecat," he said, scanning the now-seamless lake.

Durza must have hidden Muckmaw's mind, said Thorn.

"A pretty trick too. I'm not even sure how I'd go about doing that. . . . Try drawing in the scale. Let's see if that gets his attention."

Thorn obliged with some difficulty. The toes on his forefoot were too large for nimble work, and yet he managed to twist and tangle the cord about his limb enough to shorten the line yard by yard.

A new ripple, proud and wide, appeared, moving crosswise to

the prevailing current, heading toward where Murtagh guessed Glaedr's scale was. *There.* It was a long shot, especially when firing into water, but Murtagh decided to chance it. In a single smooth motion, he pressed the bow away while pulling the string to the corner of his jaw and—without hesitation—released.

The arrow whirred as it flew, and he sent with it a killing word spoken with fatal intent.

Droplets shot up as the arrow hit the lake just ahead of the ripples.

And then . . .

. . . the ripples smoothed and subsided, and from the spell he'd cast, Murtagh felt no drain of energy.

He'd missed.

He bit back a curse and nocked another arrow, fast as he could.

"Here, fishy, fishy," he muttered, sweeping his gaze across the lake. He squinted. Was that movement to the right? The water was too dark to be sure.

"Brisingr," he whispered, and released the energy in a carefully measured trickle, so as to create a dim orb of red fire in front of him. It hung over the water like a minor sun, just bright enough to allow him to clearly see the heaving hide of the lake.

He hoped the light might help tempt the fish closer.

Thorn continued to pull in the cord. Glaedr's scale was nearly to them. Murtagh could make out a golden shimmer beneath the waves, rising toward the surface.

He opened his mouth to suggest that Thorn try jiggling the line.

A great mass raced upward from beneath the scale, and blackness yawned around Glaedr's jeweled remnant, and hideously wide jaws clamped shut, disappearing it from view.

Thorn yanked on the cord. The line snapped with a wirelike *twang.*

Murtagh drew and loosed in a single motion, and with it, he cried the killing word.

A line of white bubbles traced the arrow's downward path. It was a good shot. The shaft hit somewhere on Muckmaw's yard-wide head. Murtagh saw, felt, and heard the impact.

The arrow glanced to the side and disappeared into the waves of Isenstar. Again, Murtagh felt no decrease in strength from his spell.

Then Muckmaw's bulk sank from sight, as a hulled derelict descending to its final resting place, and no hint of his pale-rimmed eyes remained. Nor of Glaedr's scale.

Murtagh lowered his bow. Nocking another arrow would be pointless. He cursed.

Beside him, Thorn shook the slack remnants of the cord off his forefoot. *The fish is formidable.*

"If we lose him, I swear, I'll drain the whole blasted—"

A V-shape of ripples formed off to the right, maybe seventy feet from shore. The ripples traced a curve about the tongue of slate he and Thorn stood on.

Thorn shifted slightly, gaze intent on the disturbance. *He has not fled.*

"No."

He is playing with us.

"How intelligent can he be?"

The ripples faded.

Thorn's glittering eyes turned on him for a moment. *Cunning enough to hunt a man.*

Cold concern congealed at the back of Murtagh's skull. Thorn was right. Most animals—most *fish*—would have fled after being attacked. But then, Muckmaw wasn't like most fish. That was the entire problem.

Murtagh set his jaw, determined. No fish was going to best him, regardless of its enchantments. He slipped his bow into his quiver, along with the arrows. The time for physical weapons had passed.

"All wards have a limit," he said. "Let's find the limits of this one. I'll need some of your strength, though."

Thorn's maw split to show his curved teeth. *What's mine is yours.*

Murtagh matched his grin. Then he returned his focus to the water. The scarred fisherman had spoken the truth: killing Muckmaw was a task for an elf or a Rider. Few others would be equal to the challenge. And by disposing of the fish, they could do some good for the common folk of Gil'ead, while also furthering their own interests. It was a gratifying combination.

Crouching, Murtagh felt around until he found a piece of loose slate. He cocked his arm and tossed the slate a few yards out into the near waters. Far enough that Muckmaw might feel safe, but close enough that Murtagh would have a clear line of sight.

A string of pearlescent bubbles appeared, rising toward the surface. He tensed, keeping firm the connection between his mind and Thorn's.

Another swell of water formed, not thirty feet away.

Murtagh focused on an area just beneath the surface, pointed, and spoke the Word, the Name of Names.

Along with the Word, he added a phrase intended to strip away the magics bound to Muckmaw, to break and end the enchantments Durza had placed on the fish more than half a century ago. Although the Word granted him complete control over the ancient language, he still found it helpful—and often necessary—to explicitly state the desired outcome.

He released the spell and, as with most uses of the Word, felt only the slightest decrease of energy. But it was enough to know the spell had taken effect. Altering existing magic by reason of the Name of Names required little in the way of brute strength. It was a subtle art more akin to adjusting the weave of a tapestry than shattering a piece of pottery.

"Got you," he muttered. Then: "Kverst!"

The word parted the swell of water as neatly as cloth cut by a razor. Underneath, Murtagh glimpsed a ridge of bladed spines and, spread to either side, a broad, humped back covered with a layer of blue-black scales glistening in the silvery light. But the spell did nothing more, and Muckmaw again dove from view.

"What?!" Murtagh's astonishment shaded into outrage. He drove a spear of thought toward the fish . . . only to strike emptiness and absence. "How?" The spell had worked. He'd felt it! And yet somehow Muckmaw remained unharmed.

Again he spoke the Word, and again he sought to break the magic bound to Muckmaw, and again it felt as if he'd succeeded. But when he sent another killing spell into the water, it passed ineffectively around the overgrown sturgeon.

He tried twice more—growing increasingly frustrated—and met with the same results.

How was it done? Thorn asked. *Wordless magic?*

Murtagh shook his head. "It can't be. The spell did what it was supposed to. I'm sure of it. It's just . . ." Counting Sarros, this made two times now that the Name of Names had failed him. It was not, he was coming to realize, the all-powerful weapon he had originally thought. That, and he had far less of an understanding of magic than he'd hoped.

He squatted on his hams and chewed on the inside of his cheek while he studied the lake. Then he laughed, quick and soft. "You clever bastard." He looked at Thorn. "I don't know if this is the answer, but one way it *could* be done would be to word a spell so that if anything changes or removes it, the spell replaces itself. *If this, then that.*" Not so dissimilar from the spells he'd experimented with during their trip to Gil'ead.

Can you use the Name of Names to stop the spell from returning?

"Maybe. Probably. But I'd have to think on it."

Then think on it.

An itch formed on his right palm. He scratched. "I don't know. It might be faster to just—" His scalp prickled, and his nostrils flared as fear jolted through him. *My hand!* He spun toward Thorn, saying, "We have to go. Get us into the—"

A splash sounded to his right and—

—he turned to see a huge, glistening mass hurtling toward him from the water. He barely had time to register a sense of disbelief before the giant fish slammed into him and he, and it, fell into the lake.

CHAPTER VI

✦ ✦ ✦ ✦ ✦ ✦ ✦

Heave and Toil

The cold water closed around Murtagh in a deadly embrace. He couldn't see, couldn't hear, didn't know which direction was up.

The impact had knocked the quiver off his back. His cloak tangled his arms and legs, making it impossible to swim.

Even through the tumult of water, he heard Thorn roaring, and a wash of red dragonfire lit the depths of the lake from above, wherever *above* was.

He ripped off the brooch that held his cloak clasped around his neck and kicked and punched heavy fabric away. Ribbons of white bubbles flowed sideways past his face. *Up!*

With a swing of his arms, he righted himself and swam toward the surface. His werelight had vanished, but floating on the choppy laketop, he saw the shape of his bow, a bright-burning crescent.

A warning instinct caused him to glance around.

From the murky depths of the lake rose Muckmaw, silt streaming from the corners of his enormous, shovel-shaped mouth: an ancient monster made of stone scales, sharpened ridges, and hateful malice.

Murtagh raised his right hand, the one with his gedwëy ignasia, and prepared to cast a spell by *thinking* the word. Even if he couldn't directly affect the fish with magic, he could still shield himself or else attack the beast with water or flame or other means.

Before he could, the monster wriggled forward with shocking speed, moving faster than any creature Murtagh had seen before, even Thorn.

The fish's mouth closed about his right arm, and he felt the bony plates within its maw grinding against his skin. Then the creature began to thrash and roll, dragging him through the water.

Murtagh's head snapped from side to side. Yellow stars flashed before his eyes, and he had to fight not to let out all his air.

His wards kept the fish from ripping off his arm. But they didn't do much more. They couldn't. He'd never thought to restrict his own movement.

He glimpsed Thorn's head and neck sticking under the water, like an enormous serpent. And he saw one of Thorn's forelegs reaching toward him, claws extended.

Then Muckmaw dove deeper, spiraling as he went. Murtagh felt himself slam into the bottom, and a cloud of impenetrable mud billowed up around them. He tried to focus well enough to cast a spell, but the fish wasn't giving him the chance.

Muckmaw dragged him across the freezing lakebed. His back, left arm, and legs banged into rocks, and the impacts left his skin numb.

Murtagh's lungs burned, and he felt his wards sapping his energy at an alarming rate.

He groped for the dagger he'd taken off bird-chest. His fingers brushed the hilt of the weapon, and then it tumbled away, knocked loose by Muckmaw's violent thrashing.

Desperate, Murtagh flailed, trying to catch hold of something— anything—he could use as a weapon.

A few seemingly endless moments of fumbling and then . . .

. . . his hand closed around a long, hard object that felt more like a rod of iron than a piece of wood.

He grabbed it and yanked it free from the sucking mud and stabbed it toward Muckmaw's broad head. *Kverst!* he cried in his mind.

A bolt of static seemed to run up his arm along with the shock of impact, and he felt himself grow faint as the spell consumed what little remained of his energy. Then new strength filled him as Thorn joined his effort, sustaining him as the spell's demands increased beyond reason.

A brief flash of light emanated from the point where the rod pressed against Muckmaw's brow, and then Murtagh felt the object sink through flesh and bone, deep into the fish's armored braincase.

The fish convulsed and released Murtagh's arm. Before Murtagh could swim out of range, Muckmaw's enormous tail slapped him broadside and all went black.

❖

Murtagh regained awareness with a panicked start. How long had he been unconscious? It couldn't have been more than a few seconds. Muckmaw was still twisting and thrashing perhaps twenty feet away.

Fire filled Murtagh's lungs and veins. He was going to burst or pass out if he didn't get air, but he refused to open his mouth. If he inhaled water, he'd have no chance of reaching the surface.

He kicked and clawed upward.

Another wash of red dragonfire illuminated the interior of the lake, and for a moment, Murtagh lost all sense of time or place. Thick ropes of water weed rose like great floating vines around him, swaying softly through the teal water. Billows of mud drifted from the track Muckmaw had gouged across the lakebed, and a mesh of shadows flickered and wavered throughout. And rising from the morass of mud and slime, like sun-bleached branches stripped of bark, was a forest of bones: arms and legs and hands hooked in claws of anguish. Bracers and cuffs and tattered garments hung from some, and scraps of tendons and withered muscle. Hundreds of dead, consigned to the deep, consumed by the fishes and insects and lesions of green mosslike growths. A battalion's worth of shields, swords, and spears lay scattered among them, the wood soft and decayed, the steel plated black with rust.

Murtagh stared with horror. Then instinct jolted him back to reality, and he tore at the water with his hands and scissored his legs until—

His face breached the surface. Air struck his skin, and he gasped, unable to empty and fill his lungs fast enough. His vision went red and dark around the edges, and he again sank under the water.

Then a rough, pointed object slid under his back and arms, lifting him. He rolled over and clung to Thorn's head with all his strength.

I have you, Thorn said.

Murtagh hacked and coughed, unable to answer, but he held Thorn even tighter.

They were over a hundred feet from the shore; the dragon lay in the water, most of his bulk hidden beneath the surface, only the spikes along his spine and the tips of his folded wings showing.

I could not reach you any faster, said Thorn.

"I know," said Murtagh, still coughing. "It's all right."

I would have rescued you and killed Muckmaw no matter what.

He hugged Thorn again and then turned to look over the lake. "You don't have to convince me. . . . I didn't think I could hate Durza any more."

What other evils has he left in Alagaësia?

The question gave Murtagh pause. "I wish I knew."

A roiling disturbance in the water twenty feet away caused both of them to tense, and Murtagh started to climb onto Thorn's back.

Then Muckmaw bobbed to the surface and rolled belly-up, his entire length limp.

Murtagh swore and brushed his wet hair out of his eyes. His heart was still pounding, and he felt ready to leap back into battle.

"Hold on. There's something I have to check." He pushed off from Thorn, set out paddling, and swam to Muckmaw's enormous corpse. Thorn followed at a slower pace, slithering through the water with sinuous ease.

Murtagh pulled himself around Muckmaw to the creature's head. Sticking out of the overgrown sturgeon's skull was—as he'd thought—a length of broken bone. A human thigh bone, by the look of it.

Murtagh's mind returned to the butchery that lay submerged beneath them, and a disturbing suspicion formed within him. The sheer number of corpses made absurd the idea that they could be Muckmaw's victims and his alone. No one would have endured the presence of such a monster. The amount of slaughter—even spread across the past sixty years—would have driven the common folk from the lake and sent word of Muckmaw throughout the land until others more fearsome still came hunting the murderous fish.

He glanced at Thorn. "I'll be right back. Brisingr!" Again he set a werelight burning in front of himself, only this one was blue white and brighter than before.

Then he took a deep breath and again dove under. The water bubbled and steamed around the ball of fire, but the glowing ball of gas still provided enough light for him to see.

Down he swam into the freezing depths, down and down until the field of crusted skeletons came into view. In the seething illumination of his werelight, the bones seemed to shift and stir with unnatural life, as marionettes badly puppeted and desperate to escape their casement of decay.

He kicked himself to the nearest skeleton and dug through the mud and silt covering the torso. The muck was cold as despair. His fingers found a tattered scrap of leather, and he pulled it free, held it up. Suspicion solidified into certainty. As he had feared, there was embossed on the leather the standard of Galbatorix's infantry.

Murtagh took one last look over the watery boneyard where so many of the Empire's soldiers lay. The weird and grotesque desolation made his heart hurt to see.

Then he pushed off and again ascended.

With a burst of spray, he broke free of the water. He gasped and clung gratefully to Thorn when the dragon swam over to him.

What is it?

Murtagh swore and banged his forehead several times against Thorn's hard scales. The water was a frigid blanket around him, heavy and constraining.

"They're down there," he mumbled. He kept his brow pressed against Thorn's neck. "Blast it. They're all down there."

Thorn's alarm increased. *Who?*

When Murtagh shared what he'd seen, Thorn's sorrow joined his own. "The elves must have driven them into the water. They never stood a chance." The last he'd seen of Galbatorix's battalions, the squares of men had been huddled together upon the smoke-shrouded plains outside Gil'ead while the ranks of tall elves marched upon them with inexorable force.

In a gentle tone, the dragon said, *It is unfortunate, but their deaths are not our responsibility.*

"They are. If Galbatorix had let us stay, we could have—"

The elves would have killed us. Even with Yngmar's strength at our disposal, we could not have withstood their combined might.

"We should have at least *tried*!"

Would you have seen the elves defeated and Galbatorix triumphant?

"No! But there must have been a way to save the men. Somehow."

Thorn's neck vibrated as the dragon growled. *You cannot force the world to be as you will.*

"Can't I?" Murtagh lifted his head to look at Thorn. "If you want something badly enough—"

Want is not always enough. Thorn nuzzled the top of his head. *The means must be there also. You know this.*

Murtagh took a shuddery breath. His vision blurred. Tears or lakewater dripping from his hair, he wasn't sure which. While Galbatorix himself had been evil, Murtagh couldn't help but pity the ordinary men who had marched under the Empire's banner, many of whom had been pressed into service. He had campaigned with them. Broken bread with them. And he knew them to be good and true. They'd had no choice whether to fight, and at Gil'ead and Ceunon, they had faced an attack from outside their lands and outside their race.

It was not so hard to understand why they spent their lives in defense of the Empire. Under different circumstances, Murtagh would have done the same.

They trusted us to be their champions, and we couldn't help them, he thought. The conclusion was profoundly depressing.

Thorn responded with firm force: *No. We did what we could, and none can claim otherwise. Do not torment yourself over this.*

A small wave struck Murtagh in the mouth. He spat out a thimbleful of water and shook his head. *It wasn't a fair fight.* He had seen how human might failed before the speed and strength of the elves. Even were they fairly matched, the elven spellcasters alone would have devastated Galbatorix's army.

Magic unbalances all things, said Thorn.

He thought about that as he extinguished the werelight and swam back to Muckmaw's floating body. *You're right. And it always has. Galbatorix had his solution. Nasuada is trying her own, by means of Du Vrangr Gata. Even the ancient language itself was an attempt at control.*

You could no more seek to control the wind or the rain than to control magic.

Then what hope has the ordinary man in a world of magicians?

The same hope any creature has when battered by the storms of fate.

Murtagh hooked a hand through Muckmaw's exposed gills and tried to pull the fish toward the shore. It barely moved. He turned to Thorn as the dragon slithered closer.

"Help."

With Thorn's assistance, moving Muckmaw to the shore was—while not easy—a fairly quick process. Once there, Thorn crawled out of the water, and then extended a paw and dragged the fish onto the bank.

Murtagh collapsed next to the fish and stared at the ceaseless stars in their slow rotation. Images of the submerged skeletons continued to pass through his mind.

Thorn kicked Muckmaw's corpse out of the way with one of his hind legs before curling around Murtagh and draping a wing over him to form a warm, safe pocket.

Murtagh closed his eyes. His wards had exhausted him even more than the strain of the fight, and his body ached from the battering he'd taken. Especially his left forearm, where the bone beneath the old cut throbbed as if bruised. He needed food, and a warm fire, and a long sleep.

Not yet, he thought. Silna still needed rescuing, and he was worried that he didn't have enough time to install himself in Captain Wren's company before the guards departed with the youngling. Assuming that Carabel's suspicions were correct. He comforted himself with the thought that Silna's captors likely wouldn't leave until morning.

A tremor passed through Thorn; the dragon was shaking, as if cold. "What's wrong?" Murtagh murmured, and stroked Thorn's belly.

The dragon growled slightly. *You're hurt.*

Not too badly. I'll be fine in a day or two.

Thorn shivered again and growled slightly. *I was too slow. I could not catch you in time.*

That's not—

The fish could have killed you.

"It takes a lot to kill me," Murtagh said out loud. The sound of his voice usually had a calming influence on Thorn. "And you too."

At first Thorn didn't respond. Then Murtagh heard rather than saw the dragon's teeth snap together. *Yes. A lot.*

"And nothing has succeeded so far."

I would rather keep it that way.

He patted Thorn and, with a groan, rolled onto his feet. Thorn's wing lifted as he stood, again revealing the night sky and Muckmaw's slumped corpse.

Murtagh rubbed his arms and wrung water from his sleeves. "This is the day that never ends."

It's already past midnight. A new day, said Thorn.

"Doesn't feel like it." Murtagh eyed the lake. Drifting some distance from the slate overhang was his bow. Or what was left of it. The string was broken, and the wood charred to a twisted cinder. The spells bound to the weapon protected it from many things, but the full heat of dragonfire wasn't one of them.

He sighed. In one night he'd lost two of his three weapons. All he had left was Zar'roc, which was formidable, but not exactly helpful if he wanted to shoot from a distance or carve a piece of bacon.

Speaking of carving . . . He went to Thorn and unbuckled the lowest saddlebag. Its contents, he was pleased to see, were still dry, a consequence of the spell he'd cast after the torrent he and Thorn had gotten caught in early last year.

Murtagh pulled out Zar'roc and walked over to Muckmaw's corpse. He stood looking at the glistening mass of flesh for a minute, judging the best place to cut. Just how much of the fish did the guards want? There wasn't a clear distinction between head and neck on the animal.

"We'll need something to wrap the head in," he said. "I don't want to use my blanket, but—"

Thorn stalked past and dipped his snout into the lake. With water streaming from his chops, he deposited Murtagh's soggy cloak at his feet.

Murtagh picked it up with one hand. Holes and long tears let moonlight shine through the felted wool. He sighed again. "I hope it's big enough."

Zar'roc wasn't a two-handed sword—at times Murtagh missed the proportions of his old bastard sword—but he wrapped his off hand around the pommel and raised the weapon above his head, like an executioner about to deliver the final, fatal blow. He inhaled, and then swung the sword down with a loud "Huh!"

The crimson blade sliced through Muckmaw's bony hide and the dark meat underneath with hardly any resistance. The fish was so large, though, that Murtagh was only able to cut through a third of its neck on the first blow.

He lifted Zar'roc again, and again slashed downward.

It took four cuts to decapitate the fish. Separated from the body, Muckmaw's head was nearly as wide as Murtagh was tall; he could barely wrap his arms around it if he tried.

The fish's giant saucer-dish eyes stared at him, pale and blank, devoid of motive force, but with what he felt was a certain accusatory expression.

"To all things an end," Murtagh murmured, and put a hand on the beast's cold forehead.

The scale, said Thorn.

"Ah." Murtagh took up Zar'roc again and pressed the tip against Muckmaw's belly, just below the fish's ribs. With a whisper of a sound, he sliced open the giant sturgeon, and a length of grey, wormlike intestine fell slopping around his boots in great slippery coils.

He grimaced and held his breath as he felt along the intestine until he found the stomach. Another quick cut, and the stomach opened to reveal a ghastly collection of smaller fish, frogs, half-digested eels, and even some branches. And buried amid the reeking refuse, Glaedr's golden scale, bright as a polished plate.

Murtagh leaned Zar'roc against the curved side of Muckmaw's corpse and fetched a piece of cloth from Thorn's saddlebags. With it, he removed the scale from the pile of filth before quickly retreating. Sickened, he leaned over and retched, though nothing came up but bile and regret.

He poured a handful of dry dirt over the scale, shook it off, and then stowed it in the saddlebags before returning to Muckmaw's head and body.

He'd just started to wrap the head in his ruined cloak when a pair of voices echoed across the shifting water. He looked up. A small coracle was approaching, and in it, two men working the paddles. Night fishers, drawn by the noise and light.

A wave of exhaustion passed through Murtagh. He was out of energy to deal with more problems. Nevertheless, he squared his shoulders and, with his left hand, reached behind the bulk of Muckmaw's body and grabbed Zar'roc, careful to keep the sword hidden.

"Don't make any sudden movem—" he said, glancing at Thorn.

The dragon had vanished. Murtagh stiffened, but then he searched with his mind and realized that Thorn had simply dropped back into the shadows behind the lake and was lying flat among the brambles that grew along the top of the banks.

For a creature so large, he could be remarkably quiet.

Murtagh looked back at the boat.

"Ho there!" called one of the men when they were about fifty feet from shore. Grey streaked his beard, and his shoulders were heavy from years of rowing. His companion put up his oars, lifted an oil lantern, and unshuttered it, releasing a key of yellow light that illuminated Murtagh, and Muckmaw's corpse beside him.

Murtagh shaded his eyes with his free hand. He could see the men gaping at him. He could only imagine what he looked like, covered in mud, blood, and fish slime.

"Wh-who goes?" said the greybeard, stuttering slightly.

The other man said, "We heard a commotion fit t' raise th' dead, but . . ."

In a soft voice to himself, Murtagh said, "But you kept away until it was over." Then, louder: "Ho there! Muckmaw is dead." He gestured at the corpse. "His head is mine, but do with the rest as you will."

The fishermen neither moved nor spoke as Murtagh leaned Zar'roc against Muckmaw's open belly—where they couldn't see—and finished wrapping his tattered cloak around the sturgeon's severed head. The length of shattered thigh bone buried in the fish's brow stuck out through a hole in the cloth.

He straightened and slung the corner of the cloak over his shoulder.

"Who . . . who are y', stranger?" said greybeard, his voice faint in the night air.

"Just a traveler," said Murtagh. He turned his back on them, picked up Zar'roc while being careful to keep his body between the fishermen and the jeweled sword, and then dug his heels into the damp ground.

Step by step, he dragged the giant fish head into the brambles atop the bank. He heard the fishermen muttering to each other behind him, followed by splashing as they started for the shore.

Atop the bank, Murtagh cast a quick spell: the same one he used to hide Thorn when they flew. It wasn't perfect—anyone who looked closely would see the air rippling like liquid glass where they stood—but it would be enough to hide them in the dark of night.

As soon as he reached Thorn, he dropped the corner of the cloak and scrambled up Thorn's side into the saddle. "Go, go, go," he whispered.

Thorn picked up Muckmaw's head in his enormous talons and, silent as a hunting owl, jumped across the moonlit field and glided on half-extended wings. He landed with a soft jolt and leaped again, this time with wings at their full spread. Two more leaps, and they were far enough from the lake that it was doubtful anyone would hear.

Whoosh! Thorn flapped once, and then again, and they were away, spiraling up into the starry sky.

CHAPTER VII

✦ ✦ ✦ ✦ ✦ ✦

In Defense of Lies

I *wanted to eat the fish,* Thorn complained as they circled over
Gil'ead.

I know, but there would have been no easy way to keep those
men from wagging their jaws about you all across Gil'ead.

Who would believe them?

Murtagh chuckled, despite himself. *Fair point. Still, do you really*
want to eat a fish that Durza meddled with?

Thorn huffed. *No magic can survive the belly of a dragon.*

Maybe you're right, but better not to test it.

Should you warn those men?

If they're so foolish as to eat Muckmaw, and they start growing ant-
lers on their heads or somesuch, they have only themselves to blame.
None of which seemed very likely to Murtagh.

Mmh. Well, I will need to hunt soon. My hunger grows.

After we leave Gil'ead, you can eat all the deer you want.

They landed several miles from the city, by the edge of a small
stream. There, Murtagh scrubbed the dirt and slime from his
hands and face. Every inch of his body felt disgustingly filthy.

Unhappy with the result, he stripped and washed again, this
time sparing no skin.

He stood on the bank of the stream, bare as the day he was
born, and looked to Gil'ead. Whipcords of smoke rose from the
lights and lanterns and chimneys within the city, and they spread
as they rose until they merged into a diffuse lens of ashen haze

that hung over the assembled buildings. The lights below painted the bottom of the haze a sullen orange, as if the sky itself were a banked fire smoldering through the night.

Murtagh wanted to return with Muckmaw's head then and there, but he knew if he went banging on the doors of Captain Wren's garrison in the middle of the night, they were as like to throw him out as let him in. It was a risk he didn't want to take when losing might mean Silna's life.

"I hate to wait," he said. "Maybe I could—"

No. Thorn slapped the ground with his tail, and somewhere a sleepy crow uttered an outraged squawk. Murtagh blinked, surprised, and turned to look Thorn in the face. *You sleep. You need sleep. Sleep now.*

"What if they move Silna, though? We might never—"

The day's hunting is done. If you go, you'll step wrong, get hurt—more hurt. Rest will help you hunt better.

Murtagh sighed and let his head fall back. "I know. I just hate to waste any time."

His head vibrated as Thorn hummed. *It is not waste if it helps.*

A wry smile formed on Murtagh's face. "You're wiser than you look, for a big lizard."

Thorn nudged him with his snout. *And you're as stubborn as you look.*

"You're right. But not tonight. Tonight I'll bend my knee to your learned advice."

Thorn snorted.

The night cold returned Murtagh's attention to the task at hand. He submerged his clothes in the creek and left them soaking there, weighted down with stones. Then he wrapped himself in his blanket and sat huddled against Thorn's warm belly while he ate one of his few remaining dried apples. His teeth chattered between bites.

When he finished, he and Thorn went to speak their true

names, as was their nightly ritual. Thorn named himself first and without difficulty, but when Murtagh tried to do likewise, he found himself unable. Something felt amiss with his name as it had been, and thus he could not speak it, for to speak it would have been a falsehood in the ancient language.

Thorn waited patiently. It was not the first time this had happened. On occasion, one or the other of them—or both—had changed, and that change was reflected in their names. Were it a small difference, new understanding was often quick to come. But when a fundamental part of their selves shifted—as it had in Urû'baen, when they broke free of Galbatorix—then understanding could be elusive and hard-fought.

Tired as he was, Murtagh had little stomach for introspection. All the same, he persisted. It was important to the two of them that they maintained a full sense of their selves.

So he thought. He had a suspicion as to the cause of his difficulty, and when he noticed he was reluctant to pursue a certain line of inquiry, he knew then he was on the right path. The change had to do with Glaedr's death, and the battle for Gil'ead, and all the lives that had been lost therein. For them, he felt a greater sense of remorse, and for himself, a greater sense of grief and shame. The realization left him diminished and far less certain about his past choices. Even though he and Thorn hadn't been in control of their own actions at the time—even though they'd been Galbatorix's oath-bound thralls—Murtagh realized he still felt responsible for what they'd done. At a certain point, the *reasons* didn't matter. The deeds remained, and the consequences thereof, and their reality was a pain greater than any wound.

The emotions were enough to alter the fabric of his character, if however slightly, and as a result, his true name. He gave voice to his newfound knowledge, and the sound of it was even more stark and discomfiting than before.

Yet as always, Thorn listened and accepted without judgment, and for that, Murtagh was deeply grateful. Then he lay beside Thorn, and they rested close together as the cold of the night pressed in about them.

~~~~~~~~~~~~~~~~~~~ ❖ ~~~~~~~~~~~~~~~~~~

Fleshless fingers reached toward him through flickering water. They closed around his ankles with an icy touch. He struggled to break free, but his strength had deserted him and the bones that bound him were as hard as iron.

He couldn't breathe . . . couldn't escape. . . .

The skeletons of the fallen soldiers rose from the torn lakebed, an army of accusers, pointing at him, reaching for him, desperate to take his warmth, his breath, his life—to tear him apart and seize what they had lost and he still possessed.

Murtagh woke with a start, heart pounding. It was pitch-black beneath Thorn's wing. His skin was coated with sweat, and he felt both chilled and hot, and the back of his throat was raw and swollen. *No, not now,* he thought. Of all the times to get sick . . . And, of course, it happened as soon as he'd entered cities and spent time around other people.

Thorn was watching him through a slitted eye. *If we stayed away from others, you would not have to worry about such things.*

"I had the same thought," said Murtagh. "But what kind of life would that be?"

A peaceful one.

"Mmh." He lay still for a moment and tried to decide whether it was worth closing his eyes again. It felt as if he had only gotten three or four hours of sleep. Maybe less.

He sat up and rubbed his face, conscious of every bump and bruise he'd taken the day before.

The sun will not show for some time, said Thorn.

"I know." Murtagh crawled out from under the dragon's wing

and looked to the east. The faintest hint of grey lightened the horizon, the first presage of far-off dawn.

He did some figuring on how long it would take to get Muckmaw's head to Gil'ead.

Holding the blanket tight around himself, he climbed over Thorn's spiked tail and—walking gingerly on bare feet—went to the creek. It ran along a gravel bed, between drooping willows and clumps of wild rosebushes, and the sound of the gently flowing water was a soothing murmur.

Despite the early hour, the trees and grass and brush were already wet with freezing dew. His breath fogged the air in front of him, and in the crispness, he could feel winter's impending arrival.

Murtagh rucked the blanket around his thighs and stepped into the creek. The water was like liquid ice. He grimaced as he reached down and pulled his clothes from under the rocks holding them in place.

As he returned to the bank, an aggressive chittering sounded on the other side of the creek. There, among the willows, was a large river otter with a thick brown pelt, waving its paws at him and baring its teeth. The otter chittered again and squeaked—as if offended by Murtagh's presence—and then slid into the water and swam away downstream.

Murtagh shook his head and hobbled on numb feet back to Thorn.

"Adurna thrysta," he murmured, and water wept from the woolen shirt and trousers, splattering the blades of grass below. He dressed in the now-dry clothes and repeated the process with his boots, which were still damp from his unexpected swim the day before.

As he forced his feet into the boots, he realized the leather had shrunk slightly, and he berated himself for not attending to them earlier. It wasn't good to let things like that slip. If you didn't take care of the little tasks, how could you be trusted to take care of the important responsibilities in life?

He rubbed some bear grease into the outsides of the boots, and then went to the saddlebags and dug out a dried apple and the last two strips of the jerky he'd bought before traveling to Ceunon. A warm breakfast would have been nice, but he didn't want to lose the time, and in any case, a pair of farmhouses and associated outbuildings were dimly visible to the north. A fire would risk attracting too much attention, even at such a desolate hour.

Murtagh didn't mind cooking, but he never liked how long it took. He thought of all the meals he'd had growing up, when servants would bring him whatever he wanted, or when he could visit the kitchens and snare a cooked pheasant or aged beef roast and a pitcher of cool milk to wash it down.

The jerky was tediously hard. He chewed like a cow on cud and stared at the ground. With every bite, he felt worse and worse. Just swallowing hurt his throat.

You should stay, said Thorn. *You'll make yourself sicker if you go.*

He coughed. "I know, but I can't give up on Silna. Not now. We've already wasted too much time. She might not even be in Gil'ead anymore."

What if she isn't?

"We'll have to track her down. Even if I have to rip the information out of someone's mind. Besides, if we don't help Carabel, I have no idea how we'll find Bachel." He made a face as he swallowed and the flatbread scraped his raw throat.

Why don't you use magic to heal yourself?

"Because there's nothing *to* heal," Murtagh said peevishly. "Nothing's broken. Nothing's bleeding. What do I fix? The bad humors in my blood?"

Why don't you try?

"Because . . . because if I cast a spell without knowing what it's supposed to do, it could consume all of my strength and kill me. You know that."

But you know what you're trying to do. You're trying to heal your fever. You're trying to make your throat feel better. That.

"I . . ." Murtagh stared helplessly at Thorn. "Haven't you ever heard that there's no cure for the common cold?"

No. A wolfish grin split Thorn's jaws. *You are a magician and a Rider. You speak the Name of Names and bend spells to your will. What can you not do?*

"Your confidence is inspiring," Murtagh said dryly. Still, Thorn had a point. "All right. I'll try. Intent *does* matter when it comes to casting spells. Maybe that'll do the trick."

Gathering his strength, Murtagh focused on himself, on his body and his growing discomfort. And he said, "Waíse heill."

A gentle warmth passed through his body, and he felt a sense of lightness, as if he'd pulled off a corselet of mail after a hard day's march. His throat grew itchy, and then the itch subsided along with the warmth, leaving him feeling cool but not chilled.

His throat was, if not entirely normal, far better than before, and his fever seemed to have vanished, along with quite a few bruises and not a little of his soreness.

Murtagh rolled his shoulders, surprised. "I don't know if it entirely worked, but . . . I do feel better."

See? said Thorn.

"Yes, you were right." With renewed vigor, Murtagh set to gnawing on the last piece of tough flatbread. He swallowed with some effort. "I *really* want a proper loaf of bread."

Thorn sniffed. *Meat is better. Why chew on burnt plants?*

"It tastes good, that's why. You should try it again."

No. It only tastes good because you put fat and salt on it.

"You have a point. All right, fat and salt taste good. Happy?"

Thorn's eyes glittered. *Bring me a mountain of bacon, and I will be happy.*

"If I were king, I would," Murtagh muttered. Their saddlebags were looking sadly depleted, and he'd spent almost all of their coin. With an unpleasant twinge, he remembered the purse he'd taken off bird-chest. He pulled it out of the pouch on his belt and cataloged the contents.

It wasn't very much. Which he'd expected. If the man had been well off, he wouldn't have attempted robbery. Still, the purse contained a handful of coppers and a single silver coin, which would be plenty to replenish their supplies.

After. Silna came first. Besides, what kind of a Rider would he be if he abandoned her?

He pocketed the coins and, as he did, noted the—again—empty sheath on his belt. With some regret, he imagined his pilfered dagger lying in the mud at the bottom of the lake. "Blast it. I don't like going anywhere unarmed."

He went to where Muckmaw's head lay on the ground, wrapped in the muddy remains of his cloak. The thick, fishy stench nearly made him gag.

Murtagh grimaced as he gathered up the hem of his cloak. "And I just got clean."

He grabbed the corners of the cloak and started to pull. After a few steps, he stopped and swore. The head was too big and heavy. If he dragged it all the way back to Gil'ead, he'd be completely exhausted by the time he arrived. . . .

"Reisa," he murmured.

Without a sound, Muckmaw's head lifted off the ground, so that it hung floating a finger's breadth above the matted grass. Murtagh waited a moment to see how much effort the spell cost him. It felt equivalent to shouldering an overladen pack: noticeable, but not so much that he couldn't sustain it for a fair amount of time.

He grunted. "Good enough."

Thorn crouched low, with a certain tightening around his eyes that Murtagh had learned was an expression of concern. *How will you open the door that is closed?*

"Carefully, I think. After our little escapade with Muckmaw,

I have an unpleasant suspicion there's more to it than Carabel said. Of everything she asked, I'm afraid this one might be the trickiest."

Even more so than Muckmaw?

Murtagh shook his head. "Muckmaw was difficult, not tricky. This, though . . . I have to deal with other people, and people are hard to predict."

Thorn hissed. *I don't like being left behind. I want to help.*

"What would you have me do? There's no changing this, not unless you want to face every soldier in the city—"

A small tongue of red flame jetted from Thorn's narrowly opened maw. *I would.*

Murtagh gave him a hug about the neck. "Be careful. I'll be as fast as I can. If all goes well, we should be able to slip away without being noticed."

Good. And then we can fly again and not worry about these people and their prying eyes.

"And then we can fly again."

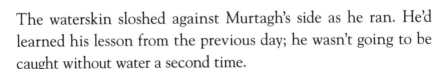

The waterskin sloshed against Murtagh's side as he ran. He'd learned his lesson from the previous day; he wasn't going to be caught without water a second time.

On his back he carried his bedroll and, wrapped in the blanket, a few basic items, such as his tinderbox, pan, some food, and the other kit a traveling soldier might be expected to have.

All part of his plan.

Behind him, Muckmaw's bundled head floated across the countryside, smooth as silk sliding over skin. A slight film of sweat coated Murtagh's brow. Keeping the head suspended was taking its toll, but far less than if he'd attempted to drag it through the brush by strength of limb.

The eastern sky brightened as he ran. Grey turned into pinks and yellows, and the blue shadows that lay across the land began to thin. The sun would just be rising when he arrived at Captain Wren's barracks, which was as he wanted.

The streets of Gil'ead were still mostly empty when he reached the city outskirts, though the smell of baking bread wafted from the buildings, warm and enticing.

His stomach growled.

With a thought, Murtagh ended the spell holding up Muckmaw's head. The head fell to the ground with a wet *splosh*. He staggered at the sudden pull of weight and regripped the corner of the bundled cloak.

Leaning forward, Murtagh started to drag.

As before, he avoided the main roads, making his way between fields and outbuildings until he was able to slip into the city proper without being seen.

A mongrel dog with reddish fur matted with mud came skulking after him, sniffing the trail of slime Muckmaw's head had left. "Go on," said Murtagh in a low voice. "Shoo. Be gone."

The cur's lip quivered, and his ears flattened.

Unwilling to risk the dog barking, Murtagh said, "Eitha!"

The mongrel uttered a small yelp-whine and ran off with his tail tucked between bony legs.

Murtagh shook his head.

From the cramped back garden of one house, he appropriated a small cart. He plopped Muckmaw's head into it, made sure the lump of fish meat was well covered by his ruined cloak, and then trundled off toward the fortress.

Long shadows speared westward from each building as the sun broke free of the horizon. Within seconds, the air started to warm, and a flock of sparrows darted across the flushed sky, chasing insects rising off the lakefront.

Murtagh's watchfulness sharpened as he neared the fortress;

an unusual number of soldiers were moving through the city, and several elves stood by the front gate of the stronghold.

His misadventure at Oromis and Glaedr's barrow seemed to have put the entire garrison on high alert.

Murtagh spotted a manservant holding the reins of a white mare by the front garden of a large house. He swung across the street and said, "'Scuse me, master. Could y' tell me where I might find th' barracks of th' city guard?"

The manservant eyed Murtagh and the cart with undisguised disdain. His hair was pulled into a short ponytail, and his shirt was made of fine bleached linen, and he stood with the poised grace of a dancing instructor. He sniffed. "Up that street, on the right. Although I'll be much surprised if they'll speak to the likes of you."

Murtagh bobbed his head. "Thank'ee, master."

He continued on, feeling the servant's eyes boring into his back until he turned the corner.

The barracks were a series of stone-sided buildings set against the fortress's outer wall and protected with a much shorter wall around their perimeter. The entrance was a narrow gatehouse with a black oak door studded with iron nails. Two pikemen stood watch at the open door.

Through it, Murtagh could see men walking about a paved courtyard, sparring, drilling, and loosing arrows at straw targets. They were each garbed in the watch's standard uniform: a red tabard over a padded gambeson stitched with the Varden's emblem.

Murtagh lifted his chin and let his stride acquire some of the regulated crispness of a marching man. *Here goes,* he thought.

The pikemen crossed their weapons as he pushed the cart to the gatehouse. He noted that their tabards were neat and in good repair, which spoke well of Captain Wren's command.

The two men looked more bored than concerned or aggravated by his presence. A good sign for things to come, he hoped.

"'Ey now," the man on the right started to say, and Murtagh whipped the cloak off Muckmaw's head.

The men's eyes widened. The guard on the right whistled. He appeared a few years older than his counterpart. "Well, blow me sideways. Is that there what I think?"

Murtagh let go of the cart and stood straight. "It is. Muckmaw himself."

The guards gave each other a glance. The older man pushed back his helm and leaned over the cart for a better view. "Son of an Urgal. It's 'im, all right. . . . An' I suppose you're the one as caught 'im, is that it?"

"Yessir. And I'd like to join up. Sir."

The pikemen looked at each other again, this time more seriously. The older one rubbed his chin and said, "Don't *sir* me. I'm as common as dirt. Thing is, I'm 'fraid Captain Wren isn't looking for no green recruit. Standing orders. You'll be wanting a different company. They're always eager for—"

The younger man tugged on his companion's arm. "It's Muckmaw, though, Sev. *Muckmaw!*"

The elder pikeman gnawed on his lip, his expression doubtful. "I don't know, now. The captain's orders were plain as day. If—"

Murtagh drew himself up and snapped his heels together. "I'm not green. And I'd like to serve Captain Wren."

The man frowned, but then, to Murtagh's relief, he turned to the yard and raised a hand. "Oi! Gert! Over here!"

One of the guardsmen broke away from sparring and headed toward them. Gert was heavy-shouldered, broad-handed, with the sort of determined stride that Murtagh had seen in dozens of veteran weaponmasters. He wore thick, short-cropped sideburns shot through with white, and his brow seemed permanently furrowed with exasperation at the stupidity of his troops.

As Gert reached the gatehouse, the pikeman said, "Look there. He caught Muckmaw!"

Gert's tangled eyebrows rose as he surveyed the slimy, gape-mouthed head. "Muckmaw, eh?" He spat on the paving stones. "About time someone put an end to him. That creature's been a blight on the lake fer an unnaturally long time."

"An' our friend here wants to join up," the older pikeman said. "Says he has *experience*."

Gert's scowl returned as he looked Murtagh over. "That so. You've carried arms before?"

"I have."

"Used them?"

"Yessir."

Another grunt, and Gert smoothed his sideburns with one thick hand. "It's against company policy, but any man that can kill the likes of Muckmaw is the sort of man the cap'n wants in his ranks. But afore I go bothering the cap'n 'bout you, you'll have to prove yourself to me, Gert. The cap'n's a busy man, you see. He has no time for nonsense."

Murtagh nodded. "Of course. I understand."

"Mmh. All right. Bring that stinking mess of a fish in here, and we'll see what you're made of." The weaponmaster strode back into the yard, and after a moment's hesitation, Murtagh picked up the handles of the cart and followed.

"Leave him there," said Gert, pointing to a spot just inside the gatehouse.

The other guards stopped what they were doing and watched as Murtagh deposited the cart where indicated. Gert led him to one of the sparring rings made of packed dirt and retrieved two spears with padded heads from a rack set against the inner wall of the yard.

He tossed a spear to Murtagh.

Murtagh caught it one-handed and slipped off his bedroll. He hadn't trained much with spears—they were the main weapon of the common footman—but he knew the basics. He hoped that would be enough.

"Right," growled Gert, taking a ready stance opposite him, spear extended. "First position. Show me what you know."

Murtagh obeyed. As Gert barked out orders, he mirrored the other man. Lunge, stab, block, thrust, deflect. Advance, retreat. With every motion, he felt the bruises Muckmaw had given him. Then Gert closed the distance between them, and they battled spear against spear for a few blows. Murtagh was fast enough that he thought he didn't totally embarrass himself, even though Gert knocked him once on the outside of his left knee.

Afterward, Gert grunted. "Not half bad. Not half good either." He held out a hand, and Murtagh gave him the practice spear.

"I'm better with a blade," said Murtagh.

Gert raised his tangled eyebrows. "Uh-huh." He returned the spears to the rack and then picked up a pair of wooden wasters made in the style of arming swords.

The other guards started hooting and shouting:

"Get 'im, Gert!"

"Show 'im what for!"

"Put a good mark on him."

"Give him stripes! Beat him black-an'-blue!"

Gert handed one waster to Murtagh.

The wooden sword was lighter than Zar'roc, and shorter too, and the balance wasn't quite the same as a real sword, but the shape was familiar, and after hefting it a few times, Murtagh felt confident he could use it to good effect.

"No head strikes," warned Gert, raising his waster.

"No head strikes," Murtagh agreed. Neither of them was wearing a helmet. He spun the sword about in a quick flourish.

Gert gave him no warning. The man attacked with a speed that belied his bulk, beating Murtagh's waster and stabbing at his liver.

If the stab had landed, Murtagh knew he would have been curled up on the ground, unable to move. But it didn't land. He parried the stab and took advantage of the resulting opening to poke Gert in the right armpit.

The man fell back a step, his expression surprised. He recovered quickly, but before he could launch a second attack, Murtagh feinted toward Gert's left hip.

Gert moved to block, and Murtagh whipped his waster around—changing directions in midair—and rapped Gert against his upper arm, near the elbow.

A series of cries went up from the onlookers.

Gert grimaced and shook his arm, and Murtagh allowed himself a quick grin. The blow hadn't looked like much, but he knew it hurt badly.

Then Gert feinted as well and attempted a short slash across Murtagh's ribs, although it was an obvious attempt to lure Murtagh into a disadvantaged position. The man was skilled, but nowhere near the level Murtagh was accustomed to.

He allowed the slash to fall past without blocking or parrying, and when Gert drew back in an attempt to regain position, he struck the flat of Gert's waster. Hard. Harder than most men should have been able to hit.

The man's blade flew wide, and Murtagh brought his wooden sword up, faster than the eye could see, so that the dull edge touched the side of Gert's neck.

They stood like that, Gert breathing hard, Murtagh's chest barely moving. *Did I dare too much?* Yet he also felt a fierce satisfaction at a move well executed, at a duel well fought and won.

He lowered his waster, and the guards watching started shouting and hollering.

"I had a good teacher," said Murtagh. He held out the waster, hilt first.

Gert shook his head with a wry expression. "That you did, boy." He took the waster and returned the wooden swords to the rack. Then he looked round at the onlookers and bellowed, "What are ye lollygagging ne'er-do-wells doing? When you can beat old Gert w' the sword, *then* you can waste the day away staring at what's none of yer business. Back at it, or you'll have scrubbing from evening to morn."

He gestured to Murtagh. "You'd best follow me. The cap'n had better see you after all."

✦ ✦ ✦ ✦ ✦ ✦

CHAPTER VIII

Masks

M urtagh scooped up his bedroll and fell in next to Gert as the stocky man headed away from the courtyard, toward a stone structure attached to one of the barracks. It looked more like a square-sided watchtower than a house, but Murtagh guessed the tower contained the officers' living quarters.

As they walked, Gert said, "Where'd you learn to handle a sword like that, boy?"

"There was a man in our village who had some experience soldiering when he was young. He taught me as I was growing up."

The guard grunted, and Murtagh wondered if he believed him. The skills Murtagh had demonstrated hardly matched those of the average foot soldier. But Gert had the good manners not to inquire further.

The interior of the tower was cool and dark, illuminated only by the occasional arrow slit or wall-mounted torch (few of which were lit). The stones smelled of damp, and the smell reminded Murtagh of the bolt-hole tunnel he had used when meeting Carabel: a mossy, moldy scent that spoke of caves deep underground and of dripping stalactites and blind fish nosing against cold rocks.

Gert led him straight through the building to a closed door by one corner. He knocked and said, "It's me, Cap'n. Mind if'n I come in?"

"Enter," answered a man from within, strong and clear.

Gert gave Murtagh a stern look. "You wait here now an' don't move." Then he pulled open the door and stepped through.

Murtagh glanced up and down the stone hall. It had an arched roof similar to some of the dwarf tunnels around Tronjheim. There was a low wooden bench against one wall, but he decided it was better to stand. Next to the bench was a planter full of artfully arranged bundles of dried baby's breath.

He wondered who had requested the flowers.

Gert kept him waiting for over ten minutes. Then the door swung back open, and the weaponmaster poked his head out. "Cap'n will see you now."

Murtagh hefted his bedroll and walked in.

The captain's study was a modest affair, as such things went. Murtagh had seen officers commission or commandeer far more ostentatious chambers in order to flaunt their family's wealth or improve their chances of climbing the ranks of power at court. Wren's tastes were more restrained, if somewhat unusual.

The walls were the same bare stone as the outside, but they were lined with racks of scrolls, over which hung maps of Gil'ead, maps of the Empire, and maps of Nasuada's new queendom, the Spine, and Alagaësia as a whole. A broad table dominated one side of the room, and even more maps—these pinned with small flags and carvings of soldiers—lay strewn across it, along with scrolls and piles of parchment covered with writing.

The captain himself sat behind the desk, marking runes on a half sheet of vellum. He looked to be in his mid-thirties, with a touch of grey at his temples and a few fine wrinkles about his eyes from years spent drilling in the sun. Lean, focused, with an intelligent and perceptive gleam to his gaze, he struck Murtagh as the sort of man who could both plan a campaign and execute it, while also earning the love of his men.

His hair was neat, his tabard and jerkin neater. Even his nails were clean and trimmed. The one flaw in his appearance was his hands; the knuckles were swollen and the fingers twisted with arthritic distortion in a way Murtagh had only seen before among the extreme elderly.

On the wall behind the captain was the room's most notable feature: two lines of wooden masks mounted on the stone. They weren't the ornate party masks of the aristocracy, with which Murtagh was well acquainted. Rather, they were rough, barbaric-looking creations that evoked the faces of different animals: the bear, the wolf, the fox, the raven, and so forth, including two animals that he didn't recognize. In style and execution, they resembled no tradition he was familiar with; if pressed, he would have said they had been crafted with the crudest of stone tools.

And yet the masks had a certain entrancing power; Murtagh found his gaze drawn to them as a lodestone drawn to a bar of iron.

Wren put down his quill and, with a slight grimace, flexed his hand. He eyed Murtagh. "So you're the one who caught Muckmaw."

At the back of the room, Gert slipped out and closed the door.

Murtagh stood at attention and nodded. "Yes, sir."

"How did you manage it, son?"

The run to Gil'ead had given Murtagh plenty of opportunity to think of an answer. As always, the best deception was the one that hewed most closely to the truth.

He adopted a somewhat abashed expression. "Truth be told, I weren't trying to. I were out fishing for eels, and Muckmaw grabbed my bait and pulled me into the water. I'm not ashamed to say, I thought my last moments were upon me. I saw the fish come at me, and I tried to use my dagger on him, but it just bounced off his hide."

Wren nodded, as if this were expected. "And then what?"

"Well, he knocked me down into the mud, and I'm pretty sure he were fixing to eat me, but I meant to make it a real pain for him. I caught hold of what I thought were a stick, and I gave him a good poke in the head. You can imagine my surprise when the stick went right in and that were the end of him. After I got out of the water, I saw it weren't no stick but a piece of bone from some unfortunate soul. You can see it if'n you want, out in the yard."

"So his weakness was bone," Wren murmured. "No wonder it

escaped discovery until now." He gestured at Murtagh's clothes. "I see you managed to dry off since your misadventure."

Blast it. Murtagh shrugged. "It were a long walk back to Gil'ead dragging that monster's head. It's bigger than a bull's."

"I see." Wren tapped his fingers against the desktop. "What's your name, son?"

For the second time in as many days, Murtagh had to choose a new name. And not just a name, an identity. "Task," he said. "Task Ivorsson."

Wren picked up the quill again and made a note. "Well, Task, you've done a great service for the people of Gil'ead, and you've more than earned your reward." From a small box on the desk, he counted out four bright gold crowns into Murtagh's palm.

Murtagh felt a small shock as he saw Nasuada's profile stamped onto the front of each coin. It was the first time he had encountered the new currency of the realm, and he allowed himself a moment of inspection, disguised as the gawking of a man who had never before held so much gold.

The likeness was an uncanny one. So skilled was it, Murtagh felt sure magic had been used in its creation. The sight of Nasuada's all-too-familiar profile—proud and perfect in resplendent relief, with a modest diadem upon her brow—set a familiar ache in his heart, and he touched the image with hesitant fingers.

Wren noticed. "I take it you haven't seen our new queen before."

"Not as such, no." It was an unfortunately ambiguous answer, and Murtagh berated himself the instant he spoke, but to his relief, the captain didn't request further clarification.

"Her Majesty's treasury issued these near winter's end," said Wren. "I understand all the coinage is to be replaced in due course."

Murtagh closed his hand over the crowns. It made sense. Nasuada would hardly want images of Galbatorix circulating throughout the land for the rest of her reign. He slipped the coins into his pouch.

"Now then," said Wren. "I understand you want to join my company specifically. Why?"

Murtagh straightened further. "Everyone says it's the best in the city, sir. And I'd like to be of some use again, aside from just guarding caravans."

"Very commendable of you. Gert seemed impressed with your swordsmanship, and it takes a lot to pry a compliment out of that old goat. He also says you have some experience. So tell me, Task, where did you serve?"

It was a question with many meanings, and they both knew it. Murtagh noted that the captain had been careful not to ask *with whom*. "At the Battle of the Burning Plains," he said quietly. "And I were also at Ilirea when it fell."

Wren nodded, keeping his gaze fixed on the vellum. As Murtagh had expected, the captain didn't inquire further. Most of the men in Galbatorix's army had been conscripts forced to swear oaths of loyalty to the king in the ancient language. Since the king's death, and since Eragon had used the Name of Names to break those oaths, the many thousands of soldiers had been free to pick their own path. The majority returned to their homes. But a significant portion opted to continue their profession as men-at-arms, and Nasuada's current regime was not so well established that they could afford to turn away so many trained men.

Besides, there were plenty of people throughout Nasuada's realm who still held sympathies for the Empire and who regarded the Varden with no small amount of ill will. It was possible that such was the case with the captain.

Either way, it would have been impolitic for Wren to press for more details as to Murtagh's past service. Knowing that, Murtagh had avoided mentioning his presence at the Battle of Tronjheim, for the only notable human forces there had been among the Varden, whereas humans had fought on both sides at the Burning Plains and Ilirea.

Captain Wren said, "How were you trained?"

"As a footman, but I'm better with a blade than a spear or pike, and I'm more than passable with a bow."

The captain nodded, making another note. "And why are you looking to serve again, Task? Yes, you wish to be of use. But why now? I assume you've not marched under a banner since Ilirea."

"No, sir . . . I wanted to see my family. I'm from a village called Cantos, in the south. I don't know if you've heard of it. . . ."

Wren shook his head. "I can't say I have."

"Well, it's not a big place, sir. Or, it wasn't. There weren't much left of it when I got there." Cantos had been the village Galbatorix had ordered Murtagh to burn, raze, and eradicate; he'd fled before obeying, but he knew the king would have found someone to commit the crime all the same.

"I see. I'm sorry to hear that, Task."

Murtagh shrugged. "It were a hard war, sir."

At that, a flicker of some indefinable emotion appeared in Wren's eyes. "That it was, Task. That it was." The captain leaned back in his chair and gave Murtagh a thoughtful look. "Have you any of your old kit?"

Murtagh gestured at his bedroll. "A shirt of fine mail, sir, but that's all."

"It's better than most, Task. There are some required items you will have to purchase of your own, but with your reward for Muckmaw, you have more than sufficient funds. The rest of your equipment can be provided, assuming . . ."

Murtagh cocked his head. "Assuming what, sir?"

Wren rested his elbows on the desk and placed one gnarled hand over the other. "If you're serious about joining my company, Task, you'll have to swear fealty to the queen, to Lord Relgin, and to this unit, with myself as its commander. Do you understand?"

A sick feeling formed in Murtagh's stomach, and the back of his neck went cold. *I should have realized.* Something of his reaction must have shown, because Wren's expression hardened. "Is that a problem for you, Task?" He picked up his quill again.

"That depends, sir. Does the queen require swearing in this tongue or . . . or . . ."

Wren's expression cleared. "Ah, I take your meaning. No, the queen does not believe in enforced loyalty. After all, a man's word should be an unbreakable bond, no matter what language he speaks. One's honor and reputation are more valuable than the greatest of riches, as I'm sure you agree."

"Yes, sir." Murtagh couldn't help but think of his own *reputation* among the common folk, and he suppressed a grimace.

The corner of Wren's mouth quirked in a partial smile. "Of course, the reality isn't always as pure or shining as the ideal, but we must trust in the goodness of our fellow men. And we must allow them to make what mistakes they will, without corralling them with magical enforcement."

What are you playing at? Murtagh wondered. It sounded as if Wren were criticizing, if only indirectly, the means and methods of Du Vrangr Gata. Or perhaps he was trying to assess Murtagh's own sympathies. Which reinforced his impression of the captain being a cautious, clever man.

"In that case, sir, I'll be happy to swear." He wouldn't be, and wasn't, but Murtagh couldn't see a way to avoid it.

"Excellent," said Wren, and started to shuffle through the sheets of parchment on the desk. "Pay is given on the twenty-first of every month. For that, you'll have to see Gert. Leave is subject to our duties, but normally you will have every fifth day to yourself, and harvest days and queen's celebrations are divided among the company. *Someone* has to stand watch, but you are guaranteed leave for at least half those days."

"Yes, sir."

Again, Murtagh found his gaze drawn to the masks on the wall, as if their empty eyes contained secrets worth learning.

There was something odd about the masks that he couldn't quite identify; looking at them was like looking at objects through a slightly warped mirror.

Wren noticed his interest. "Ah. You find my humble collection interesting, do you?"

"I've never seen anything quite like those masks before," Murtagh confessed.

The captain seemed pleased. "Indeed. They're not easily found in Alagaësia. It took me over ten years to acquire these few. The masks are made by the nomads who frequent the grasslands. Their artisans produce all sorts of arcane objects that are unknown to the rest of us."

"They seem quite lifelike, in a curious sort of way," said Murtagh.

Wren's eyes brightened. "Oh, it's more than that, Task. Look." He reached out and pulled a mask from the wall, the one carved in the likeness of a bear. Wren placed it over his face, and in that instant, his appearance shifted and warped, and he seemed to swell in size—shoulders widening, growing sloped and heavy and shaggy—and the mask moved with his face as if it were made of flesh and bone, and not wood, and an overpowering sense of *presence* made Murtagh fall back a step. It was as if the essence of *bear* had enveloped Wren, burying the man beneath a bestial cloak.

Then the captain pulled the mask away, and the impression vanished. Once again, he was just a man sitting at a desk, holding a wooden mask in his twisted hand.

"That . . . What *is* that, sir?" said Murtagh.

Wren chuckled and rehung the bear mask. "A powerful glamour, Task. I don't know why the tribes make them, but I can tell you they're not for hunting. Animals react quite badly if they see you wearing one of the masks. Dogs and horses especially. They go mad with fear."

"I see, sir."

Wren went back to searching the contents of his desk and,

after a moment, produced a sheet of parchment covered with lines of runes. "Ah, there we are." He rang a small brass bell and then dipped his quill in the inkpot. "Let's see. Task Ivorsson, was it?"

"Yes, sir."

The captain was already writing the name on the parchment. It was a form; Murtagh could read some of the upside-down words, but he pretended otherwise. A common foot soldier wouldn't be likely to know his letters.

The door to the study opened, and a young guard entered. At first glance, he reminded Murtagh of a friendly, overeager hound: jowly and red-cheeked, with a shock of straw-colored hair and a ready smile. "You wanted me, sir?"

"I do, Esvar. Task here is joining our merry band, and I need you to stand witness."

Esvar saluted and stood at attention next to Murtagh. "Sir, yes sir!"

Wren gave him a tolerant smile. Then he read from the parchment. It was a contract outlining Murtagh's responsibilities to the company and the company's responsibilities to him. He barely listened; he was familiar with the terms. What bothered him was the part to follow. . . .

"—and make your mark here," said Wren, handing him the quill and pointing to a blank spot near the bottom of the parchment.

Murtagh drew an X.

"Good. Now, Esvar."

Murtagh passed the quill to the young guardsman, who also made an X on the contract.

"Excellent," said Wren, and took back the quill and signed the parchment himself. Only he used runes; the captain had had a noble's upbringing and education, Murtagh guessed. Or that of a particularly well-off merchant.

Then Wren placed his knotted fist over his heart, and Murtagh followed suit. And the captain said, "Repeat after me. I, Task Ivorsson, do hereby swear—"

Murtagh's voice caught in his throat, and it was only with conscious effort—and not a small one—that he was able to obey: "I, Task Ivorsson, do hereby swear—"

"—my fealty to Queen Nasuada—"

"—my fealty to Queen Nasuada—"

"—and to Lord Relgin—"

"—and to Lord Relgin—"

"—and to the city guards of Gil'ead, as commanded by Captain Wren."

"—and to the city guards of Gil'ead, as commanded by Captain Wren."

"And I swear to uphold all laws and orders—"

"And I swear to uphold all laws and orders—"

"—such as I am subject to as a member of this force."

"—such as I am subject to as a member of this force."

The captain smiled, showing his strong, straight teeth, and extended his crooked hand. "Welcome to the company, Task. You're one of us now."

"Thank you, sir," Murtagh said, forcing the words past the constriction in his throat.

"Esvar will get you settled into the barracks, and then he'll see to it that you're properly kitted out." Wren gave the guardsman a mock-stern look. "Do see that he's kitted out, Esvar."

"Yes*sir!*"

"Oh, and, Task, do you know if you have any wards on you? Charms against magical attacks or a spear to the skull? That sort of thing."

"Not that I know of, sir, but then, how would I know?" Murtagh hoped the answer was vague enough to save him trouble later on.

Wren waved a hand. "No matter. We'll see to it that you're

charmed up tomorrow. I can't have my men walking around vulnerable to the slightest piece of magic."

Startled, Murtagh said, "You have a spellcaster in your ranks, sir?"

"Hardly," said Wren. "We coordinate with Du Vrangr Gata. Their magicians provide wards for everyone who follows the queen's standard."

"I see. Thank you, sir."

Wren waved a hand. "That will be all, Task. Dismissed."

CHAPTER IX

✦ ✦ ✦ ✦ ✦ ✦

Uniforms

"The captain's hands, have they always been—"

"You *don't* ask about the captain's hands," Esvar said firmly. "Not unless you want Gert to beat the tar out of your hide."

"That's good to know. Thanks."

Esvar gave a companionable nod and pointed toward the far barracks as they exited the stone tower. "Thatwise is where we're headed."

The yard had emptied during Murtagh's interview with Captain Wren, and the shadows had shrunk beneath the midday sun. Someone had removed the cart with Muckmaw's head.

Murtagh glanced at the deep blue sky. It had been only a few hours, but he already missed Thorn. They were too far apart to easily exchange thoughts, and he didn't want to risk shouting with his mind when there were those within Gil'ead who might notice. *I hope he's safe.* He could barely feel his connection with Thorn— just enough to know that Thorn was alive and not in pain.

Esvar gestured at the yard and the high fortress wall that backed the compound. "This all is ours. Captain Irven has command of the other half of the guard, at the grounds 'cross the fortress, but this here is Captain Wren's fiefdom."

"Do the captains get along?" Murtagh asked.

"Not hardly. But that's all right. Lord Relgin favors our captain, so you chose the right company, Task."

"I'm just glad to be one of you."

Esvar laughed. "Say now, you killed Muckmaw! No one in their right mind would turn you away."

Murtagh made as if he were embarrassed. "I got lucky, but thanks. So have you been part of the guard for long?"

Esvar beamed with pride. "Two months, an' I've loved every day of it, even the drilling. Even the standing watch, though it does get mighty miserable when it's raining."

"I'm sure."

"An' where do you hail from? Your tone's not from around here."

"Far to the south," said Murtagh as they entered the barracks. It was a long, half-domed room with rows of cots, each with a wooden chest at the foot. A number of men were on the cots, playing runes, napping, or oiling their boots. Shields hung on the walls, and a rack of pikes and spears stood by the door. At the back of the barracks, as Carabel had said, was a stone archway and, through it, a staircase that led down into darkness.

That's where I need to go. But finding an opportunity was going to be difficult. Either the barracks would have to be empty or he'd have to wait until the men were asleep.

A knot of anxiety twisted within Murtagh's gut. Would Silna even still be in the compound by the end of the day? He could always try to ambush any group that left the enclosed grounds, but he had no means of knowing all the ways in and out, and in any case, an open attack would make further subterfuge impossible.

He was tempted to reach out with his mind, to see if he could detect Silna's consciousness underneath them, but he resisted the urge. There were too many people around, any one of whom might notice the touch of his thoughts.

Esvar walked him through the room, introducing him to the men, who varied from friendly to standoffish to outright hostile. But they all wanted to hear the story of how he'd caught Muckmaw, and Murtagh found himself regaling them with the same account he'd given Captain Wren. The men seemed well enough impressed, but they followed up with plenty of comments about the state of his clothes, or else joked about him being fish food. He accepted the remarks with good grace, for he knew who he was. A certain amount of ribbing and gibing was normal for an outsider. Until he proved himself, the men wouldn't trust him.

Of course, he wasn't going to be there long enough to prove himself. For some reason, the thought caused him an obscure sense of regret.

Three-quarters of the way through the room, Esvar stopped by an empty cot. "You can bunk here for now. If'n Gert or the captain likes you, y' can request a change, but I wouldn't bother were I you. It doesn't serve to be too close to the front; someone or other is always getting up in th' night to visit the privy."

That could be a problem, Murtagh thought. He glanced around as he dropped his bedroll on the cot. "Where does that go?" he asked, pointing at the archway at the back.

"Down t' the catacombs," said Esvar.

"There are catacombs?" Murtagh said, feigning surprise.

Esvar bobbed his head. "Oh yes. We use 'em for all sorts. The captain an' the other officers meet down there every week, an' we use 'em for storing supplies an' such."

"I see."

A doleful expression formed on Esvar's face. "It's not so nice. Th' catacombs are dark an' full of spiders, an' the captain insists that we keep watch on th' storerooms. He says no fighting force is prepared 'less they know their weapons an' supplies are secured."

"The captain sounds like a wise man." Privately, Murtagh cursed Wren's cautious nature. It wasn't going to make it easy to find out what was behind the closed door.

"That he is!" said Esvar. "An' speaking of supplies, I ought t' get you your kit. Thisways!"

Murtagh hoped the younger man might take him down into the catacombs, but instead Esvar headed back out of the barracks and led him toward a small storehouse set against the fortress's outer wall.

Esvar was still talking; he never seemed to stop. "The catacombs were built ages ago. They say it were the elves that first quarried 'neath here, but I've never seen no elf digging in the ground or cutting stone. But Gil'ead has more 'an its share of history, yes it does. Right on th' other side of that wall is where Morzan an' his dragon were killed, near on twenty years ago." He gave Murtagh a wide-eyed look. "It were before my time, but my ma, she says the whole city shook, and there were fire and flames and lightning like a great storm."

Cold tingles ran up Murtagh's arms. *Right through there,* he thought, staring at the wall. That's where his father had died while trying to track down the dragon egg—Saphira's egg—that the Varden had stolen from Galbatorix.

Esvar seemed encouraged by Murtagh's expression. "It's true! A magician came to Gil'ead an' challenged Morzan to a duel. No one knows his name, only that he wore a hooded cape and carried a wizard's staff, like in th' stories."

"I wonder who it was." But Murtagh knew: Brom. The old man had lost his dragon during the fall of the Riders, but he had still been a clever spellcaster. *Not clever enough to ward off the Ra'zac's dagger, though.*

Esvar shrugged. "Probably one of the Varden. Or maybe a sorcerer from th' plains. Captain Wren says nomads know all sorts of magic."

The yellow-haired youth kept chattering as he ushered Murtagh into the storehouse and gathered equipment for him. It wasn't long before Murtagh found himself fitted into a new set of clothes, with a red tabard over his mail corselet and a warm woolen cloak clasped about his throat. He quite liked the uniform. It was neat and clean, and there was something appealing about the fact that folks would no longer see him as a person apart but as just another member of the guard. There was safety in numbers, after all, and he had never before felt joined to a larger group of like-minded people.

Yet he knew the truth was otherwise, and his disquiet remained.

Along with the clothes, Esvar presented him with a spear, an arming sword—complete with belt and sheath—and a deftly painted kite shield.

"You'll have t' talk with Gert about being issued a pike," said Esvar. "He won't let new recruits have one till he's gotten to train 'em." He made a face. "I'm still stuck with a spear myself."

As Esvar showed Murtagh around the rest of the compound—the privy, the stables, the mess hall, the smithy, and the small garden where they grew crabapples for cider—he continued to shower him with questions. Murtagh kept his answers short, but when it came out that he had participated in the battles of the Burning Plains and Ilirea, Esvar grew visibly excited, and his questions redoubled.

Murtagh fended them off as best he could while they went to the mess hall for the company's midday meal. The food was nothing special—half a loaf of dark-brown bread, a bowl of stew, and a mug of small beer—but Murtagh enjoyed what he now knew was the not-so-insignificant luxury of having someone cook for him. Still, it was a muted pleasure. He could not forget his purpose for being there: Silna. Frustration burned within him and dulled his appetite. He wanted nothing more than to act, but until the moment was right, all he could do was bite his cheek and wait.

So he ate and pretended at niceties.

Esvar sat on the other side of one of two long wooden tables that filled the mess hall, still talking. "Did y' see Eragon, then? And the dragon Saphira?"

"I saw them," said Murtagh.

"Were you close to them? Did you get to talk with them?"

He shook his head. "No. I only saw them at a distance."

"Ah," said Esvar, disappointed. "But still, you were awful lucky to see 'em! I'd love to have th' chance someday. Can you believe how brave they were t' face the king and Shruikan, and they killed 'em too!"

Not without my help. Murtagh bit back his annoyance and, in a mild tone, said, "I'm sure they were very brave."

Esvar didn't seem to notice. "Supposedly Eragon is only a year older'n me! How strange is that?! Can you imagine being a Dragon Rider? Can you imagine having a dragon! Why, I don't know what I'd do. Fly to the top of the sky and fight every bandit and traitor I could find."

Murtagh smiled into his mug and then tipped it toward Esvar. "You know, I believe you would."

Esvar leaned in toward him, face shining, cheeks reddened with excitement. "Did y' fight any Urgals at th' Burning Plains, or had they already joined with the Varden?"

"They'd already joined."

"That's too bad. I always wanted to fight an Urgal. But surely you saw some up closelike, yes?"

Sitting at the other table, Gert looked over from the food he was busy shoveling into his mouth with the practiced haste of a man who had been a soldier for most of his life. "Don't bother Task with so many questions. The man must be half dead from 'em."

A flush turned the tips of Esvar's ears bright red. "Yessir. Sorry, sir." And he bent over his own food.

Murtagh gave the weaponmaster a thankful nod, but Gert looked away without acknowledging it.

At the far end of the tables, several of the guards were talking amongst themselves. With Esvar quieted, Murtagh took the opportunity to eavesdrop.

"—as you will, but th' queen is still young," said one man.

"Ah. 'S never too early," said another. "Till she has an heir, the kingdom won't be settled. She'd best marry King Orrin, and—"

"*That* mewler?" broke in a third guard. "Lord Risthart o' Teirm would be a *far* better match. Or even our own Lord Relgin. At least *he*—"

"Old Relgin's wife might have something t' say 'bout that," said the first man, followed by a rather crude suggestion.

As the guards laughed, Murtagh stared into his bowl, his fist tight around the handle of the spoon. The thought of Nasuada marrying any of those men, much less some faceless stranger, filled him with an inexpressible rage.

How difficult her position is. The men were right. If Nasuada didn't produce an heir in the next few years, the crown would rest uneasy upon her head, and the continuity of her lineage and the peace the Varden had fought so hard for would be in jeopardy.

Murtagh didn't want to think about whom Nasuada might have to choose as her consort. The demands of statehood and diplomacy made no allowances for personal feelings. Nasuada would do what was best for her realm, and as for him . . . if he could work from the shadows and help keep Alagaësia stable, perhaps he could buy her some more time to consolidate her rule.

He forced himself to keep eating, even though his appetite had deserted him.

It wasn't long before Esvar started talking again. He didn't ask so many questions as earlier but instead went on about the guards, Captain Wren, and his own experience in the company (all two months of it), as well as his life in general. Murtagh was happy to listen; he'd spent so long with only Thorn for conversation, the sound of another human's voice was in itself rewarding. But he also found interesting the things that Esvar considered important.

Only a handful of years separated the two of them, and yet Murtagh felt as if he were decades older. Esvar's mind was full of dreams of daring, adventure, and honor. He nearly worshipped Captain Wren and others he considered to be shining examples of heroic accomplishment, including, of course, Eragon. And he was devoted to the guards with the fevered conviction of youth or the newly converted.

Over the course of his talking, it came out that Esvar's father had died in a storm, out on Isenstar Lake, when Esvar was only seven. At that, Murtagh felt a sympathetic pang; he understood Esvar's need to find guidance and a sense of purpose. It was an almost physical longing.

Esvar had an additional motivation for joining the guards, one Murtagh had never experienced: a need to provide. As he said, "An' this ways I can give coin to my ma, and she doesn't have to spend so much of th' day at the market. I'm able t' put bread an' meat on the table, and my sisters can get a new dress each year, both of 'em."

"That must make you proud," said Murtagh.

Esvar nodded, but his expression was serious. "It's an awful responsibility, though. If something were to happen to me while on duty . . ." He shook his head. "It doesn't bear thinking about."

"No," said Murtagh. None of them had any shield against the vagaries of fate. Not even Dragon Riders were safe from tragedy.

After they ate, Murtagh attempted to return to the barracks while the rest of the men were still in the mess hall, but Esvar forestalled him, saying, "What for? Y' have everything y' need, Task. 'Sides, Gert'll be wanting us on th' field."

Murtagh clenched a fist even as he forced a smile. "Of course. After you."

With Esvar, he joined the guards who weren't stationed on watch in drilling with spear and pike in the yard. It was an odd experience. Murtagh had always trained alone or with a single instructor, such as Tornac, and he had never fought as part of a massed formation, not even in Farthen Dûr. Moving in unison with the other men, shouting as they shouted, stamping his feet against the ground as they lunged and stabbed, advanced and retreated . . . there was a comfort to the experience. Murtagh found himself relaxing, feeling as if he could stop the run of his thoughts and simply exist.

For the first time, he realized how appealing it was to follow instead of lead. The guards could trust Gert and Captain Wren to think for them. All they had to do in turn was obey. Which, admittedly, was sometimes easier said than done. Even so, the effort of drilling or standing watch paled in comparison to the responsibilities of command.

As the sun descended, and their boots kicked up a haze of golden dust in the yard, Murtagh felt a sudden and strong regret that he couldn't stay. That he had to break his oath to Captain Wren and—yet again—prove himself a liar and betrayer.

Murtagh's enjoyment of the moment turned to bitter ashes, and his mood remained dark and dour throughout the rest of the drilling.

Afterward, as he and Esvar replaced their weapons on the racks along the yard, the yellow-haired guard said, "It wears y' down some, but it always feels good t' practice, don'tcha think?"

Murtagh grunted.

Esvar misunderstood. "Ah, don't let it get t' you. Few days of it, an' you won't even notice th' weight of a spear."

Once more, Murtagh attempted to return to the barracks, only for Gert to quickly remind him of the downside of belonging to the company: the lack of personal freedom. The weaponmaster set them to drawing water for the scullery, and then there were shirts of mail to oil and stables to muck and stocks and stores to organize.

Captain Wren, Murtagh soon came to understand, did not believe in letting his men stand idle when not on watch.

Murtagh's frustration grew. In the stables, he saw evidence for what Carabel had mentioned: a wagon readied for departure, saddles laid out, bridles being repaired. A blacksmith was seeing to the shoes of several horses, including Captain Wren's black charger, a great fearsome beast by the name of Beralt.

When Murtagh asked about the preparations, Esvar shrugged and said, "Couldn't say. Captain's business."

Murtagh took consolation in the fact that whatever was planned had yet to happen. Regardless, it hardened his opinion toward Wren and the guards. If Carabel was right, at least some of them were engaged in inexcusable villainy.

As they were shifting firewood for the captain's quarters, as well as the kitchens, Gert came by. "We had word from th' fortress," he said. "First thing tomorrow, Lord Relgin wants to see th' one what killed Muckmaw. Best make sure your boots are shined and your hair is combed, Task. Won't do to offend his Lordship."

"Yessir." An iron door seemed to slam shut inside Murtagh's mind. There was no choice now. He couldn't stay among the guards past the night. An appearance at Relgin's court would be the surest way of breaking his disguise.

Once the sun was down and the guards were asleep, he had to try to reach Silna. It would be his only chance. *Don't give up*, he thought. *I'm coming.*

~~~~~~~~~~~~~~~~~~ ❖ ~~~~~~~~~~~~~~~~~~

Evening had settled over Gil'ead, and the streets were mired in purple shadow. Warm candlelight started to appear behind shuttered windows, and lanterns and torches bobbed along the ways as late travelers and early carousers hurried to their destinations.

Murtagh trotted between the wooden buildings, nose wrinkled in distaste at the smoke that had settled across the city along with the late-afternoon chill. His duties with the guards were over for the day, but Wren's company closed and locked their gatehouse at sundown, so he had only a few minutes of freedom left.

Was that a familiar face among the knot of men and women standing by the door of a common house across the street? No . . .

no, he didn't think so. He ducked his head and hurried on, trusting that the tabard of the city watch was all anyone would see when they looked at him.

At the eastern edge of Gil'ead, he found a lone poplar tree by the edge of a barley field. After checking that no one else was in the vicinity, he sat and closed his eyes and focused on the thread of thought that joined him to Thorn.

As the window between their minds widened, the dragon's relief was a palpable sensation washing over Murtagh's body. For a time, they merely enjoyed their shared embrace, and then Murtagh said, *Are you safe? Has anyone found you?*

Only a wandering jackrabbit, who was much surprised.

I can imagine. Did you eat it?

Murtagh could feel Thorn snort. *To what end? I find larger pieces of meat stuck between my teeth. What of you? How goes it?*

He made no attempt to hide his aggravation. *They've kept me running ragged all day long. I haven't had more than five minutes to myself.*

Do they smell something wrong with you?

I don't think so. It's just how they operate. I'm going to try for the door once everyone's asleep. If all goes well, I can sneak Silna out without being noticed, and then I'll take her to Carabel, and we can be rid of this city.

Thorn noticed his grimness at once. *Why do you hate it so?*

Words were insufficient, so Murtagh shared the images and feelings dominating his mind—Esvar's comments about Eragon and Saphira; his own conflicted response to being so close to the death place of his father; the sense of unity he'd experienced moving together with the other men in the yard; his distaste at breaking another oath; and in general, the deep and growing discomfort Murtagh felt for the situation and his place within it.

This is why I prefer to avoid your kind, said Thorn. *They are too difficult, too complicated. Things are simpler when we stick to the sky.*

If only we could.

Then, too, Murtagh shared the men's comments about Nasuada and her need for an heir. And he made no attempt to hide his distress at the thought.

Thorn hummed in his mind, and in Murtagh's mind, he saw the dragon's tail wrapping around him, as if to protect and comfort him.

Perhaps you should seek her out, if you feel so strongly about whom she chooses as her mate, said Thorn.

It's not that simple.

It is as simple as you make it.

If I were a dragon, maybe.

Slight amusement colored Thorn's response: *You are as close to a dragon in human form as I have ever met.*

Coming from Thorn, that was no small compliment, and Murtagh knew it. *If only I could breathe fire like you.*

That's what magic is for. Then, changing the topic, Thorn said, *What do you make of Captain Wren's intentions?*

Murtagh opened his eyes and looked at the first few stars appearing in the orange and pink sky. *I don't know. Politics? Personal ambition? He seems intelligent and devoted to his men, but I have a feeling . . .*

The wood face masks.

Yes. Anyone who has masks like that has an interest in secrets, in hiding themselves, and in magic. It's a dangerous combination.

An image of the masks passed through Murtagh's mind as Thorn returned the memory to him for notice. *Which mask would you choose?*

A short laugh escaped him. *None. I wear too many already.*

Not with me.

No, not with you.

Then Thorn wished him luck, and they said their farewells,

and—with a strange feeling in his heart—Murtagh headed back to the barracks.

~~~~~~~~~~~~~~~~~~~~~ ❖ ~~~~~~~~~~~~~~~~~~~~~

As Murtagh sat on his cot and started to unlace his boots, Esvar came over and, in a somewhat subdued voice, said, "Look, ah, Task, I'm sorry if I were bothering you earlier."

"It's fine. Don't worry about it," said Murtagh. He pulled off his right boot.

"Well, that's kind of you to say. I just got excited t' have someone new in our ranks, 'specially one as fought with Eragon and Saphira."

"Again, it's fine." He pulled off his left boot.

Esvar shifted uncomfortably. "Well . . . I know 'tisn't easy settling in thisways. It's a big change joining the guard. Least, it were for me. But . . . anyways, I wanted you t' know you're welcome, an' I'll be glad t' stand watch with you any day, even if'n it *is* raining."

The words struck Murtagh to the bone. He stared at the boot in his hand for a moment, and then looked up at Esvar. "That's very kind of you, Esvar."

Esvar bobbed his head, embarrassed, and was about to leave when Murtagh said, "Are you standing watch tonight?"

"Me? No, no. I get t' sleep tonight."

Good. Murtagh watched Esvar walk back to his own cot. Then he shook his head, undid the clasp of his new cloak, and pulled off his red tabard.

As did the other men, Murtagh stored his clothes and belongings in the chest at the bottom of his cot. To his displeasure, the hinges of the chest made an annoying squeal loud enough to wake anyone who heard it.

It was night then, and Gert stood at the front of the barracks, looking them over with a half-shuttered lantern in his hand. He gave a satisfied grunt. "Right. Turn in. First call is two bells before dawn." Then he closed the lantern and left through the front door.

The interior of the barracks was profoundly dark, even after Murtagh's eyes adjusted to the absence of light. The only hint of illumination was a thin beam—pale and indistinct—that slipped through a crack in the shutters facing the stone tower of the officers.

Murtagh lay on his back with his eyes open, listening to the breathing of the other men. The black underside of the curved ceiling was deadly dull, but he was afraid to close his eyes, lest he nod off and lose his chance.

It probably wasn't much of a risk—the thought of sneaking into the catacombs filled his veins with too much fire for sleep to be a likely prospect—but it was best to be cautious. Any mistakes in the barracks could prove fatal. If not for him, then for the men around him, and Murtagh preferred to avoid fighting them.

As long as he did everything right, no one should know what he had done or where he had gone. He felt sorry about Esvar—the youth's optimism and enthusiasm were bright spots of positivity in the day, but some things couldn't be helped.

Time passed with creeping slowness. Murtagh tried counting the beats of his heart, but that only made the minutes seem even longer.

He was determined to wait until at least an hour past midnight before he chanced the catacombs. That would allow the guards plenty of time to fall asleep, and it might even be long enough for the man standing watch underground to nod off.

At least Murtagh hoped so.

He shifted on the cot, uncomfortable. He'd spent so long out of doors with Thorn, it felt strange to be lying on a bed again, even an unpadded cot. The canvas backing sagged beneath his weight, putting a curve in his spine that made his lower back ache. He tried shifting to his side, but that only put a painful crook in his neck.

He took a deep breath and let it out slowly. It was going to be a taxing few hours.

To distract himself, he set to composing another poem, this one not an Attenwrack, but a form of his own devising. In a silent voice, he said:

Sing of sorrows soft and sad.
Cry, O winged herald, of battles won and lost.
Who mourns for fallen men, in conflict slain?
What comfort tears when flocks of crows descend?

The words echoed in his mind as he lay in the dark. "Forgive me," he whispered. Whether the words were meant for the ghosts of his past or the men in the barracks, he wasn't sure, but when he closed his eyes, a field of drowned bones filled his vision.

CHAPTER X

✦ ✦ ✦ ✦ ✦ ✦ ✦

Softly Creeping . . .

Somewhere in the sleeping city, a black-faced owl hooted and then hooted again.

Murtagh levered himself into a sitting position on his cot. Throughout the barracks, the guards lay still and silent, their breathing slow, even, measured. One or two of them snored, but not loudly enough to wake the others.

Ever so carefully, Murtagh opened his mind and extended his consciousness to touch the thoughts of the other men. They were, as he hoped, all deeply asleep, lost in the confusion of their dreams.

He maintained a delicate contact with their collective minds as he edged down his cot and put a hand on the lid of the chest. "Maela," he whispered. *Quiet.*

Holding his breath, he lifted the lid.

It swung up and back with hardly a sound.

Relieved, he slowly pulled out his bedroll and all it contained, as well as the boots, cloak, and arming sword he'd been given.

But he left the kite shield. It would just slow him down and make stealth that much more difficult. Besides, he had his own shield, albeit with Thorn. And he left the tabard. It might have helped him to avoid unwanted attention, but he no longer felt comfortable wearing the uniform of the guard.

He wrapped the cloak around the belt of the sword so the buckle wouldn't jangle, and then slowly stood and padded on sock-covered feet toward the back of the room.

At the last cot in line—which was empty—he tripped.

He cursed silently as he regained his balance, his face frozen in a snarl.

Across the barracks, one of the guards stirred, and he sensed a twinge of awareness from the man's mind.

Murtagh remained hunched in a half crouch, afraid to move.

After several minutes, when the man seemed to again be deep in slumber, Murtagh straightened inch by inch and continued to the ink-black archway at the rear of the barracks.

He put a hand against the cold stone wall and felt his way down several steps. Then he sat and pulled on his boots, laced them tight, unwrapped the sword, buckled it around his waist, and secured the clasp of the cloak at his throat. The cloak was a gamble; it could easily get caught between his legs at an inopportune time, but it would also serve to muffle his movements. Lastly, he slung his bedroll across his shoulders. He wasn't planning on returning to the barracks—not to sleep, in any case—and there was a chance he'd have to leave in a hurry, and he didn't want to lose any more of his belongings. When you owned only a few things, they became all the more precious.

He stood and resumed feeling his way down the stairs. He wanted to cast a werelight, but it would be too risky, and besides . . .

. . . a dull orange glow appeared before him as he spiraled beneath the surface of the earth, gilding the face of the stone wall so that every pit and pock and chipped imperfection stood in high relief.

At the bottom of the stairs was another archway, this one easy enough to see in the flickering light.

Murtagh pressed himself against the outer curve of the staircase as he edged down to the archway and poked his head around the frame of mortared stone.

A long, dark tunnel stretched out to the left and right. Despite what Esvar had said, it didn't look like elf-work to Murtagh, but rather ordinary human craftsmanship. The passage to the right extended underneath the fortress, while the left-hand branch reached toward the city.

Too many tunnels, he thought. It would have been helpful to know of them when he'd been trying to rescue Eragon from the fortress. He'd had no idea that the city was sitting on a rabbit warren of underground passages.

It was the left-hand side of the tunnel that interested him the most. Several wooden doors, reinforced with bands of wrought iron, were set into the walls. Bolted to the walls between the doors were sconces that held tall candles, two of which were lit and which cast a field of dancing shadows across the stones.

A guard stood next to the middlemost door, leaning on his pike, head slumped forward, eyes half closed.

Murtagh took a moment to consider. From what Captain Wren had said, he knew the guards had wards on them. And he knew that some of the wards were intended to protect against magical attacks. But what exactly constituted an *attack* was open to interpretation.

Murtagh didn't want to harm the man. The guard was doing his duty without obvious malice. But he *did* have to get past him.

He frowned. If he cast a spell on the guard and it triggered any of his wards, the man was sure to know. The drain of energy would alert him, if nothing else. Which left only two options: either Murtagh could physically overpower the man or he could use the Name of Names to strip the man's defenses and *then* incapacitate him with magic.

He tightened his hand on the hilt of the arming sword. The Name of Names was the obvious choice, but he hated to keep using it. The Word was a powerful secret—one of *the* most powerful secrets—and every time he uttered it, he risked teaching it to some unknown listener, even if he paired it with a concealing spell, as he had done in the Fulsome Feast. And no matter how well constructed a piece of magic, there was always a chance it might not have the intended effect.

It was bad enough that he, Eragon, and Arya knew the Word.

Three was two too many to keep a secret, and every additional person who learned the Name was another chance for someone to cause untold harm.

If Murtagh had known more of the ancient language and its uses—if he'd been properly trained as a Rider and magician, as Eragon had been—he would have felt more confident of bypassing the guard's wards without the Name of Names. But as it was, he keenly felt the inadequacy of his instruction, and he resented it.

The arguments for and against using the Word flashed through Murtagh's mind, but he knew he had already made his decision. He *had* to avoid making noise, and since he wasn't going to kill the guard . . .

Keeping his voice as low as possible, he uttered the Name of Names, and with it, he said, "Slytha." *Sleep.*

Even as he spoke, he darted into the tunnel and ran toward the guard.

The man twitched and fell forward, arms and legs going limp, pike slipping from his slack fingers.

Murtagh caught the guard before his head slammed into the floor, but the pike clattered against the stones, and his helmet slipped off and bounced away, sending echoes chasing back and forth through the tunnel.

"Ah!" said Murtagh. He lowered the man to the floor and then fled down the tunnel, out of the range of the candlelight and into the shadows. There he waited, breathless, straining his ears to hear if anyone in the barracks was coming to investigate.

Long moments passed. A breath of wind tickled the back of his neck, and he watched a large brown spider crawl along the corner of the wall, a sac of white eggs webbed to its back. His lip curled.

He loosened his grip on the hilt of the arming sword. *They're still asleep.* He didn't feel safe, though. All it would take was one of the guards waking up to use the privy, and his absence could be discovered.

Moving quietly, he returned to the guard he'd put to sleep and placed a finger against the man's stubbled neck. His pulse was strong and steady, and his chest continued to move.

Satisfied that the man was fast asleep, Murtagh stepped over the pike on the ground and went to the middlemost door. It was the one the man had been standing watch by, so Murtagh guessed it was the door he wanted.

He pulled on the iron ring bolted to the wood. The door didn't move. *Of course.* He pushed instead. The door still didn't move.

Murtagh's eyes narrowed as he searched the wood planks for a keyhole. In the dim light, it took him a few seconds to find: a small round hole by one corner of the iron plate that backed the ring.

He raised a finger and touched the keyhole, prepared to use magic, but a thought stopped him.

He knelt by the sleeping guard and searched along his leather belt. The man smelled of smoke, mutton, cardus weed, and long hours spent drilling in the sun. Murtagh wrinkled his nose. He didn't understand why more folks didn't bathe on a regular basis. Cold water was no excuse to walk around stinking like a tannery.

Metal clinked as his fingers found something hard hanging off the guard's belt. He looked; as he'd hoped, a key.

He fit the key into the lock and turned it until he heard an unpleasantly loud *clunk*. With a final glance up and down the tunnel, he pushed open the door.

CHAPTER XI

✦ ✦ ✦ ✦ ✦ ✦ ✦

The Door of Stone

The chamber inside was totally dark. Even Murtagh's eyes—sharpened as they were by his bond with Thorn—could not pick out a single detail.

He returned to the tunnel and retrieved a candle. With his free hand, he grabbed the guard's ankle and dragged him through the doorway into—

—a war room of sorts. A long wooden table occupied the center of the chamber, and on it, a map of Alagaësia, similar to the one in Captain Wren's study. Backless chairs surrounded the table, and a rack of scrolls rose against a side wall. Several tall iron candelabra stood around the room, and there were soot stains on the low vaulted ceiling, which was covered with bricks.

Opposite the door he'd entered, there was another—smaller, darker, made of polished wood—that led deeper into the catacombs.

Murtagh left the guard by the table and went back out into the tunnel to fetch the fallen pike and helmet. With both in hand, he closed the door behind him, locked it, and then placed pike and helmet on the table.

He glanced around, curious. Part of him wanted to linger, to see what was written on the scrolls, to see if he could find out what sort of schemes Captain Wren was working on. But time was limited, and he had no intention of getting caught.

He checked on the guard one more time. Still asleep. The

spell Murtagh had cast was a powerful one. Barring outside interference, the man should sleep for half a day or more.

Murtagh lit several tapers in the candelabra before proceeding to the next door.

He raised his eyebrows. "Interesting."

Lines of runes had been carved into the gleaming wood, which looked old and worn, ancient even. He touched the scarred surface; it felt denser than oak, hard as metal. "Môgren," he muttered. The black-needled pinetrees that grew in the Beor Mountains, home of the dwarves. It was rare to find anything made of that wood in the western half of Alagaësia. He looked closer. The runes themselves were of an archaic design, and as he tried to read them, he realized that they were indeed runes such as the dwarves used, not humans.

He shook his head. He could read many types of writing, but Dwarvish wasn't one of them. *What were dwarves doing here, and so long ago?* he wondered. Or had the door been made elsewhere and then brought to Gil'ead at some later date?

Questions that he doubted he would ever have answers to. Perhaps the Eldunarí could have told him.

Unlike the first door, there was no keyhole cut into the Môgren, but there was an oddly shaped depression, as wide as his hand, in the center. Because of the shifting shadows of the candlelight, it took him a minute to realize what he was seeing: a reverse impression of the bear mask from Captain Wren's study. A lock, then. Possibly magic, but not necessarily.

"What *are* you up to?" he murmured.

Murtagh considered sneaking back into the barracks and over to Wren's study to retrieve the mask, but dismissed the idea as too risky.

No, what he needed was . . . He glanced around the room. Wood. He needed wood.

He went to the rack of scrolls and, after examining it, pulled out one of the shelves. He placed one end of the plank against the depression in the door and whispered, "Thrysta."

Instead of releasing the power in a single burst, he restricted it to a gentle—but inexorable—push. The plank crumpled inward as if being crushed by an invisible boulder, and the wood fit itself to the lines and contours of the mask impression.

A small, tight smile formed on Murtagh's face as he guided the spell. *Just a little more . . .*

The door broke with a loud *crack,* splitting up the middle.

"Son of an *Urgal,*" he said, teeth clenched. He ended the spell.

There was no helping it now; the guards would know someone had broken in. Literally.

Annoyed with himself, Murtagh started to pull the pieces of wood away. Once the opening was wide enough, he fetched a candle and stepped through.

Light blossomed overhead.

He winced and lifted a hand to shade his eyes. After a second, he could see.

The light came from a piece of white quartz embedded in the ceiling; it emitted a steady glow similar to that of the dwarves' flameless lanterns, which he had seen throughout their city-mountain Tronjheim.

The chamber was longer and narrower than the war room. The walls curved inward and were supported by thick white ribs. *Actual* ribs. The bones of a dragon.

A horrible suspicion formed in Murtagh that he was looking at the ribs of Morzan's dragon, buried beneath the city by whoever had made that space.

Anchored between the ribs were shelves. On those shelves, and on a stone-topped table in the center of the room, were dozens of flasks, alembics, beakers, burners, bottles, and casks, and several braziers. *Alchemy.* Or something like it.

Murtagh slowly walked through the room, stopping at times

to examine this or that. The place was a treasure house for any magician. He picked up one of several books and opened it to find himself looking at a list of words.

Words in the ancient language.

Words with definitions.

Excitement shot through him as he realized what he was holding. A *dictionary!* His lips moved as he sounded out several of the entries: "*Flauga, flautja, flautr* . . ." Of all the valuables in the chamber, a compendium of the ancient language was by far the most precious.

The book released a small puff of dust as he closed it. Hardly able to believe his good luck, Murtagh carefully placed it in the pouch on his belt and continued forward.

Two steps farther, he found a small ornate box full of faceted gems. He picked up a teardrop-shaped yellow diamond nearly as big as his thumbnail and, on a hunch, attempted to touch it with his mind. A torrent of coiled energy twisted and turned before his inner eye, constrained by the substance of the gem.

He withdrew his mind and smiled a crooked smile, bouncing the gem on his palm. After a moment's thought, he tucked the diamond into the hem of his cloak, where no one was likely to find it. Having extra equipment was always a good idea, whether it was a weapon, armor, or—in this case—energy to fuel his spells.

The more Murtagh looked, the more questions he had. The room seemed to be devoted to the study of all things magical. On a shelf was a line of bottled liquids labeled with such words as *Health, Strength, Fire,* and so forth. Potions, he guessed, enchanted to achieve certain effects.

Deep disquiet stirred within Murtagh. Was Wren the magician who used the room? Or was there another? Some unknown spellcaster who lurked in Gil'ead while engaged in arcane study? And what invidious need could they possibly have for werecat younglings?

He touched one of the ribs along the walls. The bone was cool and smooth against his hand, and he felt a pang imagining it was Thorn's. But he was not sure how much sorrow he felt for Morzan's dragon. The creature had chosen to serve Galbatorix as much as Morzan had himself; they were both culpable for their sins. *As are we all*, he thought.

He hurried through the rest of the room. Surely he couldn't be far from Silna now, though he feared what he might discover when he found her. If she was even there.

Yet another door met him at the far end, and it too differed from those that came before. The lancet structure was made of a single piece of yellowed dragon bone. Perhaps a shoulder blade or a section of enormous skull. An iron ring hung from the center of the door. Embedded above it was a decorative pattern of gems of all different colors: rubies and emeralds and rainbowed diamonds. Tourmaline, star sapphires, and banded chrysoberyl.

Wary, Murtagh touched one of the stones. As he suspected, it contained a notable amount of energy.

He lowered his hand. The door was trapped. That seemed obvious. And if he triggered the trap, there was a good chance it would alert the magician who had made the door. At least, that was how Murtagh would have done it.

Or was it? What if the magician were on the other side of Alagaësia? Alerting them might take a prohibitive amount of energy.

Murtagh scratched his chin, thinking. He could just trigger the trap and trust his wards to protect him, but . . . that was hardly the smartest path forward. The question was, what would it take to outthink the magician who had enchanted the door? If the spellcaster were clever enough, doing anything to meddle with the door or its surroundings would set off an alarm. Even the Name of Names was no guarantee that Murtagh could completely subvert someone else's spells, as his experience with Muckmaw had taught him.

Blast it. I can't waste time.

He paced back and forth, debating. What if he tunneled around the door? That would take a lot of energy; he'd be exhausted by the time he broke through into the room on the other side. And there was a good chance that the walls surrounding the next room were enchanted with some sort of warning spell as well. Again, it was what *he* would do.

Murtagh squatted and rested his head in his hands. To subvert a ward, you had to think in a sideways fashion. Which was hard—very hard—but in a way, that was the point. The difficulty of imagining a new approach was what protected the person or thing behind the ward.

He imagined inverting a sphere without breaking it. He imagined moving in a straight line down a right angle. Every impossible action that his mind could conceive, he thought of.

A small smile formed on his lips. *Perhaps* . . . Eragon had defeated Galbatorix not by trying to hurt him but by trying to help him understand the consequences of his own actions—an approach that neither the king nor his many enemies over the years had thought of. It was possible that a similar indirect approach might work on the door.

The jewels contained energy needed to power whatever enchantments were imbued into the bone door. And if that power were consumed, it would need to be replaced. So it *ought* to be possible to both place and remove energy from the gems without triggering an additional trap.

Again, it depended on how clever the mysterious magician had been.

Murtagh decided to chance it. What was the worst that could happen? A grim chuckle left him. Most people might say *death*, but dying was far from the most fearful fate. He and Thorn had already passed through the darkest valley; nothing the wards might do could approach the depths of pain, fear, and debasement they had already faced.

First he needed a place to funnel the energy; it was too much to hold within his body. He'd burn up if he tried. Normally he would store energy within Zar'roc's ruby pommel, but without the sword . . .

He retrieved the teardrop-shaped yellow diamond from his cloak. It seemed the stone was going to prove its usefulness sooner than expected.

Holding the diamond in his left hand, he pressed his right against the door. The facets of the jewels were sharp against his palm. He closed his eyes, took a breath, and slowly, cautiously, began to siphon energy out of the gems and into the yellow diamond.

For the first few seconds, the flow of energy was smooth and untroubled. But then he felt increasing resistance, and the diamond grew warm in his hand. The heat quickly increased to an unbearable level. His skin began to burn.

In an instant, he realized the stone was about to explode.

He dropped the diamond and gasped, "Brisingr!"

A bright blue werelight sprang into existence to his right: a burning ball of flame hanging at eye level, the rippling flames causing the air to shimmer and waver like crystal water.

He diverted the energy into the werelight, which grew brighter and brighter, until it was painful to look at, and waves of heat washed off the fist-sized knot of flames. Murtagh ducked his head and leaned away, but he kept his hand on the gems, and he kept drawing on them.

He slowed the flow of energy when the heat became unbearable. Beyond that, his own wards would have been triggered.

Minutes passed while the miniature sun blazed beside him, a pocket furnace suspended by invisible forces, fueled by the potential stored within the jewels.

At last, he felt the flow subsiding, and the werelight dimmed and cooled. He drained every last iota of energy from the gems, emptied them of their dregs, and left them as brittle chalices ready to again be topped to the brim.

Then he ended his spell, and wings of shadows wrapped around him as the werelight vanished.

He wiped the sweat from his brow. His heart was pounding painfully fast, and he felt shaky. The spell, he knew, had nearly killed him. If the diamond had exploded, he doubted that his wards would have been strong enough to protect him.

He picked up the gem. It was still uncomfortably warm. Murtagh had never had difficulty storing energy in a gem before. Though now that he thought about it, he'd only really used the ruby in Zar'roc's pommel, and that was a far larger stone, of finer quality too, and woven through with elven enchantments. The diamond had none of those advantages. It must have already been filled to its limit. That or there had been significantly more energy stored in the door than he'd realized.

He carefully tucked the diamond back into the hem of his cloak. It was a matter that bore more attention, when he had the time.

He squared his shoulders. Now for the most dangerous part . . .

He pushed on the door.

It didn't move.

He pulled, and still . . . it remained obstinately closed.

Angered, Murtagh said, "*Ládrin.*" *Open*, and he put the full force of his will behind the arcane word.

With an alarming *creak*, the door swung inward on hidden hinges. Murtagh waited a moment to see if he'd triggered a trap, but nothing happened, so he again took up his candle and stepped across the threshold.

Another light sprang to life from a piece of quartz set into the ceiling of the third room. By the calm, unwavering light, Murtagh saw an underground garden. Raised beds of dirt, edged with brick, lay to the right and left of a narrow path, and in those beds grew trees, flowers, vines, bushes, and all manner of small, woody herbs. The air was warm and aromatic with a heady perfume, and it was moist too, as if a bank of mist had settled across the ground. The low hum of bees sounded amid the leaves.

Some of the plants Murtagh recognized: healing plants, poisonous plants, plants for inducing visions and compelling sleep. But many were unknown to him. There was a lily whose leaf and stem seemed made of living gold and whose petals were of a whitish metal. A drooping tree with berries that glittered like beryls. Mushrooms that had purple caps and electric-blue gills.

And he saw a plant unlike any he had encountered before. It had a single stem topped with a fleshy, pitcher-shaped cup perhaps two hands high. And from the cup stood small orange tentacles, which waved gently in the air.

Even as he watched, a frog hopped past the pitcher plant. Two of the tentacles reached out, fast as snakes, grabbed the frog, and pulled it into the mouth of the cup and held it there.

The frog uttered the smallest, most pitiful screech Murtagh had ever heard. Then it made no more sounds.

His face tightened, and he gripped the hilt of the arming sword, half-minded to chop the tentacled plant in twain.

After a moment, he thought better of it. But he kept his hand on the sword as he continued down the path. *What witchery is this?*

He was so focused on the odd sights that he forgot to watch where he was walking, and he caught an ankle on the corner of a brick that stuck out. He stumbled forward a step. As he recovered, he saw a crystal case sitting between two bushes, nearly hidden by the leafy branches. And resting in the case, a blue-black oval that was half a foot wide and half a foot tall. An egg. An evil-looking egg.

He stared at it, unsettled. *What sort of creature hatches from such a thing?* Not a dragon, that seemed sure, nor any other being he was familiar with. For the first time in his travels, he wished that Eragon or Arya were there with him. Whatever the purpose of the rooms underneath Gil'ead, they had been built and furnished with serious intent, and he had a creeping feeling that whoever it was that used them was dangerous in the extreme.

His gaze turned to the door at the back of the garden—the last door that needed opening, or so he hoped.

With quiet steps, he moved toward it.

The door was made not of wood, not of bone, but of grey granite, as hard and unyielding as an oath of revenge. The surface had a dry, textured appearance, and there were veins of tarnished copper running throughout. A handle also made of granite was mounted upon the left side.

Murtagh stood before the door, wary. He probed with his mind and felt . . . nothing. No gems, no stored energy, no hidden consciousness watching him, just cold dead stone, heavy with the weight of ages.

He pushed his thoughts past the door, into the chamber beyond. Even there, he found nothing but blank emptiness.

Worry and anger hardened his mind. Had Carabel been telling him the truth about Silna? Suddenly he had doubts. *What if all this was a ploy to deceive me into coming here?* But for what reason? To gather information on Carabel's behalf? To confront the spellcaster using the chambers? Was Carabel working at Relgin's behest?

Murtagh wasn't willing to give up on the idea of Silna, though. He had to know for sure whether she was imprisoned beneath the barracks.

He grasped the handle.

The garden remained as before, bees humming in the background.

He pulled.

The door swung open in perfect silence.

The room past the garden was a bare stone cell. The walls were roughly quarried granite, devoid of windows, with a single iron bracket hung next to the door. On the bracket sat a stub of a candle.

A small sky-blue blanket lay crumpled on the floor. And that was all.

The sight made Murtagh's heart ache. For a moment, it felt as if he were back in Urû'baen, in the dungeons beneath the citadel—he and Thorn both—listening to the screams of other prisoners while the overpowering weight of the king's mind bore down upon him. The walls seemed to close in on him, and he had a sudden feeling of being deep underground, alone and isolated, trapped in the airless dark.

He picked up the blanket. It was barely bigger than a kerchief and smelled of . . . smelled of fear. Silna, or some other child, had been held captive there. That much seemed certain.

Tears welled in his eyes, but they did not fall.

He blinked and took a closer look at the back wall. Was there something on the . . . *Yes.* A faint line of white chalk. He traced it with his eyes and found that the line drew an arch from floor to head height.

An arch or a doorway. The *idea* of a doorway. A yearning for freedom.

He touched the back wall. It was hard, with no hint of movement, and when he tapped on the stone, it sounded solid.

His breath caught in his throat, and an oppressive grief collapsed upon him. Then a terrible rage began to build atop the grief, and his hands closed in fists, and he set his teeth and ground his jaw.

They would pay. They would all pay for what they had done to the werecat youngling, and he would teach them to fear him as they had feared his father.

"Curse you," he muttered, and spun around to leave.

A blur of brindled fur sprang toward him from the back corner of the cell. Weight struck him against the neck and shoulders, and hisses and yowls echoed in his ears as a flurry of white claws tore at his throat.

CHAPTER XII

✦ ✦ ✦ ✦ ✦ ✦ ✦

Pathways into Darkness

Murtagh's wards protected him from the creature's attack, but the impact caused him to stumble backward into the edge of the door. He dropped to one knee.

Despite his wards, instinct led him to keep his eyes screwed shut. He felt upward until his hands closed upon warm fur, and then he pulled the kicking, clawing, spitting creature off his neck.

Only then did he get a good look at it.

Silna!

The youngling was a mosaic-coated cat with large green eyes narrowed in anger, tufted ears pressed flat, tail puffed out, and heavy paws that scraped at the air. The werecat was close in size to a housecat, and her head had the distinctive, overly large appearance of a kitten's.

"Shh, shh," Murtagh tried to say in a calming manner, but the werecat kept twisting and biting in a desperate attempt to break free.

Finally, he said, "Silna! Eka fricai. Eka fricai." *I am a friend.*

The werecat's clawing ceased, and she stared at him with a flat, hostile gaze.

He hesitated and then carefully placed her on the floor and let go.

The ridge of fur along Silna's spine remained raised. But she didn't run. She seemed, Murtagh was relieved to see, unharmed, though she looked painfully thin.

He held out his hands, palms raised. "Can you understand me? Carabel sent me to find you."

Silna's lips retracted to bare her sharp white teeth.

"I'm a friend," Murtagh insisted. He reached out with his thoughts toward the werecat's mind. The instant he touched her consciousness, she hissed, and he felt nothing but fear on her part.

He recoiled from her mind. "I'm sorry. Sorry. Do you understand?"

The werecat's slitted eyes darted between him and the open door, and he realized he was still blocking the way. He didn't move. "I can help you out of here, but you have to trust me." He held out one hand toward her, same as he would with a skittish horse.

Silna let out a small hiss, but she didn't retreat.

It's a start. "Can you change forms?" he asked. "Then we could talk. If you can talk . . ." Murtagh wondered at what age werecats gained the ability to shift their shape. Were they born with it?

He edged to one side of the doorway, opening a space for Silna to pass through. "Come on," he said in a coaxing tone. "Come with me."

The werecat's eyes narrowed again, and then she darted forward and past him before he could react.

"Blast it!" Murtagh scrambled to his feet as Silna streaked toward the far end of the arcane garden.

Just before she reached the doorway to the alchemy workshop, a voice sounded ahead of them. Esvar's voice: "—an' I swore I heard somethin', so I came t' get you directly. Look!"

Silna slid to a stop and darted back the way she'd come.

Within the workshop, Murtagh saw Esvar, three other guards, and the nearly white-haired magician of Du Vrangr Gata. Esvar gaped at Silna. Whether from surprise that she had escaped or at seeing a werecat, Murtagh didn't know.

Nor did he wait to find out.

He opened his mouth to speak the Word and break any spells protecting the men or directed at him or Silna. But before he could utter a sound, the men spotted him, and a blade of thought stabbed into his mind—the magician attacking the very essence of his self.

Stay! Murtagh flung the word toward Silna's consciousness, and then turtled in on himself, armoring his mind with blinkered focus: "You shall not have me. You shall not have me." He dared not let the magician see his thoughts, and because of that, he dared not loosen his defenses enough to speak the Word and work magic of his own. Not until he gained control of his enemy's mind.

The werecat kitten cowered behind his back foot and hissed.

The three guards in the front charged: one in front, two behind.

Murtagh swept his cloak across their field of vision, causing them to flinch, and used the momentary cover to draw his arming sword.

The distraction allowed him to strike first. He jabbed the lead man in his right hip and—

—the tip of the blade skated off an invisible barrier a finger's width from the guard's skin.

Blast it!

The guard slashed at Murtagh with his own weapon, causing Murtagh to duck. Swordplay alone wasn't going to win the day. He had to figure out a way around the guard's wards.

His misadventure with Muckmaw leaped to mind.

Fine. Bracing himself, Murtagh slammed his shoulder into the guard's chest and knocked him across the room. The guard's wards kept him from suffering scratches or worse as he crashed into a pair of bushes, but they did nothing to keep his head from whipping to the side and striking the crystal case that contained the blue-black egg, dazing the poor man.

Cracks spiderwebbed the case.

The next soldier shouted and stabbed a spear toward Murtagh's face. He let his own wards deflect the blow as he darted forward and, still holding the sword, clapped his hands against the sides of the guard's helmet. The man cried out, dropped his spear, and collapsed.

As Murtagh had suspected. No wards against sound.

The third guard poked at Murtagh with a billed pike. He dodged and smashed the pommel of his sword against the crest of the man's helm. The blow staggered the guard, and Murtagh followed up with another clap on either side of the man's head, which sent him reeling into a bed of lilies.

The whole while, Murtagh could feel the magician trying to dig into his mind. The man's neck was corded with strain, his lips pressed white against his bared teeth, and his hands worked feverishly within the sleeves of his robe.

Murtagh started for him, but Esvar stepped in front of the magician and raised his sword.

"Move aside," said Murtagh between clenched teeth.

Esvar held his ground. His face was red with anger, but he also had a look of hurt innocence that Murtagh could hardly bear to see. "You *swore*," said Esvar. "You *swore*. I was there. An' you betrayed us!"

"I don't want to hurt you," said Murtagh. "Stand down." A bumblebee flew past his face. Its body was iridescent blue.

Esvar shook his head, his expression one of fixed determination, and took a half step forward. "Never! You attacked th' guard. I'll die afore I let you pass. *Traitor*."

Murtagh had been called worse. He spared a glance for the men lying groaning on the floor; they wouldn't be a problem. Silna still crouched low to the ground behind him, safe for the moment.

"Kill him," said the magician, his voice tight with strain.

"You're no match for me," said Murtagh. He sounded calmer than he felt.

Esvar's upper lip curled. "Don't matter. It's my *duty*." And he lunged, extending his arm in a long stab aimed at Murtagh's throat.

Murtagh parried, closed the distance between them, and smashed the pommel of his sword against Esvar's helmet. The younger man dropped to one knee, and Murtagh was about to step past when Esvar drove his shoulders into Murtagh's knees.

His knees locked out and lightning shocks of pain radiated from the joints. Murtagh stumbled back and watched with some amazement as Esvar got to his feet and shook his head. A thread of blood trickled from his left ear.

"My ma always said I had a thick head," said Esvar, grim. He lifted his sword again. "Y' can batter me deaf, Task, but you'll have t' kill me afore you get by."

Murtagh's frustration boiled over into anger, and he launched several quick jabs at Esvar's shoulders and hips, hoping that if one of them went through, the wound wouldn't prove fatal or crippling. But none of them did. Esvar's wards continued to protect him. The impact of blade against spell sent sparks flying from Murtagh's sword, and he saw the tip was bent and broken.

He wished Zar'roc was in his hand. Even if the enchanted blade couldn't cut through Esvar's wards, the brightsteel wouldn't break.

Esvar fell back before the blows. He rallied and replied with another strike, attempting to cut Murtagh across the neck and waist.

"Why. Won't. You. Give. Up!" shouted Murtagh, his fury swelling like a storm. He rained down a series of heavy cuts onto Esvar, breaking his guard and driving the young man to his knees. There was no finesse to Murtagh's attack, no art, no grace or intelligence as Tornac had taught him, just sheer brute strength. And yet Esvar's wards continued to hold. Murtagh's sword glanced off his clothes and skin as if deflected by oiled ice.

Murtagh could see that the spells were tiring Esvar, but no faster than the blows tired Murtagh.

Esvar lashed out with a blind swing toward Murtagh's legs. Murtagh let the blow bounce off his thigh and hammered at the guard's shoulder with every fiber of his being, as if he were trying to split the earth itself.

Ting!

His sword shattered, and half of it flew spinning across the room to embed itself in a length of dragon bone.

Murtagh stabbed with the needle-tipped shard that remained attached to the crossguard and—

—the jagged piece of metal sank into Esvar's upper chest, between his neck and shoulder, near his collarbone.

The guard's eyes went wide, and he fell onto his backside, stunned. He put a hand to his chest, and his mouth worked several times, but no sound came out.

In an instant, Murtagh's rage shifted to regret, sorrow, and loathing for what he had done. The distraction was enough for the magician to delve deeper into his mind, gripping and tearing in an attempt to control Murtagh's thoughts.

"Oh no you *don't!*" he growled, finally giving the spellcaster his undivided attention. He attacked the consciousness of the robed man, holding nothing back, only seeking to overwhelm, crush, and suppress.

The spellcaster's mental defenses crumbled before the onslaught, and Murtagh received a brief flash of imagery from the man—his name was Arven, and he was deeply frightened about, about . . . —and then the magician's eyes rolled back and he keeled over.

Murtagh caught him and lowered him to the floor. He'd never had someone faint on him during a mental battle before.

"Why?" asked Esvar in a guileless voice. Tears gleamed in his eyes. "Why would you? I thought . . . I thought you wanted t' be part of the watch. Why, why, why?"

"I wish I could," said Murtagh. He gestured at Silna's crouched form. "But some things are more important than oaths."

Confusion filled Esvar's eyes. "What does a *cat* have t' do with it? I don't understand."

"I'm glad you don't," said Murtagh. He hesitated and then grasped the hilt of the sword sticking out of Esvar. The young man stiffened and held up a hand as if to stop him. "Bite your sleeve. This is going to hurt."

After a second, Esvar obeyed.

Murtagh gathered his will and said, "Waíse heill," as he drew the blade out of Esvar's chest.

The youth arched his back, and cords of muscle stood out on his neck as his clawed hands scrabbled at the floor. Blood welled out around the broken blade as it slid free, and then muscle and skin knit back together, leaving behind unblemished flesh.

Esvar fell back on the floor, limp, and Murtagh sagged with sudden exhaustion. "Why?" whispered Esvar. "Y' swore an oath, Task."

Murtagh clenched and unclenched his hands. "I'm sorry. The watch isn't all you think it is."

As he turned to leave, he spotted something around Arven's neck. On a sudden hunch, Murtagh bent, dug his finger under the magician's collar, and pulled free . . .

A bird-skull amulet, identical to the one Sarros had been wearing in Ceunon.

Murtagh stared for a second and then covered the amulet with his hand and yanked it off Arven's neck. He tucked the amulet into the pouch on his belt—next to the one from Ceunon—as he stood. Looking back at Silna, he said, "Come."

The werecat trotted after him as he strode out of the garden and through the rooms beyond.

~~~~~~~~~~~~~~~~ ❖ ~~~~~~~~~~~~~~~~

As Murtagh stepped into the catacomb tunnel, he heard voices and clattering armor echoing down the staircase that led to the barracks.

What took them so long? he wondered.

To his left, the tunnel ran under the fortress. That way lay more enemies and uncertain escape.

To his right, the passageway would take him out under the main part of Gil'ead. It was his best chance of slipping away without another fight.

Silna attempted to run past him, but he caught her around the belly. "Ah, ah. I don't think so," he murmured, and scooped her off the floor.

She tried to wriggle free, but he pressed her close against his side as he turned right and sprinted into the unknown. To his relief, she didn't bite or claw.

The sound of his pounding footsteps outpaced them in the darkness.

The tunnel curved. Once the staircase was out of sight, Murtagh whispered, "Brisingr," and formed a small red flame above his head so he could see his way.

Silna growled at the light, and her pupils contracted wire thin. "Quiet."

A few hundred feet later, he arrived at an iron grate blocking the tunnel. He grabbed the bars and yanked on them. Flakes of rust showered him, but the metal held.

"Jierda!" The metal snapped like rotten wood, and Murtagh shoved the grate against one wall and hurried past.

His boots splashed in water. A thin rivulet ran down the center of the tunnel, and the walls dripped with moisture. A rat the size of a small dog squeaked when it saw him and the werecat and scurried into a hole in the stone wall.

Behind him, Murtagh heard shouts and curses and spears beating against shields. He quickened his pace as much as he could without losing his footing on the wet rocks.

Silna squirmed in his arm, and he tightened his hold.

The tunnel split in four directions. Uncertain, he took the leftmost branch. Not much farther, it split again, and then yet again, and Murtagh realized he didn't have the slightest idea which direction he was going. He didn't despair, though. Tornac had taught him a trick for besting the hedge maze at Lord Varis's estate, which was to turn in only one direction—left or right, it didn't matter, as long as you were consistent. Solving a maze in such fashion might take a while, but if there was a path to the other side, doing so would always find it.

So Murtagh turned left at every opportunity. Twice more he had to cut through iron grates, but unlike before, he took the time—a few precious seconds—to reattach the grates, both to inconvenience his pursuers and to hide his trail. He just hoped that the catacombs had more than one exit and that he wouldn't come out to find half the city's garrison waiting for him.

Even with the werelight, the darkness was oppressive, and the walls seemed uncomfortably close. Murtagh felt as if he were no more than an insect creeping through the bowels of the earth. He hated the dark and the damp and the memories of being imprisoned beneath Urû'baen.

He tried to avoid remembering, but thoughts of Esvar and the cell hidden behind the door of stone were no less unpleasant. *Oathbreaker, that's what I am.* And he knew it was so, for *oathbreaker* was part of his true name.

The werecat continued to struggle and complain, so at last he said, "Fine. You want to go down? Here." And he plopped her on the wet stones.

Silna hissed, fur still fluffed out, and she crouched and looked up and down the dark tunnel, uncertain.

Murtagh studied her. Cats weren't as trusting as dogs, and werecats were even more of an enigma than ordinary cats, but he was beginning to wonder what more he would have to do to prove himself to her. "It's all right," he said in a soft voice. When that failed to evince a response, he motioned in either direction. "What's it to be? Hmm? I don't know about you, but I'd like to escape here with my hide intact. Come with me, and I'll do my best to keep you safe."

The tip of Silna's tail twitched.

Murtagh took a step down the tunnel. He looked back.

The werecat didn't move.

He took another few steps. Still, Silna refused to budge. In the gloom, her patched coat nearly vanished, just one more shadow amid the larger darkness.

He kept walking, and as the glow from his werelight faded from Silna's position, he heard the faint pad of paws following him.

When he turned to look, Silna immediately sat and started licking a paw, as if nothing had happened.

He snorted and resumed walking. He felt sure she would stay close, but for safety's sake, he opened his mind and let out a tiny feeler, just enough to sense her presence.

In like fashion, they continued.

The two of them wandered for what seemed like hours. They should have long since left Gil'ead behind, but the tunnels were a tangled nest of intersecting and overlapping openings. *Who dug these?* Murtagh wondered. In places the tunnels almost resembled natural formations; he even bumped his head against a stalactite in one dark corner. The warren made no sense. It reminded him of the lines dug by beetles under the bark of trees.

Still, they pressed onward, and Murtagh did his best to avoid any passage that led deeper into the earth, even if it meant bypassing another left-hand turn. If they ended up on a lower level, he doubted they would ever find the way out, barring a spell to burrow back to the surface.

At times he thought he heard voices behind him, ahead of him, to the sides, but they were always phantoms. The speakers never materialized, and he began to wonder if he were imagining things.

Throughout, he didn't dare try to contact Thorn. If Arven or any other magician from Du Vrangr Gata—or even an elf—were looking for him, they would be sure to notice his mind reaching out.

So Murtagh confined his thoughts to himself, and he and Silna trotted along in silence.

Finally!

A faint silver glow brightened the tunnel ahead of them, and Murtagh heard the steady burble of running water. "Stay close," he whispered to Silna. Then he snuffed his werelight, drew his cloak around his waist so it wouldn't tangle his legs, and crept forward.

The passage narrowed until he was half hunched over, and the light strengthened until . . .

He saw an end to the tunnel. An end covered by an iron grate, which overlooked a small stream with low, muddy banks. Arching over grate and stream was a wooden bridge. Numerous footsteps echoed off the bridge.

Relieved, Murtagh sank against the curved stone wall. From the stars in the sky and the moonlight on the water, he could tell that he and Silna had been in the tunnels for most of the night. It felt far longer.

They were still in Gil'ead; buildings were visible on either side of the bridge, and men of the guard marched along the banks of the stream, shouting directions to each other. It sounded like every soldier in the city had been roused, which was to be expected.

Silna crept up beside him. Her ears stood tall, and they swiveled to track the passing footsteps.

"Wait," he whispered.

She flicked an ear and then, after a moment, settled onto her belly and tucked her tail around herself. It was the nearest she had come to him since he'd stopped carrying her. He could smell the musky scent of her wet fur, and the hairs along her tail tickled the back of his left hand.

Satisfied that she wasn't about to run off on him, Murtagh risked sending an exploratory thought toward where he believed Thorn was hiding.

He found the dragon almost immediately, and he was far closer than Murtagh expected: only half a mile or so outside the city walls, amid a patch of wild roses.

A turbulent wave of joy, relief, and anger washed over him from Thorn. *There you are!* growled the dragon.

Here I am.

I thought I would have to tear Gil'ead apart stone by stone to find you.

It almost came to that, said Murtagh.

How went it? Did you rescue the—

Yes. But it isn't safe to talk like this. What about you? Are you in any danger?

There are soldiers searching the fields, but none of them have sighted or scented me.

Despite his words, Murtagh felt Thorn nestle deeper into the rosebushes and the pain as spines tore at his delicate wings.

All right. Stay where you are, and I'll come to you once I can.

A deep hum came from Thorn's mind. *Be careful.*

Always.

They separated their thoughts, and then Murtagh wrapped his cloak around his arms and settled into a more comfortable position. Somehow he had to get Silna to Carabel. There were too many guards on the bridge and in the streets to risk going out, but if he waited too long, the sun would be up, and he'd lose his chance, and he *didn't* want to wait for another nightfall. Eventually, someone in the guard might think to check the grate where they were hiding.

He looked at Silna. The kitten blinked and stared back at him. "Why did they want you?" he asked. "What did they do to you?"

The werecat's fur bristled, and she looked away.

Murtagh didn't know why he'd expected anything else.

He closed his eyes for a second and then thought better of it. No sleep for him until Silna was safely with her own kind and he was long gone from Gil'ead. Besides, he didn't think he could relax enough to sleep.

In his mind, he could still hear Esvar asking, *"Why, why, why?"* Murtagh ground the heel of his hand against his temple, trying to press the voice from his head. He couldn't. And he worried that he wouldn't be able to for days to come.

To distract himself, he pulled out the compendium he'd appropriated—*What an elegant word for "stole"*—set the tiniest red werelight burning above the pages, and started to memorize the ancient language words. Already he'd found dozens that he could envision being useful. The realization filled him with fierce determination. The compendium alone was worth all the misadventures he'd endured over the past two days. With it, he could begin to bridge the gaps in his arcane education, a prospect that he welcomed most devoutly.

Silna sniffed the corner of the book. Her nose wrinkled.

The dull ache returned to Murtagh's left forearm as he read, and because of it, he was slow to notice a tickle on the back of his wrist and hand. At last, it became strong enough that he looked down.

A large black spider had crawled onto him. He forced himself not to react, though it took the full strength of his will. If he could not control himself, then he was prisoner to circumstance, and he refused to accept such helplessness.

Nevertheless, his gorge rose, and revulsion made him want to fling the spider away.

With tiny steps, it crossed his hand and passed onto the pages of the book. The creature's hooked feet made a faint scrabbling sound against the paper.

He tipped the book against the wall and let the spider run onto the stone. It stopped a few inches away, a huddled fist of legs. Silna eyed it, seemingly without interest.

For a moment, Murtagh again felt the weight of dozens of

fat-bodied spiders moving across his skin. Their bites had burned like fire and, when left unattended, festered into greenish sores that took weeks to heal. The creatures had bedeviled him every night in that cold underground, making it impossible to sleep, and he had been unable to do more than shake himself in a futile attempt to throw them off. . . .

He reached out and put his thumb down on the spider and pressed it flat. Yellow ichor spilled from its abdomen as it split like an overripe grape.

The werecat's ears angled backward. She stretched out her neck and nosed the dead spider.

Murtagh returned to reading.

He listened to the city as he scanned the columns of runes. When the streets quieted for a time, and he heard no sounds but the babble of water and the flutter of nightjars chasing their morning meals, he extinguished the werelight and put away the book.

"Be ready," he whispered to Silna, and edged forward.

The metal bars of the grating were no different from those he'd encountered before. "Kverst," he said in a quiet voice, and drew a finger across the cold and pitted metal.

The bars parted with bell-like *tings*, and he lifted the grate out of its setting and placed it to one side. He listened for bystanders and passersby again—he didn't dare use his mind to probe the area—and then pulled himself out of the tunnel and dropped several feet to the muddy bank below. He turned back and reached up for Silna.

The cat stared down at him without expression.

"Come on," he whispered, and wiggled his fingers.

At last, the werecat kitten walked to the lip of the tunnel and allowed him to pick her up and place her on the ground next to him.

"Worse than a dragon," he muttered. He wedged the grating back into position and then said, "Thrysta," using the spell to force the metal into place. It would take a hammer and chisel to break it free again.

Murtagh bundled the red cloak of the watch around one arm as he led Silna out from under the bridge. He glanced up and down the banks of the stream and—seeing them clear—scrambled up into the street.

He turned to make sure Silna was following.

The instant the werecat cleared the top of the bank, she took off between the buildings, sprinting faster than any human, her stiff tail tracing circles behind her.

Murtagh swore and started after her, but Silna had already vanished into the city, and he could see people staring at him from across the way. He risked opening his mind, but it was as if the werecat had ceased to exist. All he could feel were humans and dogs and the self-satisfied thoughts of a notch-eared tomcat sitting atop a plank fence.

He swore and then swore again.

There was no helping it. Silna was gone, and he had no confidence he could find her again, even if he searched for days. All he could do was hope the guards didn't spot her and that she was able to return to her own kind.

He swore once more. He had rescued Silna. But would Carabel still give him the answers he sought if he couldn't deliver the youngling to her? He chewed on the question for a time. It left a bad taste on his tongue.

If the werecat refused . . . he would insist. That much he was sure of. After everything he'd done for Carabel, he was due his answers. And if, by insisting, he ended up turning werecats as a whole against him—and Thorn—well, that was the price they'd have to pay.

There was only one way to find out.

He pulled his hood over his head and hurried deeper into Gil'ead.

CHAPTER XIII

✦ ✦ ✦ ✦ ✦ ✦

Confrontation with a Cat

It was still early dawn, and all was grey and silent except for the occasional tromp of soldiers and the cry of the watch.

A direct approach to the fortress would have been suicidal, so Murtagh skirted the center of the city and kept to alleys and side streets where possible.

The few folks he encountered gave him suspicious glances, but no more than the situation warranted. All of Gil'ead felt tense, alert, as if violence could break out at any moment. Shutters in houses swung shut seemingly of their own accord when he lifted his gaze, and he saw members of the guard posted along the main thoroughfares.

Murtagh couldn't stop worrying about Silna as he made his way through the city. Difficult and standoffish though she'd been, he hoped that she was safe and that the guards wouldn't catch her. She was so small and young. . . . *I should have done a better job of watching her*, he thought.

As he neared the fortress, he slowed to a measured walk, not wanting to rush headlong into a dangerous situation.

Without too much trouble, he found the house that Bertolf, Carabel's manservant, had brought him to before. Murtagh wondered if Carabel owned the elegant building or if she had an arrangement with whoever did. It seemed risky to be ducking in and out of a secret tunnel on a property where you didn't know who might be watching.

With quick steps, he descended the stone stairs to the well set ten feet or so below the surface of the ground. There, he pushed on the same piece of carving as had Bertolf, and the hidden door swung open.

Murtagh wasn't eager to again enter a tunnel, but at least he was familiar with this one, and it was far, far shorter than the maze they'd spent most of the night wandering. The thought reminded him of his lost sleep, and he fought back a powerful yawn. Two bad nights in a row took their toll.

He ducked beneath the lintel and walked in. Behind him, the door swung shut with a *thud* of deadly finality, and darkness swallowed him.

Somewhere ahead of him, the skittering footsteps of a mouse sounded.

"Great," he said, starting forward with one hand against the wall for balance. "Just great."

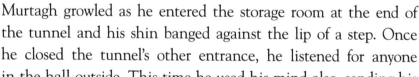

Murtagh growled as he entered the storage room at the end of the tunnel and his shin banged against the lip of a step. Once he closed the tunnel's other entrance, he listened for anyone in the hall outside. This time he used his mind also, sending his thoughts searching for nearby beings. The only one he found was a rather frightened mouse in a crack along the wall of the storeroom.

Now! Murtagh left the storeroom and hurried through the same side passages Bertolf had led him through during his last visit. He was grateful that the path had been easy to remember and that it was still early enough that most of the fortress's inhabitants had yet to wake. Plenty of the servants would already be after their duties, but he didn't think he needed to worry about running into the castle's baker that far outside of the kitchens.

Nevertheless, he was happy to reach the paneled door to the werecat's study without incident.

He didn't bother knocking; he lifted the latch on the door and pushed. It wasn't locked or barred and swung inward with hardly a sound.

~~~~~~~~~~~~~~~~~~~ ❖ ~~~~~~~~~~~~~~~~~~~

Carabel was sitting on the velvet cushion behind her desk. She was in the shape of a cat, tassel-eared, with a large mane around her neck and down her spine, and beautiful white fur that shone like satin. In size, she was perhaps three times larger than a normal cat, and lean muscles rippled beneath her hide in a way that spoke of savage strength.

She was purring and licking with her pink tongue the matted head of none other than Silna, who lay curled against her side, eyes closed in apparent bliss.

Murtagh paused at the entrance of the study, surprised and somewhat off-balance, but—for many reasons—relieved to see Silna safe. Then he moved in and closed the door behind himself.

"I take it she found you," he said. He dropped his bedroll on the floor.

Carabel looked at him, and her purring deepened. He felt the touch of her mind, as if she were attempting to communicate with her thoughts, like Thorn.

He armored his consciousness against her and shook his head. "Oh no. Not like that. We talk with words or not at all."

The werecat's ears flattened against her narrow skull. Then her form blurred and wavered, as if seen through rippling water, and after a few seconds, she again resembled a short, thin human.

Only she was without clothes.

Murtagh did not care. In other circumstances, her figure might have been distracting, but right then, it had no effect on him. He kept his gaze on the werecat as she picked up her shift from the desk and pulled it on.

"How *inconvenient*," said Carabel, showing her pointed little fangs.

Silna made a mewl of protest at being abandoned, and Carabel turned back and began to gently draw her sharp nails across the top of Silna's head. The kitten nestled closer to Carabel, and Murtagh would have sworn there was a smile upon her tiny lips.

Murtagh planted himself on the center of the knotted rug, directly before the desk. Uncomfortable suspicion soured his mouth. "The two of you are very familiar."

"Of course," said Carabel, directing a fond look toward Silna. "She is my daughter."

"Your *daughter.*"

"One of many, yes. My youngest."

"Why didn't you tell me?"

The werecat looked at him with solemn eyes. "Because names are powerful things. If you had known, it is possible our foes could have discovered the truth from you, and then they might have used Silna against me." She cocked her head. "You of all people ought to understand the danger of one's name, Murtagh son of Morzan."

"Don't call me that."

"It is who you are, human."

Murtagh fought to control his temper. "So they didn't know Silna was yours?"

Carabel shook her head. "No."

"It was just happenstance that they took her?"

"As best I can tell."

He growled and paced about the rug. "Why did they kidnap her, then? Excuse me, *kitten*nap her? And the other younglings. Has she said?"

Silna began to purr—a soft, steady rumble—as Carabel scratched along her cheek. Carabel said, "Only that the magician was involved—"

"Arven."

"Yes, that was his name. And Captain Wren too. They spoke of sending her somewhere farther south."

Murtagh's irritation with the werecat receded into the background as he stalked back and forth across the width of the study, trying to puzzle out the situation. "Lord Relgin has to be told." He stopped and gave Carabel a sharp look. "Or was this done at his command?"

Her expression grew severe. "I do not know," she said in a dangerously quiet voice. "And I would not care to hazard a guess. In this matter, safety will only be found in surety, and so far, surety eludes us. . . . I take it you did not find any of our other younglings?"

"There was no sign of them," he said, and her eyes softened with sorrow. "Does Silna know what happened to them?"

Carabel placed a protective arm around her daughter. The sight sent a pang through Murtagh. "Alas, no," Carabel replied. "She saw nothing of them. Tell me, if you would, how you rescued her. I would hear the whole of it, in every detail."

"You owe me answers, cat," he said, grim.

"And answers you shall have. But first this, if it please you."

Murtagh took a breath and did his best to put aside his impatience. He could not fault the werecat for asking.

So he described his time at Glaedr's barrow and how he had extracted the dragon's golden scale from within its earthy tomb. And he explained the steps he had followed to find Muckmaw's feeding ground, and how he had fought and killed the great fish.

The werecat listened intently, and at the point of Muckmaw's death, she went, "Sss. Good. Let the rats eat his tail and may his bones crumble to dust." By her side, Silna wiggled and looked up at her mother. Carabel resumed petting her. "The fish ate many a werecat over the years, human. It is good he is gone."

"And you got me to kill him for you."

Carabel cocked her head. "Would you have been able to gain entrance to the guard otherwise?"

". . . No. Probably not."

Smug, the cat took a sip from a chalice on the desk. "See? There was a rightness to this." She waved an elegant hand. "You may continue."

Murtagh's jaw tightened, but he did as she said and described how he had ingratiated himself within Captain Wren's company and then how he had made his way into the catacombs beneath the barracks.

The werecat spread the fingers on her free hand and dug them into the top of the desk. "Ssss. And what saw you thereafter, human?"

Murtagh gestured at Silna. "Surely your daughter can tell you."

"Your eyes see differently than hers."

He grunted. Then he described the two chambers he'd found after the war room: the magical workshop and the garden of rare and unknown plants. When he mentioned the strange egg in the garden, Carabel stiffened and her spiked hair fluffed, as if she were frightened.

"What is it?" Murtagh asked.

"An ancient wrongness that will need to be dealt with," said Carabel, examining the tips of her nails. "Rest assured, human, I will see to it that the problem is taken care of."

"And you're not going to tell me *what* this wrongness is?"

Her lips split in a sly little smile. "Every piece of information has a price, human. What would you be willing to pay for such a lovely morsel?"

"I would have thought I already earned it."

She laughed, her voice like silver coins tumbling. "No, no. Each mouse you wish to catch is different. Each mouse is new. This is a separate matter."

Talking with the cat, he decided, was like playing a game of hazard where the rules changed with each throw of the dice. *Very well, if I have to be tricksy, I'll be tricksy.* "A secret for a secret, then. Will that satisfy you?"

Carabel licked her fangs as she considered. "Is it a good secret, human?"

"As good as any I know."

"Hmm. A strong claim, that." She picked at a scratch in the desktop. "Very well. A secret for a secret. The egg belongs to the creatures known in this tongue as the Ra'zac." She added a trill to the *r* at the beginning of the name, and the sound sent a prickle down Murtagh's spine.

He swore explosively and paced in a circle before coming back to face the desk. "*Them?* Those foul creatures! How?"

The werecat raised her delicate eyebrows. "You must have known that Galbatorix hid some of their eggs about the land."

"He never spoke of it." Murtagh made a face, annoyed with himself. "I suppose I should have guessed as much. He always was devious. What is it doing *here*, though?"

A low half purr, half growl rumbled in Carabel's chest. "That is indeed the question, human."

"If I'd known what it was . . ." He shook his head. He would have melted the egg in a blast of fire fit to rival even the flames Thorn produced. As Carabel had said, the Ra'zac were a wrongness. They were the hunters of humans, nightmares of the night that fed off the flesh of people.

Murtagh remembered the moment he'd seen them crouched around the campfire where they'd caught and bound Eragon, Saphira, and Brom: stooped figures in dark hoods that hid their vulturelike beaks and round, bulging eyes, pupilless and devoid of white. He'd shot at them with his bow and driven them away. Though not before they succeeded in mortally wounding Brom. . . .

He shook himself from the shadows of the past.

"If I'd had word of it beforehand," said Carabel, "I would have said as such to you. Now your secret, if you please, human."

A rough knocking sounded.

Murtagh started, and then the study door opened to show Bertolf's broad face. He peered at Murtagh suspiciously. "Were you wanting me, ma'am? It's near time for breakfast, but the kitchens are behind today."

Carabel waved a hand. "Leave us for now, Bertolf. I'll ring if I want you."

"Yes, ma'am." The man bowed and withdrew.

The werecat focused on Murtagh once again, fierce and serious. "Your secret now."

From his belt, he removed the second bird-skull amulet and placed it on the desk. Silna hissed, arched her back, and batted the amulet onto the floor.

Murtagh bent and picked it up. Moving slowly, he placed the amulet on the corner of the desk farthest from Silna.

The kitten spat at the amulet and then hopped down to the floor and went to sit curled on the study hearth.

With an expression of distaste, Carabel hooked the amulet with a fingernail and held it up to examine. "I fail to understand," she said. "You have already shown me this unpleasant trinket. Although"— her nose wrinkled—"there is a different scent to it now."

"I took that amulet off the spellcaster," Murtagh said. And he showed her the original amulet in the pouch on his belt.

The tips of Carabel's tufted ears pressed against the side of her head. She growled then, a deep, throaty emanation that made the front of her shift vibrate. Hearing such a primal, animalistic sound coming from such a human-looking being made the hair on Murtagh's neck stand upright. "Arven. He of Du Vrangr Gata," she said.

"Indeed."

"Sss. The situation is worse than I feared, Rider."

Rider, now? She must be truly concerned. Murtagh seated himself, and he and the werecat exchanged a long, grim stare. For the first time, he felt as if they understood each other. "I think," he said with deliberate care, "that you had best tell me what exactly you know."

Carabel frowned as she again looked at the amulet. "I suppose you're right." She leaned back on her cushion. "Where shall I start?"

~~~~~~~~~~~~~~~~~~ ❖ ~~~~~~~~~~~~~~~~~~

A faint *pop* came from the bed of coals in the fireplace, and Silna flicked her ears with annoyance. Outside, in the bailey of the fortress, loud voices sounded. Murtagh kept his gaze fixed on Carabel.

"Start with the witch-woman Bachel," he said.

The werecat hissed. "*Yesss.* That one. Very well. For some years now, we have heard rumors—no more than whispers—of strange folk moving through the land. *Dreamers,* they call themselves, and the few that have been questioned claim to serve this *Bachel.* Who she is and what she wants remain . . . uncertain, but it is known that she is capable of weird magics." The werecat indicated the amulet. "We have sought this secret, human, in our own careful way. We are curious by nature, and unanswered questions attract us as moths to the flame. Five of our kind have ventured into the wilds in search of Bachel, and of those five, none have returned."

Murtagh listened with growing unease. "Where did they go?"

"Here and there," said Carabel with an unpleasant smile. "But I suspect . . . Well, you shall hear. You should know that the Dreamers have become more common. When captured and questioned, they kill themselves without hesitation, but this much seems certain: their influence spreads throughout Alagaësia like roots creeping through the soil. Their kind has been seen dealing with all the races, including the elves and Urgals, and we have scented their meddling in many a dark affair. But again, we know nothing of their goals or causes—only that their pawprints appear ever more frequently, and rarely absent blood or death."

Another *pop* sounded in the fireplace.

The werecat continued. "The amulet you found on Arven proves as much. As for *where* Bachel might be . . . Every few weeks, ships depart Ceunon and sail north in the Bay of Fundor. Even in the winter, when ice rims the bay and the waves grow steep and dangerous, even then you will find ships that take this journey. They are never gone very long. A few weeks at most, and then they return with their crew grim-faced and closemouthed. The passengers on these ships vary. Often they hide their faces and their minds, but we have seen many a notable merchant and many a scion of a titled family venture forth into the bay, and when they again alight in Ceunon, they often associate with the Dreamers, or else act in ways that seem to aid them."

Carabel pushed the amulet farther away and then licked her finger, as if to clean it. "Last year, we spoke with one of the sailors who made the journey."

"And?" asked Murtagh. His voice sounded unusually loud in the room.

The werecat lifted her chin. "He told us of a village set against the Spine. A village where the ground smells of rotten eggs and smoke rises from blackened vents. He told us of these things . . . and then he died. If your mind is set on finding the witch Bachel, seek you there, O Murtagh son of Morzan."

Rotten eggs. Brimstone. Exactly what Umaroth had warned him of. Murtagh was glad of the confirmation, and yet it left him with a deep disquiet. But he'd asked for answers, and now he had a start on them. "So the stone Sarros brought me comes from the same place as Bachel?"

Carabel shrugged. "It seems likely, but I cannot say for sure."

"And what do you think these Dreamers want with werecat younglings?"

Red fire lit her eyes, and she showed her fangs. "Sss. I do not know. Maybe nothing. Maybe this is solely the work of Du Vrangr

Gata. Maybe it is a private villainy of Arven. Or Captain Wren. I do not know, but I swear this to you, Rider: I shall not rest until I discover the truth and either rescue or avenge *all* of our lost children."

"Good," said Murtagh in a flat tone. And he meant it. Whoever was responsible deserved the worst possible punishment. If it had been Arven alone, then justice had already been delivered, but he doubted it.

The more Murtagh thought about the situation, the worse he felt. If the Dreamers had infiltrated Du Vrangr Gata—or recruited sympathizers therein—without arousing suspicion, that was alarming enough. But if what the cat said was true, they were operating upon a larger scale, and with a larger goal in mind, and they had already amassed a dangerous amount of influence. The realization made his skin crawl. How could they have escaped notice for so long? What hold did they have upon those they enlisted?

They have to be stopped, he thought. "Have you informed Nasuada of this?"

"Not as yet."

"Eragon or Arya?"

She shook her head.

"Why not?"

Carabel gave him a withering look. "Whispers and suspicions are not enough to raise a force, rouse a queen, or recall the leader of the Riders. We must have a clear understanding of the threat first."

"You mean someone needs to go to the village."

"Go. And return."

"Maybe. But I would say this"—he poked the amulet—"is proof enough that concern is warranted. That, and the kidnapping of your younglings."

Carabel's expression soured. "Again, we do not know if the

Dreamers are responsible. Still . . . perhaps you are right, and this unfortunate trinket is proof enough. Certainly it would be if you were to bring it to Nasuada along with an accounting of what we have learned."

Murtagh looked at the fireplace, uncomfortable. "You know I cannot."

"Can't you? It is said that the queen has some special fondness for you, and—"

Anger dragged his attention back to Carabel's smirking face. "It is said? Said by *whom*? You had best watch your words, cat."

Carabel shrugged, seemingly impervious to his tone. "By those with ears to hear and eyes to see."

"Well, they know not what they say, and I'll please you not to insult the queen *or* me with such slander."

After a moment, Carabel inclined her angled face. "Of course, Rider. Very well, I shall compose a message for Nasuada directly, but I do not pretend to know how she will respond. It would be best were you to pen a few words of corroboration. Will you agree to this?"

He grunted. "Fine. Yes."

As the cat collected her writing instruments, Murtagh sank back in his chair, brooding. Captain Wren's insubordination, the potential undermining of Du Vrangr Gata, the activities of the Dreamers, and the blasted Ra'zac egg—each was a serious matter. Taken together, they might represent a credible threat to Nasuada's crown.

What if . . . For a moment, he considered flying to Ilirea, but then he put the idea from his mind. As tempting as it was, doing so would be a mistake for everyone involved, including Nasuada. Her subjects wouldn't take kindly to their queen publicly treating with the traitor Murtagh.

And besides, whom would she end up sending to investigate the village? Whom *could* she send? Du Vrangr Gata was not to

259

be trusted, and at any rate, none of its spellcasters were skilled or strong enough to deal with the sort of wordless magic he had encountered. Few were. Eragon, for one, but he was busy protecting the Eldunarí and the dragon eggs, and he would not lightly leave them. Arya and the more accomplished of the elven mages were certainly capable, but Murtagh knew Nasuada would be reluctant to request help from magicians—much less a Rider—who were neither her subjects nor human.

Which left *him*. Him and Thorn.

The conclusion did not displease Murtagh, even if the unknown was, as always, unsettling. To have a clear and righteous cause to pursue was a rare treasure. By it, they could do good, and not just in a general sense, but for Nasuada specifically. She whom he had so badly hurt.

He roused himself from his brooding as Carabel gave him a sheet of parchment, a pot of ink, and a freshly cut goose-feather quill. Murtagh hesitated, unsure how to start, for he felt a weight of expectations and experiences and feelings unsaid. He shook himself then and focused on what needed saying. Wants would have to wait.

For a few minutes, the scratching of the quill was the only sound aside from the fire. He ended with:

Thorn and I will depart directly to find this village. What we might discover, I cannot say, but if it is a danger to you, your realm, or Alagaësia as a whole, we shall deal with it as need be. On this, you have my word. In any account, you may expect to hear from us upon our return.

He frowned as he stared at the last few lines. He was committing both himself and Thorn to this cause without asking Thorn. He hoped the dragon would not mind.

There was another problem besides. Nasuada did not know his hand, so how could she be sure the letter was from him? He could enchant the parchment, but to what end? She wouldn't trust a spell from an unknown source. And he didn't have a signet ring or other token on his person that she might recognize. Which left him with only his words.

He dipped the quill anew into the inkpot. Then, with special care, he wrote:

If you question the hand that scribes these runes, if you suspect my motive and wonder <u>why</u>, then I can only answer by saying—you know why.

Murtagh

The final sentence was a temerity. He knew that. But he couldn't think of anything else to write that he was confident Nasuada would believe was from him. He'd uttered those last three words to her—and her alone—in the dark grimness of the Hall of the Soothsayer. It was the closest he had ever come to confessing his feelings for her, and while it felt like an imposition to mention them now, when the situation was so much changed, he had no other choice.

He felt older than his years as he blotted the letter and wiped dry the quill. He folded the sheet and then melted a few drops of Carabel's red sealing wax onto the seam of the parchment.

"There," he said, feeling a sense of resolution.

"My thanks," said Carabel. "I am in your debt, human, as are werecats everywhere."

He inclined his head. "No thanks are required."

A small smile appeared on Carabel's face. "Perhaps not, but they're still polite. How do you plan to proceed, then?"

Murtagh rubbed his right elbow as he thought; the joint still hurt from the thrashing Muckmaw had given him. "I realize this is another question, cat, but perhaps you'll humor me and answer."

Her expression grew wicked. "Perhaps I shall," she said.

"How do you think I should proceed?"

The cat wiggled on her cushion, tufted ears perking up. The corner of her shift slid off to bare one shoulder. "*Sssah*. Very well, but I will warn you, human. Advice serves those giving it as much or more than those receiving it."

"I'll take that risk."

"Then I say this: it is better to open doors than to wait for them to be opened. And it is better to know what is on the other side of a door *before* it opens."

Murtagh understood. He rose and gave her a small bow and a smaller smile. "I thank you for your advice, werecat Carabel."

She sniffed and examined her fingernails again. "You are welcome, human."

Outside, in the bailey, shouts sounded—captains rallying their troops. To Murtagh's ear, it seemed as if the entire city garrison was being assembled in the yard.

Carabel noticed as well. She turned her head, and the thin morning light entering through the loophole window made the tufts on her ears glow. "I think you had best be off, human, lest Lord Relgin get the idea to search the keep. He's annoyingly imaginative sometimes."

"I'll bid you farewell, then, and take my leave, fair C—" Behind him, Murtagh heard a faint sifting sound, as of falling cloth. He turned to see Silna standing on two feet next to the hearth, a small wool blanket wrapped about her spare frame. She was no taller than the poker and tongs that hung nearby. Her skin was pale as snow, the veins smoke blue beneath the surface, and there was a translucence to her, as if she were not entirely substantial. Eyelids like polished shells, hair still brindled and in disordered shocks, and all about her a wild alertness, as if she had stepped from a glade within the deepest, darkest forest.

She walked to Murtagh and stood before him. He looked down into her enormous emerald eyes, clear and innocent, and knew not what to say.

He knelt before her, even as he would have knelt before a queen.

With a single bare arm, Silna hugged him about the neck. Her skin was cold against his. In a small, feather-soft voice, she said, "Thank you." Then she kissed him upon the brow, and the touch of her lips burned long after she pulled away.

She left him blinking back a film of tears. When he mastered himself well enough to lift his gaze, he saw her lying by the hearth, again in her cattish form, eyes closed, tail wrapped about her paws and nose.

His legs were unsteady beneath him as he stood. He looked to Carabel and opened his mouth and then closed it again.

For the first time, Carabel's expression softened, and her voice was husky with emotion. "I meant what I said, Rider. I am in your debt, as are all werecats. You may count yourself as a friend of our kind, and should you ever need help, you may seek us out."

He nodded and swallowed past the lump in his throat. "I am glad I could help." He drew himself up and gave her a courtly bow. "My thanks for your answers, Carabel. May your claws stay sharp, O most estimable of cats."

She bared her teeth in an appreciative smile. "Be careful where you tread, Rider. This witch is like a spider lurking at the center of a great web, and she has venom in her bite."

"Then it's good I'm not scared of spiders."

~~~~~~~~~~~~~~~~~~~ ❖ ~~~~~~~~~~~~~~~~~~~

Murtagh straightened as he exited the low tunnel that led under the fortress's curtain wall. He rolled his neck, hoisted his bedroll higher on his back, and checked the position of the sun: still low in the sky. He *should* be able to leave Gil'ead before most of the city was up and about.

He rubbed his brow. It felt as if he'd been branded. The

memory of Silna's eyes lingered in his mind, and he felt as if she had seen to his very center, every flaw laid bare before her guileless gaze. It was an intimacy he was only used to sharing with Thorn, and it left him with an uncomfortable sense of vulnerability. And yet, to be seen as he was, and accepted . . . was there any greater grace?

Troubled, he started away from the fortress. *I'm on my way,* he said, sending the thought to where Thorn was waiting. A faint sense of acknowledgment was his reply.

As Murtagh padded between the buildings, he continued to gnaw over what Carabel had said. Bachel, Wren, the Ra'zac . . . the world was out of sorts, and in ways he didn't really understand. The fact made his gut tense, as if he were about to receive a blow.

Again, Silna's eyes filled Murtagh's mind, cool and clear and full of promise. And again, he felt her kiss upon his brow.

He stopped at the side of a street, and every part of his skin prickled. His thoughts raced as he tried to solve the puzzle before him, tried to find the path of safety through a perilous maze. Had he been wrong? Bachel needed attending to, yes, but Nasuada was in danger, and his letter was hardly a proper means of protection.

He opened the pouch on his belt and dug through it until his fingers found cold metal: the coins Captain Wren had given him. He pulled one out and looked at Nasuada's embossed visage.

As perfect as the likeness was, he could not decipher her expression. She wore a mask of her own, the impassive regality that custom—and necessity—imposed. He found no encouragement in her golden features, and yet their very familiarity helped settle his mind.

He decided.

They would go to Ilirea. Despite everything he had thought and said, it was the right thing to do. He would explain himself to Nasuada and face whatever approbation came from her subjects.

Difficult though it would be, he would have the satisfaction of knowing Nasuada was safe. And once she was, only then would he and Thorn hunt down Bachel.

With the decision came a sense of relief. Murtagh nodded, put away the coin, and hurried on his way, feeling fit to face the trials of an uncertain future.

Would Thorn agree? Murtagh felt sure he would, once he shared his mind with the dragon. Unless, of course—

Someone collided with him from the side. He shoved the person away, ready to kick and punch and fight.

"Murtagh!" exclaimed a low, urgent voice.

Dismay gripped Murtagh as he saw the same unpleasantly familiar face he had spotted outside the citadel not two days past: pale Lyreth in his drab finery. And surrounding them were Lyreth's guards: six burly men with necks like bulls, the faint whiff of rotting flesh clinging to them. Ex-soldiers of the Empire, spell-warped to feel no pain.

"Murtagh, it *is* you," said Lyreth, his voice barely louder than a whisper.

Murtagh clenched his teeth. Thorn's alarm was a rising note of anxiety at the back of his mind. He considered bolting, but there were other people on the street, and he saw a squad of soldiers two houses away, marching toward them. . . .

Lyreth drew closer, his eyes darting about, the whites showing with some combination of fear and concern. "I thought I saw you a few days ago, but I wasn't certain. What are you *doing* here? Don't you know what they'll do to you if they catch you?"

"I need to go," said Murtagh, and started to pull back.

Lyreth caught him by the sleeve and held him with a surprisingly strong grip. His breath smelled of lavender and peach liqueur, but it wasn't enough to conceal the sharp stench of nervous sweat from under his arms. "You can't stay out here. The magicians of Du Vrangr Gata are everywhere, and there are elves in the city. *Elves!* Come, come, hurry. You'll be safe at my house. Hurry!"

Murtagh! growled Thorn.

I know!

The guards closed in around Murtagh, preventing him from stepping away as Lyreth pulled him up the street. And Murtagh had no choice but to accompany his unexpected and thoroughly unwelcome companions.

CHAPTER XIV

✦ ✦ ✦ ✦ ✦ ✦ ✦

Duel of Wits

Murtagh kept careful track of the streets as Lyreth hurried him through the city. If he had to run, he wanted to know exactly where he was.

Lyreth brought him to a small stone house—one of the few all-stone structures in Gil'ead—tucked away in the corner of a square that was surrounded by cramped log-built dwellings jammed cheek by jowl. The ground was dirt, and there was a watering trough in the center for horses. The whole place felt dark, sheltered, and somewhat decrepit, and the only other living creature to be seen was a bedraggled rooster pecking at the dried mud outside what looked to be a candlemaker's shop.

Lyreth used an iron key to unlock the front door of the stone house, and then he waved Murtagh in. "Quickly, quickly now."

Wary—and somewhat curious—Murtagh entered. As dangerous as the situation was, his desire to know was stronger than his sense of self-preservation. How *were* the former members of Galbatorix's nobility surviving? In a different set of circumstances, he knew *he* would have been the one hiding like a rabbit trying to escape a hungry hawk.

The building's shabby face belied its luxurious interior. Dwarven rugs covered the tiled floor. Carved balustrades lined a marble staircase that climbed to a second story. Dramatic portraits hung on the walls—portraits that were too detailed, too lifelike, to have been created without the help of magic. A gold and silver chandelier hung from the wood-braced ceiling, and cut gems dangled from the chandelier in a rainbow of tears.

"This way," said Lyreth, leading Murtagh past the anteroom into a modestly sized but beautifully decorated dining hall. Silken tapestries depicting battles between dragons, elves, and humans adorned the walls, and the candlesticks on the long table looked to be solid gold.

"Please, make yourself comfortable." Lyreth gestured at a velvet-backed chair at one end of the table.

Murtagh counted thirteen chairs around the table, including his own. The number gave him a cold chill of realization.

He took off his bedroll and set it down by the table, close at hand. Then he gathered his cloak and sat. "What is this place?" he asked. He suspected he already knew the answer.

"A place of safety," Lyreth said, seating himself. He waved at the guards, and two of them took up posts by the entrance while the others filed out of the hall. "Formora had it built as a sanctuary from Galbatorix if ever the need arose. Also"—he indicated the chairs—"as a location where the Forsworn could meet in private, away from the king's prying eyes."

Formora. She had been an elf, and one of Galbatorix's favorites among the Forsworn. By all accounts, she had been cunning, cruel, and capricious to the extreme, even as measured by the standards of her fellow traitors. Murtagh remembered Lord Varis telling him that, when she was provoked, her habit had been to cut her foes apart with magic, piece by piece . . . while keeping them alive for as long as possible. That, and she had been overly fond of candied fruits.

Murtagh glanced around the room. He'd heard of such places before. Secret hiding holes where the Forsworn could protect themselves, if not from the king, then at least from the king's other servants. Galbatorix's followers—willing or otherwise—were hardly known for their cooperative nature, and the king had encouraged their backstabbing and bloody machinations with often undisguised glee. The walls of the house would be laced with powerful wards, and more than wards: traps that would far exceed the strength and complexity of those he had encountered in the catacombs. The whole structure was probably riddled with charged gems.

"Were they ever truly free of Galbatorix's gaze?" Murtagh said.

Lyreth shrugged. "Were any of us?" He clicked his fingers, and a manservant in a fine woolen coat hurried into the hall, his polished bootheels tapping a precise tempo against the hard floor. The man placed a silver platter on the table and offloaded a decanter of cut crystal, a bottle of wine, two gold goblets, and a tiered tray of assorted delicacies: sweetmeats, aspic with candied fruit, bite-sized berry pies, and what looked to Murtagh like honey-glazed pastries.

His mouth watered. It had been well over a year since he'd tasted anything resembling proper fine food, and he found himself suddenly nostalgic for the flavors of his childhood.

The servant poured the wine, and then brought Murtagh one of the goblets as well as the tray of delicacies so that he might make his own selection.

Murtagh took some of the aspic, a berry pie, and two honey-glazed pastries. The servant then attended to Lyreth, who selected a sweetmeat and nothing more.

"You may go," said Lyreth, and the servant bowed and retired from the room.

A honey-glazed pastry was halfway to Murtagh's mouth when thoughts of poison and spells stayed his hand. Lyreth noticed and, in an offhand manner, said, "The food is safe, if you're wondering. The wine too." And he gave Murtagh a crooked smile before taking a sip from his own goblet.

Murtagh deliberated for a moment and then popped the pastry into his mouth. It melted with sweet, buttered deliciousness, and he fought to keep his pleasure from showing.

"My family acquired this place some years ago," said Lyreth, nibbling at the sweetmeat on his plate. "We kept it as a safeguard against exactly this sort of eventuality."

"Mmm." Murtagh tasted the wine; he recognized the vintage. A red grown in the vineyards of the south, near Aroughs, bottled near fifty years ago. He doubted more than a few dozen bottles remained in the land. "You honor me," he said, raising the goblet.

Lyreth shrugged. "What good does it do to hoard fine wine in these trying times? We might all be dead tomorrow."

"As you say." Murtagh took another carefully controlled sip as he studied Lyreth. The man appeared to have been under considerable stress (and understandably so); he was thinner than Murtagh remembered, and his skin had the unhealthy pallor of an invalid confined to bed. Seeing him the worse for wear was the source of some satisfaction for Murtagh, although, despite himself, he empathized with Lyreth and the difficulties he must have faced since Galbatorix's fall. It couldn't be easy, living every day in fear of being caught out.

"You smell of fish," said Lyreth abruptly.

"Baths are hard to come by on the road."

"Were you responsible for killing Muckmaw? It's all my guards have been able to talk about since yesterday. I thought it might have been you."

Murtagh toyed with the stem of his goblet as he considered how to answer. The conversation was a duel for information, and they both knew it, but the unspoken reality was that Lyreth held no power over him. If Murtagh wanted to leave, or to attack, there was little the other man could do about it. "I may have played a part in the matter."

Lyreth made an unimpressed sound. "You've certainly managed to stir up the local peasantry. They seem to think Eragon himself is wandering the land, curing their ills."

"If only."

At that, Lyreth made a face and took a deep quaff of his wine. "Blasted Rider."

Murtagh could feel Thorn's ongoing concern. *Peace*, he said to the dragon. *I have his measure.*

And it was true. Murtagh had had ample opportunity to study Lyreth and the group of eldest sons he associated with at court. To the last, they had been arrogant, cruel, overconfident, and yet also deeply insecure. There was no such thing as safety around Galbatorix, and their parents had all been born to power and influence, or else had acquired it through cunning and savagery. None of which bred kindness in their offspring. Murtagh had always been the outcast of their generation: the only known child of the Forsworn; ostensibly ignored by Galbatorix during his childhood, yet still understood to be favored by the king; groomed for power and yet powerless himself, with Galbatorix holding his father's estate in his stead until he came of age. Added to that, Murtagh's own distrust and inexperience when it came to navigating the treacherous currents of power, and he had been both an object of fear and a figure of scorn and ridicule that they had used poorly however they could. Only once Tornac took him under his wing had Murtagh begun to learn how to defend himself, in more ways than one.

He ate a spoonful of aspic. Of Lyreth, he had no fond memories. Two experiences remained in Murtagh's mind as emblematic of the man. The first was when Lyreth and a number of other boys had set out to steal cherries from Lord Barst's private garden in the citadel at Urû'baen. Murtagh had tagged along, hoping that they might let him be part of the group. They'd barely started picking the cherries when one of Barst's men discovered them and held them at spearpoint. All of them save Lyreth, who managed to slip away, only to return a few minutes later, leading Lord Barst and loudly declaiming the misbehavior of the other boys.

Despite their noble lineage, Barst proceeded to thrash the lot of them. But he spared Lyreth, which earned the young noble no end of hate from the other boys, although most of them were devious enough to hide their true feelings. Lyreth's family was too wealthy and well placed to openly oppose.

The second incident had been on Murtagh's fifteenth birthday. No one save Tornac had seemed to mark the significance of the day, but somehow word must have gotten out in the court, probably from the pages. How else to explain that, on that day of all days, as Murtagh climbed the narrow spiral staircase that led to his chambers, a group of boys had ambushed him and beaten him and left him bruised and bleeding on the sharp stone steps?

The attackers had worn party masks of a type common at court, but Murtagh could guess their names regardless. And as the fists and feet had pummeled his sides, he'd heard a semi-familiar voice cry, *"That's it! Get him! Knock him down!"* And he knew the voice as Lyreth's.

None of the boys ever admitted what they had done. They continued to treat him the same as ever about the citadel, and the only hint of acknowledgment was several snide comments made when they saw him limping the next day: "Ha! What happened? Did a horse step on your foot? Murtagh Crookshank! Ha!"

Murtagh had never forgotten. Nor forgiven.

He eyed the decorations in the hall. Despite the house's rich appointments, he guessed Lyreth found the place uncomfortably confining. For one who had grown up in the citadel in Urû'baen and on Lord Thaven's vast holdings, living in such a small house would feel like being locked in a closet.

He must be going mad trapped in here, Murtagh thought.

"How fares your father?" he asked. What he didn't say was, *Is Thaven still alive?*

Lyreth's expression remained studiously flat. "As well as could be expected."

"Of course. In these trying times." That earned him a twitch of annoyance from Lyreth. *Good.* The more he could needle the man, the more Lyreth was likely to slip and say something he shouldn't. "The Empire couldn't last forever," said Murtagh. "At some point Galbatorix was bound to fall. It was inevitable."

"Maybe," said Lyreth with undisguised bitterness. "But it didn't have to happen during our lives."

"No, but that's not ours to say, is it?"

Lyreth opened his mouth, closed it, and then opened it again and said, "Were you there? At the end? When . . . *he* died?"

"I was."

The man's gaze flicked toward him from under bloodless lids. His eyes were grey blue, like distant thunderheads. "How was it done? I've heard conflicting accounts."

"With kindness."

"You mock me."

"Not at all."

A faint frown formed on Lyreth's brow. "*Him?* Kindness? That's pre—"

"You never were the brightest," Murtagh said in an uninterested tone. "Cunning, that I'll give you. Determined, even. But not very bright."

Lyreth inhaled through pinched nostrils. "Keep your secrets, then. I'll learn the truth of it regardless. Tell me this, at least, if you would so *kindly* deign. How did you and that dragon of yours escape Urû'baen? Both Eragon and Arya were there, I understand. Surely they tried to stop you."

"Do you really expect me to explain?" said Murtagh. "Would it help you to know the spells I used? Or the dangers we braved? Does any of that matter? Suffice it to say, we escaped, and at no small risk." The truth, of course, was nothing so dramatic. He and Thorn had simply . . . left. They had played their part in toppling Galbatorix—Eragon never would have been able to work magic on the king if Murtagh hadn't used the Name of Names to break the king's spells—and after, neither Eragon nor Murtagh had the stomach to continue fighting.

Not for the first time, Murtagh reflected on the fact that if he had been in Eragon's place, he wouldn't have thought to force *empathy* on Galbatorix. It wasn't part of his nature. Perhaps that was a failing of his—Murtagh was willing to admit it was—but he didn't feel that his lack of charity toward Galbatorix was wrong, not given what the king had done to him and Thorn.

He placed the small pie in his mouth and chewed, enjoying the flavors of blueberries and blackberries admixed.

Lyreth shifted in his seat, as if there were burrs pricking him from beneath. "And since then? What have you been up to, Murtagh? Wild stories have reached my ears. Tales of a red dragon seen here or there. Whispers of magic that only a Rider or an elf might be capable of casting."

With the fine linen napkin from by his plate, Murtagh dabbed the corners of his mouth, brushing crumbs off his stubble. "Thorn and I have been traveling the land, seeing what there is to see. What of you and your family, Lyreth? How have you managed since Galbatorix fell?"

"Well enough," Lyreth muttered.

"No doubt. But how long can you continue to live in hiding? Eventually someone will realize who you are. You would be best served to surrender and cast yourself on the queen's mercy. She *does* show mercy on occasion, or so I'm told."

"Don't speak to me of that puffed-up pretender. She's a commoner, without a drop of noble blood in her veins, not from any of the proper families nor from the old lineages of the Broddrings."

"Those who conquer, rule," said Murtagh calmly. "So it has always been. You forget your history if you think otherwise."

"I forget *nothing*." A feverish gleam appeared in Lyreth's otherwise insipid eyes. "You're right, though, Murtagh. The current state of affairs can't continue. My family aren't the only ones hiding. A number of the most powerful nobles—men and women whose names you would recognize—have been biding their time, consolidating their positions for when the moment is ripe."

"Ripe for what?"

Lyreth leaned forward, suddenly animated. "What *are* you doing here, Murtagh? Muckmaw dead, and all of Gil'ead in a commotion. What is it? Are you raising troops? Killing Nasuada's lieutenants? What?"

"You've grown obvious, Lyreth," said Murtagh in a lazy tone. "You wouldn't have lasted a week at court like this."

"Bah." Lyreth waved his hand and sank back in his chair. "Events are afoot, and directness is needed. If you are too cautious, the prize shall go to another. . . . You *could* take the throne, Murtagh. You know that, yes? And all the great families would rally to your banner . . . those of us who still have some standing, that is. Hamlin and Tharos were fools. They couldn't wait, they couldn't gather the army they needed, and so their rebellions failed. Hamlin ended up with his head on a pike outside these very walls, and Tharos will spend the rest of his life in Nasuada's dungeons. Unless . . ."

Murtagh cocked his head. Nothing Lyreth said was particularly surprising, although the implications were far from pleasant. "Are you really so eager to return to the days of Galbatorix, Lyreth? Would you see me raised above you, to rule in perpetuity, undying and unchanging? Is that really your wish?"

"It would be better than what we have now!"

You mean, it would free you from hiding and again place your family in a position of power.

A sly expression formed on Lyreth's face. "Besides, think of the advantages for you, Murtagh. I know you always chafed under Galbatorix's strictures. Were the crown yours, you could rule as you see fit, with our men and gold as your bulwark. And it would be good for our kind. Nasuada cannot hold her own against Arya. A Dragon Rider as queen of the elves, who ever heard of such nonsense? Eragon is a threat as well. He's building a force of Riders out in the east. Once they're grown and trained, who can stand against him? Only you, Murtagh. And I know there is no love lost between the two of you."

The pretense to intimacy made Murtagh bristle. "Oh you do, do you?"

"I know it to be true. Come, Murtagh. What say you? All of the Empire could be yours. And more too. Galbatorix should never have suffered Surda to exist. You could break them and unite this land in a way that has never been done before. All of humanity gathered under a single standard. Then the elves might fear us, and the dwarves too."

The wine and the delicacies no longer sat so well within Murtagh's stomach. The future Lyreth described was more tempting than Murtagh wanted to admit. Were he to claim the throne, few could challenge him or Thorn, and neither Eragon nor Arya would be eager to again plunge the land into war. They would tolerate his existence and, in time, perhaps come to respect his authority. In one fell swoop, he could restore glory to his family's name and secure power such to protect Thorn and himself against all but the most dangerous of foes.

But in order to elevate himself like that, he would have to depose Nasuada, and her fate thereafter could only be exile, imprisonment, or death. And that he could not countenance. *Then I would truly be known as a betrayer,* he thought. Not just to the common folk, but to the one person, besides Thorn, who fully trusted him. Nasuada was the very reason he'd been able to break free of his bondage and help topple Galbatorix. To then act against her . . . No. It was unthinkable.

He let the idea go, and he felt no regret.

Lyreth fidgeted, seemingly on tenterhooks as he waited.

Instead of replying directly, Murtagh decided to unbalance the other man, to step sideways when a forward step was expected. From the pouch on his belt, he produced the bird-skull amulet he'd found in Ceunon. He placed it on the table and slid it to the other end.

"Have you seen one of these before?"

Lyreth picked up the amulet with forefinger and thumb and held it dangling before him, much as Carabel had done. He showed no reaction aside from bland curiosity, but Murtagh wondered if, perhaps, there was a flicker of some emotion in the man's eyes. For a moment, Murtagh debated touching Lyreth's mind, but there was no way for such an action to be interpreted as anything but an attack. In any case, as with all the children of nobility, Lyreth had been raised with extensive training on how to protect his thoughts from eavesdroppers or intruders. Success was not guaranteed even if Murtagh tried, not unless he were willing to totally break Lyreth's mind.

It might be worth it, he thought. Lyreth and his family posed no small threat to Nasuada and the stability of her realm. If Murtagh could do something about it . . .

He licked his lips, muscles tightening in anticipation of action. A few quick words, a barrage of mental violence, and he would have complete control over everyone in the house.

Surely he knows that. The thought gave Murtagh sudden pause. Why *was* Lyreth willing to take such an enormous risk?

Lyreth dropped the amulet on the table. "What a barbaric creation. I can't say I have, and I'm glad of it too. . . . But you have yet to answer me, Murtagh. Come now, what will it be? The crown, or a lifetime of skulking in the shadows until the queen's pet magicians hunt you down like a rabid dog?"

Murtagh smiled slightly as he rolled the wine in the goblet, studying his distorted reflection. "Neither," he said, gathering his will in preparation to attack. He lifted his gaze to meet Lyreth's storm-cloud eyes. "I walk alone these days, Lyreth. Thorn and I answer to no man, and we will not be beholden to anyone, least of all your family. But I *will* know the truth of what you're planning."

Lyreth's expression didn't change, as if Murtagh had done no more than make a passing comment on the weather. "You never did know your place," he said.

A powerful itch kindled in the middle of Murtagh's palm.

He opened his mouth—

Lyreth's finger pressed against the edge of the table.

Clunk! The floor dropped out beneath Murtagh, the room tilted like a pinwheel, and his stomach lurched as he plummeted into blinding darkness.

CHAPTER XV

✦ ✦ ✦ ✦ ✦ ✦

The Tangle Box

An instant of shapeless black void, a *clang*, and—
—a bone-jarring crash as his heels struck metal and his knees buckled.

He would have fallen onto all fours. He *was* falling, and then a battering ram seemed to slam into him front to back and side to side, pinning him in place, holding him upright.

The impact drove the air from his lungs, and he felt a sudden drain from his wards. He tried to inhale, but the crushing weight pressing in from all sides made it impossible.

Then the air around him vanished, and the last dregs of breath left in his lungs forced their way up his throat and out his mouth and nose.

He gaped like a stunned fish.

A high keening—eye-watering and teeth-vibrating—sounded inside his skull, so loud and penetrating it made thought itself difficult.

Time seemed to slow for Murtagh.

His lungs were burning with terrible fire. His veins throbbed. His skin was swollen like an overfilled bladder. Crimson stars mottled the edges of his vision. And the ever-present shrilling disrupted his ability to focus.

He had seconds to act, if that. He couldn't speak, and holding the ancient language in his mind was impossible.

So he did the only thing he could.

He cast a spell without a word to guide the magic. Only intent constrained the burst of energy, and that intent contained and embodied a single sentiment: *Stop!*

The energy for the spell was spent in an instant. The shrilling stopped, and blessed silence reigned. But no air returned; still his lungs were empty, and still his veins burned, and he was about to pass out.

He could see only blackness, but he knew where he was: inside a tangle box. A trap for magicians, designed to keep them from speaking or thinking, designed to suffocate them so they could be safely disposed of.

He tried to rally his strength for a second spell. If he could break the walls of the tangle box, he could let in air, precious air, and if he could breathe, he would have a chance.

But he couldn't concentrate well enough to again work magic. The glass-pane barrier in his mind was too strong for him to reach through to the flow of energy on the other side, and the crimson tunnel narrowing his vision had nearly closed.

Is this really how I die? THIS? The thought was enraging, but at the same time, he felt acceptance as awareness deserted him. . . .

~~~~~~~~~~~~~~~~~~~~ ❖ ~~~~~~~~~~~~~~~~~~~~

A thunderous crash sounded above. An earthquake-like vibration shook the metal underneath his feet, and the tremor passed up through his legs and chest and caused his teeth to chatter, rousing him back to awareness.

Stone cracked, metal tore, and then a rush of cold wind touched his cheeks.

His lungs filled with sweet air, and he gasped like a drowning man.

Bright daylight appeared overhead, dispelling the darkness. He looked up, coughing, blinking, tears streaming from the corners of his eyes.

Through petals of torn iron, he saw Thorn leaning toward him, the dragon's scales covered with chalky dust, his long, heavy jaws open to show rows of bloody teeth.

Behind the dragon, the sky was pale blue, devoid of clouds. Broken ceiling beams intruded on the bright expanse.

Thorn reached down with one taloned paw and scooped Murtagh out of the pile of muddy gravel that had immobilized him. Pebbles fell like hail as Thorn lifted him back up into the dining hall.

Murtagh's chest heaved as he struggled for air. Thorn's mind pressed against his, the dragon's thoughts sharp with anger, fear, worry, and barely leashed panic. Still, his presence was comforting, and Murtagh began to think he might actually survive.

Thorn uncurled his paw and deposited Murtagh on the debris-covered floor. He nudged Murtagh in the ribs. *How are you hurt? Tell me. Tell me! Try to breathe!*

"I'm—" Murtagh gasped. "I'm . . . trying." His lungs still burned as he forced himself onto his knees, half expecting to be attacked.

No sign remained of Lyreth in the dining hall. The fine wooden table was shattered to pieces beneath Thorn's weight, and the silken tapestries hung in tatters. By the door to the hall lay three of the bullnecked guards, limp and bloodstained, their limbs twisted at unnatural angles.

Thorn nudged him again. The dragon's eyes were wide and wild, and his sides heaved, not just from exertion. Murtagh could nearly taste his fearful agitation.

Glancing around, Murtagh became aware of how small the interior of the house was. Thorn's wings almost scraped the walls, which seemed to lean inward with ominous intent, and the timbers jutting overhead were uncomfortably similar to broken branches against a dead sky.

Newfound alarm caused him to stagger to his feet. He gave Thorn a weak pat on the nose and cast about for his bedroll. A corner of it stuck out from under the ruined table. He grabbed it and started to move toward the dragon's side, meaning to climb onto his back.

Outside the broken house, shouts and brassy horns sounded, along with a clatter of arms and armor as soldiers rushed in.

Blast it! "We have to get out of—"

A section of roof caved inward, and the slate shingles poured across Thorn's back with a dusty, deafening discord.

Thorn roared, and Murtagh both heard and felt his jolt of mindless panic. "No, wait! It's all—"

The crimson dragon reared and tried to spread his wings, only to be blocked by the walls of the house. Then he truly went mad. He thrashed like a great snake, and the shell of the building shook and shuddered, and beams tumbled down, and walls collapsed, and a thick cloud of dust darkened the air.

Murtagh crouched and covered his head with his bedroll as the house fell around them. He tried to join with Thorn's mind, but the dragon was too far gone in his fear; Murtagh could not reach him, could not calm or reason with him.

His wards deflected a mass of timbers that would have crushed him, and he gasped at the sudden loss of energy. *Zar'roc.* He needed the sword, needed the energy stored within the sword's ruby pommel.

A moment of shocking silence followed. Before him, Murtagh saw mounds of beams and rubble coated with a finger-thick layer of ashy dust. The house was no more, and beyond its confines, shadowy shapes of men moved behind the curtains of obscuring haze.

THUD.

A beat from Thorn's wings blew whorls of dust spinning into the sky and cleared the area around Murtagh. He lifted his head.

A shifting group of soldiers surrounded the square, their faces white with fear, hate, and dust. They held their spears pointed toward Thorn—as if the weapons would do any good against a dragon—and they cursed Murtagh and Thorn and shouted insults and provocations. Flights of arrows arched in from between the buildings, whistling their deadly song.

"Thrysta!" Murtagh cried, and the arrows shattered in the air and fell harmlessly to the streets.

Thorn roared again, and the men shrank back. Desperate, Murtagh pressed his mind against Thorn's, but it was like battering his head against a wall of blank stone. Fear ruled the dragon's thoughts—no other emotion was strong enough to intrude or override. In that moment, he was become a mindless beast, and Murtagh did not know how to help him.

Thorn twisted and swung his tail through the air and struck the nearby houses. The weight of his tail, and the strength driving it, broke the buildings, snapped their timbers like dry kindling, and sent doors and shutters and shingles and entire walls crashing to the ground.

Murtagh ran toward Thorn. "St—"

The dragon turned and placed a paw over Murtagh. The weight pushed Murtagh to the ground, and then Thorn's claws curved around him, and a forceful yank caused his neck to whip as Thorn loosed an unearthly bellow and sprang into the air.

Murtagh struggled to move, struggled to see, but the cage of Thorn's talons was immovable, unbreakable.

Thorn roared again. Beneath them, Murtagh glimpsed the soldiers fleeing through the streets, and he thought he saw Esvar's face among the throng, the yellow-haired youth's expression fear-stricken and accusatory. Closer to the fortress, he spotted two figures garbed in the dark robes of Du Vrangr Gata, and also a trio of elves standing by the corner of a building, the air shimmering between their hands as they chanted in what he knew was the ancient language.

No!

More arrows flew up toward them, and an enormous jet of flame shot out from Thorn's maw. Even closed within Thorn's paw, Murtagh could feel waves of searing heat rolling out from the fiery torrent.

The arrows flared red, white, and yellow and vanished like sparks in a campfire.

With another roar, Thorn bathed the buildings below in a stream of liquid fire. Yellow sheets billowed from the roofs, and the flapping of the ravenous flames drowned out a chorus of shouts and screams.

Murtagh was shouting as well, but Thorn wasn't listening.

Then they were flying across the city, and as Thorn flew, he laid down a track of burning destruction. A spell of some kind caused the air about them to grow cold and thin, but whatever the intended outcome of the enchantment, the effects soon vanished, and Thorn continued as before.

They passed over the edge of Gil'ead, and then Thorn was climbing into the sky with desperate speed, and the only sounds were the rush of air and the heavy beats of his wings.

CHAPTER XVI

✦ ✦ ✦ ✦ ✦ ✦ ✦

Aftermath

Thorn flew for hours.

Murtagh kept trying to talk with him, but the dragon's mind remained closed, armored by unreasoning fear. Helpless to do more, Murtagh strove to impress a sense of calm and safety on Thorn, despite his own upset. He wanted to rage and curse and weep, but he knew that would only worsen Thorn's state, so he crushed his own feelings and focused on maintaining an even frame of mind. Thorn needed to know that he wasn't alone and that both he and Murtagh were safe. Only then would he regain his senses.

Every wingbeat caused a painful jostle as the scales along Thorn's knobby fingers cut into Murtagh's skin. The rush of cold air was loud and distracting and leeched the life from his limbs, though he clung to his bedroll for warmth. Soon he began to shiver.

Murtagh tried to track their path, but he could only see a small patch of the ground. He could tell they were heading north and east, and that was all.

The sight of the burning buildings kept filling his mind, and he kept pushing it away, not wanting his own distress to worsen Thorn's. But he couldn't help but feel a sick sense of inevitability at what they had done.

~~~~~~~~~~~~~~~~~~~~~~~~ ❖ ~~~~~~~~~~~~~~~~~~~~~~~~

The sun was directly above them when, at long last, Thorn angled downward and glided to a stop upon a small hill by the edge of the vast eastern plains.

They landed with a jolt, and Thorn opened his paw. Murtagh dropped onto the dry grass hard enough to cause him to let out his breath in a *whuff.*

He unclamped his grip on the bedroll and slowly got to his feet.

Thorn was crouched next to him, shoulders and wings hunched as if to ward off a blow, eyes half closed, his entire body racked with tiny tremors.

Murtagh wrapped his arms around Thorn's head. "Shh. It's all right," he said, both out loud and with his mind. "We're safe. Be at ease." He repeated the words until he felt the tremors begin to subside.

It is not all right. Thorn blinked and hunkered lower. *It will never be all right.*

"The elves will have put out the fires. It's easy enough with a word or two."

Thorn laid his head on the ground and let out his breath in a great sigh. His scales felt uncommonly cold to Murtagh; normally the dragon ran hotter than a human. *How many do you think I killed?*

". . . I don't know. Maybe no one." But they both knew that was unlikely.

I hate this weakness in me. This is not how I should be. It is unbecoming for a dragon, much less a dragon with a Rider. I dishonor you and my kind.

"No, no, no," said Murtagh. The words tumbled out in a rush. "This isn't your fault. It never was."

Thorn turned doleful eyes on him. *Galbatorix is dead. My actions are my own. What he did to me—*

"What he did to *us.*"

We cannot be blamed for it, but the fault here is still mine.

A strange desire to weep came over Murtagh. He remembered Thorn as a hatchling, pure and innocent, free of any misdeed, and despite all they had done, he saw the youngling in Thorn yet. "You're not helpless," he said with fierce conviction. "You can overcome this fear of yours. Nothing in this world is mightier than a dragon."

Thorn snuffed the ground by his feet. *Nothing but a dragon's own mind.* To that, Murtagh had no answer, and his helplessness turned into coiled frustration. Thorn noticed. *But I will try, however I can.*

"I know you will. Tomorrow, let's find some trees, and we'll work on this together."

Together.

With his right hand, Murtagh stroked the scales along Thorn's jaw. They were still cold against his palm. "Thank you for coming to get me. I would have died if you hadn't."

I flew . . . very fast. Thorn shivered again, and his eyelids drooped lower, although his shoulders and wings remained hunched.

"You need to eat," said Murtagh. "Stay here. I'll be back soon."

No. Do not go. . . .

But Murtagh was already trotting down the hill.

~~~~~~~~~~~~~~~~~~~ ❖ ~~~~~~~~~~~~~~~~~~~

Thorn's approach had scared away any nearby game, and Murtagh had to range longer and wider than he wanted before he spotted a herd of red deer grazing along the banks of a creek.

He stopped some distance away. A pair of does looked in his direction before returning to feeding. They seemed entirely unfrightened; he was too far away to be a threat, and he saw no settlements in the area. The animals weren't used to being hunted by humans.

He cast about the ground, looking for a rock, but unlike the land near the Spine, the soil of the plains was rich and black and had no stones in it. What he found instead was a piece of wind-scoured bone, a fragment of a deer's thigh or foreleg.

It would do.

He concentrated on the largest deer, lifted the bone on his outstretched palm, and said, "Thrysta!"

The shard flew faster than his eye could follow. With a *thup*, it struck the doe between her eyes. Her head snapped back, and the animal collapsed, hind legs kicking.

The rest of the herd fled.

Murtagh walked to the fallen animal. By the time he arrived, the doe had gone limp and still.

He looked at the deer, contemplating what he had done. The animal's eyes were still open, and they were beautiful: round and glassy and gentle. "I'm sorry," he murmured.

Then he grabbed the deer by its legs, slung it over his shoulders, and started the long walk back to Thorn.

As he strode across the grassy plain, the weight of the animal warm and heavy around his neck, Murtagh again saw the stone cell where Galbatorix had kept Thorn imprisoned. The chamber had been long but narrow, with murder holes cut in the ceiling. Too large and cold and unfriendly of a place for a hatchling, but there Galbatorix had placed Thorn all the same and anchored him to the floor with chains of iron. Small ones at first, to match Thorn's size, but bigger and bigger ones thereafter, until the links were as thick about as a man's torso and too weighty in their combined mass for even a dragon many times Thorn's age to lift. Whenever he moved, the chains made a harsh and horrible sound. Many a night Murtagh had lain awake in his own cell, listening for the distinctive *clink*.

At first his heart ached for Thorn's isolation. It was a cruel thing to put a small creature into such a hostile place, and he could not comfort Thorn with his thoughts, for the king and his servants kept them under constant mental watch (and ofttimes outright assault). But the space was not overly large for long. Thorn's magically augmented growth meant the cell soon became cramped, and the walls kept him from spreading his wings, and the bony knuckles on the fingers that extended through his flight membranes rubbed raw against the rough stones.

Then Murtagh felt for Thorn's confinement more than his isolation. He often heard him throwing himself against the walls and chains in a futile attempt to escape, panicked thrashings punctuated by roars and growls that turned to pained whines when the guards came and jabbed spears through the murder holes or else dumped buckets of slop onto Thorn's sides, forcing him to lick the leavings off his scales.

It was no way to keep an adult dragon, much less a hatchling. A child by any measure. To spend the first few months of your life in such a fashion . . .

Murtagh clenched his jaw and quickened his pace as a familiar rage flared within him. At times, he fantasized about finding a spell that would let him bring Galbatorix back to life so that he could kill him again. But not by imposing understanding. With the sharp edge of his sword so that the man might feel the full, agonizing force of Murtagh's fury.

But it would not be enough. For revenge could not fix what the king had broken.

As Thorn had grown, he had become increasingly reluctant to return to his cell whenever Galbatorix saw fit to release him. So much so that Thorn would break into frantic, frenzied fits at the sight of the guards. He would whip his tail and snap and claw and make every attempt to escape. The sight was inspiring at first but then piteous when the king would, with a few words, reduce the dragon to a cowering heap mewling in pain.

Yet the punishment was not enough to overcome Thorn's dread of close spaces, and day by day, his aversion became ever deeper until it was an instinctual reaction.

Murtagh had only realized the full extent of the problem after

Galbatorix posted them to Dras-Leona during the war and Thorn grew frightened while walking amid the city's narrow streets. The dragon had destroyed four houses and wounded several soldiers in his sudden effort to win free.

Murtagh had hoped that their travels might help, that by avoiding cities and towns and keeping to open places, Thorn's fear would abate. And perhaps it still would, but it was going to be a slow process. If even it were possible.

He shuddered and looked to the sky for strength. He wished things had been different. But the past couldn't be changed, and the hurts they had suffered would be a part of them forevermore.

~~~~~~~~~~~~~~~ ❖ ~~~~~~~~~~~~~~~

Thorn lifted his head as Murtagh trudged up the hill and dropped the deer onto the ground in front of him.

Thorn sniffed the carcass. *Thank you.*

"Of course. Eat."

Murtagh went to the saddlebags and retrieved a waterskin. He drank and watched as Thorn seized the doe, ripped it apart, and swallowed each piece nearly without chewing.

Going to Ilirea and Nasuada was out of the question now. Admitting as much pained Murtagh, but after Thorn's razing of Gil'ead, he couldn't see how Nasuada could accept them into her court. Popular opinion would force her to deal with them harshly, and while Murtagh would have submitted to whatever punishment she deemed appropriate, he wasn't willing to subject Thorn to possible confinement. Or worse.

No. His letter to Nasuada would have to suffice, and he had to believe that she would have the wherewithal to navigate the dangers that beset her. He comforted himself with the knowledge that she was more cunning and capable than most.

Still, it was difficult to accept the change in his and Thorn's situation. For one shining moment, he had thought another path lay before them. But now Murtagh realized it had been an impossible dream. They would never be able to clear their name and attain a position of good standing among the peoples of the land. That way was forever closed.

Would Nasuada think they had turned against her? He hated to imagine her feeling betrayed. The public accounts of their escape from Gil'ead would confirm the worst aspects of his and Thorn's reputation. He could only hope that his letter would help Nasuada to understand that more was at play than was first apparent.

Murtagh drank again.

He wondered if perhaps it would be better to take Thorn farther east, to Mount Arngor, where Eragon and Saphira had established the new home of the Dragon Riders. There, Thorn would be able to live with others of his kind, far from any places where he might cause more harm. And he could receive such instruction from elves and Eldunarí as had been traditional for dragons in their order, and which Galbatorix had denied Thorn.

But Murtagh didn't want to give up. Bachel needed dealing with. And he didn't want to give Eragon the satisfaction of acknowledging his authority. Most of all, Murtagh didn't want to admit to the world that he or Thorn needed anyone else's help. His stance was sheer stubborn pride, but he could not bring himself to show their weakness to the world. Weakness was dangerous; weakness allowed others to hurt and exploit you. Weakness was the first step on the path to death.

Thorn sensed something of what he was thinking, for he said, *I will go where you want to go. As long as we are together, I am content.*

Murtagh nodded and stoppered the waterskin. "That's good, because we can't stay here or anywhere in Nasuada's realm."

I am sorry.

Murtagh avoided Thorn's gaze and did his best to bury his discomfort. "It is what it is." He replaced the waterskin in the bag. "Still, we're outcasts now, even more than before. Exiles. We'll have to stick to the wilds, keep our distance from settled spaces."

We can fly together from here on? Just us? No more anthill cities?

"Yes, we can fly together. And no more cities."

Thorn swallowed the deer's head and licked clean his chops. Having eaten, he seemed calmer, more alert. *What of you? Tell me of Gil'ead. How went things with Silna and Carabel? And how did you end up caught in a tangle box?*

"I got careless," said Murtagh. He started pulling from the bags what he needed for his own dinner. He would have to do some hunting for himself if he wanted anything to eat tomorrow.

As he worked, he shared his memories with Thorn, starting with how he'd gained admittance to Captain Wren's company. When he came to the arcane garden and explained to Thorn about the Ra'zac egg, the dragon snorted with enough force to singe the ground with a finger of flame from each nostril.

Vermin! I had hoped we had seen the last of them.

"I know," said Murtagh. He blew on the newly birthed flame of the fire he was building. "Eragon did the land a favor when he rid us of them."

The priests of Helgrind will be seeking to restore the Ra'zac to their previous glory.

At that, Murtagh gave a short laugh. "I can't see how they could. Soon there will be dragons throughout Alagaësia. No Lethrblaka could survive here." The Lethrblaka were the adult form of the Ra'zac: hideous flying monsters more akin to bats than dragons.

A Ra'zac might still work plenty of mischief before reaching full growth. Especially if a magician forces it to serve their will.

For a moment, Murtagh contemplated returning to Gil'ead with the express purpose of destroying the Ra'zac egg, but then he berated himself for the stupidity of the idea. Aside from the danger, Captain Wren or Arven would surely have moved everything of value from the chambers under the barracks.

He patted the pouch along his belt. The compendium was still there, as was—when he reached farther down—the yellow diamond hidden in the corner of his cloak.

The fire flared higher, and he continued with his memories. It wasn't long before he arrived at his confrontation with Arven, Esvar, and the rest of the guards, and Thorn tasted his regret at the outcome of the fight.

Dry grass and the stems of withered thistles snapped under Thorn's feet as he moved over and nuzzled his shoulder. *You did what you had to. No one died. Tormenting yourself won't help.*

Nothing in life is easy, said Murtagh with his thoughts, for the sound of his voice seemed unbearably harsh.

Why should it be? Life is a fight from start to finish.

A grim smile crossed Murtagh's mouth, and he patted Thorn. *And it's better to win than to lose.* The crimson fire in Thorn's eyes deepened. They understood each other.

Murtagh resumed his review, and at the end of it, he said, "I want to find this witch-woman Bachel even more than before. And I want to know what these Dreamers are about." He smashed two more turnips with the rock he was holding. He wished he'd managed to find a knife to replace his dagger before leaving Gil'ead. "Whatever they're planning, it's more dire than I feared."

Thorn hissed, and his tongue darted out between his scaled jaws. *And you still don't wish to warn Eragon or Arya?*

Murtagh dropped the smashed turnips into the pot hung over the campfire. The thought of begging Eragon for help made him want to spit. Especially since he knew Eragon *would* help. That was the worst of it. "If Nasuada wants to inform them of the situation, that's her prerogative. However, it would take too long for either of them to join us, and in any case . . . I want to deal with this ourselves. If we can. Blast it, we don't even know what's actually going on! Until we do, I say we stay the course."

A sense of agreement emanated from Thorn. Then a low cough sounded in his chest, and his tongue lolled from between his jaws.

"What?" Murtagh asked.

The dragon showed both rows of teeth. *A thought occurred to me. Carabel did you a greater favor than you realize.*

"How do you figure?"

She saved you from having to treat with Ilenna. A great boon, that.

Murtagh stared at him for a second and then started to chuckle. With a wry twist of his head, he said, "You might have a point. . . ." Then he grew grim again as he looked into the flickering flames.

What is it?

He shrugged, keeping his gaze on the fire. "I just wish I'd known to include something about Lyreth and his kind in my letter. I'm sure Nasuada suspects they're working against her, but forewarned is forearmed."

Could you use a spell to warn her?

Murtagh scrubbed the dirt with his boot, pensive. "Probably not. Urû'b— *Ilirea* is too far away for magic, easy magic that is, and Nasuada is sure to have wards protecting her against such intrusions. I could hire a courier, but I wouldn't trust a stranger with this information."

Thorn touched his shoulder again, and Murtagh forced a small smile. He scratched Thorn's cheek, and the dragon huffed. *We head north, then?*

He nodded. "Back to the Bay of Fundor. We'll follow the Spine up along the coast until we find the village Carabel spoke of."

And then?

Murtagh pounded another turnip with the rock. "And then we'll see what Bachel has to say for herself."

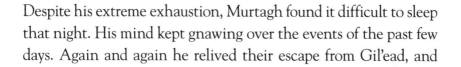

Despite his extreme exhaustion, Murtagh found it difficult to sleep that night. His mind kept gnawing over the events of the past few days. Again and again he relived their escape from Gil'ead, and he questioned what he could have done to avoid such a disastrous outcome. Images of Esvar and the field of drowned soldiers continued to bedevil him, and the faces of Silna and the two brothers from the Rusty Anchor rose up before him. The center of his brow burned, and he thought too of Essie and of the stone room beneath the barracks and the rank smell of fear.

When sleep finally took him, he dreamt of empty castles and locked doors and footsteps chasing him down endless corridors. And he heard his father's voice echo overhead with dreadful intent, followed by a remembered touch upon his cheek, soft and loving, and his mother saying, *"Beautiful boy. My beautiful boy."*

Then visions of battle filled his slumbering mind: Glaedr and Oromis over Gil'ead, swords clashing upon the Burning Plains, soldiers dying at his command, banners and pennants whipping in the wind, the smell of blood and fire, and water in his nose and throat choking him as he struggled with Muckmaw.

Thank you, whispered Silna, but he felt no relief, no absolution, and the nightmares dragged him further down, down, down to the cells beneath Urû'baen, where Galbatorix had bent and broken him, and throughout, he heard the growls and cries of Thorn, of his dragon, his beautiful, newly hatched dragon, suffering in the chamber near his.

❖

With morning came frost, and it took Murtagh a good hour or so to warm up enough to face the day. He was sore, and tired too, and the fibers of his being were frayed from use.

After a cup of elderberry tea, he practiced with Zar'roc, and the exercise helped clear his mind and focus his thoughts. And not just his, Thorn's too. How one of them felt had a large effect on the other, and Murtagh was determined to do everything he could to shore up Thorn's fortitude.

When he finished with his forms, he and Thorn left their

belongings at camp and descended from the hill to a copse of birchwood trees standing along a trickle of a stream.

Murtagh entered first. He walked backward into the copse, feeling with his heels to avoid tripping and keeping his eyes on Thorn the whole while. Once he was a good thirty paces into the stand, he held out his hands.

"To me."

A dry rustle as Thorn shuffled his wings. He shook himself, and his scales prickled along his glittering length. Then he took a tentative step forward, so his head was just under the reach of the leafless trees. The branches groaned under the influence of a passing breeze.

Thorn stiffened, and Murtagh said again, in a soft voice, "To me." He smiled for Thorn's benefit. "You can do it."

The weight of Thorn's forefoot crushed dozens of frost-shriveled leaves as he took another step forward. And another.

"That's it," Murtagh whispered. If Thorn could break his fear but once, Murtagh knew he could build off that triumph, and the fear would decrease with every success.

As Thorn's hunched shoulders moved between the pale trunks, the dragon tensed even further. He dropped into a low crouch and dug his talons into the loam, and the tip of his tail whistled as it swung through the air.

"Don't stop."

Thorn refused to meet Murtagh's gaze. He could feel the rising tide of panic swallowing the dragon's mind, and he fought it with soothing thoughts, but he might as well have tried to beat back the actual sea.

"Try!" commanded Murtagh, his tone suddenly hard. Where enticement would not work, perhaps ferocity would serve. "Now! Don't think about it!"

An anguished roar escaped Thorn, and he lurched forward on stiff legs, as a wounded animal might, and in his haste, his head brushed a low-hanging branch. Blinding fear swept the dragon's mind with such strength it sent a bolt through Murtagh's temples. He cried out and dropped to one knee even as Thorn thrashed and wriggled back out of the copse.

Thorn sat on the open ground, shivering and blinking. His jaws were open, and he panted as if from a desperate run. Then he lifted his snout and loosed a mournful howl that sounded so lonesome and eerie, the entirety of Murtagh's skin crawled.

I cannot, said Thorn. *My legs seize up, and I cannot move. It is as if a spell grips me, and I feel as if I will die.*

With an effort, Murtagh got back to his feet and, with slow steps, made his way to Thorn. "They're just emotions. Emotions aren't *you.*" He tapped Thorn's foreleg. "You can feel them, you can let them pass through you, but who *you* are doesn't change. Remember that. Remember the parts of your true name that describe the best parts of you and hold to them."

Thorn lowered his head in acknowledgment. *The doing of it is difficult.*

"It always is." Murtagh gestured at the stand of birchwood trees. "Again. Now."

Fear and uncertainty flickered at the back of Thorn's gaze as he regarded Murtagh, but then he drew himself up with a proud arch to his neck, and a puff of smoke swirled from his nostrils. *For you.*

As before, Murtagh backed into the copse, and as before, Thorn attempted to follow. The red dragon managed to force himself a few feet farther than on his first attempt, but then his nerve broke and he had to retreat. So strong were Thorn's memories of imprisonment that, for an instant, they overwhelmed Murtagh's mind, and the dungeons of Urû'baen appeared before him, as seen through Thorn's eyes. That and the dragon's visceral aversion were enough to drive Murtagh out from among the trees himself.

They took a few moments to collect themselves. Murtagh's heart was beating uncomfortably fast.

Then they tried once more with similar results.

"Enough," said Murtagh, laying a hand on Thorn's neck. The dragon was coiled into a tight knot upon the matted grass, panting and shivering as if with ague. It was still morning, and they were already wrung out.

They were both uncommonly quiet as they returned to camp and prepared to leave.

Only once Murtagh had packed up and was performing a final check on the rigging of Thorn's saddle did the dragon say, *Tomorrow, I will find another stand of trees.*

Murtagh paused with a half-fastened buckle in his hand. He finished securing it. "I'll help you." And a sense of shared determination passed between them.

Before climbing into the saddle, Murtagh wetted a scrap of cloth and wiped the sweat from his face and under his arms. He would have preferred a proper bath, but the nearby stream was too small to fit in.

"Shall we?" he asked, rinsing and wringing out the cloth.

Thorn stretched the fingers of his wings and shook them, as if to rid himself of nervous energy. *The winds are changing. We will have to dance about the clouds.*

Murtagh clambered up Thorn's side and into the saddle. As he cinched the straps around his legs, he took one last look at the peaceful expanse of grasslands and nodded. "Then let us dance. No, let us *hunt*."

And Thorn growled with approval.

CHAPTER XVII

✦ ✦ ✦ ✦ ✦ ✦ ✦

Exile

While Thorn flew and the land rolled past below, Murtagh let his mind wander. His natural inclination was to think—to endlessly turn over all that was, had been, and could be—but he fought the urge. *No remembering!* Rather, he found solace in existence without contemplation. It was a simple pleasure, perhaps the simplest of all, and yet no less profound.

High above the ground, the air was chill, and his lashes froze together if he blinked slower than normal. Murtagh used a spell to buffer the wind in front of him, to slow the loss of heat from his body. Thorn needed no such protection; his scales were sufficient guard.

From the grasslands northeast of Gil'ead, Thorn flew back across Isenstar Lake and started to follow the Ninor River northwest toward the Spine.

They made good time, but Murtagh worried that events were outpacing them, and he was likewise concerned that Du Vrangr Gata, or even the elves, were hunting him and Thorn. Unless Carabel had abilities as yet unsuspected, it would take some days for his letter to reach Nasuada. Until then, Nasuada, Arya, and Eragon—all of whom had no doubt already received word of the fight at Gil'ead—would assume the worst. Eragon and Arya might even be so alarmed, Murtagh belatedly realized, as to set out in pursuit. He half expected them to contact him, and every time he felt a touch on his mind, he fought the urge to flinch. But always it was Thorn, and the dragon said, *You are as twitchy as a mountain cat bitten by too many fleas.*

Don't talk to me about cats.

The land beneath them was beautiful, and Murtagh found himself wishing that they could ignore the concerns of queens and kings and live according to their own devices, just as Thorn had wanted. Whether that meant settling in one place—with magic as his tool, he could raise a hut or a palace, whichever suited his fancy—or searching the skies like an albatross set to wander all its days.

But in his heart, he knew neither option would work. *No one truly lives apart. We are all connected.* And ignoring their responsibilities, *his* responsibilities, would only lead to regret.

That evening, they made camp by a stand of poplar near the banks of the river. Murtagh went hunting with a pebble and spell and quickly collected a brace of hares and a large blue-footed duck that was foolish enough to swim past.

Before he started a fire and fixed himself dinner, he and Thorn went to the stand of poplar, and Thorn again attempted to enter among the trees.

In this, he was more successful than before, for the poplar were sparsely grown and Thorn had greater room about his head and sides. But in the end, the same fear caused him to freeze and then retreat, and Murtagh did not count the undertaking as much of an improvement.

The exercise furthered their end-of-day tiredness, and they spoke little through the rest of the evening.

After eating, Murtagh banked the fire and sat with his back against Thorn. For a time, he stared moodily at one of the gold crowns he'd received from Wren. Then he took up the dictionary he'd stolen and read from it while the sun set and clouds of gnats rose swarming from the treetops.

~~~~~~~~~~~~~~~~~~~ ❖ ~~~~~~~~~~~~~~~~~~~

On the morning of the second day, while Murtagh waited for what remained of the duck to finish heating, he again returned to the compendium. The words it contained represented an incredible opportunity—potential, in fact—and he found himself constantly thinking of ideas for new spells.

This time, instead of picking up from where he had left off, he flipped through the compendium at random, taking in a word here, a word there.

His gaze landed upon one in particular. *"Deyja,"* he murmured. He looked at the definition. His eyes widened. "To die. To stop living."

Thorn snorted. *A dangerous word, that.*

"Indeed," said Murtagh softly. He felt rather awed by the word. Such a simple one, and yet so profound. Galbatorix would never have dared teach it to him. In truth, *deyja* likely wasn't that useful. Murtagh guessed that most magicians would have a ward that would block its effects. And yet to see it, to *know* it, felt significant, as if he had surmounted a spire built over a measureless void.

He wondered what the word for *life* was.

He kept reading, hoping to find it. Instead, he chanced upon the word *naina*. "To make bright. Light without fire. See also *líjothsa*." He turned to the entry for *líjothsa* and read: "Light as the thing itself. See also *naina*."

His brow furrowed as he parsed the difference. Then his thoughts shifted to the light-emitting quartz he'd encountered within the catacombs and also the difficulty he'd had illuminating Isenstar Lake while in the water. Fire was a poor choice for underwater light; it created too many bubbles and too much steam.

Murtagh glanced up. The morning sky was clear and bright, filled with a seemingly endless pool of sunlit radiance. *What if . . .* The spell that he used to hide Thorn from observers worked—as best he could tell—by thickening the air underneath the dragon's body so that it bent the light around him, similar to how a lens of polished glass might.

Perhaps he could modify the spell to gather light from a large area around them and concentrate it on a single spot, to use in place of a lantern or to store for later need.

On a whim, he poured some water into his battered tin plate and then cleared his mind, chose the needed words from the ancient language—the spell was awkward, but he thought it would do what he wanted—and said, "Vindr thrysta un líjothsa athaerum," with the intent of focusing the light onto the plate.

BAM!

A flash as bright as the sun exploded in front of him, a crack of thunder echoed across the plain, and a cloud of cinders and superheated steam blasted outward. Murtagh felt the heat against his face as he fell backward, his wards activating.

Thorn let out a startled roar and reared up, spreading his wings. A tongue of red flame flickered in his mouth.

With some dismay, Murtagh saw their campfire blasted to bits: pieces of smoldering embers lay scattered in every direction, and the ground was blackened. Wisps of smoke curled up from patches of dry grass. The pan with his bacon was folded in half, the bacon itself lost somewhere in the dirt.

Cursing, Murtagh ran about and stomped out the cinders before they could start a wildfire.

What did you do? Thorn asked, his wings still slightly raised.

"I'm not sure. It was just *light!*" Then Murtagh explained what he had been trying to accomplish. He shook his head. "I definitely won't use *that* spell again unless it's at a distance."

A long distance.

"Agreed."

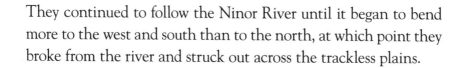

They continued to follow the Ninor River until it began to bend more to the west and south than to the north, at which point they broke from the river and struck out across the trackless plains.

Not for the first time, it occurred to Murtagh how empty Alagaësia was. For all the efforts of humans, dwarves, and elves, vast swaths of the land remained unsettled, undeveloped, and uncivilized. Part of him preferred it that way. If all the world were as cramped as Ilirea or Dras-Leona, there would be no place for those who didn't belong.

In early afternoon, Murtagh composed a stanza that he particularly liked:

Atop the tower a hollow man,
Shell of shadow, void within,
Bound by words, a villain's blade.
A name of shame, a fear of fate.
Break the bond, change the path,
The shell remains, a haunting shade.

By evening, the Spine had faded into sight far ahead of them as a line of purple jags propped against the reddened sky.

Their camp that night felt terribly alone. The land was flat, with few ridges or washes and thus nowhere to hide. Despite the lack of cover, they shared a sense of relief at the absence of copses, caves, or other enclosures. Thorn more so than Murtagh, but they were both glad to have a break, if only for a day, from Thorn's fear of narrow spaces.

They made their own shelter beneath Thorn's wing, and Murtagh amused the dragon by singing songs from court, and he even danced a step or two for Thorn's benefit.

And that was the second day.

On the third day, the eerie howls of a wolf pack woke them before sunrise. The wolves were loping across the grasslands some miles to the south, and their baying carried with surprising volume and clarity through the still morning air. Even at that distance, Murtagh could see how large the animals were; they must have been twice the size of a mastiff, with tawny coats and long, thick tails.

Shall I answer them? Thorn asked.

"If you want," said Murtagh with a smile.

Then Thorn raised his head and made a passable imitation of a wolf howl, only far louder, and far more menacing.

The pack yipped with fear, and thereafter ran in silence.

Murtagh laughed and patted Thorn.

It is good for them to know they are not the only hunters about, said Thorn, self-satisfied.

Despite an annoying side wind, they arrived at the edge of the plains late that morning, and the land rose into foothills and then the steep heights of the Spine. A dusting of snow extended halfway down the sides of the mountains, and the pinetrees glittered as if strewn with diamonds.

A band of silver water lay athwart their path, and Murtagh knew it for the Anora River, which flowed northward to the Bay of Fundor. He directed Thorn to follow the river upstream, deeper into the mountains.

Thorn did so without question; the dragon was as curious as Murtagh.

The Anora led them to a pinched mountain pass that stood at the mouth of a long, deep-set valley. Atop the mountain to the left of the pass was a ruined watchtower built in the elven style, with no path or road that led to its dark walls, and Murtagh knew it and spoke its name in the ancient language: Ristvak'baen, or Place of Sorrow. He felt both sorrow and revulsion, for it was there, in that tower, that Galbatorix had slain Vrael, leader of the Riders, following the great battle on Vroengard Island. That event, more than any, had marked the Riders' downfall.

Galbatorix had bragged of the fight more than once. Murtagh could see him still, sprawled across the fur-draped chair in his banquet hall, his harsh, eagle-like features lit by the flames from the

303

long fireplace set within one wall, eyes burning with unsavory delight as he recounted how he had felled Vrael with a kick betwixt the legs.

An urge came over Murtagh, and before he could speak it, Thorn responded, banking leftward and spiraling down to a flat rooftop alongside the ruined tower.

The presence of the rooftop was most convenient, Murtagh thought. Then he felt foolish. The tower had been built by and for Dragon Riders. Of course it would have a place for a dragon to land.

Stone scraped under Thorn's talons as he settled onto Ristvak'baen. Murtagh hoped the structure was still sound. It had held for over a hundred years; surely it could hold a few minutes more.

He dismounted, and he and Thorn looked up at the crumbling tower. A human-sized archway pierced the outer wall of the building and led to a small courtyard.

Murtagh walked through.

Patches of moss and lichen mottled the stones of the courtyard, while tufts of dead grass poked up between the joins. A stunted juniper grew from a crack in the wall higher up, its trunk a withered twist of creviced wood, and a desolate wind shook the branches. Snow clung to the corners of the yard where shadows shielded it from direct light. A single doorway gaped in the side of the tower, hinges warped, broken, rusted black.

A circle of twelve brass sockets lay embedded within the stones in the center of the yard. The sockets were each the size of a fist and as eyeless and empty as a skull. Waxy verdigris colored them green. What they had once held, Murtagh could not guess.

Behind him, Thorn hesitated and then, with a soft growl, crouched low to the rooftop and stuck his head and neck into the courtyard. His whole body was tense with strain—his lips wrinkled to show teeth—but he didn't retreat. Murtagh counted that as a small improvement.

He continued to study the yard. No evidence remained of

the fight between Galbatorix and Vrael. The place was cold and empty, devoid of all comfort, and the rattle of dry branches reminded him of a rattle of bones.

Thorn scented the air. *It is strange to think how much turned upon their meeting here.*

Heat poured through Murtagh's limbs, like a flood of molten wax. His jaw clenched, and his fists also, and tears dripped from his unblinking eyes. The surge of emotion was so sudden, so strong and unexpected, he shouted from surprise. Then he shouted again out of sheer blind rage.

Thorn flinched, but Murtagh didn't care.

He howled at the empty sky. Howled and screamed until his voice broke and blood slicked the back of his throat. The paving stones bruised his knees as he fell forward and hung his head like a whipped dog.

With one gloved fist, he pounded at the stones of the courtyard. Sharp pains lanced the bone in the heel of his palm, and great hollow *booms* echoed through the tower, as if his fist were a mallet made of iron.

A growl tore his throat, and he slapped his palm flat against the stones. "Jierda!"

With a deafening report, cracks spiderwebbed out from his hand and split the paving stones throughout the yard. Ribbons of dust drifted up from the exposed rock faces, and one of the brass sockets fell free of its setting.

Spent, Murtagh collapsed onto the broken stones and buried his face in a fold of his cloak.

The wind clawed at the sides of the tower.

Thorn's mind was a warm presence against his own, but the dragon said nothing, only watched and waited.

After a long while, Murtagh lifted his head and pushed himself back onto his knees. His cloak pooled around him in ripples of dark wool, and the sharp edges of the cracked stones cut into his shins.

He wiped his eyes with the back of a gloved hand.

"All this," he said, his voice harsh and stark in the thin air. He coughed. "All this because the Riders didn't kill Galbatorix when they had the chance. If they had—"

You would not have been born.

"Then maybe someone else would have had a better opportunity at life."

Thorn snarled and leaned forward, as if to crawl into the courtyard, but a tremor racked him, and he sank back on his haunches. *Do not say that. Never say that! Do you not want to be joined with me?*

The question cut through Murtagh's grim introspection like a razor through silk. "Of course I do. That's not what I meant."

Then say what you mean. I chose to hatch for you, Murtagh. I do not wish for another.

The dragon's fierce earnestness sobered Murtagh. "I'm sorry. You're right. I spoke without thinking. I was feeling bad for myself. It's an unfortunate habit."

Very.

"Why *did* you hatch for me?" In all their time together, Murtagh had never thought to ask.

Thorn blinked. *I was tired of waiting to emerge, and I could feel that we were a proper fit. That, and you had none of Galbatorix's madness.*

"I'm sorry I couldn't protect you better."

Now you are feeling bad for yourself again. You did as well as anyone could have and better than most.

"Mmh." Murtagh slowly got to his feet and gave Thorn a rub on his snout.

Thorn hummed and pressed against Murtagh's hand. *We survived. That is what matters.*

"I still wish we could fly back through the years and help Vrael."

Then everyone everywhere would do the same with their own regrets, and the world would be unmade.

"I suppose that's true." He eyed the cracked stones with some ruefulness. He hoped the tower wouldn't fall. "I'm going to look inside. I'll be quick."

Watch for traps. Thorn retracted his head and neck from the yard and turned to look upon the valley.

Murtagh cautiously stepped through the doorway at the base of the tower. A short, dark hall lay before him, the stone floor crusted with dirt and twigs and leaves and withered grass gathered in tangles along the corners.

From there, he made a pass through the interior of the tower—what he could access of it, that was. Fallen stone blocked several of the doorways. The rooms were dry, dead, and deserted. Some of the furniture remained: wooden chairs brittle to the touch, an iron poker leaning against the kitchen fireplace, the rotted frame of a narrow bed.

Down a flight of narrow stairs, on the floor of what he guessed had been a storage room, he found a dented brass goblet decorated with fine tracery that could only have been the work of an elven artisan. The metal was frigid against Murtagh's gloved fingers as he picked it up. He turned the goblet in his hand, studying it, wondering whom it had belonged to and what things it had seen through the long years.

On an impulse, he kept the goblet as he climbed the narrow staircase back up to the courtyard.

Thorn's tail whipped from side to side as Murtagh joined him on the flat-topped roof.

"A relic from another age," Murtagh said as he held up the goblet for Thorn to sniff. "I think I'll keep it. This cup can be the first treasure of House Murtagh. How does that sound?"

Thorn gave him a dubious look. *What about Zar'roc?*

"A curse, not a treasure." Murtagh bounced the goblet in his hand and then went to the saddlebags and unbuckled one.

Perhaps you can forge a new history for the blade, said Thorn.

Murtagh tucked the goblet beneath his bedroll and closed up

the saddlebag. "It would take an era and a half to balance out all the misdeeds done with Zar'roc." He walked back around to face Thorn.

Then I will have to make sure you live a long, long while, said Thorn, a twinkle in his ruby eyes.

"Are you sure? That sounds like a burdensome task."

Thorn huffed, and the twinkle brightened. *Very sure.*

"Mmh," said Murtagh, but he was touched. He turned and looked out over the valley. "So this is where they came from." Palancar Valley: home to Eragon . . . and their mother. The place where she had returned to give birth to Eragon, far from Morzan and the Empire.

It looks like a good place to hunt.

Some distance from Ristvak'baen, a small town was visible next to the Anora River. Therinsford, Murtagh guessed, if his memories of what Eragon had told him about the valley were accurate.

He climbed back onto Thorn and secured his legs. "Ready."

Hold on!

With a mighty leap, Thorn launched himself into the air. Then he climbed several hundred feet above the mountain peaks, where the air was thin and it was unlikely anyone below would hear the beat of his wings.

Murtagh watched with a fixed gaze as the valley unfolded beneath them. It was as much family history as geography. If events had played out only a little differently, Palancar Valley would have been his home, same as for Eragon. He wondered what it had been like to grow up in such an isolated place.

It made him wish he could talk to his mother, ask her about her childhood and her reasons for abandoning Palancar Valley to follow Morzan into the wider world. And also why, *why*, she had chosen to save Eragon from Morzan but not him, her eldest son. Had it been a matter of ability and opportunity or one of preference? The question had tormented him from the moment he'd learned of his relation to Eragon. How could a mother sacrifice one child for another?

How? It was true that Eragon had been in mortal danger. He was not Morzan's son, and had Morzan discovered the truth . . . Murtagh shuddered to imagine his wrath. So there was that. Still, Murtagh couldn't help but wonder if it had been choice rather than necessity that kept his mother from bringing him to Palancar Valley.

What was worse, to see Eragon hailed as the hero of the age made Murtagh fear that she'd been *right* to choose Eragon, and that there was some irreparable wrongness or inadequacy in himself, some flaw that their mother had perceived in him.

Perhaps it was the scar on his back. He was marked by Morzan's darkness in a manner that Eragon never had been.

Gently, Thorn said, *You do not know her reasons or situation. And regardless, I chose you.*

The words softened Murtagh's mood and dispelled some of his bitterness, though it lingered like a poisonous pool at the back of his mind. He scratched the scales along Thorn's spine and leaned forward to give the dragon a quick embrace.

Then he sat tall in the saddle and strove to bury his dark contemplations.

Halfway through the valley, Murtagh saw what he was looking for: a burnt husk of a farmhouse standing near the river, perhaps a day's walk from Therinsford. A chill crept down his back, for he knew he was looking at the house where Eragon had lived and that the Ra'zac had burned after questioning—or rather, *torturing*—his uncle Garrow.

So much from so little, said Thorn.

Indeed.

Murtagh was surprised the farm was still abandoned. He'd thought that Roran or one of the other villagers from Carvahall would have rebuilt it.

Lifting his gaze, he saw Carvahall itself, nestled between river and foothills at the northern end of Palancar Valley. The village looked different than Murtagh expected. A thick wood palisade surrounded a cluster of thatched cottages, rustic and newly raised amid the sooty outlines of what Murtagh realized must have been the original village, before Galbatorix's forces had razed it. The thought was an uncomfortable reminder of his and Thorn's actions in Gil'ead. The western flank of Carvahall butted against the Anora, and a sturdy bridge extended across the rushing water. On the far side, a wide, rutted path led to a tall hill that overlooked the rest of the valley, and upon the crown of the hill were the stone foundations and partially built walls of what appeared to be a small castle.

With his mind, Murtagh drew Thorn's attention to the unfinished castle. *It seems Eragon's cousin has been busy. He learned the hard way that safety can only be ensured through force of arms.*

Roran is your cousin as well.

Mmm. I wonder how similar we really are.

Thorn angled downward slightly. *Do you wish to land?*

Murtagh nearly said yes. He did want to talk with Roran and meet his family—he had a baby daughter, or so Murtagh had heard—for they were Murtagh's only remaining relatives, aside from Eragon. But if they did, there would be shouting and pointing of weapons and all sorts of difficult emotions. Even imagining it was exhausting.

You could go by yourself, said Thorn. And Murtagh knew how much it cost the dragon to suggest such a thing after the events of Ceunon and Gil'ead.

No . . . no, I think not. But thank you. If nothing else, he didn't want to take the time. Visiting Carvahall would delay them by at least a day, probably more, and Murtagh felt an increasing urgency to find the witch-woman Bachel.

"Someday," he muttered as Carvahall and the unfinished castle passed under them. Someday he and Roran would have a reckoning. Even though they'd never met, the bonds of blood could not be ignored.

Murtagh took one last look over the full scope of Palancar Valley, doing his best to remember every detail of the place where his mother had grown up, and Eragon too. A lonely pain formed in his heart, and then he turned his back on the vista and held on to Thorn even tighter.

Palancar Valley was the last large valley they saw. Thereafter, the mountains grew closer together and only allowed for small rifts and gaps between their forested flanks: narrow, deeply shadowed vales where, during the winter months, the sun never touched the bottom.

As they flew, Murtagh had a sense they were leaving behind the last vestiges of civilization. As rough and isolated as Carvahall was, it at least shared some connection with the rest of Nasuada's realm. Now they were entering lands that belonged to no country or race.

By late afternoon, the Bay of Fundor was visible to their right, butted up against the edge of the Spine. The mountains plunged to the water's edge, with hardly a buffer of open land, and the air acquired the taste of salt, and the cries of gulls and terns followed them along the jagged range.

Look for a wharf or a jetty. Any sort of building, said Murtagh, even though he knew they were probably still several days away from the village they sought.

Thorn coughed in agreement.

Before long, a harsh wind sprang up from the north, and Thorn's flight slowed until they were barely moving relative to the ground.

Enough, said Murtagh, and Thorn descended to a small island— no more than a hundred feet across—just off the shore. There they camped, and the wind bore down on them with unrelenting ferocity while flurries of snow obscured the mountains.

By morning, the clouds had vanished.

We should make haste, said Thorn. *The weather will not last.*

~~~~~~~~~~~~~~~~~ ❖ ~~~~~~~~~~~~~~~~~

Whitecapped water to the right, mountains beneath and to the left. A domed expanse of sky ahead. The landscape was beautiful and forbidding in equal measure, and Murtagh felt the loneliness of their position with physical force.

He kept an eye on the bay, but no ships appeared. If anyone were making the trip to visit Bachel, they were steering well away from the bay's western shore.

That day they saw great numbers of wildlife along the edge of the bay. Vast herds of bugling red elk, the animals far larger than those Murtagh had hunted on the plains by Gil'ead. Giant brown bears that trundled their solitary way through the forest. Packs of shaggy grey wolves. Hawks that screamed, and ravens and crows that cawed, and fish vultures that wheeled above the shallows and occasionally dove for the silvery bergenhed that darted through the leaden water.

Even high in the air, Murtagh felt the need to stay alert. The mountains were stark and savage, and the slightest mistake might cost them their lives, despite all their strength, spells, and experience. It was not lost on him or Thorn that Galbatorix's first dragon, Jarnunvösk, had died in the frozen reaches of the Spine.

I understand now why the Riders warned Galbatorix against venturing so far, Murtagh said.

He and Jarnunvösk were not alone, were they?

No, two others went with them. Riders both, all of the same age. Galbatorix was their leader. Always he craved power, and always it was his undoing.

A slow beat of Thorn's wings punctuated their conversation. The dragon said, *Did Galbatorix ever tell you why they flew north?*

Murtagh snorted. *For the daring of it, I believe. To show their mettle, despite their elders' disapproval.*

A sorrowful cast darkened Thorn's mind. *And so they paid the price of their folly.*

We all did.

It was Urgals who attacked them upon the ice, was it not?

Murtagh scratched his chin. *So he said. But they must have been skilled and mighty Urgals indeed to overcome three dragons and two Riders. In truth, I've always wondered about it, but Galbatorix was never inclined to answer questions.* He again looked down upon the ridged peaks. For an instant, sympathy flickered within him. *How horrible it must have been to travel all this on foot, alone, and after losing his dragon.*

It would have driven anyone mad, human or dragon.

Just before noon, they spotted threads of smoke rising from a narrow valley deeper in the mountain range. Thorn diverted to investigate, and they saw a small collection of huts—which looked like the hulls of overturned ships—in a meadow by a stream. Tall, multicolored banners hung outside each hut.

"Is that—" Murtagh started to say. But it wasn't the Dreamers. Even as he spoke, a figure emerged from one of the huts. An incredibly tall figure with grey skin and horns that curled about his enormous head.

Urgals, said Thorn with a mental growl.

And a Kull at that. No other Urgals grew as tall. Not one of them stood under eight foot, and many were far larger. Murtagh still found it impressive that the dwarves had been able to hold their own against the gigantic creatures during the Battle of Farthen Dûr.

Murtagh watched with fierce interest as Thorn circled the village, trusting his spell of concealment to keep them hidden. He saw what he took to be Urgal women—a first for him—washing clothes in the stream, and half-naked Urgal children—also a first—running about the meadow, shooting at one another with bows and padded arrows. Several males were chopping wood; others were sparring with staves and spears and clubs.

Both Galbatorix and the Varden had allied themselves with the Urgals over the course of the war, but never during Murtagh's time with either one. Before that, his only interaction with Urgals had come when he'd gone on patrol with Lord Varis's men. A band of Urgals had been raiding the holdings on Varis's estate, and it was thought that a show of force might scare them off. If that failed, their goal was to hunt down and kill the Urgals, and specifically, their chieftain, who was—according to the reports of survivors—violent, ruthless, and given to fits of insanity.

Murtagh had been seventeen and just coming into his strength. He was eager to prove himself and to use the skills Tornac had taught him. (Tornac would have argued against the expedition, but then Tornac had been back in Urû'baen.) So Murtagh convinced Varis to let him accompany his men.

The Urgals had ambushed them by a small stand of firs just outside one of the villages on Varis's lands. The fight had been short, loud, and confusing. In the midst of it, an Urgal had knocked Murtagh out of his saddle. He barely got back to his feet before the brute was upon him, swinging a heavy chopper—more like a sharpened mace than a sword.

Murtagh's shield split, and he knew he had only seconds to live. All his training with a sword was little help against the sheer strength and violence of the Urgal's assault.

But then another Urgal had pulled away the one attacking him, and Murtagh had found himself facing the leader of the band. The chieftain had a crimson banner mounted over his shoulder, and on the banner was stitched a strange black sigil.

The chieftain had smiled a horrible smile; his teeth were sharp and yellow, and his breath stank like that of a carrion eater. Then the rest of the Urgals left their kills and formed a circle around

Murtagh and the chieftain, and they'd shouted and bellowed and beaten their chests as the two of them closed with each other.

Murtagh had known what was expected of him. And he tried. But the chieftain wielded a long-handled ax, and Murtagh did not know how to defend against it. The ax was like the worst parts of a spear and a pike combined, and the Urgal quickly gave Murtagh a cut on his left shoulder, a cracked rib, and another cut on his right thigh. He'd fallen then, and he surely would have died if not for Varis.

The earl had ridden up with another, larger group of soldiers. They had driven the Urgals away, killing many, but not, to Murtagh's regret, the chieftain.

And it had been that same crimson-bannered Urgal who had led the Kull who chased him and Eragon deep into the Beor Mountains. . . .

Murtagh shook himself and brought his attention back to the village below. Ostensibly a treaty had been signed between Urgals, humans, and elves—and indeed, Eragon had even added the Urgals to the pact that joined Riders and dragons (though the thought of an Urgal Rider still gave Murtagh pause). But whether word of the treaty had reached this isolated village was an open question.

How do you think they would react if we showed ourselves? he asked Thorn.

Amusement colored the dragon's thoughts. *They would all want to fight you, to prove themselves.*

Probably. Part of Murtagh was tempted. He held no love for the Urgals—he still had nightmares about the chieftain, and about fighting hordes of Urgals during the Battle of Farthen Dûr—but he *was* curious. If there was one thing the past few years had taught him, it was the importance of knowing and understanding both himself and the world around him. And he didn't feel as if he had a good understanding of the Urgals. Recognizing his own curiosity surprised him. He really *would* be willing to sit down and talk with an Urgal, despite the atrocities they'd committed throughout the land. After all, he'd committed his own share of violence.

At the realization, some of the tension eased from his muscles, and he loosened his grip on the front of the saddle. The Urgals were dangerous enough, it was true, but so were he and Thorn. It did not mean they were not worthy of investigation.

A thread of acrid smoke streamed back from Thorn's nostrils and passed over him. The dragon said, *I would roast them with fire and eat them if they attacked us.*

Eat an Urgal? Really? I can't imagine they would taste very good. Besides, they're not animals.

Thorn snorted and turned back toward the bay. *They are meat. Meat is good.*

Once again, Murtagh was reminded of the differences between them. He made no attempt to hide his revulsion. *Would you eat a human as well?*

Indifference was Thorn's response. *If I did not like them. Why would I not?*

Because it's wrong. You might as well be a Ra'zac, then!

A sharp hiss came from Thorn. *Do not compare me to those foul creatures. I am a dragon, not a carrion picker.*

Then don't act like one. Promise me you won't eat any humans, elves, or Urgals. For my sake.

Hmph. Fine.

It was, Murtagh reflected, not without reason the elves had forged the initial bond between themselves and the dragons. He frowned as he thought of all the dragon eggs Eragon had taken to Mount Arngor. Some of them were enchanted that the younglings inside might bond with Riders, but the rest were wild dragons, unbound and free to act as they would. How well would those wild dragons fit into Alagaësia once they were old enough to return?

As the day progressed, a thick layer of clouds formed, low enough to clip the peaks of the mountains. It forced Thorn to fly closer to the ground than he preferred, lest they should overlook the village of the Dreamers.

Before night fell, they spotted three more Urgal settlements hidden among the folds of the mountains. Murtagh had always thought Urgals lived in caves. So he'd been told growing up. It was strange to learn that they had humanlike towns. *How many of them are there?* he said.

Enough for the army he raised, said Thorn.

Murtagh nodded. It was true. The horde that had attacked Tronjheim had been the equal of any army in the land. Which meant the Urgals were far more numerous than commonly believed. *They've done well since the fall of the Riders.*

Will we have to drive them out?

Only if they make a nuisance of themselves again. Eragon thinks he can keep them as allies, but . . .

You don't agree?

I don't know. Eragon sometimes has a good feel for such things, but he's also rather simpleminded when it comes to the realities of war and politics. At least, he used to be.

They landed for the night by a small mountain stream that poured into the Bay of Fundor. As Murtagh made camp, an unfamiliar roar startled him.

He spun around to see a great brown bear standing on its hind legs not twenty feet away. The beast was as tall as a Kull and far thicker and more muscled.

Murtagh's pulse spiked for a second, and then he mastered himself. The bear was no threat. A single word would be more than sufficient to kill it, but Murtagh didn't like the idea; he and Thorn were the intruders, not the bear.

Thorn snaked his head around Murtagh and growled in response, making the bear sound puny in comparison.

The animal didn't seem scared. It roared again, dropped to all fours, and then reared back up, paws and claws extended.

"What's wrong with you?" Murtagh shouted. "Are you stupid? Don't you realize you can't win?"

The bear appeared startled. It snarled at him and then looked at Thorn and let out a long, outraged bellow. On a hunch, Murtagh searched the surrounding area with his mind for cubs or other bears. Nothing.

"I think it just wants to fight."

The dragon's eyes glittered. *Then we shall fight.*

"No, please. Not now," said Murtagh. "It's been a long day."

Thorn huffed, disappointed. *Fine. As you want.* Then he loosed a long jet of red and orange fire directly over the bear's head, singeing the fur on the tips of its ears.

The bear yowled, turned, and loped down the shoreline faster than a man could run.

"Thanks," said Murtagh as he watched the animal go. "I wager it's never met anything it couldn't intimidate before."

Well, now it has, said Thorn, sounding satisfied.

Murtagh glanced at the snowcapped mountains. He hoped no one had heard the commotion. "We should be careful from now on," he said, returning to the fire he was building. "You never know who might be listening. Especially out here."

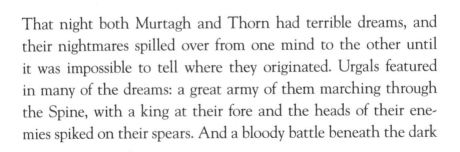

That night both Murtagh and Thorn had terrible dreams, and their nightmares spilled over from one mind to the other until it was impossible to tell where they originated. Urgals featured in many of the dreams: a great army of them marching through the Spine, with a king at their fore and the heads of their enemies spiked on their spears. And a bloody battle beneath the dark

pinetrees, with Urgals bellowing like bears and humans screaming, and Murtagh and Thorn crouched by the upturned roots of
a fallen tree, trying to hide. They were crying, crying, crying, and
the tears pattered against the dirt along with the drops of black
blood. . . .

Sleep provided no rest that night, and when Murtagh and
Thorn woke, they were still exhausted. *Those were no normal
dreams*, said Thorn.

*No. There's something strange in the land here. . . . We can't be
far, I think.*

Murtagh's words proved prophetic. In the middle of the afternoon, as Thorn rounded the flank of a particularly tall peak, a
swift-flowing river came into view, pouring out of a cleft in the
Spine and feeding into the Bay of Fundor. A blanket of low-
hanging clouds roofed the cleft, and the interior was deep and
dark and densely wooded. However, the shadows and the trees did
nothing to conceal the pall of bluish smoke crowded at the back
of the narrow valley.

And as the wind gusted, it carried a whiff of sulfurous stench
that made Murtagh's throat sting and his eyes water.

He straightened in the saddle, feeling a strange thrill.

They had arrived.

NAL
GORGOTH

~~~~~~~~~~~~~~~~~~~~~~ ❖ ~~~~~~~~~~~~~~~~~~~~~~

CHAPTER I

✦ ✦ ✦ ✦ ✦ ✦ ✦

The Village

On still wings, Thorn soared into the cleft. The soft ceiling of clouds muffled the air, and the silence only heighted Murtagh's anticipation as he leaned forward in the saddle, peering over Thorn's neck to see what lay ahead.

The mountains formed blue-white walls to either side, broken by cliffs of bare grey granite that protruded from the ranks of snowbound trees. Below, the river flowed swift and narrow along its course, the water so clear Murtagh could count the rounded rocks beneath its rippling surface.

As they neared the back of the valley, the smell of rotten eggs grew stronger, and to Murtagh's surprise, the air seemed to grow warmer as well, as if winter had yet to lay its frozen fingers upon the northern reaches.

Beneath the scrim of smoke draped over the foothills piled before them, he saw a collection of closely built stone structures. They were dark grey with domed roofs, unlike the style of construction elsewhere in Alagaësia. Some were houses, he thought, but there were other buildings as well: a narrow tower that would not have been out of place in Urû'baen and, set into the base of the near hill, what looked to be a palace or temple with a large open courtyard and a tiered roof.

Figures were visible in the streets, but distance and smoke obscured them.

The land surrounding the village was charred black like the surface of a burnt log, cracked and brittle, with tendrils of smoke rising from hollow pockets where the surface of the ground had collapsed. The few trees that stood upon the scorched earth had died, their branches bare and grey, and the bark had sloughed off the trunks in great sheets.

Wariness dampened Murtagh's anticipation. For all their powers, they were alone, he and Thorn. Not so different from Galbatorix and Jarnunvösk. If things went badly, they could expect no reinforcements. Lord Varis wouldn't ride to their rescue, Tornac wouldn't parry a blow meant for his neck, and Eragon and Arya were too far away to reach them in time.

A short growl rumbled Thorn's sides between his knees. *Galbatorix and Jarnunvösk were brash and foolish. We will not repeat their mistakes.*

"Let's hope not. Turn around for now. I'd rather not rush into anything."

Thorn banked and—without a flap of wing or sweep of tail that might have betrayed their presence—glided back toward the mouth of the cleft. There was a beaten path along the river, and Murtagh thought he saw weirs and nets set in the crystalline water.

By unspoken agreement, Thorn settled along the side of a hill one mountain over from the cleft, where a sharp-edged ridge hid them from the narrow valley.

Murtagh loosened the straps around his legs and slid to the ground. He stretched his arms and looked across the Bay of Fundor before turning back to Thorn. "What do you think?"

The scales along Thorn's neck prickled. *No village has the means to build such shells.*

"The houses? I agree. Not without a great deal of help. That or they used magic." He scratched his chin; his shave should be good for another day. Without a dagger or camp knife, he'd been forced to use a spell to remove his stubble, which made him more nervous than did a good, honest blade.

Thorn crept closer and placed his head by Murtagh's shoulder. *How long do you think you will be gone?*

"I won't be gone at all." Murtagh smiled. "This time, I think we should do things differently. This time, the situation calls for some thunder and lightning."

Thorn's long red tongue snaked out of his mouth and licked his chops in a wolfish way. *That seems most agreeable to me.*

"I thought it might."

Do you mean to kill Bachel?

"I mean to talk with her. If we have to fight, we fight, but—" Murtagh's brows drew together as he frowned. "We need to find out what she and the Dreamers are about. Whatever their goal, they're pursuing it with serious intent."

And you want to scent out how many of them are in Nasuada's realm.

"That too, although I doubt Bachel will tell us. At least, not willingly." He scratched Thorn atop his snout. "Either way, we have to be careful."

Our wards should protect us from her wordless magic, same as any other.

He gave the dragon a grim look. "Maybe. It's hard to say. If things go badly, it might be best to flee."

Flee or fight, I shall be ready.

"Then let us be at it."

Murtagh walked along Thorn's glittering length to where the saddlebags hung. He opened them and removed in order: Zar'roc, his arming cap and helmet, his greaves and vambraces, his iron-rimmed kite shield—from which he'd scraped the Empire's emblem—his padded undershirt, and his breastplate. When not marching into open battle, he preferred to wear a mail shirt for the mobility it provided, but it wasn't mobility nor even protection he was after. It was intimidation.

So, for the first time since Galbatorix had died and the Empire had fallen, Murtagh decided to substitute spectacle for subterfuge.

As he donned the armor, its familiar weight settled onto his frame with cold, forbidding constraint. Piece by piece, he assembled himself—or rather, a version of himself he had hoped to abandon: Murtagh son of Morzan. Murtagh, the dread servant of Galbatorix.

Murtagh the betrayer.

There was a circlet of gold about the helm, reminiscent of a minor crown. Galbatorix's idea of humor. He'd introduced Murtagh as his right-hand man in the Empire. A new Rider, descended of the Forsworn, sworn to the king and devoted to his cause. Before the crowds, Galbatorix had treated Murtagh as all but his son, but in private chambers, where the truth could not hide, Murtagh had been nothing more than a slave.

He placed the helm upon his head and then walked to a marshy pond lined with cattails and studied his reflection. He resembled a princeling sent to war. With the added harshness his visage had acquired during the past year, he found himself thinking he would not want to fight himself.

He nodded. "That'll do." Then he eyed Thorn. "A pity we don't have armor for you."

Thorn sniffed. *I need none. Besides, it would have to be made anew every half year.*

It was true. Like all dragons, Thorn would continue to grow his entire life. The rate of growth slowed in proportion to overall mass, but it never entirely stopped. Some of the ancient dragons, such as the wild dragon Belgabad, had been truly enormous.

Murtagh belted on Zar'roc and then closed the saddlebags and climbed back onto Thorn. "Letta," he said, and ended the spell that concealed Thorn in the air. "All right. Let's go meet this witch Bachel."

A rumble of agreement came from Thorn. Then the dragon lifted his wings high, like crimson sails turned to the wind, and drove them down. Murtagh clutched the spike in front of him as Thorn sprang skyward, and cold air rushed past with a promise of brimstone.

❖

Land in front, Murtagh said to Thorn as they flew into the cleft. *Make sure you have plenty of room. If it does come to a fight, I don't want you to get pinned or cornered.*

For a moment, Thorn's fierce enthusiasm dimmed. *You need not worry. I will not allow there to be a repeat of Gil'ead.*

I know. Murtagh patted the dragon's neck. *But let's not chance it all the same.*

Down swept Thorn from the roof of clouds, eddies of mist whirling from the tips of his batlike wings. He circled the village—his form now fully visible to those below, and shouts and screams echoed among the buildings, and bells began to clang with urgent alarm—and then down again he swept and pierced the veil of smoke.

Murtagh's eyes smarted, and an acrid taste formed in the back of his mouth.

With a threatening roar, Thorn settled on the blasted earth in front of the village. The crusted dirt cracked under his feet, and he sank inches into the ashy soil. The sight reminded Murtagh of the Burning Plains, though on cursory examination, the valley floor seemed to contain no peat or coal that might fuel an ongoing fire.

Bells continued to sound, and Murtagh saw grey-robed men and women running through the streets as they sought cover in the nearby buildings. Not that it would provide much protection against a dragon.

Murtagh drew Zar'roc then, and held it over his head. The bloody blade flashed in the dull winter light, a fitting match to Thorn's scales.

Raising his voice as if he were addressing an assembly of troops, he shouted, "Hear me! My name is Murtagh, and I have come to speak with the witch Bachel! Come forth, Bachel, that we may have words!"

The bells ceased tolling, and an eerie silence fell over valley and village. In it, Murtagh became aware of a faint hissing from the vents discharging vapor near Thorn's feet.

One by one, a number of robed individuals—men and women

alike—emerged from the buildings and gathered along the main road. They were a disparate collection: some were of pale northern stock, others were as brown as Surdans, and a few possessed the same deep black skin as Nasuada. They peered at Murtagh from under their hoods, their expressions angry and concerned, but not as fearful as he'd expected.

You would think they'd be more scared of a dragon and Rider, he said to Thorn.

The dragon licked his teeth. *I can correct that mistake.*

Murtagh hid a smile. *Later, perhaps.*

"Bachel!" he shouted. "Come forth, Bachel!"

The knot of people parted as a tall, goateed man stepped forward and, with a cold gaze, inspected Murtagh and Thorn. Two streaks of white banded his beard, and he had a pronounced widow's peak, while his shaved cheeks were sunken and pitted from pox. Murtagh found it impossible to place the man's ancestry. His brow was heavy, his cheekbones protruded, and he had a fierce, unfinished look, as if he were an earlier form of human. Unlike the others, his robe had stripes of purple sewn around the cuffs.

To Murtagh's surprise, the man bowed in a formal manner and said, "Welcome, Dragon. Welcome, Rider." His accent reminded Murtagh more of an Urgal's speech than any human tongue. "Come. This way. Bachel awaits." And then the rawboned man turned and walked back into the village, heading up the main road. As if at an unseen signal, the rest of the group dispersed among the buildings.

"Blast it," Murtagh muttered. He was no lapdog to be summoned at Bachel's convenience, and yet he and Thorn were the intruders here. Or, if he were being charitable, they were the guests. To expect Bachel to come out to meet *them* might be unreasonable, depending on the customs of her people.

And he wasn't prepared to be unreasonable. Not yet.

Still, he hated to enter the village. It would be the perfect place for an ambush, if the Dreamers were so inclined. There was also the matter of Thorn: the buildings looked uncomfortably close for him.

I will be all right, said Thorn. *Do not worry about me.*

How can I not? Maybe I should go alone.

Thorn growled. *No! I would rather bite off my own tail. We stay together.*

Are you sure? Absolutely sure?

Yes!

Fine. But if you need to leave, we leave, no matter what. Don't wait until it's too late.

I promise, said Thorn, and hummed his appreciation.

Murtagh tapped Zar'roc's blade against his thigh as he studied the village a moment more. Let the witch play her little games. It mattered not, and he refused to wait outside her doors, like a supplicant peasant seeking a favor. Now she might see them enter her domain, proud and unafraid. "After him, then."

Thorn pressed his wings close against his sides and started forward. His claws clacked loudly against the mossy flagstones that paved the road as they entered the village.

As Murtagh had feared, there was little space for them between the buildings, and Thorn grew tense beneath him. Murtagh could feel his apprehension as if it were his own. Still, for the time, the dragon kept himself under control.

Murtagh had never seen buildings such as the ones in the village. The stonework was dwarven in quality, but with an elven grace, and there were strange runes—neither dwarven nor elven—cut into the frames and lintels of the arched doorways. Sculptures of dragon-like beasts adorned the cornices, and their frozen snarls gave Murtagh an uneasy sense of being watched, as if the entire village were a living creature crouched close to the earth, waiting for its prey.

The most unusual feature of the village was the raised patterns covering walls, set into mosaics, and painted onto shutters—swirling, branching, crystalline patterns that seemed to repeat themselves as they diminished: variations on a common theme. The patterns were dangerously fascinating; Murtagh felt as if he could stare into them for the rest of his life and still find new things to see. They contained an obsessive, seemingly impossible amount of detail, and the longer Murtagh looked, the more his vision swirled and swayed. The decorations reminded him of the involuted depths of an Eldunarí . . . or of shapes that appeared only in the deepest of dreams.

With an effort, he focused elsewhere.

The curious craftsmanship of the village disturbed him. To find such accomplished, well-formed creations in such an isolated place didn't make sense. There ought to be a long lineage of like works elsewhere, but there wasn't. Not in Alagaësia, at least, and if the tradition came from across the ocean, well, that was hardly more explicable.

Murtagh shifted in his seat, feeling as if the ground had tilted beneath them. There was a deeper mystery here than he had anticipated.

Careful now, he said.

A sense of terse acknowledgment came from Thorn.

The goateed man was waiting for them halfway through the village. Seeing them, he turned and continued walking at a steady pace, long arms swinging, oversized hands nearly at his knees. Each step, he put his whole foot flat on the flagstones—a firm, unwavering stamp, heel and toes landing as one—and then pushed off in a similar fashion. Stamp, lift. Stamp, lift.

The street ascended at a steep incline toward the far side of the village. As they went, Murtagh kept a close watch on the rooflines, the alleys, the corners: anywhere that foes might be waiting. But no one showed their face, and he didn't want to risk opening his mind to search the area. That was a good way to invite a mental attack.

The more Murtagh saw of the settlement, the more he gathered an impression of extreme age. The sculptures were weathered, the steps hollowed; walls bowed from centuries of weight, and more than a few structures had collapsed on themselves and remained as crumbling, lichen-covered ruins.

I do not like this place, said Thorn.

No. Murtagh reset his grip on sword and shield. Maybe he *should* have contacted Eragon before entering the village. There were many secrets in the world, and some of them were older than even the Riders. *Nasuada has to be told of this,* he thought.

The man led them into a modest square in front of the temple-like building. A fountain stood in the center of the yard, but it was dry and full of dust and overgrown with moss, and the fluted finial atop had cracked and split sideways, leaving a chisel tip of stone pointing toward the dismal sky.

The temple—for so Murtagh had decided it was—had a two-tiered roof, with the topmost roof a ribbed dome the same as the other buildings in the village. A double row of columns guarded the shadowed entrance, while a line of dragon sculptures loomed outward from between the slitted windows. And wrapped around the columns and pedestals and the scaled statues were the same crystalline patterns seen elsewhere: a membrane of eroded veins, rotten and raveled and pocked by time.

Even new, the temple would have possessed a grim and disagreeable presence. In its current state of decay, the building's gloom-ridden bulk was all the more daunting; it projected an ancient and enduring strength—ironhard, obdurate, and devoid of forgiveness.

The goateed man stopped and took up position beside one of the pillars that framed the recessed entrance. He clasped his heavy hands in front of himself.

A horn sounded within the temple, a long, wavering note with a haunting quality, and the sound echoed with dire effect off the walls of the buildings and the flanks of the mountains. The nape of Murtagh's neck prickled, and he lifted Zar'roc to the ready. *Remember who you are*, he told himself.

Footsteps approached from inside the temple: tromping boots marching in matching time. From the shadowed entrance, a double line of fourteen armored men emerged, shields and spears held upright. Their helmets and breastplates were dented and tarnished and of an unfamiliar design. But the blades of their spears were sharp and free of rust, and they wore arming swords at their waists.

The formation parted in half, and the warriors arranged themselves on either side of the entrance. They displayed admirable discipline, moving with an alert precision that told Murtagh they weren't just ceremonial guards but warriors with actual fighting experience.

Behind them came another fourteen figures: these white-robed, with hoods pulled low over their faces so nothing could be seen of their features. Men and women alike, and each held a metal frame set with rods of iron from which hung open-mouthed bells. They shook the frames with every step, and the tongues of the bells wagged in a discordant chorus.

There was an air of ancient ritual about the procession, as if such a thing had been done for a thousand years or more.

The bell-shakers went to stand behind the warriors, where they continued their jarring cadence.

Last of all appeared four men in black armor that gleamed like lacquer. And on their shoulders, they carried a covered litter draped with diaphanous white veils.

Through the veils, a figure was partially visible.

Without word or signal, the four litter-bearers stopped upon the edge of the square and stood in place. They stared straight ahead, unblinking and seemingly unaffected by the sight of Thorn.

The bell-shakers ceased shaking.

With a whisper of sliding fabric, the veils parted.

A woman rose to stand upon the litter. She, like everything about the village, was singular. Her hair was black and shiny as obsidian and arranged in an elaborate edifice upon her head, the coils pinned and piled into a bewildering pattern. Bands of carved ivory stood stark against the amber hue of her forearms, and she wore a dress made of knotted straps. The knots traced the shapes of unfamiliar runes, long lines of them, as if she were armored with palings of words. A small dagger hung from a gilded girdle about her waist.

She was tall—taller than most men—with strong limbs, an angular face, and a dark red mouth that sat askew upon her face. Her almond-shaped eyes were rimmed with soot, which gave them the bruised look of the fruit of the blackthorn. She appeared neither young nor old; there was an agelessness to her features that made it impossible to determine her years.

So striking was the woman, Murtagh's first thought upon seeing her was: *An elf!* But then he looked more closely and realized that, no, her features weren't quite elven. However, neither were they entirely human. A deep disquiet stirred within him.

Then the woman smiled at Thorn and him with such warmth, it took Murtagh aback. "Welcome to Nal Gorgoth, O Exalted Dragon," she said. Her voice was low and melodic, and it thrummed with the power of conviction. "And welcome to you as well, Rider. I have been waiting for you, my son."

✦ ✦ ✦ ✦ ✦ ✦

CHAPTER II

Bachel

Murtagh gripped the edge of Thorn's saddle, his mind a welter of confusion. The woman before him couldn't possibly be his mother. Every reasonable part of him knew that. And yet . . . He felt as if he'd stepped wrong-footed and the path before him had vanished.

"Are you the witch they call Bachel?" he asked, attempting to feign confidence.

With an elegant motion, the woman inclined her head. "I am, my son."

A sense of imposition began to clear Murtagh's head. "Why do you call me such?"

Bachel indicated the courtyard and everyone within it. "Because you are my child, as are all who follow the Great Dream."

"I follow no one and nothing."

A faint spark of amusement appeared in Bachel's hooded eyes. "I very much doubt that, Kingkiller."

Murtagh tensed even more. "You know of me."

"Of you and Thorn both. Word of your deeds has traveled far, Kingkiller, even to this, our sacred redoubt." There was an archaic quality to her speech that reminded Murtagh of how the eldest of the Eldunarí had spoken: a remnant of past eras.

"And what *is* this?" Murtagh gestured with Zar'roc at the temple and the village.

"A place of many dreams." Bachel smiled again, seemingly without guile. "You have come to Nal Gorgoth, Kingkiller, as I foretold. Long have we waited for you and Thorn, and your arrival is most propitious."

Again, Murtagh felt lost. "Waited for us? Why?"

The witch's smile widened, and she spread her arms as if to embrace the whole of existence. "Because you are to be the saviors of the world."

~~~~~~~~~~~~~~~~~~ ❖ ~~~~~~~~~~~~~~~~~~

A profound silence reigned in the courtyard.

Thorn's confusion matched Murtagh's. But before either of them could demand an explanation, Bachel laughed, a low, throaty sound, and said, "You do not believe me. I see it in your eyes. That is of no matter. Soon you shall come to understand the truth of things. Answers you shall have, both to the questions you yearn to ask and those you have yet to conceive. But not here, and not now. It has been many an age since a Rider and dragon graced our court. We shall have a feast to celebrate your arrival, and you shall be my honored guests, you and brilliant Thorn both!"

She sat then, and snapped her fingers, and the litter-bearers marched to a stone dais on the northern side of the courtyard. The warriors followed and placed themselves on either side of the dais. The bearers continued to stand, the litter resting across their shoulders, while Bachel reclined against her carved, throne-like seat.

"Grieve," she said, "see to the arrangements. Let us have food and wine and music. Let the Vale of Dreams ring with joyful revelry, on this most fateful of days."

The goateed man bowed. "Your wish is our command, Speaker."

He clapped his hands, and the white-robed bell-shakers retreated into the temple while a rush of men and women emerged from the surrounding buildings. They seemed to need no instruction; with hardly a spoken word, the villagers brought out heavy wooden tables, and copper braziers filled with blazing coals, and iron sticks that held tapers of greasy tallow, and deer and goat hides to cover the mossy flagstones. All sorts Murtagh observed among the folk: they appeared to share no common origin. Nor were they human only. He saw two dwarves, both female, and what he thought might have been an Urgal youngling—though Murtagh only had a brief glimpse of his face. The dwarves gave no sign of hostility, but their presence heightened his wariness.

Nal Gorgoth. His brow furrowed. The name sounded Dwarvish, at least in part. As he had learned during his stay in Farthen Dûr, *goroth* meant *place* in the dwarves' tongue. Was the name of the village related to that word? Or had it another origin entirely? It also reminded him of Du Fells Nángoröth, which was what the elves called the mountains in the center of the Hadarac Desert— where the wild dragons used to live—and which was translated as the Blasted Mountains. Since *fells* meant *mountains,* then *nángoröth* meant *blasted.*

His thoughts were interrupted by the return of several of the bell-shakers carrying a heavy carved chair that they placed before the dais.

"Come, sit with me, Kingkiller," said Bachel. "And you as well, Dragon. Join me." She held out a hand, and a young, white-robed woman with flaxen hair and a devoted expression scurried up, placed a stone chalice in Bachel's grip, and filled it with wine from an earthenware pitcher. "Thank you, my child," murmured Bachel.

The young woman curtsied and withdrew.

Murtagh debated with himself for a moment. Then he slung his leg over the ridge of Thorn's back and slid to the ground, Zar'roc and shield still in hand.

Are you sure? Thorn asked.

No, but I don't see a choice. Stay close.

She cannot believe what she said.

What? About us being the saviors of the world?

Yes.

Murtagh agreed. Yet the straightforward assurance with which Bachel had spoken left him with a lingering doubt. Lies of all sorts he was accustomed to from his life at court, but he sensed no falsehood in the witch's speech or bearing. She seemed utterly convinced of the rightness of her words, and that more than anything made him uncertain.

Murtagh slowly approached the dais. Thorn followed a pace behind, claws tapping against the flagstones. The fourteen warriors attending Bachel shifted slightly. Murtagh ignored them.

With a gracious gesture, Bachel extended a hand toward the carved chair.

Murtagh hated to put himself at a disadvantage, but it would not do to completely break the rules of hospitality. So he sheathed Zar'roc—though he kept one hand on the hilt—before lowering himself to sit upon the chair. His greaves and vambraces clattered, and the point of his shield knocked against the yard's paved floor. The armor made him feel clumsy and uncouth; he never would have worn it to a high event at court, but there was a limit to how much safety he would sacrifice for manners.

The moment he was seated, two of the village men came to serve him. They set a small table before him and, on it, deposited plates laden with cheeses, sweetmeats, and fresh blueberries, along with a cup of wine and a bowl of water in which to wash his hands. The blueberries puzzled him; they were out of season, which meant magic or some form of preservation he was unfamiliar with.

One of the men bowed and left, while the other remained close at hand, ready to wait upon his needs.

There was a comfort to again having a servant attending him. It was one of the benefits of living in Urû'baen that Murtagh had not fully appreciated until leaving. Doing everything for himself—especially cooking—took far more time than he liked.

A faint smile curved Bachel's lips, and she sipped from her chalice. "I see you are not entirely at ease in our midst, but you have nothing to fear from us here in Nal Gorgoth, Kingkiller."

"Is that so?"

She inclined her head. "You may set aside your arms and armor whene'er you wish. No harm shall come to you."

"My Lady . . ." Murtagh paused while he searched for the right words. "I wish to believe you, but how can I, when I know so little about you?"

To his annoyance, Bachel answered with a question of her own: "Tell me, my son, how did you find this valley? Few there are who are aware of Nal Gorgoth's existence or where it lies."

Murtagh rolled the stem of his cup between his fingers while he considered how best to answer. Then he tasted the wine. To his surprise, he recognized the vintage as having come from the vineyards on one of the Southern Isles. *How did it end up here?*

He said, "I met several men who wore amulets of protection they claimed were enchanted by you." He fixed Bachel with a steady gaze. "They tried to kill me, but they failed, and then they told me what they knew."

A slight line formed between Bachel's brows. "I see. Then it was you met some of my Eyes. My apologies for their behavior. They would not have attacked had they known who you were. They did not, did they?"

Murtagh shook his head. "No."

"That is good. However, I must ask: my Eyes. My children. Did you kill them?"

"Those I had to. But no more." Her dark gaze lingered on him, and Murtagh felt compelled to add: "I give you my word."

"Then I thank you for your mercy. Were, perchance, the Eyes you encountered in Ceunon?"

"Some. Not all." For an instant, Murtagh thought he saw a flicker of concern in Bachel's expression. He decided to press the advantage. "Have you many Eyes?" he asked in an uninterested tone.

Bachel returned her attention to the preparations before them. "More than you would believe, Kingkiller."

It was exactly the sort of answer Murtagh had feared. "To what end, I wonder?"

"All shall be revealed in the goodness of time, my son. Worry not. But you must be patient. The secrets of the sacred circle are not lightly shared."

She spoke in such a gracious and yet commanding manner that Murtagh found it hard to dissent. It felt as if *he* would be in the wrong, despite everything he knew about the Dreamers and their activities. Yet his disquiet and his desire to know more continued to gnaw at him. *Saviors of the world . . . but how? From what? Or is she merely trying to lead us astray?*

Then Bachel turned her hooded gaze to Thorn. "O Exalted Dragon, I would ask a question of you, although perhaps you may think it impertinent. But it is this: you are larger than seems fit for your age. Is your stature born of nature, or has it another origin?"

Thorn was slow to respond, but when he did, he said to both Bachel and Murtagh alike, *I grew faster than most hatchlings, for I needed to. So I did.*

It was not entirely the truth, but Murtagh knew Thorn hated to speak of what Galbatorix had done to him, and he was not about to share those painful details with a stranger. Especially one as potentially perilous as Bachel.

The witch nodded as if she understood. "Of course. Such is the nature of dragons."

And what do you know of them? Murtagh wondered. He motioned at the ranks of scaled statues along the temple exterior. "Do you worship dragons?"

A thread of smoke came from Thorn. *What an excellent idea. All should worship our kind.*

Murtagh nearly smiled, despite himself.

A thin, cold note sounded as Bachel tapped the rim of her stone chalice. "Not as such. But we revere them, for we remember what so many have forgotten. And we count it a sacred thing to be bonded so closely with a dragon, even as you are, Kingkiller."

Before Murtagh could inquire further, the witch looked away, making it clear that, for the moment, the topic was closed.

To Thorn and Thorn alone, Murtagh asked, *What is her mind like?* He did not want to risk touching Bachel's consciousness as well. Not until they were sure of her intentions.

The dragon twitched the blunt end of his tail. *Like none I have ever felt.*

How so?

Her thoughts are as iron, and yet there is a strangeness to them. It is hard to describe. Here. And an impression came to Murtagh from Thorn, an impression of distance and desolation and distortion, as if the world were seen through a piece of polished crystal that changed the shape of every angle.

Puzzled, Murtagh looked back at Bachel and tried to reconcile her appearance with the oddness of her inner life. *She is not as she seems,* he said.

No, Thorn agreed.

Throughout the square, the villagers continued to assemble the feast. Goats and sheep were butchered, and rich cuts of meat were laid out over fires built on the flagstones. As the villagers labored, Murtagh noticed how they kept sneaking glances at Thorn. It was as if the dragon were a bloodied lodestone drawing them closer, and their bodies traced lines of force, like iron filings. Some were brave enough to reach out with tremulous hands, though none dared to actually touch him. In Murtagh's judgment, their behavior bespoke not so much *reverence*, as Bachel had said, but something closer to idolatry.

Bachel watched him watching, and she seemed to guess his thoughts, for she said, "They are enamored with the beauty of your dragon. Few there are in Nal Gorgoth who remember such a sight."

Thorn hummed, pleased by what she had said.

"But there are some?" Murtagh asked.

"There are."

"Would you count yourself among their number?"

Again, slight amusement colored Bachel's angular features. "You have questions without end, my son. But it is better to eat and then talk than to talk and then eat."

"Of course. Forgive me. The wisdom of the ages flows from your tongue." Murtagh meant his response as sarcasm, but despite himself, it came out sounding sincere.

Several men began to play lyres among the columns of the temple. The music was in a minor key and had a fierce, savage sensibility that heightened the strangeness of the setting.

Bachel raised a finger. "Alín, attend me."

The same young, white-robed woman who had served the witch earlier hurried over and bowed deeply. "Yes, Speaker?" Her voice was high and sweet.

"What think you of our guest, the great dragon Thorn?" asked Bachel.

Alín's eyes grew round, and she bowed again. "He is very splendid, Speaker. We are fortunate you have allowed him to visit among us."

Allowed? Thorn said to Murtagh, somewhat bemused.

I'll say this, Bachel does not seem concerned by our presence.

Very little seems to concern her.

Bachel looked satisfied with Alín's answer. "Yes, he is. Enjoy his presence whilst you may, my child. Such moments are rare over the long reach of years. You are blessed to live in these most momentous of times."

"Yes, Speaker."

The lyres struck louder.

"Dance for us now, my child," said Bachel. And she tapped one of the litter-bearers on the shoulder. "You as well. Put me down and join with Alín. Share with us your joy."

The armor-clad men lowered the litter to the dais and descended with Alín to stand among the tables set up before them. Then the five of them began to move in time with the music, their bodies turning and swaying with sinuous grace.

The bearers' armor, Murtagh noted, made no noise, as if it were made of felted wool rather than wood or metal or whatever was the lacquered material.

Somewhere among the columns, a drum took up the beat, and then a horn, and though Bachel's face remained impassive, a fire seemed to light her eyes, and she tapped the middle finger of her right hand against her chair, keeping time with perfect, un-yielding precision.

Murtagh watched from the corner of his eye. He couldn't decide what to make of her. Even sitting there, Bachel struck an imposing figure, tall and statuesque, like a warrior facing a gathered army, and none there were in the courtyard who could match her presence. In that, she reminded him with unexpected strength of Nasuada.

Thorn nudged his elbow, and Murtagh blinked and tightened his hand about Zar'roc's hilt.

After a minute, Bachel said, "Do you dance, Kingkiller?"

He gave her a courtly nod. "Quite well, I'm told."

"Then dance for me, if you would. Let my children see the high styles of the land."

"You make a fair request, Lady, but my armor is ill suited for such sport, and I'll not remove it."

He thought his refusal would displease her. But instead, she merely picked up her chalice again. "No matter. You will dance for me another time, Kingkiller."

"Will I?"

"It is foreseen, foretold, and thus fated." And she returned to watching Alín and the bearers.

More grey-robed servants came with platters of food: bread and milk and butter and salted meats. Grieve joined them on the dais and, after a deep bow to Bachel, said, "Dragon Thorn, we have goats and sheep and cows for you. Which would you like?"

I ate before we set off north. At the moment, I am not hungry, but I thank you for your offer.

Grieve bowed again. "Of course. As you so desire. If you change your mind, you have but to ask, and our herds shall be yours to choose from as you please."

Thorn's eyes glittered in response. *That is most kind of you.*

The dancers continued without letup, and before long, the villagers brought cooked meats to the dais and the feast began in earnest.

Murtagh was hungry, but he took only a few bites from each course, just enough to be polite, and he drank sparingly. The witch, by comparison, was immoderate in her consumption; she ate a constant stream of dishes, displaying the sort of appetite common to soldiers after days of forced marching. Her manners were fastidious, although—also to his surprise—she forwent fork and knife and devoured her food using nothing but fingers and teeth. It made for an odd mix of refinement and barbarity. Along with her food, she drank chalice after chalice of wine. And yet she remained alert and bright-eyed throughout, and Murtagh could detect no slurring of her speech.

Either she has the constitution of a Kull or she has spells protecting her, he said to Thorn.

Or some combination of both.

When Bachel held out her chalice for the seventh time, Murtagh gave an incredulous chuckle and shook his head. "You are amused, my son?" Bachel asked.

"It's only that . . . well, I've never seen man or dwarf who could hold their own with you when it comes to drink. Perhaps an Urgal might, or an elf, but I've never had chance to match cups with either of their races."

Bachel nodded, unperturbed. "It is because my mother was

indeed an elf. That is why my blood runs hot and I have the strength and quickness I do. There is no one like me in all the world."

Murtagh's mind raced. Growing up, he'd heard stories of half elves, but they were always spoken of as something out of myth and legend. It had never occurred to him that such a thing might be possible . . . though considering it now, he supposed it wasn't *that* surprising. Elves and humans were more closely related than, say, humans and dwarves—dwarves, like Urgals, had seven toes on each foot—and given enough time living in the same land, it was inevitable that some intermingling would occur.

She could be lying, said Thorn.

But then how to explain . . . her?

The dragon had no answer.

Murtagh looked back at Bachel. "Is your mother still—"

"She died long ago," the witch said in a bland tone. "She came here when she was heavy with me, and she died. Is that what you wanted to know, my son?"

He wet his lips. "And your father? He was human, I take it?"

Bachel gave a languorous wave. "A woodcutter, I'm told. He too is long since dead."

"I see. . . . My condolences."

Bachel looked at him with a glittering gaze, as if he'd grown a horn from his forehead. "Why your condolences? They are in no pain. They sleep the long slumber, and were they here, they would be honored to know that *I* of all people was anointed Speaker. That *I* was chosen by fate to read and interpret and share the truth of ages. Do not mourn for me, Murtagh son of Morzan. I have no sorrows here, only triumph, glorious and inevitable."

Then she lifted her chalice and again returned to watching those moving to the music.

In the distance, a crow uttered its harsh cry.

~~~~~~~~~~~~~~~~ ❖ ~~~~~~~~~~~~~~~~

The feast dragged on, course after course, and the players continued to weave their savage melody throughout. It was a strange celebration. None of the villagers spoke to Murtagh or Thorn, not even when they waited upon Murtagh. Only Bachel conversed with them, and she seemed more interested in indulging in food and drink than talk.

Murtagh didn't mind. The many months he'd spent traveling alone with Thorn had accustomed him to sitting and watching and thinking. And there was a certain pleasure in being served, as he had been at Galbatorix's court; he heard the careless clip of authority harden his voice when he spoke to the man attending him.

It fit with his armor.

Nevertheless, Murtagh recognized his own feelings, and he knew them for a trap that could lull him into complacency. So while he welcomed the treatment due his rank, he also made an effort to observe the villagers and attempt to deduce something of their nature.

One point in particular struck him: when Bachel issued an order, the villagers scurried about like mice before a cat, almost desperate to please her. And yet they didn't seem afraid. Or if they were, it was an odd sort of fear. Mostly, he saw deference and respect in their actions. If he could understand the reasons why, he felt he would understand the mystery at the heart of Nal Gorgoth.

Shadow filled the valley, and the stars were cold sparks in the night sky when Bachel finally pushed away her plate, dabbed her lips, and leaned back in her throne. Her skin glowed from the rubbed-in grease, and her whole being, face and body together, seemed swollen from the vast amount of food she had ingested.

"A most bounteous feast," said Murtagh. "Your cooks are to be commended."

Bachel nodded in a satisfied manner. "I thank you for your

kind words. Such a feast as this, and more besides, are your right-ful reward. Yours and Thorn's. Were it within my power, I would set a thousand days of celebration in your honor. It is only what you deserve."

Murtagh eyed her, wondering at the praise. Was it possible that the rumors about the Dreamers, and Bachel herself, were falsities? Or else misleading? Perhaps Bachel was not as he had thought. After all, were someone to judge *him* on hearsay, they would deem him a villain fit to frighten even the stoutest of hearts.

Then: "My Lady, we have eaten and eaten well. Might we now talk?"

"Of course, my son. What would you speak of?"

So many questions had Murtagh, he was almost at a loss to begin. "I have heard your people called the Dreamers. Would that be correct?"

A stillness took Bachel's face, and with a single draft, she emptied her chalice and placed it beside her litter. "It is."

"And what is it you dream of?"

"Of remaking the very face of the land." Bachel turned her dark-rimmed eyes upon him. "As has been fated since the beginning of time. And as you and Thorn are destined to help bring to pass."

The certainty with which she spoke chilled him. Partly because it reminded him all too much of Galbatorix's ironclad conviction—a conviction born of the king's own delusions and untrammeled power. And partly because he wondered if she spoke the truth.

"You speak with great confidence about our future actions."

"Of course. Because I am a seer. A soothsayer. A prophet, if you will. The gift of foretelling what shall be is mine, and before me, all paths are laid bare."

Ice poured down Murtagh's spine. Prophecy was a real thing, but rare, very rare, and—to his knowledge—limited to the near future. If the witch could see further than that, then she might very well be the most powerful being in Alagaësia.

I do not believe in fate, Thorn said to him. *We make our own way through the world.*

Yes, but if she can predict what we choose to do next, how could we possibly counter that? And what exactly has she foreseen as our future? A fierce desire to know burned within Murtagh.

"Is that why your people call you Speaker?" he asked. "Because you speak to them of the future?"

Bachel smiled slightly. "No, not quite. I am the chosen voice of the Dreamer of Dreams, from whom all wisdom flows. For the Dreamer I speak, and thus the Speaker I am."

When she failed to elaborate, he said, "And who is—"

"Some secrets are not to be shared with outsiders." She gave him a long look, her gaze hard and evaluating. "Although perhaps you shall be a rare exception, my son."

Murtagh frowned. Just because court intrigues had accustomed him to evasion didn't mean he liked it. "My Lady . . . if an oracle you are, might you provide us with a demonstration of your powers, that we may marvel at your gift?"

For the first time, Bachel did appear offended. She said, "What visions I have are granted to me for sacred purpose, and I would risk the wrath of the Dreamer were I so *presumptuous* as to demand them merely to satisfy my own selfish desires. It would be a desecration of my role as Speaker."

How convenient, Murtagh thought, but before he could voice his doubt, the witch continued:

"However, I will tell you this much, Rider, and I speak the truth, for I have seen what is to come. Ere long, you and Thorn shall fly forth, and you shall redden blade and claw in service of this cause. This I promise you."

Thorn growled slightly, and Murtagh felt his skin prickle and crawl. "And what else have you seen of our future? Why do you call us the saviors of the land?"

Bachel's mouth twisted further askew with an enigmatic smile. "We shall speak of that anon and more besides. This also I promise.

But it is late, and you must be tired from your travels. For now, you should rest. My people will see to it that you are well cared for. If there is anything you need, you have but to ask. Grieve!"

The goateed man shambled over. "Speaker?"

"Escort our guest to the chambers overlooking the Tower of Flint. Sleep well, Kingkiller, and may your dreams bring you understanding. Tomorrow we shall talk of the new age that is dawning."

Then Bachel gave word to her armor-clad servants, who lifted her litter and carried her from the courtyard back into the temple. Once she had left, the players ceased plucking the lyres, and the drums fell silent too. Soon the crackling of the fires was the loudest sound in the square.

Grieve approached Murtagh and bowed. In a condescending tone, he said, "This way, Rider."

His mind full of thoughts, Murtagh stood, stiff and unsteady. He didn't want to sleep indoors, alone and isolated from Thorn, but he feared it would be unwise to refuse Bachel's offer of hospitality.

Go, said Thorn, sensing his deliberation.

Murtagh put a hand on the dragon's neck. *I'll sneak back out once they've left me. And then maybe we can look around a bit and see what we can discover.*

Thorn hummed with agreement, but Murtagh could tell the dragon wasn't entirely happy with the plan. They'd talk more later, when there was less of a chance their thoughts might be overheard.

"After you," said Murtagh, gesturing at Grieve.

The goateed man turned and, with his heavy, flat-footed tread, led Murtagh beneath the arcade of faceted columns and through a small side door along the northern wing of the temple. The hallway inside was cool and dark; no torches or lanterns were lit, but Grieve moved with surety, and Murtagh followed the sound of his steps while probing for the minds of any who might be lying in wait to attack.

Up a flight of stairs they went, to a landing where the temple's narrow windows let through enough moonlight to see along the wall flat carvings of . . . of *what*, Murtagh did not know. His eyes refused to settle on the confusion of figures that adorned the stone. Bodies, human or beast, distorted structures, strange honeycomb patterns that melted one into the next . . . It felt as if the sculpture were an attempt to physically depict madness. The frenzied, half-formed shapes reminded him of the twisted mindscapes of the Eldunarí whom Galbatorix had enslaved, as well as the disjointed logic of nightmares. Malevolence emanated in great waves from the wall. The sensation was so tangible, it made him recoil. The sculpture was a grotesquerie—a mockery of grace and art and all things beautiful. He felt a strong urge to break it. If he were to look at the carvings for too long, Murtagh feared they would infect him with whatever insanity had inspired such a malformed creation.

"Who made this thing?" he asked. In the night air, his voice sounded as an unlovely croak.

Grieve did not pause as he lurched down the landing. "The First Ones made it when they discovered the sacred well."

"You mean the Grey Folk?" asked Murtagh. The long-dead race had been the ones to bind the ancient language and magic in the first place. He could easily imagine them building Nal Gorgoth, although he had never heard of their kind having set foot in Alagaësia. But then, there was much he did not know, and much that was hidden by the passage of years.

Grieve snorted. "I mean the First Ones. The first of the Dreamers to find this place. Many races they were, but all of them of a single mind."

"I see. And the well you mentioned? What makes it sacred?"

"That is not for me to say, Rider."

"What *is* for you to say?"

With a stiff-legged step, Grieve stopped, his shoulders and neck hunched like those of a bear readying himself to charge. "Do not expect me to provide you with aid, Rider. You are an outsider, an unbeliever, and your kind are neither needed nor wanted in Nal Gorgoth."

He turned on Murtagh. His moonlit eyes were silvered chips of ice, hard and full of hate, and Murtagh—despite all his wards and skill at arms—felt threatened enough that he put a hand on Zar'roc's hilt.

"But," Grieve continued, "in her wisdom, Bachel has chosen to tolerate your presence. That is her right."

"She *tolerates* my presence, does she?" said Murtagh, his voice deadly calm. "What other choice does she have, servant?"

Grieve's mouth split apart to show the yellow stakes of his teeth. "That you shall learn, Rider, and you will wish you hadn't. Your power holds no sway here. If Bachel wishes, she will use the Breath on you, and *then* we will see who is servant and who is master."

"I don't think I like you, Grieve."

"The words of unbelievers are as dirt beneath my feet."

"I'm glad we have an understanding. Lead on. I grow weary and would rest in my chambers."

The malice in Grieve's eyes intensified, but he turned and continued along the landing. Murtagh let the man put several steps between them before he followed. He kept his hand on Zar'roc and made sure the blade was loose in the sheath. *Jealousy or overprotectiveness?* he wondered. Or was it zealotry that fueled the hostility of Bachel's right-hand man?

At the end of a hall, they arrived at a set of closed wooden doors. "Here," said Grieve, and, without another word, departed.

Murtagh waited until he was sure he was alone and then pushed open the doors.

CHAPTER III

✦ ✦ ✦ ✦ ✦ ✦ ✦

The Tower of Flint

The corner chambers Bachel had given him would have been considered poor accommodations in Urû'baen. But by the standards of a rustic, out-of-the-way village, they were sumptuous. The inside of the temple was in better repair than the outside: the stone walls were clear of moss and lichen, the floor was well swept, and there were no cobwebs to catch in his hair.

A stone fireplace was set against one wall. Facing it was a four-poster bed of black walnut, with blankets that seemed clean and a sheepskin laid on top that smelled only faintly of the animal it had been cut from. An iron candlestick with an unlit taper stood by the bed, along with a bare side table and, a few feet past, a plain wardrobe. A bearskin with the head still attached lay in the center of the floor.

Adjoining the space was a small washroom with a stone basin, a porcelain chamber pot, and a bucket of fresh water for his ablutions. There were no carvings or banners upon the walls of either room, but the washroom floor had a mosaic made of chips of colored glass, and it contained the same branching patterns that adorned the rest of the village.

Several shuttered windows marked the walls on either side of the bedroom's outer corner. Murtagh checked to make sure that no one was hiding in the chambers, and then he went to the windows and unfastened the shutters.

The dragon sculptures that lined the upper part of the building extended past the sides of each window, the exaggerated shapes of their snouts hooked downward like overgrown corbels.

To the east, the windows opened onto the temple courtyard. The villagers had already—with unexpected speed and efficiency—cleared the tables, braziers, food, and skins from around the ruined fountain.

Thorn sat crouched on the flagstones, eyes open and alert. He saw Murtagh, and the dragon's tongue slipped out as he tasted the air. *There you are.*

Here I am. By the entrance to the yard, Murtagh spotted a pair of bored-looking villagers sitting next to a glowing brazier. The men carried spears and had swords at their waists, but Murtagh couldn't imagine that Bachel expected the guards to stop him or Thorn if they chose to leave. Their only purpose, he decided, was to keep watch and inform the witch as to the activities of her guests.

Guests. His lip curled.

The guards glanced up at him and then returned to talking amongst themselves.

One moment, Murtagh told Thorn, and went to the north-facing windows. Not far from the temple, he saw the narrow structure that Bachel had called the Tower of Flint. It stood tall and stark in the moonlight: a spear of rough-hewn stone, velvet grey, with belfry-like openings beneath the domed roof. From the tower, he thought he heard a faint murmur of sleeping birds, but the sound might as easily have been a trick of the imagination.

Past the tower stood a number of houses, and he was also able to pick out—dimly visible in the moonlight—the corner of tended grounds that extended behind the tower and temple. Their presence intrigued him. There was a path running across the neatly trimmed grass and between a double row of low shrubs, leading toward the trees along the foothills. . . .

Murtagh looked back at the guards below. Experience had

taught him caution, but it had also taught him the importance of decisive action. Whatever the truth regarding Bachel's means and motives, he didn't feel comfortable waiting for her to reveal it. He wanted to find out for himself what secrets lurked at the heart of Nal Gorgoth. That way, at least, he might be able to determine whether Bachel was lying to them.

All of which justified taking a bolder-than-normal approach.

But carefully.

Murtagh scratched his chin. The guards didn't appear to be wearing amulets like the ones he had encountered in Ceunon and Gil'ead. However, Bachel might have gifted them with some form of wards. There was no way to tell beforehand, and the nature of her wordless magic meant that the Name of Names would be of no help. And while it was possible Bachel was ignorant of more formal magic, he couldn't see how to use that to his advantage. Still . . . Whatever wards protected the guards, they might not block spells intended to help rather than harm—even as had been the case with Galbatorix.

355

He decided to risk it. As with all magic, intent mattered, so he concentrated on the fact that both of the men appeared tired. It was late, and they ought to be in bed. It would be best if they slept, for their own good.

With that firmly in mind, Murtagh cast the same spell he'd used on the guard in the catacombs under Gil'ead: "Slytha." *Sleep.*

He released the energy for the spell in a carefully controlled trickle over the course of half a minute or more. It was a gentle piece of magic, subtle enough that if a ward *did* stop it, the warriors might not notice.

The guards slumped over, and one of them dropped his spear. It clattered on the flagstones with startling loudness, and then the village was again quiet.

When no one came to investigate, Murtagh allowed himself a pleased chuckle. As much as he hated to admit it, the way Eragon had used magic on Galbatorix had been a stroke of inspiration. No one seemed to think of guarding themselves against the good, only the bad.

It wouldn't last, of course. Over the years, word would spread from magician to magician, and eventually no capable spellcaster would leave themselves open to well-meaning attacks. A contradiction, that! But a reality all the same. Regardless, Murtagh wasn't about to lament Bachel's ignorance. As long as the technique continued to work, he'd use it and be grateful for it too.

Of course, he still didn't know for sure if the guards had wards, but he would have been shocked if they didn't.

How long will they sleep? Thorn asked.

As long as needed. Help me down, said Murtagh, climbing through the window onto the skirt-roof below.

Thorn snorted and lifted his head. Murtagh stepped onto it, careful not to put a heel in the dragon's eyes. Then Thorn lowered him to the flagstones, and Murtagh straightened his sword belt and looked around.

"Thanks," he murmured, suddenly gleeful, like a fox that had broken into a henhouse while the hounds were away.

Bachel is very dangerous, I think, said Thorn.

"I agree."

Perhaps we should leave. We know where this place is now. Let Nasuada or Arya or even Eragon deal with it. This isn't our responsibility.

"Don't you want to find out the truth behind Bachel and this Dreamer of Dreams? Not to mention this supposed prophecy regarding the two of us. Aren't you curious?"

Thorn sniffed the night air and was slow to answer. *I am . . . but I am also wary. I feel as if we're sticking our paws into a dark burrow. We do not know what we might find. We might end up bitten.*

"And if we do?" asked Murtagh, serious. "Would it not be better to know if there's something here that can bite us?"

Is that even a question? The only mystery is, how large of a bite?

Murtagh cocked an eyebrow. "So far, Bachel and her people have shown us nothing but hospitality. Even if Grieve is a surly malcontent."

Yet you do not trust the faces they show you, else we would not be having this discussion.

"No. You're right."

Thorn released a very human-sounding sigh. *You will not sleep well unless you sniff about, will you?*

He grinned. "You know me too well."

After a moment, the dragon lowered his head, and the soft warmth of his breath enveloped Murtagh. *All right. But if you get caught again, I'll grab you and fly out of here, as I did at Gil'ead.*

"And if it comes to that, I'll be happy for you to grab me." He rubbed Thorn behind one of his neck spikes, and the dragon's sides vibrated with a low hum of satisfaction.

Where do you want to search?

Murtagh glanced at the tiered temple. The mountains rose high behind it, the peaks pale as the finest pearl beneath the twinkling stars. *There, but I think it would be too risky. Too many people in the building.*

Then where?

Murtagh pointed at the Tower of Flint. *It must be important for the Dreamers to have named it. And I want to see the grounds behind the temple.* He cast a critical eye over Thorn. *Some of the villagers may still be up, and you're a bit big to be sneaking around these days.*

Thorn snapped his jaws shut with a soft but definite *click*. *Then we wait until they are asleep. Where you go, I go.*

Murtagh could tell there was no point in arguing. "You're as stubborn as a mule," he muttered. *All right. But you'll have to stay behind where you don't fit.*

The dragon nodded. *That is acceptable.*

Then Murtagh nestled against Thorn's side, and the dragon covered him with a wing so he was hidden from any who might pass by. Knowing that Thorn was keeping watch, Murtagh closed his eyes and used the opportunity for a quick nap. Even in the midst of his enemies, he could still sleep—a useful, if somewhat regrettable, skill garnered over years of dangerous living.

~~~~~~~~~~~~~~~~~~ ❖ ~~~~~~~~~~~~~~~~~~

The sharp tip of Thorn's snout poking him in his ribs woke Murtagh. He reluctantly opened his eyes.

I'm up, I'm up, he said as Thorn continued to nudge him.

The dragon snorted and pulled his head out from under his wing.

Murtagh yawned. What had he been dreaming about? The memory scratched at the edge of his mind, and he had an obscure sense that it had been important. . . .

Well? Thorn asked, and lightly scratched the flagstones.

Give me a minute. Let me make sure no one is watching. Carefully, cautiously, with almost paranoid slowness, Murtagh reached out with his mind and checked the surrounding area. He felt a few people nearby, but they were deep asleep, dreaming whatever it was the Dreamers dreamed.

All clear, he said, crawling out from under the wing.

The moon was directly overhead now. The pall of smoke had dispersed, and the air acquired the perfect clarity found only on bitter winter nights. And yet the village retained an unseasonal warmth, as if summer still dwelt among the stone buildings while frost and ice accumulated on the encircling hills and peaks. Perhaps, Murtagh thought, the heat was coming from the ground itself. It would explain why the fields that fronted Nal Gorgoth were charred black.

He sniffed. He couldn't smell the stench of brimstone anymore. Was that because it had departed along with the smoke, or had he simply gotten used to the odor?

The second explanation bothered him more than he wanted to admit.

"Watch your tail," he murmured to Thorn. "Don't go caving in any of the buildings."

Thorn gave a dismissive snort. *I'm more careful than that.*

"Mmm," said Murtagh, unconvinced.

From the courtyard, he scouted down the adjoining streets before heading around the corner of the temple and toward the Tower of Flint. Thorn stalked after him, as quiet as a cat. He lifted the tips of his claws so they didn't touch the stones and walked on the pads of his paws with impressive delicacy. His tail he kept raised off the ground, and it hung behind him like a great crimson snake, headless and blindly following.

Just off the temple was a roofed well with a small winch for lifting its bucket. The well was plain enough, devoid of even the most basic decoration. Murtagh doubted it was the sacred well that Grieve had mentioned.

On the off chance he was mistaken, he leaned on the mouth of the well and peered over the edge. The black depths echoed with the faint sounds of his hands against the fitted stones. Nothing about it seemed unusual.

If he'd had a coin, he would have tossed it in for luck. He and Thorn needed more than their fair share.

"Nothing," he said to Thorn. "Do you smell anything?"

The dragon sniffed, and his tongue darted out. *Only water, wood, and sweat.*

Murtagh moved on.

A hip-high wall of mortarless stonework encircled the Tower of Flint, and there was a small wrought-iron gate blocking the way. The bars of the gate traced the outline of a dragon's head as seen from the top.

"They really seem to like dragons," said Murtagh as he unlatched the gate and pulled it open. The hinges squealed loud enough to make him pause, but no one was near to notice.

Why should they not? said Thorn. *There is no other creature or being that can match the beauty of our form.*

"Perhaps not, but you don't have to brag about it."

The truth is never bragging.

Murtagh smirked. Dragons had many virtues, but modesty *wasn't* one of them. "Wait here. I won't be long." Leaving Thorn at the small gate, he proceeded to the door of the tower. It was wood, with a heavy iron lock set into the boards.

He opened it with a subtle application of the word *thrysta* and a slight surge of energy. *Click* went the lock, and he pulled the door open.

The acrid stench of bird droppings struck him, making his breath catch and his eyes water. He screwed up his face and padded into the dark interior.

It took a minute for his eyes to adjust well enough to make out even basic shapes. He was standing at the bottom of a great cylinder, which started at the base of the tower and rose right to the top. Lining the walls were hundreds of tiny wooden coops, each with a section of a bark-covered branch protruding from the front to serve as a perch. From inside the coops, he heard a thousand little murmurs—the sounds of sleeping birds—and the silky whisper of feathered wings shuffling and readjusting. The floor was soft with a thick layer of droppings, and there were crates and barrels and other objects piled along the bottom of the walls.

Murtagh stared. The tower was as curious a space as he'd ever seen, even including the catacombs under Gil'ead. It was a demented, oversized version of the dovecotes that Yarek the spymaster had built in Urû'baen for housing his homing pigeons. But what birds were these? Not pigeons or doves, he suspected.

He cast about on the filthy floor, looking for feathers that might help identify the birds. Instead, he stepped on something hard and felt it break beneath his foot. Holding his breath, he bent to look.

Half buried in the droppings was a beaked skull. The skull of a crow. *Of course.* The tower had to be where the Dreamers raised the birds that Bachel used to make her amulets. Murtagh straightened. The sheer number of crows in the tower made him wonder just how many amulets Bachel had enchanted.

How are they fed? he wondered. It would be no small task tending to so many birds.

Keeping a hand out for balance, Murtagh felt his way around the outer curve of the chamber, intending to make a circuit and then depart. What was he looking for? He didn't know. Crows weren't used for carrying messages. There would be no writing desk with secret messages lettered across slips of parchment. No maps or magical items used for enchanting, assuming he was correct about Bachel's spellcasting. But he felt obliged to be thorough.

Three-quarters of the way around the tower, he stepped in a particularly slippery patch of droppings, and one foot slid out from under him. He flailed and caught himself with a hand on the floor. His right knee banged against the corner of a crate, sending a hot jolt through his leg, and the tip of Zar'roc's scabbard knocked against a barrel.

A muted chorus of disquiet passed through the tower as the crows shifted in their sleep, their murderous minds for a moment disturbed.

Murtagh clenched his teeth, held his breath, and didn't move. His knee throbbed. A spike of alarm came from Thorn, and Murtagh quickly reassured him: *I'm fine. Don't worry.*

Then he whispered, "Maela." It was said that the ancient language was the mother tongue all creatures had spoken at the beginning of time. Murtagh wasn't sure if he entirely believed that—he had his own ideas about how the language might have been enchanted to influence living beings—but it *was* true that animals responded to the ancient language in ways they didn't to other tongues.

Sure enough, the birds began to settle down, and shortly thereafter they were again quiet.

Murtagh made a face as he started to push upright and the droppings squished between his fingers. He uttered a single, soundless curse, as foul as the situation he found himself in.

The heel of his palm sank into the excrement and touched cold hardness buried within. He frowned. *Huh.*

Despite his disgust, he dug down until he could grasp the object. It felt like metal: oval, half the size of his hand, with carving on one side. *A coin?* But no, it was too large for that.

Keeping a firm grip on the object, he stood up and carefully made his way back out through the tower door.

Thorn wrinkled his snout and retreated several steps as Murtagh approached. "That bad?" said Murtagh, rueful, closing the small gate behind him.

If you don't bathe before tomorrow, everyone for a league will know where you've been.

"Uh-huh." Murtagh turned so the moon was behind him and held up the object he'd found. As he'd suspected, it was a flat piece of metal: electrum, by the looks of it (although it was hard to be sure in the moonlight; it could just as easily have been gold), with an iron hook on the back. It was a clasp for a cloak that would be fastened at one shoulder. Droppings were embedded in the design on the clasp's face, and Murtagh spent the better part of a minute scraping the muck away with his thumbnail before he could make sense of it.

A shock of recognition passed through him, as a bolt of lightning through a drought-stricken tree.

What is it? Thorn asked.

Murtagh shared with him a memory of Galbatorix's private dining hall, where crimson banners hung along the walls, banners embroidered with the crests of the Forsworn. The one opposite the middle of the table, facing the chair where Murtagh had so often sat, had borne the same design as the clasp.

"It is the mark of Saerlith."

A similar shock passed through Thorn. *How came it to this place?*

"I don't know." Saerlith had been a lesser name among the Forsworn; he'd done little to distinguish himself from his fellow traitors, although he had shared in their general infamy. All Murtagh knew of him was that he was human and had come from somewhere around the city of Teirm. That, and his dragon was unfortunate enough to have puce-colored scales. Like the other dragons of the Forsworn, the name of Saerlith's dragon had been lost, erased by the collective will of their species. Dragons did not forgive those they considered betrayers. A fault of theirs, perhaps, but when it came to the Forsworn, an understandable one.

Murtagh tried to recall how Saerlith had died. Not in Nal Gorgoth, that much he knew. Accounts were mixed, but supposedly Galbatorix had dispatched Saerlith to Alagaësia's southern coast, where the Rider and dragon had been ambushed and killed. By whom, Murtagh had never heard, although he assumed the Varden or their allies had been responsible.

Regardless, Saerlith had perished long before Murtagh's time.

Thorn said, *If Saerlith and his dragon discovered Nal Gorgoth—*

"Then maybe Galbatorix knew about this place." Murtagh bounced the clasp in his hand. "Or maybe Saerlith was working with the Dreamers for his own gain."

Galbatorix would have killed him for that.

"If he knew of it." Murtagh placed the clasp in the pouch on his belt. Again he felt as if the village were a living thing that was waiting and watching with unknown intent. He grimaced, knelt, and used the ground to scrape more of the crow dung off his fingers. "I don't like this," he said, straightening back up. "I don't like this at all. There's more at work here than Bachel is willing to admit."

Thorn nodded toward the pouch. *A strange people to leave makings of the Forsworn lying about.*

"It's careless, all right. Or arrogant." He paused to consider, and his skin prickled with gooseflesh as an unsettling thought occurred to him. "What if . . . what if Galbatorix found Nal Gorgoth when he was traveling back through the Spine, after Urgals killed his dragon? Or what if this is where he and my father fled after they betrayed the Riders? I've always heard it said that Galbatorix hid in an evil place, where the Riders dared not follow. What if Nal Gorgoth is that place? What if *this* is where Galbatorix met Durza and . . . where they trained my father?"

Thorn hissed, snakelike. Murtagh shared the sentiment.

If the Riders were familiar with Nal Gorgoth, why would they suffer it to endure?

"I don't know. Maybe they thought it was abandoned. Maybe they set fire to the place and drove out the original inhabitants. We don't know how long Bachel or her people have been here. The buildings are older than any I've seen. Who knows who made them."

Thorn's gaze grew more intent. *Umaroth knew enough to warn us against coming here. What if the dragons of old and their Riders—*his tongue flicked across his teeth—*were afraid?*

✦ ✦ ✦ ✦ ✦ ✦

CHAPTER IV

Dreams and Portents

Murtagh and Thorn stared at each other, an unspoken question hanging between them. What or whom would dragons or Riders fear?

"If Galbatorix and Morzan came here," said Murtagh, "perhaps all of the Forsworn did." He looked at the silhouettes of the dark rooftops and at the moonlit tip of the Tower of Flint. His discovery of the clasp put everything Bachel had said during the banquet into a new light. And yet he remained uncertain. Was he making unfounded assumptions? His gut told him there was something to Bachel's claims of fate and prophecy. He just didn't know what or to what degree. Perhaps his desire to learn more about her and the blackened land was a foolish one.

He turned back to Thorn. "Maybe you're right. Maybe we *should* leave. What say you?"

Thorn blinked, his surprise evident. In all their time together, Murtagh had never before suggested abandoning whatever goal they were pursuing. Thorn dug the tips of his claws into the cracks between the flagstones. *If this is the place that Riders feared to tread—*

"Which it might not be."

Thorn's nostrils flared. *If it is, we must know, for the sake of the hatchlings at Mount Arngor. Anything dangerous enough to threaten the Riders of old could destroy the next generation of dragons. Stay on the hunt, search the spoor. There are old secrets here, I can smell it.*

"All right. But we have to be smart about this. There's no point in getting ourselves killed."

With Thorn following, Murtagh made his way around the northeastern corner of the temple. Behind it lay a swath of cropped turf that, despite the time of year, was soft beneath his feet. A path led across the grass to a small grove of pinetrees set against the base of the foothills.

As Murtagh approached the trees, he noticed the air growing warmer. It was damp too, and the smell of brimstone again rose up to meet him. The ground around the trees was crusted black, similar to the area in front of the village, and tongues of steam drifted from the earth. And yet it was not barren. The grove seemed a garden of sorts. By the moonlight, he saw blueberry bushes and flowers—their blossoms closed and drooping downward for the night—and a vast assortment of mushrooms arranged in pleasing patterns.

He thought of the secret garden in the catacombs of Gil'ead and wondered.

Thorn hesitated at the mouth of the grove, but the path was wide—the villagers had trimmed the lower levels of branches—and there was room for him to walk without scraping the trees. So he followed Murtagh, and Murtagh was glad for the company.

"Remind me to brush out your footsteps when we head back," he murmured.

A sense of acknowledgment came from Thorn.

The heart of the grove was even darker than inside the Tower of Flint. Murtagh finally relented and whispered, "Brisingr." The werelight he created was a tiny wisp, no brighter than a dying coal. But it was enough to see where to place his feet.

The path wound between the trees, past beds of well-tended, well-weeded plants—mostly herbs and berries—until it reached the foothills.

There, Murtagh beheld an even greater darkness yawning before them, like a wound cut into the side of the hills. At first his eyes refused to make sense of the absence. Was he looking *at* something? *Into* something? Was it a shadow?

Unable to understand, he increased the flow of energy to the werelight and allowed it to brighten until—

He saw.

An open mouth of stone and earth gaping before them. The cavern was large enough that Thorn could have easily fit within, and the interior was a mysterious black depth, swimming with impenetrable shadows and unquiet with ominous sounds: the click of a falling stone, a heavy influx and outflux of heated air—as if the mountains themselves were breathing, slow and labored—the high-pitched squeaks of fluttering bats, and even, Murtagh imagined, the low, nearly inaudible groans of the earth's massive weight as it settled and shifted, constantly seeking to further collapse into the tumbled ruins time made of all things.

Along both sides of the gaping cavern was stonework of a kind with the rest of the village, and set within the stonework, a mirrored pair of iron rings, each as wide as Murtagh was tall. The rings were so stout, they could have held even Thorn, and by the wavering werelight, they appeared dark and rusted and stained black with what resembled dried blood.

An altar made of cut basalt stood to the left of the cavern, which seemed odd. Murtagh felt it would have been more impressive—and more visually pleasing—to center the altar on the opening. Compared with the altar in the cathedral at Dras-Leona, this one appeared crude, unfinished even. Still, it had a rough presence that made Murtagh think of ancient rites and sacrifices performed to appease an unkind god.

The stench of brimstone was stronger than ever. A thick wave of it rolled out of the cavern, hot and unpleasant, and Murtagh gagged at the reek of rotten eggs. He covered his nose and mouth with his sleeve.

Thorn tasted the air and then wrinkled his snout and hissed. He said, *I smell old meat and flowing water and . . .* His scales prickled. *And the stink of men. They are—*

Footsteps sounded from the cavern, faint but approaching, as two or more people climbed out of the black depths.

Back! said Murtagh, alarmed. He snuffed his werelight and retreated as quickly and quietly as he could.

Our tracks! Thorn said as he did likewise.

The footsteps were growing louder.

Murtagh hastily whispered, "Vindr!" and a small stream of wind swept smooth the path as they rushed through the grove.

Glancing over his shoulder, Murtagh thought he glimpsed a group of robed figures through the trees. His pulse quickened. Had they spotted Thorn? It was dark, and the grove was dense, so maybe not. Maybe.

The two guards were still in their enchanted sleep when he and Thorn hurried into the courtyard.

"Up, up!" said Murtagh.

Thorn crouched low, and Murtagh climbed onto his neck. He held on tightly, and the dragon lifted him high enough to scramble onto the temple's skirt-roof and thence into his chambers.

As he did, Thorn curled up by the far side of the courtyard.

Just in time. Peering out the north-facing window, Murtagh saw four men, hooded and somber, walk past the temple and disperse among the streets of the village.

He let out his breath. Then he returned to the courtyard window and looked back at Thorn. *Bachel has much to explain,* he said. *And I want to know what the Dreamers find so important about that cave.*

Thorn snorted. *Whatever it is, I think the fumes from below rot their minds.*

Murtagh scratched at his forearm, troubled. *You might be right. Either way, I'd like to know the truth.* Although, in this case, he wondered if the truth might be as dangerous as ignorance.

He and Thorn forwent the sharing of their true names. There

was too great a risk of being overheard in Nal Gorgoth, even if they confined themselves to the privacy of their minds.

Keep a close watch tonight, said Murtagh.

That I shall. If there's the slightest thing amiss, I'll wake you.

Thank you.

Then Murtagh ended the spell he was using to keep the guards asleep. The two men snorted and stirred but did not open their eyes; they were genuinely tired, and he thought it likely they would slumber straight through until morn.

Lastly, Murtagh closed the shutters to his bedroom, cloistering himself in the pregnant darkness.

Murtagh lit the taper by the bed and then went to the washroom and did his best to cleanse himself of the crow dung. Even with the help of some magic, he wasn't entirely successful. He hoped he didn't smell enough to arouse Bachel's or Grieve's suspicions.

Shirtless, he sat on the edge of the bed. The mattress was stuffed with wool, not straw. An unexpected luxury. He held Saerlith's clasp, which he had also washed, and studied it by the flickering candlelight.

If the Dreamers *had* been allied with Saerlith or the other Forsworn, did the partnership mean so little to them that the villagers would leave Saerlith's clasp to sit like a piece of rubbish in the Tower of Flint? Or had it been dropped and forgotten, the result of some accident?

Questions. So many questions.

In the back of his mind, Murtagh felt Thorn's thoughts grow strange and disjointed as the dragon passed into a troubled slumber. As always, Murtagh wished he could soothe Thorn, but he feared to wake him, so he sat and kept to himself, and the dragon's dreams only worsened Murtagh's own unease.

He leaned back with a sigh.

A day, two at the most. That was what he'd allow. If, by then, he and Thorn didn't find answers to the many questions Bachel and Nal Gorgoth raised, it would be time to apply force—by words or by action—and pry loose the information.

Murtagh shivered and reached for his shirt.

The chambers were cold and getting colder. He considered lighting a fire, but he was tired and didn't want to deal with tending the flames through the night. So he wet his fingers, pinched out the taper, and burrowed under the sheepskin and blankets.

After a few minutes, he turned the sheepskin wool-side down. *There.* Then he pulled the blankets up to his neck and closed his eyes as warmth gathered around his body.

It took him some time to quiet his thoughts enough to sleep. He *wanted* to rest; tomorrow, he suspected, would be trying, and it was important to be as sharp as possible in the event that their time in Nal Gorgoth came to violence. But he couldn't stop thinking about the Tower of Flint, Saerlith's clasp, and the cavern sitting like a great gluttonous toad behind the temple.

~~~~~~~~~~~~~~~~~~~~~ ❖ ~~~~~~~~~~~~~~~~~~~~~

Whirling darkness swallowed him, and in the center of it, at the bottom of an impossibly deep hole, at the very heart of the widdershin void, lay a formless horror—ancient and evil and from which emanated a constant, merciless hunger: never sated, all-consuming, with a particular glee for the sufferings of creatures caught between the gnashing of teeth.

His mind fled the horror, but it was a deadly riptide, more powerful than the Boar's Eye between the Southern Isles of Uden and Parlim, and the harder he tried, the slower he moved. . . .

Fear filled him. Icy, coursing fear that froze his veins and chained his limbs and turned his stomach to acid. His heart fluttered, and for a moment seemed to stop, and in the grips of his terror, he cried for help as he had when a child: "Mother!"

Then Thorn's mind touched his own, and the gaping horror receded, and for a time Murtagh felt himself lost in the vast landscape of Thorn's thoughts.

They were flying, higher and higher, until the ground faded from sight, and above and below were the same: a perfect sphere of sky, with nowhere to land and only clouds for cover. A flock of eagles screamed past, talons extended to tear out eyes, and then they were gone, and it was impossible to tell which direction was up and which down.

A timeless while passed, and then a thunder of dragons rose about them: dragons of every shape and color, their scales flashing, their wings thudding until all the air vibrated like a drum. For an instant, hope and companionship, but only an instant. The dragons turned on them and attacked them and tore at Thorn's flesh until his wings were tattered remnants and he plunged from the pale sphere of the sky into the heated depths of the earth, where the dirt was heavy and pressing and the only solace was pain and hate and the steady drip of their own hot blood.

Nasuada stood in front of him. Her dress was ripped and stained, and across her forearms, he saw the cuts and bruises Galbatorix had forced him to inflict upon her, and with them, the bloody tracks where the burrow grubs had chewed their way beneath her skin, and his guilt knew no bounds. "Why?" she said. "Why, why, why? Tell me . . . why?"

A disjunction, and then a battlefield stretched before them, from their feet to the smoke-smudged horizon. Humans and Urgals and elves struggled in their thousands: a sea of heaving bodies intent on inflicting pain on one another.

Zar'roc was in Murtagh's right hand, and his shield in the other, and Thorn stood beside him. They roared together and strode forth into maddened conflict. And Murtagh swung his sword with abandon, and he felt the familiar shock of impact as the blade sliced through flesh and bone, and his foes fell before him. A wall of rippling flame shot out ahead of him as Thorn sprayed the collected warriors with liquid fire. The smell of burnt hair and crisping skin filled the air, and the combatants screamed as they cooked in their armor.

Murtagh continued forward, Zar'roc lighter in his hand than ever before. And he killed, and he killed, and with each kill, he felt growing power.

A cloud of crows wheeled above the battlefield, and in the distance, hidden by the smoke but in presence felt, Bachel watched. And Murtagh knew she watched with approval.

CHAPTER V

✦ ✦ ✦ ✦ ✦ ✦ ✦

Recitations of Faith

The sound of bells woke Murtagh, a high, brassy *clang* that bounced off the mountains and set the crows in the Tower of Flint to cawing.

He blinked, instantly alert, and reached for Zar'roc. The familiar feel of the wire-wrapped hilt comforted him.

Grey light pervaded the bedroom. It seemed well into morning, but because of the high mountains, the sun had yet to rise.

Murtagh searched for Thorn's mind . . . and found the dragon already awake in the courtyard below.

They shared a moment of closeness, and Thorn said, *You dreamt as I did.*

It wasn't a question, but Murtagh answered all the same. *Yes. I . . . I've never had an experience like that before.*

He could feel Thorn shifting in place. *The visions were like those HE showed us, during the dark time.*

Murtagh suppressed a shiver. Of all the many tortures Galbatorix had inflicted upon them, Murtagh had hated those most of all. The king would, at his whim, flood their minds with false images that served to confuse the senses and make it difficult to resist his will.

Yes, he said. *But different too. They were more real than real.* He sat and swung his legs over the edge of the bed. He stared at the wall for a moment, and then rubbed his face in a futile attempt to dispel the memories of the night.

Umaroth was right. This is not a good place, said Thorn. *We should not linger any longer than necessary.*

Maybe not, but I want to hear what Bachel has to say for herself today. She owes us an explanation. Several explanations.

Murtagh went to the washroom and splashed his face with the last bit of water remaining in the jug. Were the ill humors that suffused Nal Gorgoth enough to explain their dreams? Or was there another force at work? Unlike with Galbatorix's coercions, Murtagh hadn't felt any mind touching theirs during the night. The dreams seemed to have arisen unbidden from the deepest burrows of their consciousness.

Thorn snorted. *Those were no dreams of mine.*

No. Murtagh well knew what Thorn dreamt of: flights and fights and their time spent imprisoned at Urû'baen.

Though it made him nervous to do so, Murtagh used the word *kverst* to remove the stubble from his face. It fell from his skin as a shedding of black dust. He ran a hand across his chin, satisfied. He did not want to appear anything less than perfectly presentable before Bachel.

Then he dried his face and belted on Zar'roc and tucked Saerlith's clasp into his belt.

As he started toward the door, a knock sounded, and a woman said, "May I enter, Kingkiller?"

Murtagh bridled at the title. Though the Dreamers seemed to use it as a sign of respect, it sat badly with him. "You may."

The door swung inward to reveal Alín, the young woman who had attended him and Bachel during the feast. As before, she wore a white robe, unlike the rest of the villagers. A tray with food rested in her hands.

She bowed slightly—which Murtagh found odd; the maids in Urû'baen had always curtsied—and carried the tray to the side table by the bed. "Breakfast, my Lord."

It gave Murtagh a discomfiting feeling to be addressed as *my Lord* again. It was his due, of course, but only because of his father's treachery. Technically, he no longer held claim to any title but that of Rider . . . and Kingkiller. And traitor.

He feigned a relaxed smile as he strode over to inspect the contents of the tray. Half a loaf of dense rye bread, three kippered bergenhed, and a tankard of watered wine. Standard fare, as such things went, but he didn't trust the food. The feast last night had been a spontaneous event, and he'd watched as the meal was prepared. However, the breakfast could easily have been tampered with. It wasn't worth the risk. He still had a bit of cooked hare in his saddlebags, and that would hold him for a time.

"I'm afraid I don't have much of an appetite," he said in a mild tone.

The woman seemed uncomfortable in his presence. She stiffened as he approached, and then ducked her head and twisted the tips of the blue ribbon tied around her waist. "Of course, my Lord. I'll remove the tray."

When she started to reach for it, he said, "Your name is Alín, yes?"

Softly: "Yes."

He nodded. "Would you be so kind as to guide me back to the courtyard, Alín? I can't say I remember the way." A lie, but he wanted the opportunity to question her.

She bowed again and, subdued, said, "Yes, sir. After me, sir."

With brisk steps, Alín led him out of the room. Murtagh followed, but at a slower pace—slow enough that she was forced to halve her stride.

"Tell me, Alín," said Murtagh, "for I much desire to know: How long has Bachel ruled in Nal Gorgoth?"

She gave him a quick, shy glance from under her pale lashes. "A very long time, my Lord. Far longer than I have winters."

Murtagh let his eyebrows rise. If Alín was telling the truth, then Bachel *was* half elf, as that was the only obvious explanation for why the witch lacked any obvious sign of age. "Would you say she has been a fair ruler, Alín?"

"Of course, Kingkiller," she answered in a reproachful tone. "Bachel is the Speaker. How could she be anything *but* just?"

"How indeed? I imagine being able to foretell the future might help avoid such a misstep. Would you say she is adept at prophecy?"

The woman nodded quickly. "Oh yes, my Lord. It is her duty to guide us, and we are fortunate she has been blessed with such great skill in augury."

"I see." Murtagh paused before the panel of stone carvings along the landing. In the morning light, they appeared no less disturbing.

Alín stopped as well. She had no choice.

"You wear white, not grey," Murtagh observed.

The woman folded her hands in front of her, and her long sleeves covered them. "I am one of the temple chosen. These robes represent our purity. So long as I serve in the temple, at Bachel's will, no man may touch me on pain of losing the hands he sinned with." She lifted her gaze to meet his, and Murtagh saw a challenge in her eyes, as if she were daring him to break the prohibition.

"And likewise, you may not touch a man."

"No, my Lord."

He nodded. Then, more gently, he said, "What is the purpose of Nal Gorgoth, Alín? What is it Bachel seeks to accomplish?"

The moment the words left his mouth, he knew he'd overreached. Alín's back straightened, and her shoulders squared, and a spark of defiant fire animated her expression. "You could not possibly understand if I told you, outsider. Such understanding can only come from Bachel herself, for she is the—"

"The Speaker. Yes, you said." Even though it was more than likely fruitless, he decided to press on. "But I wonder, for whom does Bachel speak, Alín? Who is the Dreamer of Dreams?"

The color drained from Alín's cheeks. "Please, my Lord. You should not ask me such a thing."

"But I do."

She shook her head. "I cannot say. I beg you—"

"Cannot or will not?"

She shook her head again, all defiance vanished, and turned her back to him. "You do not understand. You cannot. Please, my Lord, this way."

Thoughtful, Murtagh followed her across the landing—away from the maddening carvings—down the stairs, and through the hallways that led to the courtyard.

When they arrived at the door to the outside, Alín surprised him by stopping with her hand on the frame. In a small voice, she said, "What is it like, Kingkiller?"

"What do you mean?"

She looked back at him, her face lost in the shadows of the unlit hallway. "Out there . . . beyond. What is the rest of Alagaë-sia like?"

"What is the farthest you have been from Nal Gorgoth?"

A hint of defensive sorrow colored her voice. "I have never left this valley, Kingkiller."

It was not an unexpected answer for one of her station, yet Mur-tagh found it difficult to imagine having such a limited perspective. To be so blinkered in place could only lead to being similarly blinkered in mind.

He thought for a moment on how best to answer. Then: "Ala-gaësia is far wider and wilder than you can imagine. There are mountains so high their peaks vanish from sight. Vast deserts where dragons used to live. Forests so old no memory remains of their birth. And there are cities too: large and small, and peo-ples of all sorts. Humans and elves and dwarves and Urgals. Even werecats. And so, so much more."

A hint of wistfulness might have appeared in Alín's expres-sion, but it was difficult to tell for sure in the dark hallway. "And what do they dream of, all those people?"

Murtagh watched to see what effect his words had. "Every per-son dreams their own dreams. Some are frightening or unpleas-ant. Some are beautiful and hopeful. Some are silly or nonsense. They differ for every person."

"Even for you?"

"Why would they not?"

"Because," she said, seeming confused, "you are a Rider."

He felt equally confounded. "What does being a Rider have to do with the dreams I have?"

Alín frowned. "Surely you must know, my Lord. You are joined with a dragon, and dragons are the blood and bones of the land. They are the source of everything that was and is and shall be. I thought that, because of your bond with Thorn, that . . ."

"You thought what?" Murtagh asked gently.

"That you would have the same dreams as we do in Nal Gorgoth."

"Does everyone here dream the same, Alín?"

She turned back to the door. "It is the one thing I cannot bear. The dreadful sameness, night after night. The dreams so rarely change."

Then she pushed open the door and stepped out before Murtagh could ask another question.

~~~~~~~~~~~~~~~ ❖ ~~~~~~~~~~~~~~~

Thorn gave Murtagh a welcoming nudge as they came together in the courtyard. He scratched Thorn's snout in response.

Then he became aware that Alín was standing behind him with her hands clasped and her gaze fixed on the flagstones, her whole body stiff as if she were terrified. But when she stole a glance at Thorn, her eyes shone, and he realized that she was overawed by Thorn's presence.

"Have you ever seen a dragon before?" he asked.

She shook her head, keeping her gaze turned down. "No, my Lord. He is magnificent."

I like her, said Thorn.

You would. Would you mind if I—

You may.

With a small smile, Murtagh said, "If you want, you may come closer."

Alín gasped and looked up with undisguised joy. "Oh! Yes, please. I mean, thank you, my Lord." With careful steps, she approached Thorn.

She squeaked as Thorn arched his neck and loomed over her, a puff of smoke jetting out from his nostrils.

Murtagh smirked. *You're as dramatic as a troubadour.*

Thorn ignored him and lowered his head until he was at eye level with Alín. She stood very still, but her expression was wide and shining, and the tips of her fingers trembled.

"He won't hurt you," Murtagh said.

Alín laughed with febrile energy. "It would not matter if he did. I would be honored. It is not every day you meet a living god."

Murtagh felt his eyebrows rise. He gave Thorn a look. "Do you hear that? A *living god*, she says."

The dragon surprised him then, for Murtagh felt Thorn extend his mind until it contacted Alín's, and for a fraction of a second, the three of them were joined. Murtagh had a brief impression of Alín's inner self: a sense of warmth and wonder and overwhelming radiance.

Then Thorn withdrew the connection, and Alín cried out and fell to her knees.

Murtagh went to her, meaning to help. At the last moment, he remembered not to touch and stopped with his hands hovering on either side of her shoulders. He retreated a step. "Are you all right?"

It was a long moment before she stirred and looked up, tears on her cheeks. "I never thought to be so blessed," she whispered. She turned back to Thorn and bowed her head. "Thank you. Thank you. A thousand thanks upon you."

Murtagh wasn't sure how to respond. He watched as she gathered herself and stood. "Bachel will send for you soon," she said, her voice as thin and pale as a winter sky. "Be ready to attend her. She does not stand for delay."

"No, I would imagine not," said Murtagh.

Alín gave Thorn one last look—her expression suddenly troubled—and then fled into the temple.

Without her, the courtyard seemed cold and empty.

Murtagh turned back to Thorn. He frowned. "Why?"

With a scrape of scales against stone, Thorn wound his neck around Murtagh and trapped him in a great coil. *It seemed appropriate.*

"Because she said you were magnificent?"

Thorn coughed. *No. Because she has been told much but seen little. I was like that once. It is good to know the truth of things.*

At that, Murtagh's stance softened. "I suppose you're right." Thorn hummed, and Murtagh scratched his snout again. "Well, as long as she didn't see anything about last night, there's no harm done."

And perhaps some good.

"Perhaps."

Then Thorn uncoiled his neck and Murtagh retrieved the haunch of roasted hare from Thorn's saddlebags. He ate quickly, not knowing how long it would be until Bachel summoned them.

Voices sounded from within the streets leading off the courtyard: rhythmic chanting that seemed more ceremonial than musical.

Curious, Murtagh wiped his fingers and wandered down the nearest street, Thorn at his back.

He didn't have to go far before he saw a group of twenty or so Dreamers gathered around an alcove built within the outer wall of a house. In the alcove was a small altar—not dissimilar to the one he'd found last night—with fruits and cuts of meat piled in the center.

Another white-robed Dreamer, a man, stood facing the rest of the villagers, and it was to him the people directed their voices. The chanting was so fast, so practiced, that at first Murtagh couldn't distinguish one word from the next, but as he listened, he began to pick out repeated phrases, such as "With our hands, so we serve," "As it is dreamt, so it shall be," and "Given our earthly reward, praise be."

Between the repeated phrases, he realized the villagers were describing their dreams from that night: something to do with blood and fire and ancient wrongs. The specifics escaped him, but he caught words here and there, like silver fish flashing through a stream. Some of it reminded him of the visions he and Thorn had shared, but only in part; the rest seemed to vary wildly from what they had seen.

It was clear the villagers were well accustomed to their dreams, as Alín had claimed. The chanting was rote, ritualistic, nearly unconscious, with a trance-inducing quality, as if the drumming of their voices numbed their minds. The villagers' eyes glazed over as they swayed along with the rhythm of their words.

As he stood watching, he found himself struck by the co-hesion of the group. The villagers appeared more like a single, many-faced entity than a collection of individuals. The cause that bound them—whatever it was—seemed so strong as to erase their differences. The result was intimidating.

Even with Thorn by his side, a hollow sense of envy formed within Murtagh. He missed the moments, rare as they'd been, when he'd felt joined in common purpose with the soldiers of Galbatorix's army. The camaraderie had brought with it a certain confidence—a fortification of self, even as his definition of self had expanded to include his brothers-in-arms. He had recaptured the sense, all too briefly, while drilling with the guards in Gil'ead. And looking even further back, he had shared a similar feeling during his travels with Eragon.

But those days were long since passed.

Thorn touched his elbow, and Murtagh smiled sadly.

The chanting continued with numerous repetitions of "As it is dreamt, so it shall be," and the repetitions were so perfectly uniform, so perfectly matched in intonation and mindless recitation, that the sameness of it suddenly seemed repulsive. It felt as if he were watching a group of sleepwalking half-wits who moved without thinking, their blind, unblinking, cataractal eyes fixed upon a vague point in the distance, while their mouths hinged open and closed with synchronized precision. His envy evaporated, like mist before dragonfire, as he realized something else about the Dreamers: they were neither a conspiratorial group nor a political organization, nor even a martial one. In actuality, they were a cult, devoted to their dreams and to their Speaker above all else.

The chanting stopped.

For a moment, silence reigned in the street. Then the temple acolyte said, "Say now what differences you beheld, if any you did."

And a man with a birthmark as dark as a splash of wine across his nose said, "I saw a flight of dragons, only there was a crimson dragon in the middle. Before, there was none."

The acolyte nodded wisely. "Bachel's Ears have heard you. What else?"

A girl—no more than ten, with tresses like spun gold—said, "An obelisk of stone with a black tip and gilded carving. The carving glowed, and I heard a voice speaking words I did not understand."

The acolyte nodded again. "You will present yourself to Bachel at the morning hearing, and she will speak to you the meaning of your vision."

"As it is dreamt, so it shall be."

Murtagh continued to listen while the cultists confessed their dreams. He wondered how many of them spoke the truth and how many were inventing details for a chance to impress their neighbors or please Bachel. But perhaps that was unkind of him. The villagers seemed entirely sincere and convinced of their experiences.

They would be, he thought. He tried to imagine what it was like to grow up in Nal Gorgoth, being constantly questioned about your dreams, and if the dreams were of a like with what he and Thorn had experienced the past night . . . He shuddered.

Then a woman emerged from within the group. She was of middling age, with hair that hung in tangled skeins, and her face was drawn and dolorous, as if she'd been up the whole night fretting. She wrung her hands, the fingers twisted like roots.

"Hear me!" she cried.

The white-robed acolyte eyed her with something akin to disgust. "Speak and be heard, O Dethra."

The woman sobbed and shook her head before continuing. "I did not dream as was right and proper. My mind was empty all the night until just before waking. Then an image filled my mind, and I saw the white mountain with—"

The faces of those listening hardened, and Murtagh saw no charity in their expressions.

"Enough!" cried the acolyte. "Do not poison our minds with your false visions. You are unclean, Dethra."

"I am unclean!" she shouted, tears streaking down her cheeks.

"You are unworthy!"

"I am unworthy! Punish me! Let me atone!"

With a thunderous scowl, the acolyte pointed at her. "Dethra! You cannot regain favor in the Eyes of Bachel until you purge this heresy from your being. Go to the temple and confine yourself to the Azurite Room until such time as Bachel sees fit to bring you to the realm of the Dreamer."

The woman cried out with terror and collapsed onto the ground, where she shook and gibbered incomprehensibilities.

The white-robed acolyte stormed forward. He grabbed Dethra by the arm and dragged her toward the temple.

The crowd parted before them, men and women alike watching in stony silence. At the front of the group, the golden-haired girl chewed on her thumb, her eyes round and solemn.

In an undertone, Murtagh said to Thorn, "Is that woman most afraid of confinement or atonement?"

Or Bachel?

It was an unsettling thought. With Thorn close behind, Murtagh followed the acolyte back to the temple and watched as the man hauled Dethra into the building.

CHAPTER VI

✦ ✦ ✦ ✦ ✦ ✦ ✦

The Court of Crows

"There you are, Rider," said Grieve with heavy disapproval as he strode with a hurried pace toward Murtagh and Thorn. He made a bow so slight, it was more of a nod. "Dragon Thorn. Bachel will grant you audience now. The both of you."

Murtagh gestured at the temple. "Do you mean for us to go in there?"

"Of course. Bachel awaits you in her presence chamber."

Murtagh raised his eyebrows. "Alas, Goodman Grieve, I'm sorry to inform you that the doors of your temple are far too small for Thorn to pass through. Unless you mean for him to break them apart."

The flicker of irritation that crossed Grieve's face was satisfying. "I do not," he said stiffly. "Dragon Thorn, an atrium exists behind that will suffice if you will fly to it. Thence you may access the presence chamber."

Murtagh hesitated, glancing at Thorn. *Do you want to chance it?*

The dragon growled and, to both Murtagh and Grieve, said, *I will go so far as the atrium, but no farther. If Bachel wishes to speak with me, then she may come to me.*

Grieve's scowl deepened. "You risk offending the Speaker, Dragon Thorn."

Thorn sniffed. *So be it.* With a sweep of his wings, the dragon jumped into the air. His body blotted out the sky for a moment, and then he was above the temple, and there he hung, like a great crimson bat, before folding his wings and dropping out of sight behind the peak of the building.

In a mild tone, Murtagh said, "I'm afraid that no one can tell a dragon what to do, not even a Rider."

A grunt from Grieve, and he turned and walked with his lurching stride toward the temple's shadowed entrance.

Alert and curious, Murtagh followed, hand on hilt.

Deep between the faceted pillars, a pair of blackened oak doors stood open. The wood was chiseled with runes and inlaid with threads of gold that traced the same branching pattern carved into the face of the temple. The air within was noticeably warmer and thick with the smell of brimstone. Murtagh felt moisture collecting on his skin, tiny droplets of sulfurous dew.

They moved through a short passage lit by oil lamps. Then the way opened upon the atrium. It was large and square, with four raised pools—overgrown with reeds and floating moss— at the corners, while in the center stood a giant sculpture, nearly as tall as the surrounding roofline. The statue was made of black stone, and it was all angles and shards and misjoined edges, but when taken as a whole, there was a *shape* amid the chaos. He felt as if he ought to recognize it, but the truth eluded him, like a name or a face that he couldn't place.

Thorn had landed next to the statue and was looking at it as if he meant to knock it over with a swipe of his tail.

"What *is* that?" Murtagh asked.

Grieve continued trudging on and didn't turn to look. "A depiction of dream."

Unease made Murtagh pull his cloak tighter. *What do you think?* he asked Thorn.

An abomination.

It's a nightmare, that's for sure.

As Murtagh continued after Grieve, Thorn said, *If they are so foolish as to attack you, I shall rip apart the building from top to bottom.*

Murtagh smiled, comforted. *Good.*

On the other side of the atrium, another passage doglegged to the south. It ended at a tall lancet doorway large enough for Thorn to pass through. Ironbound doors of dark oak stood open, and past them, a great space echoed.

The chamber seemed part throne room and part inner sanctum. In its center sat a brazier of hammered copper, ten feet across and laden with a bed of smoldering coals. From it, smoke and incense—rich with the scent of sage, pine, and cedar—thickened the air, although they could not obscure the underlying taint of brimstone, which seemed stronger, more concentrated there within the temple. Beneath the brazier, a heavy cast-iron pipe joined the bottom of the metal pan to the floor.

An open-roofed pavilion, made of angled stone, ringed the brazier. From the pavilion uprights, sculpted dragon heads extended over the coals, like gargoyles on the cathedral in Dras-Leona.

The ceiling was lost in shadow. The floor glinted with pearlescent chips of a vast multicolored mosaic that swirled in ways Murtagh's eyes found difficult to follow. Blood-red banners hung from the walls, their edges tattered, the fabric mildewed and moth-eaten.

Opposite the entrance, on the other side of the brazier and pavilion, was a long double arcade with stone chairs set between the carved columns, empty save for dust and memories. The arcade ended at a wide altar of ashen stone, behind which ascended several steps to a high-backed stone chair, cold and grey and carved with arcane patterns.

And reclining upon that unforgiving throne was Bachel in all her stark, imperious glory. A single shaft of light illuminated her from above—the beam filtered through some cleverly hidden window—and it rimmed her as if with holy radiance. Unlike before, she wore an elaborate headpiece of jade and leather that was black and polished to an oily sheen. Her dress was red and, again, sewn from strips of knotted straps. Rubies and emeralds glinted from the rings on her thumbs.

She was sipping from a cup of carved quartz, her eyes liquid amber in the glow from the brazier.

In every aspect, she presented an imposing figure, and a deep disquiet formed within Murtagh. It felt as if he were approaching a source of secret power; he could nearly taste the energy emanating from Bachel, as if she were the physical embodiment of some enormous force. Even Galbatorix, he thought, would have hesitated before the witch.

Three acolytes were arrayed before Bachel and the altar, kneeling on the mosaic, hoods drawn over their faces, hands pressed together in prayer. A single grey-robed villager—a dwarf seemingly of middle age—stood in their midst, and he said, "... twelve upon twelve, and the black swan burst into fire over the field of battle, and—"

Bachel lifted a finger, stopping him. "You have had another vision of victory, Genvek."

The dwarf tugged on his braided beard. "There is yet more, Speaker. After the swan, I saw—"

"You may tell me of it later, my child," Bachel said as Grieve arrived at the altar, with Murtagh trailing behind.

The witch, Murtagh noticed, seemed none the worse for wear after her indulgence at the feast. Bachel smiled, and her teeth shone translucent as polished cowrie shells in the pale light from above. "This court has a guest that needs attending. Begone for the nonce."

Genvek the dwarf appeared put out, but he tugged on his beard again, bowed, and departed with a black glare directed toward Murtagh.

"Come now, Kingkiller," said Bachel, her voice proud and strong. "Approach that I may see you more clearly."

Murtagh obliged. He stepped between the acolytes and stood before them, though he hated to have anyone at his back.

Bachel's smile widened as she studied him. Then she gestured at the temple in a most elegant manner, the gems on her fingers tracing constellations through the air. "Welcome to the Court of Crows, Murtagh Morzansson. It has been over half a century since last a Rider stood here."

And was that Saerlith or another of the Forsworn? Or Galbatorix himself? Murtagh wondered.

Before he could reply to Bachel, she said, "And welcome to thee as well, Dragon Thorn."

Murtagh turned to see that Thorn had stuck his head into the entrance of the presence chamber. The dragon did not dare more than that, but Murtagh was still grateful to have him near.

Feeling somewhat more confident, he said, "I must admit, I see no crows, Lady."

The witch laughed, and her husky voice echoed off the shadowed ceiling. "Look closer, Kingkiller. There is much you do not see."

Murtagh hated being told that he didn't understand something. And he especially hated when it was true.

Forcing an expression of polite blandness, he turned his gaze upward while also extending outward with his consciousness. Scores of tiny minds immediately appeared above him, as rings of candles set about a ritual space. Crows. A whole flock of them perched along the underside of the ceiling, on cornices and carvings and beams of stone. Now that he knew what to listen for, he could hear the noises as they clucked and muttered and moved about on their tapping claws. And yet none of them cawed, and he saw no droppings on the mosaic below.

He raised an eyebrow. "The floor is very clean."

Bachel's smile grew mysterious. "The crows are my kin. I speak to them, and they answer. I command them, and they obey, as do all of my children." Then she raised a hand and said, "*Come,*" and he heard magic in the word: a compulsion that nearly caused him to step forward before he mastered himself.

With a soft gale of flapping wings, the crows descended in a black cloud and settled upon the back and arms of Bachel's throne and on the dais surrounding her. As one, the dire flock fixed their ghostly eyes upon Murtagh—white irises stark and staring in the chamber's gloom.

Bachel chuckled and clucked fondly at the birds. One of them hopped close to her, and she scratched it on the head and under the beak while the bird closed its eyes in apparent bliss.

"You see, Kingkiller," she said, "Speaker I am, but also am I the Queen of Crows."

There was an unreality to the image of her sitting regnant amid the murmuring multitude, a specter-like quality that made Murtagh feel as if the world had shifted sideways and he was no longer in a place where the familiar rules of nature held sway, but rather an older, wilder sort of reasoning.

He heard Thorn release a low hiss at the front of the chamber.

Murtagh made a small bow. "The extent of your power is truly impressive, Lady Bachel. It seems even the common crow recognizes your authority."

"Crows are far from common," said Bachel. She cooed at the bird she was scratching. "Did you know, my son, that the Urgals believe crows carry the souls of the dead to their afterlife?"

"I did not."

She nodded. "The sight of the crow fills an Urgal with immense dread, but an Urgal will also go to great lengths to help a crow in need or to avoid hurting one, for they think that if they anger the crows, the birds will refuse to carry them to the fields of their ancestors once they die."

"And what do you believe, my Lady?"

Bachel lifted an eyebrow. Then she said, "Go," and her voice rang with power. The birds took off in a flurry into the shadows above. "I believe that crows are hungry and they have no scruples as to how they sate their appetite, which is why you will always find them gathered on the field of battle to feast on the fallen."

Murtagh's lip curled with revulsion. "A grim reckoning and an unpleasant habit, my Lady."

The witch sipped from her cup, unconcerned. "You cannot fault them for their nature."

"Neither do I have to praise them for it."

Bachel inclined her head. "That is true." Then her eyes narrowed, and the amber in them darkened. "Tell me, my child, did you rest well last night?"

"Well enough."

Her gaze further sharpened. "And did you and Thorn dream? You must have. All creatures in this vale dream, even crows."

She asks most eagerly, said Thorn.

That she does. Murtagh toyed with the ruby set in Zar'roc's pommel as he considered. He didn't want to tell Bachel anything too personal, but he was curious how she would interpret their visions. Whatever she said could reveal more about the Dreamers than he would reveal about himself.

So he told her, leaving out but one detail: Nasuada's appearance in his dream. That *was* too personal, and Murtagh had no intention of dissecting its meaning with a stranger.

"And what of you, Thorn?" asked Bachel. "What saw you?"

Thorn growled softly. *I saw much the same.*

Then the witch tilted her face to catch the beam of light that broke upon her brow, and she let out a long sigh. "Ah, such beautiful visions, Kingkiller. I can feel their promise, like the warm touch of dawn's first rays."

"I would hardly call them beautiful."

She lowered her gaze to him. "That is because your sight is blinkered, my son, limited by your senses and the confines of your mind. As is true of all of us, even you, Thorn."

"But you can see the truth?" Murtagh asked, not hiding his disbelief.

A shake of her head swayed her headpiece. "No. I do not claim such wisdom. I am merely a conduit for understanding. An interpreter, if you will."

"Then interpret."

The corners of Bachel's mouth curved. "Very well, Kingkiller. I shall." She closed her eyes, and the acolytes bowed in rhythmic fashion and began to chant in an unfamiliar tongue, and Grieve lowered his head until only his widow's peak showed. Sparks flared in the brazier as Bachel uttered several low words in the strange language, words that lingered in the air longer than was right. For a moment, the chamber seemed to dim as if a shadow pressed in on them from without.

A chill crept into the heated air.

Murtagh held his place, but all the hair on his body stood on end. He felt as if he were in an open field during a heavy thunderstorm while lightning threatened. *How very theatric,* he commented to Thorn. Nevertheless, he couldn't deny the effect the ceremony had on him.

When Bachel spoke, her voice had an eerie, hollow timbre: "Behold . . . as it was, so it shall be. See you now the center of all things, the king on his throne, the snake in his lair. See you now past sorrows—injustices unrevenged—and future triumphs. The cleansing sword, the son freed of his father. See you this now, and know it to be true. As it is dreamt, so it shall be."

Icy dread coiled within Murtagh's core, and his whole body tensed at the word *father,* the response as instinctual as pain.

Bachel slumped slightly. Then she opened her eyes and, in a tired manner, gestured at the acolytes. They ceased bowing and chanting, and the chamber again fell silent.

Murtagh fought to remain impassive, though his muscles were as taut as so many weighted cables.

The witch straightened upon her throne. "There now, King-killer. I have said my piece."

"The Speaker has spoken," Grieve murmured.

"And yet," said Murtagh, "I understand no more than when you started."

Bachel replied: "That is because I have yet to explain the

explanation. Be not so bound by convention, my fair princeling. You must learn to see with more than your mortal vision."

Murtagh's frown deepened. "What is it you want, Bachel? Why have you seeded your servants throughout Alagaësia? To what end? And why is it you say Thorn and I are to be the saviors of the land? How? And from what?"

"Do you recognize the shape of this sanctum, my child?" Bachel asked, indicating the chamber about them.

Caught off-guard, Murtagh fumbled his reply. "No. I don't."

"You should. It has a sister beneath Urû'baen: the Hall of the Soothsayer. I believe you are well familiar with it."

For a moment, Murtagh grew weak, and he nearly sat. He trembled slightly.

He glanced around. The witch was right. If he ignored the arcade and the pillars and the open pavilion, the general layout of the space was similar, if not identical, to the Hall of the Soothsayer. And the ashen altar, that hateful slab of stone, was no different from the one where Galbatorix had kept Nasuada chained. . . .

Bachel leaned forward, hawklike. "The sacred vapors that emanate from the ground here likewise once emanated from the rocks and stones beneath Urû'baen. Then too a Speaker dwelt in that hall and breathed of them and dispensed the wisdom of dream to those wise enough to consult her."

Had Galbatorix known the truth about the Soothsayer? He had claimed ignorance regarding her origin, but if there was one thing Murtagh had learned over the years, it was that the king lied, and he lied well.

Perhaps Bachel also lies, said Thorn.

With some difficulty, Murtagh found his voice. "You claim the same mantle as the Soothsayer?"

"We are of the same lineage, in beliefs and observance, if not blood."

Murtagh glanced back at Thorn, feeling lost. Everything he had heard of the Soothsayer of old had spoken of her uncanny foresight, and there were more than a few stories of people who had ignored her advice—or sought to contravene it—to their inevitable sorrow.

Murtagh had never been able to bring himself to believe that the future was set. Like Thorn, he hated the idea that some impersonal force dictated the shape of his life. The very concept sapped all motive and responsibility from his choices. And yet . . . if Bachel were an oracle in truth, then he needed to know what she predicted for him and Thorn, if only that they might take a stand against it.

The witch seemed to read his thoughts, though he felt no touch upon his mind. "I will say this to start, my son: it was Fate that brought you here. You could no more have resisted the urge to find Nal Gorgoth—and me within it—than a moth may resist the lure of a nighttime flame. The threads of destiny may be plucked by those who know how. Plucked, and severed. Nal Gorgoth and places like it have endured for longer than you can imagine. No dragon or Rider or elf or any other creature in all the history of the land has ever succeeded in clearing our redoubts or snuffing our faith."

"Not even Galbatorix?" said Murtagh in a flat tone.

Bachel's smile widened, showing more teeth than was normal for a human. "Not even the dread dragonkiller himself, Rider. He tried, once, and soon realized the magnitude of his mistake."

Fear and frustration broke Murtagh's control. "Who *are* you?" he cried, allowing some of his power to enter his voice. He could use words to control and command just as easily as Bachel—and he had a dragon backing him to boot.

His voice resounded off the walls of the chamber, and Grieve and the white-robed acolytes stiffened. "Speaker!" said Grieve, the word coming from between clenched teeth.

Bachel seemed unaffected. She waved a hand at Grieve. "Peace, my child. You are as nervous as a spring rabbit. Our guest means us no harm." The muscles along Grieve's jaw bunched, yet he held his peace.

Murtagh was not about to do the same. "But my patience grows thin. You promised me answers, Bachel, but so far, all I have are more questions."

Her nails tapped against the arm of her throne. "Do you doubt my word?"

"No, my Lady, only the timing of its fulfillment."

She eyed him with a hooded gaze, her headpiece and shoulders haloed with pale radiance from above. "Walk among us for a day and a night, you and Thorn both. See what we are and how we live, ere you seek to pass judgment on us. Dream once more in Nal Gorgoth, and let your mind wander wide and deep."

She was being evasive. That much was obvious, but at the same time, the offer was tempting. So much about Bachel and the Dreamers was difficult to explain, and Murtagh felt it was desperately important to have a better idea of what they were and what they wanted. Especially if Bachel had the same powers of prophecy as the Soothsayer. They had to learn more. For himself. For Thorn. And for Nasuada.

What say you? he asked Thorn.

One day more is no great price.

Lifting his chin, Murtagh said, "If we do, will you forgo your riddles for plainer speech?"

The witch made a gracious gesture with her hand, as if inviting him to bow. "If you do, and you strive to see but truly, then yes, Kingkiller, I will explain my prophecy and more besides. I will lay bare the threads of fate, and you will understand both the role you have played and the role you shall yet play. A great storm is coming, Kingkiller, one that shall shake the very foundations of Alagaësia, and we must all choose where to cast our lots."

"A storm has already ravaged the land. Another might destroy it."

Fire replaced the honey in Bachel's eyes. "Then destroyed it shall be, and a new and better world will rise from the ashes!" Fast as flowing quicksilver, her expression softened. "But not today, Kingkiller." She stood then and descended from the throne, and the acolytes parted before her. "Come now. If you are to stay with us, Kingkiller, I have arranged a most amusing diversion."

Wary, Murtagh said, "And what would that be, my Lady?"

She swept past him, the train of her dress trailing across the floor. "The sport of kings, my fair princeling. A boar hunt!"

CHAPTER VII

✦ ✦ ✦ ✦ ✦ ✦ ✦

Tusk and Blade

A boar hunt would have thrilled and daunted Murtagh when he was younger. Boars were dangerous animals, and he'd known of at least four earls who had been maimed or killed by a wild hog. The danger was part of the appeal; it was an opportunity to prove your mettle, sharpen your martial skills, and—for many a man—win favor with the women at court. The first time Murtagh had gone boar hunting had been with a group of nobles, headed up by Lord Barst. It had been . . . a less-than-enjoyable experience. He'd missed his chance at a boar and ended up smeared in mud from crown to sole. Lyreth and his peers had relentlessly made fun of him on the ride back. He'd had better luck on future expeditions, but they'd always been colored by his memories of that initial humiliation.

Now, though, Murtagh found no thrill in the prospect of a hunt. His wards removed any possible danger, and with it any sense of challenge or accomplishment, leaving only slaughter for the sake of meat. It was a dour thought. There was a significant difference between a hunter and a butcher, and he had no desire to be a butcher.

Along with Bachel and her retinue, he departed the temple and returned to the front courtyard.

Dust shook from the building as Thorn landed beside them.

Bachel spread her arms in a welcoming manner and said, "A hunt, noble dragon! Join us on our venture, and you may slake your thirst for blood and hunger for flesh."

Thorn snorted and looked at Murtagh. *She enjoys making lots of noise, like a magpie in the morning.*

Do you want to come?

The dragon licked his chops. *I'll not let you wander off with her alone. Besides, she is not wrong; I do hunger.*

"Assemble, my faithful children!" cried Bachel. "Bring us horses and water and wine and all the things needed for a hunt. Quickly!"

Dozens of grey-robed cultists and white-robed temple acolytes rushed about the courtyard as they sprang to obey. Alín approached carrying two braces of broad-bladed, short-handled spears, one set of which she handed to Bachel and the other to Murtagh.

Bachel tested the edges of her spears with her thumb and then pointed a spear at Murtagh, like an accusatory finger. "There is a condition to the hunt, Kingkiller."

Of course. "And what would that be, my Lady?"

"No spells are to be used in the killing of the boars. They are sacred beasts, touched by the power of this place, and it would be disrespectful, as well as blasphemous, to do otherwise."

Murtagh likewise tested the edges of his spears. They were tolerably sharp, but the metal seemed to be rather poor iron; they would bend after the first hard blow, and the edges wouldn't stay sharp for more than a few strokes. Using them would be a challenge, as would forgoing magic.

He liked the idea.

"That seems eminently reasonable. I shall abide by your custom."

She inclined her head. "The Dreamer will look kindly upon your efforts, my son."

Then Murtagh gestured at her spears. "Do you mean to hunt as well, my Lady?"

A gleam appeared in Bachel's eyes, and she hefted one of the spears with surprising ease. "Think you that I am incapable?"

Murtagh didn't, but neither did he have a good measure of her.

In a mild voice, he said, "Hunting boar takes great strength. I have never seen a woman attempt it."

Bachel's laugh echoed off the mountains, and crows cawed in response from the Tower of Flint. "A human woman, you mean to say. 'Tis good, then, that I am not wholly human. The blood of the elves runs in my veins. Though it may not be so thick as my mother's, it is still thicker than that of the women of your kind."

"Then I look forward to seeing your prowess upon the field of action."

"And I yours, my son."

~~~~~~~~~~~~~~~~~ ❖ ~~~~~~~~~~~~~~~~~

As the cultists hurried to organize the hunting party, several of Bachel's servants brought screens and held them about her while Alín and two other women attended her. When the screens were lowered, Murtagh saw Bachel no longer in her dress of red but now garbed like a man, with leather vambraces upon her forearms and chased riding boots that went to midthigh and a peaked helm divided by lines of bright rivets. The helm had a half mask to protect her eyes and nose, and an aventail of fine mail edged with rings of brass or bronze. It was a handsome look, Murtagh thought, for war or for sport.

From among the stone buildings came men leading a score of horses—short, hardy animals that were barely taller than ponies. Their coats were shaggier than those of any horse Murtagh had seen before, as if they were wearing their own knotted blankets for warmth in the long northern winters.

The cultists gave him a mare with a liver chestnut coat to ride. She was a far cry from the chargers he'd been trained on, but the animal seemed steady enough. He just hoped the mare's nerve would hold during the hunt.

Before getting on the horse, he slipped off his cloak and tucked it into one of Thorn's saddlebags. It would only hinder him when on foot.

As he climbed onto the mare, Thorn's disapproval washed over him. *It does not seem right to see you ride one of those hornless deer animals.*

Horses. They're called horses, and you know that.

But it sounds more insulting to call them hornless deer.

Murtagh glanced over. If Thorn were human, he would have sworn the dragon was smiling. *You're enjoying this, aren't you?*

Thorn coughed in his chest. *It is not every day I see a Rider riding a horse.*

As the hunting party readied itself for departure, a realization came to Murtagh: *Dogs . . . They don't have any dogs.* Now that he thought of it, the village was surprisingly quiet. There were no hounds baying, nor were there mutts yapping in the streets or scrapping over food. It was an odd thing. In all his years and all his travels, Murtagh had never before seen a human settlement without dogs.

Are dogs so important? Thorn asked.

They are. For the common man, having a dog is the closest thing to the bond you and I share.

Do you mean to compare dragons to dogs?

No, no. Not as such, only to say that the connection a human may share with a dog can—in part—resemble the connection that we have.

Thorn seemed unconvinced. *Mmm. Did you ever have a dog?*

You know I didn't. . . . The other boys would have hurt or killed any dog I owned.

Thorn's lip wrinkled slightly, not enough that others would notice, but Murtagh saw. *They would not have dared were I there.*

Murtagh chuckled. *No. That they wouldn't.*

He coaxed his mare to sidestep over to Bachel. "I notice you have no dogs."

Disdain sharpened the witch's angled features. "And for good reason. They are blasphemous creatures."

"Dogs?"

"They refuse to accept the insight one may receive through the power of this place. No dog will stay here in Nal Gorgoth, and that has ever been the case. Crows are wiser. They understand the promise of dream."

"How will you drive the boars, though?"

Her hooded gaze grew mysterious. "You shall see, Kingkiller. We will not need such assistance as you are accustomed to."

As the group organized their provisions, Murtagh spotted Alín watching from among the temple's shadowed pillars, a furtive figure half hidden behind the carved stone.

When everyone in the party was mounted up, Bachel lifted a spear over her head and cried, "With me!" and spurred her shaggy stallion forward, away from the temple and into the village.

Murtagh was tempted to brandish Zar'roc, as if rallying troops, but instead he spurred his mare and followed at a sedate pace. The cultists trailed after, and Thorn brought up the rear, his weighted tread shaking dust from the shingles of the buildings.

Dozens of villagers gathered along the streets to watch them depart. Murtagh spotted a surprising number of children among their ranks. *It seems like there ought to be more people here, given how many children they have,* he said to Thorn. *It's odd.*

The dragon answered: *Perhaps they send the younglings elsewhere when they are grown.*

Once the party reached the edge of Nal Gorgoth, Bachel reined in her stallion and pointed toward the southern side of the valley. "Do you see that small gap between the mountains, Kingkiller? Where the trees follow a stream out of the heights? That is our destination."

"We will find boars there, my Lady?"

"Enough to feed a thunder of dragons!" Then she spurred her stallion again, bending low over the horse's neck as he sprang forward with a startled snort over the blackened earth.

Grieve scowled and lashed the side of his mare as he followed.

"Keep with the Speaker, blast you!" he shouted at the warriors who filled out their party.

With a clamor of drumming hooves and the cries of the excited men, the group headed south toward the narrow wedge of space that separated one mountain from the next.

It will be a wonder if we don't scare away all the boars with this ruckus, said Murtagh.

Thorn surprised him then by taking flight; his wings cast a crimson shadow upon the group as he soared over them. *I will scout ahead and see where our prey might be, before you drive them from their feeding grounds and watering holes.*

Murtagh watched with some regret as Thorn rose with enviable ease above the foothills. He wished he were riding Thorn instead of the mare with the coat of liver chestnut; he hated being left behind among strangers.

Most of all, he hated how familiar a feeling it was.

The air grew warmer as they neared the sliver of a side valley, and more and more wisps of smoke rose like garden eels from the crusted earth. A few times, a scrap of wind-torn smoke struck him in the face, and he gagged from the overwhelming stench of sulfur. The land had a charred and barren appearance, as if razed by fire in the recent past.

Bachel had slowed her stallion to a more measured pace, so Murtagh rode up next to her. "I've never seen a place like this before, except for the Burning Plains far to the south. And those don't smell of brimstone."

The witch nodded. "There are many such places, Kingkiller, scattered about Alagaësia, though you will not easily find them. There is another, not far south of here: the barrows of Anghelm, where Kulkarvek the Terrible is buried in state."

Murtagh fought to hide his reaction. Kulkarvek was the only Urgal known to have united their fractious race under a single banner, an event that had occurred long before the fall of the Riders, if stories were to be trusted. His resting place was one of the other locations—along with the ruins of El-harím and Vroengard Island—that Umaroth had warned Thorn and Murtagh to avoid.

But what bothered him most was the implication that there were many such places throughout Alagaësia: places where the ground was burnt and the air smelled of brimstone.

Why aren't they more widely known? he asked Thorn. *Even if they're in remote, isolated locations, surely the Riders or others would have noticed any place that smelled like this. It would be difficult to hide, especially from the air.*

A weirding veil, perhaps? A spell that hides the obvious from sight? Wards ought to block that sort of thing.

It depends on the spell. You know that. It could be an enchantment of a sort none now are familiar with. Or something akin to the Banishing of the Names.

Murtagh glanced up at Thorn. *Dragon magic? . . . Do you feel something of that here?*

I do not know what I feel, only that the land seems alive, despite the charring.

The world narrowed around them as the hunting party entered the side valley and the mountains pinched close, until the foothills were only a few hundred feet apart and dense ranks of trees blocked their sight. It was good, Murtagh thought, that Thorn was in the air and not there in such tight quarters.

Bachel led the way along a well-trodden path that wound between the tall pines.

Past the gap, the valley widened again, and Murtagh beheld what elsewhere in the Spine would have been a long alpine field where deer and bears and other wildlife would gather. Not here. Here the earth was still scorched and blackened, and the trees were dead and skeletal—bare of all but a few clumps of brittle needles. None of which made as strong an impression on Murtagh as the enormous numbers of mushrooms growing from the ground.

They came in all kinds. Brown-capped, white-capped, round as puffballs, tiered like the temple in Nal Gorgoth, broad as shields or as tall and narrow as a spear; the profusion of forms was over-whelming. There were gilled mushrooms, and mushrooms as red as ladybugs, and huge woody funguses that rose higher than a horse-mounted man. A rich, savory smell scented the area—like a cut of well-cooked beef—and thin veils of brown spores drifted upward along currents of rising air, mixing with the wisps of vapor from the ground.

Amid the field and forest of mushrooms, Murtagh spotted dark shapes moving through the shadows: monstrous wild boars, ridge-backed and covered in coarse black bristles.

"They eat the mushrooms and grow to exceptional size be-cause of it," Bachel explained, bringing her horse alongside his. "It gives their meat a taste unlike any other."

Murtagh shook his head, still taking in the sight. "I've never seen or heard of mushrooms like these."

"The ground here suits them as much as it is hostile to green growing plants."

From above, it looks as if the ground is covered with melted fat, said Thorn, circling over the far end of the narrow crevice split-ting the Spine, some miles away.

Delightful, Murtagh replied.

Bachel continued: "As you can see, we need no drivers. We are our own drivers. We will push toward the head of the valley, and the boars will gather before us. If your dragon—"

"He is only *mine* as much as I am *his.*"

Her eyelids drooped with what seemed like amusement. "Of course, Kingkiller. If Thorn wishes to hunt there at the other end, he might help us and so trap the boars between our spears and his teeth and claws."

It is a good plan, said Thorn, and Murtagh could almost hear him snap his jaws shut with finality. *I will do so.* The dragon folded his crimson wings and dove toward the far end of the valley, a burning meteor blazing.

The ranks of mushrooms hid Thorn as he descended.

Then Bachel lifted her spear. "Dismount!" The hunting party obeyed, as did Murtagh, grateful to be rid of the liver chestnut mare for the time being.

Some seconds later, a muted *thud* rolled down the valley: the sound of Thorn's impact belatedly arriving.

There were, Murtagh saw, numerous game trails wending through the expanse of overgrown mushrooms—pathways pounded flat by the passage of countless sharp hooves.

Along with the cultists, Murtagh staked and hobbled his horse and then set out on foot along the near trail. The ground, though blackened, was softer than by Nal Gorgoth, as if the entire sub-surface were riddled with fungus.

Murtagh made a face as he stepped on a shelf of brown mush-room and it dissolved into a slippery, foul-smelling liquid the color of night soil.

"Spread out," commanded Bachel. Her warriors responded quickly, forming an arching line to either side of her. Grieve re-mained close by, which she seemed to expect.

Murtagh moved away from the group toward the eastern side of the valley. He wanted space to maneuver; hunting with strang-ers was always a dangerous proposition, and doubly so here. Be-sides, he knew from past boar hunts that having room to run was often the difference between success and injury or death.

"Where are you going, Kingkiller?" Bachel called out in a gay voice.

"I hunt better alone, Lady Bachel!" he answered in a like tone.

She flashed him a savage smile. The mushrooms appeared archaic—primitive predecessors of more finely finished plants—as if they'd endured from a time beyond recorded history, and Ba-chel seemed a part of that ancient remnant. "Only remember to control your tongue, Kingkiller. You must make your kill with-out magic."

"Oh, that I shall," he muttered. No matter how poor the metal used to make the spears they'd given him, Murtagh knew he could deliver at least one fatal blow apiece.

Step by measured step, they proceeded up the valley. Ahead of them, an occasional roar sounded as Thorn chased this boar or that. It wasn't long before the dragon touched his mind again, and Murtagh found it full of blood and excitement and the hot thrill of the hunt.

The witch was right, said Thorn. *The meat is good.*

Murtagh laughed softly. *That should be all the recommendation a butcher or cook needs. A dragon said, "The meat is good."*

Thorn roared with amusement.

Mushrooms crunched and squished and snapped beneath Murtagh's boots with every step. The soft fungal bodies made it difficult to keep a steady footing. He was off any trail now, which wasn't ideal for finding game, but it allowed him to keep his distance from Bachel's group, a few hundred feet to his right.

His senses sharpened as he neared the edge of a dense stand of . . . he wasn't sure what to call them. *Mushroom trees?* Their gnarled trunks were as broad as a horse's chest and had scraps of cobweb-like membranes clinging to them. *Please, no giant spiders,* Murtagh thought. He would rather face a horde of Urgals barehanded.

The air was thick and moist and smelled fleshy and overheated, as if he were pressed close against an enormous, sweating armpit. He grimaced and moved forward with caution, eyes darting from shadow to shadow as he looked for any boars.

Would it be using magic to find the beasts with my mind?

He hadn't meant the thought for Thorn, but the dragon answered all the same: *Do you care about pleasing Bachel?*

I care about keeping my word.

Murtagh decided to rely on only his eyes and ears for the time being. It made for an even more interesting challenge.

A chorus of squeals and grunts sounded across the field to his right. He dropped into a crouch as he spotted a cluster of seven or so hogs—boars and sows alike—run out from under the treelike mushrooms and charge Bachel and her line of warriors.

Bachel sank to one knee, planting the butt of her spear against the instep of her back foot and aiming the tip of the blade toward the oncoming beasts. Her warriors did the same, and she loosed a piercing cry that captured the attention of the lead boar and drew it toward her as metal to a lodestone.

Murtagh watched, momentarily breathless, as the animals closed the distance between them and the cultists, crashing through every mushroom in their way.

Some of the hogs bypassed the waiting cultists. But three—including the lead boar—plowed straight into the hunters, impaling themselves on the weapons. One of the warriors fell, and he screamed as a hog trampled him, gouts of blood spurting from the animal's gored chest.

Bachel caught her prey on the point of her spear. The impact drove her back several inches. Then she dug in her heels, thrust hard, and forced the spear through the chest of the outraged boar. With a gleeful cry, she stood and lifted the boar upon her spear and then slammed the dying animal back down against the ground. It was a feat of astonishing strength. Even with the heightened abilities of a Rider, Murtagh knew he would have been unable to perform such an act without the help of magic.

Bachel planted a foot upon the back of the fallen boar, spread her arms and threw back her head and filled the valley with her triumphant ululation.

The sight and sound sent a savage thrill through Murtagh. The witch was as a wild beast, pure and fierce and terrifying. In that moment, she seemed more like a dragon than either human or elf.

"That is one to me, Kingkiller!" Bachel cried without looking at him. Behind her, the trampled warrior lay groaning on the ground, his broken chest heaving. The man's hog was on its side a few steps away, a wide wound in its breast, and it kicked and shuddered as it bled out.

Then a thousand more squeals seemed to sound: a tormented assault upon their ears as first dozens and then hundreds of wild pigs stormed out of the mass of overgrown mushrooms in front of Bachel and her warriors. Beyond, Murtagh heard Thorn approaching, the dragon making no attempt to conceal his heavy tread.

Distracted, Murtagh peered between the trunks of the mushroom trees in an effort to better see. He glimpsed Bachel setting her spear again, and the warriors closing in to protect her flanks.

Another grunting squeal sounded, startling in its nearness.

Murtagh dropped to one knee as a bristling shadow charged toward him through the fungal forest. Tusks flashed white and sharp in the dim light, and a reddened mouth gaped, and small eyes rolled, black and beady. The boar uttered a coughing bark that Murtagh had heard in more than a few nightmares, and then it was upon him.

The boar slammed into him with shocking force. The animal was denser than any human and many times stronger. Murtagh felt his spear sink into the beast's deep chest, and likewise, he felt the vibration along the haft as the iron blade struck a rib and snapped in two.

The boar squealed and twisted sideways as it tumbled into Murtagh. They both fell to the blackened ground in a tangle of arms and kicking legs.

Sharp, hard blows struck Murtagh along the ribs and the back of his head, and though his wards flared to life, the blows still hurt.

He yelled and tried to rise, but the boar was lying athwart him, kicking and thrashing, and Murtagh couldn't find a good angle to push himself upright.

Then more boars rushed past—a torrent of frightened, blood-maddened beasts—and their weight drove him into the slippery, slimy mire of the crushed mushrooms. A thick, rotting stench clogged his nostrils, making it impossible to breathe. Dozens of sharp hooves dug into his back, deadly as any dagger, and his wards drew even more of his strength.

The squealing and grunting were deafening. A crimson tunnel closed in around his vision, darkening the world.

Murtagh groped for Zar'roc. His fingers found the pommel, but he didn't have room to draw the sword while lying on his belly.

A word from the ancient language leapt to mind. A single utterance and he could drive the boars away or else kill them entirely. But then he would have failed Bachel's challenge, and failure was more painful than the blows battering his frame.

He managed a quick, shallow breath. It wasn't enough.

Blast it. He was running out of time. If—

He cried out in pain as a boar stomped on his right elbow. His wards kept the joint from breaking, but the pressure pushed his arm into the soft soil, and the angle caused something in his elbow to stretch or snap.

Then a black hoof came down along the side of his head, scraping his skull, and the impact whipped his neck to the side.

Stars filled his vision, and the world grew dark and hazy, and all sound faded into the distance, dimly heard and badly apprehended.

CHAPTER VIII

◆◆◆◆◆◆◆

Mother's Mercy

A black sun rimmed by black flame hung against a darkling sky. The stars were faded, guttering; the air cold and dry, and a bitter wind blew from the north.

The world was dead. All the ground was cracked and charred as by Nal Gorgoth. Bare trees stood on the flanks of slumped mountains, the sharpness of their peaks defeated by the passage of uncounted eons. No birds or beasts were to be seen; if he wandered to the ends of the land, he knew he would find nothing but bones and ashes.

Existence was a tomb wherein the sins of the past lay interred.

But no . . . not entirely.

Ahead of him, close to the dim grey horizon, an enormous section of the ground heaved upward, as if the world itself were breaking apart, but the sawbacked enormity moved and shifted as only a living creature could. Flecks of red flashed from the silhouette, like coals seen through smoked glass.

Dread consumed him. Total, thought-destroying dread that caused his limbs to go limp and his mind to go slack with unremitting fear. All had been lost, and there before him lay the instrument of their destruction.

The beast rose rampant against the black sun—a wingless dragon, apocalyptic in size, terrifying in presence. Destroyer of hope, eater of light, snake-tongued and hook-clawed.

And the beast turned, and its flaming eye settled on him, and he shrank before it, feeling death's cold touch seize his heart, feeling the *helpless, inevitable surrender before what could not be changed, what could not be stopped.*

The dragon's mouth parted, and withering flame lit its maw, and—

~~~~~~~~~~~~~~~~~~~ ❖ ~~~~~~~~~~~~~~~~~~

"Wake! Wake, Kingkiller!"

Murtagh's eyes snapped open, and he jolted upright with a panicked yell as fire coursed through his veins and his heart convulsed like a dying rabbit.

Bachel stood over him, blood-smeared, black-bladed dagger in one hand, spear in the other. Grieve and her warriors ringed them, and half a dozen dead hogs lay on the trampled ground nearby: a battlefield in miniature, but no less fraught or deadly because of it.

Before Murtagh could collect himself well enough to understand what had happened, much less speak, Thorn crashed through the forest of mushrooms, roaring as he came. He stopped directly over Murtagh and turned and snarled as he searched for foes. The sun was behind Thorn, and his scales sparked red and bright.

The sight caused Murtagh to flinch as he remembered his vision of desolation. Deathly fear again gripped him.

Thorn reached for him with a paw, as if to pick him up and fly away, and Murtagh raised a hand. "No," he croaked. "I'm fine." He wasn't, and Thorn knew it.

The dragon said, *Are you wounded?*

Murtagh got to his feet, unsteady. He checked himself. None of the blood seemed to be his, but his right elbow throbbed, and it was already starting to swell. He bent and extended his arm; it still moved as it should. So nothing torn. He cast a quick healing spell—careful to speak the words without sound—and only then noticed how deeply exhausted his wards had left him. His hands and feet were cold, and there was a gnawing hunger in his belly. *Nothing too serious. Did you see what I saw? . . . The dragon?*

No, said Thorn, baring even more of his teeth. *Your mind was closed to me.*

Murtagh was so shaken, he didn't pause to consider the wisdom of his action as he shared the memory with Thorn in all its terror-inducing immediacy. A deep hiss came from Thorn, and he dug his claws into the ground. Murtagh felt his own fear reflected in Thorn's thoughts.

It was just a dream, Murtagh hastily said.

An evil one, though. Perhaps it was more than just a dream.

A premonition? They can't reach that far into the future.

Thorn shivered and lowered his head until his eyes were level with Murtagh's. *Is that known for sure? Who has proved it?*

I—

"My son, are you hurt?" asked Bachel. She pointed with her dagger at the blood on Murtagh's chest. His jerkin was torn, and the air was cold against his skin. "You are covered in gore."

The tip of the dagger was uncomfortably close. Murtagh fell back a half step. His hand moved to Zar'roc's hilt. "Not hurt, no. Thank you for . . . helping."

The witch nodded, satisfied. She wiped her dagger on her leather vambrace and sheathed it. "It is better to hunt as part of a group than to hunt alone."

"You might be right." He shivered and rubbed his arms, trying to coax warmth back into his limbs. "When I was on the ground, I saw . . . I saw a vision. An evil one."

Bachel's expression grew intense, and she stepped forward and grasped his shoulder with her free hand. Surprised, he resisted the urge to knock her hand away. The witch's grip was like heated iron. "A vision," she said, her voice low and forceful. "Describe it to me, my son. Quickly now, before your memory fades. It is important."

Annoyed but also curious, Murtagh complied, speaking in swift, short sentences, eager to force the words out so he could stop thinking about the black sun and the impossibly large dragon. . . .

Grieve and the warriors listened with close attention, and they murmured with what seemed to be either awe or reverence as he described the dragon.

"Ah," said Bachel. "You are indeed fortunate." She released him and circled her hand above her head, indicating both the small side valley and the cleft that contained Nal Gorgoth. "All who come here dream, but few there are who receive such clear portents, and those who do often become Speakers themselves."

"Have there been many Speakers?" asked Murtagh.

"My Lady," said Grieve in a tense voice. "It is not right for an outsider to kn—"

"Tsk, tsk," said Bachel. "Our guest is no ordinary person. Indeed not." A disapproving scowl settled on Grieve's seamed face, and he pulled at the cuff of his blood-splattered robe in a nervous, angry manner, as if what he really wanted to do was wrap his thick fingers around Murtagh's neck.

In a grand voice, the witch said, "There have been many Speakers—some false, some true—through the ages. We are Du Eld Draumar, and we have lived in these places of power since before elves were elves. We were known to the Grey Folk themselves . . . known and feared."

Murtagh translated in his head. *Du Eld Draumar* was a fancy way of saying *The Old Dreamers*, but as it was cast in the ancient language, the name held more truth than it would have in any other tongue. "I believe you," he said, and he meant it. Although he doubted Bachel would give him a straightforward answer, he asked, "What, in your judgment, does the vision mean, O Speaker?"

"It is a gift. The exhalations of this land have shown you a vision of the sacred mystery that lies at the heart of our creed. What you saw, Kingkiller, is a portion of what may yet be."

"As a warning?"

She surprised him by taking his hand and pressing it flat against his chest, over his heart. Her fingers were sticky with blood. And she answered in a low, serious tone with no hint of anything but utter sincerity. "As a promise." Then she let go.

A hot-cold touch of his dream-born fear gripped Murtagh. He shrank in on himself and found he had lost his taste for further questions.

She lies, said Thorn.

If she does, she believes the lie.

Murtagh looked back at the warriors and counted. Two more were missing. Through the mushroom trees Thorn had knocked over, the open field was visible. In the center of it lay several lifeless hogs, as well as the three downed warriors. One of the men was still moving, albeit feebly. Splattered blood, human and animal alike, stained the mushroom caps in a reddened ring.

"The beasts have cost us," said Murtagh.

Bachel nodded in a serious manner, though she seemed neither sad nor upset, but rather prideful. "My men have served well today, Kingkiller, and those who fell, fell in service of our faith. Their sacrifice will not go unforgotten or unrewarded."

The warriors bowed their heads and, as one, said, "As it is dreamt, so it shall be."

At that, Murtagh thought Bachel would attend to her wounded, or at least dispatch some men to do so. Instead, she gestured at the boar he had slain. "You have taken a fine beast, Kingkiller. I expected nothing less."

In death, the boar seemed smaller, though still imposing; it must have been equal in weight to several large men. His spear projected from the center of the animal's chest, the haft a broken splinter.

With a bow and an extended hand, as if requesting a dance at court, Murtagh said, "And without the aid of the slightest charm or spell, my Lady."

"So I saw," Bachel replied. "But were it not for our help, would you have lived? Does such a victory count as a victory in truth?"

Murtagh raised an eyebrow. He did not feel like bandying words, but he could not allow her challenge to pass uncontested. "I killed the boar, my Lady, and dead he would have been no matter *what* happened to me. As that was my goal, yes, I would count it a victory."

A small smile touched Bachel's lips. "A fair point, my son." In the open field, the wounded man let out an agonized groan. The sound drew her attention, and she turned from Murtagh. "Come," she said, and strode toward the field.

The command annoyed Murtagh, but he followed nonetheless. *Should I offer to heal him?* he asked Thorn.

Wait to see what magic the witch can work. If she cannot heal the man, then offer *to help.*

A good idea.

Quickening his pace, Murtagh drew abreast of Bachel and gestured at the dead boars ahead of them. "You made a heroic kill, Lady Bachel."

She hardly seemed to react to the praise, as if it were merely her apportioned due. "It was of a kind with all my kills, Rider."

Of that, Murtagh was convinced.

As they approached the churned mess of blood and crushed mushrooms in the center of the field, it became evident that the two warriors who lay motionless on the ground were already dead.

Bachel knelt by the man who still breathed. His jerkin draped inward along the great divot in his chest where his ribs were broken. Bloody slaver coated his chin, and his breathing was hitched and shallow. A punctured lung, Murtagh guessed, if not worse.

With a gentle hand, Bachel smoothed the man's brow. He opened his eyes and looked up at her, and in his gaze, Murtagh saw utter devotion.

"Shh," said Bachel, her voice calm and vast as a windless ocean. "Be of good heart, Rauden. You have served well."

The man nodded. Tears filled his eyes, and with enormous depth of feeling, he whispered, "Mehtra."

Affection softened Bachel's face, and she bent close to him. "Sehtra." Then, with a smooth, quick motion, she drew her black-bladed dagger, placed it under the man's chin, and shoved it into his head. He convulsed and went limp.

"Shade's blood!" Murtagh swore, and started forward. Around them, the warriors raised their spears. "I could have healed him!"

Bachel withdrew her dagger and wiped it clean on the man's shirt. "He was beyond healing, my son."

"Not for me! You should have let me try!"

Bachel rose and turned to face Murtagh. Her expression was fierce and terrible but also sorrowful. "Do not think to question me, Rider! You do not know our ways! We seek to serve the Dreamer however we can, each and every one of us, and when our time is come, we *yearn* to return to He who dreams us. It is our greatest desire."

"Yes, but—"

"The matter is closed, Murtagh son of Morzan. Enough!"

Disapproval pinched Murtagh's features, and he set his jaw. As if by magic, Bachel seemed to transform before him; he saw cruelty in her features now and the stubbornness of deluded certainty. And he wondered at his own credulity. Then cold settled in his gut as he became aware of the potential danger of the situation and all emotion abandoned him, leaving him a hollow shell. He affected the same bland, noncommittal aspect that had served him so well at court. "Of course, my Lady. My apologies."

Bachel inclined her head and then turned back to the dead man and placed a hand upon his brow. She murmured something and closed the man's blank, unseeing eyes.

The witch was silent for a moment, her features inscrutable. Then: "Grieve, see to it that our kills are collected and our fallen too. Bring them to Nal Gorgoth, that we may feast upon our triumph."

"Speaker."

Bachel nodded and strode forth from the bodies and broken mushrooms toward the horses.

Murtagh watched her go. Then he looked at Grieve, who was directing the warriors to gut and truss the boars. "What does *mehtra* mean?"

Grieve gave him a sullen glare and bent to help another man with a boar. "It means *mother*, Outlander. For Bachel is as our mother in all things, and we trust her as such."

"And *sehtra*?"

"Son."

In a daze, Murtagh walked to Thorn. *She's as ruthless as Galbatorix.*

The dragon agreed. *And yet her people still care for her.*

Rauden called her mother *even knowing she was about to kill him. Galbatorix never inspired such love. Only fear.*

For a moment, Murtagh debated following Bachel and riding back upon the liver chestnut mare. But he didn't want to be anywhere near her. Not right then.

417

He turned to Thorn. "No more horses." And he reached for the stirrup hanging down Thorn's left side.

The dragon crouched lower so that Murtagh could catch the loop of boiled leather and pull himself up onto Thorn's back. *Good.*

"Can you bring my boar? I would rather not wait on B—"

The name was still in his mouth when Thorn lurched up to his full standing height, startling the warriors, who leapt away. Light as a cat, Thorn padded over to where Murtagh had made his kill.

With one foot, Thorn scooped up the hog's bloody carcass. Then he jumped skyward and flew away from the field of slaughter.

CHAPTER IX

✦ ✦ ✦ ✦ ✦ ✦ ✦

Breaking Point

I'm sorry for scaring you. The boar caught me by surprise.

A deep huff emanated from Thorn as he climbed over the flank of a mountain, heading back toward Nal Gorgoth. *You should be more careful.*

I should. . . . I might need to rework my wards. I think I've been too lax with what they allow.

Thorn executed a slow turn over Nal Gorgoth. Seeing the village once more from above, Murtagh noticed that the buildings were laid out in intersecting circles, like rings on a rain-pelted pond.

Thorn said, *Do you still wish to stay through the night?*

I don't know. An image flashed through Murtagh's mind of the black sun over a barren land, and he again felt the bitter touch of a northern wind. He hugged himself, and for the first time, he wondered if Bachel's answers were the sort he actually wanted to hear. *There's something very wrong here.*

Very, very wrong.

As they landed in the courtyard, Alín approached from within the temple, bearing a pitcher of water with a cloth and basin. It was a welcome sight. Murtagh could feel the filth on his skin, blood and dirt and the dried juice of crushed mushrooms all intermixed.

Accompanying Alín was the temple cook—a surly, heavyset woman with a stained apron and forearms as large as a baker's— and a half-dozen scullions. Together, cook and scullions braved

Thorn's close inspection to fetch Murtagh's boar and carry it away to be butchered.

Murtagh was glad to see the beast gone. He'd had his fill of boar hunting for the rest of time.

Alín placed the pitcher, cloth, and basin on the flagstones, bowed, and retreated to a safe distance.

"My thanks," said Murtagh. She averted her eyes as he pulled off his torn, bloodstained jerkin and the woolen shirt beneath. He cursed. Both garments were ruined. He would have to wear his linen shirt until he could acquire replacements.

"How went the hunt, my Lord?" Alín asked in a soft voice.

Murtagh wet the cloth and scrubbed at the blood on his skin. It clung to him with stubborn persistence. "If your only measure of success is the number of animals killed, well enough. Otherwise, I would say badly. Very badly. The beasts took three of your men."

Alín bowed her head. "I'm sorry to hear that."

Murtagh grunted. "Are you, now? Bachel stuck a dagger into one of the men. Rauden was his name. Is that how things are done among your kind?"

Pale blue eyes met his gaze and held it. "Was Rauden wounded?"

Reluctantly, Murtagh said, "He was. But I could have helped him. Or Bachel could have."

Alín's resolve and conviction never seemed to falter. "Perhaps that is true, my Lord, but I trust our Speaker's judgment. She knows what is best for us, and if it was Rauden's time to leave this life and rejoin the greater dream, then it is good that Bachel was there to ease his journey. None of us could ask for more."

"Because she is your mehtra."

A flash of disapproval crossed Alín's face. "We do not call her that lightly, Kingkiller."

"I'm not sure why you call her that at all. She doesn't seem like much of a mother."

She lifted her chin. "You must understand, my Lord, that

Bachel is the Speaker. Her concerns transcend those of normal mortals. You cannot expect to know or understand her. If what she did seems wrong to you, the fault lies not with her. She can do no wrong."

Murtagh chewed on that. There was a possibility, a very, very slight possibility, that Alín was right. If Bachel could see the future, then every choice she made might be the correct one. And yet surely killing Rauden couldn't be justified.

His lip curled. "So says everyone who wishes to hold power and not be challenged."

"You are unfair, my Lord. No king or queen has ever had as much right to rule as does Bachel, nor as much responsibility."

Abandoning the cloth, Murtagh bent and poured the contents of the pitcher over his head and shoulders. The water was shockingly cold, even more so in the unseasonable warmth that pervaded Nal Gorgoth, and yet it was a relief and a pleasure to feel himself at least partially clean.

"Is that so?"

Alín nodded, earnest. "Her burdens are immense, my Lord. The life of any one man—of any one of us here in Nal Gorgoth— is as a speck of dust when weighed against the importance of the Speaker's duties."

Murtagh didn't feel like forcing the issue. He shook his hair dry and turned to retrieve his linen shirt from the saddlebags.

As he did, he heard Alín let out a small gasp, and he knew she had noticed the scar on his back. Grim curiosity drove him to look at her, expecting to see either pity or disgust distorting her face.

He saw neither. Her face was soft with what he could only interpret as compassion. Understanding, even. The anger that had been building within him drained away, leaving him hollow and off-guard.

"Oh," she said. "In what battle were you wounded? Was it Eragon who—"

"No."

"Then was it Galbatorix or—"

"It was my father."

Her eyes grew very wide, and then Murtagh did see pity in her gaze, and he couldn't bear it, so he turned away and busied himself retrieving his linen shirt. Alín was silent the whole while.

Thorn gave Murtagh a comforting nudge on the shoulder, and Murtagh patted him without looking. Then Thorn started to lick the scales along his forelegs, and the claws too, cleaning them of the dirt and boar's blood that darkened them. His barbed tongue rasped with each stroke.

"Ah! Wait, please! I can help," said Alín. She gave a quick bow and scurried back into the temple.

Thorn paused and watched with curiosity.

"What do you think—" Murtagh stopped as he saw her returning with another basin, this one full of water, and several more cloths draped over the crooks of her arms.

Alín placed the basin on the stones in front of Thorn's forefeet and bowed again. "Please, Dragon, will you let me wash you?"

Murtagh felt Thorn consider, and then Thorn opened his mind to her and said, *You may.*

The reverberation of his words caused Alín to blink and step back, but then she bobbed her head and wet a cloth and—with as much care as if she were cleaning the jewels on a king's crown, fragile with age—began to wipe the blood and dirt from Thorn's scales.

Murtagh watched, unsure of what to make of it, but touched by her consideration. In all his time with Thorn, he had never bothered to help clean the dragon. Thorn was fastidious with his grooming, and Murtagh had seen no reason to offer aid.

He said, "So your vows allow you to touch Thorn but not me? He is as much a *he* as I am."

Alín pursed her lips as she worked the cloth under the tip of a scale. "You know better than that, my Lord. Thorn is neither human nor elf nor dwarf nor Urgal. It is different with him.

Besides, my faith would never forbid me the touch of a dragon. That would be . . . Why, that would be like locking a person underground and refusing to let them feel the touch of the sun upon their face."

"Are dragons really so essential to you and the rest of the Draumar?"

"They are. More than I can explain to an outlander."

"Mmh." Murtagh looked toward the side valley. Bachel and her retinue had yet to arrive back at Nal Gorgoth. "I had a vision during the hunt."

Startlement flitted across Alín's face, but she hid it quickly. "We have many visions in Nal Gorgoth, my Lord."

"Yes, but this one was different, I think."

Murtagh described it to her as she continued to work on Thorn's feet and legs. The acolyte appeared increasingly uncomfortable, until—as he mentioned the dragon—she said, "Stop! No more, my Lord. This is for the Speaker to hear and interpret, not I."

"And yet I would hear your thoughts," Murtagh said, and forged onward with his account.

Alín let out a cry, dropped the cloth, and clapped her hands over her ears. "This . . . No, no! I cannot hear any more!" And with her hands still about her head, she fled the courtyard.

Murtagh watched her go, frustrated. No matter how else he tried to gather information about the Draumar, all paths seemed to lead back to Bachel.

Beside him, Thorn lifted a foot and inspected his now-glittering scales. He licked at a remaining smear of grime. *Alín is not a bad person.*

"No, but her loyalty is firmly fixed on Bachel."

Then Murtagh took the last two dried apples from Thorn's saddlebags, sat upon Thorn's right foreleg, and set to eating while they waited. His mind was a muddle of indecision. He kept seeing flashes of the boar trampling him, and also Bachel shoving the

dagger into Rauden, and the black sun hanging in a dead sky. . . .
And he kept asking himself: What could be so important that the
people of Nal Gorgoth were willing to die without hesitation?

He had to talk with Bachel again. Had to try to find out *why*
she had acted the way she did. If there was a reasonable explanation, perhaps then . . . But no. How could there be?

What do you make of all this? he asked Thorn.

Before the dragon could answer, Bachel and what remained
of the hunting party clattered into the courtyard. The shaggy
mountain horses were lathered and steaming. They dragged behind them makeshift litters of branches lashed together, upon
which rested the corpses of the slain boars and fallen warriors.

Murtagh stood and started toward Bachel, determined to push
past her evasions.

He hadn't taken more than a couple of steps when a heart-
rending wail filled the courtyard as a barefooted woman ran forth
from among the houses. Her hair was undone and flew free behind her like a pennant of flame. She went straight to the litters
and fell upon Rauden's body, wailing all the while, deep, agonizing
cries that hurt to hear.

Murtagh stopped in his tracks. A crowd of villagers gathered
about the edge of the courtyard, watching.

Bachel went to the woman and placed a hand upon her head.
"My daughter," she said in a sorrowful tone. And then she spoke
to the woman in a voice intended only for her.

The grieving woman nodded, and though her tears did not
cease, Murtagh heard her say, "Thank you, Mehtra." And what
surprised him was that she seemed to mean it.

Then Bachel turned her attention to the assembled villagers.
"My children! Our dead need burying, that they may sleep, and
dream, in peace. Come with me, that we may see it done and done
rightly, and after we may celebrate their lives with this bounty the
Dreamer has given us. Come! Let us—"

A clatter of iron and a bark of harsh orders—"Move! Forward!"—among the streets of the village interrupted her.

Bachel seemed unsurprised. "Make way!" she commanded, and the people did.

Murtagh and Thorn turned to look. *What now?* wondered Murtagh.

Four spear-carrying warriors drove a line of shackled prisoners into the courtyard. Murtagh counted quickly; there were twenty-one men and women bound in irons, disheveled, dirty-faced, and dull and listless as if they had already given up all hope of freedom. They were a mix of young and old, though none were children. By their clothes, Murtagh guessed the prisoners were commoners from somewhere near Ceunon. Taken off a ship, perhaps, or captured in a raid along the Bay of Fundor.

Thorn hissed and bared his teeth slightly. *I know*, Murtagh said.

With his heavy, lurching stride, Grieve went to the warriors guarding the prisoners. He spoke with them and then returned to his mistress's side. "Your latest thralls, Speaker."

"Thralls?" Murtagh said loudly, making no attempt to hide his outrage. He was not fond of serfdom or slavery or any sort of enforced bondage. One of the first changes Nasuada had made upon assuming the throne in Ilirea was outlawing such practices throughout her realm, a change Murtagh thoroughly approved of. Though he felt she had somewhat undercut the decree by requiring magicians to join Du Vrangr Gata or else have their abilities suppressed through herbs and potions.

Bachel gave the prisoners an appraising look. "Thralls soon to join us in our high and terrible cause."

"You expect these sorry folk to swear loyalty to you?" said Murtagh.

Bachel arched an eyebrow. In her blood-spattered clothes, she had a fantastic aspect, as if she were a spirit of the forest given life and as dangerous as any wild beast. "All who serve our cause here in Nal Gorgoth serve willingly, my son. Even as you shall."

"That . . . is difficult to believe."

"And yet, so it is, my son. You must have faith."

"How can I if I do not even know what your cause is?"

Inscrutable as ever, Bachel turned away. "Soon all shall be revealed, Kingkiller, but I warn you, you may find understanding more difficult than ignorance." To the warriors guarding the prisoners, she said, "Take them away. I shall grant them audience later." And then she returned to her fallen warriors and walked beside them as the cultists carried the bodies into the temple. With them went Rauden's widow, clutching at her breast.

Murtagh watched them go, feeling helpless. He could not bring himself to intrude upon a funeral procession. So he stayed by Thorn and twisted Zar'roc's hilt until the skin on his palm nearly tore.

~~~~~~~~~~~~~~~~~ ❖ ~~~~~~~~~~~~~~~~~

Murtagh knew that he might have learned more about the Draumar from the rites attending the burial of their men, but for the present, he could no longer tolerate Bachel or the rest of the villagers. Instead, he said to Thorn, *I need to move.*

They left the courtyard, and Murtagh wandered with brisk steps through Nal Gorgoth. The village was eerily empty; all of the cultists were in the temple, and the only sounds of life came from the crows in the Tower of Flint and the livestock penned along the periphery of the village. As for the prisoners—the thralls—the warriors had marched them away from the temple and out of sight. Murtagh nearly used his mind to search for them but then decided to hold.

There would be time enough for that later.

Thorn trailed him, being careful not to scrape his scales against the sides of the buildings and destroy the aged carvings or knock loose one of the dragon-like sculptures.

Murtagh stopped and studied the sculptures. That they

resembled dragons was undeniable, but it was equally certain that the creatures depicted differed in subtle ways that made them feel like a separate race. The spines along the heads were shorter than those of Thorn or Shruikan or Saphira, and the heads themselves were longer, bonier, and thinner across the beam of the brow. Perhaps the differences were a result of creative choices on the part of the artisans, but Murtagh doubted that; the sculptures were too carefully crafted—too closely observed—for such liberties or inaccuracies to make sense.

They look more like Fanghur, he said, naming the wind-serpents, the small, dragon-like creatures known to live in the Beor Mountains.

The little worms never flew so far north, said Thorn. *Not if Yngmar's memories are to be trusted.*

Are they, though? The world is old; even dragons do not know everything of note that has happened.

It is strange, said Thorn, lifting his head above the rooftops to sniff the air.

Murtagh moved on.

The longer he walked, the more agitated he became. Between the pummeling he'd taken during the hunt and the subsequent vision, he had been in no way prepared for Rauden's killing. *No matter what Bachel or Alín or anyone else says, that was wrong.* He snorted. Eragon had said much the same to him after Murtagh had killed the defenseless slaver, Torkenbrand. But that had been different. Torkenbrand had been a threat. Rauden was no threat at all. Certainly not to Bachel.

The memory of the slaver turned his thoughts back to the cultists' prisoners. Their *thralls.*

A hard certainty began to form within Murtagh.

He stopped again and looked at Thorn. The dragon lowered his head until they were staring eye to eye. Murtagh could feel the same hard certainty within Thorn.

I don't care about whatever future Bachel sees for us, said Murtagh.

Nor I.

I just want to know what she and the Draumar are trying to do. It can't be good.

Thorn's hot breath washed over him, a comforting sensation. *You mean to press the point with Bachel?*

He nodded. *When we sup this evening. Either she'll answer us and answer well or—*

We fight?

If it comes to that. Only . . . Murtagh shivered. *The children. We have to protect the children.*

Thorn licked his teeth. *It is hard to fight in a nest without crushing eggs.*

Then we'll have to find a way to empty the nest first. It's a big enough valley. There's plenty of room to run and hide.

What if the younglings refuse to run? Thorn cocked his head. *They might stand and fight, same as their elders, and then what?*

Murtagh shook his head. *I don't know. We do our best.* He put his hands on either side of Thorn's head. *We are decided?*

We are.

And yet doubt gnawed at Murtagh. Confronting the witch seemed an increasingly chancy prospect, even if he couldn't reasonably explain why. But he was determined, as was Thorn. There was no turning aside now.

CHAPTER X

✦ ✦ ✦ ✦ ✦ ✦ ✦

Upheaval

As Murtagh and Thorn retraced their steps through the village, they came upon a toothless old man sitting by a well. The man was dressed in rags, with eyes blue white with blindness and a crude crutch cut from a forked branch. He rocked on his narrow haunches and stared sightless at the mountains while he grinned and gummed.

When Murtagh passed by, the man cocked his head and said, "Aha! The crownless prince, afoot in a foreign land. Son of sorrow, bastard of fate, sing of sorry treachery. Red dragon, black dragon, white dragon . . . White sun, black sun, dead sun."

Murtagh stopped and crouched by the man. "What do you know about a black sun?"

The man turned his face toward Murtagh. His skin was so deeply wrinkled, it hung in folds like loose leather draped over his bones. He cackled. "Dreamt it, I did. Ahahaha. Sun eaten, earth eaten, the old blood avenged and the new enslaved. Did you dream, princeling? Do you see? What? Speaker got your tongue? Ahahaha."

"No one has my tongue," Murtagh said darkly.

The man ignored him and twisted in the direction of Thorn. "Proudback, bentneck, choose, choose, choose, but can't wake from life, oh no. Serve the sire or sleep forever. What deathless lies may in eons rise, ahahaha!"

And the man said nothing more that resembled coherent speech. Frustrated, Murtagh stood and continued back through the

428

village. *This is pointless,* he said to Thorn. *They're all mad. This should be called the village of riddles.*

Maybe that is what trapped Galbatorix and the Forsworn.

What? Endless riddles?

Can you think of a better snare for a well-honed mind?

Murtagh couldn't. *I wonder if that addled greybeard is what everyone turns into if they stay in this accursed valley long enough.*

Upon returning to the temple courtyard, he and Thorn found the cultists preparing another feast. Tables and chairs and hides had again been placed around the defunct fountain, with braziers of burning coals between and bedded fires laden with spitted meat.

The food was far from ready, so Murtagh retired to his chambers for a time. He tried to nap, but his mind was too agitated for sleep. Instead, as he lay on the bed with his eyes closed, he risked reaching out with his thoughts and lightly searching the village and the area beneath it, looking to see if there were large numbers of people hidden nearby. He found a few bright sparks of consciousness where he didn't expect—one beneath the temple, and several clustered atop its highest tower—but no great hordes hidden away, no army lying in wait to storm south and overrun Alagaësia.

It should have been a relief, but he remained as tense as ever.

At last he rolled back to his feet, returned to the courtyard, and went to sit with Thorn. There, at least, he felt somewhat more at ease.

As the sun crept downward, Grieve emerged from the temple and began to oversee the proceedings. Then too came Bachel.

No longer in her hunting garb, the witch wore a dress of fine wool dyed a purple so dark as to be nearly black, and a new headpiece adorned her brow, this of gold and silver studded with ruby cabochons. A heavy woolen cloak, red as autumn leaves, wrapped about her shoulders.

She greeted Murtagh and Thorn and proceeded to her dais.

There a group of white-robed acolytes gathered in a circle about her, and they began to sway while they chanted and hummed. Murtagh did not see Alín among their ranks.

Bachel stood head and shoulders above the acolytes, her height augmented by the platform beneath her. She swayed in time with her acolytes, eyes half closed, arms raised toward the sky as if to beseech an unseen god for favor.

A strange people, Thorn commented.

Murtagh grunted.

After a few minutes, Alín scurried over. She avoided his gaze and said, "How may I serve you and Thorn, my Lord? May I bring you something to drink?"

Murtagh waved away the suggestion. "What is she doing?" he asked, motioning toward Bachel.

"She is praying for warm weather through the winter, my Lord. And she is calling forth dreams to free the minds of the thralls our warriors have brought us."

Something about Alín's phrasing bothered Murtagh, but he wasn't sure why. "And to *whom* does Bachel pray?"

Alín backed away. "I will bring you wine and cheese, my Lord, to tide you over until the feast."

"Wait, that's not—"

But the young woman was already hurrying off, her head down and her hood up.

Murtagh let out a soft growl and settled back against Thorn. *What do dreams have to do with convincing prisoners to join their cause?* he said. *If the dreams are anything like the ones we had, they'll just want to leave.*

A small puff of smoke rose from Thorn's nostrils. *Perhaps they dream differently than we do. The witch said not everyone here has such visions.*

"Mmm." Murtagh wasn't persuaded.

Bachel continued to sway and chant with her followers until

Grieve struck a brass gong, whereupon she clapped her hands and cried, "Let us eat! Kingkiller, join me." Then she sank back to her litter on the dais.

He reluctantly went to join her.

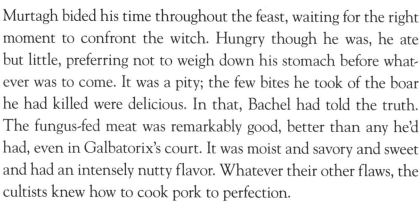

Murtagh bided his time throughout the feast, waiting for the right moment to confront the witch. Hungry though he was, he ate but little, preferring not to weigh down his stomach before whatever was to come. It was a pity; the few bites he took of the boar he had killed were delicious. In that, Bachel had told the truth. The fungus-fed meat was remarkably good, better than any he'd had, even in Galbatorix's court. It was moist and savory and sweet and had an intensely nutty flavor. Whatever their other flaws, the cultists knew how to cook pork to perfection.

As they ate, he posed a number of questions to Bachel, casual inquiries that she deflected at every turn. He might as well have been trying to extract information from a stone. In a way, he was grateful. The witch's refusal confirmed that he and Thorn were doing the right thing by choosing to confront her.

Murtagh kept a tight leash on his temper, but he felt it rising as he readied himself for action. He had never been one to sit by idly, and always restrictions and impositions had rankled. Bachel's evasions were both of those and more: she was disrespecting him in front of her people.

As the villagers served the last course of the meal—molded aspic filled with nuts and berries—Murtagh gave Thorn a discreet look and said, *This has gone on long enough. Be ready to fight or fly. If things go badly, don't let Bachel get away.*

Dark resolve colored Thorn's thoughts. *I am ready.* And he loosened his wings in preparation. No one but Alín—who stood behind Bachel—seemed to notice.

Murtagh hoped the acolyte wouldn't get in the way if words turned to violence. He gathered his will and then said, "Bachel, Thorn and I have decided: we no longer wish to wait through the night. Our patience is at an end. We would have our answers of you. Now. What is it the Draumar seek to accomplish? What is the future you have foreseen, and whom is it you serve? Who is the Dreamer of Dreams?"

The villagers playing on lyres never faltered, but he was aware of a sudden tension throughout the courtyard and of the weight of many eyes.

The witch paused with her cup halfway to her slanted mouth. Then she took her sip and placed the cup down most particularly. When she spoke, her voice cut like a sword: "You are very presumptuous, my son."

"Very. And I no longer have any stomach for these endless mysteries. You are the Speaker. Speak plainly with me, then."

She waved a hand. "Now is not the time to dwell upon such tiresome matters. It would ruin our enjoyment of this evening."

"Then let it be ruined!" His voice rang out so loudly that the musicians stumbled over their strings before regaining their rhythm. "I *insist*."

Rage flushed Bachel's face. Behind her, Alín watched, wide-eyed and terrified. In a fearsome voice, the witch said, "You *insist!*" She threw off her cloak and stood, and the players finally fell silent. "You have no right to *insist* here, O my wayward child. The traditions of hospitality protect you, but even a guest may not insult me with impunity."

"Guests or not, we will have our answers," said Murtagh.

Behind him, Thorn growled slightly and rose into a crouch. The Draumar nearest him scrambled away, scattering plates and dishes and food across the courtyard and spilling dark runnels of wine that spread like seeping blood. Thorn said: *Would you deny a dragon, witch?*

In an instant, Bachel's rage turned into equally cold contempt. "You would not understand my answers. Neither of you can. Not yet. Not so long as you are outlanders."

"Bah! Another mealymouthed nothing." From the pouch on his belt, Murtagh brought forth Saerlith's clasp and cast it down upon the dais between him and Bachel. The metal rang as it struck stone. "Whom do you serve, witch? Were you an instrument of the Forsworn? Galbatorix? Or were they your foes?"

Bachel's expression darkened as she beheld the clasp. "You have been meddling where you should not, Outlander."

"And still, you will not answer. Whom do you serve? What is it you want?"

"Whom do I serve?" The witch's voice gained in power, deepening so that her words echoed off the walls and hills. "I serve a power greater than you can imagine, Rider. I serve the Dreamer of Dreams, and I will not be questioned by the likes of you! Bow before my might and show your contrition!" Her final words arrived as a mighty blow, and the air shook loose dust and chips of stone that fell from the temple roof. A cloud of darkness gathered about her form as she lifted her arms and cried out with a wordless sound to the gloaming sky.

An attack Murtagh expected. But no attack came. Instead, he heard her cry roll the length of the valley, as a charge of cavalry rounding and repeating, and then the air went still, and the Draumar prostrated themselves with plaintive pleas. An instant later, the courtyard bucked beneath them, and all the valley seemed to heave and groan, and the very mountains shook. The granite peaks shed long slides of crusted snow, and consuming billows of white raced down the timbered flanks, and Bachel's flock of crows screamed their murderous alarms within the Tower of Flint. Owls and eagles rose shrieking from the treetops, and animals of every sort yammered throughout the valley.

Thorn snarled as the ground moved. He sprang into the air,

and the downblast from his wings only added to the confusion. The pulse of wind was so strong it forced Murtagh to squint until he could barely see.

Then the valley floor grew still again. The cries of the animals trailed off, with the last being the high-pitched yips of a fox.

Thorn drifted down and settled next to Murtagh. The dragon's scales were raised, like the ruff on a frightened cat.

Moments later, dull *thuds* and *thumps* reached them from the mountaintops, as hammer blows of giants.

Bachel lowered her arms. She looked at him and Thorn with a distant expression, as if they were of little consequence. When she spoke, her voice was hollow and void of emotion. "Do not try my patience again, Murtagh son of Morzan. I will share the truth with you when I deem fit. Until such time, partake of my hospitality, and be thou not so impertinent." Then she bent and took Saerlith's clasp and closed her hand around it. Whereas before Murtagh had felt no magic, no force or impetus radiating from the witch, now he did, and a flash of golden light rayed from between her fingers. She opened her hand to reveal the clasp crushed into a rough orb.

She dropped the orb into the brazier next to the dais, sat upon her litter, and again took up her cup. "Come, my son," she said. "Sit, and let us forget this unpleasantness and enjoy the remainder of the evening."

There were, Murtagh had learned, times when the wiser thing was to bide one's time rather than to rush headlong into battle.

This, he decided, was one of them.

He relaxed his hold on Zar'roc's hilt and warily lowered himself back into the chair where he'd been sitting. His arms were damp with sweat, and he could barely hear over the blood coursing in his ears.

Then Bachel clapped her hands and said, "Players, again."

And the musicians resumed plucking at their lyres and singing in their hidden tongue, and throughout the courtyard, the Draumar picked themselves up and began to collect the scattered contents of the feast. Behind the dais, Alín stood cowed and hunched. Her hands trembled as she clenched the front of her white robe.

Thorn settled close behind Murtagh's back, and he was well glad of the companionship. The dragon's concern mirrored his own.

We should be gone from here, Thorn said.

I agree.

Then why do we wait? A few seconds, and I can have us in the air.

And the witch can cast her magic as fast as she can think. A cultist offered Murtagh a selection of sweetmeats, and Murtagh feigned a smile and declined. *Do you want to fight her right now?*

. . . No.

A moment of grim understanding passed between them. The witch was more capable than either of them had expected, and Murtagh did not want to test their magic against hers, for fear they would fall far short. *What she did shouldn't be possible. No one is strong enough to move that much dirt and rock at once. Not even Shruikan.*

If all the Eldunarí worked together, they could.

Maybe. But I've already looked with my mind. So have you. There are no Eldunarí here.

Thorn's breath was hot against the nape of his neck. *She could have used a store of energy hidden in gems.*

Why waste it on such a demonstration, though? That much energy would be a treasure beyond reckoning. It would take years upon years to acquire. Murtagh resisted the urge to grip Zar'roc again. He wanted the sword in hand, blade drawn, and a shield upon his off arm. And yet he knew now none of it would protect him against Bachel's power. *No, she must have a source of energy that renews itself, and it can't be that far away.*

He looked up as Alín approached with a pitcher of wine and offered him a stone cup. He accepted, and she filled the cup, though she refused to meet his gaze. Then she bowed, said, "My Lord," and departed.

Still unsettled, Murtagh took a larger drink than was his wont. The wine did little to soothe his nerves. He took another sip, and a thought occurred to him that caused him to lower the cup and stare at the coals in the nearby brazier while he worked out the implications. *I think I know why Bachel keeps delaying. She wants us to sleep again. To dream. That's what she's waiting for. She said as much earlier, didn't she? That's why she asked us to stay through the night. She must believe that the dreams here will somehow convince us to join their cause. Same as with their prisoners.*

A soft growl sounded behind him. *Then we must not sleep.*

We daren't. Murtagh turned the cup between his fingers. *If we lose ourselves, I shudder to think what would happen.*

It would be good to have help if we are to fight Bachel.

The thought pained Murtagh, but he could see no alternative. *Agreed. Once we are away from this place, I'll send a message to Eragon and Saphira and to Arya and Fírnen.*

A hint of fiery excitement colored Thorn's mind. *And then the newest generation of dragons and Riders can fly forth together.*

Mmm. Before we leave Nal Gorgoth, though, I want to find out what's in that cave.

Wariness was Thorn's initial response. *Why?*

Because maybe Bachel's source of power is down there.

And if you find it—

Perhaps we can use it for ourselves. Or I can destroy it. In any case, knowing what it is would give us our best chance of defeating Bachel. We'll wait for everyone to fall asleep, I'll look in the cave, and then we'll be off. By the time the witch wakes, we'll be long departed.

Good, said Thorn.

Then Bachel proposed a toast, and Murtagh smiled and raised his cup in response. And all the while, his mind whirled with dark speculation.

CHAPTER XI

✦ ✦ ✦ ✦ ✦ ✦ ✦

Anticipation

Night had fallen by the time the feast was finished. As seemed to be her habit, Bachel had eaten all of the dishes placed before her, and more besides. She had also drunk a small cask of sweet red wine and now sat slumped upon her throne, swollen with satiation. Looking at her put Murtagh in mind of a great, overfed toad, self-satisfied with its gluttony.

At a signal from Grieve, the witch's bearers lifted the litter and carried her into the dark recesses of the temple. Then the music ceased, and the cultists began to remove the tables and clean up from the feast, and Alín came to Murtagh and offered to lead him to his quarters.

After saying a temporary farewell to Thorn, he accepted.

Alín's white robe seemed to almost glow as she led him through the unlit hallways of the temple.

"Has Bachel ever done something like that before?" Murtagh knew he did not need to specify what exactly.

A momentary hesitation—an almost imperceptible hitch—appeared in Alín's stride. "Once, a long time ago, my Lord. A woman came to Nal Gorgoth. Uluthrek was her name, which was strange, as she was human. Bachel went to treat with her outside the village. No one heard what they said, but in the end, the Vale of Dreams shook as it shook today."

"Bachel went to meet *her*?" Murtagh had difficulty imagining.

"Yes, my Lord."

"Do you know why?"

"No, my Lord."

When they arrived at the doors to his chambers, Murtagh said, "Alín, you are bound by oaths. That I understand. But I need to know: What is Bachel's source of power? Tell me that much, at least."

"She is the Speaker, my Lord. All who serve as Speaker have this power."

"Yes, but why? Where does it come from?"

A hint of exasperation livened Alín's features. "That is a silly question. It comes from the Dreamer of Dreams, as does everything in life." She bowed, then said, "Your rooms, my Lord," and turned to leave.

"Wait!" Without thinking, Murtagh reached out to stop her. But Alín saw, and she shrank from his hand as if it were a red-hot iron, and her back struck a column built into the wall.

She let out an anguished cry and arched her chest, losing all composure.

Murtagh yanked back his hand as he realized he'd nearly touched her. Then his eyes narrowed as he noticed how gingerly Alín straightened her posture, face pale as fresh-fallen snow.

"She had you whipped," he said. It wasn't a question. He recognized the way Alín moved; he'd moved the same every time Galbatorix sent him to the post.

"I should not have spoken to you as I did earlier," said Alín in a low voice.

"After the hunt?" Murtagh struggled to keep the anger out of his voice.

She nodded. "It was wrong to be so familiar. *I* was wrong." She covered her face with her hands, and before Murtagh could reply, she rushed away, her soft leather shoes pattering along the stone hall.

A thick cloud layer had formed over the mountains, rendering it a starless, moonless night. The darkness suited Murtagh; it would make sneaking around that much easier.

Still, it was hard to gauge the passage of time without a view of the sky, and he wasn't sure how long to wait before leaving his quarters. He lit a small fire on the bedroom hearth and watched the flames consume the wood.

His mind refused to rest. Images of the black sun and looming dragon kept intruding, and he found himself planning and over-planning what might happen if he and Thorn had to fight Bachel and the rest of the Draumar.

Whatever happened, he wanted to protect the children. But it would be difficult, very difficult, given the witch's abilities.

He fished out one of the gold crowns from the pouch on his belt and held it up before the fire. The metal gleamed with an almost mirror-smooth polish. There was a spell on it, he guessed, to preserve the coin from wear.

Nasuada's sculpted profile remained as mysterious as ever. He brushed a thumb across her cheek and then stopped, feeling as if he'd taken an unwarranted liberty.

She was in danger—he was sure of it—and in no small part from Bachel. And he was determined to help protect her. "If only . . . ," he murmured, then stopped. Was there a more useless phrase than that? If only he hadn't convinced Galbatorix to have Nasuada abducted. But if he hadn't, the king would have killed her instead. As had happened so often in Murtagh's life, he'd been forced to choose between a pair of evils, and though he tried to pick the lesser of the two, it was evil all the same.

Moody, he put away the coin and stared into the depths of the fire.

He wished he had thought to take the compendium from Thorn's saddlebags and bring it with him. Reading would have been a welcome distraction. Instead, he turned to composing another poem.

The words came in fits and starts, with little grace, and the lines seemed broken and unpleasant to hear. Still, he kept trying to hammer them smooth, and in the end, he recited to himself:

Fragile is the flower that grows in darkness.
Precious is the flower that blossoms at night.
Their gardeners absent, blind, or uncaring.
But bent and broken petals still have beauty
All their own. Have care where you tread, lest you
Trample the treasures scattered before your feet.

When the fire had burned for what seemed like an hour, Murtagh ground out the embers with the heel of his boot, went to the east-facing windows, and looked down at the men standing guard in the courtyard.

He swore. Instead of two, there were now seven warriors, all of them awake. And upon their mailed chests, he saw the familiar shape of the cultists' enchanted bird-skull amulet. Bachel was sending him a message. She knew he'd snuck out of his room the previous night, and now she was taking precautions to keep him from doing so again. Seven men or two—the exact numbers didn't matter. What mattered were the amulets, which might be able to block the spell he had used before.

There was only one way to find out.

"Slytha," he murmured.

Murtagh felt the slightest decrease of strength, but the men seemed entirely unaffected. "Blast it," he said between clenched teeth.

Thorn eyed him from where he lay curled upon the flagstones. *Do you wish me to remove the men?*

The idea was tempting. *Not yet. Let me think a moment.*

A puff of grey smoke rose from Thorn's nostrils. The warriors gave him nervous looks.

Murtagh retreated from the windows and paced the room while

he considered options. It was his memory of the tangle box that gave him the first hint of a solution. The box had been designed to catch and hold spellcasters who were likewise protected against magic. It had done so through a combination of brute force and by altering the things *around* an unlucky captive, but not the captive themselves.

We'll have to be quick, said Murtagh, moving back to the windows.

They won't escape, replied Thorn.

Murtagh flexed his hands, readying himself. Then he drew in his will and whispered, "Thrysta vindr." The spell was simple enough, but it was the intent that mattered.

At first the seven warriors didn't notice that anything was amiss. Then one of them made a curious face and motioned in a panicked way toward the man opposite him. His companion frowned.

Murtagh was already moving. He leapt through the window, slid across the skirt-roof below—barely bothering to slow himself— and dropped to the courtyard.

His sudden appearance startled the men, caused them to seize their spears and train them on Murtagh. But when they attempted to shout and raise the alarm, no sound came from their mouths. For, as Murtagh knew, the spell had hardened the air about their faces so that they could neither inhale nor exhale.

The men's eyes bulged with anger, outrage, and horror, and their faces turned purple as the blood congested beneath their skin. They were courageous, though. Murtagh would give them that. Five of the men charged him, while one turned to run into the main part of the village and one ran toward the entrance of the temple.

Thorn reached out with a forefoot and slapped the village-bound warrior to the ground. He did not rise.

Murtagh darted sideways and slammed his shoulder into the man running for the temple. The warrior stumbled and fell.

The five other men closed upon Murtagh. A clumsy jab of a

spear glanced off his wards, and then he managed to retreat and put the ruined fountain between him and his pursuers.

The warriors tried to follow. But they were out of air. One after another, they collapsed, faces mottled and discolored, veins standing proud along their corded necks.

Then all was quiet, save for the kicking of their feet on the flagstones.

Murtagh hurried to Thorn and checked that the saddle straps were secure. He hadn't removed the dragon's tack the whole time they'd been in Nal Gorgoth, nor had Thorn asked him to. "There's no helping it now," said Murtagh in a low voice.

We should leave before anyone notices.

"First the cave." Thorn snorted in disapproval, and Murtagh gave him a look. "It's our only chance to find out what's in there."

The dragon growled deep in his chest. *Fine, but I will be glad to be gone from this place.*

"That makes two of us."

The last of the warriors went limp and lifeless as Murtagh tightened his sword belt and fetched his cloak from the saddlebags. He debated donning his mail. The armor would have been a comfort—if only a small one—but even with a slight layer of muffling rust on the iron rings, he feared the shirt would make too much noise.

With Thorn a stealthy companion at his back—or as stealthy as a dragon his size could be—Murtagh slipped around the northeastern corner of the temple and headed across the swath of cropped turf to the grove of pinetrees. At the mouth of the grove, Murtagh paused to search with his thoughts. Finding no one ahead of them, he whispered, "Brisingr," and set a faint red werelight burning in the air above.

The arcane fire lit the way as they proceeded along the path that wound among the dark-shadowed pines. Gloom and murk pressed in from all sides, as if the only piece of reality that existed was the small circle of earth the werelight painted red.

Thorn shivered with discomfort and kept his head and tail low to avoid the branches.

Beneath the pines, the air was heavy with the scent of herbs and mushrooms, as well as the ever-present stench of brimstone. Murtagh felt as if they were in a healer's storehouse, and he wondered at the uses of the plants.

At the gaping cavern set within the base of the foothills, Murtagh saw a stain of fresh blood atop the altar to the left of the opening. In the werelight's ruby radiance, the mark was black as ink, and the sight of it filled Murtagh with an apprehension of evil.

He loosened Zar'roc in its sheath and continued forward.

Twenty feet into the cavern, he heard Thorn's footsteps falter behind him. He looked back to see the dragon pressed flat against the ground, wings tight against his body, upper lip wrinkled in a fearful snarl.

Murtagh glanced at the arched ceiling of stone high above. "Even here?" he said in a quiet voice. He had thought there was enough room that Thorn would not feel threatened.

The dragon growled equally softly. *I am sorry.*

"Your wings don't even touch the walls. You can still fight if you need, and if we have to flee, there's space for you to turn ar—"

No. I . . . Thorn put a paw forward, and then trembled violently and pulled it back. He blinked, and a glistening film coated his eyes, bright in its reflection of the werelight. *I want, but I cannot.*

Murtagh returned to him and put his arms around Thorn's neck. For a moment, they stood like that, and the heat from Thorn's scales warmed Murtagh's chest through his thin linen shirt.

"It's all right," he murmured. "Stay here. I'll be quick, and then we can be gone."

Thorn hummed, appearing abashed. *I wish I were not so faulted.*

A rush of sorrow, compassion, and regret overwhelmed Murtagh. Opening his mind more fully, he said, *My hurts are different from yours, but I am as faulted as you, if not more. You know.*

I know.

No one is perfect. No one makes it through life whole and unscathed. So do not blame yourself for what is out of your control. We are here, and we have each other. That is what is important.

Another shiver ran Thorn's length. *I will try to follow you. If—*

No, no. Stay. We'll try somewhere else, when we don't have to worry about being stabbed in the back. Stay, and I'll be back directly.

You promise?

I promise. Wiol ono.

CHAPTER XII

The Bad Sleep-Well

Murtagh advanced alone into the waiting darkness.

Despite his assurances to Thorn, he felt vulnerable and afraid. The chambers that lay buried beneath him were full of the unfamiliar, the unguessed, and the obscure. How could he ready himself to face that which he had yet to name?

He kept Zar'roc loose in its sheath as he descended along the cut-stone stairs that led into the cavern. The ceiling remained high, lost in a dome of shadow that the feeble illumination from the werelight could not penetrate. He could have increased the flow of energy to the werelight—fanned it bright as a miniature sun—but that might have attracted attention. Also, he heard the squeaks of roosting bats far overhead; more light would risk waking them, and that *would* bring the cultists down upon his position.

His footsteps seemed curiously loud as he continued down the stairs, each gritty scuff and scrape bouncing off the unseen walls and raising his pulse. The steps ran back and forth in a zigzag, and they were worn hollow in the centers from the passage of uncounted feet over the centuries. Murtagh felt a sense of not just age but antiquity. Whoever had built the stairs had done so long before Alagaësia had been a settled place. What was it Bachel had said? That the cultists had lived in Nal Gorgoth since before elves were elves. . . . He was starting to think she had told the truth.

The cavern maintained enough height and width for a dragon Thorn's size—or larger—as it continued to sink deeper and deeper

445

into the sounding earth. The air was warmer now, and moister too, and the smell of brimstone stronger still.

Murtagh wiped his palms against his trousers. He didn't want his grip slipping on Zar'roc.

The mouth of the cave faded behind him, and soon he dwelt alone in a world of gloom. He reached back with his thoughts—farther than he realized he'd traversed—and touched Thorn's mind. *All well?* he asked.

The crows are stirring, but the village yet sleeps.

Murtagh quickened his pace. *I'll try not to be much longer, but this cave . . . it seems bottomless.*

Worry not. I will guard the entrance.

I know.

Despite the heat, Murtagh shivered. The hairs on the back of his neck prickled, and he felt a disconcerting presence, as if a thousand unseen eyes surrounded him in the press of dark. His nerve faltered, and he was about to increase the brightness of the werelight when . . .

A greenish glow appeared before him, so dim that it was barely perceptible. At first he thought his eyes were playing tricks on him, but after a few more yards, he realized that, no, there was indeed light ahead.

He extinguished the werelight, and the shadows rushed in. The sickly green luminescence led him on, and with every step, it swelled in strength until he saw: the cut-stone stairs ended at a rocky cave floor that extended in unknown directions. The coal-seamed rocks were mottled with membranes of virescent slime, from which emanated the low, flameless light. Poking up among the rocks were numerous mushrooms, the most common variety being a short, purple-capped toadstool with drooping gills that resembled an oyster's inner flesh. Throughout, wisps of brimstone vapor drifted up from the cave floor, as if the earth itself were breathing and sweating.

A winding path set with flagstones like the temple courtyard extended from the bottom of the stairs and disappeared into the ringing shadows.

Murtagh swore to himself, softly, as he arrived at the bottom. He'd never seen such a place—not even in the Beor Mountains, among the tunnels and caves the dwarves built and tended. Whether or not the space was naturally occurring, he couldn't tell. No stalactites or stalagmites were visible, and the slimed rocks were broken into pieces much like quarry stones.

He pushed his cloak back from his shoulders. *I should have left it with Thorn.* The heat was becoming unbearable.

He tried to estimate how far underground he was. It had to be several hundred feet, if not more. Chiseling out that many steps would have been a monumental undertaking, even with magic, and if it had been done by hand . . . *What is so important down here?*

He started along the path.

The off-putting glow from the slime and the smell of sulfur and his underlying wariness combined to turn his stomach, as if he'd eaten a duck egg that had been insufficiently cooked. He swallowed the spit that was filling his mouth and tried to ignore the feeling, though his body was telling him to flee to open skies and fresh air.

His right foot struck something hard.

A fist-sized rock rolled away. He stepped off the path and retrieved the stone. The rock glistered and gleamed as if burning from within. It was a perfect pair to the stone he'd had off Sarros in Ceunon what seemed like half a year ago.

His heart racing, he tucked the stone into the pouch on his belt.

Perhaps a hundred feet from the stairs, a huge curving wall emerged before him, rough and creviced. Three tunnels pierced the wall, and Thorn would have fit into each had he folded his wings tight and kept his belly against the ground, like a great glittering serpent. The tunnel in the middle was edged with finished stone: a ring of rectangular blocks carved with sharp-cornered lines and the same unfamiliar runes as in the village. In the center of each block was set a cabochon of opal, which reflected the slime-glow like so many cats' eyes.

The tunnels to the left and right were plain, unfinished: rough tubes of stone that burrowed into the roots of the mountains. They did not look chiseled or hammered, and yet neither did they feel entirely natural. More than a little, they reminded Murtagh of the tunnels he'd fled through during his escape from Captain Wren's secret chambers beneath Gil'ead—only far larger.

Faint sounds emanated from the depths of the tunnels. Whispers. Moans. Soft echoing cries that had a hooting, birdlike quality. At first he thought he was hearing speech or calls of animals, but after a time, he grew convinced it was the air itself moving through the veins of the earth that gave rise to the eerie sounds.

He chose to enter the central tunnel. The unknown craftsmen who had labored upon the caves had taken special pains with that one, and so it must be of importance or lead to importance.

He continued forward. Deeper into the womb of the earth. Deeper into the black unknown, seeking, seeking, always seeking a farther shore, every sense razor-sharp and razor-scraped, skin all goosefleshed, cold sweat dripping down the back of his neck and gathering around his belted waist.

The walls of the tunnel were sheathed with diamond-shaped tiles of rough stone that were lapped like the scales of a dragon. He felt as if he were walking inside a shed skin of enormous proportion.

Not far, then. A minute of walking, no more, and the darkness again encroached, for the tiles were free of slime.

Then he saw a room before him, warm with light. A pale room. A bone-white room clad in finest marble, the veins of which were chased with hammered gold. Brass censers hung on chains from the snouts of sculpted dragon heads, which projected from the circular, column-lined walls. Small flames burned in alcoves in the wall, but the fires consumed no wicks and no fuel; they seemed to spring straight from the marble.

Several open, human-sized doorways led to yet more tunnels. But it was what lay in the center of the room that captured Murtagh's attention, for it was large and strange: a ring of rough marble, several hands high, with a lid of grey metal atop it, like a covered well.

As he crept closer, he saw a pane of clear crystal framed within the metal, and through the crystal . . . a vaporous void dropping deeper into the earth.

He frowned. Was this the sacred well that Grieve had mentioned? Was it—or what it contained—the source of Bachel's power? The well itself didn't look like much. And yet, the air seemed to thrum like a plucked string. It was true that not all magics were made by humans, elves, dwarves, or any other self-aware, thinking race. There were natural magics also, such as the floating crystals of Eoam, but they tended to be wild and unpredictable.

If the well were such a place, that could explain Bachel's prowess with magic. And if so, it wasn't the sort of thing that the Draumar ought to have dominion over. Not that he would want Du Vrangr Gata to assume control over such an important location either. This was exactly what the Riders had been created for: to oversee and mediate that which could destabilize the land.

He bent over the hammered lid and squinted as he tried to peer through the snakes of vapor swirling below. There was a hint of a shape beneath the haze: a vague outline that he could almost make sense of.

Opening his mind, he sent a cautious, probing thought into the murk. He didn't know what he expected to find, but he suspected there was *something* of interest hidden at the bottom of the well. . . .

The moans and murmurs echoing through the tunnels seemed to grow louder, and Murtagh's vision flickered as if shadowy creatures were moving about the edges. When he blinked, images flashed behind his lids—too fast to fully register—and a powerful urge to sleep settled upon his shoulders, pressing him down. He fought against it, alarmed. Wherever the urge came from, he felt sure it was the source of the bad dreams that plagued the village, as an evil miasma seeping out of the ground and infecting their sleeping minds.

The vapor below parted in places, and dimly in the dark he saw different levels of tunnels and chambers, pierced by the shaft plunging downward. And at the distant bottom, obscured by drifting patches, a pulsing glow that—

"You should not be here, my son."

Murtagh spun to see Bachel and Grieve standing by the entrance. The witch's hair was down, and it tumbled in a stormy mess around her face and shoulders to her midback, dark and lustrous. The sleeves of her dress were pushed up to expose her forearms, her feet were bare, and the soot round her eyes was smudged as if she'd been interrupted while removing it. In one hand, she carried a tall spear, the haft of which was made of a greenish material, with a long, barbed blade of strange design atop it. A faint glow surrounded the head of the weapon.

Cold lead loaded Murtagh's gut, keeping him from moving. He recognized the spear. It was a Dauthdaert—a Deathspear— made by the elves with but one purpose in mind: to kill dragons. The elves had forged the twelve Dauthdaert during their war with the dragons, prior to the formation of the Riders, and they had enchanted the weapons that they might pierce scale and bypass even a dragon's wild magic.

Moreover, Murtagh knew this specific Dauthdaert. It was the selfsame lance that Arya had used to kill Shruikan. Niernen was its name, and it was cursed and hated and coveted by every person of bloody ambition. He'd thought the Dauthdaert had been lost in the destruction following Galbatorix's death. That it had survived was surprising. That someone had spirited it out of Ilirea and brought it to Bachel was profoundly alarming.

In contrast to the lance's arcane appearance, Grieve carried a more mundane weapon: a club of hardwood shod with iron bands secured around the head.

Thorn! How had Bachel and Grieve gotten past him? Murtagh wanted to reach out with his mind to the dragon, but he didn't dare lower his mental defenses with the witch and her companion so close. Still, he felt no pain or alarm through the constant background connection that he and Thorn shared, and that was a comfort. *More tunnels,* he thought. There had to be a passage joining the temple with the caves beneath.

Murtagh's hand tightened around Zar'roc's hilt. In any other circumstances, he would have drawn, but he wanted—no, *needed*— a better understanding of Bachel's power before fighting her, especially as he was on his own, without Thorn. "I saw the cave, and I was curious."

"This is not a place for outsiders." Bachel's stance was poised but not overly stiff, the perfect way to ready oneself for violent action. Her eyes flashed with dark promise, and she held the Dauthdaert with an ease that convinced Murtagh that she was well accustomed to its use.

"And what is this place, my Lady?"

Bachel and Grieve started to stalk with measured steps around the lidded well of stone. Murtagh mirrored their movement, keeping the well between him and them.

Grieve was the one who answered, glowering beneath his heavy, unfinished brow. "It is the Well of Dreams, Rider, and none may approach it without Bachel's permission. It is the heart of all things, the source of prophecy and power, and those who defile it must die."

With the thumb of his left hand, Murtagh pressed Zar'roc an inch or two out of the sheath so that it would slide free without binding. "And have I defiled it, Bachel?"

At first he thought the witch would respond with anger. But then she laughed in a lazy fashion and took another step closer. Grieve split from her and came round the other side of the well, bracketing Murtagh.

He retreated a step to keep from being flanked. One of the open doorways was to his back; he had room to flee.

"Defile?" said Bachel, nearly purring. "No, my son, I think not. Not so long as you kneel now and swear fealty to me. For how can the servant be in the wrong if they are acting in accordance with their mistress's will? Kneel now, Murtagh son of Morzan, and your life will be spared."

Zar'roc sang as he drew it, the familiar weight a comfort in his hand. He smiled a crooked smile. "You know I will not. You have given me no reasons worth hearing. Even if you had, Thorn and I will never again kneel out of fear or desperation. If we bend our knees, it will be because of love, duty, and respect, or not at all."

Bachel's expression grew haughty. "You would not understand if I told you, Kingkiller. You would claim you did, but you would not *feel* the truth, and your heart would be empty. I had hoped to spare you this. I had hoped you would dream as we all dream here in Nal Gorgoth, and you would come to understand the truth as we all have. You would have devoted yourself to our cause, freely and willingly."

"Is that how it was with Saerlith?" asked Murtagh. "Did he follow you freely?" As he spoke, he risked sending a single blade of thought toward the surface. *Thorn!* A cry for help to the only one he could count on.

But all he received in return was fear. Fear of enclosed spaces, fear of being trapped, fear of loss. Murtagh's mouth grew sour. He could expect no reinforcement.

Bachel's lips twisted to one side. "Saerlith was a pawn and nothing more. He served our aims, even as did Galbatorix and Morzan."

The mention of his father seemed like an obvious attempt to needle him. He chose to ignore the bait. "Somehow I doubt that. Galbatorix served nothing and no one."

His words appeared to prick the witch's pride. "Your fear leads you to overestimate the king. How is it, do you think, he came to lose his dragon?"

Murtagh felt his pride similarly afflicted. "Galbatorix? He went adventuring in the north, and a group of Urgals—"

"No!" cried Bachel, and she slashed through the air with one arm, the hand flat and narrow as a blade. Then, in a more measured tone: "It is true that Urgals slew Jarnunvösk in the icy reaches of the far north, but you are mistaken as to the *reason* Galbatorix and his unfortunate party ventured forth. He lied to you, Outlander. What he told you, and everything else you have heard from the Riders of old about that expedition, all lies!"

Keep her talking. Murtagh continued to edge around the well, trying to maintain equal distance between him, the witch, and Grieve. "Then what is the truth, Bachel? Or will you only answer with more riddles?"

Bachel assumed a cold, cruel demeanor. "The truth is this: The Riders feared us, Du Eld Draumar. And they feared *me*. And, in secret, they dispatched Galbatorix and his companions to seek us out, that the Riders might later destroy us."

Just how old was the witch? "If they feared you so," said Murtagh, "why would they send Riders who were not even fully trained or tested? None of them had even a score of years. Surely you cannot expect me to believe such a tale."

"The purpose of Galbatorix's party was to find us. Theirs was not to attack," said Bachel. "Indeed, they did not even know the truth of whom they looked for, as their elders sought to keep them ignorant of the Draumar."

Murtagh's steps slowed as dozens of possibilities raced through his mind. Nothing the witch said was impossible, and if she was right, the implications were dire, for they meant the Draumar were dangerous enough to threaten even the Riders. "But they *were* attacked."

Bachel gave a curt nod. "Galbatorix came wandering back through the Spine, alone and half mad. As such, he found us, and it was as such we took him in. At first he distrusted us, even as you have, and he blamed us for the death of Jarnunvösk, but I ministered him with what attentions were needed, and in time, he came to understand that it was the Riders who were to blame for his loss."

"You turned him against them," Murtagh breathed. "And then you sent him back to confront them."

Again, Bachel nodded. "It was a test. Were the Riders as kind and compassionate as they claimed, they would have taken pity upon Galbatorix and given him another dragon. But they were not, and they did not, and so Galbatorix came to understand the truth of them."

Fear hollowed out Murtagh. It was hard for him to imagine Galbatorix being anything less than the most powerful person in the land, elves included. If Bachel had done what she claimed—whether through the force of her words or the strength of her magic or a combination thereof—then by some measure, she surmounted even the king.

In a low voice, he said, "Do you mean to say Galbatorix and the Forsworn were your thralls?"

"In part. They were useful instruments to a needed end."

He cocked his head. "Which was?"

"The eradication of the Riders."

"Why would you seek that? Are not dragons sacred to your people?"

A dismissive wave of Bachel's hand. "The lesser worms matter not. Their blood is tainted by the wrongdoings of their forefathers, and only once the Riders and their dragons were washed from the world could a new era begin."

Grieve moved a bit too close for Murtagh's liking, and he retreated a few steps. "What of Durza?" he asked. "Always I've heard that Galbatorix met him in the Spine, after Jarnunvösk died."

"That is true," Bachel said, inclining her head. "The Shade shared in our dreams, and it was because of them that his ambitions grew longer and broader than is the wont of his ilk."

"He lived here?"

"For many a year, even as Galbatorix and your father lived here after they fled Ilirea with the hatchling Shruikan." The glow from the Dauthdaert lit the side of Bachel's face with a ghoulish cast. "Your king and your father knew the truth of things, Murtagh son of Morzan. Always you were destined to follow in their footsteps. There is no other path for you."

Murtagh's mind was awhirl as he parsed the witch's revelations. And yet he remained convinced of one truth: Galbatorix would never have bent his knee to another. Not after he turned against the Riders. If he had been allied with the Draumar, it had only been as a matter of convenience. The king was no zealot, no true believer. At the soonest opportunity, he would have turned against the Draumar and attempted to undo them. Murtagh recalled what Bachel had said before their boar hunt: that Galbatorix once tried to purge their settlements. Tried and failed.

With the harsh light of insight, he realized: *Somehow the Draumar held their own against the king. Somehow she did. Bachel was a danger even to Galbatorix. But why, why, why, why?*

"I am not my father," he said in a tight voice. "Nor am I the man I once was. It is you who are mistaken, witch. I shall not bend to you."

"How unfortunate," said Bachel. But she seemed entirely unconcerned.

Murtagh lifted Zar'roc and twirled the hilt in his hand, as if he had not a care in the world. "You cannot best me, Bachel. Neither of you can."

The witch laughed, a wild, unrestrained laughter that sent chills down Murtagh's spine. She was no more scared of him than he would be of a common footpad, and his palm grew slick with sweat on Zar'roc's wire-wrapped hilt. *Should have worn gloves,* he thought. Without taking his gaze off Bachel or Grieve, he unhooked his cloak and spun it around his left forearm, and he heard Tornac's voice in his head saying, "An offhand garment may serve to distract, bind, and, in the absence of a shield, protect."

"Perhaps I cannot best you, Kingkiller," said Bachel, "though it would be an interesting contest. However, it is not I that you must overcome. I am merely an instrument of a higher power, and neither you nor I nor the wisest of elves nor the strongest of dragons yet living can prevail against that which I serve."

She touched the pane of crystal in the hammered lid, and the pane slid open, seemingly of its own accord, and a choking cloud of green-lit vapor billowed into the room.

Murtagh didn't know what danger the vapor posed, but he knew enough to be afraid. He had a half second to inhale, and then the cloud enveloped him, dimming the room and making his eyes smart.

A touch of panic spiked his pulse. He had made no wards to filter the air. An oversight. He turned to run, and the glowing tip of the Dauthdaert sliced past his ear.

He flinched and used Zar'roc to beat the haft of the lance away. Then he lunged toward Bachel, but the distance was wrong; she was out of reach, laughing amid the brimstone mist.

Grieve came at him from the side, swinging his iron-shod club with ruthless efficiency. He caught Murtagh in an awkward position, and the club slammed down against Murtagh's right arm. His wards deflected, and the club skated away amid swirls of vapor.

At the same time, cruel thoughts assailed Murtagh's mind:

Bachel and Grieve attempting to batter down his defenses and assume control over his consciousness. Their mental attacks were as strong as any he had ever encountered, including Galbatorix's. But Murtagh was no weakling, and he held fast within his inner being, secure in who and what he was.

Bachel stabbed again and again with Niernen, fast as an elf. The Dauthdaert flicked like a deadly tongue through the vapor. The edges were so sharp, they parted the cloud like cut gauze.

Only seconds had passed, but already Murtagh's lungs were on fire. He felt as if he were going to explode. He needed air, needed to breathe. . . .

He launched a counterattack against Bachel's and Grieve's minds, a desperate attempt to overwhelm them with the sheer force of his consciousness. From a distance, he felt Thorn adding strength to his own, and the realization gave him courage.

Then Murtagh stepped back, and his heel caught against the lip of a stone tile in the floor.

His stomach lurched as he fell. He twisted, intending to catch himself on one arm, but—

—too slow. He landed on his side, and the impact drove the air from his lungs. He inhaled without meaning to, and bitter, sulfurous fumes filled his nose and mouth and throat.

Coughing, he scrambled backward, keeping Zar'roc above his head to ward off blows. Bachel and Grieve were advancing on him, black shapes in the clotted clouds, their outlines bending and breaking, and he felt as if he were falling again and his body lacked substance and a horrible rushing sounded, as a wind across a desolate plain at the end of all things.

He tried to rise, tried to shout, tried to focus his will on a word or spell, but the world was dissolving around him, and his thoughts were as scattered as seeds before that horrible howling wind, and again he saw the black sun and the rising dragon, and an inexorable foreboding of doom crushed any hope he had.

Bachel's face materialized before him, wisps of vapor wreathing her angled features. Her eyes were glowing with fevered ecstasy, and her lips were ruby red as if painted with blood. And she said, "You cannot win, Kingkiller. I serve the power of dream and He whose mind conjures dream. *Sleep.*"

Murtagh fought with all his might, but blackness descended, and Bachel and the chamber and all that he knew vanished.

CHAPTER XIII

✦✦✦✦✦✦✦

Nightmare

*B*lack sun, black dragon, and an eternity of despair. He was falling toward the bottom of an incomprehensibly large void, and at the bottom lay slumbering a mind of impossible size, whose thoughts moved as slowly as the currents within an icebound sea and were just as black, cold, and hostile. He felt a presence that made him shudder and shrink to insignificance, and all of human endeavor seemed of no more importance than the accomplishments of a colony of ants.

He searched for Thorn, but the bond they shared was no longer to be found. He was utterly alone, without recourse, resource, or hope of rescue.

Then he was spinning through space, and all around malevolence pressed against him with crushing force. He saw dragons tearing at his flesh, and the bodies of his foes laid out across the mortified earth, scorched with flame, charred with soot. He saw the darkness beneath the mountains, and felt the coolness of the earth firm against his sides. Worms fed off his putrefying limbs as the smell of death wrapped him in its charnel embrace.

The void yawned wider. Amid the despair and screeching horrors, a bloody dawn spilled across a brazen land, and he saw himself triumphant: a golden crown upon his head, Zar'roc in his hand, Thorn by his side, and Bachel too . . . and a world at his feet, bowing to him as they had bowed to his father and Galbatorix.

A vision. A premonition. A dreadful promise.

Then he was in his cell beneath the citadel in Urû'baen. Stone walls wet with seeping moisture, black mold grown in veined maps across the crumbling mortar, ground mixed with droppings and urine and fallen crumbs from week-old crusts of bread. The jailers beat the bars of the cells and jeered at the prisoners—no sympathy from them, no help or kindness. And when the jailers left, terrors came crawling forth from cracks within the walls: fat-bodied spiders, pale and heavy, with furred legs and long feelers. They dragged their bloated stomachs across him and bit and bit him, and always it seemed he could feel the jittery touch of their clawed feet. The sounds of them moving about kept him awake nights, and never could he sleep in earnest.

A red egg before him, knee-high and shot through with white. Behind him, the unseen shadow of HIM. The egg cracked, and he watched, breathless, as a piece of shell fell free, and he saw the most delicate, beautiful, helpless hatchling: red and squalling and hungry, hungry, hungry. He reached for it, and snout and hand touched, and the contact was electric. . . .

He yanked against his shackles, screaming, sobbing, as he felt the hatchling's torment from the other side of the wall. HE bent over him—close-cropped beard like a black dagger, thin mouth distorted in angry delight—and said, "Swear to me, Murtagh. Swear to me, or I'll have them strip every scale from his body. Swear fealty to me as your father did before you."

He shook and shivered and raged, but he couldn't hold out. The pain of the hatchling—the pain of such a perfect, innocent creature, a pain that he felt as if each fleck of agony were his own—it was too much. Of his own, he could have endured. But not this.

"I swear," he sobbed. "I swear fealty to you."

The evil smile widened. "In the ancient language now. Use the words I gave you."

So he swore as instructed, and the words were ashes in his mouth.

Later came more oaths. And later still, HE spoke their true names, and then Murtagh and Thorn both were lost, lost, lost. . . .

Awareness returned, hazy as a cloud.

Murtagh blinked, uncertain of himself, his place, and how he had gotten there. He felt stuffed full of wool: thick, slow, and heavy.

He sat up, befuddled.

Marble walkway beneath him. Curved tunnel walls around him. And before him . . . a woman with tumbling hair, a glowing spear in one hand, and the light of triumph in her hawk-eyed face. She was fierce and beautiful and terrible. No mercy or comfort was to be found in her features, only burning passion that would sweep aside anything that barred her way.

Bachel. Remembering the name was a struggle; speaking it, impossible.

The woman bent toward him. "Rise, Kingkiller," she commanded, and her voice thrummed with power.

Her words were irresistible. In a daze, he rose to his feet, still unable to form a coherent sound.

She put her lips together and blew on him. Vapor whorled toward him, and with it, a heavy, rotten odor. For some reason, he no longer found it offensive. Rather, it was intoxicating, as if he could never breathe enough of it. Each lungful was an exhilaration that set his head spinning and prevented him from focusing on any one thing for more than a moment.

"Walk with me, my son," said Bachel. Her words echoed in his mind, soft as song but strong as iron.

She strode away through the vapor, and he followed, dumb and wildered.

A man accompanied them with a lurching, long-limbed tread. Murtagh studied his cragged face, trying and failing to place it. The man carried a red sword in one hand and an iron-shod club in the other, with a loose cloak draped over the crook of his arm.

Into a marble-clad chamber they went and along a tiled tunnel and through a slime-lit cave with a broken floor. As they arrived at the base of a set of stairs cut into the stone, Murtagh's mind began to sharpen, though he remained deeply confused.

"Where . . . where are—"

Bachel turned and blew on him again, a gentle breath of warm air. With it came a billow of vapor from a crystal vial she held on her palm. He had not noticed it before.

At the touch of the vapor, all thought deserted him.

"Close your mouth, Kingkiller," said Bachel. "It is unseemly of you to gape as a poleaxed fish."

He did as he was told.

"Good. Now come with me, Kingkiller. Come."

Up the stairs they went, and the slime-glow faded behind them. In its place, torchlight appeared above and ahead, the flames— which were not yet visible—casting a throng of shadows upon the walls and mouth of the cave.

The last step passed beneath Murtagh's feet, and then he stood on level ground again. Bachel led him toward a great red dragon crouched on the dark path before them.

The dragon snarled, and his tail twitched, and something of the dragon's presence resonated in Murtagh's mind, but he could make no sense of it. The words and impressions forced upon his consciousness were a meaningless storm filled with random bits of wind-tossed flotsam.

A roar burst forth from the dragon, strong enough that Murtagh felt the vibration against his cheek.

"Hush now," said Bachel. She lifted the vial and blew across the crystal mouth, and a cloud of vapor streamed forth and surrounded the dragon's head.

The glittering creature thrashed and quivered, and then his cat-like eyes rolled back, and his enormous bulk went slack and still.

Formless alarm filled Murtagh, yet he could do nothing.

After long minutes . . . the dragon stirred again.

Bachel walked over to him and placed a hand upon his snout. "Awake, O slave of dream."

The dragon's eyelids flicked open with a *snick*, and he arched his neck and shook his head, as if to throw off a swarm of flies. The creature stared at Murtagh, and Murtagh at him, and neither of them spoke, both equally confounded.

A set of seven crows descended from the blackened sky. They circled Bachel's head in a murderous crown and then settled about her shoulders and arms. She smiled at them fondly and stroked their feathers with the back of her forefinger while the birds peered with pale eyes, bright and suspicious, at Murtagh and the dragon.

With the birds as her companions, Bachel strode forward from the cave and into the grove of trees. "Come," she said, and Murtagh and the dragon followed.

They had no choice.

The black-needled pines stood as silent sentinels watching over the strange, staggered procession passing beneath their arching boughs. Murtagh stared up at the treetops and the velvet blackness of the clouded sky, and he tried to understand why the world felt so out of joint.

With measured steps, they walked across the cropped turf and then back into the courtyard before the temple. Rows of grey-robed people stood like hooded statues in the yard. Each held a lit torch, and their faces were turned down, so only the tops of their hoods were visible.

Bachel led Murtagh and the dragon into the center of the mute congregation, and a quartet of warriors gathered close around her, spears held at the ready.

She pointed at the dragon with a taloned finger. "Secure him," she said, her voice ringing clear in the night air. And she tossed the vial at the dragon's feet. It broke with a sharp chime. A plume of vapor expanded upward and gathered around the dragon's head, moving as if it were a living thing.

Then Bachel beckoned to Murtagh. "With me, Kingkiller," she

said, and walked toward the entrance of the temple, the seven crows still riding upon her arms and shoulders.

He wanted to object, but he could not form the words, and no sound left his throat.

The tall witch led him deep into the temple, through cold corridors devoid of light, past windows shuttered closed and empty doorways that stared like eyeless sockets. Then down again, along a snail-shell staircase, until they arrived at a series of iron-barred cells. Grieve opened one door and pushed Murtagh inside.

"Now, O Rider, drink this," said Bachel. And she handed Murtagh another vial, this one smaller, more delicate. Within was a pearlescent liquid that glowed with an unnatural luminance.

He stared dumbly at the vial, unable to make sense of what was expected. The floor and the ceiling seemed to spin; he swayed and nearly fell.

Bachel placed a finger against the back of his hand and pressed it toward his mouth. Her skin was cool against his. "Drink," she said, and her voice was a wind brushing through branches bare of leaves, needles, or bark.

He drank. The liquid burned like brandy.

Then Grieve took the vial from his hand and closed the iron door.

"Give him his cloak, that he may remain warm," said Bachel. "He is my child, after all, and I would have him treated as such."

The garment landed upon him, a heavy petal of felted wool. He pulled it off his face. The fibers rubbed against his skin; he could feel each individual one, and they overwhelmed him with the influx of sensation.

Bachel bent toward him from beyond the iron bars. "Sleep, Kingkiller. Sleep . . . and dream. . . . Dream. . . . Dream."

Her voice faded into the distance, and shadow swallowed her face as Murtagh fell backward—fell and fell and fell, and all the universe spun around him, and he cried out. But no one answered.

He was standing in the royal balcony overlooking the arena, Galba-torix behind him, looming and unseen, for Murtagh kept his gaze fixed on the sandy pit—the same pit where he'd killed his first man.

"Watch now," said the king, and his voice contained the authority of rolling thunder.

Murtagh gripped the balcony railing until his nails turned white. He wanted to shout and rant—he wanted to leap over the railing and jump into the arena—but it would only make the situation worse.

Thorn stood in the center of the pit. He was only four days old: still weak, still unable to fly, though he kept raising his thin, undersized wings and driving them down in a futile attempt to take off. He turned in circles, chirping in concern, uncertain of where to go or what to do. He saw Murtagh on the balcony and let out a pitiful whine, and Murtagh knew his own feelings were affecting the hatchling. So he hardened his heart and, despite the anguish it caused him, closed his mind to the hatchling below.

"He's too young," he said from between clenched teeth.

"No creature is too young," answered the king. "If he is to survive, he must learn to fight and feed. There is no other way."

The iron portcullises at either side of the arena ratcheted up, and from each opening, a pair of grey timber wolves loped into the pit. They growled and snarled as they saw Thorn, and the fur along their spines bristled.

Thorn shrank back, but there was nowhere to run or hide.

"Please," said Murtagh, gritting his teeth.

"No." The king's breath was warm against his ear.

The wolves circled Thorn. The dragon was longer than they were, but the wolves outweighed the hatchling by a significant amount.

After a few false starts, the wolves began to dart in and nip at Thorn's wings and tail.

The dragon twisted round to face each new threat, but he wasn't

465

fast enough, and the wolves moved together with silent understanding. Within seconds, drops of steaming blood dripped from rents in Thorn's wings, and he held his left forefoot off the ground, unable to place his weight on it.

Each drop of blood struck like a drumbeat of doom.

Murtagh felt as if he were about to explode. He tore down the barrier he'd erected in his mind and sent his thoughts hurtling toward the dragon's small but fierce consciousness.

Thorn flinched, distracted, and the wolves closed in.

Jump! Murtagh shouted in his mind, including an image of what he meant.

Thorn hesitated, still uncertain, and one of the wolves bit his tail. With a yelp, Thorn spun to face his attacker.

It was a mistake. The other wolves rushed toward him, jaws parted, foam-flecked fangs ready to close on Thorn's slender legs and delicate wings.

Murtagh forced his will onto the dragon's as-yet-unformed mind and again shouted, Jump! To his relief, Thorn jumped, and he used his wings to gain a few extra feet of height before dropping down on the other side of the arena. The walls were too high for Thorn to surmount, which meant he had to fight.

The wolves raced after Thorn, and Murtagh fed the dragon more instructions. Thorn was, like all of his kind, a natural fighter, and it took only seconds before he started to understand and respond.

Thorn sprang onto the back of the nearest wolf and sank his teeth into the beast's neck. With a sharp, vicious gesture, he tore out a chunk of hide and muscle—releasing a spray of blood—and then jumped onto a second wolf.

The wolf twisted nearly in half, snapping at the dragon, but Thorn dug his claws in and bit at the wolf's head until the creature's legs buckled and it collapsed to the ground.

The fall knocked Thorn onto his side, and before Murtagh could do anything to help, the other two wolves darted in and began to savage Thorn.

"No!"

For a few seconds, the dragon was barely visible, lost beneath a twisting knot of grey fur, legs, and tails. Growls and snarls and yelps of pain filled the arena, and fans of blood sprayed across the packed sand. Murtagh felt sharp pangs from Thorn, and he feared all was lost. He couldn't understand. Why would Galbatorix allow his newest prize to die?

"How could you?" he said, barely able to form the words.

"Watch."

The wolves fell apart. One dragged itself away, hind legs limp and useless, fur matted with spit and foam and blood. The other rolled onto its side and kicked helplessly, its belly ripped open and a pile of grey intestines spilling out. The kicking slowed.

Between the wolves stood Thorn. The small dragon was battered and torn—his wings shredded in several places—but fire burned in his sparkling eyes, and blood dripped from his razor-sharp fangs and from the large claws on his hind feet.

With a small roar, he sprang after the wolf with the paralyzed hindquarters. He bit and held the back of the wolf's neck, and the animal shuddered and went limp, dead.

Then Thorn crouched low over his kill and began to tear at the corpse, ravenous in his hunger.

"Do you see?" said the king. "He is a dragon, and dragons are meant to kill. It is what they are. It is who you are. If you learn this now, the coming days will be that much easier for you, O son of Morzan. Now go to your dragon and heal him as you will."

"I'll kill you for this."

A deep chuckle behind him. "No, you shall not. You will dream of killing me, you will plan for it, you will desire my demise with all your heart, but in the end you will see the rightness of my ways and realize that there is no opposing my power. You are mine, Murtagh, as is Thorn, and you shall serve me as your father did before you."

To that, Murtagh had no answer. He went to attend Thorn's wounds.

Nor was that the only time they visited the arena. Every time

Thorn grew hungry, Galbatorix forced him to fight for his food, and Murtagh had no choice but to watch, helpless, as the young dragon killed and killed again. Even when Thorn grew larger than the largest bear, the king still insisted on making him face his prey in mortal conflict.

Murtagh saw the sands of the pit soak through with blood, and outside the citadel, he seemed to see the sky turn red. All around he heard the sounds of prisoners shrieking and yammering their torment, and he turned and ran and ran and ran through a warren of rocky tunnels, but they kept leading him back to the charnel grounds of the arena, and each time, he saw Thorn sitting hunched over his kills, alone, frightened, covered in blood, and desperately eating.

As Thorn had his trials, so too did Murtagh have his own. And they were just as long, bloody, and inescapable.

And beneath it all—beneath the overpowering images and emotions brought forth from the unwelcome past—lay the yawning void, and within it . . . a core of slow-turning madness centered upon some unknown yet implacable purpose.

And Murtagh wept and cried out with fear.

CHAPTER XIV

✦ ✦ ✦ ✦ ✦ ✦

Uvek

Murtagh woke.

There was no slow return to reality. No gradual brightening of light, no ramped awareness of his senses. One moment, nothing. The next—

A grey stone floor lay beneath him, inches from his nose. The stone was cracked, and small filigrees of moss had infiltrated the tiny crevices in the material: a tracery of green in an otherwise bare, grim surface. The smell of moss and stone combined was like that of a high mountain stream, or else a deep cave filled with a sunless lake.

His body was cold. He was lying face down on the hard floor. His left knee throbbed, and his right arm was numb from being folded underneath him.

As for his mind . . . his thoughts were clearer, more focused than before, although he still felt strangely muzzy, and there was a sickly-sweet taste at the back of his throat that he felt he ought to recognize. . . .

He remembered the caves beneath the village, and the glowing slime, and finding the grated well where Bachel and Grieve had confronted him.

Alarm rushed through him. *Thorn!*

With his left arm, he pushed himself upright. His head swam, and he braced himself against the floor and closed his eyes until his balance returned and his right arm stopped tingling. Then he looked around.

He was in a dark cell, not dissimilar to the one he'd been confined in under Urû'baen. A narrow wooden cot sat against one wall, with a bucket for relieving himself next to it. His cloak lay beneath him, crumpled and wrinkled. There were no windows, only three blank stone walls, and iron bars where the fourth would have been. (He noted the bars especially; they represented an unusual amount of metal for such a small village.)

The only light came from a dim oil lamp near the end of the hallway in front of the cell.

Across the hall were three more cells, lost in inky shadows.

Murtagh tried to reach Thorn with his mind, but their thread of connection was nowhere to be found. Moreover—and equally concerning—Murtagh couldn't feel a single other mind in the vicinity. Either the village had been deserted or somehow his tendrils of thought were being blocked. . . . And what *was* that taste sticking to his tongue and throat? He could almost place it.

Cold fear settled into Murtagh's bones. Once again, he and Thorn found themselves overmatched, even as with Galbatorix. And once again, they found themselves bound against their will, for he could not imagine Thorn was free to fight, or else the dragon would have already rescued him.

Even in his worst nightmares, Murtagh had never imagined they would find themselves in a like situation again. *Foolish*, he thought, and cursed himself. He'd been overconfident, and now both he and Thorn were paying the price.

There would be time enough for recriminations later. For now, he had to concentrate on escape.

Murtagh clenched his hands several times in preparation. Then he gripped the cold iron, gathered his will, and whispered, "Kverst."

Nothing happened. He could not seem to breach the barrier in his mind—the thin, glass-like pane that a consciousness had to break in order to directly manipulate energy. He tried again, but he found no purchase for his will. The barrier kept slipping away, and his thoughts remained too unfocused to pierce it.

His fear deepened until it was more akin to despair. He knew then what he was tasting: the drug called vorgethan, or some compounding of it. Galbatorix had fed it to him in Urû'baen until the king had forced his fealty, Durza had used it on Eragon at Gil'ead, and Du Vrangr Gata now mandated its consumption by magicians who refused to join or swear loyalty to their organization.

For vorgethan had two very specific effects: it slowed down the movements of the body and made it nigh on impossible to cast spells.

Murtagh shook his head, dismayed and furious with himself. *How was I so stupid?* Escaping would be far more difficult now. If he could contact Thorn . . . but then, Thorn was likely chained in place, and moreover, vorgethan made it difficult to touch the minds of others.

"Your weirding words will not work, human."

The voice was deep as rumbling rocks and wild as a northern wind. It came from the cell opposite his, and the sound made Murtagh start and stumble back, hands raised as if to fend off attack.

A shape moved in the shadows: a hulking, heavy-shouldered mass with a head that was far larger than it ought to have been. . . .

From the inky darkness emerged a battered, scar-slashed face as large as Murtagh's chest. Grey skin, yellow eyes, pointed teeth, and huge ram's horns that descended in jagged turns around broad cheekbones—

An Urgal!

Murtagh's neck prickled as the Urgal studied him from across the hall, the creature's yellow eyes fierce as a wildcat's. The Urgal wore a jerkin of crudely sewn leather trimmed with bear fur. His arms were massively muscled, and the skin was scarred and tattooed with cabled patterns similar to those Murtagh had seen on the banners in the Urgal villages he and Thorn had flown over. A hide loincloth completed the Urgal's outfit. He wore no shoes, and Murtagh could see the yellow clawlike nails on his seven-toed feet.

"She used the Breath on you," said the Urgal. His mouth and chin projected from the rest of his face enough to give him a slight muzzle, and his heavy jaw mangled the words in a way that Murtagh found difficult to understand. But he *could* understand. "That is how she captured you, human."

"The Br— How do you know our tongue, Urgal?" Murtagh found it hard to string words together into coherent sentences. His mind was still strange, his thoughts kept skating in different directions, and his body felt light and unbalanced, lacking substance.

The Urgal's eyes shifted away, as if he were looking at something in the far distance. "I know many things. What is your name, hornless one?"

Murtagh knew enough of Urgals to realize the creature had just insulted him, and badly. If he were an Urgal, he supposed it would have bothered him, but he wasn't, and it didn't.

He briefly considered lying, but lies were beyond his ability at the moment. Even so, he was cautious. "Names are powerful things. It would be foolish . . . foolish to share them carelessly."

Again, the Urgal focused on him. The creature went "*Hmmm*," deep in his throat, and scratched at the thicket of black bristles that covered his chest. "You say truth, but some names are more dangerous than others. Do you not have a common name, to speak with outlanders?"

". . . I do."

"*Hrmm*. I am Windtalker and Peak-Climber. I sit in silence and listen to birds and bears and words of trees. No tribe claims me, and I claim none myself. My common name is Uvek."

"Uvek. . . . My common name is Murtagh."

A flash of fire illuminated the Urgal's deep-set eyes. "So. You are one who shares thoughts with worm Thorn. Word of you reached even farthest parts of Alagaësia. I heard tell that you fought Urgralgra in dwarf mountains, and that you then fought Urgralgra for dragonkiller Galbatorix. Is true?"

It seemed surreal to Murtagh that he was having a conversation with an Urgal—and that Uvek was asking him much the same questions that he received from humans in Nasuada's realm. "Is true," he said wearily. "Galbatorix captured us and forced us to fight against the Varden. Otherwise, I suppose I would have been shieldmates with your kind once they joined the Varden."

"*Hrmm*. Do you hate Urgralgra?"

"No," said Murtagh, again approaching the iron bars. He leaned against them, welcoming the support. "But neither do I have any love for your kind. One of your chieftains almost killed me when I was younger."

Uvek bared his large teeth in what Murtagh realized was an approximation of a smile. If not for his experience with Thorn, the expression would have been terrifying and difficult, possibly impossible, to interpret. "You say truth. I like that, human. And you are here, so chieftain cannot have been so bad. You live, he dead?"

"He's dead."

"So all good. What else matter?"

Murtagh grunted. He grasped the bars and shook them; they didn't budge. The ends were seated in deep sockets drilled into the stone, and he suspected some form of magic fortified them, for they were free of rust or discoloration.

Tonnng. Uvek snapped a finger against his bars, and the metal rang like a bell. "I cannot break this iron, Murtagh-man. You cannot break either."

"No. . . . You said she—Bachel—used the Breath on me?"

Uvek's heavy head moved up and down in a nod. "That is what she call it."

"What is it? The breath of what?"

A shrug this time. "She not tell me, so I cannot tell you."

Murtagh frowned as he tried to think. "Weirding . . . How do you know I can't use magic?"

"Because," said Uvek, hunching forward, a grim look on his bestial face, "I also cannot. They give us poison that steal our strength, make us weak and helpless. So I sit here like *chukka* waiting for knife."

Murtagh found it hard to wrap his mind around this new piece of information. "You . . . you are a spellcaster?"

"No. I am shaman. There is difference. But I am familiar with weirding ways, and I know some words of power." Uvek tugged on the tip of one horn, thoughtful. "They give you more poison, I think. Or same amount, but you smaller, it hurts you more."

A moment of silence passed as Murtagh studied Uvek again, reevaluating. He knew the Urgals had magicians of their own, but he had never met any; the alliance between Galbatorix and their kind had already been broken by the time the Twins dragged him back to Urû'baen.

His knees felt suddenly weak, and he lowered himself to the floor, using the iron bars for support. He reached back and pulled over his cloak and draped it across his shoulders. "There has to be a way to escape," he muttered.

Uvek chuckled, an unpleasant sound. "I am stronger than you, and I have more clear head, but I cannot find escape. The witch is smart, and strong too."

Murtagh blinked. He couldn't seem to clear his eyes; everything appeared slightly blurry. "If I could just talk to Thorn—"

"If wishes were real, world would end."

"The . . . the world might be ending anyway."

"*Hrmm.* That depend on what witch is want to do."

"How did you . . . How were you . . ." The light from the lamp seemed to fail, and the shadows narrowed his vision, and all grew dark and grey.

"Human? . . . Human? . . . Open eyes, Murtagh-man. Open. . . ."

The dreams this time were more fragmented. Quick flashes of images, each of which carried a charge of emotion strong enough to knock a man from his feet. Murtagh found himself whipped from the heights of frenzied delight to the depths of grim morbidity and back again. At times, he thought he felt Thorn, and their dreams seemed to intertwine, and then the whirling currents of fevered imaginings would rip them apart: strange tides leading to stranger shores.

Throughout, Murtagh tried to hold to his sense of self, but it was difficult, for he did not know what was real and he had no lodestone to set his course by. The experience was exhausting and terrifying in equal measure, even more so because he sensed a gaping chasm underlying all of the visions—and, within that chasm, a lurking presence so huge and malevolent, he shrank from it for fear of going mad.

In desperation, he cried out in the ancient language, trying to still the stormy waters of his mind. But though he could voice the words of power, he could not give them the strength needed to work a change in the sawtoothed jags of disjointed images.

Helpless, he had no choice but to ride the ups and downs of the stormy swells and hope—hope—that they would soon subside.

~~~~~~~~~~~~~~~~ ❖ ~~~~~~~~~~~~~~~~

A splash of cold water roused Murtagh from his torpor.

He sputtered and inhaled a spray of droplets. He started to cough.

A pair of white-robed cultists stood over him. One held an empty bucket, the other a wooden bowl and spoon.

"Wha—"

The men pinned him against the hard floor, holding down

his arms and legs. He thrashed, but he had no strength. They restrained him as easily as a child.

One of them produced a small crystal vial from inside his tunic. Murtagh recognized it as containing the same enchanted vapor Bachel had used on him. *No!*

He struggled harder as the cultist unstoppered the vial and blew the contents into his face. The vapor filled Murtagh's nostrils, and within seconds, his will to resist bled away, and his limbs grew slack, and he stared unblinking at the ceiling.

"Keep him upright, that I may feed him," said the other cultist.

Murtagh felt himself pushed into a sitting position. Then the man who held him grabbed his jaw and forced his mouth open while his companion spooned in slop. Murtagh gagged. A large portion spilled onto his shirt.

The cultist frowned, and after the next spoonful, he pinched Murtagh's nose and pressed the palm of his hand over Murtagh's mouth.

As the slop ran down his throat, Murtagh recognized the burning brandy taste.

When the bowl was empty, the cultists let him fall onto his side and left the cell. The door closed with a hollow *clang.*

Footsteps receded into the distance.

From across the hall, Uvek's voice sounded: "Murtagh-man? Can you speak?"

Murtagh made an incoherent sound and tried to roll onto his side. The movement nearly made him throw up. Before he could progress any further, more footsteps echoed through the dungeon, this time approaching.

The pair of white-robed cultists returned with empty hands. They opened the cell and, despite Murtagh's murmured protestations, picked him up by his arms and dragged him away.

CHAPTER XV

✦ ✦ ✦ ✦ ✦ ✦

Obliteration

Two turns of the hall brought them to a wooden door. The door opened to a stone room with a brazier full of glowing coals and a wooden slab table fitted with iron manacles.

The sight struck him with shocking force. It was horribly similar to how the Hall of the Soothsayer had appeared when Galbatorix had forced him to torture Nasuada therein. Every part of Murtagh's being rebelled at what lay before him. He rejected, repudiated, and forswore both past and future, and for a second, the searing fire of recognition burned away the effects of the vorgethan.

No! He dug in his heels and twisted in his captors' hands in a futile attempt to break free. Desperate, he bent and bit the hand of one man. The cultist yelled as hot blood pulsed into Murtagh's mouth.

The men slammed him against the table, and stars flashed across his vision as his head hit the wood. He continued to struggle even as they forced the manacles about his wrists and ankles.

"No," he growled, barely audible.

The cultists ignored him. They withdrew to the corners of the room and stood at attention, the one man cradling his hand as blood dripped from the teeth marks Murtagh had left in his flesh.

Again, Murtagh tried to use magic. Again, he failed.

The door swung open, and—with a rush of air as from a beat of giant wings—Bachel strode in. The witch wore a long, black, high-collared robe with gold stitching along the cuffs. From her brow rose a matching headdress, stiff and splayed, made of netted threads adorned with pearls and the polished skulls of crows. The dark backdrop of the headdress framed her angular face, as in a carefully painted portrait. But unlike in most portraits, a mask covered the upper half of her face, and it seemed to blend into her skin and grant the witch a strange, draconic aspect, as if the shape of a dragon were somehow imposed over her body, as a glamour or an illusion.

It was more than a simple trick; Murtagh could *feel* an additional presence in the room, a stifling, inhuman force for which Bachel was merely the vessel.

The effect of the mask was the same as . . . as . . . He struggled to remember. Then it came to him: Captain Wren. The same as the masks the captain kept in his study, and it seemed to Murtagh they must have come from the same place. Perhaps Wren had given the Draumar the mask. Or perhaps they gave him his masks.

Either way, Bachel had taken on a terrifying, outsized appearance, and every sound and movement she made acquired a heightened reality, as if he lay before a god made flesh.

As disorienting and intimidating as the experience was, that wasn't the worst of it. Not for him. For the mask reminded him, more than anything, of when Galbatorix had ordered him to wear a half mask of his own while interrogating Nasuada. Why exactly, Murtagh had never known, but he suspected the king wanted to force distance between Nasuada and him, that she might take no comfort in any look or expression of his, and he might more easily assume the role of torturer.

Murtagh had hated the blasted thing.

"Welcome, Kingkiller." The witch's words resonated as if from the peaks of the mountains: a supernatural sound that in no way resembled the voice of a human or elf.

She advanced upon the table, and Murtagh saw she wore jewelry on her hands: for each finger an onyx claw fixed to a setting of carved gold. The claws were sharp, and he stiffened as she traced them across the curve of his shoulder. Even through his shirt, they scratched him.

With an effort of will, he forced himself to say: "What do . . . do you want, witch?"

"I want *you*." She smiled, and beneath the mask, her teeth showed with feral hunger.

"Never."

"You will bow to me, Kingkiller, and you will serve me and the one I in turn serve." Her eyes glowed with honeyed light. "And you will be richly rewarded for helping to forge our fearsome future. No longer a princeling but a king fit to rule the world."

Her oversized, dragon-like bearing was crushing to be near, and Murtagh faltered before the force of it, faltered and felt diminished. "No," he said, but the word seemed pitifully weak.

"A king," she whispered, leaning down so he could feel her breath on his ear. "A king such as the world needs, and I your priestess, and we shall bring long-delayed vengeance to this corrupted land."

He shook his head, trying to block out her insidious voice. A trial was coming, he knew, and it was going to test him to the utmost.

". . . Why?"

The witch straightened, as tall and distant as a cruel-faced statue. "We are the devotees of Azlagûr the Devourer. Azlagûr the Firstborn. Azlagûr the Dreamer. He who sleeps and whose sleeping mind weaves the warp and weft of the waking world. But the sleeper grows restless, Kingkiller, and we are His eyes and ears and hands. By our doing, we shall ready the world for His dread arrival. Those who serve Azlagûr, those who well please Him— those He shall elevate above all others and grant to them power. Power such as has not existed in the world since the days of old, when magic was wild and unbound and the Grey Folk were yet primitives clawing their way out of the muck."

She bent toward him again, her expression terrible, and he

thought to see flames leaping in her eyes and blood dripping from her onyx claws. "Join me, Kingkiller. Join me of your own accord. All that you wish will be yours if you but have faith."

"Never," he gasped. The air seemed heated, and he found it difficult to breathe. He felt as if he were choking.

"So be it. I shall have you either way, for I *am* the avatar of Azlagûr, and *He* cannot be denied."

And Bachel swiped her claws across his chest. Sparks flew from the sharpened onyx tips as they struck his wards, and Murtagh grew weak as the spells consumed his strength in an attempt to protect him.

Her expression hardened, and her glamoured face was fearsome to behold. With a deliberate motion, she placed her claws in a circle over his heart and pressed downward with ever-increasing force. The tips of her claws began to glow red, and Murtagh grew dizzy and breathless.

His wards could have protected him forever . . . if he'd had the energy to power them. But he didn't. Sustaining the spells felt like trying to hold a boulder in his outstretched hands; the weight was overwhelming, and in an instant—to keep from killing him—the wards failed, and Bachel's claws sank into the meat of his chest.

Murtagh stiffened and cried out.

". . . how?" he managed to gasp.

"The might of Azlagûr is greater than you can imagine, Kingkiller. He will *not* be denied." And the witch's mind assaulted Murtagh's with a torrent of black thoughts, quick and grasping.

He had not the fortitude to hold her at bay. Not then. So he tried a different approach, one more dangerous, but no less effective. He bent like a reed in the wind and allowed Bachel's consciousness to flow around his own. Wherever and whenever she attempted to grasp one of his thoughts, he slipped sideways and turned his attention elsewhere. His distraction became a defense, and with it, he repeatedly foiled Bachel.

The witch did not give up. She had resources he didn't, and

every time a thought or memory flickered through his mind, she learned a little more about him.

"Ahhh!"

Her claws cut bloody stripes across his chest, and Murtagh arched his back. He pulled on the iron cuffs and tried to break them, but they were too thick and too well secured.

Pain focused his mind, and the witch used that to pin his consciousness in place, to hold it and corral it as she sought to subjugate him to her will. But even drugged, Murtagh knew this game. He had played it with Galbatorix more times than he cared to remember, and he knew how to bend and twist and escape her grasp.

Nasuada too had played the game with *him* during her time in the Hall of the Soothsayer. And she—fierce, proud, strong—had never broken. The thought gave him a small measure of hope.

Still, evading the witch's mental grip was exhausting work, similar in effort to physically wrestling, and compounded in difficulty by the hurts Bachel inflicted upon him.

"I have no desire to disfigure you, Kingkiller," she said, and shook a drop of blood from her onyx claws. The bead glistened in the light of the brazier as it fell, a perfect polished orb of deepest vermilion. "But it requires very little to cause agonies that will drive even an elf mad."

She pressed the tip of a claw against one of the scratches on his chest, and the point of the claw found a nerve, and electric fire shot across his torso and up his neck.

He fought to keep his face still. The more he grimaced, the worse the pain seemed. When, after an eternity of suffering, Bachel lifted the claw, he gasped. "Do you want . . . me . . . mad?"

"If mad is what I can have, then mad is what I shall take. You are a useful tool either way, Kingkiller, but my preference would be to have you as you are, whole and handsome and fit to fight an army." She laughed, and it was a disconcerting sound, emanating as it did from the draconic shadow that enveloped her. "But I think you would be most entertaining mad. You are the one who must choose, Kingkiller. Join the Draumar. Join *me*, and serve our dread master Azlagûr as have those who came before us."

"... Never."

"*Tsk, tsk, tsk.* So repetitive. So boring. You must think of more creative answers, my wayward child. Do not force me to chastise you, though chastise you I shall, for thine own good."

She lifted her clawed hand again, and he forced himself to say, fast as he could: "D-does ... Azlagûr speak to you?"

A secret smile formed on Bachel's face, and her claws paused in the air. "In a way. He speaks to all of us, Kingkiller, even you, if you but have the ears and eyes to understand. When you dream, those are Azlagûr's dreams, and by them we understand His will. As His priestess, as His Speaker, He sends dreams to me most particularly, and I share them with my people, and I interpret for them the dreams that they have. This is how we receive Azlagûr's wisdom."

"To what end?"

"That we bring about the destruction of this era and the beginning of another. That we remake the world through fire and blood and bring to fruition prophecies and plans that span millennia. Do you not understand, Kingkiller? We are the instruments of Fate. *We* have been chosen to set the pattern of history, and by it, we shall have recompense beyond mortal imagining."

Then Bachel's claws again descended, and Murtagh again gave voice to his pain.

Deep in his mind, he felt a matching agony from Thorn, and the feeling heightened his torment, for he could not help the one who mattered most to him.

CHAPTER XVI

✦ ✦ ✦ ✦ ✦ ✦ ✦

Waking Dreams

The witch tormented him for hours. Always she kept asking him to break or bend.

Always he refused.

But he gave her everything else she demanded. When she ordered him to agree, he agreed. When she told him to turn his head or say that the Varden's cause had been wrong and misguided, he obeyed. It was a trick he'd learned in Urû'baen. If he agreed, it bought him a slight reprieve, physically and mentally. If he was cooperative, that mollified Bachel to a certain extent. But on the core issue, he never budged, and as much as he could, he deflected and dissembled and otherwise tried to frustrate the witch's efforts.

Had he not been drugged, he would have attempted to seize Bachel's mind and make her his own servant. As it was, he could only endure.

Nor was the witch solely interested in his compliance. She questioned him about Eragon and Saphira, Arya and Fírnen, and specifically the state of Nasuada's realm, including the dispersion of the magicians of Du Vrangr Gata, the postings of the realm's armies, and many other useful pieces of intelligence. Much of what she asked, Murtagh had no special knowledge of, though Bachel did not always believe him and pressed him hard on every point.

Her questions taught him two things in return. First was that Bachel seemed to think a full-scale attack on Nasuada's realm was not only desirable but an actual possibility. *With what army?* And second, that Bachel and the Draumar were far better informed than their numbers or location seemed to indicate. *How many sympathizers have they?*

Such coherent thoughts appeared only in the brief respites between Bachel's attentions. Most of the time, Murtagh drifted amid a haze of pain, unable to make sense of anything but his need to escape the witch's clutches.

And . . . he was scared.

The fear did not cause him to turn coward, but the more he saw of Bachel's distorted visage, and the more he felt of her red-tipped claws, and the more her intruding consciousness pulled at the most intimate parts of his self, the greater his terror grew.

Many difficult things Murtagh had done in his life, many shameful, bloody things, some forced upon him, some born of his own weakness, but there and then was the greatest challenge he had faced. Because unlike with Galbatorix, he could not—*would* not—allow himself to give in. He knew what torments lay down that path, and they were worse than any physical pain.

Or so he told himself. But because of it, there was no end in sight, and that made it difficult to sustain hope.

He tried not to think, only do what had to be done in the unfounded, perhaps futile expectation that, at some point, at some time, Bachel would tire of him and direct her cruelty elsewhere.

Nasuada's face often filled his mind, her expression sometimes soft with sympathy, other times contorted with pain and fear, and Murtagh found himself forced to remember what he had done to her in the Hall of the Soothsayer. The suffering he had inflicted was no less than what he now endured, and the knowledge made his stomach turn. There was a part of him that welcomed his torture as penance for his crimes. But no matter how great the agony, the mistakes of the past remained a testament to his failures.

Bachel noticed, for as he struggled with his memories, she brought her face close to his and studied him with cold amusement. "What would your queen think of you now?" she murmured. "Would she pity you? No, I think she would be disgusted by your weakness, my helpless little princeling. 'Tis a fatal weakness, one you will never recover from, unless you swear fealty to me and Azlagûr."

". . . no."

Her claws descended, and he screamed again.

After an endless while, the witch grew bored with him. She drew forth another crystal vial from her bodice, unstoppered it, and blew a fresh cloud of vapor upon his face.

Murtagh held his breath, but as with Thorn, the cloud clung to him, and when at last his lungs gave out, the putrid stench of brimstone clogged his nose and mouth, and the room tilted beneath him, and everything that was solid seemed insubstantial.

Save for Bachel. She retained her sense of substance. Her face grew impossibly large as she leaned over him and said, "We shall try again tomorrow, Kingkiller. Let that knowledge fill your thoughts. In the meantime, may the Breath of Azlagûr bring you wisdom through dream, and dreaming shall you find your way."

Her face receded. "Take him to the well before you return him to his chamber. His smell offends me."

"As you wish, Speaker," replied a man from beyond Murtagh's vision.

Then the witch swept out of the room, and unseen hands removed the manacles from Murtagh's wrists and ankles. They dragged him through the building, and for a time, all Murtagh was aware of were the bumping of his legs across the stone floor, the strain in his arms and shoulders, and the bobbing of his head, which made him queasy.

Blood dripped from his body. Less than he had feared, but any was unwelcome.

Icy water poured over the back of his neck. The shock cleared his mind somewhat. He gasped and looked around; he was sitting by the well outside the temple, and the two cultists were tossing buckets of water upon him. Then they dragged him into the temple courtyard.

Thorn was there. Heavy iron chains bound the dragon to the flagstones, while his muzzle was wrapped with thick leather thongs, and his wings were pinned to his side by rounds of rope. Tar-like blood streaked the rucked membranes.

Murtagh's heart lurched. He felt as if there were words that needed saying and actions that needed doing, but he could not stir his limbs.

He stared at Thorn, and Thorn at him—the dragon's ruby eyes dull, defeated, dimmed by drugs or magic or some combination thereof. There was a sadness to his expression that struck Murtagh to the core, even in the extremes of his own distress, and he struggled to break the grip of his captors, but he could do no more than weakly thrash.

"None of that now," said one of the cultists.

Across the yard, Alín appeared—white-robed and pale-faced—among the temple columns. She seemed stricken by the sight of him and Thorn, though Murtagh could not understand why. For an instant, he thought she was about to speak, but then his captors turned and dragged him toward the temple's small side door, and the moment passed.

~~~~~~~~~~~~~~~~~~~~~ ❖ ~~~~~~~~~~~~~~~~~~~~~

Murtagh landed on his side with a painful impact, and the cell door closed behind him with a *clang*.

He lay on his crumpled cloak for a long while, trying to gather the pieces of himself well enough to make sense of the world.

Despite his efforts otherwise, his eyes slid shut. . . .

He was sitting on a throne . . . THE throne: the same black and gold monstrosity Galbatorix had held court from. Thorn was to his left, and on the polished marble floor before them knelt Eragon, head bowed so his face was concealed, his hair the same mess of tousled brown locks Murtagh remembered. There were raw red marks around Eragon's wrists, and—with the certainty found only in dreams—Murtagh knew that he had broken Eragon, and that Eragon was his to command even as Murtagh had been Galbatorix's.

Past Eragon were the kneeling forms of Arya, the dwarf king Orik, and . . . Nasuada. As with Eragon, their faces were turned toward the floor. All save for Nasuada. She looked at him with an expression of fearful devotion, and he knew that she too was his to command, and that even more than the others, she was a slave to his word.

Farther still stood endless ranks of soldiers: humans in their mail shirts and padded gambesons; elves garbed in woodland colors, with elegant bows in hand and long, graceful swords at their hips; dwarves with hammers and pikes, and battalions of spearmen mounted on Feldûnost, the proud-footed mountain goats of the Beors; and Urgals too, with their crudely fashioned weapons, Urgals of human height and others towering ten, twelve feet in total—Kull, huge, muscular, terrifying.

And he knew that every soldier owed him fealty, and that he could order them onto the field of battle, and they would die for him to the last.

Murtagh felt power to be his, and he welcomed the sense of control. With it, he could do what was right—what was needed—and, more important, he could keep Thorn and himself safe. No one could command or enslave them if they ruled the land. How simple. How direct. Why had he never thought about it before? No longer would he have to wrestle with the question of whether to keep apart from the doings of Alagaësia. By assuming his rightful place on the throne, he could sidestep the problem, and everyone in the realm might become a part of him, rather than he a part of them.

He smiled as he beheld his dominion. For the first time in his life, he felt as if he had found his place.

At the end of the impossibly large audience chamber, a trefoil window allowed for a view westward, and framed in it, a black sun descended. . . .

"Murtagh-man . . . Can you hear me? . . . Wake now, human. . . . Human?"

The dark arch of the stone ceiling was the first thing Murtagh saw. He blinked and stirred. Every muscle in his body felt sore and strained; he'd pulled against the manacles with all his might, and he was paying the price for it now. Tomorrow would be worse.

Dried blood cracked on his chest as he rolled to his knees. His mind was still bleary, his wits dulled, his vision fuzzed.

On the other side of the hallway, he saw Uvek crouched by the door to the Urgal's own enclosure, the tips of his horns touching the bars. It was difficult to tell, but Murtagh thought the Urgal appeared, if not concerned, at least of a mind to commiserate with a fellow prisoner.

"Can you speak, Murtagh-man?"

It took him longer than he liked to make a sound: "I—"

Footsteps echoed off the walls, approaching. Dread filled Murtagh, and he scooted back, away from the door to his cell. Opposite him, Uvek silently withdrew until he was hidden within shadow.

Then Murtagh saw Alín sweep down the hallway. She stopped before his cell and stared at him, her cheeks as pale as her robe. Her eyebrows narrowed, and her lips pressed together, and she trembled slightly, as if racked by a powerful passion.

She knelt and placed a wooden plate in his cell, along with a small pitcher of what smelled like watered wine. The plate held bread and hard cheese and several strips of smoked bergenhed.

Again she stood. She smoothed the front of her robe, and Murtagh noticed that her hands were shaking. Then she turned and ran from his cell, and her robe flapped like a pennant in the wind.

"You have friend, Murtagh-man." Uvek's rumbling voice preceded him as the Urgal emerged from the shadows.

". . . Maybe." Sudden hunger—ravenous, burning, unbearable—sent Murtagh scrabbling forward to tear at the bread and cheese. His own hands were no more steady than Alín's. Whether she was a friend or not, the unmistakable flavor of brandy tainted the food she'd brought—the dreaded drug vorgethan. For a moment, he considered forgoing the food, but he was desperately weak. If he did not eat, he knew his will would desert him entirely. To survive, he had to force down the very poison that kept him imprisoned.

"The witch treated you roughly," said Uvek.

It wasn't a question. Looking at him again, Murtagh saw a kindness in the Urgal's expression that he had never before encountered among Uvek's race. An image came to Murtagh, so bright and strong that he felt as if he were looking upon another time and place—an image of Uvek sitting on a high mountain ridge, near a scraggled, windblown pine . . . sitting hunched over a single blue flower, wan and delicate, a thoughtful expression on his face.

Murtagh shook his head. The Breath and the vorgethan were making reality as thin as a threadbare curtain, as if he could peek through a frayed hole and see what otherwise would be hidden.   489

"What does she want from you, Murtagh-man?"

"She . . ." He coughed. Flakes of dried blood fell to the floor. "She wants me to swear fealty to her and to join the Draumar."

Uvek tilted his head. The tip of one horn tapped the bars of his cell. "She wants same from me."

"But she doesn't torture you."

"Not since they capture you. I think she find you more interesting."

"Lucky me." Murtagh drank deeply of the watered wine and then started in on the smoked bergenhed. As he chewed, he studied Uvek. "Why does Bachel seek your fealty?"

"The Draumar seek fealty from all who cross path."

Murtagh shook his head again. He was having trouble summoning the words he needed. "Yes, but . . . No. Why . . . why you?"

"Because I was one they could find."

That still wasn't what Murtagh wanted to know, but expressing himself was too difficult, so he grunted and focused on eating.

When the food was gone, he leaned back and rested his head against the cold stone of the cell, closing his eyes while he tried to strengthen the thin, nearly indetectable umbilical cord that joined him and Thorn. Uvek watched the whole while, but Murtagh didn't care. There was plenty of iron separating him from the Urgal, and besides, he didn't feel threatened by Uvek . . . though he felt sure that Uvek was capable of great violence when the occasion called for it.

Murtagh found little success with Thorn. All he could discern were indistinct emotions, none of them pleasant. Full thoughts and words still proved impossible to exchange. In any case, Murtagh's mind kept wandering, and he noticed himself slipping in and out of awareness, as if the world were divided into short sections of consciousness, brief flashes of lucidity, and the rest madness, or worse, nonexistence.

Yet throughout, his mind kept returning to Nasuada, and the horrible intimacy of their time together in the Hall of the Soothsayer. His shame swelled, and with it, his respect for her. That she had resisted Galbatorix and endured for so long now seemed miraculous to Murtagh. He wasn't sure how she had managed. Nor how she had recovered. He feared he wasn't as strong.

He was nearly asleep—or lost in a fugue state that resembled sleep—when Uvek said, "Murtagh-man, why did you and Thorn-dragon come to Nal Gorgoth?"

"Wanted to . . . find out . . . who Bachel . . . brimstone . . . stone."

"How did Draumar catch you? Was when earth shook?"

It was too difficult to explain in full. "No . . . got careless . . . after feast . . ."

He heard Uvek shift, and the Urgal made an angry sound. "Feast! How long you been in Nal Gorgoth, Murtagh-man?"

"Two . . . two days."

"Why not kill Draumar when you could?"

Murtagh forced his eyes open. ". . . was curious. Important to know before act."

Uvek's beetled brow smoothed, and then his heavy head moved up and down. "Ah. That wise, Murtagh-man. But now you trapped like Uvek. Would have been better act sooner, save much pain, much . . ."

His voice faded into oblivion as Murtagh's eyes rolled back, and he fell away from the cell, down, down, down, through endless black, into the harsh visions of promised dreams.

CHAPTER XVII

✦ ✦ ✦ ✦ ✦ ✦ ✦

Fragments

The cultists came for him again.

The cell door banged open, and Murtagh woke with a start, confused. It felt like the middle of the night, though there was no way to tell in the windowless space. Night or day, time had lost all sense of cohesion, and for a scattered few seconds, he had no idea where he was or what was happening.

Arms lifted him off the floor, and a pair of white-robed men dragged him from the cell even as he began to protest.

The cultists carried him back to the room of torment. Coal-lit, bloodstained, the strained stench of terror clinging to the chiseled stones with dogged, unkind persistence.

Bachel was waiting for him, again bedecked with headdress and dragon-aspect mask, her figure tall and fearsome, with a crow perched on either shoulder.

Murtagh fought to no avail as the cultists chained him to the rough slab table. Murmuring softly, Bachel bent over him, and the sound of Murtagh's agony echoed off the indifferent walls.

There was a monotony to pain. Every hurt brought fresh discomfort—immediate and insistent and demanding of Murtagh's attention—and yet the pain possessed a deadly sameness that blurred into a single smear of agony. The repetitiveness was nearly as unbearable as the injuries themselves. The process was all so miserably *predictable*. He hated knowing the direction of Bachel's cruel intentions, and he hated how effective her not-so-tender ministrations were. Experience provided no protection; if anything, it made his trials harder to endure, and the continual confusion that snarled his thoughts only increased the inhuman strain of every eternal instant.

Yet for all that, he still managed to evade and confound Bachel's mental attacks. And the witch grew frustrated, and she used the Breath on him again, and time fractured around him, and he could not order the happening of events. He seemed to skip between moments, unmoored from a constant present, a castaway thrown from one chopped fragment of time to the next, as a piece of flotsam from whitecap to whitecap.

Murtagh held fast to the one thing he was sure of: his own sense of self. That much he knew. The core of what he knew himself to be—the truth of his name in the ancient language—gave him strength even in the depths of his despair.

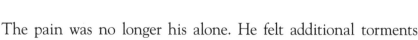

The pain was no longer his alone. He felt additional torments now, these from Thorn, and they compounded his anguish. He cursed Bachel, but the witch only laughed, as was her wont, and once more demanded his fealty.

It was a pointless exercise on her part, but Murtagh felt tears on his face—the first time he had wept because of Bachel's inflictions—and he wept not for himself but for Thorn. The dragon did not deserve the pain, had *never* deserved such treatment. *I have failed,* Murtagh thought, and the realization was crushing. Once again, he was unable to protect his friend. Once again, another suffered because of his mistakes.

He wished he could ask Eragon for help. He would have happily swallowed his pride if it meant that Eragon and Saphira would fly to their rescue. What use was pride when you were reduced to the basest, meanest part of existence? Pride, vanity, ambition, anger—none were left to him. Only the need to survive. And to somehow save Thorn.

~~~~~~~~~~~~~~~~~~ ❖ ~~~~~~~~~~~~~~~~~~

The cultists were splashing water over him, washing him as before. Old court habits made Murtagh want to thank them, to show that even though he was at their mercy, they had not stripped him of his self-possession and good manners. But the words would not leave his mouth.

~~~~~~~~~~~~~~~~~~ ❖ ~~~~~~~~~~~~~~~~~~

Thorn lay in the courtyard, beaten and bedraggled. Never had Murtagh seen a dragon so cowed—a mistreated hound cringing before its master. The sight caused something to break in Murtagh's chest, and he tried to speak.

All he could manage from between cracked lips was the softest: ". . . thorn."

The dragon's eyes stared back with a dull, lifeless gaze, and Murtagh felt a brush of his mind. For a moment, he glimpsed a dark, gloom-ridden landscape of thought, where no spark of hope shone, and grey murk pressed in from every side.

~~~~~~~~~~~~~~~~~~ ❖ ~~~~~~~~~~~~~~~~~~

Uvek was speaking: ". . . Murtagh-man . . . Can you hear me, Murtagh-man? . . . Blink if you understand words."

Murtagh tried to roll onto his side, but his muscles refused to respond. He slumped back against the wall, eyes closed, and made a sound of defeat. With one hand, he gestured vaguely toward the Urgal.

A grunt came from Uvek. Through slitted lids, Murtagh saw

him squat next to the bars of his cell. "You are strong, Murtagh-man. Stronger than most hornless."

". . . Rider." The word came as a croak from his raw throat.

"*Hrmm.* Is more than that. Strength comes from here." Uvek tapped the side of his head. "And here." He tapped the center of his chest.

A sudden cough caused Murtagh to cry out as pain lanced his side. It felt as if he had a broken rib, or near enough. He took a shallow breath. "What do . . . you know . . . of . . . Azlagûr?"

A dark cloud settled on Uvek's face, and the muscles in his forearms rippled and knotted. "Only that Draumar worship that one. I never heard name before Nal Gorgoth, but I think . . . No, I do not know what I think. Bachel is mad, but does not mean power is imagined. No."

". . . no." Murtagh grimaced as he pulled his cloak across his chest. The stones beneath him felt unbearably cold. "I keep dreaming . . . dreaming of . . ." His strength fell off, and with it, his voice. With an effort, he rallied. "Of a black sun with a black dragon. . . . think . . . it has . . . something to do with . . . Azlagûr."

The shadowed crevices on Uvek's face deepened. "Is so? I see black sun as well, Murtagh-man. Every night, it troubles my sleep. *Hrmm.* Do you know how Urgralgra think world will end?"

". . . how?"

Uvek bared his teeth. "The great dragon, Gogvog, will rise from the ocean and eat the sun and the stars and the moon, and then he cook world with his flames. Will be bad time for Urgralgra. And hornless too."

The faintest of smiles touched Murtagh's lips. "I would imagine . . . so."

"It remind me of black sun." The Urgal rolled his shoulders. "It bother me, Murtagh-man. This is a bad place, I think. Very bad."

Murtagh couldn't disagree. His eyes drifted closed, and he felt as if he was on the verge of passing out.

Uvek's voice dragged him back to awareness. "Is bad to sleep when you are hurt like this, Murtagh-man. I know. Close eyes and you not wake up again. Might be."

"Can't . . . stay . . . awake," Murtagh mumbled.

The Urgal huffed. "I will tell you story, then. *Hrmm.* I will tell you how Draumar caught me. Would you like?"

". . . yes."

"Good. Keep eyes open, Murtagh-man. Story is this. . . . Fourteen winters. Fourteen winters I sit atop mountain. I think. I dream. I *listen*. Birds and beasts, the little bees that feed off spring flowers, I listen to them, Murtagh-man. They taught me much about world, and I thought I understand, but . . . Guh!" He tugged the tips of his horns, and his heavy lips curled with disgust. "No understand. I was fool then, but I not realize. I left clan because I thought better to be alone. Only way I could learn without distraction. Only way I help Urgralgra without favor this clan or that. Only way to stand apart."

Uvek tapped a thick yellow fingernail against the iron bar in front of him. "Older I get, Murtagh-man, more I think being wise is knowing how much still unknown. Too easy to be fooled by thinking we know pattern, but the world, she like sand falling in wind. Much *zhar*. Much randomness. *Hrmm* . . . Two years ago, Clan Vrekqna came to me, told me of hornless that raid them, take prisoners, kill their warriors. They asked help, but I would not leave mountaintop, and I sent them away. Few moons later, Clan Thulkarvoc came to me with same ask. Said the hornless had strange magics they could not stand against. Said they left charms of bird skulls. Said they stole their rams and burned their huts. Still, I would not leave mountaintop. Too proud I was, far, far too proud."

A pensive silence followed as Uvek picked at his belt, and Murtagh drifted closer to sleep, lulled by the stillness of their cells.

Then the Urgal spoke again: "Two moons ago, Draumar came to my hut. They told me go with them. I say *no*. They say *yes*, so we fight, Murtagh-man. But there were too many, and I was alone.

No, not all alone. I say wrong. There was raven. She would visit me every day, and I talk to her. She listen, and I give her seeds. Twelve years, Murtagh-man, she came to me. Kiskû, I name her. She tried to help me, attack Draumar." Uvek made a deep, rolling sound like falling rock. "But Draumar kill her. That one, Grieve, he threw rock at Kiskû, hit her. Is a bad thing to do, Murtagh-man. Raven not like crow. Raven bring life and luck and tidings from afar." Uvek rocked in place, and his horns tapped against the bars of his cell. "Draumar caught me, Murtagh-man, like rabbit in snare, and they brought me here, and here I stay while dreams rot my head." The Urgal scratched underneath this chin. "There your story, Murtagh-man. Now you know how stupid I am and how I get caught. *Hrmm.* Was wrong to live apart. I could not help clans, and clans could not help me." He shook his head. "Is better to find way to be close to ones we care for, even if not always fit in easily. The bees know it. The wolves know it. Now I know it."

~~~~~~~~~~~~~~~~~~~ ❖ ~~~~~~~~~~~~~~~~~~~

Bachel was growing more and more impatient, and her methods became increasingly cruel as a result.

Murtagh knew his limits, and he was at them. His wards were gone—those that would have protected him against physical damage, at least—and his body weak, and his mind a muddled haze. At times, it felt as if the witch held his consciousness in a controlling grasp. At other times, that he was still able to evade her burrowing mental attacks. But often he could not tell whether he was free or not, and he feared that his thoughts were no longer his own.

When he grew incapable of responding as the witch desired, she wove wordless magic and healed his wounds. But never all of them, and only enough to restore him to a semblance of awareness. It was the cruelest form of care, and he hated the falseness of it almost more than the tortures themselves.

A crow cawed.

It was night. Late or early, he could not tell. The stones were cold beneath him and damp too. Uvek's breathing was a steady sound across the dungeon.

Murtagh stared into the blackness. Patterns of light formed before his eyes, an iridescent display of chaotic ornamentation, oranges and reds and pulsing blues of a purity rarely found in nature.

He could not sleep. He tried to compose a poem to still his mind, but the words escaped him. Even the very concept of the poem eluded him. What he could not name, he could not describe, and all seemed hopeless.

Again the crow cawed.

Two cultists held him down while a third forced thin gruel into his mouth. He choked and tried to spit it out, but they held his nose shut until he swallowed. The gruel burned like brandy.

His eyes jolted wider as a shiny, black-bodied spider skittered across the stones in front of him. He cried out and tried to push himself away, but pain made his arms give out, and he fell onto his side.

The spider disappeared into a crack along the wall. He stared at the narrow crevice, convinced that dozens, no, *hundreds* more spiders would come pouring out at any moment. Every touch of his clothes made him feel as if there were insects upon his body. Once a drop of moisture fell from the ceiling and landed upon the back of his neck and he scratched and scrabbled as if to tear off his own skin.

When he finally closed his eyes, spiders filled his waking dreams. Spiders both black-bodied and white, and he thought to hear Nasuada whispering in his ear, urging him to surrender. He looked and saw her there beside him, but then her face melted into Galbatorix's, and the king smiled in his vulpine manner.

Murtagh screamed.

~~~~~~~~~~~~~~~~~~~~~ ❖ ~~~~~~~~~~~~~~~~~~~~~

While in the extremes of agony, Murtagh felt a *snap* in his mind, and a flood of emotions rushed through him. Even in his dazed state, he recognized the feel of Thorn's thoughts, and he clung to them as a drowning man might cling to a passing branch.

Images of the courtyard floated before Murtagh's eyes; it was difficult to tell which part of himself was in the dungeon beneath the temple and which part was above, lying on the flagstones. Thorn was in pain equal to his own, and somehow the strength of their shared torment had overcome the stifling resistance of the vorgethan and the Breath.

499

Recognition came from Thorn, and relief and affection. Regret too, and confusion, for all was a blurred haze. . . .

~~~~~~~~~~~~~~~~~~~~~ ❖ ~~~~~~~~~~~~~~~~~~~~~

Twice more Murtagh saw Alín standing by the door of the cell. The woman seemed increasingly troubled, and she spoke to him in a voice that sounded as if at the end of a great tunnel. . . .

She gave him food. That much he remembered. Solid food, and he was grateful to eat something other than the slop the cultists had forced into him. But solid or not, the food still burned with the hated taste of brandy.

~~~~~~~~~~~~~~~~~~~~~ ❖ ~~~~~~~~~~~~~~~~~~~~~

Bachel bent low over Murtagh, her distorted, half-hidden face gilded with garish adornment by the light of the copper brazier. He could smell the sweat on her skin and feel the heat of her breath.

"You *will* serve me, and through me, Azlagûr," she whispered. "If I cannot have your obedience sworn of your own tongue, I shall have it by other means. In the end, you will bow before me, my son, and do my bidding in these, the end of days."

"Never," Murtagh managed to croak.

"No being is meant for *never*. Not even Azlagûr. We are creatures of change. Be so now, Kingkiller. Change. *Become!*"

The witch raised her arms, and her draconic aspect strengthened until it seemed as if he were staring into the eyes of a great, fiery beast. She cried out in a voice not her own, and he felt the forces of magic swirling about him. Down swung her arm. She dashed a vial against the floor, and a clinging cloud of Breath enveloped him. Then her claws dug into his torn flesh with fresh savagery, and Murtagh shouted with such violence that his voice broke and blood filled his throat.

Through Thorn's eyes, he saw heavy-browed Grieve swing an iron lash, and the dragon roared with mirrored torment.

Up and down lost all meaning. Reason and logic abandoned Murtagh—and Thorn too—leaving only feeling, and what they felt was unbearable.

What could not continue . . . did not.

Murtagh broke. He felt it, he knew it, but in the moment, he did not care. All he wanted was for the pain to cease. He could not swear fealty to Bachel, that was beyond him, but he could no longer keep fighting.

So he stopped.

He gave up, and his mind retreated from the horrors of the situation, and a strange shell of passivity formed around him, numbing his emotions, dulling his thoughts. What he was shrank until it nearly vanished.

He could feel a sense of triumph radiating from Bachel. But he did not care. It did not matter.

None of it did. Only that the pain had stopped.

And it had. For Thorn had given up also, and the two of them lay in their respective places—chained and fettered—and waited to be told what to do.

CHAPTER XVIII

✦ ✦ ✦ ✦ ✦ ✦ ✦

Without Flaw

Murtagh stood unmoving before Bachel's high-backed, fur-strewn throne. Above, the rustles and whispered caws of hidden crows echoed off the stones of the shadowed ceiling: a constant accompaniment to the doings below.

Murtagh stared without seeing as cultists stripped him of his clothes. All of his wounds had been attended to; where Bachel had inflicted her tortures upon him, his skin was again smooth and seamless.

From her raised seat, the witch watched with an impassive gaze over the rim of a dented brass goblet. Grieve stood beside her, stone-faced.

"Turn about, my son," she said.

He did.

By the middle of the chamber sat Thorn, wings furled, shoulders hunched high and tense. No shackles bound his scaled limbs, yet he did not stir.

"Stop."

Murtagh stood with his back to Bachel, eyes fixed upon the pale beams of sunlight that crept in about the edges of the distant doorway. The mosaic floor was cold against his feet. He shivered, but it was a reflex; no thought accompanied the movement.

"A most unsightly scar lies upon him, Grieve."

"Verily, Speaker."

"I wonder, ought I remove this blight from him? He is to be

our shining paragon, after all. Our faultless champion. Our king of kings."

Murtagh's lips twitched, but he could not speak.

"If you so wish, Speaker."

"Hmm." A slosh of wine in the goblet as the witch took a sip. "No, I think not. It is good for him to remember that he is not without flaw. And that he is not all-powerful."

"Very wise, my Lady."

Thorn's limbs trembled, and the slightest sound escaped his throat.

"Turn now and face me, my son."

He did.

The witch leaned forward in her seat. "You are as you deserve to be, Kingkiller. Never forget that. Your father's hate marks you, and I shall not be the one to lift that burden. Not until you bring yourself to accept Azlagûr, myself, and the Draumar as your family. For that we are, and we love you more than you know." She looked then to Grieve. "See to it that he is well fitted. After all, he is our most honored son."

Disapproval crossed Grieve's face, but his voice remained deferential. "As you say, Speaker."

"I do."

For a time, Murtagh stood fully exposed. His skin felt strange upon him, and he knew not who or what he was. An unaccountable sense of grief formed deep within him.

Then the cultists brought clothes in which to garb him. Fine woolen trousers—red and black—soft leather riding boots that reached to his knees, and a thin undershirt overlaid with a padded jerkin. Atop that, a tabard of archaic scale armor, the metal velvet grey and the tip of each scale adorned with a line of embedded gold that traced the shape of the scale. A gold-studded belt cinched about his waist, and upon his head they placed a crown-like helm, such as some long-forgotten king might have worn into battle.

"There," said Bachel, leaning back in her seat. "Now you look as you should."

Murtagh did not answer. Words seemed of no import. Behind him, he heard Thorn's heavy breath as they waited upon the witch's command.

Bachel's eyes were cold as she studied them—they her vassals, she their maternal sovereign. Her voice rang with a stony determination that overrode the soft cries of the crows above: "The time has come. We have not arrived at the end of the end, nor the middle of the end, but I say now that this day marks the beginning of the end. And it shall be a calamity to all who oppose us."

~~~~~~~~~~~~~~~~~~~ ❖ ~~~~~~~~~~~~~~~~~~~

Many things Bachel had Murtagh do. He did as he was told—listless, unresisting, his mind muffled as if bound in batts of felted wool. On the few occasions when a coherent thought came to him, he wondered whether any of it was real.

Nights he spent in the cell beneath the temple. The Urgal opposite him kept trying to speak with him, but none of the creature's words held in Murtagh's mind. They were not from Bachel, and so he did not remember them.

Days he spent sitting to the right of Bachel in the temple's inner sanctum—while Grieve glowered at him from across the chamber—or else riding beside the witch as she led him about the valley. Evenings they feasted in the courtyard: leisurely banquets of roasted boar meat, aged wine, and mushrooms cooked in every possible way. And always Bachel was talking to him: talking, talking, talking, an endless stream of words that shaped his actions and ordered the world about him.

As she spoke, she sometimes rested her hand on his arm, not with any passion, but as she might with a valued possession, and her scent mingled with that of the ever-present brimstone.

Thorn accompanied them most times, but not always. Twice

Murtagh saw Grieve climb into Thorn's saddle and ride on the dragon high into the sky above Nal Gorgoth. And once they flew out of sight beyond the jagged peaks and did not return until several hours thence.

When they did, Thorn landed in the courtyard and crouched there, cold and shivering. Murtagh stared at the dragon, miserable, though with no means to give voice to his misery.

From among the pillars along the front of the temple came Alín, bearing a pitcher of water and a basket of bergenhed and a ragged piece of cloth. She placed the basket before Thorn's head and then wet the cloth and began to wash dirt and dried blood from the healing wounds that striped Thorn's side.

Murtagh's lips trembled, and he clenched the belt around his waist.

~~~~~~~~~~~~~~~~~ ❖ ~~~~~~~~~~~~~~~~

At Bachel's command, the cultists began preparations for a grand festival to be held in a week's time. "I have had a premonition," she announced to the assembled village. "The time of the Black Smoke Festival approaches. Send forth raiding parties that we may gather the means to properly worship Azlagûr the Devourer."

Then Nal Gorgoth became a hive of activity. The cultists swarmed about in constant, frantic pursuit of their duties. Three groups of armed warriors left on horses, shouting their praise and devotion to Bachel, spears held high. Murtagh watched them go from beside Thorn, and he wished he could leave with them—to escape the valley and breathe fresh air untainted by brimstone.

That day, Bachel took him on another boar hunt. She gave him a spear to wield, and he held it without feeling, though the weight of the weapon stirred an obscure desire within him.

The witch rode before him on Thorn, her hair bound up in feathered tufts, her arms bare to the wind, her teeth flashing with fierce delight. It felt strange to have another upon Thorn with him—strange to Murtagh and strange to Thorn. But neither of them complained of it.

Bachel's honor guard followed on the ground while Thorn flew from Nal Gorgoth into the mushroom-laden valley where the boars rooted and rutted.

The hunt went much as before. At Bachel's command, Murtagh took his place by her side and set his spear against the arch of his foot and waited while Thorn drove the beasts toward their position. He waited, and no fear quickened his pulse, nor excitement nor joy nor any form of normal human feeling.

He watched what was happening as if viewing it from a great distance, as if nothing he saw could affect him or Thorn and, thus, was of no real consequence. Even his own actions felt as if they belonged to another person: a stranger without a name who wore his face but contained nothing of his self.

The boars drummed across the beaten ground, a wall of snarling, snorting animal flesh, intent on trampling a path through those blocking their way.

A shock of impact: blood and heat and the smell of viscera.

He killed his boar, as Bachel did hers.

Afterward, Bachel reclined on her litter and had Murtagh sit at her feet while her warriors tended the wounded and dressed the slain beasts. A circle of broken mushrooms surrounded them, and the air was heavy with the earthen scent.

Murtagh stared unblinking at the sky beyond the high mountain peaks, at the pale emptiness that beckoned, impossible and unreachable.

Cold fingers slid between his neck and shoulder and rested there. In a low voice that seemed to match the scent of the mushrooms, the witch said, "Can you imagine, Kingkiller, what it was like to be blessed with the full force of Azlagûr's dreams while still a child? What the power of those visions might do to you? How they might change you? . . . How lonely you would feel when you could see what others could not? When every moment was a waking dream? Can you imagine?"

He turned to her. The witch's expression was distant and contemplative, a mood he had not seen in her before. She sipped from her dented goblet. Blood lay splattered in jagged coins across her dress, same as with his hands and jerkin.

"I believe you can, Kingkiller. My mother . . . she could not. Her dreams drew her away from her people to Nal Gorgoth, but she grew jealous when Azlagûr spoke to me and the Draumar knew I was to be their new Speaker. Their mehtra. Such a blessed thing. Yet my own flesh found it unbearable. Her resentment maddened her, and she turned against me, and in time, I had no choice but to strike her down."

Another sip. "Do you judge me for it, Kingkiller? No, I think not. You would have killed Morzan had you the chance. You understand my decision, I believe. Something of it, at least. And when the time of black smoke arrives, you will understand better still."

Her words struck a false note with Murtagh, but he struggled to think why. Would he have killed Morzan? . . . *Yes.* But there was more to it than that, and the touch of Bachel's cold fingers made him want to dash her hand away and flee her presence.

He looked back at the patch of sky cupped between the snow-bound peaks.

"I am not the only Speaker, you know, Kingkiller. There have been countless others before me, stretching back to the beginning of time. Nor am I the only one now in the land. Wherever the black smoke rises, there you will find the Draumar."

That drew his attention back to her. She lifted a dark eyebrow. "Oh yes, Kingkiller. The Draumar have been part of the warp and weft of the world far more than you realize. Nor has it come about by happenstance. Why else do you think a Speaker sat in the Hall of the Soothsayer, whispering visions of what might be into the ears of the elves? Long has the will of Azlagûr shaped the course of events."

She drained her goblet. "I will tell you this, Kingkiller. There are places deep underground where Azlagûr's dreams become reality. It is true. Specters acquire substance, and the roots of the mountains seem to move, and it is difficult to know your way. Someday you shall see."

Soon afterward, Bachel stood and collected herself, and she spoke no more of such things. Then they hoisted their kills onto litters, and the cultists dragged them back to Nal Gorgoth while Murtagh and Bachel rode on Thorn.

~~~~~~~~~~~~~~~~~ ❖ ~~~~~~~~~~~~~~~~~

It was night, and Murtagh found himself staring into the dark mirror of water that filled the bucket in his cell. He did not recognize the bearded visage that looked back at him from the still surface.

An urge came upon him, and his lips moved as he attempted to speak his true name. The words were familiar upon his tongue, but they no longer rang true, and he felt a hollow despair as he realized he had again become a stranger to himself.

Anger flared, and he dashed the water aside, scattering the reflection in a thousand different directions.

The anger passed. Then he knelt and wet his hands in the water that remained in the bucket, and he washed them over and over. It seemed to him that the boar's blood still clung to his skin, and so he scrubbed until the skin was red and raw, and yet the blood never seemed to lift free.

He sat kneeling before the bucket, staring at the scratches on his hands, and he wished . . . He wasn't sure what he wished, only that it would somehow relieve the burning in his chest.

~~~~~~~~~~~~~~~~~ ❖ ~~~~~~~~~~~~~~~~~

The dreams that night were worse than before. They seemed more potent and immediate, but also more distorted and disturbing. Slaughtered villages rose before him, and memories of battle brought cold sweat to his brow. A current of deep notes—too discordant to call a melody—ran throughout, and it reminded him of the feel of a dragon's mind, only vastly larger and more twisted and alien than even the maddest Eldunarí.

Then, amid the cavalcade of bloody images, came a memory. A true memory:

The arming room smelled of rust, oil, leather, and stale sweat. Afternoon light poured like honey through the slit windows and lit the blades of spears stored in racks along the walls. It was a room of many hopes . . . and many fears.

Tornac tugged on the buckles along the side of Murtagh's breastplate, checking that they were properly tight. Then he slapped Murtagh on the shoulder. "Good to go. Keep your breathing under control and you'll have nothing to fear."

"Nothing?"

"Not from the likes of Goreth. He's fast enough, but he hasn't the technique." Tornac came around to Murtagh's front and gave him a look-over from top to bottom. "You'll do." The words were more comforting than the armor, but even so, Murtagh knew the tough-minded swordsman was putting on a brave face. Goreth was one of the most feared duelists in the king's court. He'd wounded three men in the past four months, and out of his twenty-seven duels, he'd lost only five.

Tornac read Murtagh's thoughts easily enough. He always did. "Be of good courage. It's an exhibition. The king doesn't want to see you killed any more than he'd like to see a prize horse put down."

"I know."

"Remember what I taught you and you'll acquit yourself with distinction."

Then Tornac surprised him by giving him a brief embrace. It was the first time the swordsman had shown such emotion—but then, it was the first time Murtagh was to fight a duel.

They parted, and Murtagh let out a shaky laugh.

The brightness of the sandy arena caused him to pause and squint as his eyes adjusted. It was a brisk autumn day, but expectations of combat had raised his pulse, and he already felt overly heated in his armor.

The stands were packed with nobles, there to witness the spectacle of Morzan's only-born son in an ostensibly friendly contest of arms against Goreth of Teirm, he of the silver sword. The duel had been Galbatorix's idea. He had chanced to pass the sparring yards while Murtagh took his daily instruction with Tornac, and upon seeing them, the king had proposed that a more formal test of Murtagh's skills might be appropriate. And as always, what the king desired was soon made manifest.

Murtagh saw many a familiar face in the stands, but no friendly ones. He knew Tornac was watching from the arming room, though, and the knowledge both gave him courage and made him all the more determined not to disappoint his mentor. That, and he would sooner die than embarrass himself before the current crowd. The slightest hint of weakness would earn him a lifetime of derision at court, and his position was already difficult enough.

Goreth entered through the gateway opposite him. The man was tall and clean-limbed, with the sinuous grace of a practiced warrior. Despite Tornac's assurances, there was no doubt that Goreth was a formidable fighter, and Murtagh knew he would be pressed to the limit of his abilities.

They saluted the king, who was a shadowed shape upon his throne beneath a velvet canopy. Then the heralds made their declarations, and the arena marshal read the rules of combat: No biting. No kicking while a man was upon the ground. No gouging of eyes. No striking of unmanly blows (by which was meant no striking below one's belt).

At the conclusion of the interminable talking, a horn sounded, the marshal dropped his kerchief, and the duel was begun.

Despite the fire in his veins, Murtagh felt as if he were trapped in quicksand, barely able to move his legs or swing his arms. Yet he dodged and parried and beat his opponent's blade as he should. They used no shields, as the contest was to be a test of pure bladesmanship, and Murtagh had forgone vambraces that he might move all the faster. He trusted his mail shirt to protect his arms from cuts.

Most times it would have. But the tip of Goreth's sword found the cuff of Murtagh's left sleeve, and the length of sharpened steel slid up under the gambeson he wore beneath the mail. A shivering line, hot and cold and agonizing, ran along the outside of his forearm.

Out of instinct, he yanked his arm back. He cried out as the sword cut him again on the return.

The fingers of his left hand spasmed and curled into a useless knot. If not for the onlookers, he would have conceded the duel, but pride, fear, and sheer stubborn anger forbade.

Goreth seized the advantage and stabbed again, quick. Retreating, Murtagh beat aside the attack. Goreth pressed him hard with several more strikes, and then he lunged, and Murtagh took a glancing blow to his hip, upon the skirt of mail. In a desperate attempt to recover, he replied with a swing of his own and caught Goreth's elbow with the tip of his sword.

Goreth dropped his blade.

It was a lucky strike. Murtagh could not have hoped to duplicate it in a week of sparring. He did not hesitate and followed through as Tornac had taught him and slipped the point of his sword under Goreth's arm and pricked him in the armpit, where the armor did not cover.

It was a narrow wound, but deep enough to cause Goreth to cry out and fall to the ground and to mark the end of the duel.

Or so Murtagh thought.

With blood dripping from his limp left arm, he looked to the king for the final verdict. It was tradition for Galbatorix to declare the winner of any contest he sat in witness of; the king's word was final, and until he spoke, no outcome—no truth—was official.

The shadow leaned forward on the throne, and glints of light appeared on the tips of his crown, but the king's face remained too dark to see his expression.

"Make an end of him, son of Morzan."

At first Murtagh did not believe what he heard, but Galbatorix's voice carried with unnatural force, and there was no mistaking his words. The crowd grew tense, and several gasps and cries sounded among the rows of seating, but no one spoke out against the king's command. No one was so foolish.

Goreth had not their restraint. He began to beg in a high-pitched voice. In an instant the image of the famous warrior vanished, replaced by yet another frightened soldier crawling on the battlefield, pleading for mercy from the approaching enemy.

Murtagh hesitated. He frantically searched the edge of the arena, searched for any means of escape. Then he saw Tornac standing inside the entrance tunnel to the arena, out of sight from the audience, but in plain view of Murtagh. The swordmaster's face was pale and pinched, and he looked as if he wanted to speak, but his lips remained pressed together, and his expression was severe. He shook his head, a single, short movement, and Murtagh understood. There was no escape to be had. And no help either.

"End him, son of Morzan."

Then Murtagh did as he had to, though it made him sick to bear it. He went to Goreth and attempted to give the man a quick death with a cut to the neck. But Goreth raised his arm, and Murtagh's blade skated off Goreth's iron vambrace. The man wasn't about to give up and die. Murtagh hated him for it as much as he pitied him. He lost all sense of control then, and began to rain blows upon Goreth even as the man continued to attempt to fend him off. All the while Goreth kept screaming and pleading, and Murtagh was shouting as well, nonsense sounds to drown out the man's voice.

When it was over, blood stained the packed sand for yards around them, and Goreth's horribly cut and disfigured body was finally still.

Murtagh fell to one knee and used his sword as a crutch to keep from collapsing. It was a terrible abuse of the weapon, but right then he didn't care how badly Tornac might thrash him for wrecking the edge on the blade.

A lone clapping sounded from the throne, and Galbatorix stood. *The rest of the onlookers rose in response. "Well done, Murtagh." He gestured with a finger, and Murtagh gasped and clutched his wounded forearm as skin and muscles squirmed like snakes and knit themselves whole. Then the king said, as an aside to the marshal: "Bring him to my chambers once he is washed and changed."*

"My liege."

The king departed, along with his followers, and the arena quickly emptied, leaving Murtagh alone with the corpse of his first kill. The marshal approached, but before he could speak, Tornac appeared by Murtagh's side. "I'll see that he gets to the king," Tornac said in a harsh voice, and the marshal did not argue.

As Tornac guided him out of the arena, Murtagh said, "I . . . I . . . He wouldn't—"

"You did what was necessary. Don't think about it."

But of course Murtagh did. And it was after meeting with Galbatorix in his chambers—where the king set him the task of destroying a village he believed was harboring traitors of the Varden—that Murtagh, with Tornac's wholehearted agreement, decided to flee the capital and Galbatorix himself.

He never spoke of the duel again.

~~~~~~~~~~~~~~~~~~~~ ❖ ~~~~~~~~~~~~~~~~~~~~

Some days after the cultists began their preparations for the festival, a small group of visitors arrived at Nal Gorgoth. The men came riding on proud horses, and they blew a horn to announce their arrival. They were richly appointed, and they carried pennants with colorful designs, and they were well armed and well armored.

In the temple's inner sanctum, Murtagh sat upon a stone chair next to Bachel's throne. More chairs had been set up in a double row extending from the dais with the throne, and on them reclined the visitors. The men looked to be a mix of nobles and, as evidenced by their fine garb, merchants. Their faces seemed to swim before Murtagh; he found it difficult to concentrate on their features, and remembering them was next to impossible. But there was something familiar about—

"Why, Murtagh! To think I would find you here, of all places. Whatever *are* you doing in Nal Gorgoth?"

The words came from a youngish man at the head of the left-hand row of chairs. Murtagh frowned as he struggled to focus. The man's features sharpened for a moment, and a name drifted to the top of Murtagh's mind: *Lyreth.*

Murtagh opened his mouth, closed it.

The young man burst out laughing. "My dear fellow, you look like a fish that's been struck with an oar." He moved his mouth to demonstrate.

The rest of the visitors laughed as well.

With a supreme effort, Murtagh found his voice. "I don't know why I am here."

"You must forgive him," said Bachel. Above her bronze goblet, her offset mouth lifted in the smallest of smiles. "The Kingkiller is not himself these days."

The gathered men again laughed, and the crows above imitated them with harsh, chattering cries.

Then cultists came with food. Swirls of thick, sage-scented smoke drifted from the nearby braziers, clogging the air, and Bachel and the visitors fell to talking with avid desire. Murtagh could not follow the conversation. The incense made his eyes burn and his throat fill with phlegm, and it made it even harder to concentrate, and the food distracted him, although . . . he found himself strangely reluctant to eat the cut of boar meat placed before him. The meat no longer smelled sweet and savory, and its flavor had lost all appeal.

His gaze kept returning to the faces in front of him. Aside from the one who had spoken to him, he felt as if . . . as if he ought to know the man sitting by the end, on the right. Something about the man's features lingered in Murtagh's mind—an irritant that wouldn't go away.

He put down his knife and stared at his plate, at the slices of meat that turned his stomach.

Beyond the rows of chairs, in the shadows by the entrance, Thorn sat curled on the mosaic, humming in a meaningless manner while Alín fed him scraps of boar.

Murtagh looked up. High above, in the shadowed vault of the ceiling, he thought he saw the pale circles of crow eyes looking down upon them, cold and cruel.

CHAPTER XIX

✦ ✦ ✦ ✦ ✦ ✦ ✦

Choices

I t was morning, and though the village remained warm as always, the wind from the mountains was bitter. The contrast made it seem all the worse. Curtains of snow drew across the ridged flanks of the Spine, shrouding the peaks in white, as if protecting their long-vanished virtue.

Murtagh stood next to Thorn, a cloak clasped around his neck; it felt familiar, but he could not recall where he had gotten it. A shield weighed down his left arm, and Bachel smiled as she handed him a pale sword. It was not Zar'roc—he had not seen the crimson blade since . . . since *before*—but it was the first weapon he could remember holding in . . . in . . . in . . .

He blinked.

"Go forth now, Kingkiller, and assist my men," said Bachel, commanding, triumphant, savage. Her hard hand caressed the side of his cheek, and then she looked over at Thorn. "You will serve also, Dragon. Fly as you are told, and when you arrive, you may fight alongside your master."

Thorn shivered and bowed his head. *Yes.* It was the first Murtagh had heard or felt from him since . . .

Grieve approached from across the courtyard. The man was garbed in a corselet of mail, a heavy mace in one hand and a buckler in the other.

"You will do as Grieve tells you," said Bachel. "In this, he speaks on my behalf, and as he says, you shall do."

Murtagh bowed his head.

Then the witch removed a vial from the sleeve of her black dress, unstoppered it, and blew the vaporous contents across him and Thorn. With his first inhalation of the Breath, Murtagh's head grew light, and the courtyard grew even more distant, as if he were viewing it through a dwarven spyglass.

"My Lady," Grieve said, bowing deeply.

A small smile formed on Bachel's lips. She touched Grieve upon the crown of his head, and her lips moved silently before she said, "Go now and return quickly, that I might know it is done."

"As you wish."

At Grieve's command, Murtagh sheathed the sword in the scabbard hanging from his belt and climbed onto Thorn's back. The saddle was already in place. Out of habit, he slipped his legs through the straps on either side and tightened them.

Grieve followed him onto Thorn's back and settled between the spikes behind Murtagh. The nearness of the man was uncomfortable, and even more so when Murtagh felt a sharp poke in his ribs. He looked and saw a dagger pressed against his side.

"Move with care, Rider," said Grieve between set teeth. "Else you will not move again."

Murtagh did not react. In a distracted, uninterested manner, the thought came to him that he would like to kill Grieve.

Grieve tapped Thorn's neck. "Now fly, beast!"

And with a sweep of wings, Thorn leaped from the ground, and they were airborne.

At Grieve's direction, Thorn flew out of the cleft that contained Nal Gorgoth and turned north to follow the shoreline of the Bay of Fundor. By the mouth of the valley, where the river poured into the bay, Murtagh saw a vessel docked at the wooden quay: a tall sailing vessel, trim and shapely, with a clinker-built hull as was common in Ceunon.

Flurries of snow assailed them as they continued northward. Winter was deepening; it would not be long before the mountains were impassable for those on foot.

The air smelled strange to Murtagh. It took him a long while to understand why: it no longer stank of brimstone. Rather, it was clear and cold and fresh—invigorating in its purity.

Never had air seemed so . . . so delicious.

Tracks of many animals marked the blanket of white below: rabbits and deer and bears and more besides. Their spoor traced veinlike patterns across the landscape, a map of the movements of life itself, more random than the coursing of water but more meaningful by far.

Among the game trails, a single line of dark, beaten earth ran along the shore. Too straight and regular to have been made by any dumb beast, there was no mistaking its nature: a human-made trail, cleared of snow by many feet. A group on horses, perhaps, or else travelers moving on foot, which seemed unlikely given the place and season. Whatever the answer, the group could not have been far ahead, else the snow would have obscured the trail, bleached it of color, and made it difficult to follow.

A gull loosed a harsh cry over the water and swerved away to the east as Thorn came near.

For half the morning they flew, blindly following Grieve's orders. When he said *turn*, Thorn turned. When he said *go up* or *go down*, then too Thorn obeyed. And all the while Murtagh sat bolt upright in the saddle, his face blank, the skin on his cheeks so cold he couldn't feel it.

He would act when needed—or when told—but otherwise there was nothing for him to do but *exist*.

At last, a knot of horsemen appeared along the shoreline. When they saw Thorn, they reined in their steeds.

"Land," Grieve commanded.

As Thorn descended, the horses shied before him, and the riders had to fight to hold them in place. On the ground, the truth became evident: the band of men was one of the three groups of warriors Bachel had dispatched from Nal Gorgoth.

"How close are the Orthroc?" Grieve asked.

One of the men pointed forward, toward a hogbacked ridge covered with pinetrees. "On the other side of that rise. They're gathered by a creek while they water their horses, but they'll be on the move again soon enough."

Murtagh felt rather than saw Grieve nod. "Excellent. You'll attack on my mark. The dragon and Rider will take the lead, but you must make sure to leave room for the dragon. Your horses will spook, and I cannot promise that Rider or dragon will behave as intended."

The warrior before them snorted, and the other horsemen laughed with grim humor. "They're so enthralled, they don't know where they are," said one, a short, straw-haired man with a red nose and frost on his eyelashes.

"Never mind that," said Grieve shortly. "Bachel waits on us, and we must needs not disappoint her." Then Murtagh again felt the poke of Grieve's dagger in his ribs. "Now then. You and Thorn will fly forward and attack the Orthroc on the other side of this ridge. Capture their supplies and kill all who stand before you, but should any of the Orthroc flee, you are not to pursue them. Leave that to my men. Do you understand?"

"I understand," Murtagh said, and loosened the straps around his legs.

I understand, said Thorn.

"Then go!" And to the men on horseback, Grieve motioned and said, "Charge!"

The warriors turned their horses northward, dug in their spurs, and started to gallop toward the ridge.

Thorn waited until the group had reached the foot of the rise

519

before he crouched and took flight after them. Murtagh hunched low over Thorn's neck as the cold wind blasted him head-on, forcing him to squint. Its icy ferocity cleared his mind the slightest amount, a thin layer of patina being stripped from tarnished silver.

Up the hogbacked ridge Thorn soared, over the horsemen, over the snow-laden pines, and then down again, toward a broad creek bed, nearly dry in the winter, and by the creek, a band of fur-clad figures huddled among a long train of horses. To Murtagh, the Orthroc in their barbaric garb seemed bulky and threatening, and he saw curved horns upon the heads of several of them. *Urgals!*

Thorn roared. The Orthroc quailed and started to run, but the snow hampered them. They were too slow. Far, far too slow.

Horses screamed as Thorn thudded to the ground before them. The sound was maddening, and the beasts reared and thrashed and bolted. Some fell, crushing the Orthroc who stood near. Packs slid to the ground, and lines snapped taut, pulling horses off their feet or else cracking like whips.

Murtagh did not think. He did not need to. There was fighting to be done, and a sword in his hand, and enemies that meant to kill him and Thorn. It was a simple problem.

A figure rushed them, and Thorn slapped him down with one paw, breaking the warrior.

Murtagh jumped to the ground. The impact drove him to his knees, but he quickly recovered and charged forward, buckler held high. An arrow whirred past his head, barely visible as a blurred streak.

One of the Orthroc rose up before him, spear in hand. Murtagh batted aside the spear and cut through the warrior's bearskin overcoat and into his neck. The warrior collapsed, blood spraying in a ruby fountain from his mortal wound.

Murtagh was already moving past. A pair of hulking Orthroc converged on him. A horse kicked one of them, and he fell. The other swung at Murtagh with a rusted poleax. He stepped out of range, dodged two lunges, and then closed the distance and stabbed the Orthroc in the belly and, continuing past, hamstrung him with a backhand blow.

At first the fighting seemed entirely separate from who and what Murtagh was. He watched himself move, and he felt nothing. But the instincts of flesh would not be denied. Even through the curtain of indifference, he felt the quickening of blood, and the deepening of breath, and the burn of overtaxed muscles. And a bloody rage rose within him, and along with it fear of equal strength, until his heart felt as if it were about to burst and—

thunk

An arrow struck his buckler, drove down his arm.

chink

An arrow struck his shoulder and pierced the scale armor.

He had no wards left against physical attack. The arrowhead punctured skin and muscle and sent a shocking jolt of pain through the bones of his arm and shoulder. In that moment, he went cold as ice, and his pulse stilled, and everything he saw acquired a bluish sheen. No longer was he angry or afraid. Rather, he was an instrument of pure, unrelenting violence, devoid of thought or mercy or anything resembling human emotion. He moved with a perfection of form born of practice, experience, and unconscious intent.

Above him a pennant of flames streaked the grey sky—fire from Thorn—and painted the field of struggling bodies with a ghoulish light.

For a timeless while, Murtagh fought. His left arm was numb and useless, but that hardly slowed him. He'd been trained by one of the finest swordsmen in the land, tempered in the fiercest battles in living memory, and his strength and speed were heightened by reason of being a Rider.

The Orthroc stood no chance before him. He cut them down

as shocks of dry wheat with a scythe, and his blade ran red with blood. The few Orthroc who tried to flee covered no more than a few steps before he caught them and slew them from behind, ignoring their cries.

As he killed, a terrible glee took root within him. It was as if the dreams he'd had in Nal Gorgoth were become real, and a new surge of strength coursed through his limbs. Why should he not conquer and kill? Why should he not take the throne and rule with Bachel by his side? Why could he not shape the world to his will?

At last no more Orthroc remained before him. The final one lay at his feet, gurgling a mortal breath.

Murtagh turned. A path of bloodstained snow led back to the creek. Bodies lay strewn across the splattered ground, and of the Orthroc, only their horses were still standing: long teeth bared, eyes rolling to show the whites, sharp hooves dashing at the ground.

Thorn stood crouched within a circle of corpses—Orthroc and horses alike. His snout was wrinkled in a snarl, and his teeth and claws and forelegs were gore-splattered and dark with viscera. The dragon was panting and trembling, and small spikes of flame jetted from his nostrils with each exhalation.

Grieve still sat on Thorn's back. The man looked shaken but triumphant.

The other Draumar gathered along the edge of the battlefield. None seemed to have bloodied their weapons.

A rattle sounded from the Orthroc at Murtagh's feet, then the fur-clad body went limp. The motion drew Murtagh's attention. For the first time, he looked one of the Orthroc in the face, and he saw . . . not an Urgal as he expected, but a man with wind-burned cheeks, a thick red beard, and beaded braids that hung on either side of his broad forehead. A man such as might have been found in any number of wandering tribes throughout the northern part of Alagaësia.

Murtagh raised his gaze and looked anew at the corpses of the slain. All human, and not just men but women and . . . smaller bodies too.

He began to shake as, in an instant, the fever of battle changed to sick revulsion and the seductive promises of misbegotten dreams became grim reality. Bachel had not sent them to attack a convoy of armed warriors but a group of tribespeople, and the only reason he could imagine for such folk to be on the move in the winter was because they were seeking safety—safety from those such as the Draumar.

Even in his addled state, Murtagh felt like vomiting. The pain from the arrow in his shoulder came to the forefront with crippling strength, and he gasped without meaning to. He wanted to deny the evidence of his eyes, but he was too practical-minded for delusion. He knew what his hands had done.

No, not his hands. *Him.*

He looked at Thorn, and found the dragon staring at him with a haunted expression Murtagh recognized from their time imprisoned in Urû'baen. The fires died in Thorn's nostrils, and he shuddered and let out the faintest whine.

Thorn started to take a step forward, and from his back, Grieve barked, "Stay!" Thorn froze.

As Grieve slid to the ground, Thorn and Murtagh continued to stare at each other, hopeless to break the compulsion that bound them.

Bloody snow crunched under Grieve's boots as he walked over to Murtagh. He studied the arrow in Murtagh's shoulder. "It would have been better if they killed you," he said in a flat tone. Then he took a bird-skull amulet from within his robe and pressed it against Murtagh's shoulder and pulled free the arrow.

The pain caused Murtagh's vision to fade out, and his knees buckled.

He came to on all fours. He looked: no blood spurted from his shoulder. The wound had sealed over and was red and puckered, as if a week of healing had taken place. He sat back on his heels and moved his left arm. It still had little strength, but the muscles seemed to work.

He shivered again.

"Back on your feet, wormling," said Grieve, and turned away. To the warriors on horseback, he shouted, "Gather the supplies that the dragon may carry them, and be quick about it. Bachel grows impatient. When we are gone, take what horses you can and bring them to Nal Gorgoth."

As a group, the men responded: "As it is dreamt, so it shall be."

❖

Murtagh sat next to Thorn and watched as the cultists piled bundles of supplies—food, clothes, skins of drink—before them. Grieve had spared him the task of helping, not out of mercy, but because Murtagh's injured arm meant he could be of little use.

His gaze returned to the bodies lying in the trampled snow. Then he dropped his eyes to his bloodstained hands and to Thorn's gore-splattered feet.

He pulled his cloak tighter. He still hadn't stopped shivering.

Thorn's snout touched his shoulder. The gesture seemed as if it ought to have provided a sense of comfort, but Murtagh felt no improvement. The only thought that came to his mind was: *No.* A statement of denial, of rejection. Not toward the dragon, but toward the circumstances that bound them.

The cultists used ropes to tie the supplies together. Then Grieve had Murtagh climb onto Thorn's back—as did Grieve himself— and Thorn grasped the ropes between his reddened claws and took off with labored beats of his wings.

❖

The flight back to Nal Gorgoth was cold and silent, and no slower than before, despite Thorn's additional burden, for the wind was at their backs and it eased their progress.

Murtagh wished it wouldn't.

Fingers of dull orange light were extending beneath the clouds to the west and filtering between the jags of the mountain peaks by the time the village came into sight.

Thorn landed in the temple courtyard, and Bachel came out to greet them along with her litter-bearers, warriors, and attendants. Alín stood near the witch, face pale and drawn, and her eyes widened as she saw Thorn's paws and Murtagh's hands.

Also with Bachel and her retinue were the recently arrived guests, and among them the man Murtagh couldn't place, and—

"Murtagh! You look as if you slipped and fell in a butcher's killing yard! Rather clumsy of you, I say!"

Lyreth. Lyreth in all his embroidered finery, a chalice of wine in one hand, the other pressed against the waist of a female cultist. Once his words would have bothered Murtagh. Now they were as chaff in the wind.

When Murtagh dismounted, Bachel had her warriors relieve him of his sword. Then, at her order, they took him to be washed and, after, dragged him back to his cell beneath the temple.

As the cultists left, one of them brushed against the lantern at the end of the dungeon hallway, and the breath of air snuffed out the flame, leaving the cells in pitch-black.

Murtagh lay on the stones, cold beads of water dripping from his hair onto the back of his neck. The darkness felt like a tomb for his guilt; it wrapped around him with horrifying strength, turning his insides and strangling his breath.

The force of it froze him in place for a boundless span, the gut-wrenching sense of wrongness as painful as any wound.

From it, a truth formed in the center of his clouded mind, a hard core of inescapable reality: he could not continue as he was, but neither he nor Thorn could change things. Doing so was beyond them.

A gritty scrape sounded across the hall, as of a heavy weight shifting across the flagstones. Then: "Murtagh-man, what is wrong?"

It took all of Murtagh's newly acquired mental acuity to force a word from his mouth. And he said:

". . . help."

CHAPTER XX

✦✦✦✦✦✦

Qazhqargla

"I cannot help you, Murtagh-man," said Uvek in what seemed to be a sorrowful voice.

". . . please . . . help . . . I—"

Quick footsteps approached near the entrance of the hall, and then they faltered and there was a soft cry of annoyance. After a moment, flint and steel struck.

Murtagh struggled to sit. Using his right arm, he pushed himself into a slumped position against the metal bars. The iron was so cold it seemed to burn. He tugged his cloak closer around his thin woolen shirt.

A flame flickered to life in the lantern at the head of the hall, and then Alín hurried to Murtagh's cell, carrying a bowl of watery soup with half a loaf of bread in it. She hesitated upon seeing him. "I'm sorry," she whispered, and thrust the bowl between the iron bars. "It was never supposed to be like this." And she rushed away, her footsteps light as feathers on the stones.

Across the hall, Uvek turned his massive head back toward Murtagh. Lit from the side by the lantern, the Urgal's cragged face was somber and careworn, and there was a wise sorrow in his yellow eyes. "Was it so bad, Murtagh-man, what they had you do?"

". . . yes." Murtagh cracked his eyelids open and, without moving his head, looked over at the Urgal. ". . . help . . . me. . . . I can't . . . can't go . . . on. . . ." Speaking took every scrap of strength he had, and after he went limp and had to concentrate on his breathing while he waited for the floor to steady beneath him.

"*Hrmm.*"

When Murtagh recovered enough to open his eyes again, he saw Uvek watching him with concerned intent.

The Urgal said, "Cannot Thorn-dragon help Murtagh-man? Dragon and Rider together? Dragons very strong."

". . . not . . . not this . . . time."

"*Hrmm.* I not know what to do. I am shaman; I speak to spirits. You know spirits, yes?"

Murtagh managed to nod.

"I speak to spirits. Sometimes they speak back. But they cannot hear me now. Not in this place, not with poison in stomach."

Gathering his strength, Murtagh said, ". . . if I could . . . use . . . magic . . . could . . . free . . ." The effort was too much; he couldn't maintain his mental focus long enough to keep talking.

Uvek picked at his thick lower lip with one clawlike nail. "*Hrmm.* Look, Murtagh-man." From his rough leather belt, Uvek produced a small object: a piece of carved blackstone tied with a thin strip of woven cord. "You see? I have charm here. Hornless did not take because they think just rock. *Hrr-hrr-hrr.*" It took Murtagh a moment to realize the Urgal was laughing. Then Uvek held the stone up so that it caught the lantern light. The surface glittered as if embedded with flecks of gold. "Charm is for healing. Could help with Breath, but . . ."

". . . but?"

"But no strength in charm, Murtagh-man. Charm empty. I used to heal deer with broken leg. I try give charm strength, but"—Uvek shook his head—"weirding not work. But maybe work for you. You are Rider."

The faintest flicker of hope formed in Murtagh. ". . . maybe." He struggled to sit upright.

Uvek hunched forward, cupping the blackstone as if it were fragile as a bluebird egg. "If you escape, Murtagh-man, will you free me? Will you free Uvek Windtalker?"

". . . yes."

"*Hrmm*. Urgralgra have many bad dealings with hornless. *Hrr*. And hornless many bad dealings with Urgralgra. Before I give charm, I need Murtagh-man swear oath that he never break word with Urgralgra."

". . . can't swear . . . won't . . ."

Uvek's expression remained as stone. "Then I not give charm."

Frustrated, Murtagh let his head fall back against the bars. He didn't have the strength to keep fighting, and yet he couldn't give up, no matter how painful it was to continue. ". . . can't . . . can't swear to . . . whole race . . . won't be . . . bound . . ." He paused, trying to force past the fog in his brain. ". . . bound again . . . like that." The whole reason he was in the cell, after all, was because he and Thorn refused to give their word to Bachel.

"*Hrmm*." Uvek closed his hands around the blackstone as he sat hunched, thinking. Then he said, "There is other way, if you want, Murtagh-man, but . . ." The Urgal shrugged. "Is not often done, and never with hornless. Is rite of *qazhqargla*. You become blood brother to Uvek. Then your word is mine, and mine is yours, and we share our honor."

Murtagh set his teeth as he stared at the dark ceiling. His choices were few, and if he and Thorn couldn't break free of Bachel . . . *Thorn*. He sent his mind seeking toward the dragon and, with what energy he could muster, tried to impress on Thorn the nature of his dilemma.

In return, he received a vague, unfocused response, tinged with understanding and resignation. Murtagh knew what Thorn meant. The dragon would accept whatever choice Murtagh made. He trusted Murtagh, and Murtagh never, ever wanted to break that trust. He already felt guilty enough about bringing Thorn to Nal Gorgoth and not departing earlier, when Thorn had suggested. . . .

"What say you, Murtagh-man?"

Murtagh grimaced as he pushed himself more upright. "My honor . . . is questioned by . . . many. . . . You . . . may . . . not want it."

Uvek's top lip wrinkled, showing his fangs in a grotesque smile. "I will take chance, accept burden, Murtagh-man. Will you?"

The cool underground air soothed Murtagh's throat as he filled his lungs and tried to clear his head. He didn't feel smart enough to solve the most basic problem, and regardless of how he looked at the matter, he couldn't think of another solution.

The walls he and Thorn had built about themselves could not hold. Not any longer.

"All right," he croaked. "I . . . will become blood brother."

"Is not so easy, Murtagh-man."

". . . never is."

Uvek began to mutter in his native language then, rocking back and forth. Murtagh closed his eyes and let the harsh words wash over him in rhythmic waves. After a minute, Uvek grunted. "This you will need to say, Murtagh-man." And he spoke several lines of Urgalish that, as far as Murtagh was concerned, might as well have been a convoluted exercise specifically designed to keep him from completing the rite.

For what seemed like the better part of an hour, Uvek coached him in the proper pronunciation of the words. Murtagh had to often rest, and just as often he forgot what Uvek had already taught him.

At last, the Urgal made a huff of frustration and said, "Will do. Gods will understand your intent."

A belated realization occurred to Murtagh. ". . . wait. . . . You don't have me swear in . . . ancient language?"

Uvek cocked his head. "You mean weirding words, Murtagh-man? No. They are not of Urgralgra, so why use? If man or Ur-gralgra will not keep oath in one language, they will not keep in another."

Relief and a slight sense of amusement made Murtagh chuckle. ". . . suppose . . . you're right." He had thought Uvek would have him use the ancient language, which was a large part of why Murtagh had been so reluctant.

"*Hrmm.*" Then Uvek tapped his forearm and motioned toward Murtagh. "To finish qazhqargla, must join blood and speak words. You understand?"

Murtagh gave a weary nod. "Why . . . why is it always . . . blood?"

"Blood is powerful, Murtagh-man. Blood is life. Surely hornless know this too?"

". . . we . . . know." Murtagh rolled back the sleeve on his left arm and then stared blankly at his bare skin for a moment. ". . . problem . . . I don't have . . . knife."

Uvek's heavy brow beetled. "Why need knife, Murtagh-man? Use nails." He held up his left forefinger, showing the thick, shovel-like nail growing from the tip.

Murtagh held up his own finger. ". . . too weak."

"*Ghra.* I forget how soft hornless are. What if—"

"Wait." Murtagh unfastened the clasp that held his cloak around his neck. There was a pin on the back, and while it wasn't particularly sharp, he thought it would work. ". . . use this."

Uvek grunted. "Good. Cut here." And he drew a line just below his hand. "Then we touch, share blood."

Murtagh grimaced slightly but nodded. The hall was narrow enough that they ought to be able to reach across it.

"Ready now, Murtagh-man?"

". . . ready."

In his cell, Uvek hunched over his arm, and he scraped his left thumbnail across his right wrist with a slow, deliberate movement. The Urgal showed no sign of pain as the thumbnail cut into his thick hide, and a line of black blood welled from his flesh.

Murtagh looked away. He took a breath, clenched his jaw,

and then—fast as he could, and with as much strength as seemed necessary—dragged the point of the pin across the skin of his left wrist, creating a red-hot stripe of pain.

He cursed under his breath. The pin had only cut halfway or so through his skin. He clenched his jaw again and, without pausing to anticipate the pain, yanked the pin across his wrist a second time.

Blood flooded the angry red stripe, and he let out his breath in a gasp.

Then Uvek pushed his arm between the bars of his cell—it was a tight fit, but with some force, he managed—and Murtagh did the same from his side, and they pressed their blood-slicked wrists together. The Urgal's arm was hot to the touch, and his blood burned against Murtagh's skin.

Uvek spoke his half of the oath in Urgalish, and then it was Murtagh's turn. He took his time, sounding the words as Uvek had taught him and striving to avoid mistakes. The meaning of the words was, or so Uvek had claimed, something to the effect of: "I, Murtagh Dragon Rider, join myself as brother to Uvek Windtalker. Let his blood flow in my veins even as mine flows in his. This I swear by Great-Horned Svarvok, and if I fail to uphold this sacred bond, may all manner of misfortune befall me and my tribe." The oath may not have been worded in the ancient language, but it was a serious matter all the same. Murtagh felt the weight of the words as he spoke them.

Upon completion, they withdrew their arms and tended their wounds. Uvek grunted. "The qazhqargla is complete. Now we are brothers, Murtagh-man."

". . . brothers." It felt strange to say. The only brother—half brother, really—Murtagh had known was Eragon, and their relationship had hardly been fraternal. And though Murtagh still worried about the obligations his oath imposed, he found it . . . comforting in a way, to be joined as such with Uvek. The customs of Urgals differed from those of humans, but he felt sure that if he were to call upon Uvek for help, the Urgal would answer without hesitation.

First, of course, they had to escape Nal Gorgoth.

"Here, Murtagh-man. The healing charm. Perhaps it help you."

". . . perhaps," Murtagh mumbled, accepting the blackstone pebble from Uvek. The stone was warm in his palm, and the knotted strip tied around it pleasantly textured. He tried two things then: First to draw any remaining power from the pebble. In that, he met with total failure. Uvek had spoken true. Not the slightest scrap of energy still lay in the charm. Second to imbue some of his own strength into the blackstone. Even if he couldn't directly cast a spell, Murtagh hoped that he could at least use the energy in his body to fuel the charm.

The hope proved in vain. No matter how hard he tried, Murtagh could not break the dam in his mind that prevented him from loosing the power he contained.

Uvek noticed his frustration. "Does not it work, Murtagh-man?"

". . . no . . . No!" Murtagh closed his eyes and felt tears leak from the corners. ". . . no . . . I need . . . strength for the charm, but . . ."

"You cannot give because of Breath." Uvek nodded sagely, and he appeared troubled. "I had same problem. Is there no solution? . . . Murtagh-man, are you still awake?"

Murtagh forced his eyes open. ". . . yes . . . solution? . . ." He shook his head, miserable, and lowered himself to the floor. The flagstones were cold, so he dragged the cloak over him. ". . . need to . . . think . . . sleep . . ."

"Murtagh-man. Murtagh-man! Open your ears, Murtagh-man. You . . ."

But Murtagh heard no more, and for once he had respite from the livid nightmares of Nal Gorgoth.

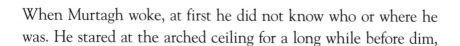

When Murtagh woke, at first he did not know who or where he was. He stared at the arched ceiling for a long while before dim, blood-drenched memories of the creekside slaughter spiked his pulse, and guilt again filled him.

He rolled over, intending to sit up, and felt something hard beneath his right hip. He looked, thinking it must be the blackstone charm, but all he saw was the folded corner of his cloak.

He patted it.

Again he felt a hard lump the size of a hazelnut. He frowned.

"What is it, Murtagh-man?" Uvek was squatting in the same position he'd been in when Murtagh fell asleep. It didn't look as if he'd moved the entire time.

At the question, Murtagh became aware of the throbbing in his left wrist. It felt as if he'd been branded. His shoulder hurt too, and that particular pain brought unwelcome memories.

He shook his head. He was getting distracted. He looked back at the cloak and felt the corner . . . worked his fingers into the hem . . . and pulled out a yellow, teardrop-shaped diamond that glittered like a bead of crystallized sunlight in the dim cell.

Uvek sucked in his lower lip and let out a low sound at the sight.

It took Murtagh a moment to remember what the diamond was . . . and where he'd gotten it. . . . *Wren . . . the door of stone . . .* Excitement began to form in him, and he held the jewel up to Uvek. ". . . energy," he whispered.

The Urgal leaned forward, his eyes gleaming with fire to match the diamond. "Is enough, Murtagh-man?"

He nodded. ". . . should . . . be."

Then Murtagh opened his mind and reached out with his thoughts toward the diamond. He could feel the knotted whirlpool of energy the gem contained: so close, so tantalizing. But no matter how he tried, he just . . . couldn't . . . get a hold of it and funnel it through his body into the blackstone charm.

He groaned with frustration and again threw his mind against the diamond. It felt as if he were trying to grasp liquid ice; it kept slipping through his mental fingers, leaving him fumbling at emptiness.

". . . it's . . . no use," he said, sitting back on his heels and shaking his head. "You want to . . . try?"

Uvek held out his paw of a hand, and Murtagh—trusting the oath they had sworn—passed him the gem.

For several minutes, Uvek sat staring at the diamond, his brow drawn, his breathing slow and heavy. The muscles in his arms tensed as if he were straining against a great weight. Then, finally, he said, "*Guh*. I cannot touch fire in gem. It keeps slipping away."

He passed the diamond back to Murtagh, and Murtagh sat against the wall of the cell and stared at the gem. After a moment, he clenched it in his fist, shook his head, and rested his forehead against his arm. ". . . has to be a way."

For a time, they sat in silence. The whole while, Murtagh battled against the ever-present haze that clogged his mind. If only he could think clearly . . .

He frowned. The Breath of Azlagûr was what disrupted his thoughts, but it was the vorgethan that kept him from using magic, although perhaps the effects of both were worse in combination. If he could remove one or the other, he and Thorn—and Uvek—might have a chance.

He sat up and looked at Uvek.

The Urgal raised his heavy brow. "What is it, Murtagh-man? You have idea?"

". . . maybe . . ."

"Is good?"

". . . maybe. . . . wait . . ."

So they waited. Without windows in the cell, Murtagh couldn't be sure of the exact time, but he didn't think he'd slept the whole night through. His body told him it was either very early or very, very late.

He remained on the floor, eyes half closed as he husbanded his strength, knowing that he would need much of it.

Finally . . . footsteps at the end of the hall.

Alín, come to retrieve the bowl she had brought him earlier. As he had hoped. The white-robed woman gave him only a brief, concerned glance before kneeling and reaching between the bars for the bowl.

". . . wait . . . ," Murtagh said, and moved to touch her wrist. At the last moment, an instinct halted his hand, though he could not have said why.

She paused, arm outstretched, her eyes wide and round, like those of a frightened doe.

". . . will you . . . talk with Bachel . . . arrange to . . . bring . . . bring me all my meals?"

He could see her tremble. "Why, Kingkiller?" she whispered.

". . . so you . . . can . . . leave out the drug." He stared her straight in the eyes, as earnest as he could be. ". . . so . . . Thorn and I can . . . escape."

Her trembling increased, and she shook her head, as if to deny his words, but still she did not pull back her arm. "I—I can't."

". . . please . . . help. . . . Bachel will . . . wash the world . . . with . . . blood . . . if she can."

Alín shook her head again, and then she did withdraw, and she fled back up the hallway, robe flying behind her.

With a groan, Murtagh collapsed back against the wall.

"Was good try, Murtagh-man," said Uvek.

". . . not good . . . enough."

"Hrmm. We shall see. It takes time to calm wild animal." The Urgal gave him a knowing look from beneath his beetled brow. "Sometimes better to let animal approach you. Otherwise, you scare."

". . . not . . . enough . . . time . . ."

"Not even gods know what future holds."

Murtagh glanced at Uvek. The Urgal's expression was impossible to read, but he seemed untroubled. Murtagh couldn't decide if Uvek's attitude was born out of fatalism or faith or some other aspect of his culture or personality, but Murtagh found it impossible to be as calm.

Calm or not, he had no choice but to bide his time and hope. And in the muddled recesses of his mind, the same two words kept repeating: . . . *please* . . . *help*. . . .

CHAPTER XXI

✦ ✦ ✦ ✦ ✦ ✦

A Question of Faith

Murtagh was not long waiting before the cultists once again came for him and escorted him to the temple's inner sanctum, where Bachel held court with her guests. The day passed much as others had in Nal Gorgoth. Murtagh served his role as silent companion to the witch—an object of derision and not some little fear on the part of the guests—while Bachel went about her business.

Once, he saw Alín among the witch's retinue, but the flaxen-haired woman avoided his gaze and quickly scurried away.

The Draumar were still preparing for the fast-approaching festival, and all the village was ahum with activity. Dark banners were hung among the patterned buildings, and carved frames placed about the dragon-like sculptures, while food and drink—much of which Murtagh recognized as spoils from the cultists' blood-soaked raid—were readied in enormous quantities.

Twice Bachel let Murtagh sit with Thorn in the courtyard, which was a comfort for both Rider and dragon. Since communicating with their minds was so difficult, Murtagh had to resort to speech, slow and clumsy and wholly inadequate to his depth of feeling. ". . . how are . . . you?" he whispered.

The dragon placed his head alongside Murtagh's thigh, and he rested his hand on Thorn's scaled forehead.

As the Draumar moved about the courtyard, Murtagh saw Thorn watching them, and in Thorn's gaze, he descried a newly found yet deeply set hate. The dragon's anger emanated from his body like heat from a forge. Once that would have worried Murtagh. Now he welcomed the feeling. He shared the sentiment, and a part of him thought there was a chance that if Thorn's emotions were strong enough, they might allow him to dispel the witch's evil influence. With dragons, you never knew just *what* they were capable of.

But Thorn made no unexpected use of magic. The two of them sat there by the side of the courtyard, often glanced at but generally ignored, and Murtagh stared at the scraps of blue sky overhead and wished . . . wished he and Thorn were far from Nal Gorgoth.

~~~~~~~~~~~~~~~~ ❖ ~~~~~~~~~~~~~~~~

That night, the cultists had barely deposited him in the cell and then departed when Alín came creeping down the hall. Her face was terribly red, the skin under her eyes was swollen, and her hair hung in a tangled mess.

She stood for a time, staring at Murtagh. Remembering Uvek's advice, he returned her gaze with an open expression and waited for her to speak.

Alín hugged herself. Then she said, "You don't understand. . . . How could you? But you don't. You can't." Her countenance grew pleading. "I believed in Bachel. I *believe*. She is no false prophet. She speaks with the authority of Azlagúr, and how can any question Azlagúr when we live with His dreams? We all share in the dream of Nal Gorgoth and the vision of what may come. And when that vision becomes manifest . . ." She shivered violently. "The world will be remade according to Azlagúr's will." She rubbed her arms as if cold. "Always I wondered at what lay beyond this valley. Always Bachel has told us of the evils that inhabit Alagaësia, of the war and injustices." She shook her head. "But you are not evil, Kingkiller. Nor is Thorn. And the way in which Bachel has treated Thorn . . . It goes against everything I know. Every tenet I believe. Everything she has preached to us over the years!"

She turned and paced between the cells, distraught. Still, Murtagh held his tongue. With a wild look, she spun back to him, her small teeth bared like those of a cornered animal. "Dragons are the lifeblood of the land, Kingkiller! They are the source of all that is good, the font of life and magic and . . . and . . . They are to be *worshipped*. Revered. Honored. Served. And yet Bachel says this mistreatment of Thorn is necessary. Needed. According to Azlagûr's will! I . . . I—" She broke off and shivered again as if with fever.

Murtagh rose on unsteady legs and went to the door of his cell. Soft and slow, he said, "What . . . do . . . you . . . want?"

A film of tears silvered Alín's eyes. "I want to help Thorn. And— No, it is too selfish of me."

". . . what?"

"I want to see the truth of the world before Azlagûr washes it clean."

"Then . . . help us."

"It is not that simple, Kingkiller. Bachel is the Speaker. She is our *mehtra!* I have sworn oaths to her and to Azlagûr. I cannot break them, and if I did, oh! If I did, my soul would be forever forsaken." Her skin glistened with a sheen of sweat, and he could smell the sour stench of her fear. "You ask me to cast away my life and condemn my eternal future for this."

". . . for what is right." The words struck home. He could see it in the misery of her expression. He struggled to order his thoughts. ". . . oaths bind, but you . . . can change . . . free yourself. . . . I . . . know. I did."

Alín looked at him with anguish. "*How?*"

He did not want to say, but he had no other resort but the deepest reservoir of truth. ". . . for the sake . . . of another."

Alín's eyes widened, and he felt as if she were seeing his innermost self. Then her shoulders caved in, and she shook her head and uttered a soft sob. "I can't. I haven't the strength."

The floor seemed to tilt underneath him and the cell spin. He staggered and grasped the iron bars for support. He took a steadying breath, trying to maintain a semblance of clarity. ". . . family?"

Alín shook her head. "No. I was found as a child. As many Draumar are."

Blood on the ground. Orthroc fallen in mangled heaps. Bodies large and small. A chill gripped Murtagh. He could guess how the children had come to Nal Gorgoth. *Orphans.* Innocents.

Sorrow overcame him, and he reached toward Alín's cheek, wanting only to comfort her.

She flinched but did not retreat.

Her skin was feverishly hot against his palm. She let out a small cry as he touched her, and he felt a tremor pass through her, but still she did not pull away. Somehow he knew that was significant. A line had been crossed that could never be uncrossed.

Tears rolled down her face. In a whisper, she said, "I want . . . I want a better dream, one of cheer and hope and love."

". . . then help us."

She stared at him with a hope as desperate as his own, and he sensed no guile in her heart. "If you leave, will you take me with you, Kingkiller?"

". . . yes . . . I swear it."

A moment, and then she withdrew from his hand and rubbed her arms again. Her lips parted, as if she meant to speak, but instead, she hurried away before he could do anything to keep her.

He turned a helpless gaze to Uvek, who was watching as always. ". . . did I scare . . . her?"

The Urgal grunted and scratched at his neck. "*Hrmm.* Maybe yes, but—"

More footsteps sounded, and Alín reappeared carrying a bowl and pitcher. She avoided Murtagh's eyes as she knelt and placed the dishes just outside his cell. Then she bobbed a quick curtsy, as she might have to Bachel, and rushed off again.

"Is always rushing, that one," said Uvek.

Murtagh didn't answer as he pulled the dishes into his cell. He cautiously tasted the watered wine in the pitcher and then the bread and soup in the bowl. None of them burned like brandy as he swallowed.

He looked to Uvek and nodded.

The Urgal grew very still, as if readying himself for action. "How long, you think, Murtagh-man?"

"I don't . . . know. A day? . . . maybe more . . . depends . . . how much . . . gave me."

"The black smoke time is only day or two away. I think it bad if we still here when it happens."

". . . that soon?" He hadn't realized the festival was so close.

"*Hrmm.* Heal faster, Murtagh-man."

~~~~~~~~~~~~~~~~ ❖ ~~~~~~~~~~~~~~~~

Every meal thereafter, Alín brought Murtagh food free of vorgethan. He had hoped that his body might purge the drug within a few hours, but to his aggravation and disappointment, the process was far slower.

Other cultists continued to feed Uvek, and the Urgal remained under the effects of the vorgethan. Murtagh asked Alín if she could help Uvek as well, but she shook her head and explained that a man by the name of Isvar prepared Uvek's food, and that Isvar had been specially appointed by Bachel and would not surrender the honor.

So they waited, and every few minutes that Murtagh was awake, he tried to access the energy in the yellow diamond, that he might transfer it into the blackstone charm. At some point, he *had* to succeed. The question was whether that would happen before the time of the black smoke.

He was growing increasingly concerned about the festival. From certain fragments he overheard, it seemed to him that Bachel was planning something particularly dramatic, and he worried that her plan would involve him and Thorn.

Even though Murtagh was no longer receiving the vorgethan, his mind felt as clouded as ever. The witch continued to use the Breath on him whenever they met, and the stench of the swirling miasma never seemed to leave his nostrils.

The following morning, Murtagh noticed that a goodly portion of Bachel's guests were departing. They gathered in the courtyard on their fine horses, carrying their colorful pennants, and they saluted Bachel. The man Murtagh felt he ought to recognize said, "Fare thee well, Bachel. We shall send you tidings of our plans ere long."

The witch picked at the rim of her dented goblet. " 'Twere best if you stayed for the time of the black smoke."

The grim-faced man inclined his head. "We'll leave such things to you and your followers." He looked at Murtagh with an expression of mild disgust. "And to whatever you have made of *him*."

"Ah, but I and my companions shall stay and keep you company, most honorable Bachel," said Lyreth. He stood at one corner of the courtyard along with four other men. They all had ruddy cheeks, as if from drink.

Bachel did not seem impressed. To the first man, she smiled and gestured, as if giving permission. "Go, then, and safe sailing upon your journey. Let the culmination of our plans arrive most swiftly."

"My Lady."

And with that, the group trotted out of Nal Gorgoth, heading for the Bay of Fundor and the ship Murtagh knew was docked thereat.

With every hour that passed, Murtagh felt as if his body were becoming lighter, more responsive. Unfortunately, his mind failed to follow suit. Every thought took work, and it was difficult to hold on to one for any length of time. And yet he could tell that the drug vorgethan was slowly working its way out of his limbs.

But not fast enough for his liking. The villagers were growing more excited by the prospect of their festival; even the heavy-browed Grieve seemed enlivened.

Bachel dismissed Murtagh early that day, as she was preoccupied with preparations for the festival. He didn't mind. The less he saw of the witch, the better.

Once back in his cell, he did not sit or lie down. Despite his sluggish mind, he forced himself to stand and pace. Movement, as Tornac had told him, always cleared the blood. So he moved, with the hope of speeding the passage of the vorgethan from his veins.

Uvek watched with impassive patience. Only once did he ask if Murtagh had succeeded with the diamond. Aside from that, the Urgal seemed content to wait. Seeing him squatting in his cell, the flickering light casting deep shadows from Uvek's horns, Murtagh could imagine the Urgal situated in a high mountain cave, as still and silent as a statue, an oracle waiting for the faithful to flock to his feet.

And still, Murtagh paced.

He was getting close to being able to access the energy in the diamond. He could feel it: a delicate tickle, like an itch high in his nose. If only . . .

A noise at the head of the hallway. Alín, bringing him his evening meal. Bread, a soup of boar meat, and watered wine.

Before she left, he said, ". . . wait . . . can you bring me . . . my sword, Zar'roc?"

She shook her head, hair hiding her face. "I can't," she whispered.

". . . where?"

"Bachel keeps your sword and armor in the temple, in her presence chamber."

That made sense. He nodded slowly. "I'm nearly . . . free. Can you . . . help ready Thorn? . . . water . . . food . . . saddle . . . shackles?"

She hesitated. The hair still covered her face, and she made no move to brush it aside. Soft as a falling petal, she said, "I will try, Kingkiller."

". . . thank . . . you. . . . We could use . . . supplies of . . . our . . . own . . . as well."

Again a pause, and then she turned away and departed.

Murtagh remained where he was, watching.

"She still uncertain, Murtagh-man." It was the first thing the Urgal had said in hours.

Murtagh grunted as he lowered himself onto the stones. "She'll do . . . what's right."

Uvek's head swung from side to side. "Depends on what she thinks is right."

". . . always . . . does." Murtagh looked over at the Urgal. He felt inexpressibly tired. Worry, guilt, and the constant fight to think had consumed his limited strength. Just for a moment, he wanted to forget Bachel and everything about Nal Gorgoth. ". . . tell me a . . . story, Uvek."

The Urgal's heavy forehead wrinkled as he lifted his brow. "What sort of story?"

". . . of your people."

"Hrmm. I have many peoples. My family. My clan that I left. My fellow Urgralgra."

Murtagh waved a hand. He was too tired to bother with details. ". . . you . . . pick."

For a minute more, Uvek was silent, ruminating. Then his brow cleared. "I know. I will tell you of son of Svarvok, Ahno the Trickster. This was in time of red clover, when rivers tasted of iron. Ahno had changed himself into deer, and Svarvok sent wolves to chase him, nip at his heels, but Ahno laughed at father and changed himself into wolf instead. Seven winters Ahno ran with wolves, lived as wolf, ate as wolf. Was part of pack. *Led* pack. You hear, Murtagh-man?"

". . . I hear."

"Good. *Hrr.* Problem was, wolves did not choose Ahno. Did not want him. But could not drive him from the pack. Ahno was too strong, even in shape of wolf. But—" Uvek's eyes gleamed with sly delight, and the tips of his fangs showed between his lips. "Wolves are cunning. A black-skin she-wolf known as Sharp-tooth went one night to gathering of wolves beneath full moon. Was bright as day with light from moon on snow. Wolves howl and growl and Sharptooth convinces pack to help her. Next day, Ahno's pack goes hunt red deer. They run deep in forest, where shadows and big antlers live. Then Sharptooth came to Ahno and lured him away from pack." Uvek's expression grew rather goatish. "He liked her shape, her fur, and her teeth. You under-stand, Murtagh-man?"

". . . understand."

"*Hrr-hrr.* Sharptooth ran and ran, and Ahno followed, until they arrive at cliff. All packs wait there, hidden in bush. On cliff, Sharptooth let Ahno approach. Then she bite Ahno, and other packs come and snap and growl and run at Ahno, and they drive him"—Uvek made a diving swoop with his hand—"over edge of cliff. Fall not kill him, Murtagh-man. Wolves know this. Ahno son of Svarvok very hard to kill. At bottom of cliff was cave, and in cave lived *ûhldmaq*. You know?"

Murtagh shook his head. ". . . no."

"Is Urgralgra who became bear. Very dangerous. Is told of in the stories of before times. This *ûhldmaq* was named Zhargog, and he was very old, very hungry. He came at wounded Ahno and fought with him, and ground shook and rocks fell, and at last, Ahno had to give up wolf form and return to being Horned. Then he fled, and Svarvok spoke to him, say, 'Ho! now, Ahno! You have given up your teeth and paws and fur. What have you learned from this, my son?' And Ahno laugh despite hurts and say, 'It not good to run with pack that does not want me. I will find pack that does want.' Then he change into eagle and fly away. And how Svarvok dealt with son then is another story entirely. *Hrmm.*"

Murtagh returned his gaze to the ceiling. ". . . are there . . . many . . . stories of Ahno?"

"Oh yes, Murtagh-man. Entire winter's worth. Ahno was very clever, got into much trouble. In end, gods put him on mountaintop, tie him to stone so they not have to listen to his constant talk."

"Did he ever . . . find his pack?"

"For a time, Murtagh-man. For a time."

~~~~~~~~~~~~~~~~ ❖ ~~~~~~~~~~~~~~~~

That night, the dreams that came to Murtagh exceeded all bounds of normal constraint. They possessed such vivid, horrific immediacy that reality itself seemed to have broken into blazing fragments: each an image that contained an epic's worth of meaning—meaning that was understood perfectly and utterly and without words.

He careened through hallucinations of the highest order, where the air seemed to twist and bend, and every emotion, every fear and hope and joy, was given its shining instant beneath the black-sun sky.

The night felt endless, but even eternity itself could not endure, and at last the visions grounded themselves in something Murtagh knew far, far too well and that—given the choice—he would have rather forgotten.

The air was cold with winter's last breath, and steam rose from the droppings in the stable. He was trying to be quiet as he and Tornac hurried to saddle their horses. The animals nickered and pawed impatiently, eager to be gone. They hadn't been ridden for over a week and were excited for release from the city.

"Easy there," said Murtagh, petting his charger.

His sword kept getting in the way, tangling with his legs, as he wrestled the saddle onto the charger's back. Both he and Tornac were armed, and under his cloak, Murtagh wore a coat of fine mail.

They moved with hurried fear. Blankets, saddles, harnesses, bags laden with the supplies they'd need to get far from Urû'baen.

"What if he comes looking for us?" Murtagh whispered. He still couldn't believe they were leaving the capital once and for all, leaving behind everything he'd known for the last fifteen years.

Tornac looked over the back of his horse, a roan mare with a white star on her breast. The swordmaster's lean, tanned face was deadly serious, but there was a light to his expression that bespoke anticipation and, perhaps, a portion of excitement. Danger always quickened the blood. "Then we hide. Dragon eyes are keen, but even they can't see through leaves or branches, and the king can't take the time to search every copse and grove in the Empire. As long as we get enough of a head start, he'll never find us."

Murtagh was still troubled. "What if he uses magic? He must have spells to search. And I've heard he can reach out with his thoughts and find a person, even if they're on the other side of Urû'baen."

Then Tornac gripped Murtagh's shoulder and fixed him with a firm gaze. "The charms I had off the hedge-witch will protect us from any sort of spying. The king is not all-powerful, Murtagh. No one is. Were every whisper about Galbatorix true, the Varden would have long since fallen to his might. As would the elves and dwarves."

Murtagh pulled on the charger's girth, tightening it the appropriate amount. "You shouldn't have said his name," he muttered.

Tornac paused in his own work. "Do you not want to leave?"

". . . I do."

A nod from Tornac as he returned to adjusting the roan's saddlebags. "Then enough of this. We need to be well gone before dawn breaks." Murtagh grunted, and Tornac gave him a considering look. "We agreed. You can't stay. If you do, the king—"

"If I do, the king will turn me into my father. He'll make me into another one of his bloody-minded lackeys, same as Barst or Yarek," said Murtagh, with no attempt to hide his bitterness.

"It's not just that," said Tornac. "Even if you weren't Morzan's son, this isn't a good place for you, Murtagh. Those leeches at court will ruin you if you stay."

Pride made him reply, "I'd never let them."

Tornac stopped and stared at him over the back of the roan. "You say that now, but they'll keep grinding you down, year after year. That sort of attention cripples a man's soul. I've seen it happen." He returned to working on the horse's tack. "You need to be free. Free of Galbatorix. Free of court. Free to make your own choices. Only then will you become the man I know you can be." The care in his voice surprised Murtagh, but Tornac's face was hidden behind the horse's side. "You deserve a chance to find your way, and blast it if I'll stand by and let them make you into something resembling Lyreth or his like. Trust me. Leaving is for the best."

Only then had Murtagh realized that Tornac's true motivation had nothing to do with opposing the king, and he felt a sudden sense of gratitude. "I trust you."

Once their steeds were ready—their hooves muffled with rags—they departed. The boy who slept in the stables was still asleep, and the watchman whose duty it was to walk rounds through that part of the citadel was at the far end of his route. Tornac and Murtagh had planned their escape most carefully.

Out they went through the side gate of the citadel keep, open and unguarded during festival week, and headed toward Urû'baen's outer curtain wall. The clopping of the horses' hooves was a soft accompaniment as they made their way between the rows of sleeping houses. The sky was nearly black, and the great shelf of stone that hung over the eastern half of the city blocked any view of dawn's first light.

The relatively short distance to the wall seemed at least a league, for their nerves were stretched to the point of breaking, and at every slight breath of wind, Murtagh expected Shruikan's black form to burst from the citadel as the king came to accost them.

They soon arrived at the postern gate set within the back portion of the city's defenses. Murtagh had bribed a watchman to leave it open, and so it was. He held the reins while Tornac unbarred the door, and then, together, they hurried through the dark, tunnel-like exit that led through the enormous curtain wall.

Then dismay. Fear. Hopelessness. Waiting for them in the field outside was a group of soldiers. Twelve spearmen, with a proud captain at the fore, his white-plumed helmet catching the last remnants of starlight.

At first Murtagh had a wild, horrible thought that Tornac had betrayed him. But then he saw the swordmaster's face; Tornac was as distressed as he. Perhaps more so.

"So, the wayward sheep have been found," said the captain with entirely too much glee. "The king will be pleased. Release your steeds, Murtagh son of Morzan, Tornac son of Tereth, and drop your weapons, and you shall not be harmed. This you have on my word, and as royal decree."

There was no choice. Murtagh let go of the reins, as did Tornac, and reached for the buckle of his sword belt.

If he had not known Tornac so well, he would have missed the man's intention. The slight shift of the swordmaster's stance as he grounded his feet, balanced his weight—it was all the warning Murtagh got.

Tornac feinted with his hand, first appearing to grasp his own belt, but then, with deadly speed, diverting to grasp the hilt of his sword and draw the blade.

The captain barely managed the first note of a high-pitched screech before Tornac caught him in the throat with a perfectly placed lunge.

The soldiers yelled and scattered while Murtagh scrabbled to draw his own sword. It snagged in the sheath, and freeing it took precious seconds.

In that time, Tornac wounded two more soldiers and had begun advancing on a third. The men found their courage then and closed in around the swordmaster with their spears a ringed thicket of stabbing points.

Then the sheath released Murtagh's sword, and he fell upon the soldiers from the side, and for the second time in two days, he fought, and he killed.

Never before had Murtagh let loose with such a combination of cold-minded ruthlessness and desperate savagery. But he was not only fighting for himself—he was fighting to help Tornac, and he would have sooner taken a blow than see the swordmaster harmed.

The soldiers were veterans all: trained fighting men who had been rewarded for their loyalty and doughtiness with a post guarding the citadel of Urû'baen. But they had been surprised, and the quick felling of several of their number confused them, caused them to fall back, and every time they faltered, Tornac or Murtagh extracted another life in exchange.

For the most part, they fought in silence, save for grunts and clashes of metal and the occasional quick cry. No one had the wind to speak. They were panting and fearfully focused, and sweat dripped into their eyes.

And yet . . . for all of Tornac's skill, and Murtagh's too, the numbers were badly against them. Twelve against two. Even with surprise on their side, it was hardly a fair fight. Murtagh glimpsed a blot of blood on Tornac's right shoulder and more streaming from a cut on his scalp, and he felt a burning line somewhere on his own hip.

The swordmaster fought like a cornered cat, twisting and bounding and lashing out with blinding speed. Gone were the stylized forms used at court duels. Gone were the perfect angles and distances of sparring. And yet it was a dazzling, daring, dashing display that would have won applause from even the most jaded audience. At that moment, Murtagh truly believed that no man could have stood before Tornac.

But like all perfect moments, even in dreams, it could not last.

Murtagh tripped, and he felt the point of a spear jar his ribs as a soldier rushed him. He fell. Before he could make sense of what was happening, Tornac was standing over him, sword buried in the soldier's side.

Then another soldier came at Tornac from behind and, with a long-bladed knife, stabbed him between the shoulder blades and bore him to the ground.

Murtagh scrambled free and slew the soldier before he could pull the knife out of Tornac's back. Then another minute of desperate fighting followed as he contended with the last four soldiers.

The men were no match for Murtagh, but he knew they were sworn to Galbatorix with the most solemn of oaths. They could no more retreat than he would surrender.

In the end, in the grey predawn light, only he remained standing amid the scattered bodies. The roan mare had run from the field, but his charger stood by the gate, snorting and pawing.

Anguished, Murtagh staggered over to Tornac and turned him on his side. Frothed blood dripped from the swordmaster's lips, but his eyes were still open, and he smiled as he saw Murtagh. "Did you end them rightly?" he asked.

Murtagh nodded, struggling to find enough breath to speak. "All dead." He grasped the swordmaster's hands. They were startlingly cold.

Tornac smiled again. "I taught you well, Murtagh." Then his expression caught, and his grip weakened. "Tell . . . tell Ola I'm sorry. . . . If you get the chance."

"Of course," said Murtagh. He couldn't bear to think how the pleasant, round-cheeked woman would take the news.

"She's going to hate me for this." Tornac's eyes wandered, and then his gaze sharpened again, and for a moment, he was as lucid as Murtagh ever remembered. "Go. You have to go, blast you. Take my charm and leave me. I'm done. Go and be free and forget . . . me. . . ." A harsh rattle sounded in his chest, and his body went limp, and the gleam faded from his eyes.

Then Murtagh wept, and he was not ashamed.

. . .

A disjunction, and Murtagh once again found himself cowering on the desolate plain, at the end of all things, with the black sun rippling with tendrils of black flame while the monstrous, mountainous, humpbacked dragon rose wingless against the horizon, blotting out light and hope.

. . .

Another disjunction. A field of golden grass blanketed the gentle curve of a hill. Standing amid the grass was Nasuada clad in a dress of red velvet. She turned to look back at him, and she held out her hand toward him, but her expression was sorrowful, and no matter how he reached for her, he could not close the distance.

Then the sky darkened, and the sun lost its luster, and land and sky both became the color of tarnished pewter. Tears traced lines down Nasuada's cheeks, but he felt them on his own, hot with regret and the pain of parting.

Stars pricked the blackened sky, and a sense of impending and unavoidable doom hollowed out his chest. And far in the distance, a humped mass stirred along the horizon and began to ascend to eat the guttering sun. . . .

~~~~~~~~~~~~~~~~~~ ❖ ~~~~~~~~~~~~~~~~~~

Murtagh woke covered in cold sweat, disoriented, uncertain of what was real and what wasn't, and yet consumed by a sudden conviction that time was desperately short.

The clash of chimes and bells and brazen cymbals sounded outside the temple, loud enough that the commotion filtered through the stones of the building. And wild, barbaric cries too, as if the entire village had gone mad.

Across the hall, half-shadowed Uvek looked out with a grim, heavy-lined expression. "Time of black smoke has arrived, Murtagh-man."

Fear spurred Murtagh to action. He pawed through his cloak until he felt the yellow diamond hidden within the hem. Where was the charm Uvek had given him? Where? Where? Where? For a moment, he couldn't remember. Then he recalled: tucked deep in his left boot.

He grasped the charm and reached for the energy stored in the diamond. The swirling vortex tickled his brain, tantalizingly close. He could *almost* touch it. The drug vorgethan must have been nearly purged from his body, but try though he might, he couldn't quite unlock the flow of energy.

Clang!

The unseen door at the end of the hall opened, and boots tromped toward the cells. Cultists come to fetch him.

Murtagh yanked his hand out of his boot and stood. He cursed to himself. He'd been too slow. Time had run out. Now he had to face whatever the Draumar had planned.

Black smoke. Black sun. *Doom.*

CHAPTER XXII

✦✦✦✦✦✦✦

Black Smoke

"**A**re ye going to th' festival?" asked one of the cultists, a red-bearded dwarf who leered at Murtagh through the bars of his cell. "'Course you are, Kingkiller. 'Course you are."

The dwarf and the man who was his companion dragged Murtagh from his confinement. Murtagh put up no resistance. Until he could move and think of his own accord, he was at Bachel's mercy . . . and she possessed precious little of that particular virtue.

Uvek remained squatting and watching as the cultists removed Murtagh, and Murtagh gave no look or sign of acknowledgment to the Urgal. Best the Draumar did not know they had even spoken.

As the cultists escorted Murtagh up the worn stairs and through dark corridors to the front of the temple, he noticed that the ever-present stench of brimstone was startlingly stronger. The miasma lay on the village, as heavy as a blanket, and it made his eyes water and the back of his throat sting. Every breath threatened to make him retch.

Bloody light broke across him as the dwarf and man guided him between pillars into the temple courtyard. Smoke filled the valley. Black smoke, rising from the vents in the ground, and it acted as a curtain upon the sky: a red and orange scrim that diminished the sun to a dull disk no brighter than an ember in a dying fire.

The courtyard was transformed. Bachel's carved throne had been moved into the yard and placed upon the dais at one end.

A long table stood at right angles to the dais, and in the center of the yard, before the ruined fountain, the cultists had placed the great ash-colored altar. Murtagh could not fathom how they had moved such an enormous block of stone, unless Bachel had employed magic in the effort.

Banners hung upon the patterned pillars that lined the temple, and streamers of knotted fabric—similar to those the Urgals made—hung from the eaves of the surrounding buildings.

At the table sat the remaining guests. Lyreth had a chalice in one hand, while his other hand wandered across the back of a village woman seated on his lap.

All the villagers were gathered around the courtyard, packed into the streets as so many pickled bergenhed in casks. They were chanting and moaning and beating drums and ringing bells and striking brass cymbals that jarred the smoke with their brazen crashing. Their clothes were different: a complete change of raiment such as Murtagh had never known commoners to possess. Instead of their usual robes, they wore sleeved jerkins cut and sewn out of dish-sized scales of thick boiled leather dyed dark brown. The effect was between that of a closed pinecone and the belly of a dragon. The scale pattern continued along their arms and trousers, also of leather. On their faces, the Draumar wore molded half masks that resembled Bachel's, though theirs possessed none of that mask's transformative power. Even the children were garbed as such, furtive figures amid the forest of legs.

Bachel herself sat upon the hide-strewn throne, her hair raised in an edifice of ragged tufts, her lids and eyes blackened with soot, her lips red as blood, and the hated claws of onyx upon her fingers.

A flock of restless crows roosted on the eaves behind the dais, cawing and cackling in response to the cacophony the villagers produced. They formed a dark crown above Bachel's head: a shadowed symbol of her supreme authority.

To the left of the witch stood Grieve, and for once the dour man had an almost pleasant expression. The festival seemed to suit him.

But of everything Murtagh saw, it was Thorn he had eyes for most. The dragon was chained next to the dais, wings pinned by cabled ropes, a muzzle of wrought iron locked about his long jaws. Murtagh could feel the dragon's fetters as if they were tight against his own body, and their touch seemed to burn with icy cold.

Soon, Murtagh said to Thorn, and the word was a promise, an oath, an apology. But it was like pushing his thoughts through a wall of wool. Still, the dragon's eyelids flickered, as if he understood. Murtagh hoped he did.

The two cultists brought him before Bachel, and she inspected him as one might inspect a prize horse. "You look as though the night treated you badly, Kingkiller." She gestured with one elegant hand to her right, and he obediently took his place.

His gaze kept drifting back to Thorn. The dragon was still suffering the effects of the drug vorgethan; Alín could not bring him clean food or water without arousing suspicion. Murtagh could feel a low, dull sense of misery emanating from the dragon. *Misery.* He hated the word. . . .

Once again, Murtagh attempted to access the power in the yellow diamond. *Almost.* But almost was never enough.

Then Bachel stood and clapped her hands over her head, and after the crowd quieted, she proclaimed, "Let the recitation begin!"

A line formed outside the courtyard, and one by one the cultists presented themselves to Bachel and told her of the visions they'd had that night. The dreams were far more varied than usual: fantastic images and narratives that Murtagh would have hardly credited as true had he not experienced something similar himself. Yet there were commonalities of theme among the visions, promises of bloodshed and vengeance claimed, premonitions of a world razed and rebuilt—a world where every living creature worshipped Azlagûr the Devourer, or else died.

557

The recitation took hours. Every member of the village came before Bachel and had their say. At the table in front of the throne, Lyreth and the other guests grew restless, and they often stood and left for a time, only to return later and resume eating.

Once Lyreth came to Murtagh and stood before him while gnawing on a leg of lamb. The young nobleman was fever-eyed and disheveled, and his movements had a sharp, birdlike quality, as if he were overly excited. "Did you enjoy those dreams last night, Murtagh? Eh?" And he poked Murtagh in the chest with the end of the leg. The meat left a grease stain on his woolen jerkin. Lyreth took another bite, his eyes wandering across the courtyard. "It was a *singular* experience. That's why I wanted to stay, to see if what Bachel said is true. I dreamt of my father and . . ." A strange smile lifted one corner of his mouth, and he looked back at Murtagh. "Enough of that. How do you like this, Murtagh? Here you are, a faithful servant to the throne again. Even if you sit upon the throne in Urû'baen, yours is ever to be the slave and not the master. You and your dragon both." He laughed in a most unpleasant way. "How do you like seeing the foundations of the future, Murtagh? These *Draumar* may be inauspicious material from which to alter the course of history, but from small seeds may tall trees grow." He poked Murtagh in the chest again and then, with a smirk, returned to his seat.

For his part, Murtagh stood. He stood and he kept trying to force his mind to access the energy in the yellow diamond. Surely the vorgethan couldn't still be in his body!

The dull disk of the sun arced across the sky. The smoke never lessened, and no breath of wind arose to give them relief. Beneath the stifling blanket of haze, it grew increasingly warm—as if the earth itself were heated—and the whole village seemed to labor beneath an obsessive presence. Murtagh could not shake the feeling he'd had in his dream, of cowering on the blasted plain before the rising abomination, far in the distance. . . .

The ceremonies went on. Endless rites, obscure and meaningless to Murtagh, but clearly of deep value to the cultists. Bachel spoke at times, in the same manner she often did, of the riches and rewards destined to those who followed their faith. The discordant music continued, and between that and the smoke, a pounding headache formed at the base of Murtagh's skull. His eyeballs throbbed with every beat of a drum or crash of a cymbal.

Then the observances came to an end, and the villagers fell to feasting. That, at least, Murtagh was familiar with. Great servings of food were brought forth from the temple kitchens and from dwellings throughout Nal Gorgoth. Boar meat and venison and mushrooms prepared in a dizzying variety of dishes. Wine too, and mead, and bergenhed, and aspic, and loaves of fresh-baked bread, and more besides. Pies, savory and sweet. Deep dishes of creamy soup, wedges of hard and soft cheeses, berry tarts. All manner of sumptuous food.

Bachel's servants filled her dented brass goblet with wine, and with his thoughts now clearer, Murtagh recognized the goblet as that which he had found in the tower of Ristvak'baen. His neck stiffened, and he clenched his jaw. The witch continued to pile presumption upon presumption.

Throughout the evening, Murtagh ate when ordered to. He knew it would help keep up his strength, but he had no stomach for food.

He saw Alín on occasion, moving about the courtyard, tending to the guests, helping with the serving, rushing to obey Bachel's orders. As with the other Draumar, she wore a scaled outfit, and it gave the acolyte a darker, more serious appearance than Murtagh was used to.

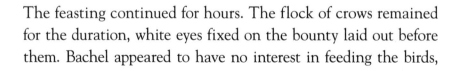

The feasting continued for hours. The flock of crows remained for the duration, white eyes fixed on the bounty laid out before them. Bachel appeared to have no interest in feeding the birds, but they did not defy her and take flight. As she ordered, so they obeyed.

Lyreth and his companions consumed cup after cup of wine. They seemed to view the entire festival as a lighthearted affair, no different from the themed parties so common among the nobles of Galbatorix's court. Murtagh knew better, but he would not have warned them even if he could. Some wisdom, he thought, was best acquired through experience.

As the orange smoke-darkened disk of the sun approached the peaks of the western mountains—which were visible only as dusky silhouettes beneath the sinking orb—the villagers cleared the food from the courtyard and lit the braziers.

Then Bachel did say, "Bring in the offerings!"

A parade of gifts followed. Wooden carvings, small and large, plain and painted, simple and complicated. It seemed as if the villagers had spent the entire year chiseling away at a piece of hardwood in their spare time. The sculptures would have horrified most any artist in Alagaësia, no matter their race, for they were the shape of dreams: distorted, angular, structured according to flawed, uncomfortable logic. In them, Murtagh recognized fragments of his own brimstone-born nightmares.

Each sculpture, Bachel accepted with grace and thanks. She made no distinction in quality; simply creating a piece seemed sufficient to satisfy the traditions of the Draumar.

When the last villager had presented the last carving, Bachel's warriors gathered the sculptures into a pile behind the basalt altar set before the ruined fountain.

Bachel stood and cried out, "For another sevenmonth, Azlagûr has gifted us with His dreams of prophecy. Now, during the time of black smoke, we repay His generosity with these gifts. With these sculptures born of dream. Azlagûr is well pleased with your efforts, O Draumar! You have proved your devotion, and we make now this burnt offering that Azlagûr may continue to look upon us with favor.

In return, we serve Azlagûr with our lives, and may destruction strike us and all we care for if we break this sacred covenant."

She lifted her pale arm and pointed at the mound of carvings. She spoke no word, but her body grew tense as a bowstring drawn taut, and then the tension released, and a bolt of liquid fire leaped from her hand and flew to the sculptures.

Yellow flames engulfed the carvings. In an instant, a year's worth of work was lost to fire, charred and seared and soon to be reduced to ashes. But the villagers were not dismayed. To the contrary, they cheered the eruption, and Bachel seemed gratified by the display.

Then once again she clapped her hands. "Bring forth the initiates!"

Murtagh expected to see a line of younger villagers, ready to assume the responsibilities of their elders. Instead, Bachel's warriors ushered into the courtyard the same sorry-looking prisoners they'd herded into Nal Gorgoth before . . . before the Breath of Azlagûr had fogged his brain and sapped his will.

Among the prisoners was Uvek. The Urgal's wrists and ankles were shackled, his lips pulled back to show his fangs. The sight sent a spike of alarm through Murtagh. As far as he knew, the cultists hadn't taken Uvek from his cell in all the time since Murtagh and Thorn had arrived at the village. That they had done so now presaged nothing good.

The prisoners were herded into a block before the dais. The mound of burning statues backlit them in a writhing thicket of flame and sent their famished shadows stretching off to the north.

Bachel looked the prisoners over with exaggerated care. Then she took a small crystal vial from within the sleeve of her dress, descended from the dais, unstoppered the vial, and blew the swirling contents into the faces of the flinching prisoners. The vapor clung to their heads, and Murtagh saw it pour into their mouths and noses as they inevitably inhaled.

He instinctively held his own breath, hoping that no scrap of vapor would be blown his way.

With a satisfied look, Bachel returned to the throne. Lifting her husky voice, she said, "Dream now, unbelievers, as do all who live here in Nal Gorgoth. Those of you who are prepared to swear loyalty to Azlagûr the Devourer, and who are prepared to join us as faithful members of the Draumar . . . step forward now."

The prisoners shuffled and shifted and looked at each other with dazed expressions. Then a full three-quarters moved forward in a single staggered group. Uvek was not one of them. He remained standing at the back, teeth bared, arms pressed outward against his shackles, his fingers locked in claws.

The corners of Bachel's lips curved. "Excellent. I applaud your wisdom. You shall be inducted into the mysteries of our order, and the veil of common life shall be torn from your eyes by the truth we share. Come. Swear to me and to Azlagûr."

One by one, the prisoners who had stepped forward knelt before Bachel and swore their fealty. Though they did not use the ancient language, the stifling sense of presence increased, and the hairs on Murtagh's arms and neck stood on end, and he felt a thrum in the air, as of a great power passing through Bachel into her new followers.

An eerie light brightened the eyes of the men and women as they finished their oaths. With each, Grieve removed their shackles, and they went to stand with the rest of the assembled cultists, an expression of wonderment and—Murtagh thought—fear upon their faces.

"What of these recalcitrant stragglers?" Lyreth asked, his voice ringing out over the courtyard. He gestured toward Uvek and the other prisoners who had refused to budge.

"A sacrifice to Azlagûr," said Bachel. "In which you are included as well, Uvek Windtalker! Your time is at an end, and I shall no longer waste my energies upon you. Not now that I have a Rider to do my bidding."

She rose and put a hand on Murtagh's shoulder and tightened her grip. Even through his clothes, the tips of her sharpened onyx claws hurt. "Come, Kingkiller. Join me in presenting this sacred offering to Azlagûr. Today we shall appease our dread master, you and I together. You shall watch me wield the dagger I had of Saerlith, and then you shall wield it in turn, and the blood will flow and flow and the earth will turn black with it even as it shall when Azlagûr rises from His repose and wreaks His vengeance upon the land." Her eyes were burning with excitement. "Come. Now."

Murtagh's heart began to hammer as the witch took his hand and led him to the altar. The cultists and prisoners parted before them; the sight reminded him of the weddings that had taken place at court, with Galbatorix presiding, a dark and foreboding figure waiting at the head of the great presence chamber to deliver his royal benediction.

Across the courtyard, Thorn stirred in his shackles, a futile protest of movement. Without looking at him, Bachel said, "Stay," and he subsided, but his eyes sparked with restrained fire.

No, thought Murtagh when he saw the stained surface of the altar. He couldn't do this, couldn't be forced to do this. He wouldn't allow it. Wouldn't—

Bachel clapped her hands, and her warriors dragged to her the first of the remaining prisoners. The man was a ruddy-faced commoner garbed in a rough, homespun smock. He had a short, untrimmed beard that made his chin and upper lip look as if they had been rubbed with dirt. His jaw was set, and his brow furrowed, but he was obviously frightened, and the Breath of Azlagûr still held him in its power and seemed to have left him with no will to fight or flee.

"Hold him down and bare his breast," said Bachel, her voice loud and clear.

The warriors hauled the prisoner onto the altar and pinned him down. One of them used a knife to cut open the smock to expose the man's chest, and the man let out a small groan.

Murtagh gripped the edge of his cloak with his right hand and began to pull the fabric up with his fingers, feeling for the diamond hidden within the hem.

The cultists started to chant, and the combined power of their voices was like a great drum beating through the air and ground. The sound was seductive, transfixing, overwhelming; it made Murtagh want to join the rhythmic recitation, to lose himself in the cry of the crowd and to become one with the group.

Moving in time with the chant, Bachel drew the black-bladed dagger from the sheath on her girdle and raised the weapon above her head. From where Murtagh stood, the knife was outlined against the sinking disk of the sun, as sharp as a serpent's poisonous tooth.

His finger touched the diamond in the hem.

Bachel's dagger descended, fast as a falling arrow.

The prisoner let out a low grunt as the blade pierced his heart, and his whole body went rigid. He thrashed, but the warriors held him in place.

Blood sprayed skyward as Bachel withdrew the dagger. Then she moved lower, and as the man gurgled and gasped his last breath, she began to cut open his belly.

Murtagh watched. He had no choice. Gore in and of itself did not bother him. He had butchered his share of animals while hunting, and he had seen—and carried out—more than his share of bloody deeds on the battlefield. But to watch a man killed so coldly, without a chance to defend himself, was horrific. It gave him visions of Goreth of Teirm lying before him in the packed-sand arena. . . .

The diamond was hard between his fingers as he seized it with crushing strength through the hem.

He drove his mind into the gem, trying once more to free the energy contained within. The swirling store of power trembled beneath his mental grasp, an electric whirlpool that sent tiny shocks through his consciousness. He strained with all his might, but the barrier in his mind continued to hold.

Bachel spread out the prisoner's bloody intestines across the ashen altar, and she made a show of studying them. Then she raised her stained hands and cried, "Azlagûr has blessed us!" The cultists roared with approval. "The time of the Draumar is at hand! Hark! I see our people stepping forth from the shadows and marching across the land! I see the sons and daughters of Azlagûr's betrayers brought to heel! I see the Dragon Thorn and the Rider Murtagh flying at our fore! Yea, and even shall they cast down the false hero Eragon, and by their claw and tooth and blade shall they usher in the end of this age. All shall bow before Azlagûr's might, and His reign shall take hold, and so shall we endure, yea even unto the end of time. As it is dreamt, so it shall be!"

"As it is dreamt, so it shall be!" the villagers chanted.

Then Bachel stepped back from the altar and gestured at the corpse of the man. "Take him to the deep and deposit his body in the Well of Dreams, that Azlagûr may know we have served Him."

Two of the warriors dragged the corpse away, leaving black streaks across the altar.

With a wicked smile, Bachel advanced on Murtagh. He froze, and his heart jumped as she took his right hand in hers. She lifted his hand, and the diamond slipped from between his fingers, and the cloak fell straight. Her smile deepened as she pressed her black-bladed dagger into his palm and wrapped his fingers about the hilt. The blood on her skin stained his own.

"Now it is your turn to prove yourself a faithful servant to Azlagûr the Devourer," she said, and a tone of unhealthy delight colored her voice. "Bring another!"

The warriors grabbed the next prisoner—a short, brown-haired woman—and carried her to the altar. Despite the stultifying effects of the Breath, she was clearly terrified. Her nostrils flared, and her lungs rasped like overworked bellows, and a fine sheen of sweat coated her ashen skin.

Even though Murtagh wasn't touching the diamond, he should have been able to draw the energy from it. Under normal circumstances he could have. He felt sure that if he just tried hard enough . . . but even in that moment, with his heart pounding and the smell of blood and death filling his nostrils, he could not bring his full strength to bear.

One of the warriors cut open the front of the woman's tunic. Bachel savored the sight before turning back to Murtagh. "Now, Kingkiller. You know what is to be done. Now, by my word, my will, my command, sacrifice this unbeliever to Azlagûr the Devourer! Do this, and you shall be favored above all others."

A scrap of black smoke blew into Murtagh's face as he inhaled, and the smoke choked him and unbalanced his thoughts. The world distorted, and the festival and Nal Gorgoth itself seemed to thin and waver.

His hand trembled around the hilt of the dagger.

For the slightest moment, he imagined accepting. No longer would he and Thorn be outcasts. They would belong to the Draumar, and the Draumar would belong to them, and wherever they went, whatever they did, they would be able to rely upon the Draumar for help, even as the cultists might rely upon them. He would lead the Draumar to victory against the rest of Alagaësia. He knew how. Bachel was not wrong in that. And in victory, he and Thorn might at last be truly safe.

The prospect was enormously tempting.

Yet he could not bring himself to take the first step along that path. The costs were too high. He and Thorn would still be Bachel's thralls, servants to her grim cause, and there was no certainty they could ever overcome her. Besides, to pursue an absence of danger beyond all other considerations was its own form of madness. And as much as he yearned to belong, the question of to whom mattered. The Draumar, he deemed, were unworthy of his loyalty. He had rejected what Galbatorix offered—and through that rejection won his freedom. Likewise, he now rejected Bachel.

"Kill her, Kingkiller!" Bachel insisted. The leaping flames of the bonfire gilded her hollow cheeks with liquid gold. The chanting of the cultists surged in response to her words, rising to a demented frenzy.

Murtagh lifted the knife. He had to. Bachel's words left him no choice. But in his mind, he continued to rebel. Time was nearly gone, and yet he still failed to breach the barrier and access the energy in the diamond.

He couldn't do it alone.

The thought struck him with clarifying force. In an instant, he diverted his mental energies to Thorn—and then to Uvek—and threw himself against the unnatural haze that separated their minds and pierced it through the strength of his will. *I need your help!* he said.

The knife began to descend.

Thorn blinked, and Uvek snarled, and yet Murtagh felt nothing from them. Despair sank its teeth into him. They had lost, and Bachel had triumphed. If only—

New strength poured into him. Thorn's and Uvek's both. Their contribution was limited—neither was able to fully overcome the restrictions of the Breath or the vorgethan—but it was more than he had on his own.

With them backing him, Murtagh again drove his mind into the diamond. It took every scrap of their combined might, but he was able, just barely, to prize open the bottled store of energy.

The torrent of potential rushed into him.

He directed it into the blackstone charm. At the same instant, he mouthed the Urgal word that Uvek had taught him: "*Shûkva.*" Heal. It felt strange to work magic without the ancient language, but the word served its purpose nonetheless, and the charm triggered.

A sense of lightness passed through Murtagh, and a cloud seemed to lift from his mind as his sight and hearing sharpened and his thoughts grew swift as a high-spirited stallion. It occurred to him that he was lucky his remaining wards hadn't blocked the effects of the charm.

He stopped the downward motion of his arm. The tip of the black-bladed dagger hung a hair's breadth from the center of the woman's chest.

Bachel looked at him, and her angled eyes began to narrow. "Do not hesitate, Kingkiller. Finish the deed!"

Murtagh knew the odds were against him. His wards that protected him from physical harm were exhausted. All he had was the force of his mind and the strength of his body, and Bachel and the entirety of the Draumar were arrayed before him—and they were well protected by amulets and enchantments.

His lips curled. *A good fight, then.*

The first flash of alarm crossed Bachel's face, but before she could act—

"*Vindr!*" Murtagh shouted, and stabbed the dagger toward the witch's heart.

CHAPTER XXIII

✦ ✦ ✦ ✦ ✦ ✦ ✦

Fire and Wind

The Draumar were warded against magic, but they were not warded against the *effects* of magic.

At Murtagh's shouted command, a torrent of ferocious wind knocked the cultists and prisoners off their feet, and even sent a number of them tumbling across the flagstones. Behind him, the bonfire roared to sudden heights, the flames leaping twenty feet or more into the air, and a cloud of swirling embers filled the yard while writhing shadows stretched to the surrounding buildings.

Summoning so much wind ought to have been beyond Murtagh's strength, but he drained the yellow diamond empty, and he drew upon Thorn and Uvek, and his might was more than that of any single man, even a Rider.

The tip of the black-bladed dagger bounced off Bachel's breast, stopped by a spell, and the weapon flew from his hand.

Then the witch was shouting in a guttural, unfamiliar language as she jumped back. One of her onyx claws pointed at him.

"Skölir!" he shouted. *Shield.* It was a generic ward, so vague as to be dangerous, but it was all he had time for.

Gouts of inky darkness poured from her finger and flowed around Murtagh as water around a stubborn boulder, deflected by his counterspell.

Another word, and she could kill him. His makeshift ward could be bypassed in any number of ways. So he did what always ought to be the first thing in a duel between magicians: he attacked Bachel's mind with his own. Now freed of the Breath and the vorgethan, he knew he had a chance of overcoming her, if he could just—

Bachel laughed, and there was no humor or levity in the sound, only cruel, scornful mocking.

She stepped back, and a cloud of flapping wings and clattering beaks and stark white eyes obscured her as the murder of crows descended into the yard and surrounded the witch. Then the birds darted forward, and Murtagh heard and felt them everywhere around him, and they blotted out the light.

In the distance, Uvek bellowed, and fear shaded his thoughts.

From within the storm of crows, Murtagh sensed the witch's mind slipping away, like a wisp on the wind. He tried to find her again, but to no avail. The minds of the flitting birds confused his inner eye, and he felt himself lost and uncertain of his balance.

It was an untenable position. At any moment, a blade or spell might end him.

Desperate, Murtagh thought back to the compendium, and he uttered the simplest, and greatest, of the killing words: *"Deyja."*

Die.

The crows fell as dark, heavy rain.

He stood alone beside the altar. The female prisoner had rolled off the block of basalt. Around him lay a rosette of slain crows, their feathers pressed flat against the flagstones, as so many green-black petals.

Bachel was gone. Vanished. As was Grieve, and half the guests at the long table.

Blast it. He needed to catch Bachel before she could work more evil. But first—

The cultists were massing at the side of the courtyard, warriors and common Draumar alike gathering themselves for a charging attack.

"Vindr!" Murtagh drove them back with word and wind as he strode to Thorn. Once more the dragon's strength served as his own. With another arcane command—"Kverst!"—he struck the shackles and muzzle from Thorn, and then he took the blackstone charm from his boot, pressed it against Thorn's snout, and again said, "Shûkva."

The change in Thorn's demeanor was instantaneous. He arched his neck and roared, and a glittering ripple flashed along his sinuous length. *At last!* he said. And the feel of his mind, once more whole and sound, filled Murtagh's eyes with tears.

It was the work of seconds to effect a similar cure on Uvek and to free him of his fetters.

The Urgal rolled his massive, rounded shoulders and let out a roar to match Thorn's. "Is good, Murtagh-man. Has been long time since I fought. This I think I enjoy."

"No younglings," said Murtagh in a hard tone as he handed the blackstone charm back to the Urgal.

A rippling sheet of flame shot from Thorn's mouth, driving back the surging mass of cultists. *The same goes for you,* said Murtagh with his mind. *Leave the younglings alone.*

I will try.

Uvek lifted his horns to show his throat. "As you say, Murtagh-man. And I ask you not kill more crows. Is bad fortune."

Murtagh nodded in return. "I promise. Now let's—"

He stopped when he saw Alín appear deep among the shadowed pillars that fronted the temple, running toward them with Thorn's saddle and bags piled in her arms. As she staggered beneath the weight, Grieve and two armored acolytes darted up from behind and seized her.

The saddle and bags fell, and Alín thrashed in a frantic attempt to free herself. But Grieve and the acolytes dragged her back into the depths of the temple, and they vanished from sight even as Murtagh readied a spell.

He shouted in anger and started after her.

After two steps, he swung back to Thorn and slapped him on the side. "Go! Break! Burn! Tear this place to the ground."

Thorn's jaws parted in a toothy snarl, and the tip of his tail twitched. *I thought you would never ask.* Then he roared again and leaped into the air with a thunderous sweep of his wings.

The backdraft sent swirls of embers through the air, each one a tiny whirling firestorm.

As Thorn cleared the buildings that edged the courtyard, he laid down a wall of fire between Murtagh and the massing mob. A clutch of arrows pierced the wall and streaked past his head, trailing pennants of flapping flames.

Murtagh sprinted toward the temple even as the flames died down and the cultists surged forward. Behind him, he heard Uvek loose a mighty bellow: a battle cry fit to make even the bravest man quail.

Then Murtagh was among the dark rows of faceted columns. He ran through the open doors of blackened oak, down the alcove-lined passage, and into the atrium with the nightmarish statue of *dream*.

A deafening crash sounded behind him, and an enormous *thud* vibrated the ground. He spun around to see a cloud of dust rising above the front of the temple. A dark shadow swept over him as Thorn swooped overhead.

There, said Thorn. *None shall reach you from the entrance. I blocked the doors with stone.* As he spoke, the dragon alit upon the Tower of Flint and began to tear at the slate shingles that roofed it. A twisting stream of angry, frightened, cawing crows flew up through the holes and dispersed into the smoke that darkened the valley.

Murtagh smiled tightly. *Thanks. Be careful.*

Thorn roared in response.

Then Murtagh turned left and started out of the atrium,

heading toward the temple's inner sanctum, where he was most likely to find Bachel, Grieve, and Alín.

Along the way, he ended his shielding spell. It was too broad to be truly effective, and although it *was* a ward, the way he had cast it was as an ongoing effect, which was costing him precious energy that he knew—or rather, feared—he would need to overcome Bachel. Better to start fresh with proper wards, which would only trigger when actually needed.

As he passed among the pillars along the southern edge of the atrium, he struggled to remember the exact wording of his earliest wards. It had been some time since he cast them, and it wouldn't do to accidentally curse himself. *Ah, that's it,* he thought, and opened his mouth to—

A heavy weight slammed into his back, between the shoulder blades. His head whipped back, pain shot through his neck, and he fell forward onto the paved floor. White sparks flashed behind his eyes as his forehead bounced off the stones.

A boot rammed into his ribs, knocking the air from his lungs. Then again. And again.

"There! That's right! You never were any better than a piece of gutter filth!" shouted Lyreth.

The sound of his voice and the feel of the blows filled Murtagh's mind with memories of being ambushed on the spiral staircase at the citadel of Urû'baen. An instinctual sense of panic and helplessness gripped him, and he curled into a kneeling ball, trying to protect his head and the back of his neck.

Magic. That was the answer. If he could just cast a spell—

Something hard struck his temple. His vision flickered, and the ground seemed to tilt and turn beneath him. Dazed, he tried to recover, but it was impossible to think, impossible to move—

He lost his balance and rolled onto his side. He saw Lyreth standing over him, a bloodstained brass goblet in one hand, a vicious, snarling expression on his face. Lyreth raised the goblet again and—

Something yanked Lyreth to the side and sent him tumbling across the floor. The goblet fell and bounced with several high-pitched *tings*.

Then Uvek was standing over Murtagh, offering him a huge grey hand. In the other, the Urgal held a spear taken from the Draumar.

"Thanks," Murtagh managed to gasp as he accepted Uvek's help and the Urgal pulled him onto his feet.

"Of course, blood brother."

Several pillars away, Lyreth stood somewhat unsteadily. He glanced between Murtagh and Uvek, and fear widened his eyes. He made to turn, as if to flee, and Murtagh said, "Don't even think about it, Lyreth. I could kill you with a word."

The noble's face went even paler. He wet his lips. "Nonsense. Bachel's magic protects me."

Ah, he has an amulet.

"Do you really think that can stop me, Lyreth? Me? Even Galbatorix could not stop me with his oaths. If not for me, you'd still be a slave to his will." It was a bluff, but Murtagh somehow believed his own words. If forced to, he felt sure he could find a way past the amulet's wards. *Somehow.*

Lyreth lifted his sharp jaw. "So then kill me. What are you waiting for?" When Murtagh didn't immediately answer, he smirked and began to back away. "That's what I thought. An empty b—"

"No," said Uvek, and his voice was like grinding rocks. He pointed at Lyreth with one hooked nail. "You stay." Lyreth froze. There was no chance he could outrun an Urgal, and they all knew it. "Do you want I should kill this hornless stripling for you, Murtagh-man?"

Murtagh was sorely tempted. But he shook his head. "No. Leave him. He'll make a better prisoner. We'll take him back to face Nasuada's interrogators."

Fear again animated Lyreth's face, but then he assumed the same haughty, contemptuous expression that Murtagh had learned to hate growing up. "Do you think it's so easy to make me a prisoner? You never could best me at court, Murtagh."

"And you could never best me in the arena. Goreth of Teirm could attest to that."

Somewhere in the village, a building collapsed amid shouts and roars. Murtagh resisted the urge to look. He felt no pain from Thorn; the dragon was safe enough.

Lyreth made a dismissive motion. "You don't have a sword now, Murtagh son of Morzan, and if you have that pet Urgal of yours catch and bind me, you're a bigger coward than I thought. I wager you can't make me bend a knee. I wager upon my life."

It was a provocation, and Murtagh knew it, but neither could he let the challenge pass unanswered. "It might very well be on your life," he said darkly. He wiped a line of blood from his throbbing temple. "No one calls me coward without a fair answer."

Uvek nodded approvingly. "I will watch, Murtagh-man. Is good to fight. Clears the blood, adds honor to your name."

"And my honor is your honor. Yes."

The Urgal moved back several paces as Murtagh and Lyreth began to circle each other among the pillars. Lyreth's unexpected courage puzzled Murtagh; he never would have thought of Lyreth as brave. Cunning, yes. Charming, when need be, yes. Cruel, most certainly. But not the sort of man who would jump at the opportunity to lead a charge in battle.

He must really want to avoid being captured. The thought gave Murtagh pause. If that was Lyreth's true motivation, then—

He sprang forward. If he was right, delay would be deadly. With two steps, he closed the distance with Lyreth and, before the other man could back away, grabbed him by the shoulder with one hand while striking him in the jaw with a fist.

Lyreth took the blow better than Murtagh expected, and a second later, he felt an answering blow against his left kidney. The pain made Murtagh's eyes water, and his whole body went rigid, save for his knees, which buckled.

Then Lyreth pushed against him, and they were falling together.

A jarring *thud* as they collided with the floor. For a minute, the only sound was their ragged breathing as they wrestled across the flagstones. Up close, Lyreth smelled of wine and a cloying, peach-scented perfume that Murtagh found distinctly off-putting.

The other man fought with desperate strength, but desperate or not, he was far weaker than Murtagh, and Murtagh soon gained the advantage. Lyreth seemed to realize his plight, for he resorted to the lowest of tactics and drove his thumbs into Murtagh's eyes.

Pain caused Murtagh to jerk his head back, and his vision flashed white and red, and sparkling stars exploded at the points where Lyreth's thumbs contacted.

They separated, and a second later, they were both on their feet, fists raised, hair tousled, teeth bared. Murtagh blinked. The world throbbed with reds and yellows, every line and angle outlined with a glowing halo.

Several quick jabs followed, and then Murtagh grew impatient and rushed Lyreth. He was no longer a youngling, and he'd be thrice cursed before he let Lyreth again use him badly.

He slammed Lyreth into a pillar, and the man's head cracked against the carved stone.

For an instant, Murtagh thought he'd won. Then a flash of silver by his belt caught his attention: Lyreth fumbling to draw a short-bladed dagger from under the hem of his tunic.

Alarm spiked Murtagh's pulse. He jumped backward, but too late: a burning line slashed across his ribs as Lyreth lashed out with the weapon.

Murtagh resisted the urge to disengage. Instead, he stepped forward again and trapped Lyreth's arm between their bodies. He caught the man's wrist with his hand and bent it inward until the dagger pointed back at Lyreth, and before Lyreth could drop the weapon, he shoved the knife deep into Lyreth's chest.

Lyreth stiffened and let out a grunt, but he kept struggling against Murtagh, seemingly unwilling to acknowledge the wound. Murtagh knew he'd hit the man's heart. He'd bleed out given enough time, but that could be a minute or more, and Lyreth was fighting with the same stubborn tenacity as a buck that had been struck in the chest by an arrow and refused to fall.

This is taking too long. The thought came to Murtagh with cold clarity. Alín needed rescuing. More importantly, Bachel was still on the loose, which meant Thorn was in danger, even if some of the dragon's wards remained. The contest with Lyreth was an unnecessary distraction, and a dangerous one at that.

All anger left him then, and he stepped back and pulled the dagger free of Lyreth's chest. A spray of crimson blood hit him, and the color drained from Lyreth's face. The man flailed and scrambled after Murtagh, only to collapse into his arms.

Keeping a firm grip on the dagger, Murtagh lowered Lyreth to the ground. Already he could see the light fading from Lyreth's eyes. His first instinct was to let the man die. But he didn't want to lose all that Lyreth knew.

"Waíse heill," he said, and placed his left palm against the wound in the man's chest. It was a risky spell; he could be attempting to heal something that was beyond his strength or ability, but it was all he had time for.

The spell had no effect.

Lyreth chuckled. He sounded genuinely amused. Blood stained the corners of his mouth. "I'm charmed, remember? Your spells . . . won't . . . work."

Murtagh ripped open the front of Lyreth's tunic, convinced he would see one of Bachel's bird-skull amulets hanging around Lyreth's neck. But all he found was pale skin and the red-lipped line that was the wound into Lyreth's heart.

"What did you do?" he said, angry.

Lyreth chuckled again, more weakly this time. "Bound wards to . . . me. . . . No need for . . . amulet." His gaze wandered for a moment, and then he rallied and looked at Murtagh with undisguised spite. "You always were a . . . bastard."

And then he went limp, and his last breath left his body.

Murtagh stood and looked down at the corpse. "No," he finally said. "Eragon's the bastard. Not me."

"A good kill, Murtagh-man," said Uvek.

Murtagh grunted. He motioned to the Urgal. "We'd better hurry."

CHAPTER XXIV

✦✦✦✦✦✦✦

Grieve

As Murtagh ran with Uvek toward the temple's inner sanctum, he quickly cast a basic ward against physical damage, and he was just beginning to formulate a ward that could protect him, or others, against the Breath when they arrived in the echoing room.

There, waiting for them in the presence chamber, was Grieve and seven acolytes in their armor of leather scales. Grieve carried his iron-shod club; the acolytes carried spears and wooden round-shields.

Neither Bachel nor Alín was to be seen.

Uvek stomped his feet and bellowed, and the sound of his war cry echoed a dozen times off the high ceiling.

"Where is Bachel?" said Murtagh, raising his voice over the echoes. He regripped Lyreth's dagger. It was the only physical weapon he had.

"That is none of your concern, Outlander," said Grieve in his harsh tone.

"I disagree. Tell me, and tell me where Alín is."

Grieve smiled grimly. "With the Speaker. She shall see to the little traitor. Now surrender, Outlander, or you shall surely die."

"You know I'll never surrender." Murtagh was already preparing for the mental assault he was convinced would follow.

Grieve snorted. "Of course, but formalities must be observed. I'm glad for the chance to be rid of you, Rider. And you as well, Urgal."

Uvek let out a low growl. "You owe me blood, *shagvrek*, for death of Kiskû."

A disdainful sneer crossed Grieve's face. "Was that your bird? Annoying thing. Uvek Windtalker, the greatest shaman of his people, and yet you chose to sit atop a mountain and talk to a bird for years on end. What a waste."

Rage darkened Uvek's face, and he lowered his head so that, for a moment, Murtagh thought he was going to charge. "You are slave to dream, *shagvrek*. Is wrong-think to worship Bachel or Azlagûr. You crawl before them, happy for attention. Like dog."

Grieve snarled, his expression hateful. "I am no slave, *Urgral-gra*." He spat out the word as if it were invective. "I serve those who accepted me."

Uvek spread his broad arms. "Then let me give embrace. See how long you can stand welcome. *Hrr-hrr-hrr*."

Grieve lifted his club and pointed it at Murtagh and Uvek. "Kill the unbelievers." And he drew forth a crystal vial and threw it at the mosaic floor.

Murtagh had been expecting exactly that. Even as the vial flew through the air, he cried, "Drahtr!"

The vial swooped back up, just missing the floor, and gently arced into Murtagh's left hand. Grieve's face contorted with rage, and he bellowed as the seven acolytes charged Murtagh and Uvek.

Murtagh didn't have time to slip the vial into the pouch on his belt before the first cultist was upon him. He sidestepped a jab of the man's spear, sprang forward, and drove Lyreth's dagger through the man's temple.

Good thing they're not wearing helmets.

He left the dagger where it was and snared the end of the cultist's spear as the man fell. Holding it one-handed, he waved it at the other cultists while retreating. That bought him time to put away the vial, and then he had both hands on the haft of the spear. A fierce glee overtook him.

Beside him, Uvek caught a man's spear and used it to smash the cultist against the brazier in the center of the chamber. Sparks and glowing coals flew like a shower of meteors. Another of the Draumar jabbed Uvek in the upper arm, but the Urgal's hide was so thick, the cut drew no blood.

For the next minute, Murtagh and Uvek fought side by side. They were fit companions. The Urgal's size and brute strength—as well as his unexpected speed—allowed him to break the line of Draumar and keep them on the defensive, while Murtagh felled his opponents with practiced ease.

As they fought, Grieve stalked the perimeter of the battle, hefting his iron-shod club. But he continued to hold himself apart, content for the time to let his minions strive unassisted with Murtagh and Uvek.

When just two of the cultists remained, and the glittering mosaic was slick with blood, then and only then did Grieve attack.

His assault came as a surprise. Murtagh was focused on the Draumar in front of him—a stocky, slump-shouldered man with a streak of grey along his brow—and he nearly missed Grieve's club as it swung toward him.

Murtagh twitched and managed to deflect the devastating blow with his spear. At the same time, he felt the man's mind driving against his own. And not just his; Uvek snarled and said, "You shall not have my thoughts, *shagvrek!*"

The addition of Grieve to the fight shifted the advantage back to the cultists, for the witch's adviser and right-hand man struck with a power Murtagh had not anticipated—he seemed nearly as strong as a Kull—and though ungainly, he was swift on his feet. Fending him off was like trying to fence with a savage animal, fierce and untrammeled.

The five of them maneuvered around the pillars and the brazier in the center of the sanctum, each seeking to land a mortal blow. Murtagh stabbed his spear into the brazier and tossed a clump of coals at one of the remaining acolytes. The man ducked, and Murtagh moved in, only for Grieve to drive him back with swings of his heavy club.

A painful stalemate held as they struggled to and fro. Their blows, parries, and occasional shouts echoed through the space, and a pair of dispossessed crows fluttered about near the crown of the ceiling, screaming at the combatants below.

Then Uvek uttered a growl of frustration, and with one hand, he grasped the lip of the burning-hot brazier and flipped it over. Coals cascaded across the gory floor, and the heavy copper dish landed on the shoulders of a cultist, crushing him. A gong-like tone sounded.

"Desecrators!" cried Grieve.

Murtagh seized the opportunity to lunge forward and took the other acolyte in the throat. As the man sank gurgling and gasping to the floor, Uvek slipped his spear under the overturned brazier and stabbed the man struggling beneath its weight. The man went limp, and the brazier moved no more.

"By Azlagûr, I curse you," said Grieve, and spat on the floor.

Murtagh snorted. "I've been cursed by better than you and lived to see them become food for worms." He pointed his spear at Grieve. "Come now, dog. Meet your fate."

Grieve drew himself up, squaring his hunched shoulders, and his eyes rolled back to show white. "Azlagûr, hear the plea of your follower, Grieve the First. Let me defeat these unbelievers, and I shall—"

Uvek did not let him complete the contract. The Urgal shouted, "No!" and rushed forward and struck at Grieve with the haft of his spear, using it as if it were a staff.

The wooden pole snapped in two against Grieve's robe, seemingly broken by the immovable fabric. But Murtagh knew the truth: a ward. Unsurprising, but unfortunate.

A grim certainty settled over him: Grieve would be no easy opponent.

He tried then to seize the man's mind, even as Bachel and

Grieve had attempted to seize his. But Grieve's mental defenses were formidable, and in any case, the man gave Murtagh little time to concentrate, for he answered Uvek's attack with a shower of blows from his club.

Uvek caught one blow against his forearm. The force of the strike would have shattered a man's arm, but the Urgal merely grunted and fell back while swinging the remnants of his spear to gain himself room to recover.

Murtagh took the lead then, but he met with no more success. He jabbed, and Grieve parried. He feinted . . . and Grieve nearly caught him upside the head with the club. Every attack Murtagh made, Grieve seemed to perfectly anticipate.

The same proved true as Uvek attempted to flank Grieve. Even working two against one, neither of them could slip past Grieve's guard, and he kept landing blows with his club. The blows did not hurt Murtagh; he had his ward to protect him, but he was tiring and did not know how long he could maintain it. And they *did* hurt Uvek; the Urgal was limping now, and a plate-sized bruise marred his forearm.

It occurred to Murtagh that he was treating Grieve as if the man were also a magician. But so far, he'd seen no evidence to that effect. If Grieve couldn't cast spells, then there was no reason not to attack him with magic. But if he could . . . doing so might prompt a desperate and incredibly dangerous response.

Crack! Grieve smote the middle of Murtagh's spear. The wood snapped like dry straw, and he fell back.

Shade's blood! Enough with caution; magic was worth the risk! "Kverst," said Murtagh, aiming his will at Grieve.

He felt a quick drop in strength—as if he'd sprinted up a hill—but the spell had no effect on the man.

Grieve laughed. It was a thoroughly distasteful sound. "You cannot break my mistress's power, desecrator!"

With Thorn, Murtagh felt sure he could, but Thorn was otherwise occupied, and Murtagh didn't dare open his mind to reach out to the dragon. Regardless, he felt sure that Grieve had given him the answer: they had to defeat the man's wards. And that required energy, magical or physical. In the end, there was no difference. When cleverness failed, *effort* was the key to overcoming spells.

Murtagh threw his broken spear at Grieve and shouted, "Hold him off!" as he dashed toward the back of the chamber.

Behind him, Uvek roared, and the Urgal's footsteps thudded as he closed with Grieve.

Bachel's throne was missing from the dais—removed so that she might sit in state during the festival of black smoke. Where it had stood, the floor was dull and hollowed from uncounted years of bearing the heavy stone chair.

At the back of the dais were a pair of shallow steps that descended to a recessed area where various ceremonial items were stored: robes, tapers, brass censers, the headpiece the witch had worn when he first met her. . . . Also, there was a chest of dark walnut, and Murtagh hoped it was where he would find—

He threw back the lid of the chest.

Yes!

Zar'roc lay before him, a gleaming length of metallic beauty, red as blood, strong as hate, sharp as his will. The hilt found his hand, like an old friend, and he tore blade from sheath with a steely, slithering sound.

Finally, Murtagh felt ready to confront their enemies.

Nor was the sword just a sword. It was also a repository: a storehouse of energy that he had carefully gleaned in dribs and drabs, hoarding morsels in the great ruby of its pommel.

He drew upon that repository now, and he said, "Brisingr!" At his command, the blade burst into a profusion of crimson flames.

With the burning blade held at his side, he strode to Grieve, each step weighted with approaching doom. He swung, and the searing, incandescent edge came down upon Grieve's brow—and stopped a hair's breadth away, blocked by the man's wards.

Murtagh held Zar'roc against the slippery surface and pushed harder while pouring even more energy into the fire rising from the colored steel. The heat was blistering, and he narrowed his eyes as the stench of burning hair filled the chamber.

"Now, Uvek!" he shouted.

The Urgal lowered his horns and bulled forward, taking a heavy blow from Grieve's club against his armored forehead. The impact would have killed any human, but Uvek did not even react. He grabbed the club with one enormous hand and held it motionless in the air while he beat Grieve about the ribs and shoulder with the broken haft of his spear.

Grieve bellowed with anger, his face a mass of shifting shadows beneath the fiery blade. He wrenched at his club, fruitlessly trying to free it from Uvek's iron grip. Then Grieve abandoned the club and made as if to duck out of the cage of their arms.

"Brisingr!" Murtagh shouted again, and redoubled the strength of the spell. The flaming blade shone with blinding light, and drops of liquid fire fell onto Grieve's wards, where they danced like beads of water on a hot skillet.

Uvek struck once more at Grieve's ribs: a mighty blow that shook the man and that Murtagh felt transferred into his hand through Zar'roc's hilt. At that, Grieve's skin went grey, and his ward collapsed.

Murtagh sensed an instant of overwhelming terror from the man's mind, and then Zar'roc sliced down through Grieve's head, the enchanted blade burning its way through flesh and bone as if they were no harder than fresh-formed cheese.

The sudden removal of the ward made it difficult for Murtagh to control the sword's path. He struggled to arrest the swift descent of the blade even as Uvek released Grieve and twisted away, but Zar'roc's blazing, razor-sharp edge severed the tip of

Uvek's right horn and touched him on the shoulder, near the collarbone.

Uvek's breath hissed between his teeth, and he growled as if meaning to attack. But he stepped back and clapped a hand over the cauterized wound.

What remained of Grieve collapsed to the floor.

Darkness compressed around them as Murtagh ended his spell, extinguishing Zar'roc.

"Gzja!" said Uvek, and spat on Grieve's body. "You no more throw rocks at birds. Now Kiskû rest easy."

Murtagh gestured toward Uvek's shoulder. "Let me see. I can help."

Uvek grunted and shook his head. "Is not bad, Murtagh-man. An Urgralgra wears his hurts with pride. I will live."

"Are you sure?"

The Urgal seemed offended that Murtagh would question his word. "Sure, sure. This small hurt. I had much worse from bear. I will live."

"Good."

With the toes of his bare foot, Uvek nudged the fallen tip of his horn. "Not good to lose horn, but horn grow back."

Murtagh started back for the chest behind the dais. "I suppose you'll just have to live in a cave until you're presentable again."

"What means *presentable*, Murtagh-man?"

"Fit to look at." He was relieved to find his armor neatly stored inside the chest. And with it, the ancient language compendium, which was more valuable to him than any gold or gems.

The Urgal laughed as Murtagh pulled on his corselet of mail. "I no longer look for mate to live with, Murtagh-man. Broken horn will not be big problem."

Moving with haste born of need, Murtagh donned his arming cap and helm, and then strapped on his greaves and vambraces. He decided against the breastplate; mobility was more important than protection from war hammers or the like. For that he had his ward. He belted on Zar'roc's sheath and tucked the ancient language compendium into the pouch where he had stored the vial of Azlagûr's Breath.

Then he scouted across the mosaic floor until he found one of the acolyte's shields. Taking the shield, he returned to Uvek where he stood beside Grieve's remains. "What is *shagvrek?*" Murtagh asked.

"Hard to say. Is hornless from before."

"Before what?"

"Before hornless fill land. Before elves have pointed ears. Before dwarves were short. Before dragons had wings. Before that."

Startled, Murtagh peered at him. "I've never heard of such a thing."

Uvek nodded. "Shagvrek old. Live in caves. Burn meat and eat dead."

Before Murtagh could ask more questions, dull *thuds* sounded outside the temple, and a thin veil of dust sifted from the ceiling. Opening his mind once again, he could feel Thorn's delighted, bloodthirsty rage as he tore apart the buildings in Nal Gorgoth. It was a shame, Murtagh thought, to lose such ancient structures (their carvings were well worth study), but he wasn't about to let that stop him or Thorn from flattening the place. Nal Gorgoth and those who lived there were an abomination Murtagh was determined to see cleansed from the face of the earth.

He felt some pain from Thorn—arrows through his wings—but otherwise the dragon seemed unharmed.

Do you need help? he asked.

Only if you wish.

Uvek gave a restless glance toward the direction of the sounds. "Murtagh-man, there are other Urgralgra in Nal Gorgoth. Some prisoners. Some Draumar. Maybe Draumar will not listen to me, but I have duty to try."

"Go. If you need aid in battle, call for Thorn."

Uvek grunted and started to leave. Then he strode back to Murtagh and bent down and gently bumped foreheads with him. "Is good to have you as qazhqargla, Murtagh-man."

An unexpected upswelling of camaraderie filled Murtagh. "And you as well, Uvek Windtalker."

"*Hrmm.*"

Then the Urgal trotted away, his footsteps surprisingly quiet for his bulk, and Murtagh stood alone among the scattered corpses.

He ignored them. Closing his eyes, he sent his mind ranging through the village as he searched for Bachel, determined to find the witch and, once and for all, bring her to account. The thought of breaking her power held dark appeal. As she had done to him, he would do to her. She had brought him low, and he wanted revenge.

That, and he wanted to help Alín. No, *needed.*

Throughout Nal Gorgoth, he felt a confused chorus of pain and terror as the cultists fled before Thorn or else attempted, in vain, to halt the dragon's rampage. But nowhere among the panicked minds of the Draumar did he detect the familiar shape of Bachel's thoughts.

He delved deeper. Extending his consciousness into the depths, he searched under the buildings, down among the rot of tunnels that corrupted the roots of the mountains.

There. A cluster of sparks, as errant fireflies trapped far below the surface. He reached toward the brightest one, and the spark flared in response, and then pulled inward and shrank as Bachel shielded her thoughts from his.

Dread certainty congealed within Murtagh. The witch knew he was coming, and she was not alone. They would be ready for him. Ideally, he would take Bachel prisoner, that he might finally have his answers—most specifically about the activities of the Draumar in Nasuada's realm—but Murtagh suspected the witch would sooner die than submit. That was acceptable too. Bachel was so dangerous, keeping her captive would be like trying to restrain a rabid beast with his bare hands. Nor would killing her be much easier, if even he could.

For a moment, doubt assailed him. *We could still leave.* There was nothing to stop him and Thorn from flying away. They could fetch reinforcements, and with Eragon or Arya by their side, the witch would hardly stand a chance. But there was no guarantee Bachel or the Draumar would hold in Nal Gorgoth while they were gone.

And in any case, he couldn't abandon Alín. He'd made her a promise.

At least Bachel won't shake the mountains while she's under them, he thought, and felt grateful for the smallest of mercies.

Shield in one hand, sword in the other, he trotted out of the temple sanctum and toward the back of the building. There, he found the door that opened upon the cropped sward abutting the western side of the temple. Thick plumes of black smoke rose from vents in the ground.

A terrific crash caused him to flinch and turn. One side of the Tower of Flint had just collapsed inward, reducing the structure to a mound of rubble.

Past the tower, flames lit Nal Gorgoth. Half the buildings had their roofs torn off. Loose stones lined the streets, and bodies too.

Thorn swooped past, scales shining, threads of hot blood trailing from his wings.

Murtagh saluted, and the dragon roared in return. Then Murtagh started across the sward, heading toward the grove of pinetrees beyond. *I'm going to find Bachel,* he said.

Grim concern was Thorn's first response. *It is too dangerous.*

I know, but I must.

Do not go alone. Take Uvek with you.

He has duties elsewhere, and I need you to keep the Draumar occupied out here.

Across the village, Thorn roared again, this time with frustration. *You won't ask me because you know I'm too afraid.*

Murtagh stopped for a moment, his own emotions a conflicting welter. *I didn't want to trouble you. That is all. You're as brave a being as any I know.* Then, more gently: *You probably won't even fit in the tunnels down there.*

You don't know that.

Then come if you want! I'm not trying to stop you.

An uncomfortable silence followed, and Murtagh could feel Thorn's mind churning with a mix of shame and anger.

Finally, Murtagh said, *I have to go. Guard yourself well.*

. . . And you the same. Then a snarl echoed across the tumbled rooftops. *Make the witch sorry she ever thought to chain us.*

"I'll try," Murtagh muttered, starting forward again.

A pair of sword-wielding Draumar sprinted toward him from the grove. He cut them down, one after the other, with decisive swings of Zar'roc. The elven-forged blade shattered the sword of the second cultist into silver shards.

Murtagh let out a shout as he hurried forward. It was more a battle cry than anything: a release of the furious energy coursing through him. He knew the feeling well; it was an old companion. Some men fought while in the grip of an icy calm, and he appreciated the value of that, but calm held no appeal for him at this moment. He had been bound, and now he was released, and every bottled bit of rage boiled out of him, as steam from a heated rock.

More Draumar attacked as he entered the grove. Five of them, armed with spears and swords and a single bow. Murtagh caught an arrow on his shield, and then he was among the cultists, beating and cutting and stabbing with deadly intent.

Dangerous as it was, Murtagh found the fight exhilarating, and he laughed at the fear of the men. *Good.* It was only right that they quailed before him.

The skirmish did not last even a minute. As the last body fell to the ground, he was already moving past, heart hammering, lungs heaving. His lips were drawn back to bare his teeth in a bloody grin, and he felt a sense of power gathered about himself, like an invisible cloak.

But even then, he knew his battle-born confidence was a falsity. Bachel would not be so easily overcome as her thralls. Cunning was needed, as much as strength, were he to have any chance of prevailing. So, as he exited the grove and advanced upon the yawning cavern set within the base of the foothills, he looked in the compendium for the words he needed to compose a spell that would protect him against the Breath of Azlagûr. The magic would filter the air, as a cheesecloth might filter water, and keep the poisonous vapor from entering his lungs.

Once he was well satisfied with the phrasing of the ward, he cast it, and a grim smile touched his lips. "Let us see how you like that, O Speaker of lies," he muttered.

Fresh torches burned on either side of the ominous cave, and there were many tracks leading into the opening. Murtagh took them as evidence that Bachel had brought a contingent of warriors with her.

He hefted Zar'roc again, preparing himself, and then strode forward and allowed the darkness to swallow him.

OTH ORUM

~~~~~~~~~~~~~~~~~~~~~~~~~ ❖ ~~~~~~~~~~~~~~~~~~~~~~~~~

CHAPTER I

✦✦✦✦✦✦

Creatures of the Dark

The air in the cave was hot and stifling, and the heat seemed to be increasing as Murtagh descended along the cut-stone stairs. He did not remember it being so warm during his previous venture into the warren hidden beneath Nal Gorgoth. *It must be because of the black smoke,* he thought. But, of course, that failed to answer the question of what caused the black smoke itself.

As he hurried downward, he dipped his mind into the ruby mounted within Zar'roc's pommel. A fair amount of energy remained stored within the faceted gem. Less than he'd hoped, but more than he'd feared.

He debated casting a spell to light his way, but he didn't want to make himself an obvious target. Besides, he remembered the glowing fungus that populated the depths of the caves. He could wait for that dubious illumination. Better to be a hunter stalking in the dark than prey standing in a moonlit clearing.

Beads of sweat began to run down his brow and into his eyes. He wiped them away with the inside of his forearm, the rings of mail hard against his skin. Fighting was hot work, and the sweltering temperature of the cave only exacerbated the lather he'd worked up on the surface. As did the corselet of mail. Iron rings were the very opposite of a cooling fabric.

With his outstretched consciousness, he detected a flicker of life ahead of him, off to the side of the stairs. A man, he thought, but—

A whirring noise crossed the cave, and an arrow bounced off the air in front of his nose.

Murtagh flinched. Even after long acquaintance and deep familiarity with magic, instinct still made him react as if the arrow had been about to hit him. It was a sobering realization to know that, were he not a spellcaster, he would have just died.

He did not dwell on the thought.

Kneeling, he placed Zar'roc on the stairs and felt about until his fingers found a small, sharp chip of rock. He held it up on the palm of his hand and whispered, "Thrysta!"

The rock shot through the air, faster than any eye could see, and—aimed by his will—intersected with the consciousness of the cultist who had shot the arrow.

A flat *smack* echoed through the cave, followed by the unmistakable sound of a body falling.

Grimly satisfied, he continued onward.

~~~~~~~~~~~~~~~~~~~~~ ❖ ~~~~~~~~~~~~~~~~~~~~~

When Murtagh arrived at the vast, slime-lit cave at the bottom of the stone staircase, three more Draumar came rushing out of the shadows to attack him.

The lead cultist jabbed a spear at his hip. Murtagh parried and lunged and ran the man through. Zar'roc pierced the man's leather-scale armor as if it were no thicker than gossamer.

He withdrew blade from flesh, pivoted, and cut the next Draumar through the neck. The man's head fell to the ground amid a shower of green blood and bounced away, hair flying in a tangled mess.

A high *clang* jarred Murtagh's hearing as he caught the spear of cultist number three on his shield. The man jabbed again, his face a rictus of anger. Murtagh sidestepped and neatly chopped off his right arm.

The cultist howled and staggered back.

Murtagh gave him no quarter. He followed up with two quick thrusts: one between the man's ribs and one up under his chin.

"Pathetic," said Murtagh as the cultist collapsed. Grieve had been formidable enough, but if this was the quality of Bachel's ordinaries, Murtagh was far from impressed. They had neither technique nor magic, only blind faith to fuel their violence. Tornac would not have approved.

A frown settled on Murtagh's brow. Why were the cultists bothering to attack in such limited numbers? They had to know they stood no chance of stopping him.

They're trying to delay me, he realized. Either so Bachel could escape or so the witch and her minions might prepare for his coming.

With a flick of his wrist, he shook the blood off Zar'roc's blade. In a detached manner, he noted the liquid's unusual appearance; it resembled the dark, iridescent green of the water beetles he would find around Urû'baen. Somehow the sickly glow emanating from the membranous slime on the cavern's rocks had altered the color of the gore. His skin didn't look normal either; it appeared horribly unhealthy, as if the slime-glow had leeched him of all vitality.

He hurried along the path of flagstones, eager to reach the Well of Dreams.

His steps quickly brought him to the three tunnels bored into the far wall of the enormous cave. As before, he took the central one, and rushed down the tunnel shingled with scalelike tiles.

Extending his mind, he searched for Bachel and her retinue. But he felt no tickle of thoughts, and his inner eye saw no bright sparks of being amid the surrounding darkness.

When he broke into the marble-clad chamber that housed the Well of Dreams, he found it empty, devoid of motion, save for the flames flickering in the alcoves along the walls. The well itself was open, the grated cover pulled aside to expose the shaft that plunged into unknown depths.

The stench of brimstone poured out of the well with sickening strength. Even as Murtagh took a step toward it, a column of black smoke erupted from its depths, billowed against the arched ceiling, and then ascended through narrow slits cut along the crown of the ceiling, and which he had not noticed before.

They built this in expectation of the smoke, Murtagh thought. He tried to imagine what lay below. Heated vents full of molten stone, or something of that like. He had heard of such things among the Beor Mountains: places where the mountains breathed fire, and hot smoke and ash often made the surroundings miserable to endure.

He risked a quick glance over the lip of the well. The hole beneath seemed bottomless. For a moment, his balance wavered, and he imagined falling and falling . . . forever lost in the bowels of the earth.

With an oath, he pulled himself back and looked around. "Where are you?" he muttered.

Once more, he reached out with his mind. When he was assured that no one (and no *thing*) was close enough to ambush him, he closed his eyes and focused on his inner eye.

He had to range farther and deeper than he expected before he again located Bachel's white-hot spark of consciousness. She was below him—almost directly underneath the top of the well—and at such a distance, he thought it would take a rock many seconds to fall to her.

"Blast it." He eyed the human-sized doorways leading out of the chamber. The prospect of getting lost underground appealed to him no more than it had in Gil'ead. But there was no helping it; he had to find Bachel and stop her from escaping.

Right. He started toward the corresponding doorway. Most folks were right-handed, so if either passage was to lead somewhere important, he guessed it would be that one. And if he were wrong . . . He wondered how difficult it would be to use magic to blast his way straight through the rock. Even Thorn would struggle to muster enough energy to burrow more than a short distance. Rock was heavy, and no amount of chanting in the ancient language would change that.

He ran onward.

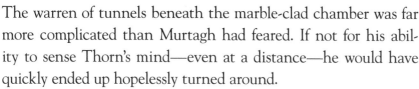

The warren of tunnels beneath the marble-clad chamber was far more complicated than Murtagh had feared. If not for his ability to sense Thorn's mind—even at a distance—he would have quickly ended up hopelessly turned around.

Not far from the chamber, he again found himself in passages large enough for Thorn to have moved through. The wending shafts ran in seemingly random directions, through chambers natural and otherwise—many times he chanced upon what appeared to be shrines or altars or abandoned guardrooms—but always they led downward.

Although the slime-glow was often bright enough to illuminate his path, more than a few of the spaces were as black as the void between the stars. To keep the patches of blinding darkness from unduly slowing him, Murtagh relented and created a red werelight that floated some feet above and in front of his head. The combination of colors from the werelight and the slime painted objects the most hideous shades. So much so that he sometimes had difficulty recognizing the substance of what he saw. He nearly altered the werelight to the pure white of the sun's noonday radiance, but he valued his night eyes too much.

The air grew thicker as he descended, until it lay heavy and moist in his nose, throat, and lungs, and it took a conscious effort to breathe. At times, clouds of smoke wafted over him, and then he was grateful for his wards, for they seemed to filter some of the stench.

The weighted presence Murtagh had felt in the village was even stronger in the caves. It pressed in around him like old honey, and he had an unaccountable urge to crouch and hide or else to

601

flee far, far away. There was nothing concrete to which he could attribute the feeling, but it was as inescapable as the stifling air.

His attention began to wander, and his vision too. Focusing on any one thing for more than a few seconds seemed . . . not impossible, but his gaze kept slipping, and a few steps later, he would find himself wondering what he had been looking at and what he had been thinking about.

Strange . . .

He shook his head to clear his mind. The motion was a mistake. The world tilted around him, and he fell to one knee, planting his shield against the ground for balance.

After a moment, he felt stable enough to stand.

Could there be drink in the air? Mead or strong spirits sprayed in a fine mist? He tasted the air: brimstone and nothing more. Nevertheless, he cast another ward to purify the air around himself.

It didn't help.

Concerned, he staggered onward.

Phantasms began to plague him: flashes of shimmering rainbow colors, dolorous moans that snaked through the tunnels, and—rare at first, but then with increasing frequency—visions that appeared before his eyes and that, for those timeless moments, seemed as real as the rocks.

He saw Tornac standing before him, wooden waster in hand. The swordmaster had just been assigned to Murtagh, and they were about to spar. . . . The clash, when it came, was quick, and the outcome was Murtagh on his backside with a bruise forming across his left ribs. He expected scorn and derision from Tornac. Such had always been his lot at court. But no ridicule was forthcoming. Instead, Tornac walked over to him, offered a hand, and in a matter-of-fact tone said, "It's a start."

The lack of rancor opened Murtagh's heart. He was slow to admit it to himself, but at that moment, he learned to trust, and he clung to

Tornac's instruction—no, his leadership—as the only steady rock in a storm-tossed life.

Murtagh blinked, disoriented. Whatever strangeness was affecting him, he wasn't about to turn back. "Is this what you count on protecting you, Bachel?" he asked, his voice small in the vastness of the cave. "Well, it won't. This I swear."

With dogged steps, he continued.

—black-sun plain scoured by a howling wind that chilled flesh to bone . . . A man lay hunched in the barren dirt, arms wrapped around his head as he rocked back and forth, screaming in a high, broken tone—

The tunnel Murtagh was following angled steeply downward. His steps quickened as, relieved, he allowed himself to be pulled along by the descent. He kept his gaze fixed forward, hoping to see the tunnel's end, for it ought to lead him close to where Bachel was waiting, if not the very location.

—a thunder of dragons flew past, so numerous that they blotted out the sky. Their scales flashed with every conceivable color, a profusion of terrifying beauty, and the air beat like a drum from the force of their mighty wings—

Murtagh broke into a trot. He tried to block out the visions by reciting a scrap of verse. It helped for a time, but then his attention wandered for an instant and—

—Nasuada lay before him, chained to the ashen slab in the Hall of the Soothsayer, even as the prisoners had been held upon the altar in Nal Gorgoth. The pleading in her eyes was as loud as any speech, but they each had their roles to play, and he could not help her. The king commanded, and he obeyed, and she suffered because of it. They all suffered.

"No, no, no," Murtagh muttered. He banged the rim of his shield against his forehead. The impact helped dispel the images still playing behind his eyes.

The tunnel opened up into yet another cave. As with so many

603

of them, it was lit by slime, and ranks of purple-capped mush-rooms edged a small pond far to his right. Rings spread across the surface of the water, as if something had just jumped into—or out of—the pond.

A thicket of larger mushrooms stood before him, like so many stunted, unwholesome trees.

As he picked his way between the woody stems, a sharp chit-tering caught his ear. He stalked quietly between the mushrooms and soon saw . . . an odd *shape* crouched over the body of a fallen cultist.

As the red glow from the werelight touched the creature, it twisted to look at him with the face of a nightmare. A glisten-ing black tongue as long and thick as his arm lolled from narrow, shrewish jaws, which were too thin to entirely contain the muscle. Loose, sagging skin as pink and pale as a piglet—bare of fur, save for an occasional white bristle sprouting from warty growths—hung in repulsive wrinkles over protruding bones. From the nar-row skull stared lidless eyes no bigger than a fish egg and seemingly too sensitive to bear the soft glow of the werelight, for the creature squinted and recoiled as if in pain. Most disturbing of all were the beast's front paws, or rather . . . *hands*. It had long, humanlike fingers with broken, grime-packed nails smeared with the blood of the dead cultist, and the fingers opened and closed as if to squeeze the life from another unfortunate victim. Dragging behind the beast was a thick rope of a tail, as limp as a dead earthworm.

Revulsion filled Murtagh. The creature—the *fingerrat*, as he thought of it—seemed wrong in a fundamental manner, as if its very existence were a perversion of all that was good and right.

He reached out to the fingerrat's mind. What he discovered only increased his aversion: a gnawing hunger dominated the ani-mal's consciousness, and all it seemed to think about was the plea-sure of eating the warm man-flesh below it and its anger at being interrupted. The others would be coming soon, and—

Others?

More chittering sounded in the shadows. A horde of pale finger-rats crept closer, feeling their way with their long fingers, their tails sliding across the cave floor like so many scaleless snakes.

The creature squatting over the corpse uttered a descending moan—Murtagh recognized the cry as one of the many sounds he'd heard filtering through the underground complex—and it returned to tearing at the body, using its tongue to flense skin and muscle from the man's chest.

"Begone with you, foul creature!" Murtagh shouted, and sprang forward, waving Zar'roc.

The fingerrat shrieked like a pained infant as it cowered. Then it hissed, showing rows of translucent needlelike teeth, and—with shocking speed and agility—jumped toward Murtagh's throat.

He fell back and slashed the air in front of him, hoping to hit the creature.

Zar'roc struck, but Murtagh's edge alignment was off, and the hilt twisted in his hand, and he almost dropped the sword.

He staggered as the fingerrat crashed into him and hot blood gushed over his corselet of mail. Teeth snapped at his throat, stopped only by his wards. Then he threw the creature off, and it fell to the ground, nearly cut in half, squalling and thrashing in its death throes.

The stench of offal made him gag. No help from his spells there.

The squeals of the wounded beast did nothing to deter its approaching kin. They continued to crawl closer through the mushroom thicket while uttering harsh laughing sounds that raised the hair on Murtagh's neck. Something seemed desperately wrong with the creatures, as if they were half mad from living underground, or else so crazed from the constant smoke that they had no sense of self-preservation.

"Don't do it," said Murtagh, keeping Zar'roc at the ready. "I'll kill you all."

More of the fingerrats appeared out of the darkness. How many were there now? Thirty? Forty? He tried to count, but it was impossible to keep track of any one individual as they moved amongst themselves.

"Naina," Murtagh said, and the werelight above him flared in intensity until it was so bright, it banished all shadows beneath it.

The fingerrats screeched and spun in circles as if a bee had stung them on their sunken flanks.

"Begone!" Murtagh cried again. It was a mistake. The sound of his voice focused the attention of the creatures; they turned toward him, tongues extending like so many feelers, bleached whiskers twitching, knobbed hands reaching.

"Kv—"

The horde rushed him, their hands and paws scrabbling against the dirt and stones of the cave floor.

Murtagh struck down the lead rat, but then the rest of the creatures swarmed him, snapping and clawing and lashing him with their heavy tongues. His wards flared, and his strength ebbed with alarming speed as the spells struggled to protect him.

He tried to speak, but the warm hide of a fingerrat pressed against his face, preventing him from uttering a sound. Nor could he draw in a breath.

The animals smelled of must and musk and warm dung.

Enough! He focused his will and, with his thoughts, said, *Kverst!*

The bodies of the fingerrats dropped from him like so many sacks of flour.

Murtagh shuddered. It would not have taken much more to deplete his immediate reserves of stamina, and then his wards would have failed in order to keep him from losing consciousness. If the fingerrats had pressed but a little harder, or if he had hesitated a few seconds longer, they would have overcome him.

A sense of satisfaction filled him as he stared at the mound of bodies. He had no love for such slaughter, but had he the time, he would have hunted down the rest of the carrion eaters and seen to it that their like never bothered another person.

More chitters sounded in the distant shadows.

But not now. He reduced the brightness of the werelight to its previous level and hurried away. Maybe the corpses of their kin would distract his inhuman pursuers, give them enough food that they would not bother following him. It was a hope.

As he trotted along, Murtagh reviewed all the animals he knew of in Alagaësia. He had never heard of such grotesque beasts. Had they a name in the ancient language, he was ignorant of it, and none of the old stories spoke of creatures of that kind.

Do they only live here, *or in all the places where the Draumar worship?* Was there a chance he might have encountered fingerrats somewhere beneath Gil'ead? The possibility disturbed him.

Still, he ran. And though the chitters faded, they never entirely vanished. Twice more, a fingerrat darted out of the darkness and attempted to bite him. Both times he slew the creature with a single blow from Zar'roc.

Murtagh couldn't shake the feeling that he was trapped in a waking nightmare. The constant sounds echoing around him— and now he began to question whether some came from other creatures stalking through the underground warren—the seemingly endless tunnels, the shimmering distortions floating before his eyes, and the heat and sweat and crushing sense of presence . . . all of it combined to give him a pounding pressure at the back of his skull and a conviction that he couldn't trust anything around him.

—a body of a dragon draped across the land, spikes as tall as mountains, teeth as long as towers, blood flowing like rivers across the withered plains—

He shook his head and pressed on.

Amid the chitters and moans, a new set of sounds became noticeable: a scissorlike slicing and a tiny tapping as of iron nails dancing across stone.

He froze when something large and angled ran out of a side passage and darted halfway up the curved wall of a tunnel. The thing stopped and clung there, unnaturally still.

"Naina," Murtagh whispered, though he almost didn't want to see whatever the creature was.

The werelight brightened to reveal . . . *what*, Murtagh didn't know. The creature was the size of a large wolf. A *very* large wolf. But it more resembled an insect than any furred or feathered animal. It had four double-jointed legs with spikes at the joints, and then another set of legs—or rather, arms—held close against its narrow chest, just beneath its mouth, which was a butcher's collection of cutting blades. Similarly, the arms ended in razor-sharp pincers, and the creature opened and closed them with the same slicing sound Murtagh had heard moments before. Flat, tick-like head, segmented body, jagged limbs: all of them were clad in black plates of naturally grown armor, no different from a beetle's shell. The creature had no eyes to speak of: only a double row of pits—no bigger than seeds—along both sides of its head.

The monstrosity looked as if it were made out of sawtoothed lengths of shadow welded into an unlovely whole that reminded Murtagh entirely too much of a spider.

Murtagh straightened from his crouch. He didn't feel like cowering before this particular horror. "I don't like you," he said in a matter-of-fact voice. "If you attack me, I *will* kill you."

The creature cocked its head and mashed the blades in its mouth. Then it darted down the wall of the tunnel and—before Murtagh could do more than take a half step back—skittered out of sight.

"Shade's blood," Murtagh muttered. How many unnatural horrors lurked beneath Nal Gorgoth?

Gooseflesh prickled across his neck and arms as he hurried onward.

CHAPTER II

✦ ✦ ✦ ✦ ✦ ✦ ✦

Freedom from Misery

Not a hundred feet down the tunnel, the giant spider attacked him from behind.

Murtagh heard the iron-nail tapping seconds before the creature struck. He spun around just in time to block a spear-tipped leg plunging toward his heart. Zar'roc's blade rang as it glanced off the spider's carapace, same as if he'd caught another sword against the edge.

The spider struck again. It was faster than any human. Faster than any elf. His wards blocked the attacks, but then the spider swept a limb across the ground and tangled his legs.

Murtagh fell. By instinct, he covered himself with his shield, and as he landed, he again cast the killing spell: "Kverst!"

The magic had no effect.

He was so surprised that, for a moment, he failed to act. Then he used his shield to heave the spider off him. It was incredibly heavy, as if it had metal in its shell. Still, he threw it back, and as it scrambled on bony legs to again attack him, he swung Zar'roc far harder than he would have against any human foe.

He struck the spider across the flat of its head. The carapace cracked beneath Zar'roc's crimson blade, and black blood oozed out, thick as warm tar. The spider clicked in distress, and the cutting surfaces in its mouth stabbed and gnashed.

Murtagh swung again, and this time, Zar'roc split the creature's head in two. Its legs gave way, and it collapsed against the ground.

He stared at the monster as he regained his breath. Why hadn't the spell killed it? A ward? On an animal so deep in the ground? It wasn't impossible, of course, but the only explanation that made sense was that Bachel herself had enchanted the spider. The question was, why? So the creature might hurt or delay him, same as with the cultists? Were the creatures likewise her thralls?

Chittering echoed in the distance.

He straightened, grim. Whatever foul minions Bachel had amid the caves, they weren't about to stop him; of that, he was sure.

Determined, he resumed his course.

As he made his way through the underground chambers, the fingerrats and shadow spiders continued to attack. One here. Two there. A rat dropped on him from a crevice hidden high upon a slime-infested wall. A spider leaped out at him from within a dark chasm. And more. Many more.

He beat back every assault, meeting savage fury with equal force. Zar'roc's blade was constantly awash with blood, and his boots grew wet with gore, and his eyes stung from dripping sweat. Fatigue slowed his steps, and he began to worry what would happen if he could no longer keep up his wards.

It was hard to track time or distance. Thorn's consciousness had faded from his mind, and when Murtagh reached for him, he realized he could no longer feel the dragon's thoughts. Too much stone separated them.

Alarmed, he searched instead for Bachel. If he could not locate her, then he was truly lost. . . . But no, he again felt the witch's life force. Only she was not just below him, she was also behind him by what felt like a good quarter of a mile. Despair touched Murtagh. He must have gotten turned around during the fighting.

The path seemed endless. And always the chitters and the tapping and the swish-swash-scissor-slicing haunted him. He dared not lower his guard for even a second, and the constant state of watchfulness was of itself exhausting.

Even with his magic and his sword, Murtagh felt as if he were a child alone in the dark, afraid of unseen monsters waiting to pounce. But this time, the monsters were real, and no less terrifying for it.

Visions and phantasms continued to bedevil him. He managed to ignore most of them—even when they occurred at inopportune moments, such as in the middle of a fight—but at last:

Dark ceiling, dark walls, floor of patterned wood . . . a fire roaring in the stone hearth along one side of the great hall. Dishes scattered across the banquet table, which all the guests had long since fled. . . . At the head of the table, the dark shape of his father, still wrapped in his travel cloak, hunched, brooding, the ever-present goblet of wine grasped firmly in his hand. Hovering behind him, the slim figure of his mother, speaking in low, tense tones.

Murtagh sat on the edge of the hearth. The sounds of his parents talking distracted him at times—his father's voice was loud, brusque—but then his attention returned to the wooden horse he was playing with. It was painted brown and white, with crisp black hooves, and it had a mane and tail of real horsehair. He ran it back and forth across the hearth, making little sounds as he did. He jumped the horse over imagined rocks and hedges, and then, by accident, he brought the horse too close to the fire, and a spark landed on the tail.

A flame kindled in the hair. Frightened, he shook the horse, and the flame went out, but the smell of burnt hair stung his nose, and the tail was ruined.

He started to cry. That much he remembered. The horse was so handsome, and now it was ruined, and he had no others like it.

His father's voice rose in an angry shout. "—don't stop that brat and his mewling, then I will!" And there was the scrape of a chair being shoved back and a cry of terror from his mother, and a heavy weight struck Murtagh in the back and knocked him flat against the hearth.

Zar'roc fell beside him with a clatter, the blade's edge so sharp it was invisible.

Murtagh knew he screamed, but he felt no pain, only a sense of cold and weakness as blood spread in a pool around him. His mother's face appeared over him, her expression pinched with fear, and that disturbed him more than anything. He didn't want her to worry, didn't want her to be afraid.

Then the hall grew hazy, and the last thing he was aware of was his mother murmuring in an unfamiliar language as the dreadful chill settled in his bones.

Murtagh stopped by a mound of mushrooms and gasped as if he'd taken a blow to the stomach. He clenched his jaw and stared at the rocky ceiling for a time as tears spilled from his unblinking eyes. "That's not for you," he muttered to whatever force inhabited the caves. Why had he been compelled to relive that particular moment? He went to great lengths to *not* think about it, although the knotted scar on his back had been re-minder enough: a memento of both his father's cruelty and his mother's love. The latter part was why he'd kept the mark. Re-moving the scar would be easy enough with a spell, but to do so felt like repudiating his past to such a degree, he might as well have declared himself nameless and kinless. Perhaps he should have. Morzan's legacy had brought him nothing but pain. But his mother's . . . was more complicated. From her he had life and love, and just because his life had been difficult, that did not negate her love.

Quick *tip-taps* circled him in the shadowed distance. He heard, but he did not care.

Murtagh looked at Zar'roc. He scowled with barely contained disgust, and his hand shook. Scar or not, he hated the sword, hated what it represented. *Zar'roc. Misery.* His father's choice of name, and a fitting one, given Morzan's history. That wasn't what Murtagh wanted for his life, and yet he had taken the blade from Eragon, to claim it as his own, as if somehow it would protect him.

Instead of it protecting, he felt as if it were defining him. *Zar'roc.*

Misery. Names were important, even for the smallest thing. By naming, one might gain understanding. Even more, one might re-cast the very nature of a thing. Had he not experienced that himself in the citadel of Urû'baen when his true name had changed?

An idea occurred to him. A bright, promising idea that brought with it fierce determination. He knew the Name of Names, the very key to the ancient language and its arcane power. By it he could use or define or even change the words of the language.

Which meant . . . he could rename Zar'roc. If he so wanted.

Murtagh did not have to stop to consider. He wanted.

But rename to what? If not Misery, then Happiness? Hardly the right meaning for his or any sword. Besides, Murtagh had never tended toward happiness—he wasn't sure he knew what it really was—and he would have felt ridiculous carrying a blade called Happiness.

Even though time was short, he stood still in the dark and let his mind range wide as he sorted through dozens of possible names. At its core, the question was simple: What did he want Zar'roc to represent? That was, what value did he want to give pride of place in the center of his being?

All around, he continued to hear the *tip-taps* of the marauding shadow spiders. But they held their distance, and he paid them little attention, for the problem he was wrestling with was all-encompassing and, he felt, crucial to his survival.

In the end, the answer came from within, as it must—from his memory of Morzan hurting him, and from his own true name, which he saw with new clarity: what it had been, and what it now was. For he was a changed person. The pain he had clung to so assiduously no longer held sway over him; he had new cares and new values, and he was determined to pursue them.

Fired by inspiration, Murtagh opened the pouch on his belt, took out the compendium, and, one-handed, flipped through the parchment pages until he found that which he sought.

He studied the short line of runes. Was he sure? *Yes.* More than ever before.

The spell required energy he did not have to spare, but nonetheless, he drew upon his body and, soft as a falling feather, spoke the Word and, with it, renamed the sword:

"*Ithring*" . . . *Freedom.*

As he spoke, the barbed glyph stamped upon blade and sheath shimmered and shifted into a new shape, a new understanding. And he recognized the glyph as that which the elves used for the sword's new name.

The hate and anger that had been boiling inside of him cooled into calm determination. He nodded. *Freedom.* His father had chosen to spread *misery* through life and land. Perhaps Murtagh could do better.

A crooked smile crossed his lips. He had no delusions. He knew he had responsibilities that bound him. To Thorn, if nobody else. But they were responsibilities he had accepted for himself, not ones imposed from the outside. Freedom had always been what he aspired to, and what he would always cherish. His blade could stand as a symbol for that. And when he fought, as he knew he would soon need to, then it would fall to him to grant his foes their final release. And besides, he might use Ithring to help those, like Alín, who could not help themselves. To cut their bonds and set them loose, even as he and Thorn had freed themselves of Galbatorix's oaths.

His mother, he thought, would have been proud of him for it.

"Ithring."

The word felt strange upon his tongue, yet fitting also. The sword itself seemed different: an ineffable change that left the blade brighter and cleaner.

Murtagh felt different as well. He stowed the compendium and resumed his journey with a new sense of lightness, as if renaming the sword had somehow helped drive back the oppressive presence of the caves. And when the dark denizens of the undercroft again attacked him—the shadow spiders and their gnashing blades, and the fingerrats reaching for his throat—he dispatched them with a calm efficiency that had previously escaped him. For he knew who he was and why he was there, and he no longer sought to fight with misery, but in pursuit of freedom.

CHAPTER III

✦ ✦ ✦ ✦ ✦ ✦ ✦

To Hold the Center

A pale glow appeared ahead of Murtagh—spilling out from behind a fold of rock—and his pulse quickened. At last! Bachel was near. He could feel her. And not just her, others besides. Thirteen of them, by his count.

He readied himself with a long, slow breath and a drawing in of his mind. Bachel might not have a legion of Eldunarí to command, as had Galbatorix, but she was no less dangerous. Murtagh had no intention of underestimating her. She'd gotten the best of him before; it wouldn't happen again, regardless of her source of power. That he swore to himself.

He spared a quick thought for Thorn and then continued.

His boots were soft against the stone as he rounded the fold of rock. Beyond it, he beheld a vast, circular chamber that looked as if it had been scraped out of the granite by a great millstone. He hardly noticed the slime-veined walls, for a cluster of white crystals thrust upward at various angles from the ground. The crystals were semi-opaque and translucent along their sharp edges, and they varied in size from small protrusions no larger than the thorn of a rose to enormous pillars as thick around as an aged oak. Large or small, the crystals glowed with a natural radiance, white and pure and beautiful to behold.

In the center of the chamber lay a wide clearing with a gaping hole at its heart: a void twenty paces across that opened to yet further depths.

At the height of the chamber was another opening, and he

had a sense that it led up, up, up to the Well of Dreams. For all his walking, he'd merely ended directly below where he'd started.

Bachel stood waiting for him by the void.

He hardly recognized her. The witch still wore the enchanted half mask that transformed her aspect to that of a dark, draconic being. But she had exchanged her dress for a suit of armor that encased every inch of her body, and the armor was made not of leather or metal but rather of dragon scales.

The scales were reddish black and glimmered with an oily sheen. They emitted a dim glow, dying embers still pulsing with contained heat. The scales must have come from an old dragon, for some looked to have been cut from even larger pieces. Seeing the armor, Murtagh realized that the leather garb the cultists had donned for the festival of black smoke had been made to resemble Bachel's fantastic suit.

In her hand, the witch held the Dauthdaert Niernen. Its blade matched the light from the slime along the walls.

Six acolytes stood to Bachel's left and six to the right, as if two great wings extending from she who served as their central body. The impression was marred slightly by the pair of acolytes who held Alín between them, their hands firm around her arms and wrists as they kept her kneeling upon the stone.

A reddened bruise discolored Alín's cheek, and blood spotted one corner of her mouth, but her neck was unbowed and desperate hope filled her eyes as she beheld Murtagh. "My Lord!" she cried.

Dark rage gripped Murtagh as he saw her plight. He welcomed the emotion, knowing it would serve him well in the fight to come.

The acolytes carried neither swords nor spears but tall staffs of knotted wood, each embellished with strange carvings. For the oddest moment, Murtagh was reminded of Brom. Then the cultists stamped the butts of their staffs against the ground, and the sound echoed again and again from the domed ceiling, and they began to chant in a low chorus that filled the chamber with building urgency.

Murtagh picked his way between the crystals, careful to avoid their sharp edges.

As he approached, Bachel lifted Niernen and pointed the lance at him. She seemed entirely unafraid, and she said, "I am impressed, Murtagh son of Morzan. The power of Azlagûr's dreams drives to madness most who venture into the depths below Nal Gorgoth."

"But not you or your servants."

"I am the Speaker. I am Azlagûr's chosen mouthpiece. His protection grants certain privileges to me and those I choose as my attendants."

Murtagh wasn't so sure about that. He affected a casual expression and spun Ithring in his hand as he paced forward, keeping a close watch on the cultists. "What of those . . . *things* in the caves? Are they your doing as well?"

Beneath the mask, Bachel's mouth twisted with amusement. "Not mine, Kingkiller. Mites and fleas of Azlagûr are they. Useful tools, nothing more."

He nodded in a pretense of understanding. The twelve acolytes couched their staffs toward him as he stopped some ten paces in front of Bachel. If he could somehow maneuver behind them, he could drive Bachel toward the hole in the floor, and it would limit her movement. . . .

A column of thick black smoke jetted up through the hole, as loud and fast as a giant waterfall, only in ascent. Heat followed, so intense that Murtagh fell back a step, and the stench of brimstone was overwhelming.

Bachel seemed unaffected. She extended Niernen and let the tip of the lance enter the flow of smoke. The glow from the blade illuminated the dense haze from within, giving it an unearthly hue.

Then, just as suddenly as it had started, the torrent ceased, and what remained continued upward, lifted by the heated currents of air. It vanished into the shadows above, but Murtagh knew that, in a few minutes, it would arrive at the surface and thence would seep through the ground and into the polluted air around Nal Gorgoth.

"What is this place, witch?"

Bachel drew herself up, eyes bright with fury, and her mask lent her voice terrifying power. "You will address me by my rightful title, desecrator! This place is Oth Orum, the hidden heart of the world, the very center of all being, and your presence is an affront to Azlagûr Himself. No outlander has set foot here, not in all the thousands of years the Draumar have guarded it. To come here unconsecrated is to invite death, and death you shall have unless you realize your error and kneel before me."

"I shall not kneel. Not to you. Not to Azlagûr. Not to anyone."

Bachel's fury increased, but she mastered herself and, in a cold tone, said, "Why, Kingkiller? I have offered you everything, and still you scorn me."

"No, you have taken, not offered." Murtagh did not blink as he met her gaze. "I am my own man. By my will, I make my way. I will let no one steal that from me, least of all you, witch. Surrender now, or I swear the worms will feed on you this very day."

"Desecrator!" she declared. "Defiler! You will rue those—"

The ground shook beneath them, and a thunderous rumble echoed through the caves and tunnels. Flakes of stone fell from above, and billows of grey dust clouded the chamber.

Murtagh dropped into a half crouch, alarmed. Was this Bachel's magic again?

But no, the witch and her minions staggered, as if surprised, and then Bachel laughed, low, throaty, delighted. "Do you feel that, Kingkiller?! Do you? That is Azlagûr come to purge the unbelievers! He shall sweep aside the unworthy, like maggots before the flame! Submit!"

Worry gnawed at Murtagh's confidence. He still did not fully understand the forces he was dealing with; whatever lay at the bottom of the hole, it was concerning.

Raising Ithring, he pointed at Bachel, even as she had pointed

619

at him with Niernen. "Let Alín go," he said, and his voice rang loudly. "She has no part in our quarrel."

"Oh, but she does," said Bachel. "She is my vassal, and you have turned her against me, and against Azlagûr Himself. She shall pay for her sins, Rider. She shall pay most dearly. Her blood will be a welcome sacrifice to our dread god."

"Liar!" shouted Alín. "Hypocrite! You broke our creed! You went against everything you told us was sacred!" She spat on the floor in Bachel's direction. "*You* are the defiler! *You* are the desecrator!"

Bachel turned, the slightest smile upon her distorted features. "Foolish girl. There are deeper truths than you know. Everything I have done has been in service of Azlagûr's will. You dare question *me*? She whom He has chosen as His Speaker?"

Hair flew wild about Alín's face as she shook her head. "How can you say that? All my life, we worshipped the dragons, as you taught us. You said—"

"The *dragons*?" said Bachel, her voice so loud that Alín quailed into submission. The witch laughed, and there was nothing pleasant in the sound. "You wish to understand that which is above your station, *wretch*, but I will indulge you this once. Azlagûr has no regard for the little worms. They may serve Him or not, and if not, the calamity of His arrival shall sweep them aside. *That* is as He desires. *That* is as it shall be. The little worms are not gods. They are noisome spawn, weak, blind, and benighted."

The twelve staff-wielding Draumar seemed unsurprised. Murtagh wondered if they were Bachel's inner circle, privy to information kept from the rest of the cult.

"No," said Alín in a small voice. She was shaking. "That cannot be. Why w—"

Bachel rapped Niernen against the stone. "Because! The little worms are aspects of Azlagûr, but they are *not* Azlagûr Himself. It is the Great Devourer we worship above all else." The witch shook her head, as if disgusted, and held out her off hand toward the nearest of the Draumar. "Give me now your knife."

The acolyte obliged by producing a short-bladed dagger from within the sleeve of his jerkin. The iron blade appeared as grey velvet in the light from the crystals.

Bachel took the dagger and strode toward Alín.

"No!" shouted Murtagh, and he launched his thoughts at Bachel's mind in a furious assault.

The witch's steps faltered, and then she stopped, and Murtagh strove to hold her in place as he charged forward.

Bachel motioned at the Draumar. Their chanting increased, and Murtagh stumbled and fell to one knee as the full force of twelve more minds crashed into his. Their voices filled his ears with a throbbing rhythm. His head seemed to pulse with the same tempo, and darkness crept in about the edges of his vision.

Moving was impossible. Murtagh's awareness of his body shrank as he focused inward and armored himself against the onslaught. His sense of self became the center of his existence; it was all he allowed himself to think of, all he allowed himself to imagine. What he saw, he observed without judgment or reaction, as if he were watching events without meaning.

Bachel raised an arm and threw a vial toward him.

The glass shattered on the stone by his hand. A cloud of pearly white vapor floated up to his face and wrapped itself around him. But he smelled none of it, and it had no effect on him—his wards at work.

The witch bared her teeth. "Your magics will not—"

Another tremor passed through the mountain, and for a moment, the ground seemed to rise beneath him.

The disturbance provided a useful distraction. Two of the Draumar lost their concentration, and Murtagh seized the opportunity to drive deep into their minds. But only for a second. Then the combined might of the cultists forced him to retreat within himself.

621

Bachel abandoned Alín and advanced upon him. The butt of Niernen tapped against the ground in time with the witch's every step. Her guards followed, two of them dragging Alín between them.

Bachel stopped in front of Murtagh, and the staff-wielding acolytes closed in around him, forming a tight circle. Their chanting increased in volume again, a dozen voices drumming against his ears, a dozen minds battering against his consciousness.

"Why do you strive so?" Bachel said, her voice a low purr. "Surrender to me, my son. Join us. Join us in service to Azlagûr, and never again will you be tormented by doubt. Your place in the world will be secured, and your name will be sung for a thousand generations."

Join us, the cultists' thoughts chanted, a constant, maddening refrain.

Murtagh felt physically trapped, hemmed in too tightly to move or even to think. Bodies all about him and voices also, and every member of the group assaulting him in the same fashion until it seemed he was dealing with a single, massive creature determined to defeat and constrain him.

His hand trembled about Ithring's hilt. Even the idea of standing and striking was enough for the cultists to gain purchase on his consciousness. The weight of their minds pressed him down, flattening his being until his identity thinned and nearly vanished, and it was difficult to tell whose thoughts belonged to whom.

Yet even then, he refused to surrender. He was sovereign to himself, and he would sooner die than be otherwise.

A sudden movement: Alín twisted and wrenched free of her captors. She tore something from the neck of the man to her right, and then she sprang toward Murtagh.

Bachel shouted and pointed at Alín. A spear of fire leaped from the witch's clawed finger and struck Alín in the chest.

The fire passed harmlessly around her.

With a desperate cry, Alín collapsed against Murtagh with her arms around his shoulders. Her fingers fumbled against the back of his neck and—

Clarity. Sudden relief. The pressure upon his mind vanished, and he jumped to his feet.

A bird-skull amulet bounced against his chest.

Ithring sang through the air as he swung at the nearest cultist. The man had no wards to protect him; the sword's crimson blade passed through him with hardly any resistance.

The chanting dissolved into panicked discord.

Murtagh quick-stepped to the next Draumar and clove head from body. The cultists were crowded close to him, and he moved with ruthless efficiency among them, chopping at arms and legs and stabbing where he could, determined to keep them so busy they could not again immobilize him.

Bachel snarled. A torrent of flame shot from her to Murtagh. As with Alín, the flames wrapped around him without harm. Nor did the arcane fire touch two of the three Draumar behind him. However, the third cultist was the man from whom Alín had stolen the amulet, and him the fire harrowed, and his skin cracked and his hair vanished in a flare of orange sparks. He ran away screaming as a blanket of flames enveloped him.

In his blindness, the man ran off the edge of the great hole in the center of the room and fell into the black void, the flames trailing like flapping flags from his body.

Murtagh did not pause to watch, but hurried about his butchery, eager to put down the rest of Bachel's guards before they could regain the advantage.

Several of the cultists attempted to block or parry his attacks, and a few even struck at him in turn. But they were not trained warriors—not as he was—and he outfenced them with ease.

As he spun about, he saw Alín grappling with one of the cultists. The man struck her with his staff, and she fell to the stone, limp and unmoving.

The sight spurred Murtagh to even greater speed. By his hand,

Ithring traced a fatal cutting line from body to body, a bloody blur too fast to follow. The Draumar toppled like scythed stalks of grass.

A grinding rumble passed through the floor of the cavern. More dust sifted downward, while shards broke loose from the crystals and landed in a tinkling cascade throughout.

Murtagh stumbled and paused, arms outstretched.

Before the shaking subsided, Bachel came flying toward him—a dark shape piercing the curtains of dust, the ancient lance held before her.

He was quick to respond, but the witch was faster still, for she had the reflexes of an elf. The tip of Niernen struck him in the side and, to Murtagh's astonishment, punctured his shirt of mail and stabbed him between the ribs.

Bachel pulled the lance free, and he fell back, clutching his side. Fire burned in his chest, and blood spattered his lips as he coughed. Then he went cold with fear, and his thoughts grew hard and simple. The blade had touched a lung. It was a deadly wound, if not immediately fatal. He had seen such injuries on the battlefield. His lung would collapse or else fill with blood. Either way, he would die from lack of air unless he could heal himself.

The witch crowed. "You cannot triumph in this place, King-killer. Here I reign supreme, for I am Azlagûr's champion."

One of the acolytes charged at Murtagh from the side. He dodged a swing of the man's staff and ran him through the neck.

The cultist fell, gurgling and kicking.

Murtagh glanced about, expecting another ambush. There was no one left standing in the chamber, save him and Bachel. Dark slicks of blood coated the stone surrounding the crumpled bodies of the eleven fallen cultists—the twelfth having cast himself into the hole.

The witch raised her left hand and made a crushing motion. The bird-skull amulet about his neck cracked and disintegrated in a pale powder that ran down the front of his mail. As it did, the amulet's protection vanished, and he felt the witch launch a renewed assault upon his mind.

He steeled himself against the invasion.

A smile pulled Bachel's mouth further askew. "Did you think mine own charms could withstand me, Kingkiller?" As she spoke, she stalked toward him, as a great cat walking down its prey.

Despite his pain, Murtagh kept his mind calm, clear—emotionless. Panic would not help him. The witch lunged again, and he parried. The wound in his side made it impossible to move smoothly; he hitched as he deflected the Dauthdaert, which provided Bachel with ample opportunity to evade his counter-strike.

"This resistance will bring you only death! Kneel before me!"

"No."

Again the witch came at him, and Murtagh retreated around the gaping hole in the floor, attempting to maintain distance between the two of them while also drawing Bachel away from Alín's motionless form. Bright spots of blood fell from his side, leaving a trail of splattered blotches, as a line of red coins strewn behind him.

Never before had Murtagh felt such a sense of desperate struggle. Not even during the fight against Galbatorix and Shruikan. At least then there had been others to help. Here he was alone, without even Thorn, and the slightest mistake would mean death.

He might already be dead.

His breath wheezed through his punctured lung. Even now it was difficult to get enough air.

Forward strode Bachel, and she jabbed at him with furious intent: a half-dozen quick stabs, which left Murtagh with a small cut on his calf, just above his greaves.

His wards couldn't stop the Dauthdaert. No ward could. Galbatorix had claimed the lances were the only weapons dragons feared. Murtagh believed it. He had learned to fear them himself.

He feigned a stumble, and when Bachel moved to take

advantage of the supposed opening . . . he sidestepped and slashed underneath her outstretched arm.

Ithring glanced off a protective spell. Even without her armor, Bachel would have been well shielded against his blade.

Murtagh reassessed. He wasn't going to defeat the witch through force of arms, unless he could somehow break her magical defenses.

As Bachel twisted around to again face him, he drove his mind against the witch's with every mote of strength he could muster. The invisible assault was so strong, it stopped Bachel in her tracks. Her face went rigid with strain as she struggled to repulse his intruding thoughts.

Neither of them moved; they had not the attention to spare.

Bachel's mind was uncomfortably familiar to Murtagh. How many nights had she spent torturing him, trying to break his will in the room of horrors beneath the temple?

But this time it was different. He was himself again, and though he was no elf, his strength of mind was the match of anyone's, as was his determination. Bachel could not easily fend him off, and every triumph he had against her—no matter how small—further fueled his attack.

Still, the witch was strong and devious. Trying to restrain her consciousness was like trying to hold on to a beast that kept twisting and snapping. The slightest of openings allowed her to shift the attack back to Murtagh, and then he was on the defensive until he could again begin to pin her down.

Though they did not move, their breathing grew heavy, and sweat dripped from their faces and onto the floor. And Murtagh felt and heard the all-too-swift patter of blood falling from his side. Each inhalation was more difficult than the last.

Hard as it was, he made progress against Bachel. Every time she wriggled out of his mental grasp, the space he gave her to move was smaller, and bit by bit, he cinched tight the fetters he was binding about her being.

When Bachel realized what was happening, she panicked. He had expected as much. But instead of thrashing or stabbing or doing anything so reasonable, she lifted her hand and pointed at Murtagh, and to his shock he felt a surge of energy in her mind, and—

—jagged shards of ice shot up toward him from a suddenly frost-covered ground. The needle-sharp tips shattered against his wards, but the air on his lips grew painfully cold.

He snarled. The witch refused to adhere to the only rule of a spellcasters' duel: which was to *not* use magic until one had established control over their opponent's mind.

Murtagh's first instinct was to lash out with the most dire spells he knew—spells that would draw so much energy from him, they might kill him, but that also might be his only chance of stopping Bachel before she accomplished the deed herself. Still, he hesitated. Suicide held no appeal—and it occurred to him that Bachel was undisciplined, untrained. She didn't use the ancient language because she didn't know it, and she wasn't adhering to proper dueling protocol because she was likewise ignorant of it.

That didn't make his position any safer, but it did mean that if *he* used magic, she wasn't likely to react with suicidal force as would any trained magician.

At least, so he hoped.

Maintaining his pressure on her mind, he shouted, "Brisingr!" and allowed a stream of sparkling crimson flames to pour forth from the tip of Ithring. The spellfire flash-melted the icicles before wrapping around Bachel with intrusive intimacy.

He ended the spell to see the witch unharmed and laughing. "Bow, infidel!" she shouted.

Another tremor shook the ground. The distraction allowed Bachel to wrest her mind even further from his. Then she pointed Niernen at him, and he felt a sudden and drastic decrease in strength as his wards fended off an onslaught he neither felt nor saw.

"Thrysta!" was his reply, and the spell had a similar effect on Bachel; she slumped as his attack depleted her reserves.

They cast spells with wild abandon, each trying to overwhelm the other. Murtagh uttered words in the ancient language as quickly as he could: once he'd exhausted the most obvious means of defeating Bachel, quantity became more important than quality. Speed was of the essence.

In that, Bachel had the clear advantage. Murtagh had never truly appreciated the power of wordless magic before. The witch did not need to stop to think of *how* to phrase her enchantments; she simply willed them to be, and they were. Concepts that would have been tedious or impossible to express in the ancient language were a trivial matter for her, and indeed, many of the attacks she launched at him were of a sort he would have struggled to replicate.

The limitation for both of them, of course, was the energy at their disposal. Murtagh quickly depleted what remained in Ithring's ruby, leaving him with only the reserves of his body. And it was easy to overtax those.

Whether Bachel had hidden stores of energy herself, he didn't know. But her lips soon grew grey, and she tottered slightly as she advanced on him. Murtagh felt no better. Every spell consumed another portion of vitality, and a deadly lethargy dragged at his limbs and mind.

Between them flickered staggering blows of heat and cold, light and dark. Wind howled in brutal gusts, only to vanish a second later, replaced by tendrils of liquid night, or else invisible forces that sought to cut or crush or inveigle themselves into the fragile flesh of their foe. Once a double of Bachel appeared next to Murtagh—lifelike in every respect, even down to the pores of her skin—and the illusion so startled him, the real witch nearly managed to stab him again.

Murtagh had spent many an hour over many a day thinking of attacks and counters to use when fighting another magician. But none of the schemes he'd devised succeeded against Bachel. Nor were spells he'd used with success in the past effective. He even tried bypassing the witch's wards as Eragon had done with Galbatorix's: by helping her. That too failed.

Indirect attacks seemed to have the most effect. If a spell did not work upon Bachel herself but on the environment around her, then he was able to more consistently stress her wards and, sometimes, bypass them to a degree.

The realization gave him an idea.

He glanced around. On the other side of the clearing, an enormous white crystal leaned out over the open space, like a windblown tree near to falling. However much the crystal weighed, he guessed even Thorn would struggle to hold it up.

Fast as he could, he scoured his scrambled brain for the words he needed and then muttered, "Ílf kona thornessa thar fíthrenar, thae stenr jierda." It was a gamble, but just maybe . . .

Bachel snarled, her mouth pulling further off-center. "Your magic has no effect against me, Kingkiller. Abandon your pride and kneel! Do you not yet understand you cannot resist Azlagûr or His disciples? Surrender and serve!"

Another jet of black smoke shot up through the hole in the center of the cave.

"I would rather die." Murtagh began to retreat toward the leaning crystal. He affected a limp and moved as if his strength had nearly given out and he were about to pass out. It wasn't entirely an exaggeration.

"Bah!" Bachel's face distorted into a hateful visage as she strode toward him, head held high, planting the butt of Niernen firmly against the stone floor with every step.

Good. She was confident. Too confident.

As the witch neared, Murtagh cast another spell, this one an attempt to blind her by bending the light around her face. The magic succeeded, but only for a second, and then Bachel waved her hand, and her strength surged against his. He did not fight it.

629

He released the spell. But it had served its purpose to distract the witch, and to fulfill her expectation that he would continue to fight until the bitter end.

The soft radiance of the crystal appeared above him as he edged underneath it.

He paused there for a moment, just long enough for Bachel to close within a few yards of his position.

She strode forward, a cruel, triumphant smile upon her lips.

He stepped backward.

As Bachel's foot touched the stone directly underneath the crystal, a great CRACK sounded, and Murtagh's knees buckled as his spell exacted its price.

The crystal snapped off near the base and came crashing down.

Bachel started to jump out of the way, but—fast as she was— the huge trunk of faceted stone caught her across the hips and legs and drove her to the ground.

A lightning-like flash surrounded Bachel, and in the same instant, her wards gave out, and the thousands upon thousands of pounds of crystal crushed the lower half of her body.

The impact shook Murtagh off his feet. He landed on his backside with a painful jar, nearly deaf from the sound of the felling.

Bachel screamed. She was pinned, trapped, and butterfly wings of crimson blood spread about her. A piece of the crystal had struck her on the head and knocked her half mask askew. The repositioning seemed to have disrupted the mask's effect; no longer did the draconic glamour cloak Bachel in its dreadful aspect. She seemed merely a woman again—smaller and diminished, but still as angry as ever and far from dissuaded.

"Kverst!" Murtagh said, even as the witch cried in a malevolent tone, "*Stop!*"

Their spells clashed. One against the other, and neither he nor she was willing to give way. A black veil gathered around Murtagh's vision as the heat fled his body. Nevertheless, he dragged himself upright and took the two steps necessary to close the distance between Bachel and himself.

The witch's face was twisted with effort, her grey lips pulled back in a snarl. Her neck was corded, and veins stood out like tangled rope beneath her skin. She still held Niernen, and as Murtagh approached, she drew back her arm and stabbed with the lance.

He had not the strength or speed to evade.

The tip of the Dauthdaert glanced off his helm with a metallic squeal, and his head snapped back as he absorbed the force of the impact.

Then he was inside Bachel's reach. She could no longer attack him with the spear.

Their eyes met, an instant of calm amid a storm, and he saw in her gaze recognition and, he thought, acceptance. He felt a sense of closeness with her, as if she were as dear to him as Tornac or Thorn, for the arrival of death destroyed all boundaries and pretenses.

With his last dram of strength, he swung Ithring. A single, perfect blow, which struck Bachel upon the crown of her head and split her skull.

Her opposition vanished. His spell, *kverst*, took effect, and the witch fell away from him, pulling Ithring's hilt from his hand.

Cold blackness washed over Murtagh, and the cave tilted around him as he collapsed, unconscious.

631

CHAPTER IV

✦ ✦ ✦ ✦ ✦ ✦

Islingr

A deep, grinding rumble and the sound of uprushing smoke were the first things Murtagh was aware of.

Then pain, and a cold so intense it went to his marrow, and an immense weakness. He needed food and drink and time to recover. None of which he was about to get.

He opened his eyes. The domed ceiling was dark with smoke. It had thickened since he'd passed out.

Setting his teeth, he rolled onto his right side—where it hurt less—and pushed himself into a kneeling position.

He looked at what remained of Bachel: her lower half pinned beneath the crystalline rubble, her neck twisted at an unnatural angle, Ithring still embedded in her skull, honey eyes wide and lifeless. He felt nothing, thought nothing, only looked at what he had done. It was important.

From far above, he felt Thorn touch his mind, a distant yet urgent contact. As Murtagh's strength ebbed, their thoughts merged, and for an instant, the differences between them dissolved, and he beheld the world as did Thorn:

The two-leg-nest turned below as he dipped his wings toward the fang-tooth-sunset-mountains. Many of the stone-wood-shells were broken and on hot-tongue-fire, and the flames cast flickering shadows on the surrounding hills. White-eye-crows screamed, and goats too, and a steady stream of bad-dream-two-legs fled on foot along the banks of the clear-water, heading toward the Bay of Fundor.

His wings hurt from many arrow-bite-holes, but the pain was of no matter.

Concern came from Thorn. The dragon gave him a plea and a command cojoined: *Heal yourself!*

I—

Another rumble shook Murtagh, and from the hole in the center of the cave came sounds as rock being crushed and broken. Apprehension gathered in him, and it occurred to him that haste might be called for.

Getting to his feet took a concentrated effort of mind and body, and he nearly fainted again as he rose. He stood for a moment, swaying, until his vision cleared and his balance steadied. He'd dropped his shield at some point. Picking it up seemed more trouble than it was worth.

The eleven Draumar lay on the other side of the hole, their bodies fallen like broken dolls amid the broad, oil-slick splay of blood. There too lay Alín, still motionless.

Murtagh! Thorn's frustration was palpable.

"Can't. Alín. Have to . . ."

Pressing a hand against his wound, he stumbled over to the witch. He braced his left foot against her head and pulled on Ithring. The blade stuck, and he had to yank twice more.

Distaste and pity made Murtagh turn away from her remains. "May you dream forever," he muttered.

More grinding sounded from beneath the hole, and another jet of black smoke shot up through the opening.

With halting steps, he made his way around to Alín. He let out a cry as he dropped to a knee next to her and the jolt sent pain through his side.

Blood matted the woman's hair, but she still breathed.

Murtagh placed Ithring on the ground and pressed his palm against Alín's head. "Waíse heill," he whispered.

His vision flickered as the spell took effect. He swayed and fell sideways, barely catching himself before his head hit stone. His eyes drifted shut.

. . .

Air whistled past his head as he dove toward burnt-black-ground, legs tucked close to chest and belly. He landed with a crash of thunder. The horned-two-leg-no-sword turned to look at him, surprised, afraid.

Help.

Horned-two-leg understood and ran to him. Climbed onto his back. He wolf-ran toward foot of grey-rock-mountain.

. . .

Murtagh started as he came to, disoriented.

By his knees, Alín moaned, and her eyelids fluttered.

More sounds of crashing stone emanated from the hole, as if the mountain were gnawing itself to pieces, and there was a great grinding commotion painful to hear.

The ground shuddered beneath Murtagh as he grasped Ithring and forced himself to his feet. He coughed. Gobs of blood sprayed forth, wet and sticky.

He wanted to also heal himself, but he had not the strength. Not yet. But he knew that if he did not attend to his stab wound soon, he would lose the opportunity.

A violent tremor made him stagger. Throughout the cave, crystals cracked and shattered, crashing against the ground with bell-like notes: a cacophony of disjointed music.

Apprehension shaded into fear as Murtagh tried to imagine what could cause the mountains to shake. Bachel was dead, so . . . Was there some reality to the beliefs of the Draumar, something that went beyond the foul fumes that seeped from the rocks surrounding Nal Gorgoth?

He fixed his gaze on the hole. He had to know.

Ithring's tip dragged against the stone as he started toward the gaping void. Every step cost him, and he felt increasing reluctance to look over the stony lip and see what lay below.

But still, he crept closer, his whole body taut with pain and dread.

The ground spasmed beneath him. He pushed Ithring away as he fell onto his side. Hot pain clamped about his limbs, and his vision went white and then black.

. . .

The mouth of grey-rock-mountain yawned before him. He hesitated. Inside lay pain and fear and cold-net-chains and close binding. But Rider-Murtagh was in danger, needed help.

He stepped forward, only to stop and whine. The fear was too great. His stomach felt sick-bad-food-burn.

"What do you wait for?" bellowed horned-two-leg.

He snarled and roared and then shook his head and spun away from the loathsome hole. Two bounding leaps, and he again took to the air and rose circling above the hard-gaping-mountainside.

And he hated himself for it.

. . .

Murtagh gasped. Where was he?

A fist-sized piece of crystal skittered across the ground near his head. He flinched. Using Ithring as a crutch, he pushed himself to his feet, holding his side. Thorn wasn't coming. The thought was nearly as painful as his wound. He wished he could soothe the dragon's distress, but there was a greater worry at hand. Still, the thought remained, a barbed needle in his mind.

He dragged himself forward, desperate, gasping.

A prismatic shimmer passed across Murtagh's vision. For a moment, he felt he was elsewhere, else*when*, on a withered plain scoured by endless wind—

He shook his head. *No.* With the last of his strength, he staggered across the final few yards to the hole and collapsed on his knees before it.

He peered over the rim, wary.

Blackness yawned below, soft as dragon wings and with an impression of immense depth. At first his eyes could find no purchase in the void, but then he discerned motion, barely visible, as of a great, shadowy river flowing past.

Smoke pillared up in a roaring column.

Despite his best effort, the hot cloud enveloped him, stinging his eyes and clogging his nose and throat.

He fell back and struck the stone, and again his surroundings deserted him.

. . .

Horned-two-leg was shouting at him and beating against his shoulder. He paid the two-leg no mind as he kept his gaze fixed on the mouth in the mountain. Rider-Murtagh was hurting, and that made him hurt.

The two-leg shouted louder, and this time, he heard the words: "What manner of beast are you? Are you dragon or crawling worm?! Turn back! Go!"

His scales bristled, and he roared as outrage fired his anger. Then he tucked his wings, dove, and landed on break-bone-ground at the foot of the mountain.

Before his nerve could fail him, he ran forward into black-moist-egg-smell-hole.

Grey-stone-walls surrounded. Air thick, choked. The space was too small, not move, not think, too close. Like prison in Urû'baen. Dragonkiller bending over him, showing little teeth, hard-iron-rings, sting of whips . . .

He could not continue. He lashed stump-tail and whimpered.

Then horned-two-leg stroked the side of his neck and said, "Your Rider needs you, dragon. Think of him. Do for him, not yourself. For other we can be strong."

The words sank into his mind, settled there. He clung to them with desperate strength. Rider-Murtagh needed help. And Rider-Murtagh had always helped him.

There was only one choice. It was the only choice there had ever really been, but he had feared to truly face it until that moment.

The first step was impossible.

The second was nearly so.

The third was only horribly hard.

The fourth came quickly, and then he was crawling forward like four-legs-no-wings, scenting for prey. The cave-fear did not leave, still felt like hot-blood-heart would break, but he could move. He could fight. He could help.

He roared again.

. . .

Bitterness coated the back of Murtagh's throat, sharp, acrid, poisonous. He came to, coughing and hacking, and each purging convulsion caused him agony through his chest.

He blinked back tears, barely able to focus. Thorn was on his way. The realization brought as much fear as pride and relief. If what was in the hole could hurt Thorn, Murtagh wouldn't be able to protect him.

He rolled back onto his knees and again peered over the rim of the abyss, dreading what he might see. As before, he had a dim sense of ponderous motion within the murky, smoke-filled space beneath the mountain.

He reached out with his thoughts. No living thing lay below. And yet . . . He widened his search, opening his mind and spreading his consciousness as far as he could through the deepness. Wider and wider he went, until he was spread as thin as a film of soap, and he felt . . .

He felt a mind.

A mind as vast as the mountains themselves. A consciousness so far removed from his own, he might as well have been an ant clinging to the side of an unimaginably large beast. The thoughts of the mind were cold, slow-moving things—dark islands of ice drifting along a listless current. Pervading all was a sense of dire intent, an ancient, calculated malevolence that pulsed outward like the beat of a monstrous heart. From the mind he felt hunger, immense and endless, and a coiled rage that knew no bounds.

637

Shocks of freezing fear shot through Murtagh's limbs.

At his touch, the mind stirred, and the tremors and rumbles beneath the cave intensified, and Murtagh felt the mind turning toward him, focusing the enormity of its consciousness upon the single point of his being. When it found him, when it had him within his grip, he knew he would be helpless.

He did not think. He did not wait. He drew upon what was left of his strength and cried out the spell he had used once before, on the windswept plains between Gil'ead and the Spine: "Vindr thrysta un líjothsa athaerum!"

The air above the glowing crystals rippled like glass, and in an instant, all the light in the cave bent into the hole and flash-formed a single bar of blinding, white-hot illumination: a fiery lance forged from the sun itself.

A blast of superheated air struck Murtagh with the force of a thousand hammers. It slammed him into the ground, and he felt his organs shift as the world exploded beneath him.

❖

He blinked.

Everything had gone cold and silent. Ash drifted down from the stone ceiling, soft grey flakes that fell like snow.

He pushed himself onto his forearms.

The hole in the center of the cave was twice as large as before, and the edges glowed a dull red. Through it and below . . . nothing was visible. No hints of movement beside the falling flakes. *Empty.*

A piece of rock dropped from the ceiling and bounced across the floor several feet from him. It made no sound he could hear.

He tried to stand, but his arms and legs would not hold his weight.

He tried to reach out with his mind, but that too was beyond him. His throat was tight, and he felt as if he were choking. Darkness feathered the edges of his vision.

He tried.

He tried to try. . . .

He couldn't . . .

As awareness slipped away like water between fingers, the stone beneath him shook with the hurried tread of something huge and heavy approaching. . . .

His last thought was one of regret. *If only . . .*

~~~~~~~~~~~~~~~~~~ ❖ ~~~~~~~~~~~~~~~~~~

Glittering redness moved above him, and white jags that resolved into claws and teeth.

Thorn. He tried to rise but had not the strength.

Then the horned shape of Uvek was kneeling next to him. The Urgal muttered in his guttural tongue and pressed the cold hardness of the blackstone against Murtagh's brow.

Welcome relief as the pain in his ribs faded, but his breathing felt no easier, and he remained as weak and helpless as before.

The Urgal's voice sounded as if muffled by woolen batting: "He has too much blood in lungs, not enough in body. You must take him to one of your healers, dragon. And quickly too."

There was jostling and shifting then, and the shapes of the chamber tilted as the Urgal picked him up and climbed onto Thorn's back.

Murtagh struggled against the Urgal's hold, wanting to speak, but the words would not form. Frustrated, he groaned, for there was something that needed saying, something important.

The world rose beneath him as Thorn stood, and his eyes rolled back.

The familiar pounding rhythm of Thorn's trotting jarred Murtagh to wakefulness.

A dark stone ceiling swept past overhead, faster than a man could run. Deep booms echoed through the tunnel—as if from an enormous drum—and alarmingly loud cracks, and the mountain shook about them.

Flakes of stone fell as thick as snow.

"Faster!" growled Uvek as stones clattered about his head and horns.

~~~~~~~~~~~~~~~~~~ ❖ ~~~~~~~~~~~~~~~~~~

Flames billowed out before them as Thorn swept the interior of a cave toothed with stalactites and stalagmites. Fingerrats in their hundreds squealed as the fire seared them. The vomitous stench of burnt hair filled the cave.

More of the grotesque creatures swarmed up Thorn's sides. Uvek swung at them with a hammer-like fist, and they fell broken to the beslimed ground.

Thorn snapped and tore, and then he was moving forward again.

Amid the shrieking of the fingerrats, Murtagh remembered what needed saying. "Alín," he murmured, but no one seemed to hear or care.

~~~~~~~~~~~~~~~~~~ ❖ ~~~~~~~~~~~~~~~~~~

Time had little meaning. He was awake, but reality faded in and out around him: a series of disjointed impressions that gave him no sense of place or progress, as if he had been and would forever be caught upon Thorn's back, subject to events without reason or explanation.

He felt as if he were choking. Every breath was a struggle, and when he failed the struggle, darkness would encroach, and another island of reality would wink out.

In his brief moments of awareness, he kept trying to talk to Thorn, but he could not seem to catch the dragon's attention, and the failure was greatly distressing.

He saw caves and tunnels without end. Vaulted chambers filled with rotting mushrooms. Shadow spiders darting about the creviced stone, avoiding Thorn's seeking fire. Pillars of crystal and walls of strange carvings that looked older than even the dwarves' ancient works.

The paths Thorn followed were different from those Murtagh had, and he did not recognize their surroundings.

The mountain continued to shake. Twice he heard huge falls of stone, and Uvek shouting, "Turn, turn!" And always Thorn's rasping breath, as if the dragon himself were struggling to breathe.

~~~~~~~~~~~~~~~~~~ ❖ ~~~~~~~~~~~~~~~~~~

The faintest light appeared above them, orange and sooty, as a bonfire high upon a hill. Murtagh squinted, tried to raise his head.

A line of rough-hewn steps ascended the stone face before Thorn, rising toward the ruddy mouth of the cave. Salvation. Freedom.

Uvek bellowed something, and Thorn raced forward, grunting as he scrambled up out of the depths of the mountain. Hollow *booms* echoed throughout the widening cavern, louder than ever before—deafening crashes of thunder that vibrated through Murtagh's bones.

He gasped and coughed. Clotted blood stopped his throat; he couldn't cast it clear, couldn't get the air he needed.

Steps shattered underneath Thorn's weight. The cavern shuddered, and boulders plummeted from the raw ceiling and cracked and bounded around them. A piece of stone as large as a cart glanced off Thorn's left shoulder, knocking the dragon to one side. He lurched, and Murtagh's head whipped around at the impact.

Stars spangled Murtagh's vision as black gauze wrapped close around the edges.

The whole cave seemed to be collapsing. Entire sheets of stone fractured free and tipped downward until they disintegrated into a shower of splinters and tumbling rubble. The sound was numbing, staggering, impossible to comprehend.

"Faster, dragon!" Uvek shouted.

The clots in Murtagh's throat slipped the wrong way, and he inhaled them. The breath stopped in his chest. He couldn't cough, couldn't make a sound, couldn't . . .

His head snapped back as Thorn leaped forward again. The mouth of the cave was shrinking as the ceiling collapsed, the orange light of freedom diminishing.

A particularly large boulder crashed down in front of them, and Thorn slipped and fell forward onto his chest.

The impact was brutal. Murtagh's vision went white, his chest seized, and he felt himself sinking into oblivion even as thunder descended around them.

No! he thought.

The world ceased to be.

REUNION

~~~~~~~~~~~~~~~~~ ❖ ~~~~~~~~~~~~~~~~~

CHAPTER I

✦ ✦ ✦ ✦ ✦ ✦ ✦

Acceptance

He was warm, and a soft weight lay upon him, holding him down with comforting closeness. That much he knew.

A haze of milky brightness formed in front of him. He blinked, unable to make out any details within the smear of light.

It seemed important to rise, but his limbs refused to respond. He lay limp and slack, save for his breathing.

The flow of air into his lungs was smooth and unlabored.

Again he tried to move. His arms stirred slightly, and a small groan escaped him.

A hand—dark and smooth—descended to press against his chest.

"Stay. You were badly hurt. Rest while you can." The voice was gentle, reserved, but still firm.

He knew the voice. How many times had he heard it in his dreams? How many times had he yearned (and feared) to hear it again? . . . Yet he wondered: Was he dreaming still?

Once more he struggled to sit, but the effort defeated him, and he sank back into softness. Despite his inner protest, his eyelids descended, and the waiting darkness embraced him.

And he knew no more.

~~~~~~~~~~~~~~~~~ ❖ ~~~~~~~~~~~~~~~~~

The golden light of late afternoon fanned across the plaster ceiling. A sweet smell of flowers pervaded the air, and water—as of a small brook—trickled nearby, while soft coos of drowsy doves sounded among rustling leaves.

A gentle breeze stirred a pair of white muslin curtains.

Murtagh lay beneath a heavy blanket, on a large four-poster bed. He felt no desire to move. His whole body was relaxed to the point of immobility.

A frown formed as he continued to stare at the ceiling. He *knew* that ceiling. He had grown up looking at just such a ceiling, and seeing it again made him feel as if nothing of the past few years had really happened.

He almost believed it.

Ilirea. I'm in Ilirea. His stomach knotted at the thought of again facing . . . her. *But how?*

He started to rise and heard, "Ah, ah! Please take care, King-killer."

His eyes widened, and he turned his head to see a young woman sitting next to the bed. Flaxen hair fixed in a neat braid, and a simple servant's gown of green. Pale skin surrounding eyes the color of a summer sky. A ripening bruise and a pair of scabbed scratches marred her left cheek and temple, but otherwise she appeared fresh-faced and well fed, if somewhat worried.

"Alín," he breathed.

Behind her, Thorn sat crouched by the sill of a great dormer window, large enough for the dragon to pass through. Even as Murtagh saw him, the dragon lifted himself off the floor and stalked over dwarven rugs to the end of the bed.

Alín stood and smoothed her dress. "You must be famished, Kingkiller. Rest here, and I will fetch you something."

Before Murtagh could object, she hurried from the room, her skirt swishing with each step. The chamber's heavy oaken doors creaked as they opened and shut. In the hall outside, Murtagh glimpsed a pair of guards standing at attention.

Thorn extended his neck until his nose touched Murtagh's outstretched hand. *You live,* the dragon said.

As do you. . . . You came for me. Into the cave.

Thorn hummed, and his eyes glittered with ruby light. *Of course. You needed me.*

Tears threatened to spill down Murtagh's cheeks. *Thank you.*

Thorn dipped his head. *You will never again have to crawl into a cave alone. Not so long as you are my Rider and I am your dragon.* And then Thorn spoke his true name, and Murtagh heard and felt the difference in the dragon's self. His heart near to broke with relief, and pride too, that after so very long, his closest friend and bonded partner had finally won out over his fear.

Then tears did fall from Murtagh's eyes, and he wrapped his arms around Thorn's head and held him tightly. *Ah, that makes me happy. There is something you should know as well.*

Oh?

I am not who or what I was either. And Murtagh spoke his true name, in all its flawed extent, so his very essence was laid bare.

Thorn's inner eyelids *snicked* closed, and he gently licked Murtagh's arm. *You are free.*

We both are. . . . I'm sorry. I should have been more careful in taking us to Nal Gorgoth.

A slight growl sounded in Thorn's chest. *The deed is done, the fight is ended, and we still have our freedom. It is not so bad.*

Grateful, Murtagh laid his chest against Thorn's scaled brow and savored their closeness. All felt right between them, and that, more than anything, mattered.

At last, he released his hold on Thorn and looked around the room.

It was one of the large chambers in the northern wing of the citadel, where the structure had been relatively undamaged by Galbatorix's explosive self-immolation over a year ago. Murtagh vaguely remembered the room being used by the head of the royal mint, but he couldn't recall for sure.

Then he looked down at himself. A white linen shirt hung upon him, smooth against his back. No bandages were wrapped about his chest, and although he felt sore and tired, he wasn't in pain.

When did— he started to say.

The doors to the chamber swung open, and Alín entered, carrying a platter with bread, fruit, and cheese, as well as an earthen pitcher alongside a crystal chalice. She walked around Thorn, placed the platter on the small side table next to the bed, and again seated herself.

Then Alín took the pitcher and poured watered wine into the chalice, which she handed to him. "Here. A drink will do you some good, my Lord."

Murtagh obeyed. She was right; his throat was painfully dry.

"Four days," said Alín. "That is how long you have been in Ilirea, Kingkiller." She smiled slightly. "I thought you might wish to know."

He placed the empty chalice on the side table. "It would be best if you refrain from calling me Kingkiller here, Alín. As a title, it will earn me no favors."

Her cheeks colored, and she ducked her head. "My apologies."

"That's not . . . How did we get here? How did *you*? I thought you were left behind in Oth Orum."

"No, not quite," said Alín. "Uvek found me and had me climb onto Thorn behind him. I was with you the entire time."

"I didn't see you."

She shook her head. "You wouldn't have, my Lord. You were delirious from your wound."

Murtagh glanced around. He half expected to see the Urgal step out from behind a tapestry. "And Uvek? Is he here?"

No, said Thorn, and Murtagh could tell that the dragon was speaking to both of them. *He went to help his people, but he bid us welcome to his hearth and home whenever we might so wish.*

A pang of regret surprised Murtagh. He would have liked to thank the Urgal in person. "I see."

From her skirt Alín produced a small length of knotted rope, rough, brown, and frayed, but formed with obvious deftness. She handed it to Murtagh. Puzzled, he turned it over.

She said, "Uvek gave this to me that I might keep it safe for you. He said that it means *brother* in his tongue."

"Brother." Murtagh glanced from the knotted rope to the inside of his left wrist. There, the cut that marked his blood oath with Uvek had been healed. But not entirely. A small white scar remained as a permanent reminder. *A new scar to go with an old one.* It was not an unpleasant thought.

With a sense of gratitude, he tucked the knotted rope into his shirt. He knew he would keep it safe for the rest of his life. Family, it seemed, came in many forms, and odd as it was, he thought of the Urgal as such. Then he returned his attention to Alín. "You were very brave in Oth Orum. And also before. If not for you, none of us would have escaped."

"You're too kind, my Lord." She pressed her lips together. "Bachel betrayed our beliefs. Even if she was being true to Azlagûr, even if she was still serving His will, I wanted no part in it."

"Still, what you did wasn't easy. Thank you."

Her cheeks colored again. "What you had to endure was far harder, my Lord."

Uncomfortable, Murtagh changed tack. "Have you been well here? Have they treated you fairly?" *Has she?* But he did not voice the thought.

Alín nodded, serious. "Oh yes. Very well."

"And is Alagaësia everything you hoped it would be?"

"Everything and more. Only . . ."

"Only what?"

Her expression grew troubled. "I worry about the Draumar. I know Bachel is dead, but a new Speaker will be chosen, and . . ."

Murtagh thought he knew the true source of her unease. He shared it. "And what?"

She looked at him with open earnestness. "I fear . . ." She swallowed and lowered her voice to a whisper. "What if Azlagûr is truly risen?"

A chill crept into Murtagh's bones. "Worry not. Thorn and I will see to it the Draumar are dealt with. As for Azlagûr—"

A creak of iron hinges interrupted him as the chamber's doors swung open—pushed by a pair of handmaidens—and Nasuada strode into the room.

As always, the sight of her had a physical effect on Murtagh: his pulse quickened, and his muscles tensed, and he felt an apprehensive gladness. The light from the windows framed Nasuada's face as she gazed at him with a serious, watchful expression. Her dress was red velvet with gold trim—as fine a garment as had ever graced Galbatorix's court—with sleeves tailored short to show the ridged scars on her forearms. And unlike when he'd last seen her, in the courtyard before the half-destroyed citadel in Ilirea, a shining, beautifully crafted crown rested upon her brow.

Old habits made Murtagh pull back the blanket and descend from the bed to stand upon unsteady legs. He was, he was relieved to see, wearing soft trousers. He bowed as well as he could. "Your Majesty." The words were an unsettling echo of the formalities he had observed with Galbatorix.

"Murtagh." Her expression was impossible for him to read. Then she gestured at her servants. "Leave us now."

The handmaidens curtsied and departed. Likewise, Alín rose from her chair and, with a slight apologetic glance at Murtagh, hurried from the room.

The doors closed with heavy finality.

You do not expect me to depart, hmm? said Thorn, sharing his thoughts with Nasuada.

The queen's expression didn't change. "Of course not. You are a welcome guest, Thorn."

Murtagh wondered if the same were true of him.

A spate of lightheadedness caused him to sway, and Nasuada said, "Sit before you fall over."

With some gratitude, he lowered himself onto the edge of the bed.

He watched, wary, as Nasuada approached with perfectly measured steps and settled into Alín's recently vacated seat. "You should be careful. It was no sure thing that you would live. You were fever-blind and raving when Thorn brought you here. My spellcasters had to labor long and hard to save you."

He winced. The attentions of Du Vrangr Gata were hardly what he would have wanted, but then, he was alive, and for that he was grateful. "Then I am in their debt. And yours." Later, he would have to use the Name of Names to remove whatever unwanted enchantments the queen's pet magicians might have placed upon him. *As well as Bachel,* he thought with sudden alarm.

Nasuada inclined her head. "The work was not entirely theirs. I am told"—her eyes flickered toward Thorn—"that your companion, the Urgal Uvek, used a charm that was sufficient to keep you from dying on the spot."

"He did a lot more than just that." Murtagh spoke his next words with care. "Who else knows that Thorn and I are in Ilirea?"

She turned and plucked a dried apricot from the platter on the side table and took the smallest bite.

"If you are asking whether the people of the city are currently assembled outside these walls, clamoring for your head . . . you may rest assured, they are not. Thorn was careful in his approach. He found my mind, at night, and I saw to it that no one might hear his wings as he brought you to this very room." She waited as he took another drink. "Only I, my handmaids, and a select few of my spellcasters know you are here, and they have all sworn to me oaths of utmost secrecy in the ancient language."

That made Murtagh feel better. But only a bit. "And what of

you?" he asked. "Do you wish to claim my head, Your Majesty?" He trembled slightly, and he was not sure why. He hoped it went unnoticed.

The queen took her time answering. "That depends." Her bearing softened somewhat then, and for the first time, a deep well of concern appeared within her eyes. The sight of it left him unbalanced. He was not used to such consideration. "Murtagh . . . what happened? Thorn has given me some of it, but not all he said made sense, and Alín insisted it was not her place to say. I would have the rest from you. The truth."

"The truth . . ." Murtagh reached over, took the platter of food from the side table, and placed it on his lap. "If I may."

"As you will."

He tore off a piece of bread and paired it with the hard sheep cheese. He chewed without thinking, without feeling, simply seeking the strength to say what was needed.

Nasuada waited without complaint. She contained a stillness not unlike Uvek's: a patient, careful watchfulness, as of a hunter observing a dangerous animal.

Murtagh knew he was that animal.

He swallowed. "Did you receive my letter? I sent you one from Gil'ead."

Nasuada nodded. "It arrived two days before you did. I must say, it raised more questions than it answered."

"Ah. Well then . . . Where to start?" He started at the beginning, on the day they had parted—on the day Galbatorix had died—when Umaroth had warned him of brimstone and fire and not delving too deeply in the depths. He spoke slowly, haltingly, at first, finding it difficult to frame things with the proper words. Nasuada did not press him, and the words came more easily as he went. At least for a time. He told her of his suspicions and the reasons he'd pursued them, and how that pursuit had led him to Ceunon and thence to Gil'ead.

He told her of all that had occurred in Gil'ead, of Carabel and Muckmaw and Captain Wren and the traitors within Du Vrangr Gata—of Lyreth and the tangle box, and the destruction that had resulted thereof.

Nasuada listened without interruption, but he saw her expression alternately soften and harden, and often he could not tell why.

Then of his and Thorn's great flight north, he spoke. Of the mountains and the herds of red deer and the villages of the Urgals. He drank and ate as he could, but his appetite deserted him when it came time to speak of Nal Gorgoth.

Murtagh faltered then, and the words again grew difficult. Yet he persisted. He spoke unsparingly of the village, and Bachel, and his mistakes that resulted in the witch ensnaring and imprisoning both him and Thorn.

He made no attempt to hide what had happened to them while in Bachel's thrall. He told Nasuada every sordid detail, and as he spoke of their torture, she placed her hand on his, and the understanding in her eyes caused him even more pain than his recollection.

"You must hate me for what I did to you," he said in a thick voice.

"At first, but only at first. It wasn't your choice."

He squeezed her fingers, a silent thanks. Still, his guilt remained. "I don't know how you endured. I . . . I couldn't."

"It helped to know you cared."

Tears again filled his eyes, and he looked out the window, unable to bear Nasuada's gaze. "She broke me. And there was nothing I could do about it. I . . ." His voice hitched, and his throat tightened like a clenched fist.

Then he spoke of the raid on the Orthroc. The images that filled his head were worse than any nightmare, and when he attempted to explain whom he had slain—attempted to describe the fallen bodies, large and small—his emotions burst forth, and he wept openly, without shame.

Nasuada stirred, and he felt her hand upon the back of his head, and he bent toward her as his grief ran its course. She held him, and her presence was a balm for his soul.

In time, he found the strength to continue.

~~~~~~~~~~~~~~~~~~ ❖ ~~~~~~~~~~~~~~~~~~

"Do you think that the creature you felt was Azlagûr?"

They were sitting by the dormer window, looking out over a small atrium with an ash tree growing in the center and an artful stream that wound among beds of perennials. Rock doves roosted among the branches of the ash, and a cheeky red-tailed squirrel ran up and down the trunk, chattering at every movement above and below.

After speaking for so long, Murtagh couldn't bear to remain in the bed, so they had moved to the sill, next to Thorn. Murtagh's legs had been stiff and weak, but Nasuada had helped him, without comment, by wrapping an arm tight around his waist.

Her scent was completely different from the stench of brimstone: sweet and clean and healthy. It made it hard for him to concentrate.

"I don't know. If nothing else, I believe it was what the Draumar *believe* to be Azlagûr."

Nasuada looked out over the walls of the atrium toward the western horizon. The sun was setting, and the buildings of Ilirea cast long shadows back toward the citadel. The serenity of the city stood in stark contrast to how it had last appeared to him: covered in smoke, lit with fire, and echoing with the discordant clamor of battle. Not unlike his final visions of Nal Gorgoth. . . .

"Do you think you killed it?" she asked.

"I hope so, but . . . I fear not."

She looked back at him, and he saw his concern mirrored in her eyes. "How could a creature so large go undiscovered for so long?"

"I'm not sure it has. The Draumar know of it, and the dragons too, it seems. Some of them, at least." He scratched his beard. It was getting longer than he liked. "I need to talk with Eragon, to warn him. And I want to question Umaroth and find out exactly what he and the other Eldunarí know. I'd ask you to send a courier on my behalf, but I wouldn't trust this to a scroll or to someone's mind. Besides, a courier would be too slow, and— No, once I'm fit, Thorn and I will go to Mount Arngor."

"That may not be necessary."

"Oh?"

Nasuada gestured toward the main part of the citadel. "Before he left, Eragon enchanted a scrying mirror, that I might communicate with him more easily than by courier. He did the same for all the kings and queens of the land."

Murtagh allowed himself a rueful smile. "Of course he did. He's getting clever, that one. . . . Have you spoken to him of me?"

"Not since you arrived."

He nodded. "I see. Well, perhaps your mirror will suffice. I would prefer to avoid having to fly all the way out to Arngor. Not if this *creature* is loose in Alagaësia."

Concern darkened her expression. "How great a threat do you really think it is?"

"I don't know, but . . ." He shook his head. "If even half of what I saw is true, Azlagûr may be more dangerous than Galbatorix ever was."

Nasuada pressed her lips together, and for a few minutes, they watched the sunset in silence. She, of all people, had a true understanding of Galbatorix's cruelty and depravity, and she had witnessed firsthand the staggering extent of his power. The king had humbled them all. It was only through the greatest of luck—and not a little skill—that they had overcome him.

She turned to Thorn. "What of you? Did you feel anything of this Azlagûr?"

No. I was too busy razing Nal Gorgoth, and by the time I found Murtagh, the caves were empty of all but vermin.

"The thing to do," said Murtagh, "is to find El-harím and the barrows of Anghelm and wherever else black smoke might rise from the ground. Perhaps we will chance upon Azlagûr at one of them, or at least we may learn more of note."

"El-harím," mused Nasuada. "How strange."

"You know of it?"

"A name from an old rhyme." She paused for a moment, considering, and then recited:

In El-harím, there lived a man, a man with yellow eyes.
To me, he said, "Beware the whispers, for they whisper lies.
Do not wrestle with the demons of the dark,
Else upon your mind they'll place a mark;
Do not listen to the shadows of the deep,
Else they haunt you even when you sleep."

The words struck Murtagh with unexpected familiarity. At first he could not place them, but then he remembered: the Hall of the Soothsayer, when Nasuada had allowed him to touch her mind, that he might prove his intentions. "Ah! You used that poem to shield your thoughts."

Nasuada nodded, and he could see a shadow of the memory in her eyes. "I learned the rhyme as a child in Surda, but I cannot recall anything of its origin."

He made a wry face. "I only caught snatches of it before. I'd forgotten until now." He shook his head, grim. "Yet more proof that something of the Draumar has been known for many a year. If we'd but had the eyes to see and the ears to listen, we could have discovered their existence long ago."

"Your mention of eyes makes me wonder," said Nasuada. "I don't suppose Grieve's were yellow?"

"No. That they were not. One thing is certain—the Draumar need rooting out, and the children they've stolen need rescuing. I also want to have a talk with Captain Wren and put a stop to the whole business with the werecat younglings, whatever that is. As soon as I'm able, we'll set out."

Nasuada lifted her chin. The diamond set in the center of her crown glinted in the sunset's ruddy light. "You forget, I have not given you leave to depart Ilirea."

Murtagh studied her, uncertain what game she was playing. In a casual-seeming way, he allowed his gaze to wander around the chamber. Were there soldiers or spellcasters hidden behind the walls? He nearly went searching with his mind, but then decided he didn't want to know. If Nasuada were going to turn against him, he would rather leave that for the future. Even so . . .

Thorn, were you able to retrieve Ithring when you rescued me?

I was.

Did you bring it here?

I did.

Murtagh looked back at Nasuada and, in a bland tone, said, "I don't happen to see my sword. Do you know where it is?"

A slight smile touched Nasuada's lips. "I thought you might ask." From within a fold of her dress, she produced a small silver bell that she rang twice before putting it away.

Once more the oak doors swung open, and Alín entered. Crosswise in her arms, she carried Ithring and Niernen. And not just them. Atop the weapons lay the cloth-wrapped bundle that Murtagh recognized as containing Glaedr's scale, and beside it, a familiar dented brass goblet.

Alín brought the items to Murtagh. One by one, she handed them to him, and then curtsied to Nasuada and said, "Your Majesty."

She started to depart, but Nasuada held out her hand in a

commanding gesture. "A moment, Alín. Tell me, have you had any cause for complaint here in Ilirea?"

Alín made a slight curtsy. "Oh no, Your Majesty. Not at all."

"And would you be willing to accept me as your queen and to serve as one of my faithful subjects?"

Murtagh caught a quick, uncertain glance from Alín, but then she said, "If you will have me, Your Majesty."

"Excellent," said Nasuada with aplomb. "Then it is settled. To-morrow you may swear to me formally at court. However, there is another matter. Murtagh has told me much of your history, and it seems to me you are a person of uncommon spirit and fortitude. It would be foolish of me, as queen, to overlook such virtues. Thus, I ask: Would you also be willing to accept a position as one of my royal maids?"

Alín grew very still, and when she answered, her voice was small: "This is a great honor you offer me, Your Majesty."

"It is."

A faint tremble passed through Alín's frame. "And what if I decline, Your Majesty?"

"Then I will bid you good fortune, and you may follow your heart's desire wherever it leads."

Alín lifted her head, her eyes shining. "In that case, I would be proud to accept."

Nasuada nodded in acknowledgment. "The head of my reti-nue, Farica, will speak to you then about your roles and responsi-bilities."

Again Alín curtsied. "Thank you, Your Majesty."

"You may go now."

As she withdrew, Alín bobbed to Murtagh and murmured, seemingly out of habit, "Kingkiller." Murtagh winced, and her cheeks paled as she realized what she'd said. She ducked her head and hurried away.

Once Alín was departed, and the doors closed, Nasuada turned her gaze on Murtagh. He found it difficult to meet her eyes, but meet them he did. "Was it well done?" she asked.

"It was," he said. Of her own and with no standing to her name, Alín would have found it difficult to make her way outside Nal Gorgoth without patronage or protection of a sort Murtagh was in no position to supply. Elevating her to a royal maid was an act of charity on the part of Nasuada, but he knew there was more to it than that. Kings and queens could not afford to think of charity alone. Alín was their strongest link to the Draumar, and their best source of information on the cult. It was wise of Nasuada to keep her close, and to earn her loyalty that others might not turn Alín against them. *Very well done indeed,* he thought.

"She holds you in high regard," said Nasuada, and there was no mistaking the slight edge to her voice.

In an unaffected manner, Murtagh replied, "And I hold her in high regard. If not for Alín, Thorn and I would still be at Bachel's mercy."

"Mmm."

"And because of that, I thank you for the kindness you have shown her."

After a moment, Nasuada relented. "It was only right."

"Alín was most devoted to Bachel, but Bachel betrayed her trust. She will not give her loyalty again so easily, I think, but once she sees your fairness and honor and goodness of character, I am confident she will be likewise devoted to you. She needs someone whom she can respect and believe in."

"Are you that person?"

He turned to face her square on, his expression frank. "I have neither the reason nor the desire to command her or anyone else. Those days are long since behind me."

"Is that so?" Nasuada picked up one of the chalices resting on the sill and sipped from it. "*Kingkiller.* I've not heard that title before."

"I never aspired to be called so."

"Didn't you? You wished Galbatorix dead many a time. And you chose to kill Hrothgar."

Before her bluntness, he had no defense. "I did. I was . . . angry."

She nodded. "My father and Hrothgar were friends. Did you know that? Even when they were at odds, they respected each other, and they often found time to talk on subjects unrelated to the responsibilities of rule. I knew Hrothgar nearly all my life. In many ways, he was the closest thing I had to an uncle."

There was no accusation in her voice, only a straightforward statement of fact underlaid with sadness.

Murtagh looked down at Ithring and Niernen. "Do you blame me for killing Hrothgar?"

She was slow to answer, but her voice was firm when she spoke. "Yes. I do." His heart sank, and he looked up to see her facing him with the same level of frankness he had displayed. "But I understand."

He wasn't sure how to respond.

To his relief, she shifted her attention to the sword and reached out to touch the crimson sheath. "The crest here is different than I remember."

"It changed when I renamed it."

Her eyebrows raised. "Zar'roc? You can do that?"

"I can. I did." And he told her the new name.

Her expression softened then, and she murmured: "Ithring. *Freedom* . . . It is a good name. Better than Zar'roc."

Murtagh was surprised by how much her approval meant to him. Pensive, he slid a hand across the smooth coolness of the sheath, still unaccustomed to the new meaning associated with the weapon. Then he placed the sword, Glaedr's scale, and the brass goblet on the floor next to his chair and held up Niernen, so the tip pointed toward the ceiling. "I fear we may need the Dauthdaert more than my sword."

Nasuada gazed up at the lance's glowing blade. "Will you carry it?"

"I think so. Along with Ithring."

"A Rider wielding a spear meant for killing a dragon. The elves will not approve, I think."

"Why shouldn't they? As long as it does not bother Thorn—"

Carry as many teeth or claws as you need, the dragon said.

Murtagh tipped Niernen toward Thorn in acknowledgment. "Then so I shall."

A frown drew together Nasuada's brows. "You did not explain how this weapon ended up in the clutches of the Draumar."

"If I knew, I would have— Ah!" Murtagh made a face as another memory rose to the front of his mind. "Wait." He carefully placed the lance on the floor, next to Ithring. "I saw someone among the visitors who came to Nal Gorgoth. Someone I recognized from among the Varden. Someone in your circle of advisers."

Nasuada's frown deepened. "Who?"

"I don't know. I don't. I've tried to remember, but I can't. The effects of the Breath were too strong. Thorn, do you—"

The dragon shook his long head. *No. I know the one you speak of, but I can no more name him than can you.*

"Barzûl," said Nasuada. She stood and paced before the sill, forearms crossed, picking at the lace cuffs on her shortened sleeves.

"Has anyone in your court gone traveling in the past month?"

Nasuada stopped by her chair. "Far too many, I'm afraid. And I can hardly go around accusing my most trusted ministers without an ironclad reason. Are you *sure* you can't remember?"

Murtagh spread his hands. "If I could, I would."

She tapped the sill. "Were you to see this man again, do you think you could point him out?"

Murtagh considered. "I think I might."

Nasuada nodded. "Then I will see about finding a place of concealment from which you can view my court."

He stood as well and joined her at the window. His legs felt stronger than before. "There's no telling who might be working against you."

"Do you think I don't know that?" said Nasuada. "These Drau-mar seem to have infiltrated my entire kingdom. Some number of Du Vrangr Gata have allied themselves with the cult, and now I do not even know if I can trust the captains of my army. At every turn, I see plots and schemes and knives lurking in shadows."

She remained as controlled as ever, but her distress was pal-pable. Murtagh was not sure how to respond. Unable to think of anything to say, he dared to put a hand on her shoulder.

A quick intake of breath from Nasuada, and she unfolded her arms and looked at him with such an expression, he was not sure whether she found the gesture comforting or whether she was about to call the guards to have him dragged away.

He dropped his hand.

"Stay," she said in a calm, quiet voice.

"What do you—"

"Don't go searching for Azlagûr. Not for the time being. Let me send my men instead. Stay here, in Ilirea."

His throat tightened. "As what?"

"Not *as* what. *For* what. For me." Her gaze burrowed into him, as if searching for some hint of his reaction. "You are the only one I can rely on in these matters. The only person whom I don't have to worry about being corrupted by gold or magic or promises of power."

He found it as hard to breathe as in Oth Orum. "Nasuada . . . How would that work? Your people hate me, especially after what Thorn and I did in Gil'ead."

"No one need know you are in Ilirea. There are ways. Trust me."

A harsh laugh escaped him. "Shall I be your secret shame, then? Your pet spellcaster kept locked away in a tower, hidden from all? And what of Thorn? He can't—"

She stopped him with a hand on the center of his chest. Her skin was warm through his shirt. "I have no desire to cage you, Murtagh. Neither you nor Thorn. I only suggested concealing your presence because I thought it was your desire. If you wish to make yourself known, I will vouch for you before the whole of Alagaësia."

"Would you?" His question brought her up short. "Have you told your people how we helped kill Galbatorix?"

Speaking carefully, she said, "I have made it clear you are not our enemy, but it takes time for word to spread, and people tend to believe what is easiest. Stay in the shadows if you wish, but if, or when, you are comfortable stepping into the light, you may, and no one—least of all I—will stop you. The choice is yours. Likewise, if you wish to leave, leave. But for now, stay."

A moment's pause, and then, in a softer voice still, she added, "I do not ask for reasons of state alone."

The words were formal, but he recognized their intent, and his heart raced beneath her hand. He placed his own hand atop hers. "I will not swear fealty to Du Vrangr Gata."

"I know."

"Nor to the crown. Not yours, not anyone's."

She stepped closer. "That too I know."

He shook his head but did not push her away. "You ask me to trust you, but how can you trust *me* after what I did to you?" He made no attempt to hide his anguish.

She tipped her head back. Her eyes gleamed with tears. "Because I can. I do."

He pressed his lips together, every muscle in his body tense, as if to flee. A slight tremor ran through him, and he felt a similar quiver through the back of Nasuada's hand.

They stared into each other's eyes, not speaking. A new understanding came to Murtagh then, unfolding within him layers of revelation.

663

He looked at Thorn, and in response to his questioning thought, the dragon hummed. *Yes.*

Trepidation gave Murtagh pause. He feared to speak, to step into the unknown. But it was necessary, so he put aside his concerns, though he felt raw and defenseless, vulnerable to the slightest scratch.

"What is it, Murtagh?" she asked in a gentle tone.

He nearly laughed, his pain was so great. "*Murtagh*. Son of Morzan. So the world knows me and curses me because of it."

"That is because they do not know you as I do."

"And yet it is who I am. That is who you want to st—"

Her fingers tightened against his chest. "It is not all you are."

"No." He took a shuddering breath. "No, you are right."

She nodded. "It is a good name. Murtagh. I like it."

Words failed him. For a timeless while, they stood as such, neither willing to part, and nothing else existed but the two of them. Then Thorn huffed, and Murtagh blinked. There was wetness at the corners of his eyes.

Nasuada lowered her hand. He felt the lack of her touch with almost physical force, a cold absence that sent a pang to his heart.

She turned and went to the window and looked out over the rooftops of Ilirea. Her neck and back were very straight, but the slightest waver colored her voice.

"How will you decide, then?"

Murtagh joined her. They stood looking out, side by side.

The city was nearly lost in shadow. The high outer walls blocked the evening light that straked westward, and candles and lanterns sparkled among the dusky streets, where bands of barefoot children played with dogs. Far beyond Ilirea's outer bounds, the red-rimmed sun sat low upon the flat edge of the plains, and the land seemed strangely desolate, an uncomfortable reminder of his visions in Nal Gorgoth.

He had a premonition then of the danger gathering against them. Difficult times lay ahead. Of that much, he was certain. Yet, despite the prospect, he felt a sense of rebirth, there in the rebuilt ruins of his past. And a sense of comfort too, for those he cared about were close, and that was a new, and welcome, thing.

. . .

"I will stay."

ADDENDUM

Names & Languages

◆ ◆ ◆ ◆ ◆ ◆

ON THE ORIGIN OF NAMES

To the casual observer, the various names an intrepid traveler will encounter throughout Alagaësia might seem but a random collection with no inherent integrity, culture, or history. However, as with any land that different groups—and in this case, different species—have repeatedly colonized, Alagaësia acquired names from a wide array of unique sources, among them the languages of the dwarves, elves, humans, and even Urgals. Thus, we can have Palancar Valley (a human name), the Anora River and Ristvak'baen (elven names), and Utgard Mountain (a dwarven name) all within a few square miles of each other.

While this is of great historical interest, practically it often leads to confusion as to the correct pronunciation. Unfortunately, there are no set rules for the neophyte. You must learn each name upon its own terms unless you can immediately place its language of origin. The matter grows even more confusing when you realize that in many places the resident population altered the spelling and pronunciation of foreign words to conform to their own language. The Anora River is a prime example. Originally *anora* was spelled *äenora*, which means *broad* in the ancient language. In their writings, the humans simplified the word to *anora*, and this, combined with a vowel shift wherein *äe* (ay-eh) was said as the easier *a* (uh), created the name as it appears in Eragon's time.

To spare readers as much difficulty as possible, I have compiled the following list, with the understanding that these are only rough guidelines to the actual pronunciation. The enthusiast is encouraged to study the source languages in order to master their true intricacies.

PRONUNCIATION

Alagaësia—al-uh-GAY-zee-uh

Arya—AR-ee-uh

Azlagûr—AZ-luh-goor

Bachel—buh-SHELL

Brisingr—BRISS-ing-gur

Carvahall—CAR-vuh-hall

Ceunon—SEE-oo-non

Dras-Leona—DRAHS-lee-OH-nuh

Draumar—DROW-mar (*drow* rhymes with *cow*)

Du Weldenvarden—DOO WELL-den-VAR-den

Eragon—EHR-uh-gone

Farthen Dûr—FAR-then DURE (*dure* rhymes with *lure*)

Galbatorix—gal-buh-TOR-icks

Gil'ead—GILL-ee-id

Glaedr—GLAY-dur

Hrothgar—HROTH-gar

Ithring—ITH-ring

Lyreth—LIE-reth

Murtagh—MUR-tag (*mur* rhymes with *purr*)

Nal Gorgoth—NAL GOR-goth

Nasuada—nah-soo-AH-dah

Niernen—nee-AIR-nin

Oromis—OR-uh-miss

Oth Orum—OTH OR-um

Ra'zac—RAA-zack

Saphira—suh-FEAR-uh

Shruikan—SHREW-kin

Teirm—TEERM

Tronjheim—TRONJ-heem

Umaroth—oo-MAR-oth

Urû'baen—OO-roo-bane

Uvek—OO-veck

Vrael—VRAIL

Zar'roc—ZAR-rock

GLOSSARY

THE ANCIENT LANGUAGE

Adurna thrysta.—Thrust water.

Atra esterní ono thelduin.—May good fortune rule over you.

brisingr—fire

deyja—die

drahtr—pull

Du Eld Draumar—The Old Dreamers

Du Fells Nángoröth—The Blasted Mountains

Du Vrangr Gata—The Wandering Path

Du Weldenvarden—The Guarding Forest

eitha—go; leave

Eka fricai.—I am a friend.

Eldunarí—the heart of hearts: the gemlike stone wherein a dragon can store its consciousness

entha—still

flauga—fly

flautja—float

flautr—floater

gedwëy ignasia—shining palm

Halfa utan thornessa fra jierda.—Keep this fork from breaking.

hvitra—whiten

Ílf adurna fíthren, sving raehta.—If water touches, turn right.

Ílf kona thornessa thar fíthrenar, thae stenr jierda.—If this woman touches there, then break stone.

islingr—light-bringer/illuminator

ithring—freedom

jierda—break; hit

kverst—cut

Kvetha Fricai.—Greetings, Friend.

ládrin—open

Lethrblaka—Leather-Flapper

letta—stop

líjothsa—light

lyftha—lift

maela—quiet

naina—make bright

reisa—raise/lift

Reisa adurna fra undir, un ílf fíthren skul skulblaka flutningr skul eom edtha.—Raise water from below, and if touch dragon scale, carry scale to me.

skölir—shield

slytha—sleep

sving—turn

Thrífa sem knífr un huildr sem konr.—Seize that knife and hold that man.

thrysta—thrust

Thrysta vindr.—Thrust/compress the air.

vindr—wind; air

Vindr thrysta un líjothsa athaerum.—Compress air and gather light.

Waíse heill.—Be healed.

Wiol ono.—For you.

zar'roc—misery

DRAUMARI

mehtra—mother

sehtra—son

DWARVISH

Arngor—White Mountain

barzûl—curse someone with ill fate

Beor—giant cave bear (borrowed from the ancient language)

Fanghur—dragon-like creatures native to the Beor
  Mountains. Smaller and less intelligent than dragons;
  related to the Nïdhwal

Farthen Dûr—Our Father

goroth—place

Môgren—black-needled pinetrees native to the Beor
  Mountains, noted for their hard, dense wood

Tronjheim—Helm of Giants

URGALISH

chukka—marmot-like creature native to the northern reaches
  of the Spine

ghra—exclamation used to express doubt or a sense of mild
  disapproval

gzja—exclamation used to express contempt

qazhqargla—rite that joins two Urgals as blood brothers;
  may also refer to blood brothers as such

677

shagvrek—ancient race of hornless

shûkva—heal

ûhldmaq—Urgals who, according to legend, were transformed into giant cave bears

Uluthrek—Mooneater

Urgralgra—Urgals' name for themselves (literally, "those with horns")

zhar—randomness

HUMAN RUNES

Here set out you may see the system of runes as employed by the humans of Alagaësia during the time of this tale. There are exceptions to its use—notably among the wandering tribes of the southern reaches and the great grasslands to the east—but these are the runes one may expect to most commonly encounter throughout the lands of humankind.

The originating genius behind this system is unknown, and will likely remain forever lost to the depths of time. It is possible that no one individual is responsible and that this mode of writing emerged via an amalgam of accident and exigency—rather than being assembled by conscious design—as wrack and wreck may gather against a crag of stony strand.

The runes are referred to by many names, but their primary one is the Ullmark. Prior to humanity's arrival upon the shores of Alagaësia, their race was far more savage and uneducated than in latter ages, and they employed an entirely different system for recording information, one that bears more resemblance to the knotted banners of the Urgals than to any mode of writing that is native to Alagaësia. Of this earlier system, few examples remain—scraps and fragments littered about the ruins of barrows and long-abandoned hill forts—for under the leadership of King Palancar and his many and divers successors, humans quickly adopted and adapted the dwarven runes, known as the Hruthmundvik.

Humans, being as they are, made no attempt at faithfulness to the Hruthmundvik and freely altered and rearranged the runes to suit the needs of their own tongue, even going so far as to invent wholly new ones. Still, some similarities remain. The runes for *g*, *k*, *m*, *n*, and *y* are the same in both the Ullmark and the Hruthmundvik, although the Ullmark contains several unique runes, as well as runes for sounds not found in Dwarvish, such as those for *þ* and *x*. Also—and here the guiding hand of one or more scribes seems apparent—runes of similar shapes were assigned to sounds that, likewise, share a close resemblance. Thus, the mirroring or echoing between *a* and *o*; *u* and *y*; *c*, *k*, and *q*; *s* and *z*; *b* and *d*; *f* and *v*; and *m* and *n*. From this and other pieces of intelligence, certain clues as to the pronunciation of the humans' language in the time of King Palancar may be gleaned.

For the sake of general understanding, all of the words (and some of the names) on the maps in this volume have been translated into English and either written as such or transliterated into the Ullmark to help convey the proper look and feel of Murtagh's world.

As for the actual language that the humans of Alagaësia use, that is a matter for examination elsewhere and elsewhen.

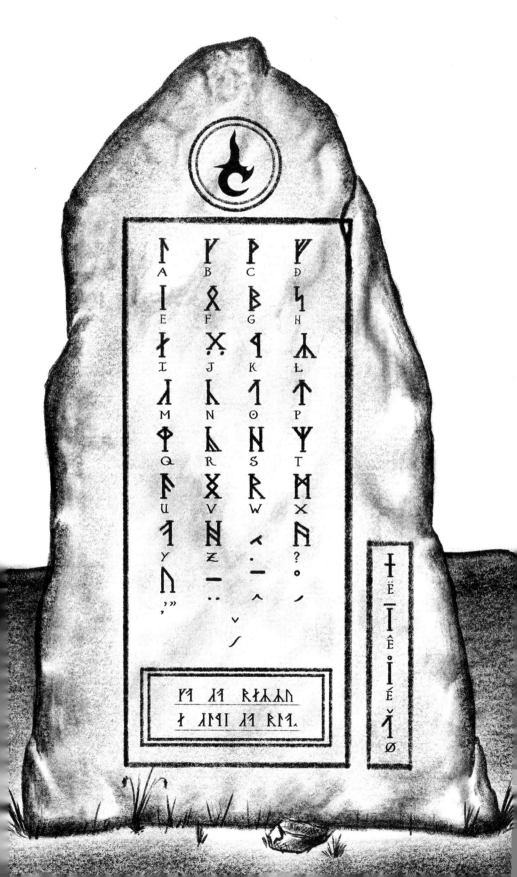

Afterword &
Acknowledgments

✦ ✦ ✦ ✦ ✦ ✦ ✦

Kvetha Fricai. Greetings, Friend.

You made it. Congratulations. Take a breath, put your feet up by the fire, let your emotions settle out. I hope this tale of Murtagh's journey affected you as much as it affected me.

Perhaps you have some questions. Allow me to attempt some answers. . . .

The initial inspiration for *Murtagh* came from, of all places, a tweet. A number of years ago, when I was in the midst of rewriting *To Sleep in a Sea of Stars*, a fan asked me what Murtagh was up to at that moment. It was way past my bedtime, and I was feeling a bit punchy, and as a result, I replied as follows:

> At one point (after *Inheritance*), Murtagh enchanted a fork to be as deadly as any sword. He called it Mr. Stabby. Thorn was not amused.

Absurd though it was, the idea stuck with me, and in 2018, when I decided to finish a collection of short stories set in Alagaësia, I thought back to that tweet. With some adaptation, it formed the basis for the first story in what became *The Fork, the Witch, and the Worm*, the first volume in Tales from Alagaësia. (Will there be a second volume? Indubitably.)

That story, as many readers will recall, was written from the point of view of Essie, not Murtagh, but even so, I could fee[1] outline of a larger tale coalescing around that core, one that might serve as a proper, full-sized return to Alagaësia.

And so it proved. After *To Sleep in a Sea of Stars* was finally released, and after I spent a few months revising and editing *Fractal Noise* (a prequel to *To Sleep* that I originally wrote in 2013), I felt ready to return to Alagaësia.

As I fleshed out the plot and delved ever deeper into Murtagh's and Thorn's characters, I found rich earth to work with. Indeed, the richness surprised me. My first conception of *Murtagh* was more in line with the sort of old-fashioned adventure novel that Edgar Rice Burroughs might have produced (and which I still very much enjoy).

But the more I thought, plotted, and wrote, the more I felt for Murtagh and Thorn, and the more I realized that this book provided a perfect opportunity to explore the issues they were dealing with following the events of the Inheritance Cycle, as well as those of Murtagh's own tragic childhood.

The writing itself proceeded with pleasing swiftness. Having a clear plan makes all the difference. I started in October 2021, and the first draft was done by January 30, 2022. Not too bad, all things considered. Of course, there were tweaks and changes and edits to follow, but the major pieces were in place.

I quite enjoyed returning to Alagaësia with an extra twelve years of life and writing experience under my belt. And as with *The Fork, the Witch, and the Worm*, revisiting these characters felt like coming home after a long absence. It was good for the soul, is what I'm trying to say. To have this book released in the twentieth anniversary year of *Eragon* only sweetens the experience.

Now, there are two additional points that need addressing:

First, although *Murtagh* acts as a stand-alone entry into this world, you will have no doubt noticed that certain storylines are far from concluded. This is on purpose, and although I can't reveal my exact plans at the moment, rest assured, I have much more to write in (and around) Alagaësia.

Second, although *Murtagh* is the fifth full-length novel I've written in this world, it's not *the* Book V. Or rather, the book I've always thought of as Book V. That particular story takes place a bit further down the timeline, and I still have every intent of writing it.

So yes, lots more to come, both in Alagaësia and in the Fractalverse. I have stories to tell, folks!

~~~~~~~~~~~~~~~~ ❖ ~~~~~~~~~~~~~~~~

As with every novel I write, *Murtagh* wouldn't have been possible without the help of a great many people. Some of you have been here from the very beginning; others are new to the team. But together I owe thanks to:

At Home: My wife, Ash, for your love and support, and for giving me the time and space I needed to write, edit, and promote *Murtagh*. Thank you! I know it was a push. Also, our two children, who, though they didn't understand what I was doing, provided so much joy every day.

My mom for your usual keen eye when it comes to editing, as well as for helping with business and family. And my father for keeping everything running, month after month, so I could stay head-down in the book.

My astoundingly competent assistants, Immanuela and Holly, for your own (very helpful) editorial comments, as well as all of your hard work on websites, social media, merch, and so much more. Couldn't do it without you!

At Writers House: Simon Lipskar for being such a wonderful agent. Twenty years and counting! Here's to twenty more. (I still owe you a sushi dinner for losing my bet that I could keep this book under the word count of *Eragon*.)

Also Simon's assistant, Laura Katz, who does such an excellent job of facilitating this whole process. And, of course, much appreciation to Cecilia de la Campa and the whole rights team at Writers House for securing all of the many publishing deals for *Murtagh* around the world.

At *Knopf/Random House Children's Books:* First and foremost, my amazing editor, Michelle Frey. Your intimate knowledge of Alagaësia and the characters who populate it helped me elevate this book beyond what I thought possible. I am forever in your debt. No author could ask for a better working relationship. Hard to believe we're lucky enough to still be doing this after so long.

Also in Editorial: Knopf publishing director Melanie Nolan, Andriannie Santiago, and veteran reader Michele Burke.

Copyediting: The incomparable Artie Bennett, the dedicated and eagle-eyed Alison Kolani, Janet Renard, and Amy Schroeder (masters all of grammar, punctuation, and continuity).

Managing Editorial: Janet Foley and Jake Eldred, heroes in managing (and re-managing) all the moving parts required to keep the book on track.

Design: April Ward and Michelle Crowe (the book is beautiful, inside and out!).

Marketing: John Adamo, Kelly McGauley, Jules Kelly, Regina Andreoni, Katie Halata, Mike Rich—for masterminding a campaign that far exceeded the already sky-high bar you set with the Inheritance Cycle.

Production: Tim Terhune—sorry for cutting things so close to the wire. Just keeping you on your toes!

Publicity: The indefatigable Dominique Cimina and Josh Redlich for your enthusiasm and energy in getting the word out about *Murtagh*.

Publishing Office: RHCB publisher Barbara Marcus, longtime friend and advocate Judith Haut (what a journey from Luling!), Gillian Levinson, Erica Henegen, and Rich Romano for fine-tuning all the publishing logistics.

Sales: Amanda Close, Joe English, and the entire (and *tireless*) sales team. From the big stores to the little, and every venue in between, thank you for being my champions all these years. Murtagh and Thorn couldn't be in better hands.

And there are *many* more people at RHCB who have worked on the Inheritance Cycle and the World of Eragon over the years, and who have contributed to *Murtagh* specifically. A veritable army, in fact. My heartfelt thanks to each and every one of you. I'm enormously grateful for your efforts. None of this would be possible without you!

Special Thanks: To Rebecca Waugh, Amanda D'Acierno, Orli Moscowitz, and Taro Meyer in Listening Library for your work on producing and recording the audiobook. And, of course, Gerard Doyle, who has returned to narrate *Murtagh*, even as he narrated all of the Inheritance Cycle. What a treat!

Music is to an audiobook what the maps and illustrations are to the print version, and Malte Wegmann did a wonderful job of bringing Alagaësia to life for the audiobook via his compositions (you can find the tracks online for free). That makes three books in a row, Malte!

John Jude Palencar for once again producing a stunning painting to grace the cover of my book. This makes the . . . tenth(?) painting he's done for me over the years (there have been a lot of alternate covers and pieces of interior art). What a privilege.

And last but not least, Alex Lopez, Mike Macauley, Hellomynameis99, ibid-11962, and all of the other readers who have done so much for the Inheritance Cycle fandom. You've helped foster a lively, welcoming, and thriving community, and I appreciate it.

~~~~~~~~~~~~~~~~~~~~ ❖ ~~~~~~~~~~~~~~~~~~~~

So. Once more we have come to the end of the road. A huge thanks to *you*, my faithful readers, for joining me on this journey.

687

It's been an honor and a pleasure. I hope life is treating you well and that you defeat whatever might bedevil you in the dark. Remember that you aren't alone. We each have a light inside of ourselves, and it's important to share that light with others.

Go forth, be awesome, and as always . . . Atra esterní ono thelduin.

Christopher Paolini
November 7, 2023

CHRISTOPHER PAOLINI

Author of the Inheritance Cycle (*Eragon, Eldest, Brisingr, Inheritance*). Creator of the World of Eragon and the Fractalverse. Holder of the Guinness World Record for youngest author of a bestselling series. Qualified for marksman in the Australian army. Scottish laird. Dodged gunfire . . . more than once. As a child was chased by a moose in Alaska. Firstborn of Kenneth and Talita. Has his name inscribed on Mars. Husband. Father. Asker of questions and teller of stories.